ENVOY TO LAN'LIEANA

Let he who desires peace prepare for war.

BOOK ONE: NO HONOR IN GLORY

Nicole Mann

TLS

ISBN13: 978-1-959350-39-2

SET IN: IRONWORKS 48/32 PT, GEORGIA 11PT
©THE THREE LITTLE SISTERS
USA/CANADA

I joke that I do all things through spite which strengthens me only because there is no explaining the relentless ambition and drive it takes to turn a dream into reality.

Accordingly, this book is dedicated to everyone who has insisted over the past 25 years that they would 'read it when I finished'.

Guess what...?

It's go time.

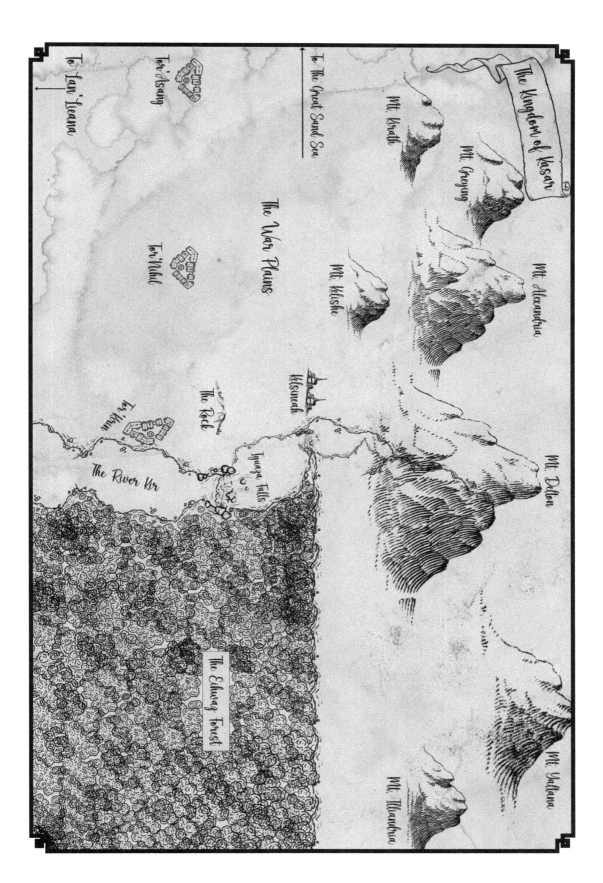

DRAMATIS PERSONAE

KIERNAN, Seventh
Counsel Lord / Lord
Seventh

VINICIA ('Mother',
'Vin'), Soldier Tyro
Barracks Mother

RYLAN,
Conscripted Soldier
Tyro, Son of the
Great House of the
Northern Lights

THE LORALAE (Lora),
former Val'Kyr assassin,
suspected sorceress,
prisoner of war

MICAH (Micahleia), Conscripted Soldier Tyro

WESTLY, Conscripted Chiurgeon, Kindred Dryad

NICHI (Andronicus), Soldier Tyro, Son of House Windover

SERA (Seraleia), twin sister to Micah

KAITLYN, Dame of House Windover, Aerie Branch

LENAE, Consort to the King, Kiernan's former betrothed

KREYCHI (Krecentius), former Shadow Guard Primarch to Lord Seventh, Heir to House Windover

TYRSTEN (Tyr), Soldier Tyro Primarch, Son of House Windover, Borean Branch

DYLAN, Street Crew Leader, Son of the Great House of the Northern Lights

VOLUME 1: THE MEN OF KOSAR

The end of a war is a thing long crafted,
Handed down to each Seventh Counsel Lord
Every seventh cycle, in a line stretching back
To when the Gods were men.

CHAPTER 01: SOLDIER TYRO RYLAN SU'DELTON

Wednesday, 19:00
"Four days and a wake up!"

Rylan scoffed to hear the celebration being repeated among the eighty-strong formation of officer candidates. Obnoxious as the saying was, there was no denying the excitement among his fellow tyros. After four solar cycles spent training at the Delton Military Academy, in four more days the dawn would rise on their graduation and the beginning of the rest of their lives. All they had to do was prove they Honored the men who had come before them with a mock battle over the capital, claim the Glory of being one of the few to challenge and conquer the gale-force Ice Winds that defended the Palace grounds, and then present themselves to the Seventh Counsel Lord's officer corps to receive their coveted rank pauldrons.

Four days and a wake up and they would be the newest Prefects in the Kosaran Legions, deployment ready and eager to begin a life most had been dreaming of since they had fledged. A day Rylan had once dreamed of himself, only to hate the fact that he stood here now. After everything that had happened in the three and twenty cycles he'd been alive, Rylan was only a tyro because he had been conscripted.

Two cycles ago, Rylan and his street-crew brothers had been forcibly inducted into the Delton Academy in exchange for Micah's twin sister Sera being saved by a Palace-trained chiurgeon. The same Ice Winds everyone looked forward to now had nearly killed her and despite having a dryad for a mother, Westly hadn't been able to heal her.

Asking for help from the Palace chiurgeons had been a desperation move and while Sera had lived, the three of them had paid with their freedom.

"It's only four more days," Micah said, realizing Rylan was muttering about what the tyros could do with their so-called Honor and Glory. "I thought you'd be excited."

"They've been counting down the days for a moonturn," Rylan grumbled, returning his friend's blue-grey stare with an irritated one of his own. "I'm sick of it."

Micah made a face, unable or unwilling to press him further, though he didn't look away. At a head shorter than most of the men of Kosar, it wasn't like Micah had anything else to look at beyond the row of white-feathered wings in front of them. With a markedly round face, olive skin, and night-black hair, it was only because he had spent his life living on the streets of the capital city that he was as pale as a proper Kosaran. Given his mixed heritage, he just considered it lucky that both he and his sister had been born with wings.

Unlike their Ehkeski mother, that meant they had an actual place in Kosaran society, not that Micah had ever expected to be conscripted into the Warhost. He was a bard, sure, but he had never wanted to be a warbard. Like Rylan, though, he would call Orders for the Warhost whether he liked it or not, and there wasn't a thing they could do about it.

"It's not four days. It's four more solar cycles," Rylan argued, shifting his weight as he resettled his wings. "And that's if they even let us resign our commissions. Westly is a Palace-trained Chiurgeon now and he'll serve for life if they get over his sorcery. Speaking of which, they might just keep you for life as well. You won't be able to hide how strong a warbard you are once you're outside of Delton and the Cantullus Preems never retire," Rylan insisted, angry all over again as Micah rolled his eyes.

"And you?" Micah prompted, since he could tell Rylan was going to say it anyway. "Why won't they let you go?"

"Because Lord Seventh thinks I'm some sort of good-luck charm for the Host," he swore. "Gods, I should just kill the man myself before he leaves. That would get me right out of this fucking conscription and—"

"And into the High Cells," Micah cut in, rolling his eyes. "His seven cycles are over once he graduates us, you know that. Then no one will care who you are or why he wanted you."

"He's done with the War, but he's not done being a Seventh," Rylan insisted, shifting his weight with his irritation. "Once he isn't Lord Seventh he becomes the Envoy Seventh, which just means he has to leave Delton or he'll start going crazy. That's what happens when you're a priest to a war god too long. Founder Noventrio's Gift eats them alive from the inside out. Blood and Ice, I've told you this before."

"And I still don't believe you," Micah scoffed. "Lord Seventh is a warpriest, sure, but that doesn't mean he can literally see through the eyes of his soldiers whenever he wants," he said, mocking the words Rylan had used the last time they had argued about this. "And you saying he can makes you sound like Kait fussing over one of her fae stories, except you actually believe it's true. Am I right?"

The last he threw over his shoulder, pulling their friend Nichi into the conversation whether he wanted to join or not. Kaitlyn was Nichi's near-sister and even if Micah was sweet on her, both believed that her stories of fae were just that: stories. No matter what Rylan had said about things he had learned as a fledgling from his family's archives, nothing would convince Micah that he was telling the truth about the sorcery of the Seventh Counsel Lords.

When Nichi finally looked over at them, wincing with a desire to support Micah even if he knew he couldn't, Rylan counted it as a win. He at least suspected Rylan was right. Nichi had been raised in one of the Great Houses of Kosar as well and like him, Nichi's House's Founder was also a Founder of a capital city-shelf, if on Mount Alexandria instead of Mount Delton. As a result, both he and Rylan had the tall, lean figures and platinum hair that marked them as nobility. Most common-born or Guild families had darker hair, though very few ever had Micah's black.

The only other people Rylan had seen with black had come off the streets like them. Most men on the streets of Delton were from fallen Houses and hated to be reminded of what they had lost. Rylan had kept up the practice of dying his hair even while conscripted, if only to keep himself from looking like the sireling Nichi was. Like the princeling Rylan himself used to be, since Rylan's own House had stood higher than Nichi's before it had fallen. Before Founder Noventrio had abandoned it, since they had sired a fledgling like Rylan with sorcery enough to disgrace the House at large.

"He sounds perfectly reasonable compared to Kait," Nichi had to admit. "Even I know enough about the stories of Founder Iskander to make me sound insane," he said, looking to Rylan. "I just keep it to myself."

"Yeah, well you'd complain too if your ancestors were trying to ruin your life," Rylan grumbled. "I mean, even if Lord Seventh goes on Envoy, I'm sure he'll leave explicit instructions for his Counselheir to continue ruining our lives. Mark my words, this shit about not being able to see Sera for Family Day? It's just another blicing straw to break us. I swear if he—"

"Rylan, I don't care!" Micah cut in, his wings flaring as he turned to face him. "It's only four more days. We'll see her in four more days."

"But we haven't heard from her in four *moonturns*," Rylan insisted, turning to match him with equal frustration. "Not even a *letter!* He's kept her like a hostage these past two cycles, and now this? He's doing this to us on purpose."

"Blood and ice," Micah swore, throwing up his hands to shove Rylan back a step. "Do you really think Lord Seventh is going down to check the post every morning to make certain no letters from my sister reach us? Do you think he doesn't have anything better to do? Nothing at all!"

"Not if he's going on Envoy, he doesn't," Rylan shot back, though it was the last word as Nichi stepped in to separate them.

"Guys!" Nichi hissed, pushing Micah into his spot in formation before they could come to blows. Everyone else was trying to ignore them, given how often Rylan and Micah had been at each other's throats. Crew-brothers or not, they certainly knew how to hate one another when it came to Sera.

As Micah swore under his breath, muttering an apology to Nichi for having to get between them yet again, Rylan just looked away. Not that there was anything to see from the back of the formation. At eighteen stories above the ground, the rooftop of the stone Soldier Tyro barracks was empty of anything but the stairs down and an equipment shed off to their far right. The rest of the roof was left open for these sorts of formations and with the way they were set up, they were just staring into the sharply sloped forest of the Delton Mountain.

If they turned around they would have the whole rest of the massive Palace to look at. Standing at a height with the barracks, the nearby Sires' Wing was capped with an ancient crystal roof and that was something.

Then again, the sun wasn't quite down so it would just be glaring in their eyes, which was the true reason they were facing east to begin with. That left all of them to stare at the emerald nothing as they shifted in the bitter cold, watching the antics of the platinum haired Primarch of their century, Nichi's far-cousin Tyrsten, as he talked with the men at the head of their files.

From what Rylan could hear over the wind and wing rustling, they were being peacocks about the new uniform jackets they had been required to put on before coming upstairs. Unlike the worn indigo of their wool tyro jackets, these were true flying leathers, made to last a lifetime on the War Plains rather than a few cycles as tyros. That meant that in addition to being made from a top grain, indigo-died leather, each jacket also had a soft, suede patch on the left shoulder and upper arm that would protect it from the hard leather rank pauldron.

As Prefects, most of the suede would still show since their pauldrons were just a fancy epaulette with a cross-body strap to hold it in place. It was the Praetor's pauldron that covered your upper arm and a Primarch's pauldron that covered your upper arm and your left chest that needed the rest of the suede. For a man of the Host, either serving under Lord Fifth as Vanguard and constantly on the Plains or serving under Lord Sixth as Home Guard in rotations to and from your home shelf, that softness wouldn't be very noticeable since you broke in the whole jacket before ever getting a rank pauldron.

As Delton Tyros, however, the fact that you received both at once meant your shoulder would always give away how naïve you were, no matter your rank. How 'blue' you were, and that wasn't a compliment. In truth, it was only the reputation of Lord Seventh that kept the men of the Nine Legions of the Warhost from disobeying any order you gave them. Just the rumor of the Seventh's supposed sorcery, his 'Gift' from Founder Noventrio that let him see through the eyes of any soldier on the Plains, kept those men in line.

The Lord Seventh was the ruling Warlord for a reason, both a warbard and a warpriest without peer, and from the stories Rylan had grown up reading as a fledgling in his House, the strongest warbards that served Lord Seventh were considered nearly omniscient themselves.

Rylan had also grown up with the knowledge of what happened when a man held that Gift too long or used it too much, and that was the madness that Micah had scoffed at before.

Micah, who was acting like he didn't give a damn that he hadn't heard from Sera in four moonturns. Rylan knew that was a lie, especially when the reason Micah had been able to keep in touch with her before was because of his own gift as a warbard. Twin that he was, he had been communicating mind-to-mind with her like the Cantullus Preems were said to do since the day they were born.

"Fine," Rylan conceded, looking past Nichi to see if Micah was still pointedly ignoring him. "If we can't go down to see her, then she should at least be able to come up here for the night. Mother can go get her from the Live Oak. You know she offered to get her if you're worried about her coming up alone."

Micah's dark look was full of fire. They had argued about this before, but now that they were so close to graduating, Rylan just couldn't let it go. He needed to fight someone to settle his nerves and Micah was a good enough target.

"I don't care what the Barracks Mother said," Micah growled, his voice low and angry as they heard a commotion at the front of the formation. "*My* mother said to never go anywhere near the Palace—me or Sera—if we could manage it. I only pass among the veterans because they cut most of my hair off. Sera?"

Sera looked exactly like their Ehkeski mother, Rylan knew. The Southern Ehkeski, a wingless people who allied themselves with the Matriarchy of Lan'lieana that Kosar had been fighting for generations. Micah had claimed their mother had been taken as worse before, that she had been seen as one of the Lan'lieanans herself and been beaten for it. From the few drawings of Lan'lieanans that Rylan had seen, it wasn't like he could deny the similarity. Unlike their mother, though, both Sera and Micah had been born as windwalkers when they had taken on their Kosaran father's white-feathered wings.

While that was good for living in the mountain kingdom, they were still clearly outsiders. Micah had been able to pass because no one knew what the men of Lan'lieana looked like. Sera, however? Sera had worried her entire life about being mistaken for one of the black-haired, copper-skinned Lan'lieanans. As a result, she had never gone into the sun, had never worn her hair uncovered, and would never do anything that might put her at risk, like their mother had asked.

But if Micah, Rylan, and Westly were about to leave for war for the next four cycles, what was she going to do? She had assured Micah that she was doing fine in the tavern that she had been put in, which worked well enough, but Rylan knew better.

Every few moonturns since they had arrived, he had managed to slip out of the Palace to go check on her, and Rylan knew for a fact that Sera had people from the other street crews harassing her. Trying to get at her, because Rylan, Micah, and Westly were so far away.

Sera had insisted she was fine, but Rylan didn't believe it. Not when the last people stalking her had been from his older brother Dylan's street crew. Given that—given everything—Rylan had no idea how Micah could be so calm when it was driving him mad. If Sera knew she could come up here, just for the night, wouldn't she want to? Wouldn't she want to see all of them before they deployed?

"He was born on Mount Delton," Rylan muttered, knowing at least Nichi could hear him. "He's as Kosaran as either of us."

"It doesn't matter," Nichi said, mollifying him. "What matters is what they will do to her if they think she is a Lan'lieanan. Mike is right. She is safer in a tavern than in a Palace full of veterans."

"She's in a *veteran's* tavern," Rylan countered. "Tell me why the blicing Lord Seventh had the Palace chiurgeons heal her at all, just to put her there?"

Nichi was about to say more when he realized Micah was glaring at him, blue-grey eyes full of fire. "Because healing her put the last son of House blicing Northern in his Warhost," he said, his voice flat and hard. "Your House is dead, Rylan, but you aren't. When you agreed to commission into the Host, he made them not care, but he sent her away as soon as she was stable. She is only alive because the Host believes you are Lord Seventh's omen, so they leave her alone. But the more you fuck with them, the more you call this a conscription, or a punishment, or whatever you go on about, the more you put her at risk. So stop trying to help. Just shut it, put your head down, and graduate already. The only way out of this is to get through it."

Rylan had to bite his tongue to keep from snapping back at his crew-brother. It wasn't like Micah was wrong, but they had no idea what Sera was going to do while they were deployed. That was the last thing they had been trying to figure out before something about Micah's warbard training had messed with his ability to talk with her. It had been getting bad for moonturns before that, sure, but the worst he had gotten were headaches. Now, though? Now he could barely think about her without a massive migraine, a backlash headache Westly had called it, and it just wasn't worth it. Everyone knew whoever was chosen to lead their squads for the graduation tournament was going to use him as his Canto Preem, or lead warbard, to issue orders.

Surprised at Rylan's silence, Micah shook his head to see Rylan's thoughts had turned inward. Micah hated reminding Rylan of why they were here. That bardic talent also let him sense how deeply it cut at Rylan's own emotions, but he had been spinning himself into a panic. Given that they were waiting in this formation for their headmaster to show up and give them their assignments for the graduation tournament, he shouldn't be acting like such a prick right now.

Still, the reminder hurt more than Rylan could put to words. When he had been eleven cycles old, there had only been whispers of the financial ruin plaguing House Northern. Rylan had therefore been raised to attend and excel at the Delton Academy, as if that alone could somehow rebuild the gravitas of the House's name. Surprising even his family, Rylan had been honestly excited to attend. Worse, he had been ravenous for anything he could get his hands on related to their Founder and the Seventh's Seat, going so far as to pledge before his family's altar that he would become a Counsel Lord before he knew anything about the madness involved.

Glory to the House of the Northern Lights and all that...

Unfortunately, by the time Rylan was twelve, the rumors had become a reality, and Rylan had watched as his family tried to salvage the honor of their bankrupt House. Realizing what was happening, Rylan's next-eldest brother Dylan had left on his own, choosing a life of poverty on the city streets rather than being chained to a woman to improve the family's finances. Rylan had been the last, desperate hope that they might find Glory at war, but at the barest hint of Rylan showing the kind of sorcerous talent that had made the kingdom fear the Seventh Counsel Lords, he had been thrown to the streets to follow Dylan. As far as the House was concerned, if the Gods of their Ancestors really wanted him for military service, they would find a way.

Rylan had hated all of it, especially watching as his family sold off everything that wasn't made of the stone foundations to pay off their debts. Eleven cycles had passed as the House fell into ruin and no one should have known or cared until the Seventh Counsel Lord had realized who Rylan was. Micah and Westly had brought Sera to the Palace for healing over Rylan's own protests and while Sera had lived, they were still paying a terrible price. Two cycles into their conscription, they now had to survive four more on the War Plains in exchange for her life.

Because if we're going to train you, we're going to use you.

That was what Headmaster Counsel Lord Aaron had said when they had commissioned. Two cycles in training, four cycles at war, all the while leaving Sera at the mercy of the Palace's protection. And the Counsel Lord who had made it all possible was now leaving on a suicide mission for peace. That was the true madness, Rylan knew: thinking that this war might ever stop when men corrupted by his family's vicious, unforgiving war god of a Founder could do anything at all in the name of peace.

"Rylan," said a voice beside him, soft and pleading. "Stop."

Rylan's breath caught as his other crew-brother, Westly, was falling into the rear of the formation on his left side. Rylan hadn't realized he had been muttering out loud, though from the look Westly was giving him, he clearly had been.

Clenching his jaw, Rylan tried to look apologetic as he met Westly's gaze. Unlike Micah, Westly was almost half a hand taller than Rylan himself and largely androgynous. Birch-pale like a Kosaran, he had willowy arms and legs beneath the tunic and sweater he wore, making him an even more conspicuous recruit into the Tyro Legion than Micah. Given his bright green eyes and dark emerald hair he usually kept hidden under a slouchy knit cap, there was absolutely no denying that Westly's mother had been a dryad. With a windwalker for a father, though, Westly had been born with feathered wings and so ended up in Kosar while his mother, wingless and bound to her grove in the Eihwaz forest, remained at the base of the Kihara mountains.

All things considered, Westly was quiet and reserved most of the time. He would have even fit in with the soldier tyros, if it wasn't for how he wore his garnet Bloodcloak, the mark of a Palace Chiurgeon, like a shield. That cloak was meant to defend him from men who viewed his sorcerous talents as an insult to those who truly studied medicine, but it just drew more attention to him the longer he wore it.

The chiurgeon tyros he lived with coveted the Bloodcloak just as much as the soldier tyros wanted their pauldrons, and to see it so close was torture for most of them.

It's not Westly's fault that Lord Second had been forced to give him the Bloodcloak in the first place, Rylan thought, glaring as he caught one of the other chiurgeon tyros in their formation looking back at Westly. No, the fault lay with Lord Seventh.

Before their conscription, Westly had been the healer for their small crew, but when he had taken the Warhost commission, the Second Counsel Lord overseeing the Palace Chiurgeon training hadn't known what to do with him. It had taken Westly all of three moonturns before Lord Seventh had needed to get involved, forcing Lord Second to remove him from a program he clearly didn't need. There was nothing anyone could teach Westly about plants that he couldn't intuit with his talents, and nothing about medicine that he couldn't just heal with his mother's dryad magic.

While that had made him a pariah within the chiurgeon community, he still had his required service to provide, and so he remained trapped in the Palace like Rylan and Micah.

All because he's waiting for us to graduate so we can serve our boon together, Rylan thought, turning his eyes forward as he heard the warning of 'Stand By!' rising over the shifting of eighty sets of feathered wings. *Gods, I hate this place so much. None of this makes any blicing sense.*

Not that anyone cared.

"Easy On!"

Seeing the Canto coming within ten paces of their formation, Rylan echoed the 'Easy On' call as he took an informal position of attention, wings tucked back to let the canto officer see everyone in the group. When there was silence among them, the man got his headcount and then waved them out of the bracing with an '*As you were*'.

"Call them to proper attention, Tyro Primarch," the Canto went on, speaking to Tyrsten directly.

More than ready to get this over with, Rylan was already moving as Tyrsten raised his voice over the wind.

"Fall In!" Tyrsten barked, the tone of his voice changing to hold the uncanny intensity that meant he was calling true Orders. When the tyros had shifted to ensure they had enough space to make a flat-footed launch no matter their flock, Tyrsten called out again: *"Eighteen!"*

"Eighteen!" The head of the files repeated, heads turning to the right as everyone else held still.

"Wings!"

"Wings..." They echoed together.

"Up!" Tyrsten commanded.

All at once the eighty-strong formation came to braced attention. With their head and eyes snapped forward, they drew their wings tight behind them again, tips crossed just so as they stood with their hands in fists at their sides. No one moved, no matter the wind howling across the barracks.

The formation called to order, Tyrsten pivoted in place, moving his right fist to his left shoulder with the salute to acknowledge the cantullus officer who had overseen their discipline and instruction for the past four cycles of training.

"Good evening, Tyro Primarch," Canto Xavier said, returning Tyrsten's salute.

"Good evening, Canto," Tyrsten responded formally. "Eighteen is ready for final inspection."

"Nice try, but you still have four days with me," the Canto chuckled, shaking his head as he looked beyond Tyrsten. "Put your men Easy On so we can talk until Lord Third arrives."

"Hoi, Canto," Tyrsten acknowledged before shifting his head to the right. *"Eighteen!"*

"Eighteen!" The men said behind him.

"Easy..."

"Easy..." they echoed.

"On!"

Now the whole formation shifted, each man stepping out their left foot to a more relaxed position again, their hands moving to the small of their backs. They still looked sharp, the angles of their wings now matching the angles of their arms, but their heads were free to follow the Canto as he paced at the front of the formation.

"How are we feeling tonight, boys?" Canto Xavier asked, relaxed as he took in the sight of the young men before him. Most were only three and twenty cycles old, but compared to the sixteen cycle boys who were recruited directly into the Legions, they were ancient. "Are you ready to see who will be leading your bevies for graduation?"

The chorus of 'Hoi, Canto!' That echoed the question made Rylan shift his weight uneasily. He didn't care who would be heading the two forty-man bevies, which bevy he would be assigned to, or even what tasks he would do for the stupid tournament. Once it started it could be over and then he would be one step closer to the end of his conscription.

"I'm glad to hear it," Canto Xavier said, turning to pace in the other direction. "Especially since the Ice Winds are expected to pick up tonight. When the storm breaks in four days, you flock will really learn what it means to fly."

Someone—some idiot—actually called out *'four days and a wake up!'* in response to that. Rylan rolled his eyes as the rest of the Tyro century laughed. They were excited. He was not.

"That does seem to be the case," the Canto said. "And for that reason, I expect you to keep to the barracks unless you are required to be present at Court. Either way, you will need to sign in and out so we can keep track of you. Otherwise, we will have a final revel to feast you before the tournament starts, but that is it. Am I understood?"

"So we get drunk tonight, Canto?" Someone on the far side of the formation called, causing more laughter throughout the group.

"Better tonight than in four days if you intend to wake up and graduate," Canto Xavier warned, glancing at the rooftop entrance as the door opened and shut. "Ultimately, while you remain in residence, you will respect Mother's wishes on decorum in the barracks, hoi?"

"Hoi, Canto!" Called a few folks in the group.

Rylan shifted to see his auburn-haired Barracks Mother as she stalked towards the formation in the dying autumn light. She was dressed like them in an indigo leather uniform, but she was also hard bodied. All whipcord and muscle after ten cycles of keeping fledgling officer candidates in line. If the Tyro Legion feared any woman, it was not a Lan'lieanan. Until they left for the War Plains, the only woman they feared was the Dragon Lady of the Warhost: Barracks Mother Vinicia.

Smirking to himself, Rylan stood a little taller. Mother was the person he was waiting on with this formation, not the Canto or Lord Third. He was going to ask Mother about going to see Sera, no matter what Micah thought.

"I'm sorry, Canto," she called, raising her voice so everyone could hear. "Were you addressing just a few of those men?"

"I was not, Mother," Canto Xavier said, shaking his head with disappointment. "I meant to remind them of your rules about revels before graduation, but only a few seemed to hear me."

As she resettled her wings in vexation, pulling them in tight against the wind, no one could miss the red and green leather scripts that held the fate of two men in their ranks. Those pace-long cylinders would go to the two bevy commanders, giving them the information they needed to start the chaos of planning for their graduation tournament. Once those were in hand, it was one enormous step closer to the Ice Winds flight and then finally their pauldrons.

Turning to look at the group, the light in her eyes was wicked She was not about to hand over the scripts to a group of men who could not even sound off, but they could earn her forgiveness. Of the many things she could do to discipline a group so large, however, one was her absolute favorite.

"Perhaps they need a reminder of what it means to obey a command," Vinicia said, and the Order she barked had the whole century swearing. "Half-right, *face!*"

As the formation shifted forty-five degrees to the right, Rylan just laughed. This woman could be evil incarnate, but he adored her all the same.

"DROP!"

As one, the eighty-strong tyro legion dropped onto their bellies, hands tucked under their shoulders. Wings tight behind them, every man in the formation hoped he would have enough space for the foxdrops she adored.

Every man but Rylan.

"Tyro!" Vinicia snapped, seeing Rylan still on his feet. "I said *Drop!*"

Rylan shifted his weight onto one foot, arms crossed under his chest.

"Blood and ice," Micah groaned. Chiurgeons were exempt from her physical corrections, but both Micah and Nichi had moved with her order. To see him standing in defiance, though?

::*"DROP!"*:: She said again, wings flaring as she threw the weight of her warbard's gift behind the command.

Now Rylan dropped.

Thought to be a blessing passed down from Founder Noventrio through the Seventh Counsel Lord, the uncanny ability to rattle a man's soul with an Order was unique among the cantullus officers. Not only did the words get vocalized like a normal shout, when a true warbard leaned into the command, they could also whisper the words into the back of your mind. That whisper was the only reason most soldiers heard orders on the wind, and every single officer recruited to serve under Lord Seventh had to prove they could receive orders this way in order to graduate.

Men like Micah who showed a spark of that Gift were coveted among the cantullus corps because they could send those orders as well. There were already rumors that he was going to be sent to train in Kirath as a true Cantullus officer when he graduated, which would have been an honor if he had wanted the work. Instead, Micah was terrified it would mean being separated from his sister even longer.

But compared to Mother…?

Barracks Mother Vinicia was a stronger warbard than any canto who had ever overseen their tyro training, no matter that she was a woman. Because of that, every time she dropped them, Rylan made certain they remembered that fact. If Rylan was some second coming of House Northern in the Tyro Legion, then Rylan wanted them all to know that she and her Gift were the only reason he would ever fall in line.

Woman or not, she led and he followed.

"One!" Vinicia called, arms crossed beneath her chest as she struck a pose at the head of the formation. In unison, the formation began the hated foxdrops, exploding off the ground with their arms as they backwinged to their feet. Wings tucked back with speed, they leapt up, piked, and then landed on hands and toes in the position they had started from, dropping back down to the ground to conclude the pattern.

"Two!" She called again, giving them no time to pause.

Rylan was happy enough to follow along as she took them through a full twenty-count. Just enough to exhaust them, but not enough to ruin their night or Warhost flying leathers.

"All right, Mother," the Canto said, interrupting her with a raised hand before she could say 'one and ten' to keep them going. "I think they get the idea."

Vinicia allowed herself to be placated, hands on her hips as she addressed their group. "Tyro Primarch," she demanded. "Why are your men on the ground?"

Tyrsten did half a foxdrop, coming to his feet and landing at his position of attention. "All the better to honor you, Mother," he said, struggling not to pant. "Eighteen! Wings up!"

Most of the men managed one last drop to get back to their feet. Some of them were not so lucky, crawling back up instead. Still, the Canto and Vinicia waited until they were at their silent position of attention before speaking again.

"Will Lord Third be joining us, Mother?" the Canto asked, seeing her shifting the straps of the scripts off her shoulder. Like the other men in the formation, he also didn't miss the blanched face she couldn't hide or the uneasy way she stood now that the theatrics of their foxdrops were done.

"No," Vinicia said, pushing past the moment of weakness. "I have been told Counsel Lord Kiernan will be taking his place, as it is his wish to give these tyros their first Orders and name them soldiers before the war game commences."

Even the Canto looked surprised to hear that. Being named a soldier was a change in legal status, not just bragging rights. For men like Rylan, Micah, and Westly, it offered protection they wouldn't have had otherwise. Lord Seventh was clearly doing something else to affect them, not that Rylan knew what it was. Still, he hated it. The man was insane.

"Will you be staying with us?" the Canto asked, taking the scripts from her as she coughed into her elbow.

"I will not," she said simply. "Lord Third has requested my presence elsewhere. Once Lord Seventh has said his peace, the boys are dismissed to their families for the evening. I will be in my office if anything is required. Muster is at nine marks," she said, turning to look at the greater formation. "No exceptions."

As the Canto nodded to confirm her words, the tyro century gave the one up, three down salute, stomping their right foot in unison. Satisfied, Vinicia gave a curt nod before moving to retreat down the stairs from the rooftop, leaving the group in silence.

Their Barracks Mother hadn't been gone two heartbeats before the Canto looked beyond their formation, calling 'Wings Up!' with such a sharp snap that there could be no doubt who he was calling it for. As the whole century came to attention, Rylan caught sight of wings moving over their formation and then men in fitted black uniforms backwinged into a defensive position on the roof.

Once they were set, a second wave of men joined them, the seven cloth-of-silver stripes on their right arm and left calf marking them as Shadow Guard as they caught the light. When the last man dove in to set down next to Canto Xavier with a flourish, Rylan knew exactly who it was.

Seventh Counsel Lord Kiernan su'Illiandria flared his wings as he settled onto his feet, showing the heavy black wing-bars granted to him by Founder Noventrio when he took up the Seventh's Seat on the King's High Counsel. Unlike his Shadow Guard, Lord Seventh was in the same indigo leather as the soldier tyros, though what could be seen of it had gone sky blue from wear over the past seven cycles. Covering the fitted uniform was the more formal draping that men of the Warhost wore for special occasions or appearances at Court.

Called a 'kama', the wide-sleeved, cross-body tunic and high-waisted, voluminous pants were made of silver brocade and indigo silks. Most of the kingdom relegated the kama to the solar festivals or other high holy days for worship of Shelf, House, or Guild Founders, but the ancient style meant something different for the Warhost. The war they waged against the women of Lan'lieana had been going on since the time those garments had been commonplace and so the Warhost wore them in remembrance.

This was the garment of their forefathers, and they Honored their memory and gave Glory to their sacrifice, even as they sent more sons, brothers, and fathers to die. If a tradition of killing was instilled in tyros, the memory of those who had died was instilled in the Host. It was everything wrong about the war in one place, just like Lord Seventh himself.

Rylan set himself for a fight as the Counsel Lord turned to look over the collected century. Kiernan su'Illiandria was a lean man with a sharp, hawk-nosed face and a slim, if chiseled jaw to match. He was also clearly descended from a mix of House and Guild families for all his hair was a dirty blonde, though it was well known that he was a guildson. However, given that the Guilds on the Illiandrian Mountain had more influence, money, and power than the Houses, he was as noble as a guild-born man could be.

He is also clearly not all there, Rylan thought, watching as the Counsel Lord's head tilted as he observed them. It looked as if he was listening to the wind, that or looking through them, rather than at them. From the way the man's Shadow Guard was watching him as much as they were watching the air around the barracks, Rylan wasn't the only one who had noticed that Lord Seventh wasn't entirely present in the moment. Then again, the Sevenths never truly were, what with their minds being filled with the Warhost at all times. Any commander could look distracted, but this? This was something else entirely.

"My Lord Seventh," Canto Xavier said, calling the man's attention back as Rylan realized Kiernan was looking straight at him. "You have come to give the assignments for the war game, Ser?"

Kiernan's dead-eyed stare turned from Rylan back to the Canto with interest. "I have," he said, touching his left shoulder to release the Canto from his braced attention. Unlike the Praetor's pauldron that Canto Xavier wore, a middle-weight piece that covered his left shoulder and upper arm, the Lord Seventh's pauldron was a masterpiece of sculpted leather. Rather than looking and acting as armor, Kiernan's pauldron was made of sections that, when put together, formed the quicksilver dragon that was the heraldry of the Seventh's Seat. With its head resting on Kiernan's left chest while the rest of it twined down the man's arm, it clung to him like a wild thing.

"Easy On, soldiers," the Lord Seventh said.

The Eighteenth Century shifted like clockwork, the files of eight men switching to stand in an ever-so-slightly relaxed posture, hands held on their low backs. Their eyes could follow the activities before them as well, which only made it more obvious that the Lord Seventh was staring directly at Rylan again. Rylan met his stare, his face making it clear he hated the man, even if he bit his tongue to stop himself from speaking. Micah would have been proud.

"You have, Ser," Canto Xavier confirmed, shifting to take the long leather scripts from his shoulder. "Do you mean to make the announcement, or shall I?"

"You may," Lord Seventh said, head tilting as the wind through the formation picked up.

"Hoi, Ser," Canto Xavier acknowledged, picking up the green script to read the name. "The first bevy will consist of even numbered squads and will be commanded by..." He said, pausing for effect as he handed the script to Lord Seventh. "Tyro Fionn su'Greying! Tyro, post!"

Rylan winced as half the tyros tightened their wings to let Fionn step back and exit the formation. When he came back to braced attention before the Lord Seventh, Rylan could tell he was ecstatic. After a quick handshake, hand off, and congratulations, he saluted Lord Seventh and followed the Canto's gesture to return to the formation.

As he got settled in the back row, Rylan saw Micah glancing to where their century's Primarch had moved to stand on the other side of Westly once the Canto had arrived. Tyrsten was clearly the choice to lead the red bevy and odd numbered squads, his and Micah's included. Tyrsten had been in command of their century for almost two full cycles; if he could handle all eighty of them with their training schedules, he could handle forty during a war game.

The formation hushed as the Canto handed the red script to Lord Seventh, who read the name stenciled on the leather before nodding. "The second bevy will consist of odd numbered squads and will be commanded by..." Canto Xavier said, pausing for effect. "Tyro Rylan su'Delton!"

You could have heard a feather fall in the stunned silence.

Rylan's heart was racing as he realized the Counsel Lord's eyes had narrowed with the challenge as everyone in the formation turned to stare at him. Rylan in turn glanced at Tyrsten, who had gone white as a sheet.

"Tyro Rylan," the Canto called, his voice edging close to the snap of command the barracks mother had used with him earlier. "Post!"

Habit alone made him move. Stepping back with his left foot, he pivoted to move around the side of the formation. He was always in the rear, always ready to leave, and now this?

"He's the last son of House Northern," someone muttered as he passed. "Of course he's going to lead a bevy."

Rylan swallowed around his angry response, driving himself forward.

"I guess you really can be a shit bag and survive if you have a Counsel Lord for a sponsor," another man said, and this time Rylan caught eyes with him. He was a heartbeat from turning on him, at screaming at them all that he didn't want this, but he held his tongue. Instead, Rylan just came to full, braced attention before the Lord Seventh as the sick sense of dread ate him alive.

"Honor and Glory, soldier," the Lord Seventh said, turning the red leather script to show his name burned into the side.

There is no honor in seeking your glory, you asshole, Rylan thought, taking the script with his left hand as he gripped the man's hand with his right. All he said was: "Honor and Glory, Ser."

With that, with his whole world gone silent and still, Rylan saluted, pivoted, and started for the back of the formation. Fionn was there as well. Him and Tyrsten. Tyrsten, who had been his friend despite every terrible thing he had done to try to get thrown out of the Soldier Tyro program despite his conscription.

"I'm sorry," Rylan started to say. "I didn't—"

"This isn't about you," Tyrsten said, his voice rough with emotion. "Nothing is ever just about you. It's about all of us being able to work together. The moment we graduate we work for him whether you like it or not and people's lives will depend on our ability to do our job, no questions asked."

Rylan swallowed around the knot in his throat as Tyrsten finally turned to look at him. He was absolutely furious, but not at Rylan. He was angry because he hadn't seen it coming. He wanted to be a Cadre Primarch to a Lord Seventh one day and he should have seen this coming.

"Hoi," Rylan said, hating himself even more as Tyrsten's attention turned back to the voice of the Lord Seventh.

"The Host is watching, soldiers," the man said, and Rylan swore to realize Kiernan's eyes had gone silver-white as he stood before them. Warpriest that the man was, the silver godseyes were the undeniable proof that the Lord Seventh's sorcery was more than rumor. If he was showing them openly, if he was flaunting the fact that he was not only a warpriest but a sorcerer like legend claimed, the man truly was mad. "For Honor and Glory."

"Honor and Glory," they called in return, right hand to left breast as the Counsel Lord flared his wings. A few moments more and he released them from the salute, taking off with the flat-footed launch that was a part of their combat flying. As his Shadow Guard followed, the century of tyros let out a collective breath.

"On my next command, return to barracks and stow your flying leathers," the Canto said, wasting no time. "I will see you for muster at zero nine. *Fall out!*"

Chapter 02: Seventh Counsel Lord Kiernan su'Illiandria

Wednesday, 19:30

"**M**y Lord Seventh?"

Kiernan looked up from the stack of letters he had been about to read, surprised to hear anyone calling for him. Given the heavy guard Lord Sixth had gathered around him in the days leading up to the Soldier Tyro graduation, only a select few individuals would have been able to interrupt him, much less unannounced long before this.

As the man leaned against the threshold of the room, Kiernan grinned despite himself. Though he was dressed like proper House nobility, all fitted black leather with gold piping along every seam and tailored curve, the man had been the Primarch of Kiernan's fumentari of bodyguards for nearly half of his seven-cycle term as a Counsel Lord. The second half of that time he had technically been at Court to see to the administration of his House's affairs in support of an ailing sire, but he had continued working for Kiernan all the same.

"Kreychi!" Kiernan greeted, making to stand only to have the platinum-haired man wave him off. "Gods, it is good to see you. I was just about to get into this letter from my father, but—Wait, shouldn't you be having audiences with your House?"

"I am on my way," Kreychi assured him, finally moving into the room. "But I saw you returning with your guard and had no idea where you'd been, so I thought I'd drop in. You weren't off causing trouble, were you?"

"I was assigning the tyros to their bevies for the war game," Kiernan said, a twist to his lips as Kreychi came to a stop beside his desk. Most of the room was barren at this point, nothing but empty bookshelves, tables, and the massive map of the War Plains affixed to the wall behind him. Kreychi noticed, but then again, Kreychi's men had also been subtly moving Kiernan's personal effects out of this room for moonturns to prepare for his leaving on Envoy.

"So just giving them all a heart attack," Kreychi laughed, looking down at the letters and reports scattered across Kiernan's desk. "Don't you have anything better to do?" he added, reaching past a stack of tyro reports towards the rather large pile of letters addressed to one Tyro Rylan.

"You're stealing mail, now?" Kreychi asked, suspicious as Kiernan winced. "This is from a woman, Kiernan."

"He does not need the distraction," Kiernan said, shrugging. "Especially not about his House's old estate and more Court nonsense than even you would want to deal with."

"Court nonsense?" Kreychi scoffed, opening one of the letters for inspection. As he skimmed, Kiernan watched the man's eyes go wide. "The Kirathy nobility are doing... Gods above, this is serious. Kiernan, who is this woman?"

"No one of consequence," Kiernan said, gesturing to the pile. "You can take the letters if you want. I'll be gone before any of it matters."

Kreychi shot a hard look at him, doing just that, but Kiernan couldn't be bothered to care. He had cared about so much for so long that the idea of leaving it all behind was the only thing seeing him through now. If Kreychi wanted to catch what was slipping through the cracks, so be it. He was the spymaster, after all.

"Anything else I should know about?" Kreychi asked, his look softening as he found Kiernan rubbing at his temples.

"Hest'lre has gone into the Lower City to check in with the Primarch overseeing the veterans on the detail to remove the Sires and their families from the Wing," Kiernan said, shrugging. "I think it was just to get away from me, though. You know how superstitious he is and my eyes keep shifting when I'm not thinking about it..."

"It will get better once you give your hawkeye to your counselheir and leave Delton," Kreychi agreed as Kiernan picked up the letter he had been reading when Kreychi had come in. "Though I won't complain that he isn't here when I come to check in on you, either," he said, moving between Kiernan's wings to settle his hands gently on either side of Kiernan's head. "Now, what's in this letter you're supposed to have?"

"It's from my father, but every time I look at the script my vision blurs," Kiernan said, closing his eyes as the man's hands slipped beneath the long length of his warcrest. After ten cycles at war, the short crest of hair Kiernan had begun as a Delton tyro had grown extensively. After his first fighting season, Kiernan had begun the boxed-braids that marked him as a veteran and for all his long service they were now plaited together to keep them out of his way. Still, that didn't do anything to lessen the weight of it as it hung down between his wings.

"With that small of a script, I can't say I blame you," Kreychi said, his interest caught as Kiernan struggled to focus on keeping the paper lifted. Kreychi knew exactly how to release the tension along the shaved sides of his scalp and as his fingers worked their magic, Kiernan forgot what he had been saying.

As Kreychi's hands caressed down the cords of tension in Kiernan's neck, Kiernan let the letter drop into his lap. Kreychi had always been able to slip under his skin, forcing him to relax no matter the pressure Kiernan had been under. After all their time together as tyros, it made sense that they had eventually become wingmates on the War Plains. That and as his bodyguard, sharing Kiernan's nest made it impossible for Kiernan to ghost him like he did the rest of his fumentari guard. When you wanted to always be around someone, they didn't have to worry about you wandering off.

A solid quarter mark passed before Kreychi's hands stopped moving. By that time, Kiernan's head had dropped back against Kreychi's torso and he was having trouble keeping his wings in place for all the tension the man's touch had stripped away. When he was finally done, Kiernan sucked in a breath as he felt Kreychi's hands gliding along his jaw, holding him in place as he shifted back to set his lips on Kiernan's own in the silence.

Shivering with the feel of the man's affection, Kiernan froze in the moment. His racing heart was a stark reminder of just how starved he was for touch, anyone's touch. Kreychi knew it as well, though he had given his word. He would do nothing—nothing serious—unless Kiernan asked. When Kreychi eventually pulled back, hands sliding to Kiernan's shoulders, Kiernan knew all he would have to do was look towards his nest in the next room and Kreychi would have stripped him down to his flesh and feathers without a word.

Kreychi was in love with him. If there was anything Kiernan wanted done, in the world or in a nest, Kreychi would do it for him. Despite that, or perhaps because of it, Kiernan felt it would be a disservice to what intimacy they had shared on the War Plains to take him up on the offer now. After Kreychi had resigned his commission to serve his House instead, Kiernan had told him that their own intimacy was through.

It was Kreychi's duty now to find a wife and begin his own line of heirs—not that the man cared. So long as Kiernan focused his own life to the duty of the Seventh's Seat, Kreychi remained devoted to him. Worse, now that Kiernan was so close to leaving for his Envoy, Kreychi was convinced that the man Kiernan needed the most protection from was himself, not some assassin.

"I wish you would let me take care of you again," Kreychi said, the words full of sorrow as Kiernan picked up his head.

"You care for me too much already, Kreya," Kiernan defended, pulling in his wings to put a proper space between them.

"I would not have to if you took care of yourself," Kreychi countered, moving to pluck the letter from Kiernan's lap.

When Kiernan looked to him again, he didn't miss the twist to the man's lips as he saw Kiernan readjust his position. Yes, the man could still light a fire in him no matter the rejection and that would have to be compliment enough.

"Let's see what this says," Kreychi said, smiling to himself as he rested his hips back against Kiernan's desk.

Kiernan took a deep breath, trying and failing to look at anything other than the finely turned thigh and calf that showed through Kreychi's courtier's garb beside him. Exhaling with a sigh, Kiernan set his hand against Kreychi's thigh for the simple comfort of the contact, shifting to rest against the thin back of his chair. He could enjoy the play of lamplight along the man's angled face as he skimmed the letter without feeling too much guilt, at least. Kreychi would never begrudge him that.

Brilliant as the man was at politics and spycraft, as he began to read his father's letter with a more than amusing affectation of importance, Kiernan's laughter was genuine:

> For the eyes of the Hawkeyed,
> High Wing Commander at War,
> Sovereign of the Seventh Seat,
> Dedicate of His Majesty, King Braeden,
> Heir to the Throne of the Windwalkers,
> Avatar of the Gods of our Ancestors,
> Blessed be his reign,
> And His Warrior Consort, the Dame Lenae,
> For him, these words have been written.

"Oh, good," Kiernan laughed, settling into his ease as his friend looked up. "I was wondering where he was going with that."

"Hush," Kreychi scolded, moving on to the actual letter.

> My Son,
> It has been a long three winters since we saw you last. Your mother fears you may have lost your bearing or let some War wind carry you away and I must echo her concern. Though you may be a Counsel Lord now, you were born to be my closest confidant.

Kiernan winced as Kreychi looked over to him, about as impressed with Kiernan as his father had been with those opening lines.

"You haven't been home in three winters?" Kreychi accused.

"I haven't had time," Kiernan said, waving off the guilt trip. "Besides, he's just drowning in fledglings. I told him to expect me to come before I went on Envoy, so I don't know why he's trying to insist I come now."

"Maybe because your letters never have more than ten words to them no matter what you get in return," Kreychi said, shaking the long letter in his hands. Now the accusation was personal.

"I'd rather talk face to face," Kiernan protested, matching Kreychi's look with a flat one of his own. "Of all the men who have served me, you should know that much."

When Kreychi only rolled his eyes, Kiernan waved at him to go on.

*When you left for Delton with Lenae at your side, I was as proud as a
father could be. As the seasons passed, the son I knew turned into a soldier
and that soldier turned into a veteran I grew to respect. In those times your
letters were a comfort, full of heroics on the War Plains, and I lived through
you as you grew into your command. When they named you as the King's
Seventh Counsel Lord—Warlord over all Nine Legions—I went mad with
pride. Though your sisters had long fought me over their choice for suitors,
I changed my heart and wed all but one of them into the Illiandrian Houses
who had named you a favored son.*

"Didn't one of your sisters marry into Borean?" Kreychi asked, looking up in
thought. House Borean was a branch of Kreychi's ruling Windover House in
Alexandria, but the marriage would have happened while Kreychi was still at war.

"Kaylee did," Kiernan said, sighing. "But her husband passed last winter and she's
been in mourning ever since. She's the other one that writes me novels for letters
these days, nagging me to introduce the two of you. You wouldn't believe the letters
I get from her about what a scandal it is that you aren't married yet."

"And you can't tell her it's because I'm still running your Shadow Guard, can
you?" Kreychi defended.

In addition to his role acting as proxy for his ailing father in the Kosaran House
of Lords for Windover, Kreychi had refused to let anyone else manage Kiernan's
personal guard while they were both in Delton. As far as Kreychi was concerned,
he might as well have been on rotation back from the Plains rather than out of the
Warhost entirely. The fact that he still wore his platinum hair in a long braid down
the back of his head was not something missed by many. Kreychi may not have the
warcrest braids anymore, but he hadn't shaved his head when he had returned,
either. Instead he had simply brushed out the length, so it was presentable for his
duties at Court.

"I never asked you to keep serving me when you resigned your commission,
Kreya," Kiernan said, if softly. "That was your choice."

"I swore an oath, Kiernan," Kreychi said. "There has not been a Seventh that has
survived to go on their Envoy in almost thirty cycles. For all you have done for the
Host, you will survive to start your Envoy if I have anything to say about it."

"And if I don't come back?" Kiernan asked, his voice softer than he had intended.
Every man who had ever set out on the diplomatic mission to talk peace with the
Lan'lieanans had died trying, if not for the reasons people thought.

"Then your father is going to be livid," Kreychi said, gesturing to the letter as he
laughed to break their tension. "Not to mention Lenae. I would take the fumentari
into the Eihwaz with you if you would let me, but—"

"Kreya," Kiernan warned, steeling himself as his old wingmate looked ready to
argue the point. "Don't do this. I've made my decision. I have to go alone."

For as long as it had been Kreychi's duty to ensure Kiernan's safety on the War Plains, Kreychi would never lose the instinct to protect him. Kiernan's Envoy was the one mission that he meant to accomplish all on his own. The very idea of a diplomatic envoy flew in the face of the success he had led with the Nine Legions for the past seven cycles, and for good reason. They were winning, weren't they?

Only if winning meant dying, Kiernan knew. *And I do not mean to die. I will not let anyone else die either, if it is in my power.* Terrifying as peace *might be, it is time Kosar learned to live.*

"Go on," Kiernan said, gesturing for Kreychi to keep on with the letter.

> *Perhaps it was that season of weakness that brought me to this day, but I am here nonetheless. Long I have heard word from my men that the sirelings are craven, but their talk has turned dark with the speculation that you mean to attempt your diplomatic Envoy. Duty that it is for your Seat, you know you have our full support. Peace on the War Plains is what I have prayed for since the day you left my side. If any man can do it, surely it is you. However, it is clear to me now that the Houses believe that the wealth of our Guild will flounder like one of their bankrupt estates when you leave, and that I will not abide.*

"And now he gets to the point," Kiernan said, making a face as Kreychi looked up. "I usually skim all that part before."

"He's proud of you, you idiot," Kreychi said, shaking his head. "You could at least let him tell you."

"I did and you have," Kiernan insisted.

Kreychi just rolled his eyes.

> *Kier'n, you have always had a talent for dealing with quarrelsome men regardless of your own position. Though you are not a lawspeaker, your Counsel Seat demands much respect in these matters of inheritance. I write now to implore you attend this last union of your sisters, if you do mean to set out on Envoy. At this time, young Kiera has been offered a ring by the youngest son of the Spinner's guild and against the insistence of your brothers-by-law, we have set their intentions in the Hall of Records to bless their union.*
>
> *With this alliance, I mean to set your inheritance rights to my title as Guild Master in Kiera so that she may hold them in trust for your return. Given the messengers Lenae sent to her Spinners Guild, I think it best to wait until after the Ice Winds have come to host the celebration. I regret that your travel will be at the most difficult of times, but as you must oversee the tyro graduation and have yet to name a Counselheir, my wings are bound.*

*When the day is done, you have been absent far too long and there are
more than a few fledglings who would know their Great Uncle Kier'n as
more than some figure of state. When all is ready, send a courier to hail
your coming and we shall arrange the exchange of rings accordingly. May
you do honor to Kiera as her most illustrious guest and support my decision
to grant her inheritance Seat with the gravitas of your own.*

By my troth,
Sire Tiernan, High Guild Master at Illiandria
Scribed by the hand of his youngest, Kiera

As Kreychi began to settle the papers back into their original order, Kiernan let
out a long breath. So that was why his father had written. Another man asking him
to throw the power of his seat behind his own goals before he left. Granted, it was
his father, but still.

"It is hard to believe that Kiera is old enough to marry," Kiernan said aloud,
watching as Kreychi set the letter on his desk.

"Ten cycles at War will turn any sister into a bride," Kreychi said. "I only have a
near-sister and even I know that."

"Yes, but would Dame Kaitlyn be allowed to rule your House if you and your
brother were still at war?" Kiernan countered.

"Of course not," Kreychi said, even as he realized that was exactly what Kiera was
meant to do in Kiernan's place. "Wait. You mean—"

"Kiera will be the High Guild Master for the Weavers and Spinners on Mount
Illiandria while I am on Envoy," Kiernan said, amused as Kreychi gawked. "When I
return, when Lenae and I return and can be wed as our Guilds originally intended,
we will have more influence than even your own Windover House on Mount
Alexandria."

Kreychi was speechless.

"I told you I mean to return from this Envoy and not as some Spirit trapped in my
Founder's temple," Kiernan said quietly, pulling his wings in to turn and face him.
"My father wants my Seat behind his decision to stop them from trying to break up
our Guild. The Houses don't believe I will come back, but the guilds do. They all do,
or they would be the ones pressuring my father to not let Kiera and Lenae's brother
wed. Don't you see?"

"They believe you will return," Kreychi said, just as quietly. "All of Illiandria?
Well," he amended. "Most of it, at least."

"This is why I want to go home before I set out on Envoy," Kiernan said, relaxing
with just the thought. "I need to be around people who believe in me."

"Kiernan, you know I do," Kreychi said, ready to defend his own actions even as
Kiernan raised his hand.

"You are a rare gem, Kreya," Kiernan said, meaning it. "But for as many people
want to kill me for even thinking of leaving, there are so many more who are done
with this war. Perhaps not on the Delton mountain, but elsewhere. Places where
people's lives don't revolve around sending their sons to die for Honor and Glory.
We can do more than that—live for more than that."

Kreychi looked like he wanted to protest, but Kiernan's raised eyebrow stopped him. Flushing, Kreychi tore his eyes away, looking beyond the small corner office and lounges meant for entertaining that anchored the other side of the room. The doorway into his private residential suite was open, however, letting in the blackness beyond. Having seen all of it hundreds of times before, it wasn't long until Kreychi's attention came back to Kiernan and the enormous oaken desk he sat at.

"Who do you mean for your Counselheir, then?" He asked. "Who will come into this place and hold it for you like Kiera will do for your guild?"

Kiernan didn't even flinch. "You know I'm not going to answer that."

"Is it me?" Kreychi went on, crossing his arms over his chest. "You asked me to do it cycles ago, but I refused. I still refuse, if you care."

"You can't refuse an appointment to the Seventh Seat if Founder Noventrio chooses to mark your wings," Kiernan reminded, flaring his own to show his seven dark wingbars.

Kreychi sucked his teeth in annoyance. "Fine then," he said, trying a new angle. "Answer me this: does the man you mean to name Counselheir even know?"

"Why would that matter?" Kiernan asked in return.

"Well, if I was given ultimate power over the Warhost, I would like to know I could stay in control of it for at least seven cycles," Kreychi said. "But if you mean to come back, does that mean you intend to continue as acting Seventh? How would that even work?"

"I will happily retire as soon as I have Lenae released from Founder Kerowyn's service to the kingdom," Kiernan said with a smile.

When Kreychi just rolled his eyes at his non-answer, Kiernan's laughter was genuine.

"Has Hest'lre been after you to ask me again or are you finally putting money in the betting pools?" Kiernan asked, resting into the slim back of his chair as he started after his Illiandrian ice wine once again. After a massage and the man's company, the distraction of the Warhost in his mind had finally settled to a dull roar.

"Neither," Kreychi said, sighing as he moved a few steps to pick up a nearby stool. When he returned with it, he took a seat that let him rest his wings against one of the more stable bookshelves next to the desk and Kiernan waited for him to go on. "But Hest'lre does need to choose his own Heir so he can begin teaching him as well, not to mention Hest'lre needing to study under Ninth Counsel Lord Shayan," he went on. "In case you've forgotten that Shayan intends to retire. He's only what, nearly seventy cycles old now?"

"Hest'lre will know when it's time for him to know," Kiernan said evenly. "And it won't be time until after the Ice Winds have come, that much I promise you. So if you can tell me when this rain will turn to ice, I will tell you."

"If I knew that, I would be betting on tyro pools," Kreychi said, his look turning grim. "What I do know is that if you keep stringing the veterans along, they will mutiny before you get a chance to leave at all. At that point, there will be nothing Hest'lre or I can do to stop them coming for your throat."

"Once I confirm I am going on Envoy, I'm as good as dead anyway," Kiernan warned, his gaze shifting towards his half-packed war chest tucked into the far corner of the room. Monstrous as the thing was, Kiernan was tempted to just pack a haversack full of food and leave with nothing more than his rank pauldron, a flight cloak, and the clothes on his back. "Why else do you think the men before me didn't name their Counselheirs until they left?"

"Those men still left a few hints for their Sixth as to the pool the person would come from," Kreychi argued. "After the fight you had with Lord Fifth over that damned loralae, Hest'lre is lucky anyone in the Vanguard even speaks with him if he does not order it. As far as I can tell, you aren't picking someone from his Home Guard, so what does that leave him with? One of your Cadre Primarchs? Decius?"

"Decius," Kiernan scoffed. "I'm surprised he hasn't just declared himself my Heir for all he has done to undermine me these past few turns. Roder is even impressed," he said, shifting to refill the wine glass he had emptied earlier while listening to his father's letter. "But if I told him—if I told anyone—their sudden change would let the whole kingdom know."

"And whose fault is that?" Kreychi insisted, waving off a glass for himself. "After everything you've done as Seventh you have changed the whole course of the war. You won us vengeance for the Fall of the Kirathy shelf and have spent the last seven cycles devouring the land they took from us for generations. We are so close to victory now that the men on the front can taste it and you're about to abandon everything just to wander through a blicing dryad forest? Every man in your Seat that has ever gone through there to skirt the War Plains has ended up dead."

"Not Eirik," Kiernan insisted. "Eirik survived."

"Eirik came back a blind fool with that horrid gryphling on his shoulders," Kreychi argued, scowling as Kiernan hid his face in the wine glass. "Maybe you don't remember how badly people reacted to that, but I certainly do. Ninth Counsel Lord Shayan had to give the creature its own Shadow Guard detail before the veterans finally stopped trying to kill it."

"That 'horrid gryphling' is a dryad's familiar and whatever dryad Eirik was working with got him back here alive," Kiernan argued, setting the glass aside for all the heat in Kreychi's tone. "I actually mean to ask Eirik if I can take it with me before I leave. I know he depends on it to see, but if it showed him the way out of the forest, maybe it can show me the way through it."

"Do you realize how insane you sound?" Kreychi scoffed. "Kiernan, the Lan'a are so routed that Lord Fifth has seen Ehkeski cities throwing them out without our help. They are inviting our Vanguard in and pushing the war front forward through the winter without contest. Lord Fifth is only waiting on orders to press the advantage and as much as you two can't agree on what color the sky is, he is still willing to work with you. You just want to give that up? Trade the might of the Warhost for a gryphling?"

"I have to," Kiernan said, resigned. "You just have to trust me."

"Gods," Kreychi sighed. "Do all Sevenths go mad or is it just you?"

As the accusation hung heavy between them, Kiernan watched his former wingmate check his anger. After fifteen solar cycles together, refusing his help when he meant to go on the most dangerous mission in his career was one of the hardest things between them. Kiernan's only response was to look down to the silver spiral pendant that hung from a leather thong on his neck. Trapped inside the cage was the blue-black hawkeye stone that had been the symbol of the transfer of power from Ex-Counsel Lord Eirik to himself.

With that power came the blessing of Founder Noventrio and the great ancestral Gift that made the Seventh Counsel Lord the pillar of command for the Kosaran Warhost. With that Gift, he could know exactly where any man was any time he wanted, no matter where they were in the world. If Kiernan knew the man personally, he could even see through his eyes for a time. Such an ability to coordinate men and supplies to counter whatever the Lan'lieanans threw at them was an incredible boon and had nearly won them the war at large.

Unfortunately, for as much as the caged stone was the symbol of his duty, the leather cord it hung on was also inclined to strangle him in his sleep. There was a reason that the Seventh Counsel Lord's term was only seven solar cycles, while almost every other Counsel Lord had the ability to serve for life. That kind of power came at a terrible price, but it was one Kiernan was willing to pay if it meant he could bring an end to the war. Step one was fleeing Kosar once his Counselheir was named in order to cut himself off from that power. If he didn't, if he tried to stay like so many foolish men before him, the presence of the Legions in his mind would drive him into madness.

"I should get going," Kreychi said, looking to the time candle in the room as Kiernan's thoughts turned dark. Clearly there was no arguing the point.

"I should be going as well," Kiernan agreed, refilling his wine as Kreychi gathered himself to leave. "Straight to Illiandria. Tonight."

Because walking these halls knowing that half these men want to put a knife in me the way they did Hewn is enough to drive anyone mad.

"Not before you speak to Lenae, you won't," Kreychi warned, but Kiernan waved him off. "Lord Sixth would have my head if I let you leave before you spoke with her again."

"He's not your commander any longer, you realize?" Kiernan said, even as Kreychi scowled. "And she is the one avoiding me, I'll have you know. She always does this—always pulls away before I deploy. It's nothing new, Kreya. She knows I am leaving after I graduate the tyros and hand over the Host. If you say I need to speak with her before that, fine. I'll go down tonight."

Kreychi looked as if he was about to say something, but ultimately stopped. They had argued more than once about Lenae over the past few days, but Kreychi kept insisting he needed to speak with Lenae before he left. His refusal to explain why meant that Lenae had ordered him to silence. Considering the Consort to the King was the one woman who could give orders to anyone in the Kingdom, it wasn't like he could argue with her.

"Once you have the last of your things packed just send for me and I'll have my boys move it," Kreychi said, touching his right fist to his left chest. "Discretely, of course."

"Thank you," Kiernan said, raising a hand as Kreychi disappeared down the hall.

Kiernan waited until he heard the door leading out into the Sires' Wing open and close. When Kreychi passed by his suite, Kiernan heard the man knock twice on the wall and let out the breath he had been holding. Despite having to leave his side on the War Plains, Kreychi had always been a presence in his life as a soldier. When Lenae couldn't be there for him, his Kreya always was. Whether or not it was in the man's best interest was his own concern, but for now Kiernan didn't care either way. Couldn't care.

Kiernan swallowed around the knot in his throat as he felt Kreychi moving away, though his hands brushed the corner of his mouth as he remembered the feel of the man's lips. Beautiful as Kreychi was in face and form, he had been just a friend while they had been tyros. Truly, Kiernan had never thought to take a wingmate at War for how devoted he had been to Lenae all his life, but that first summer on the Plains he had been so utterly alone.

The next fighting season when Kreychi had graduated and come to his unit, suddenly the idea of taking a wingmate had made so much sense. The moment Kreychi had reappeared in Kiernan's life they had taken to nest and Kiernan had lost himself in his friend. As he grew into his command, Kreychi had followed him as well, eventually becoming the only man Kiernan could trust to keep him sane when he became the youngest man ever named to the Seventh Counsel Lord's Seat at eight and twenty.

Now, with days to go before he left on Envoy, it would be so easy to let Kreychi be the reason for his sleepless nights. It still wasn't right, however, no matter the strangeness of the situation. The intimacy men shared as wingmates on the Plains was not the same as what men shared with women in the mountains. Sure Kiernan might not be an ordinary man and the woman he loved might be conscripted to serve as Consort to their King, but his time with Kreychi had ended four cycles ago.

Still, the man's offer remained, just as the man did in his life. As far as Kreychi was concerned, if Lenae could not be the partner Kiernan needed until he made peace with Lan'lieana, there was no reason he had to be starved of affection. Heart in his hands, Kreychi would wait until Kiernan was dead and burned before he ever gave up hope of being able to return to Kiernan's side. Given how numb he felt with the weight of duty on his wings, Kreychi's kiss had been a lifeline. For the first time in moonturns he had actually felt alive as his heart raced with memories of summers past. Given how he could still sense the man's hands on his skin, lingering with an asking Kiernan couldn't deny, Kiernan knew that if his wingmate asked again, he wouldn't be able to turn him away.

Kiernan took a shuddering breath as he tried to move past the thought, even if all he was left with was anxiety and the threat of rain.

Turning back to his desk, Kiernan looked to the map of the Kosaran range he had pinned above it for his planning, retracing the route in his mind to calm himself, even if nothing else would. Back when the kingdom was founded, their ancestors had created cities on the huge, shelf-like areas of these mountains. Over the span of two thousand cycles, the humid summers and icy winters had eroded whatever the range had been into the landscape they knew today.

The city-shelves remained on the angular and fertile peaks, while the foothills of the mountains had all but vanished, leaving towering pillars of forgotten stone between them. While the terrain was perfect for a windwalker like himself, it was almost impassible for any other people. The wingless Ehkeski that lived on the War Planes would have no hope of scaling the wet walls and should an actual dryad venture out of the Eihwaz, they would find a clutch of harpies before they ever found one of the shelves. And the Lan'lieanans? They had his Legions to get through first.

As incredible as their stunt had been attacking the low-lying peak of Kirath nine cycles earlier, it had been just that: a stunt. Though it had crippled their military infrastructure and forced thousands to resettle all over the range, Fifth Counsel Lord Roder had learned that the attack had been done against orders by a rogue force of Lan'lieanans. Whatever their reasons, the attack had shaken Kosar to its core and when Hewn, the Seventh Counsel Lord in charge during the Fall, was assassinated for the abject failure of defending the Kirathy Citadel, Kiernan had been given the Seventh's Seat and a Warhost ravenous for revenge.

Fortunately for him, Kirath was in the exact opposite direction of the course he meant to take leaving Delton after he named his Counselheir. Looking over the map, Kiernan followed the way-stations along their secret path to the next major city-shelf. Given that the capital of Mount Yaltana sat like a cat on top of the snowy mountain, it would be hit with winter far earlier than Mount Delton, so the chance of running into someone lying in wait for him were slim to none.

Once he had pinpointed the few way-stations beneath Yaltana, Kiernan moved further along the path, double checking the course he meant to take from there to his native Illiandria. Just thinking about it he could smell the sweet scent of the river weed, rasha, that supported his guild. It would be a relief to return home to Illiandria this winter, but there was no denying that it would be a treacherous flight after the Ice Winds.

If worse came to worse, he could always go on foot, but the vegetation was thick along the lonely paths between the pillars. Moreover, a few days in the air would turn into moonturns on the ground, and any provisions he needed he would have to carry himself.

It would be worth it though. Anything would be better than the gale he had to navigate here at the Palace. Of all his planning, the one thing he hadn't predicted was having to spend his last days pretending that he wasn't about to leave. Kreychi had been right to challenge him about the officer he would name as his Counselheir. It was an injustice to his long-time partner and Sixth Counsel Lord to refuse to tell him, thus delaying Hest'lre choosing his own heir in return.

And now, on top of it all, his own sweet Lenae was keeping a deliberate secret from him. No matter how much love he had for her and the fact that returning to her was the driving force behind why he had to attempt this Envoy, he did not mean for his carefully laid plans to change on the verge of his departure. If there was any wisdom to the old proverb 'words of want quickly change to words of woe' Lenae would never say, but she had paid a high price for begging the Gods to let her go to Delton with Kiernan when he had first become a tyro.

The night before his departure, Consort Telessa had succumbed to sickness and Lenae, hysterical about losing her Kier'n to War, had been granted the one thing that would let her stay by Kiernan's side: the silver-eyed blessing of the Founder who named the Consort for the realm. Though it had seemed a miracle at the time, the gift was truly a curse. With her betrothal to an infant king and the only hope of either one returning to Illiandria rooted in an end to the War, they had suffered ever since.

Kiernan swore as he realized he was pulling at the long braids of his warcrest and forced himself to let go. All things considered, he had been lucky that when he finally went to War, his time away from her had not lasted long. In his three solar cycles on the War Plains, he had risen from a Delton Prefect to a Vanguard Praetor and then assigned as one of Seventh Counsel Lord Hewn's cadre Primarchs all on his own. When Sixth Counsel Lord Magner had been killed during the Fall, Kiernan found himself back in Delton almost overnight, working to help Hewn's team sort through the chaos until his assassination two cycles later.

The appointment of Kiernan to the Seventh's Seat had come as a surprise to everyone. Most had whispered that Consort Lenae had pressured the still-living Counsel Lord Eirik to choose him, but Kiernan hadn't cared. No matter how it looked, it meant they were guaranteed the next seven winters together, wrapped around one another in his Counsel Lord's suite whenever she could find an excuse to step away from her entourage and he from his fumentari guard.

However, when the Ice Winds finally hit, it would be time for Kiernan to leave. The fact that Lenae had no control over whether he would return both frightened and infuriated her, but if he succeeded in his diplomacy, this would be the last goodbye ever spoken between them. If he came back with a Lan'lieanan wife for King Braeden, Lenae would be released and they could return to Illiandria at last.

For love of her, he had to leave. He had been given no other choice since the day her eyes had turned silver, but with this Seat he had a chance to free her. All he had to do was the impossible.

CHAPTER 03: RYLAN

Wednesday, 20:00

"This is impossible," Rylan swore, shoving the papers he had pulled from the red leather script away from him as he sat back in his chair. The desk was absolutely covered in intelligence, none of which made sense.

"It's only impossible if you try and do it all yourself," Micah said, not that Rylan had asked for his input. "That's why you have to name your cadre. Then we can help."

"Cadre," Rylan scoffed. "I should just give the whole blicing thing to Tyrsten and beg his forgiveness for stealing this honor from him. He loves this shit. I just—"

"Hate everything," Micah interrupted, silencing Rylan's rant.

Rylan glowered as he looked over at his crew-brother in the small room. All they had inside it were two desks, two built-out platforms for the bowl of their nests, and the two massive lockers that held their gear. Micah was over near the lockers, putting his indigo Warhost jacket away like they'd been told. Rylan was still in his, but he also wasn't going anywhere so it wasn't like he needed to change.

Micah was apparently going over to the Sires' Wing for the Windover revel with Nichi whenever the sireling came by to grab him. Westly had come down with them initially to check on Micah and his headaches, but he had left some time ago to check on their Barracks Mother as well. His only words to Rylan had been to warn him not to do anything unwise. Given that Rylan couldn't think of doing anything at all, well, anything other than fleeing from the Delton shelf into the wilds of the Kihara range to hide, that wasn't likely. It was too blicing cold and he really hated sleeping outside.

By contrast, Micah was standing near the open window puffing on a twist of terra like he didn't have a care in the world. Smoking the dried leaf was supposed to be banned in the Tyro Barracks, but given how often it was used by vets on the Plains to level out their moods after a hard fight, Westly had taken a special interest in it while he had been in Delton. He had given a twist of it to Micah when he had started having headaches whenever he spoke with Sera mind-to-mind, which had helped for a time.

Now it was the only thing keeping Micah's ears from bleeding, he claimed, and he had his head in the clouds more often than not thanks to Westly's ability to grow the plant. The terra was probably the reason Micah didn't care about Sera the way Rylan thought he should, which just served to piss Rylan off. How did you tell someone the thing possibly saving their sanity was making them forget everything else important in their lives?

"I cannot believe how obsessed you are with Lord Seventh," Micah said, exhaling a burst of azure smoke with his sudden laughter. "It's so dumb, Ry."

Rylan looked up, about to snap at him when the door to their room opened in a rush, dragging the smoke towards the hallway. They both panicked for a heartbeat, only to relax as Nichi Windover snuck into the room, his eyes lighting up with the subtle smell. As he moved towards Micah, though, Rylan sighed as Micah sucked in a deep breath of the terra and crooked a finger at Nichi. Nichi closed the distance between them in a few steps and when Micah was ready to exhale, Nichi sealed their lips together to breathe in the azure smoke in a slow, deliberate exchange.

Rylan rolled his eyes as they shared the breath of terra between them, Nichi going hands-all-over in thanks until Micah pulled away laughing. Dizzy as the terra made Nichi, the stupid grin he wore just served to amuse Micah further as he put out the twist of terra. Micah still had half of it left, but for as hard as it was to get ahold of, he guarded it jealously.

Nichi was the only one he shared it with and only to torture the sireling. Nichi had wanted to find Micah's tail feathers ever since they had joined the academy in Delton. Unfortunately, Nichi had also taken Micah to his House's suite of apartments to do it and had ended up introducing Micah to Nichi's near-sister Kaitlyn in the process. The rest, including Micah's falling madly in love with Kaitlyn, was history.

Micah and Nichi still messed around, sure, but Delton tyros were forbidden from starting any sort of wingmate relationship until they were properly part of the Warhost. Relationships with men were fine on the Plains, but relationships with women came first in the mountains, especially for a prince of House Windover. Princelings were also given an incredible amount of grief for having relationships with men in general until they had sired fledglings of their own, but given that Nichi had three, Micah would be fair game in just a few dawnings.

"You ready to go?" Nichi asked as Micah stepped back from him to pick up the bent-necked, fretless lute he played at the Windover revels. Unlike most of the warbards in the Lord Seventh's service, Micah could play more than war drums.

"I am," Micah said, grinning as he looked towards the door.

"You sure you don't want to come with us, Ry?" Micah asked, moving to let Nichi step out onto the small balcony so they could leave. "It's open to everyone."

Rylan had never come before, so why Micah thought he would come tonight was just absurd. "No," he said. "I'm not a sireling."

"Yeah, but you are a bowen," Micah said as he backed away. "Maybe if you actually let someone find your tail feathers you'd be less of an ass all the time."

"Why don't you go fuck yourself and find out for me?" Rylan threw back, making a rude gesture. "Tell me if it makes you less of an ass."

"Sorry, Ry," Nichi called, laughing as he caught Micah's wing with his own to keep him from stepping off the balcony. "If anyone's fucking him, it's me."

"Uh, no," Micah scoffed, closing the thick glass of the balcony door behind them. "That would be Kaitlyn. Come on…"

Rylan put his head back in his hands as their words trailed off. Staring hatred down at the red script, he was paralyzed with panic. He didn't want to do this. He had managed a four-man crew, sure, but not forty men he barely knew. Forty men he didn't want anything to do with, much less lead.

He was still staring at it a candlemark later, completely inside his own thoughts when he heard a soft knock on his door. After a heartbeat, he heard a voice as well and sat up straight as the door opened to let in his Barracks Mother. For as terrible as he felt, the usually powerful woman looked like death warmed over.

"Mother?" He asked, shifting in his chair to come to his feet.

Vinicia waved him off, moving past the two desks into the room to perch on the edge of the platform of Rylan's nest that stood between the desk and their gear lockers. The fact that she was taking a seat with him made him worry more, not less. Westly had gone down to check on her, but from the guarded way she moved and the dark circles under her eyes, if there wasn't anything Westly could do to help her, they might have real cause to worry.

"This is the last thing I will do today before I find my nest," she defended, looking down to the slip of parchment in her hands. "You, however," she went on. "Have a lot of work ahead of you."

"Mother, why do I have this?" he asked, shifting away from the script as if it might bite him. One of the worse secrets of the tyro Legion was that she was the one who wrote the reports for the Third Counsel Lord, Headmaster Aaron su'Yaltana, regarding their progress over the cycles, so he knew that she knew that he hated his conscription. She also knew how much he wanted out of the Warhost, not further inside of it, and yet….

"Because you've earned it," Vinicia answered gently. "I wrote your recommendation myself. You are respected among the tyros and as much as you think they aren't worth your time, you have been worth all of mine."

"But everyone hates me because they know I don't want this," he protested. "Why can't I just give it to Tyrsten? It should be his."

"We work with what we are given, Rylan," she said. "And you have been given a gift beyond imagining with this chance. Succeed as the bevy commander, actually win this tournament, and it will make this application for the title for your House's old estate that much easier to manage."

"You're the reason I am doing it at all," he said, looking away from her. "Buying the title to the Estate."

"You are rebuilding your House," Vinicia corrected softly. "The House that was founded on the Seventh's Peace, not this obsession with war. It is that kind of peace that the Warhost needs, especially in its officers, and you can do that. I know you can. You are one of the very few who truly believes in that peace, Rylan."

"And you," he insisted. "I know you were the one who bought my family's library when they sold it. You had to, if you also mean to put the House's Estate in trust for me while I'm at war. I don't know how you'll keep it up while I'm gone," he said, slowing with the thought. "Just what kind of Daughter are you that you can afford this, Mother? The title for the estate is ten thousand crowns, but the upkeep is what bankrupted my House."

His Barracks Mother just smiled. "My family moved from the Kirathy Shelf seeking their own peace before I was a fledgling," she answered. "All you need to know is that my family believes in the Seventh's Peace as well. We will make the estate into a Seventh's Library the whole world can access if that's what it takes, but it will be safe for you when you come home. Sera will be safe as well, living with me as you do your work on the War Plains. You must be at War to put a hold on the Estate's transfer and that means you must graduate. There are more people than myself who have a use for the Estate, I fear."

"What people?" Rylan asked, suddenly defensive. If he was going to war, no one was going to mess with the only reason he had to come back.

"Courtiers," Vinicia said, waving a dismissive hand. "And I will deal with them. My uncle was a lawspeaker for the Host and has given me advice on what needs to be done. I will see to this tomorrow when the justiciars take new meetings. I just need your signature."

Rylan sat up straighter as his Barracks Mother came to her feet to hand him the paper. Taking it from her, he read through the neat script before shifting to open his drawer to pick up the quill and ink he needed for his signature. As he shifted the paper, though, he saw the space where his name was needed and realized the 'soldier' requirement.

"Lord Seventh called us soldiers," Rylan said, looking up at her. "Was that all for this?"

His Barracks Mother just winked.

"You have far more power on this shelf than anyone gives you credit for, Mother," he said, signing his name and title to the sheet: Rylan su'Delton, House of the Northern Lights.

"No, I do not have any power of my own," she argued. "I just know how to move those men who do. It is all I am allowed in my life, I fear."

Rylan frowned as he looked at her, hating to see her exhaustion and knowing there wasn't anything he could do to help it. He was the cause of part of it, clearly, if she was chasing after his signature when she should be in her nest. Vinicia didn't seem to notice, instead looking over the information he had spread out on his desk related to the war game.

"All you need to do tonight is name your cadre," she said, setting a gentle hand on his wing to encourage him. "And ask Tyrsten if he will help you, do not just assume. His pride was wounded with this, true, but he has already proven to Lord Seventh that he can lead. Now you must help him prove that he can be led as well. Can you do that for me?"

"Of course, Mother," Rylan said, meaning it.

"And remember, Rylan," she added, flexing her hand on his wing before taking it back. "The Lord Seventh does not fight the entire War on his own. He identifies what needs to happen and sets those orders in motion. Use your cadre well and you can do the same."

"Hoi, Mother," Rylan said, letting her pick up the parchment he had signed now that the ink was dry.

"As for tonight," she went on, one eyebrow raised as she watched him. "Why don't you go visit Westly for the evening? He is working on something for the chiurgeons, but I know he isn't one to revel either. You two are family."

"I want to visit Sera," Rylan said, not looking up. "Why can't I go out to see her just this once?"

"Because the Lord Seventh gave you an Order," Vinicia said, gesturing with the paper he had signed. "And I don't care if you have managed to sneak off Palace grounds before," she said, this time with a warning. "There is a fifty crown bounty on the head of any tyro leaving the Palace tonight. The Lord Sixth means it for your head, so don't give him the satisfaction."

"Hoi, Mother," Rylan said as she started for the door.

"Rylan," she said, letting her true exhaustion show as she studied him. "Perhaps this won't mean anything to you, but in case it does... You should know that I knew the Lord Seventh when he was a tyro in these barracks. He was far more clever than anyone gave him credit for, given how distracted the Court was with Consort Lenae being part of the tyro system, emeritus or not.

The fact that he helped her become a true warrior when all they wanted from her was a pretty face took cunning and tact. But War changes a person," she went on. "He is not the same man I knew in this place and while the Seat may be wearing on him, he does see something in you. I think it is the part of himself that he lost."

"The only thing he has lost is his mind, Mother," Rylan insisted, though when she just looked away, he wished he had the words back. She had done so much to help him, to make the system work for him despite how it had ruined his life, and of all people, he shouldn't be fighting her.

Vinicia let out a slow breath as she pulled the door closed behind her, either not willing or not able to press the point further. As the sound of her boots clicked softly down the hallway, Rylan shifted on his seat, eyes going to the bowl of his nest. The square platform it rested in was filled with downy feathers, scraps of fabric, and other stuffing, which made it a perfect hiding place for just about anything a tyro could want. As far as Vinicia was concerned, if she didn't have to look, she wouldn't, but give her a reason and she would tear your room apart and see you pay for every bit of contraband she found.

Rylan pushed away from his desk with purpose as the silence of the nearly empty barracks made his ears start to ring. Given the late harvest sun, night had fallen in the candlemark since formation and if everyone was gone now, no one would notice him leaving either. Well, no one would notice a man dressed in pitch black and covered in soot, so long as he could manage his fly-by-night trick one last time.

He *had* to talk to Sera and he was going to talk to her, winds be damned.

As he pulled up the lip of his nest from the platform to retrieve the clothing he would need to wear on the streets, though, he hesitated. He was still wearing his Warhost jacket and while he hadn't earned it quite yet, it did make him look an awful lot like a true soldier and the whole Lower City was bursting with soldiers right now. Chewing his lip, Rylan put a hand to his tyro's crest, wondering if it was long enough to pull off the disguise. Everyone had changed back into their uniform or other court garb for tonight, but if that was what was expected....

Rylan exhaled a laugh, running a hand through his hair. He had needed to blacken his hair again, which meant most of the dye was gone. If he just cleaned it, though, he wouldn't look like himself. He'd look like the son of House Northern he had been ages ago and he could braid what hair he did have into a crest. He'd only need it to stay plaited until he was out of the Palace, right?

Rylan took his hand back from the lip of his nest with purpose, moving to his locker instead to grab out the three-paneled flight cloak and cotton flight hood that matched his Warhost jacket.

Those in hand, he made a quick stop in the washroom to scrub out his hair. Once the sides of his scalp were shaved back to regulation, he braided his tyro crest into the three-strand plait that would keep it flat against his head and then tied off the tail at the rear. Once it was set, Rylan got into his flight hood, a yoke of fabric that cinched under his arms to hold an oiled canvas hood and internal cowl on his shoulders. With that pulled up against the cold and his lack of a pauldron hidden under his flight cloak, he should be able to blend in anywhere in the city.

With both in place, Rylan stuck his head out into the hallway and, seeing no one, hurried the few steps it took to get to the lame-man's stairwell that led to the roof of the barracks. Once successfully on the roof, Rylan steeled himself and slipped outside, forcing himself to walk towards the eastern side of the barracks as if he wasn't in a hurry at all. Given the freezing winds, there were no palace guards in the sky as he made his way towards the small shack that had been built up against the rooftop embattlements, slipping inside without issue.

Heart thundering in his chest, Rylan pushed through the cleaning supplies and other tools stored in this place to crouch down on the western wall. With his fingers hooked into the crease he had carved into the stone wall two cycles ago, he jostled the wood shelving above it and then shifted to brace himself before pulling at the pace-wide stone with all of his strength. Slowly, very slowly, Rylan dislodged the cube from the wall and with it came in the wind that was whipping around the Soldier Tyros' Wing.

Though it had taken him almost a fortnight to carve this way out of his prison, Rylan thanked his once-noble father for teaching him at least some part of their family's talents. The ancient House of the Northern Lights had been one of the first families to settle the capital city and because of that, they had played a critical part in carving the two-tiered city-shelf into the side of Mount Delton. Though the sorceress talents of their Ancestors had been lost to time, House Northern had leaned on that legend of stone masonry until recently.

Focused again, Rylan threw on his flight cloak and cinched the ties of his flight hood around his face before maneuvering himself into the space he had created. Turning to push his wings out of his new hole in the embattlement, he grabbed onto the handles he had carved in the back of the cube and, with painstaking slowness, crawled both himself and the cube back into position.

Now clinging to the side of the Palace wall, all he had to do was wait. During his effort to move the stone, he had heard the unmistakable, piercing call of a warbard cutting through the winds, warning the guards in the area that they were changing duty status. Loud as the man was, Rylan's ears were ringing as the message boomed just beside his position and whispered inside his skull.

::"Shelter the light! Pull inside your towers! No sane man will fly in this weather."::

As the call echoed around the Palace, Rylan shook his head free of the ringing in his ears. With his feet pressed firmly against the wall, he released his grip and pushed straight out with all of his strength. Once he was clear of the eighteen story building, he twisted in the air and flared his wings, gaining enough lift to glide along the eastern wall of the barracks with little effort.

Gathering his luck, Rylan made his way towards the low, southern embattlements that marked the edge of the Palace proper and the two massive torches between them that lit up the sky. Rylan's ancestors were with him as two small blossoms of light separated from the torches with his approach. When both guards turned to make the trek towards the safety of their respective towers, Rylan powered between the fires. Distracted by the warmth waiting for them, the guards were once again oblivious as he soared past.

Rylan's next obstacle was a long stretch of barren white stone that kept the Palace a respectable distance from the rest of the city. Unlike the other mountain cities, Delton had been carved in two parts: one main shelf for the city and the vaulted Palace shelf that overlooked it—protected not only by its height, but by the tremendous updraft that had helped his ancestors carve the shelf in the first place.

Before he had been disowned, Rylan had taken his warrior's flight in this wind as a test for admission into the officer's academy. The first time he had challenged this particular updraft, it had felt like he hit a wall of force. It had also thrown him nearly a league into the air, releasing him with just enough time to come to his senses, cut back through the updraft with intention, and land on his face before the previous Seventh Counsel Lord, Hewn su'Greying.

Even today, Rylan still remembered the look of pride the Lord Seventh had given him. It was the look he had always wanted from his father, the look his brother Dylan would give him whenever he managed some other feat of cunning or secrecy stealing sweets from the House's kitchen.

To see it coming from the commanding Warlord of the Nine Kosaran Legions, knowing all it could mean for his House to have a son once again serving the Seventh's Seat, Rylan had been speechless.

"Well done, son," Counsel Lord Hewn had said, waiting for Rylan to find his feet. "It looks like we'll be seeing more of you soon."

After a lifetime of being groomed for the position, Rylan had wanted nothing more than his chance to work towards the Seventh's Peace. All of that had changed when Rylan's House had thrown him to the streets. He had honestly forgotten most of it until suddenly his little family had needed a true chiurgeon to heal Sera instead of a dryad-kin and his wild talents.

Face to face with the Counsel Lords again, Rylan had found himself bound to a commission sponsored by Counsel Lord Hewn's successor, Kiernan su'Illiandria, and he would have left long before this if it hadn't been for his Barracks Mother making him see what good he could do because of this terrible place.

What she couldn't see, though, was how everything hinged on Sera being able to have a say in what they were doing. He had asked her about it, both through Micah and through the post he was allowed to send to the Live Oak, but he had never gotten any sort of response. All of her messages had just stopped when Micah had stopped hearing from her and though Micah seemed to not care at all, Rylan had been quietly losing his mind thinking she was dead.

That was the only reason she wouldn't be contacting them, wasn't it?

Free of the updraft, Rylan set himself against the humidity in the chill night air and cut a hard left over the twilight expanse of the Lower City. Even in the dim light, Rylan could make out people still making last-minute preparations for the first of the winter ice storms. His ancestors might have helped build the stone city on stilts to keep the front doors above the snow levels, but the roof decks were a different story. All of them served as guides over the massive city, each marked and coded with colored landing mosaics to guide windwalkers like Rylan along their way.

In daylight the markers were simple enough to read, flowing as they did along the ripples of commerce, but the overcast evening blended them all together, disguising both distance and direction. Fortunately, the great Estates of Delton were a blazing ring of lanterns in the night, so he at least knew where to aim for now. Having grown up in the Estates himself, he could count across the swath of them from the bank of the dark River Kir and find his way.

When the long stretch of curving buildings finally gave way to the brightly lit tavern district, Rylan dropped down into the tight alleyway to continue on. Here the winds buffeted him less, but he had a greater chance of being seen. By their very nature, Palace funded taverns were full of Palace paid veterans and with a fifty-gold bounty on his head, it was in Rylan's best interest to remain discrete.

As the sky above flashed a brilliant white, Rylan was glad he had made it this far. With the clouds opening to release their weight upon the city, he could manage better speed without the strong crosswind, not that it wouldn't take everything he had to power through the water. Rain, no matter how soft it fell, hurt like fire when you flew through it at traveling speed.

If he weren't so exhausted, Rylan would have been happier about touching down on the Live Oak's back deck half a candlemark later. Instead, he just pounded on the door and tucked his hands beneath his arms as the driving rain plastered his flight hood against his head and hair. Shivering with cold, he finally just shook his head free, letting the rain streak through his hair as his attempt at a plait fell apart. He was going to have to fix it before heading home, so what did it matter?

When at last he heard the bolt of the tavern door slide free, Rylan's heart leapt into his throat.

"Sal'weh?" A woman called as her eyes adjusted to the night.

"Uh, sal'weh," Rylan said in return. He didn't know this woman at all. "I was looking for Sera?"

The woman scoffed, clearly irritated. "I'd like to know where she is too," she said. "That girl has been gone for a season, not that she told anyone where she was going. Just vanished one day after some cast-off nobles came by talking nonsense to her about a House. Who ever heard of a noble House forming from street trash like them?" She said, laughing for how ridiculous it sounded.

Rylan had so many questions, though he bit his tongue on all but one.

"House Northern?" He asked. It couldn't be, but...

"No, House Kirath or something," the woman said. "But they're going to use whatever that big empty one is on the east of the city. You one of those street idiots, too?"

"No," Rylan lied, glancing down at his Warhost gear. "Just trying to deliver a message."

"Well, next time use the front entrance," the woman said, hand on the edge of the door to close it in his face. "Then maybe I won't think you're chasing the tail feathers of a whore."

Rylan's jaw clenched as he fought to keep from sniping back at her and she shut it as he stood there. "Thank you," he muttered as he heard the locks sliding home. Sighing to himself, he flared his wings and glowered at the sky, shifting to take off once again.

House Northern was part of the central ring of estates, with the taverns and meeting halls on the inside near the Palace and the merchants and other cargo things on the outer ring where the gondola lines were positioned on either side of the shelf. He could fly another half candlemark in the rain and get there easy enough, but if that was where Sera had gone, why hadn't she said anything? Why had she just left? And who, gods forbid, had come to tell her of it?

Rylan took to wing with acid boiling in his stomach, terrified of just what that might mean. If his elder brother's crew had come for her, then she would have gone with them to not make a scene, right? Sera was brilliant and clever, and not above playing people for fools if she wanted information out of you. Like Micah she also had a bit of a bardic talent, though where Mike had the active ability to read people's emotions, Sera had a more passive ability to get people to tell her more than they ever intended.

All that in mind, Rylan made the flight from the Live Oak Tavern to House Northern in record time, rain be damned. When he got there, he came in close to the low wall before backwinging down beside the great stone temple on the estate. The massive building was a shell of itself now and black as pitch for the rain pouring outside, but it served well enough as shelter. For as much time as he had spent playing inside and around it as a fledgling, though, he knew what it looked like, or what it had looked like, before the ancestral carvings and statutes had all been removed.

As he reached out a hand to orient himself, his anger ignited the spark of fire in him as he realized how much had changed in this holy place. That spark had once told him that he was a true legacy of his House, an undeniably direct descendant of Shelf-Founder Noventrio, but embracing it in anger was what had gotten him disowned. After everything he had done to become the Son his House had wanted, acknowledging his gift had turned Rylan from the House's last hope of salvation into its greatest abject failure.

Pleading with himself, Rylan flexed his palm, struggling to bring the spark into manifestation so he could see what had become of the temple. He was furious at the hollow emptiness of this place, freezing with the rain and cold, and this spark had saved his life more than once lighting kindling on the Streets.

He just needed to want it, needed to make it come to life, but no one had ever explained how it was supposed to work. Instead, they had just thrown him to the streets before he could set part of the Estate on fire a second time.

At this point, while it was true his Barracks Mother had managed to save the books from his Estate as it collapsed, he wasn't about to ask her if she could look through them to find something for him. He was most definitely not going to ask her to find one about supernatural stone cutting with fire magic. For all he knew, her own House had already donated the books to the Seventh Counsel Lord's Library for all the Glory it would earn them to add to the collection. Rylan shivered as he gave up the attempt, though he nearly jumped when lightning cracked overhead.

Looking up, Rylan's whole world became the tower of empty shelves rising above him, though as the light flickered through narrow windows, he froze as he realized there was one statue left in this place. Rather, because it had been built into the walls itself, the nine-winged figure of Founder Noventrio still loomed within the space. As the lightning flashed again, crossing the sky with a deafening crack, Rylan was able to make out the image of Founder Noventrio's own Guide, the quicksilver dragon the Founder had allegedly made a pact with during the birth of Kosar.

Ancient as the history was now, it had been the mountain dragons that had allowed the windwalkers sanctuary in their home after their people had fled here some two thousand cycles ago. Though they were relegated to myth and legend now, the dragon coiled around Founder Noventrio's own statue in this place was the reason the Seventh Counsel Lord's heraldry was still a quicksilver. According to Rylan's family's lore, 'Noventrio' had actually been the dragon's name, calling to mind the nine winds that he ruled over in the Kihara range before the windwalkers had arrived. Their own Founder had been called by another name, though they had no knowledge as to what that was.

Rylan's growl of frustration echoed like haunted laughter as he stood in the abandoned temple, staring at the absolute nothing that was left of the glory of his House. All of his brothers—all of his family—they had just given up. If he really was the last son of House Northern, then it was up to him to make certain the kingdom remembered the true purpose of the Seventh's Seat. Standing in this hollow alter, though, Rylan felt the weight of the burden he had taken on like a crushing against his chest.

Why do I even care? he demanded of himself, closing his eyes against the burn of frustrated tears. *I don't want to care. I don't want any part of this, but I can't just give up. For the life of me, I can't quit.*

Quitting was easy—*war was easy*—but peace? That was the only thing worth fighting for.

::The peaccce that wasss promisssed.::

Rylan's eyes flew open as he heard a voice on the wind, a whispered hiss that had his wings dropping low and his eyes searching wildly around the temple.

"Who said that?" he demanded, pivoting around the space in a rush.

When only the rain and roaring wind answered him, Rylan felt the spark of fire magic in him starting to catch. He wanted to see—needed to see—if only to save himself.

::Kenrhysss' promisssed peaccce,:: the voice said again, growing in strength as Rylan's breath caught. He wasn't alone in the temple. He wasn't a priest, but he wasn't alone. He had come into this place for sanctuary and now he would answer to the Gods of his Ancestors that his family had abandoned.

"Who's there?" Rylan demanded, as a howling rush of wind surged into the empty temple.

::He mussst not take hisss own tail,:: the voice answered, and Rylan froze as he realized there was a bright, white spark crackling in the air at the center of the temple. Right where he had been standing before the stone altar. ::Be on your guard, fledgling,:: the voice said, swelling into the vaulted space. ::Only the windsss can sssave you from men ssseeking peaccce.::

Rylan wasn't sure when he fled the temple, but when he stopped he was securely inside his family's old kitchen, door slammed shut behind him. As he leaned on his wings against it, gulping down air to ease his panic, he opened his eyes to realize that the House he had thought empty was anything but.

Worse than that, there was a woman standing over a kettle just three paces from him, gaping as openly as he was to see her there. Something was wrong about her, though.

For one thing, she was short for a Kosaran and for another her pale olive skin looked like it never lost the glow of summer. She also had smoky, blue-grey eyes that could swallow him up with a glance.

"Sera?" He whispered. He had just seen a blicing ghost so now he must be hallucinating. There was no way Sera was in his old House cooking over a kettle big enough to hold stew for twenty people.

"Holy shit, Rylan," Sera swore, setting a wooden ladle to the side as she looked deeper into the House. Seeing no one, she moved towards him, grabbing onto the front of his sodden cloak to drag him away from the door.

"What are you doing here?" she demanded in hushed tones.

Rylan was speechless. Though Sera was usually dressed like a tavern worker in a long woolen tunic with a thick waist belt, she wasn't wearing that now. No, now she was in some sort of court styled bodice made of violet suede with red piping. The shirt she was wearing was red silk, too, and though her hair was still wrapped up in her scarf, it looked styled rather than hidden. She was as formal as Nichi had been to head to the Windover revel, strange as that was. Why, though? What in the winds was she doing here?

"You weren't at the Live Oak," Rylan panted. "The girl said you had gone to the big empty estate and I just... Sera, why aren't you talking to Micah?" he asked, his voice growing louder as his surprise gave way to angry panic. "I thought you were dead!"

The last he said through gritted teeth as she clamped a hand over his mouth to silence him. "I'm not dead," she insisted. "Blood and ice, I told you not to come. I specifically wrote you and told you not to come here. I can handle myself."

Rylan's pleading look finally got her to take her hand off his mouth.

"I haven't gotten a letter from you in moonturns," he said, which seemed to surprise her. "Micah hasn't heard from you in that long, too. Sera, what's going on?"

"We're too far apart right now and every time I go back to the Live Oak, his mind's in a fog," she swore, pulling her wings in tighter. They were in a pantry, he realized. A fully stocked pantry. Granted, the things inside weren't the best quality, but if she had spent so much money on new clothes, why would they be? "It's okay. I'm okay, but you can't be here, Ry. I'm trying to keep these assholes from stealing the House out from under you, but if they find you here, it will just make everything worse. That's why I told you not to come."

"Well, I'm here now," he said, taking hold of her upper arms to stop her from trying to drag him out of the pantry. "Can I at least say sal'weh?"

Angry as she had seemed to have found him on her doorstep, Sera's panic stalled as she saw the hesitant smile he was giving her. A moment more and she threw her arms around his middle, burring her head in his shoulder. Soaking in her warmth, Rylan rested his chin against the top of her head as his world righted itself with her in his arms.

"Sal'weh, sweetness," she murmured, sounding as relieved as he was, if only for the moment. Sera laughed as she squeezed him, not caring about the water on his cloak, but it faded as Rylan released her.

"Gods, but I've missed you," he said, smiling as she reached up to tousle his hair.

"Of course you have, soldier boy," Sera teased, enjoying the mess she had made of his tyro crest.

"I'm not a soldier yet," Rylan countered. "Not until I graduate."

"Then why are you dressed like one, tie-row?" She asked, picking at his flight cloak to see the jacket he wore beneath. His Warhost jacket, she realized, looking up at him with a sudden light in her eyes.

"Tyro," he corrected, grinning as she confirmed everything he was wearing was Warhost gear. "Like the tea Westly makes from all his flowers. Teer-row."

Sera ignored him as she smoothed a hand across his broad chest, chewing her lip. She always did that, always had to be touching him, and he honestly couldn't figure out why. Well, he hadn't been able to until Tyrsten had cornered him and demanded an explanation for where he was going when he snuck out. Rylan had eventually told him, but the fact that he was breaking the rules for a woman made all the sense in the world.

When Tyrsten had asked if they had taken to nest, though, the look of confusion Rylan had given him had Tyrsten doubled over with laughter. He hadn't even realized Sera might feel that way about him—or him her—until Tyrsten had even asked. He then only let Rylan go after he promised the next time he snuck out, he would tell Sera how he felt.

That had been almost six turns ago, but now that he was here his heart was racing as he realized he had to ask her. Coming down here wasn't just about losing contact with her, or his House, or any of it. If Lord Seventh had his way, this might be the last time he could see her before he deployed.

"So are you going to tell me why you're dressed like a Court Daughter or do I have to guess?" He began, pressing into the shelves of the pantry to get a better look at her in the dim light. "Not that I mind."

She really was as beautiful as he had described to Tyrsten, all brilliance and cheeky cleverness while still being able to put him on his wings. Given all that, this bodice just set everything in perfect proportions.

"You better not mind," Sera laughed, hands settling on his arms as she kept close to him. Any further away and her wings would be hanging out of the pantry. "I don't mind if you like it, though."

"I do like it," Rylan said, not about to be distracted. "But I still want to know."

"Stubborn," she accused, tugging at the hem of his jacket. "There were some vets at the Live Oak talking about the House Northern estate a while back. After that letter you sent me about what you wanted to do once you were a soldier, I wanted to see what they were talking about. Someone saw me and asked if I was still running with a crew and when I told them no, they invited me here. More than a few of them have been squatting in the Estate for a while, but it's only because some noble is paying them. I got them to trust me enough to let me cook for them, so I earn my keep. Speaking of which," she said glancing back to her stew. "I was almost done. I need to get it out to them, sweetness, or they'll come get it themselves. You can't be here when they do."

"Why?" Rylan asked, shifting to look as well. "Who is it?"

"It doesn't matter who it is," she said, pressing him back into the pantry. "What matters is that you stay safe and let your Barracks Mother work her magic for you. I can handle myself. Micah isn't the only bard in our family," she reminded. "All it takes is a smile and a little mental nudge and everyone ignores me. If they don't, I send them on their way with a slap, which works well enough. I am done trading flesh for coin and they know it, even if I did turn a pretty copper once."

"You turned over most of it to Wenda, is what you did," Rylan muttered, only to watch as Sera's beautiful smile turned into a scowl.

"Wenda," Sera scoffed, rolling her eyes at the mention of her old crew-leader.

"I'm just lucky that Wenda set such a high price on Micah and I. We wouldn't take anything less than double what my mother pulled. Micah made sure of that."

"That's because you're not a whor—a, uh, courtesan, I mean," Rylan said, nearing embarrassment with the misspoken words. "But you're better than all of that and you know it."

"I only know it because you got us away from that place," Sera smiled, flushing as Rylan watched her. The red scarf she had wrapped around her hair had threads of sapphire in it, making her own blue eyes that much brighter. "With you and Westly, we were happier than at any other time in our lives."

"Which is why I want us back together," Rylan said, changing the subject.

"But it seems like the whole blicing world is against us. Vin has a plan, though."

"So she's Vin now?" Sera smirked. "Have you finally taken your esteemed Barracks Mother to nest to thank her for all her help?"

Rylan nearly choked.

"Hah!" he said, answering her confused look. "Mother is about the last person in the Palace any man could take to nest, second only to the King's Consort."

"Ah, well then," Sera chuckled. "I never thought you'd turn soft for a woman anyway."

Rylan's heart skipped as he realized Sera had given him the perfect opening for Tyrsten's question.

"Well, reputations are distracting," he shrugged, trying to stay casual as his heart raced. "But with so many people out for my head, I haven't had time for anything else."

"I may have noticed," Sera laughed, and the unusual quietness of her tone dared him to hope.

"It's worse now," he persisted. "Lord Seventh named me as one of the two Tyro Primarchs of the bevies that will compete in the war game. If I can win, Mother says it will look good for my request to stay the title to the Estate while I'm at war. Then when I get back, the House can really be ours. I just..." He said, stalling as he watched her face lighting up with glee. "What?"

"You're one of the Bevy Primarchs?" She asked, her voice low and quiet. "You're serious?"

"Well, yeah," he said. "They told us at evening formation. Why?"

"You just made me twenty crowns!" She said, hitting his chest with a laugh. "I put in for a pool at the Live Oak before I left. No one believed me when I said it would be you."

"I still don't believe it's me," he said. "Why did you bet on me?"

Sera's smile nearly stopped his heart. "Because you're brilliant, Rylan. I've told you for cycles and even if you can't see it, everyone else can. Impulsive, but brilliant."

Rylan didn't know what to say. Sera was the brilliant one. He had just forgotten more than the Delton Academy had ever taught him about warfare, tactics, strategy, and the histories of the Seventh Counsel Lords. Staggered as he was by her accusation, Rylan could only watch as her wings shifted and flared as she looked up at him with a pout.

"What, no witty observations?" She chided. "No wonder you don't pull people into your nest."

Rylan could barely hear her for the pounding in his ears.

"I don't want people in my nest," he defended.

"That doesn't mean they don't want in yours," Sera said, her posture changing as he watched. Shoulders back, wings fanned ever so slightly, she looked like an actual Goddess. "There must be plenty of lonely Court daughters ready to nest with a tyro such as yourself."

"Not my type," he insisted, retreating just enough to catch her attention.

She leaned in, looking him in the eyes as she set a hand on his chest with all her casual grace.

"Oh, so you have a type?" She asked. "I would have never known."

"Well, that's understandable," Rylan said, shrugging. "You're one of a kind."

Three heartbeats passed as Sera stared at him, smoldering in her surprise until her olive skin turned a beautiful shade of scarlet. Now Rylan had his answer. The one thing Tyrsten said Rylan had to know before he left for War. If Sera was his reason to make it back, something other than his House or the Seventh's Peace, then she needed to know he felt that way.

"Why in the world didn't you ever say anything!" she accused, embarrassed and flustered at the same time.

"I didn't know!" He said, defending himself as she swatted at him. "Gods, with the life I've led, it's not like I ever had the chance to think about stuff like that. One of my boys, one of the tyros in my squad, he got so mad at me for not telling you that he said he'd drag me here by the downy if I didn't say something the next time I saw you. So I did. I have, I mean. Sera, I think I love you."

That stopped the assault, though her annoyance was still sharp.

"You think?" She scoffed, though there was fondness in it. "You'd burn down this city for me if I asked! That's so much more than love, Rylan. In the Houses they want romance and nonsense, but you've killed men for looking at me wrong when I couldn't do it myself. You traded six cycles of your life to the bloody Warhost just to see me healed. Of course..." She insisted, her whole demeanor softening as she looked up at him. "Of course you love me."

"I would do anything you asked of me," he said, meaning it.

"And I, you," she said, her smile giving over to laughter as she looked at the pantry they stood in. "I mean, I'm not risking my wings in a House full of our old enemies for nothing. I'm doing it for you—for us. I want a life with you, Rylan, and I know how much this place means to you. The only reason you hate it is because it hurt you, but we can fix that. We can make it better. Once you return from war..."

As she faltered, Rylan knew her 'once' was truly an 'if'. There was no guarantee that any of them would make it back. Watching her realize it truly for the first time, Rylan could see how trapped she felt.

"I'll come back," he swore, catching her around the waist before she could flee. "I'll bring all of us back."

"I know you will," she said, putting a hand to her eyes. "Gods, I just—"

She stopped herself as there was a noise near the threshold of the kitchen.

"Kitchen girl!" Called a woman's voice, annoyed. "Where did you go?"

"Sweetness, you have to leave," she whispered, putting her hand over his mouth to stop him from speaking. "Fifty crowns is a lot. Any of them would kill for less than that."

When he nodded, only kissing her palm with the promise, she took her hand back.

As she looked up at him, her eyes suddenly pools of sadness, his heart ached. In her he had found the silence of his hidden shelter, the strength to power away from the Palace grounds, and the undying affection that kept him flying in that downpour. She was the only reason he had to keep going. She always had been, no matter how long he hadn't realized it. He knew it now and she did as well. Seeing that longing reflected back at him, he found the courage to close the distance between them.

Rylan was ecstatic when Sera wrapped her arms around him, dragging him down to kiss her a second time and a third. He hadn't been joking when he said she wielded her wiles like a weapon and as she unleashed it on him he could have died happy. But as they came up for air, Rylan stopped to feel her putting a hand back across his lips as she panted. When he closed his eyes, going completely still, she pulled up his flight hood and grabbed a bag of salt from the shelf next to them, moving out of the pantry with her game face on. She hadn't been talking to anyone at all.

"I'm here," Sera said, raising the salt as proof of why she had wandered off. "Did you mean to help me bring it out to serve?"

Whoever had come in to ask after her scoffed. "No," she said, already turning away. "Just get it ready. They're going to want to celebrate after this meeting is done."

"Of course," Sera said, throwing her voice just enough to let Rylan know it was safe to leave.

Rylan didn't say val'weh as he slipped out the door, though he caught Sera's smile as she watched him go. He also didn't get back on the wind given the lightning he had seen earlier. Instead, he stayed on foot, moving around the building to see if he could figure out where this supposed 'meeting' was happening. It didn't take him long, given how he could see from the light pouring from the window that had once led into his father's study.

Moving up to the window, Rylan dropped his wings to disguise his shape and peered inside, glad for the break in the glass that allowed him to hear what was being said inside.

"We only have a fortnight left to wait," came an excited voice as someone closed the door to the study from the outside. "Lord Dobren says that the period to claim the Estate is going to lapse before winter and then we can make the petition."

There was a pause as several bodies moved into the room. "Oren, Ulyn, I told you idiots to go get the food. This shouldn't take long and I'm blicing starving."

Rylan froze to hear those names, caught between fear and a sudden, blinding rage as he recognized his elder brother's voice. Dylan was inside the house.

"Are you sure we should even talk about moving the crews right now?" Said a new voice, older and female. That was Wenda. Wenda had effectively owned Sera and Micah before Rylan had persuaded them to abandon their mother's brothel and join up with him. As far as Rylan knew, Wenda was still keeping a tally on how much Rylan had cost her for the loss of her blue-eyed twins.

"It's now or never," Dylan went on, pacing before the hearth. "We're moving the rest of the crews into the House when the Court changes over. No one will notice another hundred more folks moving things out of the streets if we do it right."

They were moving into the House? All of them?

"What makes you think we can pull this off?" Asked another voice, echoed by the grunts of at least four more. Rylan recognized this voice as well. Was everyone beyond the wall a crew leader? Were they actually negotiating with one another? Banding together like... like civilized people?

"House Northern abandoned the Estate nearly a cycle and a day ago," Dylan said. "But House Kirath needs an Estate on Delton in order to petition for a patent of nobility here. If I secure the Estate, they've agreed to adopt me as a Son and let anyone I approve into the new House."

"Do you even have a claim to this place?" Wenda asked.

"It's my fucking House," Dylan shot back. "I'm the only Son left who hasn't died at war or married into another family, so I'm the only one with rights to it still," Dylan insisted, though he hedged under Wenda's stare. "I've also had people living here long enough to argue I'm in possession of it again, so yes, I do. Legally, I do."

"What about your brother?" she challenged. "Rylan?"

There was true fire in his brother's eyes at just the mention of Rylan's name. "Either the War kills him or I do," Dylan said, his voice hard and cold. "Lord Dobran only wants him to live long enough to graduate so the price will drop at the sale. If they let one exiled Son have it for that price, they'll have to let me have it for the same."

"Can't you just enlist as well?" someone asked, though Rylan couldn't see who it was. "Join the host and serve a three-cycle rotation? If it'll drop the price by five thousand crowns-"

The man's voice cut off at the look of pure murder in Dylan's eyes. Of all the things not even Rylan talked about with his brothers, it was why they had failed the exams when Rylan hadn't.

"Only being a Seventh's man drops the price," Dylan said, his voice dangerously quiet. "And you only get to serve Lord Seventh if you can hear the warbards."

"And you can't?" This time it was Wenda again, unflinching.

"Ten of my uncles, my father, and six of my brothers have all failed that fucking exam," Dylan said, turning on her as his wings flared. "Which means they paid off everyone in that Palace to keep us from being officers until my family raised the coin to pay a canto double what he was getting in order to pass Rylan. But not a cycle after passing, Rylan threw a tantrum that nearly burned down this Estate. He's been dead to all of us since he proved he was a sorcerer and I will kill the corpse that still walks to take back my House. Got that?"

The silence in the room confirmed that they did.

As Dylan went on with his planning, Rylan tasted bile. If that was the lie Dylan was telling himself, fine, but it was still a lie. Rylan *could* hear the cantos and he always could, though no one in his family had believed him. They had just assumed he couldn't like the five generations of men before him. If the cantos had been paid off to let him into the academy, though, that price might have actually bankrupted the House...

But with the financial backing of another House, Dylan would be in a position to buy it back. The only reason Rylan had any chance of making the claim was because of his Barracks Mother, wasn't it? She was from a House as well and had the money to move into this place herself after the title was settled. She would hold it in trust for Rylan until he returned from war, setting up a Library to rival the Seventh Counsel Lord's own with the books Vinicia had saved from his family's collection. Other than Sera, this Estate was the only reason he had to graduate at all.

"So who's in?" Dylan asked.

Picking himself up in silence, Rylan shifted to get a better look through the warped glass that had betrayed their meeting. As he memorized their faces in the dim light, his anger roiled inside of him. Dylan with his lethal self-confidence, Wenda with her arms crossed under her sagging chest and all the others swaying to take the risk...

Rylan's vision went red with the influx of light as someone shifted, but he refused to look away. As the silence grew heavy among them, the air around Rylan grew still and he focused on the roaring flame of the hearth.

If only it were larger, he thought. *If only it was reaching out towards them, consuming them and everything else inside. That would solve everything. The only thing that kept that fire controlled was the stone hearth and in their hubris they had built it so large already. Fire to consume them. To brand them as vipers.*

Desperation fueled his need and the hatred he felt twisted with his desire for the roaring flame to consume them where they stood.

Rylan inhaled deeply as he felt an icy sensation creeping up the back of his legs. Strangely, the higher the ice moved, the brighter the flame burned, but he wasn't about to question it. He flinched when a sharp pain shot up his neck and across his shoulders, but he couldn't stop now. The more he focused, the more it burned. Burned and grew and strained until, all at once, the fire in the hearth exploded with power, sending flames out in a violent arc across the room.

Rylan staggered away from the window as the scream of panic and pain roared up on the other side. As much as he reveled in it, a part of him was fighting against the chill he had brought down on himself with its making. Worse, as he tried to move, he realized that he was as stiff and frozen as Sera when she had been caught out in the Ice Winds.

Blood and ice, not again...

Even if Rylan's talent for fire-starting had saved his life more often than not, whenever he manipulated something too large this backlash happened. Though he would never admit it, a fire larger than his fist still terrified him and he knew that was part of the problem.

He had started the fire that burned the estate after Dylan had first abandoned him to the family, and the ice in his veins now was almost as bad.

Despite everything, though, Rylan had never thought to want a fire as badly as he had wanted it now and even if had sucked the life out of him in the process, he wouldn't have cared. Like some story of the fae, he had called to the fire and it had answered. He would do it again in a heartbeat, too, having managed some portion of revenge on the men who thought to ruin the very last part of his life before the streets.

And then in a small corner of his mind, Rylan realized that the fire was spreading like it had in his youth. Unconfined by the hearth, the fire was lapping at the walls of the room and people were tearing down the curtains to smother it. His cover gone, Rylan staggered back to feel the press of heat reaching through the glass, only to have one of his knees buckle. He would have fallen on his wings if it hadn't been for a sudden, icy burst of wind keeping him upright.

Staring through the glass, Rylan gaped as he realized the tone of the crew's screaming had changed. Given all the people, they had managed to put out most of the fire, but now there was something else. Rylan couldn't hear what they said, but he could hear Dylan's bellowing response.

"He's right fucking there!" he said, pointing straight at the window. "Get him, you idiots!"

Rylan managed to pull his mind out of its fog just as Chaes and Uln came bursting out of a side exit of the house. Despite his cold, despite every bit of reason he had, Rylan's anger flared again. It wasn't enough, though. His body was moving in slow motion, frozen in ice, and when his brother's crewmen neared, Rylan swung his fist only to swear as it was caught mid-swing. Instead a hand crashed into the left side of his face and he went down hard.

"Did you hear the plan, little brother?" Dylan laughed, moving to stand over Rylan's body as Chaes and Uln stepped on Rylan's wings to hold him in place.

Rylan couldn't say a word, his jaw clenched against the ice burning in his veins as he tried to call the fire again. Call to it and kill Dylan once and for all.

"Did you realize there's a bounty on your head, too?" he asked, looking up between his two boys. "I say we play a little catch and release. We'll beat the shit out of him and then take him to the Guard. Then they'll give me fifty crowns for turning you in and beat the shit out of you some more. If you can still fly when they're done with you, maybe you can try and graduate, but if you can't... The House is mine," he said, laughing. "If you can, then you better believe I will be the first man in line to put a knife in your back. An unmarried bowen's inheritance falls to his next-eldest brother but it would save my friends a lot of coin if you died a soldier, rather than a blicing tyro."

Rylan meant to swear at him, meant to say anything at all, but as he opened his mouth to speak, Dylan knelt down, his fist already headed for Rylan's face. As Rylan's vision filled with stars, he was hit again, and then a kick knocked the wind out of him, leaving him gasping for air as his vision went black.

Chapter 04: Kiernan

Wednesday, 23:00

Kiernan came awake with a start, surprised he had been able to sleep for all the roaring of the Warhost in the back of his mind. Glad to be conscious once again if only so he could finish reviewing the tyro reports, he remembered he had wanted to speak to Lenae before it was too late. Finding the strength to stand despite muscles gone stiff in the cold room, Kiernan rose to move towards the common area of the suite of apartments that he shared with Sixth Counsel Lord Hest'lre. From there, he went towards the double doors to the ante-chamber, only to find the formal entrance already propped open.

That, and the current Primarch of his fumentari was peering into the cavernous Sires' Wing with his hands braced on the balcony railing as his second rolled his eyes. For all that Kreychi had said about the Home Guard men being ready to mutiny, Kiernan could trust that these two had loyalties only for him. Kreychi had vetted them personally on the Plains and they had followed him back to attend his Seat as his personal guard. In the seasons since, they had served as some of his most trusted allies.

As Kiernan walked past the threshold of the suite's main entrance, both men came to rigid attention. No matter the darkness of his own suite, the massive crystal roof that capped the vaulted ceiling of the Sires' Wing let in a spectacular view of the moonlight that bathed the mountain peak now that the storm had passed. Given all the white marble that lined the walls, most of it taken from the mountains deeper into the Kihara range, it was an almost supernatural trick of light that the area was so brightly lit with so few lanterns.

Moving out into the Wing properly, Kiernan glanced down through the balconies that allowed entrance to the other suites until he saw the commotion that had drawn his Primarch's attention as he had walked out.

"My Lord Seventh," Primarch Henrick greeted, saluting with his right fist to his left breast. Across from him, Henrick's partner, First Praetor Lyonel, did the same, straightening as he did so. Kiernan returned both men's salute with one of his own before they relaxed.

His curiosity sated for the moment, Kiernan shifted back to see the two men, still surprised by the immaculate black uniforms. Unlike Kreychi's own fitted leather, the clothes they wore as part of his Shadow Guard fumentari was all relaxed black leather, though instead of the gold piping that declared his House allegiance, the left forearm and right calf of these men's uniforms were decorated with seven cloth-of-silver slashes that marked them as his Shadow Guard. They had heavy braided warcrests as well, both decorated with an unmistakable number of metal bands throughout that marked their own personal acts of valor throughout their Warhost service. Given how clean it all was, though, it wrankled Kiernan to no end.

These were the men who had fought and nearly died for him just to take one of his most ambitious Lan'lieanan assassins into custody not but four cycles ago. Most ambitious, if only because she was one of the sorcerous loralae who had been trained by some unknown allies of Lan'lieana to move unseen through his camp and catch him unguarded in his own tent. Having managed to survive such overwhelming odds, Kiernan had made the woman a sort of tribute to the crown, though he did allow Lord Fifth access to her so she might be a case study in the type of women who had brought the Kirathy shelf to its knees with the Fall.

Despite all of that, the only thing Henrick and Lyonel wore now that showed their true experience were the bruised rank pauldrons strapped over the Court finery. Made of a hardened leather that covered their left breast from neck to shoulder, the leather capped their bicep and then carried on in bands down to just above their elbow. The largest piece of the arm was embossed with a soft copy of the quicksilver dragon that was Kiernan's heraldry as Seventh. Given his greater rank as Primarch, Henrick's pauldron had the addition of a metal quicksilver riveted to the center of the leather that covered his chest to mark him as Kiernan's personal cadre.

Kiernan envied them both, since his own clothing and pauldron looked nothing like the armor the two men wore. Instead, his fitted indigo leather was covered by a set of silken kama that honored his Seat-Founder and all the men who had come before him.

Though the story itself was lost to myth and legend, the Warhost remembered that they had entered these mountains wearing the voluminous pleated pants and wide-sleeved, cross-body tunics of their ancestors. They wore the same clothing now whenever they were at Court, even if they also wore their more modern War Plains uniform beneath. Given Kiernan's position and connection with Founder Noventrio, it was his duty to bring an end to that war with the collected wisdom of those same ancestors.

Thus, the massive Library to his right and the fact that he was expected to be in the formal kama more often than not.

Compared to Lyonel and Henrick, he felt as if he was swimming in a sea of indigo silk. The movements of his legs were all but hidden by the swishing fabric and if he crossed his arms, he could have hidden a short bow within the wide sleeves of the tunic. The sculpted quicksilver of his Counsel Lord's pauldron kept at least the left sleeve tamed with the strap around his bicep, though he still had to fight with the two straps that crossed over his chest to hold it in place.

It wasn't uncomfortable, but it did limit the movement of his arm to some extent. Or maybe the kama did? His whole Seat had been strangling him for so long that he honestly wasn't sure.

Still, Kiernan had always liked the idea of the Seventh's Pauldron when he had been in the Legions, though after so many cycles wearing it he was just as often irritated by it. There was just something unnerving about the heraldry of a Seat-Founder clinging to his arm, always waiting for its chance to glare disapprovingly if Kiernan looked to the left.

"Henrick," Kiernan acknowledged, forcing himself into good humor as he brought his right arm up to tap his fist against his shoulder in a flourish of indigo silk. "Lyonel."

But just as he took his salute back, releasing the men from their braced attention, a scream sounded from the mass of Courtiers below. Not a scream; a shriek? "It's a bit late for trouble, isn't it?"

"Not for the younger court, Lord Seventh," Henrick answered, and his seriousness broke as he grinned. "One of the Daughters from a Yaltanan house has been berating one of the Alexandrian soldier-tyros for a good five beats. We can't tell who he is, but the Daughters are in a tizzy and the girl is clear out of her mind."

"It's his own fault," Lyonel observed, setting his hand to his collar bone to do his best impression of a distraught Court Daughter. "They were promised and still he was faithless. Taking one of the Sons as a wingmate was all well and good, but to nest with one of the other Daughters? And from a first tier House?!"

Kiernan let his amusement show as Lyonel's theatre came to an end. "Only the best intelligence from you two, I see."

Lyonel gave a trouper's flamboyant bow, wingtips fluttering as his hand rolled to touch the ground with a flourish.

"Did you see Heir Kreychi among them?" Kiernan asked, unable to keep the laughter out of his voice.

"Hoi, Lord Seventh," Henrick said. "When Heir Kreychi left, he returned to the Windover suite, but someone must have called for him since he came out a few moments later. From the way he dove into the crowd you'd have thought he was still our Primarch."

"Well, I do need to get to the entrance of the Royal's Wing," Kiernan said, sighing. "And they are gathered just where I mean to go. Perhaps I can scare them off and give Kreychi some assistance?"

Henrick and Lyonel came to attention as Kiernan looked out into the Sires' Wing once again. Kiernan had been attempting to stay in and around his Counsel Lord's suite until Graduation, but if he was going to move among the courtiers, he might as well not be seen as hiding.

"You're a braver man than I, Lord Seventh," Henrick said, though Kiernan could only shrug. Bravery was facing a Lan'lieanan in single, ground-based combat. This Court drama was intellectual torture. As far as he cared, the younger court's proclivity towards coupling produced soldiers for the Legions and pleasure in the process. Whose nest you shared only became important if you were the heir to a noble House.

"We'll be shadowing you, then?" Lyonel asked, respectfully imposing himself. "Lord Sixth did say to, ah, 'not let you wander off again' before he left for the Lower City."

"Hest'lre would say that," Kiernan said, looking back to his men with a laugh. "I suppose the three of us will be more imposing than just myself," he relented. "And Kreychi will doubtless appreciate it."

"Hoi, Lord Seventh," Henrik agreed, leading the way towards the end of the Sires' Wing where the railing opened at the corner.

From this vantage Kiernan could see all eighteen stories of the apartments and suites which housed the Courtiers during the summer fighting season when the Warhost was largely in Kirath. Given that the winter was upon them, all the finery was about to be traded for the uniforms of his own officers as they prepared for the next fighting season under a new Seventh, but for now it was all merriment and ignorance of the changes to come. They had two more days of revelry until the Graduation Tournament and then they would all vacate the Palace and return to their Estates, either on Mount Delton or the other cities throughout the mountain range.

"Into the breech, boys," Kiernan said, exhaling a weary laugh as he unfolded his wings and dove into the open space. There were three white landing mosaics he could use, and since the path to all of them was clear, he and his two shadows took the one closest to the commotion.

To say they were noticed as they backwinged onto the flight circle in unison was an understatement. With his seven black wing-bars and two fumentari shadows, the courtiers scrambled to make space despite the lounges on the ground floor of the Sires' Wing. Usually the collections were meant to host groups as they met for drinks or other entertainment, but given that the two young courtiers had been called out by Heir Kreychi near to the flight circle itself, the space for folks to gather and gawk was rather impressive.

Once they landed, Kiernan refolded his wings with emphasis, letting his shadows take their place at the edge of the still-growing crowd. As more than one courtier closed their wings to not risk drawing Kiernan's attention, the hysterical Court Daughter swallowed her tongue.

"Heir Kreychi," Kiernan greeted, extending his hand with all the formality expected between an Alexandrian House Prince and a King's Counsel Lord. "What seems to be the cause for alarm?"

"Simply a misunderstanding of etiquette, Counsel Lord," Kreychi greeted, grasping his forearm in return. "These two were in the process of making their apologies. Isn't that right?"

Kiernan turned his look from Kreychi to the cause of the commotion. On the right was a Court Daughter in such a deep curtsy she might as well have been kneeling before Kiernan and Kreychi both. Of greater interest was the eye-straining chartreuse gown she wore, which was far too cumbersome for flight and marked her as minor nobility.

On the left was a young man Kiernan easily recognized, given the boy's long-held position as the Tyro Primarch within the Soldier Tyro program. As Tyrsten snapped to attention, Kiernan looked him over. Though the young man might not know it, Kreychi had brought him to Kiernan's attention long before Headmaster-Counsel Lord Aaron had recommended him for his current rank among the Tyro Legion. The boy was cunning as any other Windover Kiernan had ever known, but apparently Tyrsten also had a gift for navigating wounded prides and unbridled passions that had reminded Kreychi of Kiernan himself.

Unfortunately, Tyrsten was decidedly out of uniform at the moment, dressed in the same fitted black leather doublet of Windover, if trimmed in the more familiar Illiandrian blue. Then again, if the graduation tournament was to happen in three days, then this was their revelry night, so he supposed he didn't have to lean quite so hard on the lad.

"A simple misunderstanding, My Lord Seventh," Tyrsten answered tactfully. "She believed I had the privilege to promise a ring."

"And what did you do to discourage her belief?" Kreychi asked flatly.

"Nothing, Heir," Tyrsten admitted, glancing away from Kiernan as his tone gained a hint of fear.

"So her anger is justified?" Kreychi pressed.

"Hoi, Heir," he said.

Kiernan examined the tyro with thought. "How long did you manage this?" He asked, neutral despite his honest curiosity.

"Over a cycle, My Lord Seventh," Tyrsten admitted and there was an uncanny light in his eye.

No wonder the girl had turned into a screeching harpy, Kiernan thought, managing not to chuckle as the Daughter, still in her curtsey, shook with rage. Given the encouraged promiscuity of the younger Court, exclusive pairings with anyone—especially a soldier tyro—was taboo. Kiernan had violated that particular norm himself, surviving as an unattached figure of state only because his own celibacy was a ruse.

Fortunately, the Court could neither substantiate the rumor that he had long made a cuckold of King Braeden or the one that he had taken his famed Lan'lieanan prisoner to nest, only one of which was true.

"I am glad we were able to clear the air," Kiernan concluded, looking to Kreychi with a nod. "You'll see to the rest?"

"Hoi, My Lord Seventh," Heir Kreychi responded and gave a veteran's salute despite his status at Court. As the other nearby veterans did the same, Kiernan put his right fist to his left breast and dismissed them all with an upward palm and sweep of his arm.

"It would be unwise to come to my attention again, tyro," Kiernan added as Tyrsten remained at braced attention. "You wouldn't want to know what happens to men who disobey my direct order."

As Tyrsten reset his salute, Kiernan raised an eyebrow at the girl, who dissolved into a gaggle of her friends with the dismissal.

"If that is all," Kiernan began, his shadows closing around him once more as the last of the Windovers scattered.

"A word, My Lord Seventh?" Kreychi said as Kiernan looked towards the Royal's Wing.

"Walk with me," Kiernan prompted. He would never turn away the man's company, but whatever this was, it was all for politics and not pleasure.

"Thank you, Ser," he said, still formal despite the history between them. As more than one of the courtiers they passed began to eavesdrop, Kiernan gestured for him to continue. If Kreychi wanted this bit of information to be public, Kiernan respected his choice. "I wish to request an audience with your Chiurgeon Westly su'Kelsineah, if you would allow it. I have it on good authority that Second Counsel Lord Gallen will object to this request, but we are at our wit's end. The Palace chiurgeons under his command have no answer for us, but we must continue to try."

"And so you wish to talk to my dryad-kin," Kiernan finished, coming to a stop a few paces away from the entrance to the Royal's Wing. Former primarch or not, Hest'lre's palace guards knew that Kreychi was a civilian now. He could only enter the suite if sent for, not as a guest of Kiernan's.

As for the Chiurgeons' Counsel Lord, Gallen would be more than displeased, but young Westly had only tended the glass garden while he had been at the Palace. He was only under Kiernan's protection because of the bigotry of some of the chiurgeons in residence against Westly's kindred talents.

"Only by your leave, My Lord Seventh," Kreychi insisted.

"The young man wears his own Bloodcloak," Kiernan reminded, glancing to the entrance of the Royal's Wing once again. "He does not need my permission to work with you, nor do you need my permission to speak with him."

"While that is true," Kreychi agreed, realizing Kiernan's impatience. "I would rather not upset the chiurgeons of my House with the asking. Your blessing should help me better navigate the issues that will arise."

"Then you have my blessing," Kiernan said, as if the words were magic.

"Windover is in your debt, Counsel Lord," Kreychi said, reaching into one of the pockets of his doublet before offering his hand.

"Only because you insist on it," Kiernan acknowledged, gripping Kreychi's hand. In the press, he felt the token that was the boon that Kreychi had requested, a small stamped piece of silver with the Windover House crest. "Good winds to you, Heir Kreychi," Kiernan said in parting.

Hand still gripped in Kiernan's own, Kreychi's eyes narrowed as he saw a courier coming towards him with a hurried step. "Heir Kreychi?" the man echoed, stopping to salute Kiernan and Kreychi both. "I have a letter for you from Lord Sixth. I was told the matter was of the utmost urgency."

"I'll take it, then," Kreychi said.

The letter exchanged, the courier saluted once again and then turned to be on his way. Curious, Kreychi looked to Kiernan as he opened it. Hest'lre had been known to send messages to Kreychi that were actually meant for Kiernan, if only to be certain Kiernan would read them. With a moment to glance at the writing, Kreychi handed the note over without a word.

It was from Hest'lre, that much he could tell from the script, but the words it contained were a dagger in Kiernan's pride.

❦

Your little idiot is in the High Cells.
You owe me fifty crowns to pay my men.
Lucien has cleared the Cells for you.

❦

Kiernan refolded the letter as his heart started to race.

"Do you need an escort somewhere?" Kreychi asked, seeing Kiernan pale as he looked between the entrance to the Royal's Wing and the exit from the Sires' Wing.

"It seems I need to speak with Lord Eighth before I speak with Lenae," Kiernan said, as if nothing was wrong. "Henrick and Lyonel will serve as my guard. Get back to your nest, Kreya," he added quietly. "I will be fine."

"You will not be fine," the man insisted sharply, one hand up to stall Kiernan's shadows from joining them. "If you do not take care of yourself, you will be worse than fine."

"I—" Kiernan began, only to have his breath catch as Kreychi set a hand on his arm before he could respond. The hard grip was nearly enough to make him wince, though it buckled his nerve faster than anything else. "I hear you, Kreya. Come..." he said, his will breaking for all the fire of purpose in his old wingmate's look. "Come find me with the dawn. The Gods seem to be keeping me from speaking with Lenae, but I would speak with you again if it can be managed."

"Your will is my own, Lord Seventh," Kreychi said, releasing his arm with the dismissal. "I will see you at dawn."

Gods be good, Kiernan sighed, letting Kreychi step out of his way and out of his thoughts for the moment. *Rylan, if you would just keep your head down this could be over for both of us that much faster. The more you fight me, the more chances they will have to realize what I am doing and we may both end up dead.*

"Lord Seventh?" Primarch Henrick asked, coming up on his right side.

"Follow me," Kiernan replied, stepping off as the two men fell in beside him.

Given how close the entrance to the Royal's Wing was to the Sires' Wing, they had a short walk to reach the Long Hall. Pausing to make certain the path was clear, Kiernan started across the marble hallway with the same intensity, leaving the two men in his wake for a heartbeat before they were with him once again. Recognizing his formal kama and the quicksilver rank pauldron, the four men guarding the thresholds to the Sires' Wing and the Hall of Justice directly across from it came to rigid attention as he passed.

"Wings up!"

Kiernan gave them a curt nod as he moved onto the long stretch of rugs which buffeted the sounds of their footfalls as they strode down the empty corridor. When they finally reached the end of the hallway, now halfway across the Palace from where he had been in his own suite, he came to a stop before a large circular desk.

Having seen him coming, the night bailiff was already on his feet.

"My Lord Seventh," the man said, right hand to his left shoulder in salute. "The Cells have been cleared of all but the one who was brought in and your Loralae, who cannot be moved."

"Not without my approval, no," Kiernan said, returning the man's salute. "Are you showing me down?"

"No, Ser," the man said. "Lord Sixth said to allow you the Cells in privacy."

"As you were, then," Kiernan said, taking the keys the man offered. "Are you coming with me?" he added, glancing back to Henrick and Lyonel.

"We made a blood oath to never leave you alone with that woman, Ser," Henrick said for both of them. "If she is there, we will be as well."

"Come on, then," Kiernan said, sighing as he started towards the iron door to the High Cells. "I don't have all night."

After a slow decent down ten stories into the bedrock of the Palace Shelf, they reached the first level of the holding areas that served the Palace and the Halls of Justice. This deep into the mountain, it took a trick of engineering to allow in fresh water and clean air, but their Founders had managed it. Letting Henrick and Lyonel each pick up one of the daystar lanterns, Kiernan passed by the empty guard station and started after the heavy iron locks with his set of keys.

Once that was closed behind the three of them, it was another two doors before Kiernan rounded a corner to where the true Cells began.

"Are you here to talk to her or...?"

Henrick's words fell away as Kiernan handed him the keys, moving before the first set of bars that held his Val'Kyr prisoner. They had apparently placed Rylan across the hall from her, likely thinking it poignant to make him stand between two people he was certain wanted him dead, but he ignored it all the same. Gestures were fine; a dagger slipped into his pocket to give him one last warning was the only thing he feared right now.

After confirming the woman was asleep, Kiernan turned to Rylan, arms crossed over his chest. It took a moment for Henrick and Lyonel to hang their lanterns on the hooks in the stone wall, but once they did it put Rylan in a pool of light through the bars of his cell. Seeing him, though, made Kiernan grimace. The boy looked as if he had fallen down the mountain face first.

"On your feet, Tyro," Lyonel barked when Rylan made no move to stand. Before the young man could say anything in response, Kiernan raised a hand to call off the First Praetor. Given his injuries, Kiernan would not insist on formalities.

"Tell me, Rylan," Kiernan said evenly. "Were you so eager to begin the Tournament that you could not wait four days?"

The heat of Rylan's stare was impressive.

"Fuck you, Ser," Rylan said, pressing his wings back into the wall to sit up straighter. "And fuck your tournament."

"Tyro!" Henrick snapped, taking a step closer to the cell.

Kiernan's raised hand stopped him as it had stopped Lyonel.

"That tournament is the only hurdle you have left before you graduate," Kiernan reminded, patient in the face of the young man's anger. "If you do not want to be here, finish and be gone."

"If it wasn't for you, I wouldn't be here at all, you asshole," Rylan said, furious as he wrapped an arm around his torso to brace against some unseen pain. "I never wanted to be here and yet—"

"And yet the reports I have from Counsel Lord Hewn say differently," Kiernan said, cutting off the young man. "Rylan su'Delton, last son of House Northern and yet the first in five generations to dominate his warrior's flight," he quoted from memory. "Full of cunning and fire, he was as promising as he was eager to prove himself. He will be an officer without peer, honoring both his House and the Seat itself with a gravitas our line has not known in an age."

"Some gravitas if they let men like you sit on the Seat," Rylan scoffed, looking away from Kiernan as he did so.

Kiernan's steady gaze never faltered. "The Founder of my Seat is the God of your Ancestors, son. If He wants you for His purpose, there is no force in this world that can stop Him," Kiernan said evenly. "Though you may test the truth of my words at your leisure."

"Some warpriest you are," Rylan challenged, dodging all of it. "Two cycles I've fled this Palace and it takes until now to catch me?"

"You alone may understand just how easily I could have you brought back to this place because of our Founder's blessing," Kiernan countered, his look hard. "The only way out of the Host is to pass through it, tyro," he added quietly. Dangerously. "Has your time in this academy taught you nothing?"

"For the thousandth time, no!" Rylan spat, suddenly pushing to his feet. Pain or no, Rylan threw himself at the bars, slamming his hands against it as he screamed. "Everything I ever needed to know about the Warhost I learned from my House! Everything this blicing academy teaches is why we will never win! We can't, not even if all the men in Kosar served you at once. But you still fight them," he said, gesturing beyond Kiernan to where he could hear the Lan'lieanan prisoner stirring from her sleep. "What did she ever do to you, huh? What makes it okay to trap her in this place? To trap me for not wanting to murder women who have never done anything to me at all?"

Now the woman truly was awake, swearing under her breath as she lifted her head to see what was causing such a commotion. Kiernan kept his eyes on Rylan, not about to stop the tirade. He had wanted the young man to hate him and it was a confirmation of his efforts with the venom Rylan showed now.

"Maybe she has a home you're keeping her from, too," Rylan went on, seething. "All I ever wanted was the scrap of a family I actually managed to have after I was thrown out of Northern. All Sera ever needed was to be healed, but now you're holding her hostage. For what? For me?" He accused. "What did I ever do to you to end up in a *cage*?"

Kiernan was impressed. This was the hate he had seen beneath the surface of Rylan's look when he had accepted the position of Bevy Primarch this afternoon. No matter his physical pain or emotional fury, Rylan was ravenous both for an answer and for revenge. It had taken two cycles to get the boy to this place, but now he was perfect. Rylan was absolutely perfect.

"Responde puero, Draco Dominus," said an irritated voice from behind him. "Conatur ad somnum." *Answer the boy, Dragon Lord. I was trying to sleep.*

Kiernan didn't have to look to know his Lan'lieanan prisoner was speaking to him. Of all the men on this shelf, he was one of the few who was fluent in the only language she would ever use. The Old Tongue was close to the dryad language after all and the woman had been taught her loralae sorcery by dryads.

Realizing the woman had spoken, Rylan's attention shifted to her. Silent as she moved, she had come to her feet and was standing just behind Kiernan at the bars of her own cell.

Taking a breath, Kiernan stepped back to see them both at once as Henrick and Lyonel moved onto the balls of their feet. They had no idea the woman was harmless, but given her reputation, they didn't trust her. She still looked every bit the berserk Val'Kyr assassin who had come after him four cycles ago on the War Plains. Shorter than Kiernan by almost a hand and a half, she still wore the rags of pants and a knee-length kurta, which was a tight fitted dress with an open back that had to be frigid in the Kosaran winters. Her hair had grown nearly to her waist in the time no one had trusted her with a knife and the mess of around her face just brought out her sapphire eyes that much more.

"Have you considered my offer?" Kiernan asked, speaking the Old Tongue to keep the words between the two of them.

"I would rather kill you here and take my chances through the War Plains than set foot inside that dryad forest ever again," she said, rolling her eyes.

"And I still have just as much reason to kill you as this one does," she said, gesturing to Rylan.

"He has reason enough," Kiernan answered, shrugging. "I made certain of that."

"You're worse than a Great Tor Mother," the woman scoffed. "You do realize that if he leaves this place, you'll have yet another man hunting your wings. Is that what you want? More assassins? You do not have to torture a fledgling for that, Dragon Lord. Release me and I will end you properly."

Kiernan narrowed his eyes at her.

"Or I could teach him," she went on, smirking as she looked at Rylan. "This one has a talent for fire-starting and I still remember my spells, even if you stole my focus stone. I am not as harmless as you believe."

"If you do not come with me on Envoy, you will be left at Lord Fifth's mercy," Kiernan said, ignoring her threats. "I can at least give you the chance to go home. Take me as a prisoner when you cross the front, I don't care. All I ask is that I am able to speak with your Matriarch. We can end this. Our people do not need to fight any longer."

Lora's sputtered laughter was apparently too much.

"What are you saying?" Rylan demanded in Kosaran. "What are you two blicing talking about?"

"He wants to go all the way to Lieana," Lora said, answering the boy even if he couldn't understand her. "Thinks he'll survive more than the time it takes to shear off his wings and hang them in Tor'Nihil. For all you've done, Dragon Lord," she cackled as Kiernan rolled his eyes. "I could bring them your wings and be forgiven my mother's exile. I could be forgiven having a Blackwing as a father, even. Twenty cycles hunting you on the War Plains and I could live with such Honor and Glory that even your Host would sing my praises."

Kiernan closed his eyes, covering his face with a hand. When he had calmed himself, he looked up again to see Rylan watching him.

"Know this, tyro," Kiernan said, ignoring the laughter of the woman behind him. "There is only one choice for a man who serves the Host and that is either to bend to my will or be bent by it."

That got the boy's attention.

"If I do no other thing before I leave on Envoy," he went on, the threat thick in the air between them. "I will make you understand at least that much."

With that, Kiernan had one parting glance for the Lan'lieanan and then pivoted to leave. Henrick and Lyonel fell in behind him, opening and closing the doors as they made their way back to the start of the High Cells. Kiernan outpaced them as they turned over the keys, the Warhost coming to life in his mind, feeding and fueling on his anger as he stalked through the Palace. The courtiers he passed were a silent blur, and he was glad when he found the doors to his suite already open.

Once inside, Kiernan came back to himself in a rush, realizing he was alone in the darkness of his room. Henrick and Lyonel were gone, which meant he had somehow ghosted his two best shadows and in doing so…Kiernan grimaced as he reached into the pocket of his doublet and flinched to discover three sharpened daggers waiting for him. Someone had gotten close to him, three someones to be exact, and if he had doubted it before, he was certain now.

The scrawled engraving of his name on the blade told him he was marked. The 'seven' on the other side made their message clear. They would kill him if he didn't stay to lead the Warhost. They didn't care at all that staying would kill him just as fast as the men themselves. Anger flooded him as he stared at the crude markings and he made a fist around the handles of the blades.

With his other hand he took hold of the hawkeye pendant around his neck that was the symbol of his Seventh's Seat and cut the leather cord he had worn without fail for the past seven cycles. Once he was free, he threw all of it as hard as he could against the map of the War Plains with a scream of sobbing rage. As the token of his Seat and two daggers scattered behind his desk, he flinched when he heard the third strike true. It sent a shiver down his spine to watch the blade slip out of the wood and the sound of it hitting the stone nearly did him in. After all he had done for Kosar, everywhere he looked there were people that wanted him dead.

Worse, somewhere in this Palace the woman he loved was trapped in a cage far stronger than the bars of the High Cells, put there by the Gods themselves. In order to be released from her duty to their King, Kiernan had to make peace with Lan'lieana. If he could bring back a Lan'lieanan woman to be Braeden's queen, the two of them could finally be done with the War, but without a guide—without any instruction on the politics of a Lan'lieanan court—he might as well be committing suicide like everyone before him.

But still he persevered. If this was the way the world treated men who truly wanted to help, he would make certain his Seventh's Peace brought both Kosar and Lan'lieana to their knees. By the end of this, by the end of everything, the Gods themselves would beg his forgiveness as the whole world burned.

Chapter 05: Rylan

Thursday, 00:30

"I'm not an idiot," Rylan insisted, matching the dark skinned Lan'lieanan woman across the hall from him gaze for gaze. "I know you two were talking about me. What did you say? Did he answer my question?"

The woman didn't respond, just tilted her head to the side as if his words confused her. Or was she confused why Rylan was talking to her? Either way, he wasn't an idiot. He had studied the Old Tongue when he was in House Northern so he could read the ancient histories, but he hadn't ever heard it spoken before. By the time the woman and the Counsel Lord had made their exchange, he had been lost, but he had recognized some of the words. They had been talking about him.

"And I know you can understand me now," Rylan said again, wondering if he should try speaking the woman's Lan'lieanan. He had been taught that by House Northern as well, though the Academy had brought more of it back than he had expected after ten cycles. If he was nearly first in his class for speaking the stupid language, it should be good for something.

"Or am I not slinging silver well enough for you to sail by?" he added, only to see her pull back in surprise. "Sing to me, woman, or take your eyes back to your own ocean."

The woman's snort of laughter gave him hope. She had understood his use of her mother tongue.

"Tu tantum loqui lingua antiqua?" he said, finally remembering a bit of the Old Tongue. *Do you only speak the ancient language?*

The woman smiled at him, white teeth flashing in the dim light as she set a finger to the side of her nose.

Rylan gave an exasperated sigh, leaning back against the wall of his cell. His ribs hurt too much to stand for long but if he sat, then the weight of his wings made them scream in pain. At least his wings seemed to be intact, even if they were bound.

"Okay, well I don't," he said in return. "I speak Kosaran, some Lan'lieanan, and I can read the Old Tongue, but it's been a long time. You can understand me, though, so talk to me. What did he say?"

The woman pursed her lips, glancing down the hallway where the Counsel Lord had come from before. Finding no one, she turned her wicked smile back on him.

"What?" he demanded.

She touched a finger to her temple.

::Nashtae.::

Rylan froze as he heard a voice echoing all around him. It felt like the trick the warbards used, sounding orders aloud but also in the back of your head so you could hear them on the wind. The Cantullus Preems, the strongest of the warbards, were supposed to be able to send orders without opening their mouths at all, but this woman... This was different.

"Nashtae?" Rylan returned, confused. It was a Lan'lieanan greeting, but had she really just spoken into his mind?

The woman's grin deepened.

::Calm your thoughts and I can speak with you, boy,:: the voice said again.

"What did Lord Seventh say about me?" Rylan asked, hesitant as he felt a presence sifting through his mind. His heart was absolutely racing.

::That Dragon Lord only ever talks to me about one thing,:: she sent, brushing the waves of her long, red-gold hair from her face with the thought. ::He demands that I take him back to the islands so that he can talk with our 'Great Matriarch', which is ridiculous. We have nine Matriarchs, but he would not even make it past the war front with his wings intact,:: she said, matter of fact. ::The idea that he means to do this warmongering for peace does not make any sense at all.::

"Are you talking about the Envoy?" Rylan asked, confused. "The Seventh Counsel Lord's Envoy?"

::Obviously,:: she sent, annoyed. ::You are a man of the Host. Explain it to me.::

"It's part of what the Seventh's do," Rylan answered, not sure where to begin. He knew far too many stories of previous failed Sevenths, especially of the Ancestor Sevenths from his House, but they all ended the same. They were either assassinated, had accidents on the way to the front, or died throwing themselves on the mercy of the Vals. What they were supposed to do, though, was a whole other thing.

"The Seventh Counsel Lord is the commanding warlord over the Legions for seven cycles and then he has to leave Delton," Rylan began, since she clearly wanted to know. "If they can't win by force, they're required by the Gods to try and make peace with your people. Most of them have gone through the Plains to do it, but the past fifty years or so they've been going through the Eihwaz Forest to try and get around the Warhost. As far as the Host is concerned, if the Seventh isn't going to go out in a blaze of glory, they'd rather kill him and keep him from becoming an intelligence risk."

::That is some honor you have, killing a man for seeking peace,:: she scoffed, rolling her eyes.

"As far as I'm concerned, there is no honor in glory," Rylan snapped, angry that this woman would assume he did. "And even if you do have honor, they expect you to use it to die for some other man's glory. For his glory," he said, glowering. "The fucking Lord Seventh."

::Great Mothers,:: The woman sent back, shaking her head as she began to pace along the length of her cell. ::I can't even see the man without wanting to slap him. If he thinks he can just storm Tor'Nihil and demand anything, he'll die just as fast as those others. This is why we leave our own men on the islands, I'll have you know,:: she said, stopping as she looked at Rylan. ::There, at least, their strength can be put to good use bringing in nets or crafting or caring for energetic fledglings. On the Plains, all you men can do is wave your privates around like we should be impressed.

All that Dragon Lord can do when I tell him to stop being so rude is throw a tantrum and demand I cooperate with him. Why?:: she insisted, glaring at Rylan now. ::Why do any of you think the same tactics that fail you on the Plains will work for any kind of peace? Goddess, but you men are so bloody emotional!::

"Emotional?" Rylan repeated aloud, watching her stalk to the rear of her cell to burn off her frustration. "We're emotional?"

When the woman pivoted towards him again, a finger on her lips to silence him, Rylan just clenched his jaw.

::You want to know what that Dragon Lord said about you, son?:: she said, clearly still angry. ::He thinks that the things you do in the passion of youth have enough weight to shake the foundation of his entire war planning,:: she sent, coming to a stop at the center of her cell to take hold of the bars. ::As if a butterfly landing in the Eihwaz could explain why his own countrymen are out for his head. How is that not emotional? How is that not so absolutely ridiculous to him? You are a fledgling, not a war fighter. Nothing you do matters until you have spilled blood on the Plains.::

Rylan couldn't argue with that. Even he knew that until he earned his warcrest, until he got his first confirmed kill or did something else of merit no woman of the Vals would look at him twice no matter where he was on the Plains. Like some strange code of honor, they would not touch an unblooded soldier. Once you made the choice to kill their sisters, fine, but until then you might as well have been an innocent. Clearly, the woman thought the same of him. Given how much he didn't want to go to War at all, it wasn't like she was wrong.

Seeing her calming down, Rylan looked at her in a new light. This might be the only time he ever got to talk to a Lan'lieanan this candidly and she seemed like the kind of woman who would go on for candlemarks if he gave her a topic to fly with.

"Who are you?" He asked. "What's your name?"

The question itself seemed to annoy her, given her hard stare.

"My name's Rylan," he said, holding his hands up for peace.

::Your Lord Fifth calls me The Loralae,:: she said in return, begrudgingly. ::That will do.::

"Lora, then," Rylan said, smirking at her look of annoyance. He could be a brat too, if that was her game. "So where are we, exactly? You look like you've been here a while."

During all his time on the streets, Rylan had only been taken in and wingclipped three times. Each of those times he had stayed in the catacomb of cells that the Guard maintained at the base of the Palace shelf. Those were usually teeming with folk, with little enough silence to let you sleep at all. Here, though...

::I am told these are the High Cells,:: Lora sent, resuming her pacing as she looked around her cell. It was all carved stone, but for a prison cell it was well appointed. She had a raised nest of rasha with pillows and comforts, what looked like a desk, paper, and a number of books, but her clothes? Her hair? All of it looked like she refused to play their game. She was a wild animal in a gilded cage, lest they forget.

"So we're below the lawspeakers," he said, which made sense. But he hadn't gotten arrested, so why were they holding him? *Holy gods, Mother is going to be so mad.* Sighing, he tried to pull his thoughts back into focus. The woman was clearly following along in his head, skimming for any information she herself could use.

"Why are you here?" He asked, deflecting.

::Why do you think?:: She shot back. ::I'm from the Lans.::

"Well, yeah," he said, making a face. "But just being from a place doesn't make you a criminal."

::Are you sure about that?:: The woman asked. ::As far as I can tell, you are in this place because you are from the streets.::

"I'm here because I'm a tyro that left the Palace without permission," Rylan said.

::But you are a tyro because you were from the streets, are you not?:: She asked and Rylan shoved at the feeling of her rifling through his mind.

"Why do you care?" he asked.

::The guards were talking about having to clear a pool last night after you had been caught,:: she explained, coming to a halt at the end of her cell. ::You're something of a celebrity, if you didn't know. Care to tell me why?::

As she considered him, Rylan studied her in turn. The kurta that she wore seemed big on her now, which meant she had been here a long time. She also didn't have any marked hem or cuffs, or possibly she had torn them from her kurta before she had been captured to guard which part of the Vals she had been from. Long hair or not, she was not one of the Val'Corps women who used ballistas, lances, and heavy armor in her daily life. She was too light on her feet for that, too clever with her words.

She was probably Val'Kyr, all things considered. A kyree woman, which meant she was a spy and a certain threat no matter her cage.

"Only if you tell me why you're in here," Rylan returned, matching eyes with her. As used to seeing the grey-blue of Micah and Sera's eyes as he was, neither one of them had the same sapphire violence just beneath the surface. She did seem to have the blank expression that the twins could get when they didn't want to give anything away, though Rylan was sure he had picked up on the cues they had used to talk to one another with their eyes and hands while they performed.

::I should be dead,:: Lora said and seemed more annoyed than relieved. ::But your Dragon Lord didn't have the decency to put me down after I failed to kill him. That was... four summers ago? Five?::

Rylan's eyes went wide as he suddenly knew who he was talking to. *She's that kyree?* Rylan realized. *The one that tried to kill Lord Seventh. Talk about a celebrity*, he thought and then swore as he realized she probably heard that as well, if she could hear the rest of his thoughts.

::Don't be shy, boy,:: she sent, intrigued. ::What have you heard of me?::

"Only rumors," he said. "Some folk were saying he had taken you to nest, but that just seemed ridiculous," he added, seeing her ire in the way her eyes narrowed when he looked to the freestanding nest in her cell. "Most folk just thought you were someone that he had caught to answer for the attack on the Kirathy Citadel."

::Oh, that,:: Lora scoffed. ::No, I was not there for that. I saw the other kyree moving in, but I wasn't a part of it. I heard it was quite the slaughter, though.::

Rylan's uneasiness returned with the casual approval he could see in her. "It doesn't surprise me about Lord Seventh," he continued, moving away from the subject. "He's the reason my brothers and I are tyros. We couldn't pay to have one of our sisters healed when she got caught out in the Ice Winds, so they conscripted us instead."

::Was she worth that price?:: The woman asked, noting the loathing in his thoughts.

"She would be worth any price," Rylan answered immediately and the woman's opinion of him seemed to visibly rise. So did her posture, which made him think of Sera and all her dancer's grace. Seeing her now, realizing everything that Micah had ever said about how afraid their mother had been for Sera before she died... He never would ask Sera to come up to the Palace again. This Val'Kyr woman could have been her near-sister.

::So you tyros are not supposed to leave the shelf, then?:: she asked. ::Or just you three, because of the debt?::

"Just us," Rylan said. "They think we won't come back. Two solar cycles I've been leaving and coming back, but that is still their story. It's almost over, though," he said, even if the prospect held no joy for him. "I am supposed to fly the graduation tournament in a few dawnings, but I can barely breathe with these daggers in my side. I think they broke something."

Now the woman looked concerned. ::What will that mean for her?::

"I don't know," Rylan confessed, hating himself all over again. "All I can do is hope our Barracks Mother might be able to help me."

The woman's approval of him seemed to grow again. ::You're not half bad for a Kosaran,:: she declared. ::You are the first I have encountered in this place who seems to understand where a man's priorities should be.::

"Thanks?" He said, not quite sure how to take that.

She looked about to say more when she suddenly glanced down the hallway, her eyes narrowing again. ::Someone is coming for you.::

Rylan followed her look, though he couldn't see or hear anything on his own. The tyro program had taught them that being confined in solitary too long could crack your mind, but that wouldn't explain her uncanny senses. Maybe there was something he was missing? Some sound of them approaching that he just couldn't hear?

"Who's coming?" He whispered back at her.

::The Guard,:: she said and then tilted her head to see as far down the hall as either of them could manage. Her eyes unfocused for a moment and then came back as fast as they had shifted. ::They're here to take you somewhere,:: she added and then backed away from the cell door. ::It has been interesting speaking with you, boy. I wish you well.::

Rylan wasn't sure what to make of that as he watched Guard Johan moving into the cells. As he worked the keys, Guard Traver looked at the woman the way a fledgling looked at a caged plains cat. He was safe from her, if only on this side of the bars.

As Johan opened Rylan's cell, Traver turned to look Rylan over.

"You would have died of shame by now if you had any sense," Johan said, grumbling as he worked.

Rylan restrained himself from responding. This guard's only problem was that he actually had to work. No wonder veterans had such contempt for the Palace Guard; they were all just a bunch of aged, lazy sirelings.

"Can't complain about that one, though," Traver said, laughing. "Her, we don't mind."

Rylan could understand the rancid response just beyond his thoughts.

When Traver had the manacles fastened around Rylan's wrists, he brought the chain up between his wings and clamped the heavy collar around his neck. Satisfied, he picked up the lead chain of the front of the contraption as Johan looked into the woman's cell.

"I'll be back for you, honey," he said, blowing her a kiss.

::I will kill him,:: the woman growled as Rylan was shoved down the hallway. Rylan didn't doubt she would, given the chance.

As Traver pushed him onward, Rylan did his best to walk without limping, but his whole body ached from the night he had been through. Knowing the two guards weren't about to slow for him, Rylan put his head down and focused on one step and then the other, finding the numb center that his tyro training had drilled into him. In that place he could get through anything.

Soon enough, the cells vanished behind them and Rylan was choked to a stop. Clearing his throat as quietly as he could, he waited for Johan to open the door at the end of the hallway. Once Johan was out of the way, Traver gave him a shove and Rylan staggered forward. As his wings tried to flare in their bindings to keep him on his feet, his whole body spasmed and it was all that Rylan could do to drop to his knees in the bright holding cell, tears in his eyes again.

"Welcome back," a voice said from just beyond him. It was the Sixth Counsel Lord, heavy flight cloak folded over his arm as if he had just come in off the winds.

Rylan bit back a response and dragged himself off his knees. Finally seeing the room he was in, he realized that it was only half as big as he thought, with a set of iron bars stretching from floor to ceiling in the middle of the otherwise barren expanse. There were three chairs on the other side, with Lord Sixth sitting in the one on the far left. Surprisingly, it looked as if the man was as exhausted as Rylan felt.

"While I want to say that you had every bit of this coming," Lord Sixth went on conversationally. "It won't change the fact that every guardsman in a league of here wants one of your feathers as a trophy."

Rylan scoffed without meaning to and the Counsel Lord shifted in his seat, causing his wings to flare and show their dark markings.

"Do you honestly think I want you in here?" He said, coming to his feet in a surprising show of exasperation. "By all the gods of Earth and Sky, boy. If you had just stayed in the Palace, you could have avoided all of this. It was four blicing days until you could be granted a proper leave."

Rylan only half trusted what Lord Sixth was saying, but as they stared each other down there was nothing he could read that made him think the man was lying. That, or the Counsel Lord's northern-Ehkeski heritage and angled eyes made for a nasty face at cards. Regardless, there wasn't anything Rylan could say in response, so they both waited in silence until two more voices could be heard on the other side of the door.

When it opened, Rylan was unsurprised to see his Headmaster, Counsel Lord Aaron, coming in, though he winced to realized he looked as pleased to be here as Lord Sixth. He was also wearing his rank of office, a silver braided king-chain with crossed scrolls emblazoned on the dangling pendant. Fortunately, given that his Headmaster was not a warlord, he didn't have the rank pauldron to make him look as if he was spoiling for a fight.

Behind him was his Barracks Mother and if Rylan hadn't just seen the look from the Lan'lieanan moments before, he would have doubted he had ever seen a woman so enraged. By comparison, Vinicia's ire as she greeted the Lord Sixth came a close second.

"Is it your practice to brutalize officer candidates, or just your men's?" She demanded, with a biting tone Rylan had not expected a woman could use with a man of the King's High Counsel.

"A pleasure to meet you as well, Mother," Lord Sixth answered evenly.

Vinicia looked as if she had a choice set of words she meant to share until his Headmaster put a hand on her wing. "Vinicia," he said, his voice soft but demanding her attention. "This is not the time or the place if you mean to help the boy."

Vinicia's grip on the red script over her shoulder clenched into a fist as she took control of herself. As the two men watched her, both leaning back just enough to make Rylan think they were as wary of her as he was, Vinicia looked past his Headmaster to where Rylan was watching them beyond the bars.

"Tyro Rylan," Vinicia began, calling his attention back to them. "What did I tell you about leaving the Barracks?"

Rylan came as close as he could manage to military attention, hearing the fury in her voice.

"That I would regret it until the end of my days, Mother," he answered.

"And now you will know why," she said, shifting her attention to his Headmaster.

"Before this business with your traveling to the Lower City had become such an issue," Counsel Lord Aaron began, hands behind his back. "I had arranged with Lord Seventh that you would serve out your boon as a member of the Palace Guard. I had intended for Tyro Micah's twin to receive room and board for that time, but that is no longer an option."

Rylan remained silent as his Headmaster continued, though he was gutted to realize that the Lord Seventh had meant what he'd said about changing the terms of his conscription. But if someone had just told him—if they had told Vinicia, even—none of this would have happened. Obviously, he would have waited!

"Furthermore," Counsel Lord Hest'lre went on, clearly gathering himself to leave. "As you have seen fit to make yourself the enemy of my Palace Guard, the Lord Seventh has ordered a change in your commission. While the orders have not been cut as if yet, it would not be wise to cross him further."

"Which is why you will be focusing your attention on the Tournament from now on," his Headmaster finished, gesturing to Vinicia and the script she held. "And as my Cantos have gone for the season, your Barracks Mother will be overseeing your preparations personally."

"Honor and Glory, Mother," Rylan said, about to salute her until he saw the hard look from the Sixth Counsel Lord. Instead, he pressed his right hand flat against his shoulder in a civilian courtesy.

"Aaron," Lord Sixth said, nodding to Rylan's headmaster as he turned to leave. "I will see you this evening."

Rylan came to braced attention, changing his salute from the flat palm to the fist even if the man paid him no mind. Once he was gone, storming out of the room, Rylan watched as his willowy dryad-kin crew brother took his place at the door.

"Mother?" He asked, only to see Lord Second and stand even taller out of respect for the man. "Oh, sal'weh, Ser."

"Chiurgeon Westly," Lord Second acknowledged, motioning for him to enter the room. "Thank you for coming."

"Your will is my own, Ser," Westly said, inclining his head as he stepped inside, collecting the bag of his medicinal supplies and the excess of his Bloodcloak as he did so. "Honor and Glory."

"Honor and Glory," Counsel Lord Aaron returned before taking his own leave.

When it was just the three of them in the room, Vinicia moved towards the bars that stood in the center. There was a door of sorts on the far left, though as she neared it without any sort of keys Rylan wondered how she was going to get through.

"Mother, the Guards are coming to release him. It will just be—" Westly said, raising a hand as Vinicia grabbed onto the handle and twisted, snapping whatever mechanism controlled it without a second thought. "A moment," Westly sighed.

"How...?" Rylan asked as his Barracks Mother opened the door and moved through it. She had just snapped the lock with her bare hands. As he took a step back, eyes going wide, his attention shot to Westly.

"She is kindred," Westly explained as Rylan gaped. "Like me. She's been teaching me for cycles. I just—"

"I know you hadn't told him," Vinicia said, only to look at Rylan with irritation. "But you should have realized it by now. Honestly, son."

Rylan flushed with the unexpected reprimand as she came to a stop in front of him, glowering at the manacles, chain, and wing bindings he wore. Her eyes were white all over as she stared through him with the same sort of healer's sight that Westly used.

The sight Westly had begun to use after they had come to the Palace, Rylan realized. He knew that kindred usually died young—either killed because of their wild talents or as a result of their inability to master them—but Westly was ancient for a kindred. Vinicia had to be older, though. Much older. If she had been teaching Westly, then she had survived 'coming into her power' or whatever it was that happened when a dryad-kin reached maturity.

"You're a force of nature, Mother," Rylan said, raising his hands what little he could to defend himself. "But I didn't realize—"

Westly's hand went to his face as Vinicia waved hers before Rylan, causing the locks on his bindings to release. Unfortunately as the wing binding gave way, the pain searing through his back and torso drove Rylan to his knees.

"Come over here and watch the door," Vinicia said as she kicked the metal aside so Rylan could fold his legs beneath him with her help.

"Yes, Mother," Westly called, jogging over to do as she ordered. Apparently Vinicia was using Westly's presence as the chiurgeon in the room about as much as Westly used the bag of 'medicine' at his side: not at all. Westly had said that using the herbs could help strengthen his sorcery, but it was the latent energy inside of a windwalker that he accessed.

That, and something about how giving someone a tea was much less likely to terrify them than direct healing. Considering what Vinicia looked ready to do, Rylan might have preferred the tea. If Vinicia could heal him back to health, she was stronger than Westly had ever thought to be.

Taking a breath, Vinicia came out of her healer's sight with a sigh. "Two broken ribs, a fractured cheek, bruised bones in a multitude of places, and more scrapes than I care to count," she concluded. "Rest is the only thing that would heal this kind of damage, but as we don't have time for that, I will make this quick. I am leaving the bruising, however," Vinicia warned, reading his hesitancy as she took his head between her hands. "And you will act as if you are still suffering through graduation, am I understood?"

"Hoi, Mother," Rylan said, ducking his head to hide his uneasiness.

If she meant to heal that much of him directly, a thing Rylan had only seen Westly do a few times on sprains or minor cuts, then he was going to be ravenous for a fortnight. Even the simpler things Westly had done had left him feeling peckish for days...

"He has not come into his power," Vinicia said, tipping up Rylan's chin to get him to focus. "I came into mine long ago. You will be fine."

Exhaling in a rush, Rylan closed his eyes. He might still have been wincing, but he gave up the pretense at holding himself together. As Vinicia's hands went to his temples again, Rylan hissed air through his teeth, bracing himself.

"Are they coming?" Vinicia asked, throwing her voice in Westly's direction.

"No," Westly confirmed.

"Then come here and watch the working," Vinicia said. "I will do this quickly, but this will help keep you safe if you must heal a grievous wound on the Plains. Large injuries, general exhaustion or malaise, those you cycle through yourself and reset the body's harmony. Poison or disease is different. If you pull it through yourself, you will end up with a sour stomach, but this," she said, shifting the hand on Rylan's head to brush across the split lip and blackened eye he must have. "This has to remain, even if they feel fine. Blood magic heals at a different rate than your herbs, but if you use it, it is important to leave the superficial injury. Understood?"

"Hoi, Mother," Westly said.

"Very well then," she said, setting her hand back on Rylan's temple. "Hold on, love. I need to make this look good if we're going to convince Lord Seventh not to send your brother to Kelsineah thinking he can heal the entire Warhost overnight."

Rylan grit his teeth, nodding as he felt all his pin feathers standing on end throughout his wings. As he braced against the feeling of ice racing through his veins, the woman's sorcery slid under his skin, masking the searing sensation of his body piecing itself back together. Whatever Micah said about the nearly erotic feel of Westly's magic, whenever Westly did anything to him, he always paid for it with pain. It was worse with Vinicia, freezing him like he had dropped into the River Kir at midwinter, but it was over in an instant.

Taking her hands back, Rylan collapsed forward onto his hands and knees, leaving him to shiver of his own accord. As she came to her feet, Westly took her place, offering him a small disc of dried herbs.

"Suck on this," he said quietly. "It should take the edge off of, well…"

"Everything?" Rylan hoped through chattering teeth.

"For a while, at least," Westly said. "Come on, Ry," he went on, offering his hand to help him stand. "Just come back to the Garden with me. I've got food there to see you through the worst of it and you can use my workspace to get started. We can head to the Barracks at dawn when I meant to check on Micah."

"Dawning is three candlemarks from now," Vinicia warned, moving to set the long leather scroll on its end before him. "Your cadre will need to oversee your soldiers getting their gear tomorrow. By the time they are finished in the Armory, you will have their team assignments finished with the cadre and complete a briefing for the mission at large. Once you have done that, then you may sleep. Am I understood?"

Rylan shook himself as he pushed back onto his heels, wanting to glare at her with the same defiance he had shown Lord Seventh in the Cells but managing to hold himself in check. Unlike the Counsel Lord, she meant to make sure he got through this challenge. She wasn't the one setting him to it.

"Understood, Mother," Rylan said, composing himself. "But there is one thing you need to know. My brother Dylan is at the House Northern Estate. He is doing something to try to steal the House and I don't know what it is. I have to stop him—"

"Just what do you think that paper you signed this evening was for?" She asked. "I told you my uncle was a law speaker, but my father is worse. We will make certain that House belongs to you, Rylan, no matter who tries to take it."

Rylan considered her for a long moment, unsure.

"Have some faith in me, son," she said, stepping back to gesture to the door. "I may work in mysterious ways, but I have gotten everything I have ever wanted in my life and I want this for you. All you need to do is graduate. Am I understood?"

"Hoi, Mother," Rylan said, feeling a weight lifting off his wings as the woman nodded.

"Who is your cadre, then," she asked. "Tell me now."

"But I don't—" Rylan began, only to look away. "Mother I haven't even asked them."

"Trust yourself, Rylan," she insisted, not about to take no for an answer. "Tell me who will understand the orders you give them."

Rylan let go of a ragged breath, looking down at the script in his hands. "Tyrsten is my second," he began. "Nichi and Tyrren will take the shooters, Westly will organize the chirons, and Micah will have the warbards and heavies."

"And I will handle the Estate," she confirmed. "If you think Sera is in trouble," she added. "I can check in on her as well. I can do that much from here if it's needed."

"Sera can handle herself," Rylan said. "It's me I don't trust. I'll just take off without telling anyone, apparently."

"Do you trust me?" She asked, offering her hand to help him rise at last.

"With my life, Mother," Rylan said, taking the help.

"Then don't set down that script," she said, a smile twisting her lips as she steadied him. "Every cycle I see good men forget how important it is to hold onto what matters. Remember the duty to your men, Rylan, and they will do anything you ask of them."

CHAPTER 06: KIERNAN

Thursday, 01:00

"Remember your duty," Kiernan repeated, head in his hands as he fought through the swirl of the Warhost in his mind. The swirl of Tyro Rylan's thoughts in his mind. No matter how he tried to force them away, they were hounding him now. "Hold onto what is important. Gods, did I ever fuck that up."

As he sat staring into the black depths of the Seventh Counsel Lord's Library from his perch on the crystal roof, Kiernan wished that the chill of the night was doing anything to cool his flesh. Ever since he had taken off the hawkeye he had had to contend not only with the Warhost, but the seething rage flowing up from them as well. In a twist of fate, that now burned in him as strongly as any fever he had ever suffered in his life.

"Gods forgive me," Kiernan muttered, mopping his brow even as the wind chilled his flesh. "I only took it off for one blicing moment."

That was the reason for everything wrong in his life: that damn hawkeye. It was why Rylan had mutinied, why his Sixth Counsel Lord was now first in line wanting him dead, and why he couldn't do a blicing thing to help either of them. It was also why he hadn't cared if he left his suite after two full bottles of Illiandrian wine hadn't been able to drown out the Warhost in his mind. No one ever set foot on the ancient crystal ceiling of his Library for fear of it breaking, but in his current state, falling to his death would be a blessing. If nothing else, it would at least be memorable.

Before tonight, Kiernan wouldn't have considered himself a superstitious man. The Gods he gave praise, his Ancestors he respected, and ever since he had been forced to work with the Founder of the Seventh's Seat, he thought he knew what to do with that. Before he had been a Seventh, Kiernan had given more credence to a fool's luck at cards than the idea that your familial ancestors were actually watching over you. The idea that some of them watched you only to see if you would disgrace their memory was absurd. What sane person would cling so much to their life after passing just to exact revenge?

As a tyro, Hest'lre had sworn to him that it was true, but Hest'lre was also half-Ehkeski, relying on his Father's Founders and his mother's clan elders instead of a House or Guild. Still, Hest'lre had honored them as they were due and look where it had gotten him: Sixth Counsel Lord on the King's High Counsel and the second most powerful Warlord in Kosar.

And Kiernan? Kiernan had that and more, but only for seven cycles. It was his own hubris to think he could throw the hawkeye away as if nothing would happen. As if the shades of the Seventh Counsel Lords in the Library wouldn't come after him. As if there were no consequences at all to anything he did in the world.

'We control the strings over too many lives for you to just turn your back on your ancestors', Hest'lre had said. Screamed, really. Hest'lre had a Founder overseeing his Seat too, though from what Kiernan could tell, his friend was doing much better than Kiernan was at working with it. And it was an 'it' singular, because unlike Noventrio, Hest'lre's Founder did not trap his Counselheirs inside a blicing Library when they died, as if they were new books for his collection.

To be honest, Kiernan couldn't remember a time in their long friendship when Hest'lre had been as furious with him as he was now.

But after hearing what had happened over the marks since he had thrown the hawkeye against his chamber wall, Kiernan was now drowning in the shame that should have kept him from taking it off in the first place.

No matter what he thought, knowing that it was possible for the Founders to act on the world was just as insane now as it had been back then. With the hawkeye on, Kiernan had at least been able to placate Noventrio by being under his control, but without it—without having the shielding that his hawkeye had provided against his Seventh's Gift—Kiernan was learning why his predecessors had only survived seven cycles. He was barely managing one day before losing track of which thoughts were his own inside his head. So many angry, violent, hateful voices were bubbling up into his subconscious and most of them had no other thought where he was concerned but the hope that he would die soon.

Tyro Rylan was the worst though, seething in his rage somewhere from the Glass Garden. Even if he was focused on graduating once again, it was clear to Kiernan that Rylan had a powerful Gift and not just for commanding men.

His crew brothers had gifts as well: Tyro Micahleia, who was a warbard that the Cantullus Corps suspected was stronger than he had ever let on, and Chiurgeon Westly who the Second Counsel Lord would rather dead than thriving for all he was a disgrace to the true work of chiurgeons. All of them were suffering so much in this place and it was his fault.

He had done this to them. He had bent and broken their world around them on purpose and while he knew he had been doing it for the greater good, it wasn't enough. Realizing what he had done, feeling Rylan's furious hatred inside his head, it was molten steel searing along his veins. Without the hawkeye to protect him, he couldn't even remember why now. He could barely think at all. In his deepest heart he knew he had needed to break the boy, that the whole blicing war had depended on it, but now that it was done Kiernan was coming apart at the seams.

"I'm sorry!" Kiernan sobbed, gripping at his warcrest as he hid from the roaring wind. The only reason he could think of was that he had felt this way once when he had realized what it truly meant that Lenae was to be the King's Consort. Fighting to get her back was the only way he had survived being apart from her and Rylan was a part of that somehow. As the last son of House Northern, he had to be. He just couldn't remember why.

With his own self-loathing rising like bile in the back of his throat, Kiernan uncurled from the tight ball he had made to take another long pull from the wine he had cradled in his lap. In the seven cycles he had been a Counsel Lord, Kiernan knew now that he had somehow become the monster he had always feared. Whether it had been the Gift going to his head or the power of his Seat, there was nothing to change that now. No, now he was just a dead man and after everything he had done, he deserved it.

That was the true reason he had come out on top of the Library. With his vision trapped inside the white fog of power, the only thing he could see were the spirits of the ancestor Sevenths moving in the library like so many silver-blue fish as the Palace around him became a stone blur.

::Is this how you've chosen to die? Some tribute to my Ice Winds?::

Kiernan clenched his jaw against his angry retort as the voice of his Founder overwhelmed all others in his mind. Since he was far too drunk to be afraid of the shade, Kiernan simply watched as the God of the Ancestor Sevenths passed through the crystal at his feet. As Noventrio's shade joined him at the apex of the roof, he flashed with light and was suddenly made of flesh and feathers before him. It was supposed to be impressive, but the contortion of nine full-sized wings splayed out behind him just seemed... Ridiculous.

It's not even symmetrical, Kiernan thought to himself. *And after all this time it still just looks ridiculous, all of them going this way and that. He's just a vain, self-important—*

"You do realize I can hear you?" Noventrio said flatly, shrugging his shoulders in a way that folded the wings into the two Kiernan's mortal mind preferred to see.

"I never forget you can," Kiernan muttered and went back to his third bottle of wine. "Even if you have forgotten that life has moved on without you," he added, giving the Founder a sideways look at the ancient garb he insisted on wearing.

Dressed like Kiernan himself in the formal kama, the wide sleeves and billowing pants that hid Noventrio's legs caught in the breeze chasing across the roof. So did his unbound silver hair and long mustache, reminding Kiernan once again of just how ancient the creature was. In this man's time there had been neither warcrest nor need for aerodynamics in flight.

This man had wielded pure sorcery on the Plains before becoming tethered to the Kosaran mountains, though why his great Temple Tree was encased in the stone of the library rather than being open for worship like all the others, Noventrio had never said.

"What do you want?" Kiernan prompted, picking up his bottle as he shifted position.

"To talk," Noventrio said, reaching to pluck the wine from Kiernan's hand. Kiernan released it without protest, though he gaped as he watched the Founder take a sip. That was new.

"The shield on the hawkeye works both ways," Noventrio explained. "If I am going to have to drain your power directly to keep your Gift from eating you alive, then I must do something with the excess. Taking a more solid form works well enough and it has been an age since I have felt the wind on my wings."

"With nine of them I think you would just fall over," Kiernan observed and the Founder rolled his eyes as he handed the bottle back.

"My sister Celenae has six," Noventrio observed.

"Sure, but they splay out nicely in statues," Kiernan defended. The Shelf-Founder of Illiandria was Lenae's namesake after all, so he knew her well. "It is her spiritual prowess, not chaos behind her. Is that what yours are for? Do they show how absolutely insane you are?"

As Noventrio's look darkened, Kiernan realized that maybe he should be more frightened of what a war god could do with an ability to touch the material world. "There is a reason for order in her agricultural workings," Noventrio said with quiet ire. "And a reason for chaos in mine. War is chaos. Perhaps you could have my mastery of it if you had not forsaken our bargain."

Kiernan ducked his head to avoid the Founder's menacing look. "What bargain?" he asked, feigning ignorance.

"That you would not take off the hawkeye until you named your counselheir," Noventrio reminded, glowering. "The only way you can lose it is if you take it off."

Kiernan's retort was to finish the last of his wine. After three bottles in only twice as many candlemarks, he was going to need to find some water before he killed himself hanging over a basin with the dawn.

"Good Guides," Noventrio sighed, looking to the east. "I do not have time to coddle you further. Your Sixth is looking for you and his heart might give out if he finds you up here. I gave my word to Founder Talon that his Shayan could retire when you left for Envoy and I am in no mood to irritate him," Noventrio said, reaching over to take hold of Kiernan's arm with an icy grip. "Now stop trying to drown yourself and get back to work."

Kiernan had just enough time to flinch before the world lurched around him and he found himself standing in the middle of his room wondering what in the world had happened. The first thing he knew at once was that he was suddenly sober, but the Founder had done more than heal him. Somehow he had taken the fever from his skin as well and his eyes had lost the fog of his godseyes entirely...

Not that any of it helped. Kiernan winced as he looked around the absolute havoc he had created in his Counsel Lord's suite since he had returned from the Cells. His clothes were strewn everywhere, his weaponry in warring piles, and the papers were scattered to the winds. He was lucky most of the furniture of his office was too heavy to move or he might have overturned them as well trying to find his hawkeye.

Gods, can I really survive three more days of this? Kiernan thought, hand gripped against his warcrest as he panted for a breath, trying and failing to bring up any kind of shield against the Warhost that was screaming inside his head again. He couldn't live like this, couldn't live with the feel of the Warhost buzzing in his mind like a hive of murderous hornets. Not for long.

Maybe Kreychi can find me some terra, he thought, desperate as he gave up the grip on his hair and washed a hand over his face, spinning in a circle to see the chaos of his office. That had helped after Kirath, at least. When he had first taken up the Seat and learned the true power of the Seventh Counsel Lord was an acutely terrifying knowledge of Warhost operations. Only the numb calm inside a cloud of terra had let him figure out how to use the shield the hawkeye had set over him.

For now he just took a steadying breath, closing his eyes as he tried to remember what the shield had felt like under the hawkeye. Given how long he had manipulated it, he felt like he should have been able to figure out how to set one, but it was like something had wedged that part of his mind fully open. Or maybe it had been open this entire time and the hawkeye had allowed him to close it? Not only did he have no way of figuring that out, but he had no way to stop it either. He was just going to burn himself out no matter what he did.

I was lucky my eyes were only starting to grey into godseyes when I got back from the Cells. If I go out again everyone will know I have taken off my Hawkeye and think I have given it to a Counselheir.

Swearing at himself, Kiernan groped for his missing hawkeye. It wasn't there of course, so he just turned to the last case of Illiandrian wine he had from home. Neither a sea nor a horde of angry Lan'lieanans could surmount the fear of the death he might perish at his own people's hands.

And if it happens in front of Lenae?

Kiernan picked up a new bottle, only to realize that he had taken his key for opening it out onto the roof with him and it was still there. Swearing to himself, Kiernan gave up the bottle and returned to his desk, dropping his head in his hands for all the sick sense of dread he felt.

Could he even leave if he had no hawkeye to pass on to his Counselheir? Would he have to stay, just to dissolve into madness in Delton? The hawkeye was the only key to the Library of war history stretching back to the founding and the living Seventh the only keeper of it. There was a much larger version of the hawkeye stone outside the Library—this one actually shaped like a hawk—that was said to have been put in place to bind Founder Noventrio to the original duty to end the war, but that wasn't exactly the key to getting in.

After Counsel Lord Hewn had been assassinated, it had been Ex-Counsel Lord Eirik who had named him Counselheir and gifted him the stone, so there hadn't been a need to find out what happened to a Seventh who died without an heir-apparent. For that matter, after what Eirik had said of the meddling ancestors trapped inside the Library, Kiernan had been hesitant to go in at all.

It had only been Lenae's prompting that had gotten him inside and he had been astounded to find that the Library had been built around Founder Noventrio's enormous temple tree. At eighteen stories tall, the tree was stunted compared to Founder Celenae's temple tree in Illiandria, but for all the volume of paper and text surrounding it, it could have doubled in height.

Unfortunately for Kiernan, there was more than a dead tree and a hundred thousand books inside. Waiting for him on the very first day he thought to enter the Library was the shade of every single man who had ever served the Seventh's Seat, their spirits tied to this place by a duty unfulfilled.

Kiernan wasn't just a warpriest, but a continuation of a line of men who had anchored themselves to this cause, willing or not, all ready and waiting to assist him with planning.

The root of the power of the Warhost, the root of Kiernan's own Seventh Counsel Lord's Gift, was the pool of pure spiritual prowess created by these men. Once linked to that power, Kiernan's own budding ability as an empath had grown from an all-too-accurate intuition into true mind-speech. Because of these men, because of Founder Noventrio's claim to them, there was no man of the Host that Kiernan could not reach. Worse, while most of the Ancestor Sevenths could only link the warbards they led to Founder Noventrio's power to make certain their Orders were heard over the winds, Kiernan's own strength had produced more Cantullus Preems than had been seen in a dragon's age.

With those men under his command, Kiernan had led the Host on a warpath that beat back the women of Lan'lieana to territory that Kosar hadn't held in two hundred cycles. As he grew in power, Kiernan had pushed into his strengths, and had gained an ability to truly sense his men. It had trickled down first with his cadre before flowing into their cohorts and the men they commanded who were the sources of his reports. With his Gift he was able to find the men who had told the men the information they had eventually reported to the ones who had committed it to paper.

Once he had realized that connection, Kiernan had pressed even further, following the minds of those lower enlisted long before the reports came. Any time they faced overwhelming odds or risked defeat, Kiernan's attention was drawn to them and he was able to direct reinforcements to their position, saving far more lives than he might have otherwise managed from the Citadel in Kirath.

The back edge of that blade had been that he was also drawn to the losses. Any time one of those men died, a part of Kiernan died as well, but it was a worthwhile fight. They Honored him with the loss of life, sought his Glory as they served a purpose greater than themselves, but as he neared the end of his time drowning in that power the feeling had changed. He hadn't been able to place why, but he had known he had to let go of the Gift and soon.

Now, having thrown off the hawkeye before another man could take that Gift from him, he was left to drown in the violence of every single emotion that surged towards him. The stone he had thought just a token of his seat was actually a sink for the bloodlust and rage he could feel coursing along his Gift.

Founder Noventrio apparently fed on that, gained power and purpose from that, and though he sent the Seventh Counsel Lords to do his bidding, he tamed the wildness of their spirit from the chaos of war to the sharply ordered perfection of a calculated plan. A winning strategy. A brilliant tactic.

Or a man so full of himself and his own importance that he cast off the only protection he had three days too soon, Kiernan knew, hating himself for his own hubris.

Left to wallow in the chaos of all he had done as a Seventh, Kiernan tried to force himself to calm. He was angry with himself, angry with everyone who he could feel bubbling up through his Gift, and in his panic he was raising more energy than he could control. As he stared down at his shaking hands, he stretched his fingers apart as wide as they would go to find the web of minds calling out to him. Closing his eyes, he let the strongest part of his Gift burst into life.

In the darkness of his mind Kiernan saw the bright points of power that marked the veterans pooling around the base of the Delton Palace. Most were the men of his cadre when he was in Kirath for the fighting season and his familiarity with them made them resonate with incredible strength. If he pulled back from that initial pool, he found the emptiness at the end of the shelf and pulling back further still, he saw the glistening tower that was Yaltana where his most hardened veterans lived over the winter. Another stretch and he found his native Illiandria to the east and Alexandria to the west.

As that steadied in his mind, he fought through the chaos of thoughts from his cantullus men who could sense him searching and took a ragged breath. For as much strength as this was taking, it still wasn't enough to burn through the power that was boiling beneath his skin. Without the hawkeye to absorb it, without something to do with all that power...

I've never tried to feel the whole Host at once, Kiernan thought, squinting against the sweat as it slid down his temples. *I suppose there's a first time for everything.*

His nerves steadied, Kiernan reached out once again, gathering the mountains of Kelishe, Greying, Kelsineah, and finally Kirath into his thoughts. With all the space gathered in among the white fire of minds in the black, he started to breathe easier. Now he could choose who he wanted to listen to and who could reach for him. For the first time in candlemarks he could even hear himself think, though drunk as he was with relief, that wasn't much.

This peculiar Gift of far-seeing the positions of his veterans was the reason he had been such an effective leader. If he tried, he could target and follow any soldier on a battlefield or any agent behind enemy lines. If he knew them well enough, the most incredible part of his Gift let him see through their eyes. After seven cycles of honing the ability, if he absolutely needed to know something right this instant, he could. That was the power of the Seventh Counsel Lord.

::My Lord Seventh?::

Kiernan's eyes snapped open at the sound of one of his primarchs echoing in the unsteady silence. For as strong as Kiernan was, those who remained close to him throughout his term had gained strength as well. All ten of the men he had elevated to Primarch in his service were blisteringly strong in speaking to him through his Gift, but Decius su'Yaltana was the greatest warbard among them. It helped that the man had been a Cantullus Preem serving the Seventh's Seat long before Kiernan had ever thought to add him to his cadre.

::We have been waiting for your summons, My Lord Seventh,:: Decius called once again, patient but only just. ::If you do mean to leave on Envoy, there is still the matter of your Counselheir. Shall I call the cadre?::

::Uh, that won't be necessary,:: Kiernan sent back in a rush. ::As you were, Preem.::

Struggling to focus with his panic, Kiernan stretched out his arms as he opened his wings. Once both were fully tense, he took a breath and then snapped them back towards him in a rush of power. There was an audible pop as energy pulsed away from him and off into the mountain peak, and the few things still standing on the bookshelves in his suite vibrated and fell to the ground. His mind, thankfully, remained humbled and alone.

Gods, why did I even do that ? Kiernan thought, his heart racing as his sanity returned without the distraction of the Host. *Now he's going to know. He's going to call a counsel. If he gets them all together, he's going to kill me.*

I did what I had to do, Kiernan reminded himself, and forcefully. Better to risk being hounded by his cadre than losing his mind without his hawkeye. The energy Founder Noventrio had granted him access to was just a touch weaker than the raw force of the River Kir. If he didn't use it, if he let it fill him instead, he would die like so many other Sevenths who had lingered too long in Delton when they should have set out on Envoy. At its core, the whole reason the tenure of a Seventh Counsel Lord lasted seven cycles was because that was how long it took a man to literally burn himself out with that power.

Trying to focus his mind once again, Kiernan set his palms on the top of his oaken desk.

One thing at a time, he told himself. *If I take it one thing at a time, I can conquer the world. That's what Lenae always says.*

Steady in his purpose, Kiernan reached for his father's letter so he could begin writing his response. That would be the start. If he was going to go home for the winter, he would have to finish making arrangements soon. Once the letter was ready, he would need to send a courier to his Guild. A courier was easy enough to find, given how many guards he had posted at the exit of his suite.

Harried, Kiernan let his leg take over the shaking that had been in his hands as he tried to set to his task. Kiernan opened one of the few drawers that remained in the desk and fished out a piece of parchment. As he laid it flat, he reached for the ink pot that normally sat at his left hand, but no...

Kiernan closed his eyes as he realized that the only thing on his desk was the letter. The rest had been swept off with that rush of power. Cringing as he moved, Kiernan looked down to the left side of his desk. Had he put the cap back on? Yes, thank the gods. With some stretching, he managed to retrieve the pot without moving from the chair and set it on his desk. The quill that went with it was lost, but if there was one good thing about being a windwalker...

Kiernan curled his right wing around him and slipped his fingers in between the feathers, preening through the mass. He cursed as his hand struck a tender spot and then craned his neck to see the feather more clearly. When he found it, he nearly swore again. He was sure he had seen the same long, wide feather two cycles ago. He would be lucky if it only bled when he pulled it out.

Spreading the other feathers out of the way, he wrapped delicate fingers around the shaft, and winced as the pressure he applied began the flow of blood. He pressed harder where the stalk met his skin, and with a strangled yelp, slid it free. As soon as it was out, he pressed his two unused fingers against the wound before it colored his wing. If he was smart, he would take himself to a chiurgeon for assistance now, but that was out of the question without his hawkeye.

Stubborn, Kiernan pressed on the swollen mound and sliced into it with a fingernail. He was surprised to find the delicate new feather intact, even if it was dyed red with his procrastination. When the mound was drained, Kiernan spat on the back of his hand and used that to wipe the new feather clean. He could already hear Lenae taunting him:

The longer you leave things untouched, the more they'll hurt when you finally deal with it. Preen, fool, and not just your feathers!

Here in this mess, it meant so much more than her drawing some vast conclusion about his lack of cleanliness. She always did have her ways of getting her point across where others failed. It was why he still loved her after all these cycles and why he had forsaken all others for just the hope that, at the end of the War, they could still be together.

Kiernan opened his desk once again to grab his quill knife, queasy with the thought of leaving her. After a few precision cuts, he whittled a nib into place and then split the shaft. He didn't have time to temper it properly, but it would do for now.

As he dragged off the excess ink from the tip, he knew what he would say.

T'n - It would be my honor to stand with you. When the soldiers are made, I will come with the snows. K'n

With that, he used the end of the feather to worry over the wet ink until it was set and then folded and sealed it without making his mark. Best to let Lenae's announcement obfuscate his simple, anonymous note to a Guild Master at Illiandria.

Next, he needed to deal with the last of his packing so he could transition peaks. Though tempting, the thought of what might happen if he simply abandoned his things and flew off right now kept him firmly in his place. Every man who thought he could get money for Kiernan's head would be on him in an instant. Given that they waited for him even now, what kept him from doing it anyway was nothing more than self-preservation.

That, and making sure Lenae would never have to see his body.

"Kier'n?"

Nausea washed over him at the sound of Lenae's searching voice as she travelled the short hallway between the joined sitting room and his private apartments.

"Lenae?" Kiernan called in return, twisting to see her. As she put a hand on the side of his open door, waving off her entourage, Kiernan came to his feet. "Lenae, you shouldn't be here. How did you—?"

She smiled as she moved to step inside and for a moment the sun burst through the pitch and mire of his thoughts.

"Is this your idea of packing?" Lenae chided, trying and failing to push the door open enough to slip by.

She will notice, he realized at once. *Even in this dim light, she will see my eyes have gone grey and know the stone is gone. She will try to do something, but there's nothing she can do. There's nothing anyone can do.*

Kiernan got up from his desk to assist her, which meant dragging his warchest full of the old Seventh Counsel Lord journals out of the way.

"Is there a better way?" Kiernan answered, only to look past her and see his former wingmate raising a hand towards him in the hall. Desperate as he had been the night before to drag Kiernan into a nest, Kiernan had told Kreychi to come back at dawning. He hadn't even begun to hope he would see Lenae.

Gods bless you, Kreya, he thought, the fear and panic releasing from around his heart as the man turned to give them privacy. Having stopped him from speaking with Lenae the night before, Kreychi had traded a possible moment alone with him for what he knew Kiernan truly needed: Lenae herself.

Once Kiernan had closed the door with her inside, Lenae's hands slid around his neck, pulling him against her. Kiernan was clay in her hands, submitting to the mercy of her most ardent affection as the world righted itself.

Given how long it had been since they had been truly alone, when her hands found the front of his hip he came alive for her at once and suddenly he was glad he hadn't moved the warchest that far off. He had her lifted onto the tall box and was tearing after her laces before he heard her laughter.

"Kier'n, I am not dressed for a dalliance," she pleaded, hands going into his warcrest. "Besides, you'll never get this off without my help. I swear, I can't even get it off without my ladies' help."

Kiernan tried to pretend he hadn't heard, not wanting to stop his searching for how to remove the strange new court garb she wore. Some wildly tempting high-low skirt that had a seam attached... to her bodice? He would cut it from her to get at the soft flesh beneath, if that's what it took. She did this sometimes, confounding him to raise the tension between them, but right now he couldn't stand it. He wanted to worship her, to devour every part of her before it was too late, but when her fingers in his hair tightened to command his attention, he had to obey.

Kiernan stilled as she clicked her tongue at him, though when he looked into her eyes, he knew the moment was lost.

"Kier'n?" She said, panic knotting in his stomach as her eyes went wide to see his own. "Kier'n, your eyes!"

Kiernan flared his wings, his hands sliding from the outside of her thighs as he let her put him on his knees before her. Free hand to her mouth, Lenae let go of his warcrest to find his collarbone. His bare collarbone, for all his hawkeye was gone.

"Where is it?" She whispered. "Kier'n, you're not supposed to take it off until you've named your Counselheir. Not until you're ready to leave. If you've named him then you have to leave. Now. This instant! Your Gift—"

"Lenae," he pleaded, taking hold of her trembling hand with both of his own. "I haven't named anyone yet, but I don't know where it is. I lost my head last night for all that was happening and I just... I'm sure it is here somewhere. I haven't left since I threw it against the wall."

"Kreychi said you went into the High Cells," Lenae remembered aloud as Kiernan kissed her palm to beg her forgiveness, even as her tone sharpened. "You didn't go to speak with her, Kier'n, did you? Oh, that terrible woman. You know she will still kill you if you give her the chance," she said, pulling back from him. "Kier'n why did you go down there? I told you not to speak with her again."

"I did not," Kiernan insisted, putting his hands up in surrender. "There was another matter that called me down to the Cells, but she was nearby and gods can she ever get under my skin. Lord Fifth can have her when I am gone and that will be the end of it. She is not coming with me."

"You should never have asked her in the first place," Lenae said with force. "Lord Fifth should have had her in Kirath all these cycles and you know it. The entire Warhost knows it!"

As she turned to move away from the door he had to duck Lenae's wings, though he had a sudden thought as he saw the hard-soled slippers she wore. Coming to his feet to follow her, Kiernan picked up one of his bottles of Illiandrian ice wine from the crate sitting next to his desk, only to see her glowering.

"Have you lost your key to that, too?" She observed and then sighed as she handed her slipper to him. Kiernan thanked her and turned the bottle on its side, using the shoe to rap at the bottle until the cork was freed. With his practice, it didn't take long. There were benefits to growing up next to a vineyard.

"Care to join me?" He asked sheepishly, returning her slipper.

"It is not even dawn, Kier'n," Lenae said, unimpressed.

Shrugging, he took a hesitant sip as she worked her way towards his desk. Ignoring his chair, she picked up the letter he had just written to his father and took its place, sitting with her wings draped over the back.

Kiernan took a second sip off the icewine as he sat before her. Though she didn't intend it, Kiernan had to steel himself as he watched her crossing her legs before him. He was aching with need and even if she loved him dearly, she was here for business, not pleasure.

"I thought your eyes were supposed to turn silver like mine when you went on Envoy," she said quietly, studying his face. "But your eyes are just clouding with white."

More than anyone, he knew that she understood how unnerving it was to suffer such a change. Not only did she have the silvered irises of the King's Consort, something less than true godseyes that let her still see, but with them came the ability to channel energy as well. Where his Seventh's Gift let him oversee the Host, though, hers gave her the strength to bear a fledgling whose ancestors stretched back to two Kosaran Founders: Aluvinor and Kerowyn.

When he didn't say anything more, her real concern came out.

"Maybe you should go speak with Counsel Lord Eirik," she said, her tone softening. "His eyes had this same fog when he came back from the Eihwaz."

"I just need the stone while I'm in Delton," he defended, even as he dared to reach a hand towards the calf nearest to him. She was so close to him and yet still so very far away. Lenae didn't quite kick him in response, but the way she flinched back broke his will to ask at all. She always did this when he was about to deploy, so he wasn't sure why it hurt so much more this time, but it did.

Tucking the hand beneath the arm holding his wine, he took another drink before going on. "The hawkeye will suppress the coloring until I can name my heir and leave," he said. "Once I am beyond Delton, the fog will fade."

"And if you can't find it?" Lenae asked, all logic and reason.

"Then I'll have the Dragon Mask brought up from Kirath," Kiernan said and Lenae did not like his attempt at a joke. "The veterans would love that, for all it would mean I was staying another cycle. They sure will be confused when they realize I'm just wearing it to sneak out of the city."

The flat look Lenae gave him was not encouraging. The Dragon Mask was what Seventh Counsel Lords wore while working within the Kirathy Citadel. While some thought the mask only for show, the sculpted crystal headpiece was meant to keep the Host from seeing the godseyes the Seventh showed while using his Gift. With his hawkeye on, the godseyes only changed the brown of his eyes to silver so it wasn't terrible, but without the hawkeye, his eyes were completely white. More than one Seventh had been killed for revealing the truly sorcerous nature of his Seventh's Gift, and he considered it lucky no one but tyro Rylan had realized the change the day before during the tyro formation.

"Fine," he said, taking another sip of the wine to hide from his failed joke. When he looked back to her, she had unfolded his note to his father. "Can you send that home for me?"

"Of course," she said. "It may take some time, though. Melody and Phaedra have told me they wish to leave my service and return to their families this winter. They broke the news to me yesterday evening."

"I didn't realize they had come back," Kiernan said, surprised.

"They said they saw you returning to the Sires' Wing last night," Lenae said. "They did say you were deep inside your thoughts, however."

"Deep enough that I didn't notice that I was having marks set on me," Kiernan muttered. "I ended up with three daggers when I got back. It's why I took the hawkeye off. I was so angry that I just threw all of it against the wall."

"Which wall?" Lenae asked, and then turned as Kiernan pointed to the map behind his desk where she was perched. "And the blades? Where did they end up?"

"I really wasn't paying attention," Kiernan answered and took another drink. "When I couldn't find the hawkeye... I got distracted."

"You panicked," Lenae corrected, taking the bottle away from him so he couldn't hide behind it anymore.

"You were saying something about your ladies?" Kiernan asked, turning the conversation back to her. "You will have enough for Winter Court, yes?"

"I'll have a few," Lenae said. "But I need at least two more women and I haven't had enough time to find them."

"Well, don't worry about me," he said, crossing both arms over his chest now. "You'll have some young blood around you before the fortnight is through and a new Seventh besides."

"You have decided on an Heir, then?" She pressed. "Hest'lre said that Kreychi refused cycles ago. Something about the Alexandrians already tithing too much?"

"So you've been gossiping with Hest'lre?" he accused.

Lenae rolled her eyes. "It is his partner that you're replacing," she reminded. "As Ninth, he'll have to work with both the new Sixth and Seventh, and you haven't given him any idea of who that is. If you know, you should tell him."

"I only just managed to get the choice down to two," Kiernan lied. "When I know, he'll know. But," he said, moving on. "Who have you considered for new ladies?"

"Melody and Phaedra are both from Illiandria," Lenae said. "I could call up one of your sisters? I heard Kaylee's husband from Borean had passed, but she will be out of morning by Spring. Do you think she would like that?"

"She'd be a cat in cream," Kiernan said, nearly laughing. "Especially with Kreychi as the House Heir and still scandalously single. Gods, she's hounded me for cycles for not introducing them, but he was my Primarch. I wasn't about to give him up for the politics of a ring."

"Not until you absolutely had to," Lenae said, attempting to console him. "I've heard rumors he's being made Patriarch soon."

Kiernan let out a rough sigh. "So his Sire really is that bad. Well, I suppose that makes sense why he was asking after Chiurgeon Westly," he said. "Gods, after all his time with me, I'm afraid Kaylee wouldn't be to his taste. She used to boss me around the Guild the way Kreychi bossed me around the Plains. I suppose I could ask her when I get to Illiandria, but that's not helpful for the Announcement. What if I gifted you a woman tomorrow? Would that be enough time for them to assist you?"

As Lenae considered him, Kiernan glanced at the wine as his mouth went dry. Walking back his pressure on Tyro Rylan might take the edge off the feel of violence flowing up his Gift, too. The boy's seething hate was still enough to make him want to hide in that bottle.

"I thought you had cleared your boons," Lenae said as his thoughts wandered. "Who else do you owe before you leave?"

"I don't owe anyone; Windover owes me, but that's beside the point," Kiernan said, sitting up a little straighter. "No, I'm talking about the girl I've been keeping in the vet tavern on the Lower Shelf. I could have her in your hands before the announcement," he added as she made a face. It wasn't like the girl could be with Rylan and Micah if she was in the Royal's Wing, right?

Gods, one day gone wrong and I'm pivoting from cycles of planning just to save myself from a backlash headache, Kiernan thought, groaning. *I'm not going to make it very long in Lan'lieana at this rate.*

"I think you've got that warcrest braided too tight," Lenae accused, watching him flow in and out of his own thoughts. When he was focusing on her again, she sighed. "Kier'n, a tavern girl wouldn't know the first thing about assisting me with the High Court. I need women who can stand with confidence, not terrified maids."

"I've read her letters to Rylan, Lenae," he laughed. "That girl has information that had Kreychi gawking last night. She is dangerously clever and if you could earn her loyalty, she might be exactly what you need in a handmaiden."

With Lenae's interest caught, it looked as if she was going to say something when they both heard the main door of the Counsel Lords' suite slam open and closed.

"Kiernan!" Hest'lre yelled, nearly shaking the walls. "Dammit, man, where are you?"

Lenae sat up at the sound of their old friend storming towards Kiernan's blockade. Kiernan just waited for him, staying seated.

"Kiernan, I'm going to kill you," Hest'lre said, storming into the room in a swirl of indigo silk. Barrel-chested and busy as the man was, he had his right arm out of the kama sleeve to give him a greater freedom of movement that Kiernan envied. The long sleeve of it was tucked into the waist belt and away from his wings, but the whole look of it set Kiernan on edge. Hest'lre was on a warpath, that much was clear, and he was coming for Kiernan.

"Good dawning, Hest'lre," Lenae said, deflecting the man's attention as she flared her wings.

"Lenae," Hest'lre acknowledged, still fuming. "Maybe you can knock some sense into him. I told you he was harassing the tyros, tyro Rylan to be exact, and now the whole blicing situation is boiling over."

"Hest'lre, I know. I—" Kiernan began, but Lenae's hand on his wing made him hold his tongue.

"What's going on?" She asked, patient as ever.

"Do you realize it took your dryad-kin chiron to piece Rylan back together after you left? From what I saw, Rylan is lucky he's even alive," he said, coming to a stop in front of Kiernan's desk as Kiernan realized the man's anger for closely guarded fear and panic. "From what Henrick told me, you're lucky *you're* even alive. Lyonel said you ghosted them coming back from the Cells. Are you out of your blicing mind?"

There wasn't anything Kiernan could say. With all the minds and emotions of his veterans creeping into his consciousness, he clearly was. As Kiernan's own fear surfaced, Hest'lre actually looked at the room he and Lenae were in. Surrounded by the toppled chairs, strewn weaponry, and a sea of paperwork, it was not the same room he had seen just a few marks before.

"Shit, Kiernan. What happened in here?" Hest'lre demanded. "Did someone actually come after you?"

"No," Kiernan said, placating the avalanche of panic. "I made this mess myself."

"Truer words have never been said," Hest'lre agreed, retreating back into his anger. "Lord Ninth never had to deal with this madness when he held my Seat. Eirik may have had his indiscretions, but you?" Hest'lre said, real loathing coming through. "I thought you were better than this."

As Hest'lre stared him down, demanding an answer, Kiernan waited for him to realize that the hawkeye was gone. It didn't take long.

As Hest'lre lifted a hand to point, Kiernan could see the whites all around his dark brown eyes. Lenae had been the first person he had told about the curse of his Seat, but when Hest'lre had been named his Sixth, he had been the second. No hawkeye. No pendant. No protection.

"You didn't!" Hest'lre balked. "Kiernan! Why would you ever take that off?"

Kiernan just looked at him, unblinking in his shame.

"By Earth and Sky," Hest'lre swore, palming the air in front of him in a circle of warding. Of all the shelves, Alexandrians were the most superstitious and his partner was no exception. If anything, Hest'lre was worse because he knew magic and demons and curses were real. Kiernan's especially.

"I can't," Hest'lre said, his voice cracking as he backed out of the room. "I can't help you. When you find the blicing thing, send for me."

Kiernan hung in that numb sense of shock for a long time, staring as not only his Sixth Counsel Lord, but his brother-at-arms and best mate actually fled from the sight of him.

Fled.

When Lenae slid off his desk to leave as well, he couldn't even look at her.

"He will calm down," she promised, even if the words were weak. As she pulled him to his feet, enveloping them both in her wings, he felt more vulnerable than he had in an age.

"I know," Kiernan said, his words hollow as he breathed in the rose and honey scent of her golden curls. Lenae was his life, and he was leaving her. He had to leave her. He had to. "But will I survive the time it takes?"

"I will always be here for you, Kier'n," Lenae insisted, but he could hear the hesitancy in her voice. "And if you need anything, you know Kreychi-"

"Kreychi's father is dying," Kiernan murmured. "I can't ask anything of him that might take him from his House."

As his stomach knotted around itself, Kiernan's resolve buckled under the weight of despair. Lenae must have sensed it, for she pulled back just enough to kiss him whether he wanted it or not. Kiernan yielded eventually, heart thundering in his chest.

I can't do this alone. I can't do this with anyone else. I can't leave this room and I can't stay. I have the power of a blicing God at my command and it will destroy me if I cannot find a way to control it. I never wanted any of this, but they put you in a cage. They put us both in a cage and we have no way out...

Kiernan didn't know how long she held him, but by the time he came back to himself, he could tell she had taken his numbness for strength in the moment. Not wanting to let the world crash down around her as well, he didn't fight her parting kiss.

"One thing at a time, beloved," she said, picking up his folded note. "Sending this is step one. Sending your things to the Guild Hall in Delton is the second. Once it is there, I will see that it gets delivered to our family back home."

"And then I graduate the tyros and return as well," He said, as if it was that easy. No matter the words, though, his heart broke as he remembered when he had first come to Delton with her. When he realized they would never be married. Not if she was the Consort.

"And don't finish that bottle by yourself," she added, attempting humor. "You never could hold your icewine."

Lenae didn't look back as she left; she never did. They had to believe they would see one another again, never acknowledging that this time might be the last. With less than a fortnight to go, only habit kept him from calling after her. Kreychi, however, was a different story.

"Kiernan?" He asked, moving to the threshold of the room once Lenae was gone. "Can I get you anything?"

It was such a simple question. Kiernan looked up, agony tracing every line of his face as he felt the minds of the Warhost closing in around him. Lenae needed him to be strong, but he was going to War again, perhaps for the last time. He couldn't have her with him, couldn't have anyone, and Kreychi could see it written all over his face.

"I don't," he began, fear choking his words. "I don't think I can do this, Kreya. It's killing me."

Kreychi didn't say a word, just slipped inside the room and took three gliding steps to close the distance between them. Kiernan's heart ached as Kreychi took hold of his jaw, steadying him as he set their lips together and breathed life into the black pit of Kiernan's soul. As Kreychi steadied him on his feet, gripping him with a strength Kiernan had lost when Hest'lre had fled and Lenae had walked away, he hated himself for needing the man just to survive.

Kreychi didn't care, however. He would piece all the shards of Kiernan's spirit back together if that's what it took.

"I'm sorry," Kiernan sobbed when Kreychi embraced him. "Kreya, I'm so sorry."

"Just tell me what you need," Kreychi insisted, setting a hand over Kiernan's lips to silence his apology. "Let me take care of you. That's all I have ever asked."

Kiernan nodded just a hair before closing his eyes, kissing the man's palm before it slipped away. "Terra," he whispered, gulping down air through a waterfall of tears. "I need terra and another case of wine. Then maybe I can hear myself think."

"I can do that," Kreychi promised, releasing him from the hold to take him by the shoulders. "I will ask Borean about the wine and if Henrick can't find me terra, my brother can. I will be back as soon as I source it."

Kiernan nodded, taking a shuddering breath as he tried to collect himself. Kreychi's confidence didn't waver, though he did set his lips on Kiernan's one last time before he was on his way out the door.

Three more dawnings, Kiernan promised himself. *Three more dawnings and then I can leave. If I cannot drown myself in wine or smoke, perhaps Kreychi will let me drown myself in him.*

CHAPTER 07: SOLDIER TYRO MICAHLEIA SU'DELTON

Thursday, 02:00

"What do you think Rylan's doing?" Nichi asked from his indelicate sprawl as Micah moved to take a seat once again. They had both been trapped beside the circular stage within the lavishly appointed entertainment suite for House Windover for the past few candlemarks, but with a changing of acts, Micah had managed to slip away to be rid of all the ale he had drank without realizing it.

"Sleeping, probably," Micah said, flexing his aching hand as he took up his double-stringed lute once again. "That man can sleep through anything, including a revel."

"You don't think he tried to leave?" Nichi pressed, about to say more until he heard something ringing in the distance. Swearing, he sat up on his lounge as the sound of coin belts jangled just outside the entertainment suite.

"Damn," Nichi said, shaking his head as Micah saw the gaggle of scantily clad court-daughters at the threshold of the room. "I thought they weren't coming tonight."

"Of course they're coming," Micah said, picking through his cords to alert the drummers in the room that they would be needed soon. "We haven't been subjected to their newest choreography in at least..."

"Two days," Nichi finished for him. "We saw this same dance two days ago."

"Would you rather be with Tyrsten right now?" he asked, shooting Nichi a warning glance. "Last I saw him he was off to apologize to that first tier daughter again just so he didn't have to show his face here. Everyone keeps telling him how much of a travesty it is that Rylan stole his chance at being Bevy Primarch as if he hasn't been our Century Primarch for two cycles."

"Tyr will be fine," Nichi argued. "And everyone knows he's going to be on Rylan's cadre, so we'll be fine as well. All we're doing tomorrow morning is getting issued gear and sorted into teams. Once Rylan does that, it isn't even his job to plan anymore."

"No, then it's our job," Micah said, sighing. "You know he's making all of us his command cadre, not just Tyr."

"What, so Rylan will put you on Overwatch, I'll take the Sharpshooters, Ren will take the Heavies, and Tyr will actually coordinate everything through your Warbards?"

Micah's laughter seemed to be the expected response. "Tyrren couldn't win a thumb-wrestling match with the Heavies, let alone lead them," he said as the sound of coin belts moved closer. "I'm taking the heavies and the warbards. You and Ren can take the shooters. Westly is going to be coordinating the chiurgeons we need and Tyr will be Rylan's second."

"You're sure about that?" Nichi scoffed. "Rylan will make Westly cadre?"

"Of course he's cadre," Micah said. "Someone has to organize the chirons."

"But Westly isn't even a tyro," Nichi said. "I didn't think they'd let him fly the Tourni with us. I'd think he'd use Chiro Raleigh, if anyone."

"You got a problem with Westly flying the Ice Winds?" Micah asked, watching as Nichi shifted back in his seat. "You never really talk to him when he comes around."

"Not at all," Nichi insisted, perhaps a little too quickly. "I just... Well, Kaitlyn says older dryad kin tend to settle when they find a good glass garden. Maybe he doesn't want to leave."

"Yeh, but this is Rylan we're talking about," Micah said, strumming through his chords. "And Wes will do anything Rylan asks, even if it kills him."

"At least he doesn't have to listen to this," Nichi said, sinking lower in his seat as the Daughters and their obnoxiously loud coin belts moved into the room at last. "Gods, you think they'd give up after a few cycles, but no..."

"They have gotten a little better," Micah defended, even if it was half-hearted.

It wasn't better. It could never be better. These girls had no idea what they were doing with the dances and he should know. His mother had taught his twin sister Sera everything she had known about the intricate Ehkeski dances. If you didn't know what to look for, then the show the Daughters put on was fine, but after a lifetime of seeing it done properly...

I'd show them how it's done myself, but to the winds if I'm going to admit that I know how to dance, too! It was bad enough that the younger court knew his mother had been Ehkeski, but he had been an idiot when he had opened his mouth about the first terrible performance. He had only gotten away with his hide because he had said it was really the music that was off, and that if he only had a proper instrument he could prove his point.

Two solar cycles later he still regretted letting them know he could play, but he had been so long without a set of strings that his hands had been itching just being in this place. It was Rylan's fault he ruined his last lute, anyway. Rylan was usually the reason everything in his life got ruined, even if he loved the man like a brother.

Taking one last drink from his ale, Micah set the cup at his feet.

"Need any more?" Nichi asked.

Micah glanced up to see his best mate giving him a look that was anything but innocent. Matched with the overly inviting way he was strewn out on his lounge, wings relaxed on either side of the padded backing, Micah didn't have to guess why his cup had never run dry this night.

Micah raised an eyebrow at him, unimpressed, and Nichi laughed as he ran a hand through his platinum tyro's crest. Micah was matching his friend's movement before he realized what he was doing, and Nichi smirked as Micah tried to play it off as unintentional.

I should have never taught him how to read body language, Micah swore, putting his hands back to his strings. *He already knows he's too bloody attractive.*

Sighing, Micah checked the time candle at the far end of the room and saw it burning well past the mark for two past midnight. Given the heat in the suite, it might have been midsummer rather than long past harvest. Trying to cope, Micah had stripped out of his heavy tyro's jacket, leaving him in his indigo shirtsleeves. For how he stared, Nichi was enjoying the way the fabric stuck to the curves of Micah's arms, even if Nichi refused to even open his black court doublet to return the favor.

Despite being just as much of a soldier tyro as Micah was, Nichi was far too aware of his rank to be caught wearing anything but his Windover Blacks while in the suite. Micah was perfectly happy to stay in the tyro uniform wherever he went, but then again, the clothes were free and it wasn't like he owned anything else. Fortunately, the indigo the Palace used to set the soldier tyros apart from the crimson of the chirurgeon tyros and the yellow of junior lawspeakers did a killer job of setting off the grey-blue of his eyes, so he wasn't about to complain. He might not be a House prince like Nichi or Rylan, but he could break hearts with the best of them. Growing up in a brothel had made him an expert in that much at the very least.

"You could get me some water," Micah answered, wiping the sweat from his hands on his woolen pants. "Any more ale and you'll have to pour me back into the barracks," he laughed. "Though I think you're half again as bad as I am."

"I've no idea what you're talking about," Nichi said, following Micah's look as he scanned the circular entertainment suite. Only about half of the room was paying attention to the dancers as they circled the room. The rest were all paired off, wings pulled up for privacy as they devoured one another's faces.

"You know," Nichi said, and Micah looked up to realize Nichi had gotten to his feet and moved to the side of Micah's lounge. "If we're too wet-winged to make it back to the barracks, we could just stay here. My sire keeps a suite for me with a double nest in case I want to entertain."

Micah rolled his eyes as Nichi leaned onto the lounge, his own wings flaring to give them privacy in the moment. "Oh he does, does he?" Micah challenged, one eyebrow raised as Nichi began to close the distance between them.

"Mmm hmm," Nichi confirmed, matching the stare of Micah's blue-grey eyes with one of his own. There was real desire in that look, but the smoldering challenge Micah gave him in return always made Nichi hesitate.

Nichi might have been raised in the Tyro Court, but Micah had actually traded flesh and feathers for coin before they met Rylan on the Streets.

"You realize you're a terrible flirt when you're drunk, right?" Micah said, calling his bluff as his friend hesitated. Two cycles Nichi had wanted to drag him into a nest, but he could never bring himself to do more than steal a kiss here and there. Now it took the terra just to temp him, and for as skittish as Nichi was about having sex with men because of the rumors of his elder brother's singular affection for the Lord Seventh, he was still a fantastic kisser. Micah honestly didn't mind, especially when they shouldn't have been doing any of it. Wingmates were for the War Plains, not for the mountains.

"So what," Nichi defended, pulling back as he flushed. "You're just— I mean, come on. Who has eyes like that? How dare you be so fucking gorgeous."

"How dare I?" Micah laughed, shifting his lute in his hands so he could pick out a sorrowful chord to make a true martyr of his friend. Ever since they had met, Nichi had been insisting that he was more than willing to take poor, street-born Micah to nest, but Micah had a very good reason to refuse.

"Gods, fine," Nichi scoffed. "That's what I get for trying to lure you up here to make a wingmate out of you," he complained, pulling back to sulk as he leaned more heavily on the lounge. "You do know that there's nothing wrong with branching out a little, right?"

"I am branching out," Micah argued, shifting to play one of the progressions that his golden-haired Kaitlyn loved to hear. "Even if she is your near-sister, she's still from a branch of your House."

Nichi was not amused by the sideways humor. Kaitlyn and Nichi's fathers were brothers, making them near-siblings even if they had been raised as first-siblings. Besides, Micah wasn't from the Houses at all so no one cared that they both happened to think Micah was gorgeous. Most of the House would have shared a nest with him if he'd been up for it, to be honest.

"That's not what I meant," he argued, even as he laughed. "You do see how insane you make the other Daughters by letting Kait claim you, right?"

"About as insane as you went exclusively nesting with that harpy from Kirath for a cycle?" Micah replied, and then Nichi really did give him a sour look. "It's not like I need some half-wit Daughter trying to show me how it's done. Not having to show folks how it's done is a blicing relief."

"To the winds with idiot Daughters," Nichi agreed. "I was talking about me."

"I don't have time to show you either. You obviously need a lot of help," Micah said, cackling as he dodged Nichi's attempt to smack him.

"Piss off, Mike," Nichi laughed, standing tall as the dancers began to move towards the circular stage set at the center of the room. "Oh, and that's my cue," he added. "I'm going to need another bottle of mead if they're doing more than one dance."

Micah wished him well as his friend made his way towards the exit. Turning his attention back to the dancers, he picked through each of the four sets of double strings until they sang together and then rounded out the sound against the deeper bass of the final two. Once he was set, he lifted his chin and caught the attention of the other warbard-trained soldier tyros scattered around the performance circle and then the shuffle of palms on stretched hide created the hiss that got everyone else's attention.

When the last of the courtiers found their seats, Micah could see the circular dance area once again. With everything moved aside, it was obvious this particular space was meant to be a stage. Not only was the oak floor waxed and buffed to a dull shine, but hanging directly above the circle was an enormous wrought iron chandelier. Capping the arms of the black monstrosity were twenty lanterns meant to brighten the stage while the rest of the large room remained dim. On top of that, someone had carefully pinned a huge cloth-of-gold fabric to tame the brightness into the warm glow that set the mood.

Once his audience was settled, Micah stilled his strings and looked up to the lead dancer, a blonde haired Daughter named Makayla. As her troupe came into position behind her, she blew him a kiss to let him know they were ready. Micah forced a smile and then the group lifted their hands up in front of them, arms crossed at the wrist to frame their faces as their costumes settled. True to the Windover colors, they were still in the black and gold, but it was the amount they wore that was the most surprising. Tonight they had forgone the black cropped undershirts in favor of wearing only the gold brocade half-vests that left next-to-nothing to the imagination.

The only other thing they wore were their feathers and the sheer cloth-of-gold skirts that were slung so low you could see the top of their thighs. Micah frowned as he looked at the matching triangular belts, realizing that they were actually strung with gold coins that would ring against one another as they moved.

Obviously, Makayla's belt was the most heavily adorned, with at least five rows of the coins across her hips, while the others had the coins hanging off the bottom edge.

Micah almost stopped playing. Looking between the gold on the ceiling and the gold they wore, he could have bought his way out of his conscription with the amount they ruined just for a night's entertainment. Seething but doing his best not to show it, Micah waited for the chorus of comments to die down before starting the slow introduction of "Stella Solemque"—or 'Sun and Stars' in the Old Tongue—which was the name of the song the Daughters always wanted him to play.

Micah felt the burst of their happiness in the postures they took when Makayla glided forward to stand with him. The other eight girls followed her lead, creating a circle with their wings on the inside as he picked through the meandering notes. Then each girl set her wings to form a backdrop behind them and did their best to move with the slow, isolated grace that created the illusion that each of them was, for that moment, an Ehkeski woman standing before their portion of the circle.

To be honest, Makayla was the only one who could pull it off, and for as poor as she was in comparison to his mother and sister, her ability to follow along with his playing had vastly improved in two cycles. It still hadn't earned her a place in his nest or drawn him into her own, but that didn't stop her trying.

As the taxingly slow introduction finally came to a close, Micah gave a low-to-high whistle that caught the attention of the other warbards in the room. With a nod, they grinned back at him and the drummers around the circle came up in unison to join him. That was part of the show after all, since the warbard training could enhance not only orders from the men of the Host, but revels as well.

Taking their cue, the girls turned to face one another and Micah set out the rhythm he wanted as they returned to the center of their performance stage. When they were finally together, Micah set his palm against his strings and let one of the other sirelings take up the solo work.

That sharp-handed drumming was the signal for the girls to change how they were standing as well, turning out to their audience as they raised their hands slowly before them, palm up as they encouraged the other watchers to carry the heavy down beat of the rest of the drums.

With the room clapping along, the drums skittered off on their own missions and Micah set his hands back to his strings to start the melody in earnest. As he cycled through his progression, the girls followed along with hips and hands. Whenever he went up in notes, their movement increased. Whenever he went down into the bass strings, they bent their knees to crescendo with him back into the heart of the song.

Order slinger, bardic singer, all of it came from the same source and as he hit the fast-fingered bridge, the girls moved through a new pattern and the crowd burst into cheers. Coming up onto the edge of his chair, Micah's excitement overcame the ale that had been fogging his thoughts. Confident that the dancers were now taking his cue, Micah wondered if they could handle the sort of push he had once given to Sera as she danced.

When he had first started to play as a fledgling, his mother had explained that every good dancer had grace, but not every dancer had the ability to transfix an audience. That was where his music came in, his music and his subtle, bardic Suggestion that the only thing in the world that mattered was the dance. Captivated by it, they lost track of time and in the process turned over more and more coin to ensure it continued.

That was a reason that their little street crew had never been truly poor. How could they be, with his bardic magic and Sera's dancing? Given two cycles of a warbard's training, which went into far more theory about harmonics, music, and the pure force of will than Micah had ever believed possible, he wanted to see if he could make these women truly come alive. That, and Westly had said that using his talents during something other than class might be able to make his headaches go away.

Taking a moment to shake off the rest of his ale, Micah rolled his head about his neck and resettled himself in his seat. As the drums played through their part, he inhaled deeply, shifting his hands around the fretless lute until he could depress the strings with true precision. When they began to fall back into the rhythm of the song, Micah began his work.

As the gut-string cords cut into his fingertips, he made the shift in tones more overt. Makayla yipped at him from her place among her troupe, accepting his challenge with one of the Ehkeski call-and-response tricks he had taught them. With a grin, Micah nodded and came to his feet, the crowd roaring with approval to see the duel for what it was.

As Micah played for them, the girls seemed to light from the inside with energy, strong and confident and alive. When they were in unison with his melody, he began a cascade to accompany their fluid movements and poured the strength of his will through his hands and into the music that resonated from the bent neck, fretless lute. Makayla in turn raised her right arm to signal her dancers and the troupe shifted their arrangement. Micah punctuated the music with a triple beat and Makayla changed the shape of her upheld hand to signal them to pivot through the movements. Micah was leading their dancing now, playing them as another extension of his instrument.

Micah's pulse was racing as he played through his notes. As he fought for breath, his vision blurred with concentration as the dancers began to tire under the strain. In one last burst of energy, Micah set his hands to begin the spiraling arpeggio that brought the song to a close. The women looked relieved, all of them stepping and turning together, and the flourish of their skirts rose just high enough to entice.

It was a perfect ending.

Micah gave a victorious cry as the girls spun out of the grip of his bardic magic, twirling freely about the room. He dropped back onto his chair, trilling out of the song so that only the breathy, throbbing drums remained. Those beats would sustain the dancers as they moved into the crowd towards individual targets.

"For Honor and Glory!" Nichi called, giving the cry of the Warhost as Micah looked up to realize that the entertaining suite was now packed with people.

"Honor and Glory!" all the tyros in the room returned, and Micah raised a fist overhead to thank them as he caught his breath.

"Well done, Micah," added a voice from behind him and Micah's gut clenched as he recognized just who it was. Trying not to wince, he turned and pulled his lute against his chest so he could give the right-handed salute to Canto Xavier who led their century. "It seems like my suspicions were correct, however. You have been restraining yourself in class."

Micah flushed, glancing to the man standing to his Canto's right. While Canto Xavier was still dressed in his uniform flying leathers, the man with him was dressed in the formal, brocade kama that all Warhost men wore when they were present in Delton on official business.

Seeing him, Micah came into a full salute as he recognized the heavy Primarch's pauldron and quicksilver concho on the left breast that marked him as Lord Seventh's personal cadre. On his right shoulder he wore a pauldron as well, a flared extension of a leather epaulet that acknowledged how he was the strongest warbard in Kosar, second only to Lord Seventh. This man could send orders to an entire Legion without vocalizing at all.

"Tyro Micahleia," Canto Xavier began, making the introduction. "This is Cantullus Cadre Primarch Decius su'Yaltana. He could feel your efforts from where we were speaking with Lord Sixth in the King's Suites and he insisted I make the introduction."

Micah's heart was thundering in his chest.

"Well met, young canto," Decius complemented, returning Micah's salute to free him to move. "I must confess, I was suspicious of the reports I received of your strength, but now it all falls into place. You may have trained your talents to an instrument, but such a crutch will not hold you back in Kirath. I am certain the new Lord Seventh will enjoy a bit of fanfare and your playing is brilliant."

Micah's tongue turned to ash, though he managed to duck his head with the praise.

"You are meant to serve as the Red Bevy Canto, I've heard?" Decius asked.

"Hoi, Preem," Micah confirmed.

"Let me set you a true challenge, then. If you can call to me during the tourni without your toy," he said, meaning the lute. "I will make certain that you are assigned to my personal chain of command. The Host needs men to serve the new Lord Seventh, and I will accept nothing but the best."

"Honor and Glory, Preem," Micah managed, saluting again as the men returned it and turned to walk away.

Heart still pounding, Micah looked down at his lute in amazement. He knew he hadn't tried in class, not really, but to think a Preem had felt just his force of will from the bottom of the Sires' Wing. Gods forbid if he actually tried!

"Mike!" Called a voice from behind him. "Holy shit, Mike! Was that Canto Decius?"

Micah looked up as Nichi took the place the two men had vacated. "Yeah," he said, shaking his head. "Yeah, it was."

"Blood and ice, I told you!" Nichi laughed. "I told you that you could get a proper commission if you just tried for once. Gods, just imagine being his apprentice! You'd never have to be on the Plains at all, following Lord Seventh around like he does."

And I'd never see Sera again, Micah knew. He hadn't wanted anyone to know what he could do, hadn't even wanted to know himself, and now?

"Kait!" Nichi called, looking past Micah's wings as someone moved up behind him. "Kait, did you see that!"

No matter everything that had just happened, when Micah felt the two slender hands of his beloved sliding around his middle as she kissed between his wings, the world righted itself.

"I did see," she said as Micah laid his hands on her own, pulling her closer so her arms were tight around his middle. "And it is wonderful, as long as he wants it."

"What do you mean, as long as he wants it?" Nichi scoffed. "Of course he wants it. That's a Cadre Primarch he just impressed."

Kaitlyn's lips on his neck made Micah shiver. As the world around the two of them went silent, it was only because his eyes were open that he saw Nichi was still rambling on.

"Hello, sweetness," Micah said, shifting his head so he could nuzzle back her golden curls. "What kept you?"

"I was caring for a few of the House chicks who wanted one of my fae stories before they would sleep," she whispered, kissing his cheek before pulling away so he could turn and embrace her properly. "But I did catch the end of your performance," she said, her dark brown eyes full of pleasure. "You were pulling people in from the hall you were so wonderful."

"I would rather be entertaining you. Alone," he whispered, flexing his wings around her as he made her certain-sure of just who held his heart.

Beside them, Nichi groaned to hear their exchange, though he waited until they had made one another breathless before butting back in. "Are we heading back now?"

Micah frowned at him, looking around to see that the other tyros were starting to pack up their things. It was late, sure, but it wasn't so late yet that they needed to head back. Then again, with the tournament coming up they should probably get some actual sleep.

Sighing, Micah folded his wings behind him, only to catch Nichi preening at one of his own with a pained look he immediately tried to hide.

"We probably should head back," Kaitlyn answered and Micah smirked at her as he set his hands at her waist. She was still in her own version of the Windover Blacks and the place where the peplum on her bodice flared was just at the start of her snug woolen leggings.

"We?" Micah asked, sneaking his thumbs between the fabric to get at her skin. "Should I be expecting company tonight?"

"I have a fledgling in my nest, remember?" Kaitlyn said, eyes mischievous as she felt his caress.

"And you don't want to wake her," Micah smirked.

"As it turns out, I do not," Kaitlyn grinned, taking her time as she felt down the length of his muscled arms. Micah flexed for her as she did and when she tried to hide her pleasure by chewing her lip, he just grinned. When she was quite done, Micah tugged her against him and no groan from Nichi could stop him from stealing another kiss or three. It was Kaitlyn he wanted to take to nest and as deep in his ale as he was, she knew he was easily distracted from Nichi's attention, House prince or no.

When they finally parted, Kaitlyn stepped away entirely, giving Micah the space to pack up his lute from where he had rested it against the back of the lounge. Intoxicated or not, Micah got the instrument back into its proper case and slung between his wings without a problem. He could and had done it in his sleep a few times when he and the rest of his crew had still been on the streets.

"Whose fledgling was it you were taking care of, anyway?" Micah asked as they moved out into the main receiving room of the lavishly appointed Windover apartments. "I didn't think it was good to have them at Court."

"It's not," Kaitlyn said, though she shot a shadowed look at Nichi. "But this one insisted on seeing her before he left for war. Said it would look good if he was seen doting on the girl, even if her mother is still in Alexandria recovering from the birth of her son."

Nichi's grin was wicked. "What?"

"You had your fledgling brought here?" Micah scoffed.

"Only one of them," he defended. "And if I intend to marry her mother, it lets me see what kind of heirs I'll have. The worst kind of ringing is finding out your wife's House has raised a flock of brats that will spoil the fortune you've built."

"I thought princelings weren't supposed to see their fledglings until they got back from war," Micah frowned, now looking to Kaitlyn.

"They're not," she agreed. "But with Kreychi without a wife and about to become our Patriarch, it isn't a bad idea. Dame Andrea even supported it, knowing it would help buffer the rumors about the foundation of the House weakening. It's..."

"Political nonsense?" Micah supplied. "Gods, but the Houses are strange," he went on, which amused both Nichi and Kaitlyn as they took the lead down the hallway once again. It wasn't the first time he'd made such a comment. "Where I'm from, chicks are a deficit."

"It's not about where you came from," Nichi assured him as they moved towards the exit. "It's where you're going that counts."

"We're going to the War Plains," Micah reminded. "I'm pretty sure chicks aren't a good thing to have down there either."

Kaitlyn actually giggled at that, but Nichi was having none of it. "Chicks that get made on the Plains stay on the Plains," he said, trying to change the subject.

"Unless they're born with wings," Kaitlyn added. "Then they go to Kelsineah."

"Like Westly?" Micah asked and watched as Nichi's interest caught on his crew-brother's name.

"Westly is a rather different case," Kaitlyn said as Nichi wandered off through the scattered lounges to find a bottle filled with water rather than mead, he claimed. "His father was actually from Kelsineah, right?"

"Apparently," Micah said, sidling up next to her. Of the three of them, only she hadn't indulged and he could use something steady at the moment. "His mother was the dryad."

"Well, obviously," Kaitlyn laughed, gathering him up into her arms. "A greenman isn't going to tempt anyone across the River Kir. They don't look nearly so pretty."

"And you would know, how?" he asked, squinting at her.

"I have an illustrated manuscript from the Eastwatch Clan," she said, matter of fact. "And it's worth quite a few crowns. Eastwatch is the Clan that goes into the deep woods to help—"

"—Guide the Seventh Counsel Lord on Envoy. Yes, you've told me," he said, talking over her until she flushed. "About twenty times. This moon," he added, laughing. "Oh, and did I mention—"

"That it is Westly's father's Clan," she said, doing him the same favor as she laughed and pushed out of his arms. "Well, it's not every day someone actually knows something about the fae," she added, pouting. "I forget you know so much sometimes."

"Did I ever tell you that Westly says the Ehkeski call us all fae: dryads and windwalkers?" he said, curling his wings around them as if he was telling secrets. "You go on about Gifts and Talents and dryad magic, but they have nothing for themselves, so we're the supernatural ones."

"I can't say I disagree with them," she said, trading another kiss before embracing him fully. Dizzy as he was, Micah set his head on her shoulder and closed his eyes, taking the moment to enjoy the soft lavender scent in her hair. It was almost like his sister, just close enough to make his heart ache, but different enough that he remembered who it was he was holding. Kaitlyn didn't say a word, though she did kiss his temple before they relaxed into the embrace in the quiet.

That silence was always the hardest part, he knew biting into his lower lip to stop himself from speaking. Both Kaitlyn and Nichi knew why he had overindulged tonight, though he had done it so often with them that it almost seemed normal. It hurt almost physically being away from his sister, but if he could drown himself in merriment, he could almost forget how much.

When his head was finally steady, Micah pulled back from Kaitlyn's shoulder, curious why it seemed to be taking Nichi so long to forage. When he found him again, Nichi was walking out of the third hallway in the suite of apartments with his far-cousin Tyrsten in tow. Unlike Nichi's black and gold court clothing, Tyrsten had on an ill-fitting indigo uniform.

"What?" he greeted, seeing Micah's dubious look.

"Kayla take you back?" He asked, reaching up to touch his neck where Tyrsten was starting to show a lover's mark just above his uniform collar.

"Eventually," Tyrsten laughed, rubbing at the spot despite his chagrin. "This is what got me in trouble, though, so she had to make it worse before she went off dancing. The whole troupe jumped me just to steal my Blacks. This was all I could find to wear to get back to the barracks. Blicing women, am I right?" He said, looking to Nichi.

"You have no idea," Nichi agreed, though he rolled his eyes as well. His last bit of trouble with the House had gotten him in hotter water than the Seventh Counsel Lord. The last woman to come chasing Nichi's wings had been the Daughter of the branch of their House that had defected from Windover to join the rumored 'House Kirath'. That was a new House entirely, forming to take in the exiled nobility of the Kirathy shelf that had been ravaged by the Lan'lieanans some eight cycles ago. If Micah hadn't dragged Nichi out of that particular woman's nest by the scruff of his neck, House Kirath might have been able to gut the power of Windover itself because of a chick Nichi might have gotten on her.

Sighing, Micah looked towards the door. "Is there anyone else in the suite from our century, or is it just us?" He asked, ready to leave.

"Just us, I think," Tyrsten said, frowning. "Ren is at a party with the chirons—Oh, blood and ice. Nichi," he said, wincing. "Your brother said he needed to talk to you this afternoon. Something about your sire? Did you talk to him?"

Nichi's look darkened. "Yeah, I did," he said, looking away as he started to head for the door. "And I can do it tomorrow morning."

"But the chirons are going to be running the gear-issue tomorrow morning," Tyrsten protested, following after him as Micah and Kaitlyn separated from their embrace. "It would be better if you talked to Westly now. Mike, he'd be up, right?"

"He should be," Micah said, looking between the two of them. "Why? What's going on?"

Nichi ignored the question. "It's almost three past midnight, Tyr. If you really think Rylan is going to make us cadre, then I want an actual night's sleep to deal with him," he said, grabbing one of the indigo tyro cloaks hanging next to the suite's double doors. It didn't matter which one he took, since the whole tyro system worked like one large commune. If it fit, you could wear it. If you wanted a specific one, you better keep an eye on it. "Come on, Mike."

Micah made a face as the two sirelings looked at him. "I was actually going to stop by the Garden before I went back to the barracks," he said, confused. "If you want to go on ahead, go with Tyr. I'll just catch up."

"No, we signed out together, so we have to sign back in," Nichi said, groaning as he tossed Micah one of the cloaks. "Tyr?"

"I don't have to sign in with anyone," he said, grabbing up a cloak of his own as he followed Nichi towards the exit of the suite. "But you need to talk to him, Nichi."

"What's this about?" Micah asked, looking between the two of them.

Tyrsten pursed his lips, looking away with a distinct 'this is House business' sort of unease. Sighing, Micah didn't press him. "Well if we're going back, we should go. Kait, I—" Micah said, only to stop as Kaitlyn picked up one of the ebony and gold House cloaks for herself. "Wait. Are you coming, too?"

"There is a chick in my nest," she reminded, smiling as she dropped the heavy silk between her wings and over her shoulders with a bit more delicacy than the three tyros. "Remember?"

"Oh right," Micah grinned, much to her pleasure. "So maybe I don't need to talk to Westly either..."

Nearly a cycle ago, Kaitlyn had turned the House signet ring on her right hand for him, which had signaled to the members of the younger court that she would put off others' advances despite the fact that Micah could not and did not claim her. It meant more to him than he had realized at the time, but over the course of the cycle, he found himself settling into the rhythm of her companionship.

She reminded him of his sister—intelligent, curious, and beautiful because of it— and now she was starting to spend most of her nights in his nest in the Tyros' Wing when she didn't have House duties to manage the next dawning.

"Need help with that?" Micah asked, watching as she tried and failed to catch up the cloth-of-gold ribbons attached to the panel between her wings. Finally giving up, Kaitlyn pouted as she stepped up to him.

Micah smirked as he slid his arms around her waist and took hold of the two thick ribbons. As he brought them around to the front, he drew her closer, bringing her in for a kiss until Nichi had to remind them of his presence.

"We're ready whenever you two are done," Nichi said, nosing in between the crests of their wings. As Kaitlyn flushed and pulled away, Micah finally tied the ribbon in a bow around her waist. With Nichi walking out of the suite to join Tyrsten, Kaitlyn caught his eyes with a look and it was almost as if he could hear her thoughts like he could his own sister's.

I am not done with you yet.

Once they were outside of the suite, the four of them moved down to their left to where the balcony railing opened at the corner of their floor. They didn't have to walk far, given that the Windover suite was at the very end of the long Sires' Wing, set up against one side of the Seventh Counsel Lord's Library. The Library itself was the full eighteen stories tall, and as they approached it Micah was certain Kaitlyn would have given her left wing to get inside the place just once.

When they reached the opening, Micah and Nichi stopped to allow Kaitlyn and Tyrsten space to spread their wings and check the chasm for traffic before tipping off the edge. As Kaitlyn spiraled down the sixteen stories to the flight mosaic reserved for those landing or taking off from the ground floor, Tyrsten cut a straight path, pulling up at the last moment with a backwing that sent a crack of air through the nearly empty Sires' Wing.

After a moment to let them clear the space, Micah looked back to Nichi and sputtered with laughter to see his mockery of the smoldering look Kaitlyn had given him back in the suite. Micah shoved him unceremoniously out into the chasm for his efforts, to which Nichi shouted back: "It was worth a shot!"

Surprisingly, Nichi actually twisted into the slow spiral as well, so when Micah tipped off, he managed to beat Nichi to the flight circle since he could still manage the sharper dive and backwing they were required to use with their combat flight, drunk or not. Usually Nichi could as well, if only because the rush of free fall could overcome the mead for at least a few wingbeats.

"You all right?" Tyrsten asked, watching as Nichi messed with his wing again, only to see a few feathers fall away for his effort. "You've been preening all day."

"It's just an itch," Nichi replied, dismissive as he caught up with them. "Someone probably pranked my doublet and it got on my wings. Come on, let's go."

A quarter mark later, they were back in the Soldier Tyros' Wing. As they hit the landing of the tenth level, Tyrsten stalled at the desk where two tyros were sitting, bored out of their minds. They did at least have something of a meal and what looked to be an ale for each of them, but desk duty waited for no revel.

"Everything quiet?" He asked, signing Micah and Nichi back into the floor.

"Hoi, Primarch," said one of the two, toasting him with his mug.

Tyrsten skimmed the list on the bit of flatboard they had handed him, frowning. "Mother signed Rylan out?" He asked.

"Yeah," the tyro said, shrugging. "Apparently he left, but he's down with Westly."

Tyrsten made a face, glancing to Micah. "He'd rather sit with plants than the women of our House?"

"He's a bowen, Tyr," Micah said, shaking his head. "He wouldn't even know what to do with a woman."

"He's a what?" His friends gawked. Even Kaitlyn.

"Well he certainly isn't fucking my sister," Micah insisted. "I think I'd know about that."

Tyrsten just chewed his lip to hide a smile.

"Who needs him, anyway?" Micah said, rolling his eyes. "Why do you think I go to revel with Windover?"

When the four of them looked to Kaitlyn, gorgeous in all her court finery, Micah remembered himself. Before he could say anything, though, she spoke up in his defense.

"I'm so glad you think I'm prettier than Rylan," Kaitlyn laughed, batting her eyelashes.

"And a sight better in a nest, too, I'd think, if Rylan's a bowen," the second tyro on duty said, only to flinch as both Nichi and Tyrsten glared. Not that they were wrong.

"Rylan would take Mother to nest before he'd ever take a man," Micah laughed, raising a hand to wave goodbye. "And he'd die trying at that."

With laughter following in his wake, Tyrsten waved as well, though he remained with the two on duty to chat. Micah, Nichi, and Kaitlyn continued down the hall, though Micah stalled at Nichi's door given his mate's sour look.

"What?" Micah asked, even as Kaitlyn tugged at his wing to keep moving.

"You don't happen to have a twist on you, do you?" he asked, opening his door, only to turn back and rest his head against the threshold.

Micah glanced down the hall where he could still see Tyrsten talking with the others before answering. "I'm running low, but yeah, I mean..." He looked to Kaitlyn as well. "Why? What's up?"

Nichi chewed his lip, his thoughts clearly inside his own head.

"This about Wes?" he asked, sensing the thought even if he couldn't quite explain how. All that warbard training through the Academy had been messing with his ability to read people, making it easier somehow. "Why do you need to talk to him?"

Nichi's look made it clear he wasn't about to talk with Kaitlyn there.

"Heyla, sweetness," Micah said, catching her look. "Why don't you go on ahead? I'll be right with you."

Kaitlyn's smoldering look went to Nichi. "Don't you dare keep him too long."

Nichi exhaled a laugh, pulling back from the door to nod. "Course," he said, watching her move a few rooms down before slipping inside.

Micah stepped into Nichi's room when she was gone, pulling out the tin of terra he kept in a secret pocket in his uniform. Banned though the plant might be, Westly had given him a supply of it to dampen his abilities through the warbard training.

With the issue he'd had contacting Sera recently, it was also the only thing either of them had found that could ease the headaches he was getting the closer they got to graduation.

"You need a talk with this or can I...?" Micah said, fingering the half-burnt twist he had been working through over the past few nights. He was going to need to smoke the rest of it given all he'd done at the revel. Still, he could spare a little.

Nichi just moved over to where he had left an oil lantern burning low in his room, turning it up enough so Micah could remove the glass and catch the twist. That done, he let Micah work at getting the twist truly lit as he stripped out of his court clothing. He had his flight boots, court doublet, and silk shirt thrown in a pile by the time Micah gave him his full attention.

"I can't do this, Mike," he said, sitting down heavily on the platform that held the bowl of his nest. "I just can't."

"Can't what?" Micah asked, confused as Nichi dropped his head in his hands as his wings relaxed behind him. "Talk to Wes? You talk to him all the time, man."

"No, I don't," Nichi said, not looking up. "I specifically don't."

Frowning, Micah sucked in a thin stream of the azure smoke from the twist as he waited for Nichi to gather his thoughts. Exhausted as he was, he seemed to be trying to wring out whatever he meant to say from his platinum tyro crest.

"What are you talking about?" Micah asked, squatting down in front of Nichi to offer him a drag of the twist.

"I mean yeah," Nichi said, his anxiety bleeding through. "I'll say sal'weh and work together, but with Kreychi still working for Lord Seventh at Court, I couldn't do more than that. But now Kreychi is hovering over Lord Seventh again, like actually going to see him every blicing day and everyone is noticing, and I just—" Now he looked up, close to frantic. "Micah, what if he's going to name my brother Counselheir?"

Micah's jaw dropped open in surprise. "I thought you said he refused," he insisted.

"He had! Or I thought he had, but the Founders take who they want for that Seat," Nichi said, groaning as he washed his hands over his face. "But he came back when I started on my own commission and he was trying to not make my life harder, no matter his connections. And our matron started trying to have both of us make sure we threw chicks on proper Daughters…I mean, I have three, but he doesn't have any. Do you know how many Lord Seventh's have offspring, Mike? None of them because they're too focused on the blicing war. That, or they can't throw because they become a Founder's Priest or—Gods, who knows!"

Micah sucked down another thin line of the azure, realizing now why Nichi had every reason to be so upset. However, if he wasn't going to smoke the terra, Micah certainly was. His own nerves were on edge now. This was insane.

"So you really think he's going to be Counselheir?" He asked. "Or has been the whole time he's been here?"

"What other explanation is there?" Nichi insisted, looking up again. "That he's just been in love with a man he met as a tyro all this time? That he's let it ruin his entire life?"

It is possible, Micah wanted to say, not that Nichi wanted to hear it.

"So what if he is the next Lord Seventh?" Micah said instead. "What does that have to do with Westly?"

"Nothing? Everything?" Nichi swore, covering his face with his hands. "Kreychi wants me to go talk to him, to have me ask if he will heal our Sire. He says it has to come from the House, not from Lord Seventh or him, and I just—If he isn't going to lead the House and he wants my father well, that gives me time for my four cycles at war before I come back and become Patriarch. I don't want to do that, Micah. I've never wanted to do that. I'm supposed to be able to serve, but not if he's going to be Lord Seventh. They won't even let me, knowing we don't have an heir to the House."

"What about Kait's dad?" Micah said, setting a hand on Nichi's knee to try and calm his friend. "He's acting as your Patriarch right now, isn't he?"

"Yeah, but all three of his sons died at war. My near-brothers... Gods, it's like they never existed. He doesn't even talk about them anymore and Kait barely remembers them. That's why they came to live with us, Mike. Because it broke him to lose everyone so soon after losing Kait's mom. I mean, I was a fledgling, but I still remember when they moved in. That's why he's only going to be Patriarch until Kreychi takes his place, but Kreychi refuses to do anything until Lord Seventh goes on Envoy. But what if he's saying that just to hide the fact that he's going to be the Counselheir? Mike, I'm so fucked. Kait can't even help me."

"Because Kait would marry out of the House, not in," he finished, realizing just how trapped his friend might actually be. "Blood on my ashes..."

"So *why* does he want me to talk to your brother?" Nichi insisted, angry now. "I've done exactly what my Matron asked of me, staying away from Westly all these cycles. I just—Mike, she was so worried when she realized Westly was part of our squad that she made me promise I wouldn't talk to him any more than necessary. She didn't want anyone to think I was like my brother."

As Nichi caught his breath, Micah just shook his head. Nichi wasn't making any sense at all. "Why would she care who you talked to?" He asked. "He's just a chiurgeon. People aren't going to talk about you going to see your best mate's friend who's a chiron, especially if I go with you."

Nichi's hands were shaking, even if he was trying to hide it as he wrung them together.

"No, he's not," Nichi insisted, shifting away from him as he readjusted his wings over his nest. "Gods, he so much more than that. Mike, he's like a greenman out of a fae tale. He's the woods come to life and blicing brilliant and I..."

Micah's incredulous look halted all the words suddenly pouring out of his friend. There was real passion in him and absolute wonder just talking about it. Micah's jaw dropped open as Nichi started swearing at himself, covering his face with his hands.

"Nichi, do you like him?" Micah asked, only to have Nichi's awe turn into panic.

"No!" Nichi insisted, realizing what he had said—how he had said it—as he scrambled back from the precipice of what was clearly a confession. "Fuck, no. I just—I used to live for the woods before all of this tyro shit and someone's going to think—someone's going to realize. No, I can't, Mike. I can't get any closer to him. If I get any closer to him someone might come after him."

"Nichi, what are you talking about?" Micah insisted.

"After everything Kreychi has put the House through," Nichi said, hands going to his hair. "If I'm in love with a dryad kin, they might kill Westly because they think he made me like my brother. They might think he's trying to destroy the House."

Micah stuck the terra between his lips so he could grab at his friend's hands. At this rate Nichi was going to tear his hair out just to stop himself from shaking.

"You don't know how crazy the Daughters can get, Mike. They mask it at court, but back home? Oh, Gods… Gods, if Kariin found out? If this rumor about her being in House Kirath is true, I just—"

"Nichi, you need to calm down," Micah pleaded.

But Nichi wasn't listening. He was holding his breath, shaking with the force of his panic. Having seen enough, Micah gave up his hold on Nichi's arm and sucked down a breath of the ashing twist in his hand. That done, he got down on his knees, grabbing either side of his friend's face and when Nichi took a ragged breath, Micah closed the distance between them.

Nichi froze as he felt Micah's lips on his own. When he inhaled in surprise, Micah exhaled the breath of terra in a slow, intentional exchange, keeping them together. Once Nichi figured out what was happening, he had his own hands on Micah, more than willing to re-share that breath as the affection sent all other thoughts out of Nichi's mind.

After what seemed like an age, Micah finally drew back from the dizzying exchange. Nichi looked dazed as well and as they both recovered, Micah took another deep pull off the terra to calm his own nerves. Sensitive as Micah was to other people's emotions, Nichi was still a maelstrom, no matter his efforts.

The sudden, gentle knock on the door behind them startled them both back to their senses. Micah was on his feet as soon as he heard Kaitlyn's voice at the door. "Everything all right in here?"

"Uh, yeah," Nichi said, pulling back as Micah stepped away. "Sorry, I…"

"It's okay, Nichi," Kaitlyn said, holding her hand up for peace. "I just wanted to make sure you were okay."

"I'm fine," he said, looking over to her only to duck his head as she moved into the room. "Gods, I'll be fine. I just need to sleep."

"Wes is going to come here in the morning," Micah said. "Just come to my room and you can talk to him there, okay? No one has to overhear anything."

"Yeah, okay," Nichi said, shifting so he could fall back into his nest as the terra started to work its magic on Nichi's nerves.

"Thank you for that," Kaitlyn said as Micah moved to join her at the door. She wasn't wearing more than her leggings and silk undershirt at this point, but she also knew what kind of pressure Nichi was under. What kind they both were, with graduation just a few days away.

"For what?" Micah asked, curious as she took hold of the open front of his tyro uniform.

"Taking care of him," Kaitlyn said as she walked him across the hall to the room he shared with Rylan. "Think you could try that breath again with me?" She asked once they had slipped inside. "It looked like fun."

"You want to try my terra?" Micah asked, honestly surprised.

"I want you," she whispered, pulling him close. "Breath or body, I will take what I can get."

Kaitlyn gasped as Micah took hold of her waist, picking her up with the tyro's strength she loved so much before tossing her gently towards his nest. Wings flaring as she found her feet, Micah put the last of the twist in his lips, stripping out of his uniform as she watched him with a hunger he could readily see.

After one last drag of the terra, he set the ash of the twist aside and stalked after her, closing the distance between them to share the sweet azure smoke with the woman he adored. When the breath was spent, Kaitlyn dragged him down over her in his nest, blurring what little time was left in the night with the press of her body and the breath of hot azure smoke between them.

Sometime near to dawning, Micah came awake all at once as he heard a knock on his door. With his head still pounding from too much ale, his heart raced with panic.

Oh Gods, not a nest check...

As he struggled to come back to his senses, Micah realized that there had only been the one knock. If it was a nest check, one of their Cantos would have thrown open the door by now with their Barracks Mother at his heels spreading the fire and fury of readiness as they went.

"Rylan?" Micah called out, hoping it was just his crew-brother.

"No, Micah," answered a woman's voice.

"Mother?" Micah yelped, trying to orient himself as he looked beyond the curve of Kaitlyn's body. It wouldn't do to keep his Barracks Mother waiting, even if she didn't sound like a harpy at the moment. Given how sharp she could be during the nest checks, any tyro in their right mind made sure to keep her happy at all times. But now? Now she sounded worried and that was more frightening than any face she had ever put on for show.

"Kait," he said, touching Kaitlyn's shoulder. "Kait, you have to go."

Kaitlyn murmured in sleepy protest, pressing herself against him as if to convince him otherwise.

"I know, sweetness," he told her, brushing her golden curls from her face. "But Mother is here..."

"Oh," Kaitlyn said, waking more quickly as she realized why it was she needed to go. "Oh!"

Micah held still as she lifted herself onto the flat surface beside his nest. Watching her slide beyond it, Micah fell back into the remaining warmth and rolled his head around his neck, trying to stop the pounding. Kaitlyn squeaked as her bare feet met the cold stone floor, but she made quick work of dressing again.

After a moment, Micah followed suit, dragging himself onto the platform beside his nest as he waited for the room to right itself. Once he was steady, he put a bare foot to the stone and let the shock of it wake him. A second foot and he could think more clearly, though he was no less intoxicated.

Cursing the cold, Micah got back into at least his uniform knickers before looking towards the door again. After the night he'd been through, he didn't trust himself to walk more than it would take to escort Kaitlyn to his threshold. It was a wonder Kaitlyn was so dexterous, but she always made it a point to keep watch over him when Rylan was gone and be ready to manage him if he over indulged. It had, embarrassingly, already happened more than once.

When they were both ready, Micah opened the door, letting lantern light flood the room. As the lean, strong-winged figure of his Barracks Mother stood out in silhouette, Kaitlyn made a respectful curtsey.

"Mother," she said, demure despite her own higher social status. There was something about women in their respective territory that was beyond Micah's comprehension.

"Oh Kaitlyn, you are here," Vinicia said with surprising relief. "Could I borrow you please?"

"Of course, Mother," Kaitlyn said and made another small curtsey.

Micah looked between the two women in confusion. Though his Barracks Mother looked to be the same age as Kaitlyn—somewhere around three and twenty— Vinicia was as hard-bodied as a woman could come. Even though she tried to hide her strength beneath a set of working leathers died indigo like his own, every man who had been a tyro in the past decade knew not to cross her without very good reason. Her auburn hair held fire in it, and as the saying went, you didn't want it to light up her wings.

Despite all of that, he would have never known it to see her now. Rather, as she stood with her arms crossed under her chest to wait for Kaitlyn to join her in the hallway, everything about her was wrong. In addition to still looking like she was being taken by a wasting sickness, she was worried, almost panicked, and if she was coming to his room in the middle of the night to find Kaitlyn of all people... Had something happened to Rylan?

"This isn't about Rylan," Vinicia began, answering the first of Micah's unspoken questions. "But I will need to speak with your crew at some point soon."

"Hoi, Mother," Micah responded, even more confused.

"I take it from how you reek of terra that you had a good night?" Vinicia went on, shifting her weight as she glanced into the dimness of the room beyond him.

"You could say that, Mother," Micah answered, and then took the chance to speak out of turn. "Has something happened?"

As the woman exhaled slowly, considering her response, Micah knew he was right. When she looked back down the first side of the hallway, Micah did a double-take to see how her eyes unfocused in a way that reminded him very much of Westly.

"It is women's business," Vinicia said when she refocused on him. "Which is why I need Kaitlyn's assistance. Everything will be fine, but it will take a dawning. Maybe two."

Micah answered her look with respectful silence, if only because he wasn't sure what to make of her answer. He knew that Westly had sworn to the woman's compassion for their conscription and that she had earned Rylan's respect after she had thrown him in a linen closet the first time he had tried to get thrown out of the academy, but he could never get a true read on her. For as strong a warbard as he was, she put all of it to shame.

Now he had no idea what to think, though staring at her just made him realize that it wasn't the room that was spinning. As he relaxed out of his braced attention to grab onto the threshold for support, Vinicia's worry was for him alone.

"Are you all right, son?" She asked, just now realizing that he had a belly full of ale in addition to a head full of smoke.

"You may find me hung over a wash basin in the morning," Micah said and gave her a sheepish grin. "But that's all from me, Mother."

"Do you need help getting back to your nest?" she asked, looking past his wings to the line of clothing he had shed earlier with Kaitlyn. Micah turned his head to follow her gaze and then cursed as the room started to spin again. Before he knew what was happening, he felt both Vinicia and Kaitlyn's strength beneath him as his own gave out.

"I think maybe I do," Micah groaned, and let them help him stagger back to his nest. As he fell into it, Kaitlyn stepped away to grab the pitcher and basin they kept in the room so she could set it on the flat area beside his nest.

"I don't want you getting up until you've drunk at least what is in here," Vinicia said and then waved off his efforts to find his blanket. "That will help your head. Westly can see to the rest when he comes to check on you come dawning," she added.

Micah started to assure her and Kaitlyn both that he would do as she said, but his words fell away as she moved to tuck him into the large nest. She wasn't exactly making a fuss over him, but then again.

In the dark, the thick braid over her shoulder and her slender strength could have been Sera's, he realized and his eyes were suddenly burning with tears. *Oh Gods, Sera.*

"Hey, now," Vinicia said, her voice a whisper as she realized he was shaking. "Love, it's going to be all right," she insisted, smoothing back his tyro's crest to calm his nerves. "I'll do what I can for all of you, and you know that. Just get some rest, okay?"

Micah let out a ragged breath, cursing the ale and smoke and unexpected kindness that had brought him to the pit of sorrow he had been trying to avoid all night. As she came back to standing he watched her move towards the doorway. Both she and Kaitlyn looked back at him once, just to be sure, and then closed the door behind her and was gone.

Micah's strength vanished with the light and he hated himself as tears burned like fire down his cheeks. All he wanted in the world was his sister close at hand, but it seemed that everything was set to keep them apart.

I can't think about this now! Micah screamed at himself, and his hands went into his hair, straining against it to draw his attention away from his own dark thoughts. *I spent all night not thinking about this and I can't give in now. Three more nights and I can be with her again. Gods, it's only three more nights.*

It was an eternity.

Chapter 08: Chiurgeon Westly su'Kelsineah

Thursday, 04:00

*I*s *it three days and a wake up now?* Westly thought, shaking his head as he washed his hands over his face to clear his head. *Or is it still four if you haven't slept? One long, endless day? Great good gods...*

Westly had been working since mid-meal on documenting the changes he had made to the chiurgeons' glass garden, only to get a missive from Lord Seventh near to midnight to let him know his assistance had been requested for one of the noble houses and that it was okay to respond to them. Then he had spent the next candlemark working until Mother had come to the Garden looking for him. All she had needed was someone to stand guard while she worked and even if he hadn't minded, he also hadn't expected to have to spend the following candlemark bribing Rylan with roasted caffea to get him to do what Mother had asked.

Now that he had Rylan focused, Westly himself had lost the ability to do anything at all with his workspace, but they still had a candlemark before they could go back across to the Soldier Tyros' Wing. He needed something to do to try and keep himself awake and the only thing he could focus on was the fact that he would have to try and actually talk to the chiurgeon tyros today.

After two cycles spent trying to avoid them, he was not looking forward to it. Hearing his sigh, Rylan gave him a flat look. He knew why Westly had been pacing for the past candlemark, not that he'd wanted to talk.

"Go sleep if you don't want to think about it," Rylan said. "Or do something. I can't focus if you keep trying to summon the nine winds every ten steps."

Westly just scowled at him. "Move, then," he said, starting towards the desk. "Micah needs more of his terra, anyway."

"Yeah, sure," Rylan said, stepping off the stool.

When Rylan was out of the way, Westly reached under the lip of his workbench to flip the hidden latch, releasing a small spring behind the drawer that held the collection of seeds he wasn't supposed to have access to. Terra would take the most concentration, so he pulled out the vial, uncorked it with his teeth, and shook out one of the small seeds onto the desk.

While smoking the dried plant did nothing for him, or at least nothing like it did to windwalkers like Micah, growing it from a seed was a high in itself. Usually he would grow plants the old-fashioned way with water and soil, but every once in a while he indulged himself in pure sorcery.

With the seed in hand, Westly put the vial back in its hiding spot and secured the drawer before looking towards the room with his nest.

"Just grab me when the time candle hits the fifth mark and we can go over," he said as Rylan sat back on the stool. "Micah should be up by then."

"Yeah, sure," Rylan said, returning to the notes he had spread across the massive workbench as Westly started for his room.

Despite the flora that filled the garden, the Palace chiurgeons were lying to themselves if they believed he only nurtured the earth as they did. At one time it had taken almost a full cohort of chirons—what everyone called the chiurgeon tyros—to keep the Garden at optimal growth. Westly, however, managed it all by himself, a fact that the chiurgeons were starting to remember now that his crew brothers were graduating. Raleigh had said something about a similar schedule being created for his absence, but that request had stalled in the Green. Second Counsel Lord Gallen seemed content to let him vacate the premises before determining how they would repair the 'devastation' he had created by using the space as his permanent quarters.

Westly really hadn't made any change that wasn't absolutely necessary, and that included creating a modest space for his own privacy. After moving one of the bookshelves a few paces out from the wall, he had encouraged a thick climbing vine to cross the space, creating both a roof for privacy and a wall to close it off from the main room. What they should have been concerned with was the nest he had created inside. Rather than resigning himself to the dirt floor as was expected, Westly had taken a page from Counsel Lord Kiernan's rasha guild and grown himself the long lengths of river weed with the same trick he was about to use and encouraged it to weave itself into the heavy, freestanding nest that he had enjoyed ever since.

After his success with that project, he had gone on to craft a whole room of furniture and shelving from the river weed, and when he had finished, he had encouraged a resilient moss to cover the earthen floor with its fuzzy softness. That way, if you were really wary of a dryad-kin, you wouldn't even want to set foot in the place. So far, the precaution had worked splendidly.

Pushing past the curtain of vines, Westly climbed into the soft embrace of pillows that cushioned his nest. As it cradled his form, he moved to splay his wings out and leaned back to rest himself against the edge of the nest. When he was comfortable, he closed his eyes and cleared his thoughts, taking deep, slow breaths as he worked to dismiss the exhaustion he felt.

Once he was centered, he raised his left hand to chest level and placed his right hand flat beneath it. He held the pose for a long while, breathing with purpose until he felt the tension in his body starting to fade. When the steady hum of the garden's energy had soothed his nerves, his mind came into perfect, weightless clarity.

Despite the small scope of his life, there were few forces in the world he had yet to encounter. Though he had never met her, his mother had been a dryad, a woman whose spirit was intertwined with the energy of the land she protected. In her life before meeting his father she had tended her own garden, except that the 'garden' was an uncountable amount of acreage in the Eihwaz forest and there were no demands on her time or forced cultivation.

His father had been a windwalker given Westly's own wings, but Westly hadn't had the chance to know him at all. The people who had raised him had all been the wingless Ehkeski of Clan Eastwatch. They had lived below the Kosaran's chiurgeon citadel at Kelsineah, which overlooked the flood plains that bordered the River Kir at the entrance into the Kihara mountain range.

For work, his father had been a deep wood's ranger for the dryad just on the other side of the Kir. His work had been to guide the clansmen to areas where lumber could be collected from various wildwoods that buffered the grove, at least until Westly came along.

Surprisingly, the most interesting thing Westly had ever learned about Eastwatch had not come from the clan itself. That information had come from Counsel Lord Kiernan, who had told him that Eastwatch also guided the Seventh Counsel Lords through the Eihwaz whenever one managed to make it to the entrance to the woods somewhere between Yaltana and his own Illiandria.

Considering that it had been almost thirty cycles since Eastwatch had heard from a Seventh, the man had joked that Westly was welcome to come as his guide on the first part of his Envoy if he felt so inclined. Westly hadn't known what to say, and though Kiernan had seemed amused by the idea, Westly was certain the man wouldn't have minded the company. From the few moonturns he spent in the rear corner of his suite recovering from the other chiurgeons' attempt on his life, Westly had seen just how isolating it was to be the Seventh Counsel Lord.

As for the start of Westly's life with Eastwatch, he had been raised among the clan just outside of Kelsineah until he had fledged, a thing that took dryad-kin quite a while longer to manage than a normal windwalker. Once the clan was confident that he had his mother's talents under control, the Elder had started to talk to him about returning to his mother's woods. Having grown up wingbound inside the clan territories and itching to learn how to fly despite every admonition against it and his nature, Westly had realized that he had to leave.

Once he made his way into Kosar proper, wanderlust and a long life had brought him to Delton, and that had eventually led to this garden where he had finally set down roots again. Here among the herbs, he could tap into the power he cultivated like he had done for his Clan and it suited him far more than he ever thought it would. Then again, when you didn't stay anywhere for more than a few solar cycles, it felt strange to enjoy staying anywhere for any significant amount of time.

Westly loosened his grip on the seed and turned his thoughts to the River Kir, ready to begin his working. As the energy of the river pushed all other thoughts from his mind, he split his attention to hold the river in one part as he reached for the energy of the dense forest with the other. Though the ground was frozen in the world around them, the land beneath was rich with life that lay dormant. Like the seed in his hand, it too waited for the measure of life contained in the energy of the Kir. As he connected the two in his mind his lower hand dropped like a weight into his lap as the great force of the earth pulled it home.

Moving forward, Westly turned his thoughts to the seed in his raised fist, a vast empty nothing that wanted to consume, grow, and expand with life. As the river tore through the woods in his mind, the seed blossomed in his thoughts, triggering something deep and raw and completely beyond him. When the in-pouring of river and earth matched the immense draw of the seed, he unclenched his fist, dropping the seed into his open palm.

The shock of it was incredible.

Heady with the sensation of channeling the raw elemental power, he forced his palms together and buried the seed between the energy he had gathered. The two met in the seed as naturally as in the ground itself and as they filled the great void of potential, Westly began his final task: drawing from within the delicate seed the plant that existed at its core.

His arms shook as he raised his top hand with frustrating slowness. When his hands parted, Westly felt tiny roots digging their way through the spaces between his fingers, nourished by the energy coursing through his arms. Soon enough he felt a leaf brush against his palm, and as he held his focus, he let the energy feed the tiny plant until it was two leaves, then four. As the plant took on a life of its own, drawing what it needed without Westly's prompting, the roots doubled in size. Now they clung to him deftly, twining around his wrist and snaking down his arm towards the solid, natural earth.

Westly relaxed then, comfortable in his place as a conduit, and watched with fascination as the plant continued to grow. It would take half a candlemark at best for the plant to reach maturity and as far as he cared, he had all the time in the world.

Sometime during the exchange, Westly lost consciousness. At least, that's the only thing that would explain the lapse of time and the sharp head-pain that came from working with far too much energy. Raising his pounding head from where it had fallen against his wing, Westly grimaced as he opened his eyes into the great mass of the terra plant that had grown while he was asleep. Heavy as it was, it had dragged Westly's arm down by his side, finding support in the pillows and rasha structure of his nest so it could better leech energy from Westly himself. Making a face at the innocent plant, Westly spent a few moments plucking the roots from his nest until he freed himself enough to come to his feet.

With the root ball of the excessively leafy plant held in one hand, Westly used its weight for a counterbalance as he came out of his nest and yawned as he shuffled back into the Garden proper. Unsurprisingly, Rylan was still bent over the workbench, his once empty parchment now covered in a chaos of scrawled writing. Focused as his crew-brother was, it took until Westly was standing next to him before Rylan realized his presence.

"Holy shit, Wes," he said, jerking back in surprise. "Did you turn into a plant when I wasn't looking?"

Westly moved the terra from between them to give him a flat, annoyed look.

"Gods, it's just a joke," he laughed.

"I'm glad you're in a better mood," Westly said, waving him away from the desk.

Taking his cue, Rylan grabbed up the last of his caffea before moving so that Westly could get at what he needed. After a moment groping under the desk, he managed to catch hold of the tall box he kept there. Inside the box was a ceramic pot already prepped with soil and as he pulled it out, he was glad to see that he had remembered to leave a hole in the dirt so the roots would have somewhere to go.

"You can't stay on my arm forever," he admonished, gathering the pace-tall branches with his other arm so he could free himself. That done, he knelt and settled the plant's rump into its more appropriate home. Even if the branches were all pressed together, the terra would be fine this way for a few candlemarks, sustaining itself on dirt and water until he had time to harvest it. As it was, he was ravenous to break his fast and Micah was going to be waking soon.

"I just have to water this and we can go," Westly said. "Can you be ready when I get back?"

"Yeah, it's all dry now," Rylan confirmed. "I'll get it back into the script."

Nodding, Westly grabbed his bucket and turned to the spring that waited on the other side of the garden. On his left, the back wall was lined with wooden storage shelving that rose for almost three stories.

At the top, the crystal roof of the garden soared another story upwards as it slanted to the stone wall between the two chiurgeon buildings. The other walls of the garden were made of the same material, which dazzled with color as the sun refracted off ten thousand chips in the ancient roof. Without fail, the sight of dawn pouring through it always made him smile.

Reaching the other end of the garden, Westly dropped the bucket into the large stone pond. Fed by one of the off-shoot aquifers that brought water into the Palace from the Kir, whoever had managed this creation must have been far more skilled than himself with directing and blending energy. No matter the freezing weather or ridiculous summers, the temperature of the water was always the same. That was good, as the pond nurtured both the garden and the water-loving plants like rasha that thrived with their roots submerged.

His bucket filled, Westly stepped to the side of the plants climbing the wooden lattice behind the pond and hazarded a look at his reflection in the crystal. Normally, there were two things that set him apart from his fellow Kosarans: his bright emerald eyes and the dark-green, almost black color of his hair. It was possible that he might have had the normal Kosaran browns at one point in his life, but as soon as he began experimenting with his kindred talents they had taken on the vivid color. Even so, something seemed off this dawning.

Frowning at his reflection, Westly set the bucket on the wide lip of the pond and moved to the edge that connected to the crystal. After he, Micah, and Rylan had been conscripted into service, his two crew brothers had their hair cut into the short tyro crests. His promotion from chiron to full chiurgeon meant that he could keep the style that he preferred, so he had kept it in the so-called street crest he had worn for cycles before ever setting foot in the Palace.

While the sides of his head were still shorter than the top, he usually just left it to its own devices instead of trying to use beeswax or resin to keep it in place. As he had been distracted of late, the crest that he did have had grown out so much that it was just a tousled mess that Rylan had said made him look like a plant himself the day before. Thus the crack about being a full plant now, not that it amused him. More striking, though, was the fact that the shorter sides, which had been dark the day before were now streaked with white.

I wonder if Mother knows anything about this...

Of the very few kindred dryads he had met in his life, Barracks Mother Vinicia was the only one that didn't have hair or eyes like his own. Instead, her hair was a deep auburn of the Palace walls, which went to show just how long she had been working among the wood and stone of the barracks, rather than herbs like him. Somehow she also managed to keep her eyes the dark brown of her Kosaran father's, a feat that Westly envied.

Now that he was thinking about it, she did have some small streaks of silver-white mixed into her hair, though she wasn't old enough to have the silver by age. Maybe the white in his hair meant he was coming into his power? She did keep warning him that it was about time. He would just have to ask her, he supposed, now that his body was starting to change.

Sighing, Westly went back to his desk and found that Rylan had moved the massive terra plant into Westly's room while he was away.

"I figured you'd want it somewhere out of sight," he said, pausing as he packed up the last of his papers into the red leather script.

"You're not wrong," Westly acknowledged, pushing past the vines to enter the room and dampen the soil until the terra was satisfied. That done, he retrieved a few of the dried compost plugs he had made and pressed them deep into the soil, giving the plant a bit more than normal to feed on while it adjusted to the earth. This plant would be hungrier than most and there was no true way to gauge how much nutrient it still needed. Terra plants were not known for being small, even if he had worked out a way to condense them and their properties over time.

Finished with that, Westly readied himself to leave, picking up the long, heavy sherpa lined jacket he wore, settling the piece between his wings before finding the waist belt and securing it in place. Once that was done, he slipped his journal inside the breast pocket and put the teas in his chiurgeon's shoulder bag. Knowing that Micah had indulged, he had prepared an antidote to the toxins that he hadn't quite figured out how to remove from the plant yet. Much to Rylan's pleasure, he also picked up the tin that held the last of the ground caffea, handing it to Rylan for safe keeping. Rylan had a pour-over carafe in the barracks for when Westly brought him the grinds after a long night out visiting the Lower City. He might not be leaving any more, but he certainly would need the brew if he was going to make it to graduation.

With both of them ready to leave, Westly picked up his heavy woolen Bloodcloak and the matching knit cap and gloves he carried with him to ward off the worst of the cold. The Bloodcloak was the closest he would ever come to the crimson uniform most Palace chiurgeons wore. For one thing, the emerald in his hair was proof enough of his talent and for another, he would never really be one of the Palace chiurgeons. The only time they even acknowledged his abilities was when some tyro had half-ripped his wing off during a sortie. Even then, after Westly had stitched the fool back together, he still had to suffer a fortnight of gossip about the fae-bargain he had struck to do it in the first place.

"You really need all that?" Rylan asked, worrying at the split in his lip as he watched Westly pull the hat on over his mess of long hair. "I'm dying from all the heat in here. It'll actually feel nice in the Palace for once."

"You try living in here all the time and then go into the Palace," Westly countered. "I never get used to the cold anymore."

Rylan shrugged, ready to go whenever he was. Westly hesitated, though, hating the look of bruising that still marred his friend's face.

"Gods, come here," he said, moving up to Rylan as he waited. Rylan didn't go anywhere, though he did close his eyes as Westly set his hands on his temples. A few moments more and he shivered, muttering about already being hungry enough to eat a yak.

"Well, I have to look at you all day and I don't want anyone to think I can't heal you," Westly explained, taking his hands back as the dark purple and sickly yellow faded from Rylan's pale face. "They're already going to think I'm the one who fixed you, so I might as well."

"You sure Mother won't mind?" he said, hesitant.

"If she asks, I'll explain," he said, sighing. "She knows how I feel about bruises."

Rylan just nodded.

To say Westly hated bruises was an understatement. The only time he had ever had to deal with bruises on himself was right after their crew had been conscripted. He had known that Kosarans harbored suspicions about his talents, but on the streets and in Kosar at large they had never sought to do more than give him a wide berth. These boys who studied to be chiurgeons took his very existence as a personal insult and made certain he knew it.

To avoid their brutality, Westly had tried keeping to himself by using his sorcery to seal the door to the room he had been given in the Chiron Tyros' Wing whenever he was inside.

That was fine until he had to leave to eat and bathe, and no task was completed without some insult or fist swung at him in the halls. At first, he had healed himself from the bruises and ignored them, but when they realized what he was doing, it only made things worse. When he started to defend himself, which meant wiping the floor with most of them, the chirons had started coming after him in groups. Eventually, all their anger and fear had culminated in a full attempt on his life.

Counsel Lord Kiernan had been the only thing that saved him. Too exhausted from the fight and too drained to use even the barest of his magic, Kiernan had given him sanctuary when the Green refused and for three moonturns he had healed the old-fashioned way. Though he had been fevered through most of it, Westly could have sworn that Kiernan must have had some healing talent of his own. There was just no other explanation for his survival. None of the Palace chiurgeons would have helped him and the chirons were the ones who had put him there in the first place.

When Westly was finally able to leave, Lord Seventh had made certain everyone knew that Westly was under his direct patronage. Kiernan had also forced through Westly's promotion to full chiurgeon and given him his rank robes and access to private quarters in the Chiurgeons' Wing, not that grown men were any kinder towards him. Doubly insulted by his youth and unmerited promotion, it was a wonder he survived the time he spent in their midst. Fearing the same sick cycle about to repeat itself, Westly had gone back to him with another idea.

Unable to seek refuge in the Soldier Tyros' Wing with Rylan and Micah for lack of space, Kiernan had made the Garden into Westly's sanctuary. Lord Seventh seemed to have had a very personal dislike for Second Counsel Lord Gallen, headmaster of the chirons, even before Westly had been involved and the feud had redoubled how Lord Second and his Palace chiurgeons had treated Westly.

In the end, Lord Seventh had somehow forced Lord Second's hand into removing the chirons that tended the Garden so that Westly could have the chance to prove himself. If he could manage the Garden alone, by whatever means, then Lord Second would let him be while his crew brothers were part of the Tyro Legion. It had been Westly's idea to install tables in the hallway outside of the Garden where chiurgeons could leave requests for herbs, and that buffer had allowed him the peace he needed to live in the hostile space.

Sometime after the process had proven itself, Lord Second had blown a lot of hot air about how the whole transition had been his idea. Something about Westly being 'with the plants, where he belongs'. Westly didn't care and Kiernan seemed happy that he was safe, even if he continued to blame himself for not foreseeing the problem it would eventually become.

In all honesty, that move was probably the best thing that had happened to him since coming to the Palace. Now that they left him alone, he was free to let the garden become his entire world. The simple task of tending such a large space provided the needed rhythm to his life once again, which is why having Rylan suddenly insert himself into his revere had so thoroughly upset him.

Westly sighed, dismissing the thought as he turned from his workbench to nod to Rylan. As much trouble as his crew brother was, he was still family. "Let's go."

Their morning sortie begun, Westly took the lead as they passed through the Chirons' Wing to make certain they wouldn't be stopped. After that it was down the Long Hall, passed the entrance to the great Courtiers Hall, the Sires' Wing, and the Hall of Justice with the lawspeakers until they found the door to the Soldier Tyros' Wing standing open at the far end. After that, it was a moderate flight up the large, spiraling corridor and then a little less than half of the length of the Palace again to Rylan and Micah's room.

Westly let Rylan get the door when they arrived, shutting it behind him once they were both inside. Micah was waiting for them, sitting on the edge of the platform that held the bowl of his nest.

"You spend the whole night in the Green?" Micah greeted, not believing.

"What do you think?" Rylan said, moving past the two desks near the doorway to throw the red commander's script in his nest.

Westly just sighed, dropping the tea he meant for Micah into the mug of water on the desk.

"I think Mother came by looking for you some time past four, but she's supposedly the one who had signed you out," Micah said, turning his look on Westly as he worked to bring the tea to boiling so it could steep.

Rylan didn't say a word, just stripped out of his uniform tunic. As Westly grimaced to see the purple bruises along his back and torso, Micah's mouth fell open.

"Holy shit, Rylan," he said, eyes going wide.

"He did go out, and he got caught," Westly finally said. "By Dylan's crew and then the Palace Guard. Mother got him out of the Cells."

"How are you walking?" Micah said, still gaping. "Gods, Rylan. How are you even standing? Did you heal this?" He finished, looking to Westly in disbelief.

"No, Mother did," he said, only to flush at Micah's further surprise. "I thought I told you she was kindred," he defended. "I mean, she's female so it's different, but she's still a healer. She works with blood magic, healing wounds and injuries on people without having to use herbs. She's been trying to teach me so I can take care of the Warhost men in Kelsineah, if that's where they're going to send me."

Micah didn't know what to say, other than to look at Rylan as he ducked into a clean shirt. "So you're fine, then? Except for the bruises?"

"I'm starving," Rylan muttered, looking over at Westly. "But yeah, I'm fine."

"Holy shit, Rylan," Micah said again, watching as Rylan leaned against the platform of his nest to wash his hands over his face. "Tell me it was worth it."

"It was," he said, groaning. "I found Sera, but she wasn't at the Live Oak and hasn't been for turns. When I saw her she said she's too far from the Palace to reach you, but she has been writing us. She specifically said for me to not come find her, fearing this would happen," he went on, crossing his arms over his chest to hold his bruised rib. Even if it didn't hurt, the memory of the abuse itself was still fresh in his mind. "Not that I knew. Not that any of us knew. Someone is keeping her letters from us."

"Yeah, I asked about that," Micah said, wincing. "Nichi says they hold back letters from tyros the moonturn or so before Tourni so we can focus. I don't know where they go, but it's not uncommon."

"So I was right," Rylan sighed, looking up. "And I was right to go to her. Micah, she said she heard something about the House Northern estate, the one Mother is helping me get the title to, and she went to check on it. The blicing crews are meeting there. My fucking brother—"

As his words cut off, Westly could feel the tension in the room thicken.

"If your brother lays one hand on her, I will kill him," Micah said, his voice low and angry.

"Get in line," Rylan swore. "With as many men as he has now, though? It would take this whole blicing century to drive them out."

"What about Sera?" Micah pressed.

"She was in the thick of it with them," he said. "Just cooking for them, like it was no big deal. She was dressed like some blicing House woman, too, but I've never seen those colors. Violet and red?" As Micah made a face, Rylan went on, running his hands through his tyro crest as if it could spark memories of when he had been a prince of House Northern. "I wasn't there long, but she said some Lord was paying the crews to be there. She didn't know why, but if Dylan is there, they may be trying to put a claim to the Estate too. He has a right to it, same as me. I just have priority because I'll be a soldier when I graduate."

"Mother said you're both soldiers now," Westly said, cutting in. He wasn't a genius for House politics like his crew-brothers, but he knew that much. "You'll be a veteran when you come back from war, but it takes a soldier status to stay the auction."

"When did you become a lawspeaker?" Rylan scoffed, looking up in surprise.

"When Mother explained what was going on to me," he said, shrugging. "I went down to check on her yesterday, remember?"

Rylan nodded, pulling out of his own thoughts as Micah chewed his lip. "Is Mother going to be okay, Wes?" he asked for them both. "She looks like death."

Westly let out a slow breath. Vinicia was kindred, that was true, but she was different as well; older by ten cycles and female at that. Without a garden to cycle power through, she sustained herself on the ambient energy of the eight hundred strong tyro legion she oversaw. Unfortunately when they graduated, when there were only eighty bodies instead of eight hundred, it meant she was starved for power. From what little she had said, the past few cycles had been worse with him on the shelf with her, but she didn't begrudge him his space or his life. She had taught him how to work with blood and bone in addition to his own talent with herbs, and for as strong as it had made him, it had also weakened her.

Female kindred—female dryads—the stories said that they always had greenmen with them to balance their need for power against what they used in their groves. Greenmen were creatures who could gather power elsewhere and fill themselves with it, bringing back that overwhelming potential to be shared and balanced between them.

All the tyros acted as her greenmen in some small way, giving her life and purpose with their work, but when they graduated it was very hard on her. Every autumn they cut down her grove, but every spring they filled it again. New life would always come in to replace what had been lost, if only because of a war that never seemed to end. The war that she hated to see go on, for all the innocent lives it ended.

Looking between his brothers, knowing how much Vinicia was doing to not only help give them a place to come home to after the war, but a place for her as well, what he said was: "Being on the Palace shelf isn't good for her with as strong as she is. It's been hard to share it between us, but the problem is how drastically the energy of the Palace changes when the tyros leave and the vets come in. She needs something stable, so if we want to help her, we need to get that House. She'll keep it safe for when we come back and it will keep her safe while we're gone."

"I didn't realize it was that bad," Rylan said, crestfallen. "Gods, I thought she loved it here."

"What she loves is us," Westly said. "The tyros. She hates what this place makes of us, though, just as much as you do."

Rylan let out a rough breath, affirmed in his purpose once again. "I know what I have to do, then," he said, coming to his feet. "But first I need to eat something before I gnaw my wing off. You're going to see to him?"

"Yeah," Westly said. "Then we'll be down."

Rylan pushed away from his nest with a sigh, moving to his locker to trade his Warhost leathers for his actual uniform jacket. Once he had that and his tyro cloak in hand, he nodded to them both before grabbing up the red leather script and heading out the door.

Once he was gone, Westly's attention turned to Micah with concern. "How are you doing?" He asked, watching as Micah rubbed at his temples.

"I swear it's not anything more than I've had before," he said, trying not to complain. "But I'm bloody famished, too, even if the thought of food makes me want to sick up. I don't even know where to start sorting myself."

"Well, it's only dawning," Westly said as Micah looked up from the tea in his hands. "Why don't you go ice your head in the bathing chamber and come back? First formation isn't for another few candlemarks and I can bring food up when Ry and I go down."

"No, I need to stay up," Micah admitted. "But I don't think that's what caused this. Wes, I think it's one of those backwards headaches or whatever you call them..."

"A backlash headache?" Westly corrected, surprised. "I thought you weren't doing anything more with the warbards until after graduation?"

"I told you I was playing for the revel last night," Micah said. "And I got so into it I started to play like I would for Sera, just to see if I could..."

"And now you've given yourself a headache," Westly said, sighing. "Do you have anything else until the Tourni?"

"No, thank the Gods," Micah said. "I might start bleeding from the ears if I had to try and do anything else today."

"If it's that bad, then I should have a look," Westly said, moving to stand in front of his brother as he sat on the edge of his nest.

Blinking into his secondsight, Westly moved close enough so he could set his hands lightly on Micah's temples. With a little focus, Westly extended his perception into, rather than at his crew brother and saw the deep sapphire aura that surrounded Micah like a double image. Interspersed within the blue, he saw the lighter color the terra left behind and grimaced as he realized that the antitoxin he had made was not going to be strong enough. That, and the inner light Micah clung too was darker than before, as if his encouragement of the dancers had literally sucked the life out of him.

Westly took his hands away, blinking a few times to shed the white film that overtook his eyes whenever he used the secondsight. Micah put a hand out to steady him, since that transition usually made Westly light headed, but he actually felt fine for once. Energized, even.

"What did you see?" Micah hesitated to ask.

"Enough to know that you're running yourself ragged," Westly answered. "You've been spending time with Kaitlyn like I suggested, yes?"

"Yeh," Micah agreed. "But it's not the same. She's not Sera."

Westly could tell there was more to be said, but from the look on Micah's face, he wasn't going to talk about it. Not yet, anyway.

"I should get to the latrines," Micah said, dodging the tension. "I promised Mother I would drink that pitcher of water when I woke and it's talking to me. I probably should have some more, anyway."

Westly stepped back to give him room, turning back to check on his remedy as Micah went to his locker to find a clean uniform. Westly handed him back the tea that had been steeping, drawing out a bit of the heat into his hand before handing it back to Micah. He had long since learned that Micah would rather shoot the whole thing down at once rather than drink it over time.

"You look like shit, too, you know?" Micah said, taking the concoction and doing just that. He made a face after he swallowed, but Westly didn't apologize. If he wasn't going to taste it for long, why waste the sweetener?

"Yeah, well, I didn't get a lot of sleep either," Westly said as Micah set aside his leather flight boots and tossed a clean uniform out to wear when he got back from the washroom. "And what sleep I did get was with your favorite plant growing around my arm."

Micah stopped in the middle of his work, looking up in disbelief. "How do you just doze off doing that?"

"The same way you fall asleep with Kaitlyn in your nest," Westly shrugged. "Working with energy feels amazing. Better than sex, I'd wager," he added, attempting Micah's sense of humor.

"I find that hard to believe," Micah laughed, which made Westly feel better as he closed his locker at the far end of the room. "Especially when you don't know what you're missing, what with you being a thirty-cycle bowen."

"Well, you don't know what you're missing," Westly returned lamely. "Working with energy feels good because it is good for you," he said, and then added more rationally: "Besides, how would I ever help someone if my magic just hurt them more?"

"Fair enough," Micah admitted. "So you're like me then. You seduce them."

"No," Westly scoffed. "If I did, wouldn't I have had a partner by now?"

"Oh, you could have a partner," Micah said, though he grinned as he seemed to realize something. "Speaking of which, I had a favor to ask of you."

"What kind of favor?" Westly asked, suspicious.

"Look, I know you've already got a rough day ahead of you, but would you answer a question from Nichi?" He asked.

Westly's heart was in his throat. Nichi Windover wanted to talk to him? Aloof, mysterious, absolutely gorgeous Nichi Windover? Sure they saw each other often enough when their squad had to work with a chiurgeon for flight maneuvers, but they never really talked. Not that Westly could ever find the words to do more than answer his questions with a yes or no.

Sensitive as Westly was to magic, just being in the presence of someone so intimately connected to a Founder was intense. Rylan might have felt the same, but given how much he pushed his House and birth-family away, it was embers compared to Nichi. Nichi's family honored and revered the Alexandrian shelf-founder above all others and that power just sang in his soul.

"Why?" he asked, managing to keep his voice steady despite his nerves.

"It's something about his House—his Sire, I mean," he explained. "I don't know what it actually is, but Kreychi wanted him to ask you and it's probably because of something Lord Seventh said."

Westly remembered to breathe. He had gotten a missive from Lord Seventh about that, hadn't he? A note saying that if someone from the Houses asked for his assistance, they had cleared it with him first to be certain it wouldn't be a problem with Lord Second.

"I don't see why not," Westly said, even as his heart pounded in his chest.

"Great," Micah said, moving for the door with a towel wrapped around his waist. "Do you want to stay here while I wash up? I mean, he's probably hung over a basin, so I can just grab him when I come back?"

"Sure, I guess," Westly said, exhaling his nervous laughter as Micah left. "I mean, I don't have anything else to do for the next three days."

CHAPTER 09: MICAH

Thursday, 05:30

When he arrived at the washroom, Micah was nauseous from rolling out of his nest after so little sleep. He was still a little drunk, too, but rising early was the only way he would make it to muster on time today.

Once he was inside, Micah massaged his temples and kept his eyes down, trying to keep to himself. Without Sera around, every day started off feeling like the whole Palace was trying to talk inside his head at once. It was as if they knew Micah could hear their rhetorical muttering and expected him to provide the answers they couldn't find themselves.

I'm an empath, Micah thought sourly. *Not a mind reader.*

After a stop behind the short privacy wall to relieve himself, he continued towards the outer wall where there were a number of down-spouts waiting to be used. This close to winter most of the tyros avoided them, but the cold water did wonders for his head on days like this. So it was with some relief that Micah tossed his towel on one of the nearby benches and worked the lever to let the water come flowing out. Hands against the wall, Micah dropped his head and let the water fall against the back of his neck.

I don't care what Westly calls my bardic gift, Micah thought, shivering as the water slid down between his wings before swirling around the rest of him. *Without Sera it's nothing but a curse.*

When they had both been very little, his mother had seen Micah's bardic talent for what it was and had given him the fretless lute so he had a way to focus it safely. Fretless, because it was harder to master. The ability was supposed to be a blessing, since an acute awareness of a person's emotions gave you the chance to affect them. In his case, his talents had been what kept them flush with coin.

With a little training in body language and mental impressions, Micah was able to tell who would be willing to pay out after a performance, point them out to his mother and sister, and then they would dance or sing to entice them. Sera's own abilities then heightened those people's emotions, redoubling his in the process, and it became almost too easy to suggest that their audience leave a significant tip.

But the older Micah got, the more his sense of a person's emotions started to gain images and sounds, until it felt like he could almost hear a person's thoughts. It was an intense experience, but his mother had assured him that as long as he was with his sister, she would be able to balance him out. Any time he felt overwhelmed, he could just go to her and she would make the world go silent. Any time they were happy, that joy was shared in a way he had never found with anyone else.

To live and breathe purely on emotion, to exist without words...

Micah coughed as his chest tightened around the hole in his heart. It wasn't until he'd been conscripted that he'd realized just how strong his abilities had gotten after their mother had passed. With Sera gone, the only thing he had to help him was Westly's terra. The smoke numbed his bardic and empathic gifts, but it also made him that much more sensitive when it wore off, making mornings like this into torture. That was the real reason he insisted on getting up so early; the fewer minds that were active, the less he had to deal with and the faster he could recover.

But being this close to graduation there were always tyros awake, be they on the end of an all-night revel or getting up early to slip back from Court before first formation. Technically everyone in their century had already graduated, but they would never earn their coveted rank-pauldrons if they didn't fly the Ice Winds challenge in three days.

And yet the first thing he does is leave the shelf and get the shit kicked out of him? Micah thought as his anger flared. He immediately regretted it.

Micah doubled over on himself as the lance of pain shot through his eyes, his own anger spiking inside his mind even as he tried to shove it back down. But the more he tried to keep calm, the stronger that anger and hate became. After two cycles of strangling it back, the only place that was safe for him was inside that cloud of terra or at the bottom of an ale. So while he still might be drunk and disoriented, his mind was at least quiet.

Or so he thought.

Just as he got himself under control, the band of tension around his head sharpened and made a valiant attempt to shatter the right side of his skull. He was lucky he was already crouched against the wall, as only the sheer force of will kept him on his feet. When he got his eyes open enough to see where the projected agony was coming from, Micah saw Nichi coming over to drown himself sober.

"You all right, man?" Micah said as Nichi came to a stop a few paces away to drop his towel on a bench.

"I can't do this," Nichi groaned, moving towards the down spout Micah had used. "Gods, I couldn't even sleep. What do I even say to him?"

Micah picked up his towel as Nichi let the lukewarm water pour over his head. As his wings drooped with exhaustion, Micah did his best to project calm over his friend in much the same way he projected energy at the dancers the night before. Without his lute, though, there wasn't much he could muster. Nichi just kept his head against the stone wall, brooding so fiercely that Micah could feel the pressure of it gripping him by the back of the neck.

By the gods... Micah thought, putting a hand to his temple as Nichi just stood there radiating agony. But as Micah thought to say something—anything—to distract his friend, he heard someone hailing Westly from behind them. Micah raised a hand to greet him, but as he turned back towards Nichi, the look of fear distorting Nichi's face made the pain between Micah's eyes nearly blind him. As a cascade of Nichi's feathers went scattering to the floor, Micah was sent staggering back to his senses.

"Hey, Wes," he managed, looking to Westly who was slowing as he recognized Nichi. "I thought you were going to wait..."

"Tyr came and grabbed me," he said, hesitant as he stopped at the benches just past the privacy wall that blocked off the showers. "He said he thought something was up, but he had to go talk to Ry... Oh, Nichi you're molting," he said, keeping his voice low. "Is this what you wanted to talk about?"

Nichi's suddenly panicked look went to Micah behind him as he shut off the water. "I'm not molting," he defended. "And I don't want to talk to you, kindred."

"But Micah said..." Westly began as Nichi turned to pick up his towel.

Micah's vision blurred under the feel of confusion and anxiety emanating from his friends. Whether Westly knew it or not, when he had moved around the low wall that blocked off the downspouts from the rest of the bathing room, he had trapped Nichi between them. Nichi clearly knew it, wings flaring to keep Westly away from him.

"Micah needs to keep his mouth shut," he said, angry as he covered himself with his towel and tucked it around his waist. Westly wasn't looking at him, though, his eyes going wide as he saw the feathers on the floor where Nichi had been standing.

"Nichi, there is something wrong with your wings," he insisted, taking a step forward. As he reached the other side of the low wall, however, Nichi's angry look kept him at arm's length. "Nichi, don't be a fledgling," Westly insisted. "I'm a chiurgeon."

"You think I don't know that?" Nichi threw back.

"Then talk to me," Westly insisted, shifting his weight under Nichi's stare. "If you need help, I'll help you. I'm not—I won't hurt you, Nichi. I promise."

"I said I don't need your help," Nichi insisted, drawing himself up, even if Westly still had the true height between them.

"Then explain why you're molting," Westly said, gesturing to the wet floor behind them. Nichi just scoffed, tightening his wings as he prepared to walk around Westly. "I wouldn't be here if Tyr hadn't seen you shedding feathers in the hall."

"No," Nichi said, even as Westly moved to block Nichi's path. "I'm not molting and even if I was, it's none of your business."

"Nichi, the Ice Winds will rip feathers from healthy wings," Westly said, reaching out to him again. "Just let me look at them. If there's nothing wrong, fine."

"And if there is?" Nichi asked, his wings flaring in a clear threat. "You're going to do something about it?"

"You were already going to ask me to do something, weren't you?" He asked, matching his ready stance. "What exactly do you think that was?"

"Both of you calm down," Micah said, desperate to stop the physical violence building between them. Westly would wipe the floor with Nichi if it came to it and that would just make everything worse.

"What's your problem, kindred?" Nichi challenged, scowling as Westly came within arm's length.

"You're my problem," Westly said, flaring his wings. "Or do you need me to drag you to Mother before I have you blacklisted from the tournament? I've already seen enough to have you grounded."

"You wouldn't dare," Nichi spat. "My brother—"

"Answers to My Lord Seventh," Westly said, driving over Nichi's words. "So do not think for one moment that you can out-influence me, Andronicus Windover."

Micah's jaw went slack as Nichi shifted his weight to throw his fist in response to the words. Nichi absolutely hated when people used his full name. Only his mother ever used his full name.

Westly's hands came up between them faster than Micah could follow. As Nichi's fist neared his face, Westly deflected the blow to the side with his left hand as he shifted to the left. Still moving forward, Nichi's eyes went wide as Westly's right hand came up from under the deflection and shot out in front of Nichi's neck. Before Nichi knew what was happening, Westly had circled his right leg behind Nichi's forward foot and shifted his weight to throw Nichi bodily to the floor.

This was the reason Westly had survived by himself for so long before joining their crew. Peaceful as he was otherwise, if you threw a punch at him, Westly would put you on your wings. If he had to keep you there, you were as good as dead.

"Okay!" Micah called, grabbing at Westly's arm as he stood over the princeling, fuming. "You've made your point!"

That was apparently the wrong thing to do. Just as Micah tried to pull Westly back, his brother pivoted in place, flipped his wrist free and dropped his open palm on Micah's chest to send him staggering backwards with the wind knocked out of him.

"Stay out of this!" Westly said and then blinked into the white-eyed healer's sight that meant he was using his dryad magic. "If the only thing he'll listen to is brute force, then by the Gods he has this coming."

As Micah fought to breathe, Westly dropped a knee onto Nichi's chest, trapping him on top of his wings before he had gotten his bearings back. With everyone in the room realizing that there was a fight, Micah was sent staggering again.

"No shit—It's Westly!" one of them realized, in a voice so loud that it got everyone else's attention. "Wes just put Nichi on his wings!"

As the force of violence radiating from his friends was redoubled by the bloodlust of the other tyros coming to watch, Micah thought he was going to be sick.

This is not happening. This cannot be happening.

"Stay still, you idiot," Westly cursed, flinching as Nichi tried to knock their heads together. Westly freed one of his hands, keeping Nichi's arms locked with the other and the press of his chest. The free hand he used to grab the length of hair on the top of Nichi's head, trying to get a good look into his eyes, but Nichi had suffered enough. For as dexterous as Westly was, Nichi had the sheer strength of a soldier tyro to push through it. As Westly tried to figure out what was wrong, Nichi managed to free one of his hands and shoved off the knit cap he wore to grab onto Westly's longer street crest.

More than surprised to be out-muscled, it didn't take much force to drag Westly's head back enough to relieve the tension on his wings. As Westly grabbed at Nichi's hand to save himself, his knee slid from where it had been pinning Nichi's other arm, allowing the princeling to counter-attack. With his free hand, Nichi swung for the only target he had and Westly's pallor went white as he doubled over in agony. With both hands free, Nichi shoved Westly off him and came to his knees.

"Nichi, stop!" Micah demanded, pushing off the wall to try and rush in between them. "You'll be grounded!"

"He started this," Nichi answered, committed to his madness as he climbed on top of Westly. "But I'm going to finish it."

Still reeling from the hit to his groin, Westly brought up a weak guard. As the onlooking tyros dragged Micah away from the fight, Nichi took his revenge, grabbing Westly's arms like Westly had done to him and pinning them to his chest as he landed a battery of blows against the side of Westly's face. By the third hit, Nichi's hand was coming away bloody.

::"NICHI STOP!":: Micah screamed, throwing the weight of his warbard gift behind the plea.

The whole room froze as Nichi's head snapped up in his rage, but he did stop. Exhausted as he was from the effort of their struggle, Nichi just sat there, panting as Micah realized to his horror that Westly wasn't moving at all.

Chirons weren't taught to fight, which is why threatening to strike one could get you expelled. Obviously, Westly could hold his own. Nichi would likely graduate because of it, but no one had expected Nichi to be quite so brutal.

In the silence of the room, Nichi back-winged off Westly and matched Micah's furious look as he put a hand to his lip. He came away with blood, though if it was his or Westly's, there was no way of telling. After a long moment, Nichi swore at no one in particular and turned to storm out of the washroom.

Westly's groaning back to life was the only thing that broke the silence. The shock of seeing his crew-brother alive might have been the only thing keeping Micah from tearing off after Nichi.

"It's over," Micah snapped, knowing he had all the tyros in the room under his Suggestion. Lute or not, the adrenaline he felt was more than enough to let him wrap the need for silence into the sending. As the tyros around them stumbled away in a daze, Micah moved to help Westly get off his wings. Working together, they got Westly back onto his hands and knees until Westly was spitting out blood onto the cold stone floor.

"I wus wight," Westly managed, trying to stem the line of blood from his nose. "Someding's wong—"

"Of course you were right," Micah swore, offering his hand to assist Westly in standing. "But why in the name of the gods did you have to jump him?"

"'caus 'es a' a'hol," Westly muttered, wobbling on his feet. Micah couldn't argue with that. "Are you o'day?"

"No," Micah hissed, not that it made much difference. "Gods, just get cleaned up. I'll see what I can do to calm him down. I don't think I can protect you from his family if this gets out."

"You dun have to," Westly answered, and Micah watched as Westly's composure darkened. "I can dake care of mydelf."

"Like you just did?" Micah asked, and then regretted saying it as Westly turned the dark look on him. Broken nose or not, there was more to sorcery than manipulating plants. From the stories his mother had told, some kindred could bind men with air and cause wounds with unseen and wholly unstoppable forces. Brother or not, chiurgeon or not, if Westly lost control of the dryad in himself, he could bring the Palace down around them.

Westly shook himself as Micah took a step back, releasing him from the stare. It wasn't hatred Westly felt, but fear, and it was Nichi who had truly started the fight. As long as it stayed that way, they were safe.

"If you didn't beat enough sense into him," Micah promised. "I'll do it myself."

"Dun kill him," Westly warned, breathing easier as Micah went chasing after Nichi. "Not even Mother is dat good."

Chapter 10: Westly

Thursday, 07:00

"I'll just... Clean up," Westly said as Micah left. Most of the tyros in the room seemed to be ignoring him and Westly suspected that was Micah's bardic Gift at work.

Sighing, Westly found his way back to the basin next to Nichi's molted feathers. He was covered in blood and for all Micah's Gift had done, he wasn't sure what was going to be worse: walking through the hallway answering questions about a broken nose or using his sorcery to recover from the fight in front of the tyros here.

If I can even use them...

Just thinking about Nichi had been enough to fluster him this dawning, but now the memory of the press of their bodies in the fight had set him on edge in a way he had never felt before. Even if it had been a true fight, Nichi was still gorgeous and no one had ever set hands on him so intently, well... Ever.

Swearing as he picked up his discarded cap, Westly shoved it into a pocket before folding back the sleeves of his sherpa coat so it wouldn't get covered in blood. Moving to the basin, he put his hand in the water only to hesitate as the surface began to glow with a strange azure light.

Apparently some of the blood that had been on his hand had been Nichi's and since it wasn't from his own body, he might be able to use it to heal himself. Westly remained cautious, though. While it was true that the blood of a windwalker could be used as a source of power, from what little he knew of blood magic—if that's even what this was—using it always came with risks.

Unlike the energy from the River Kir which could be directed and channeled like true water, blood magic just went everywhere. Without precision, it could manifest indiscriminately and corrupt everything you were working with. Not that he had any choice at the moment; he wasn't about to walk back to the Garden to access his power there.

"This better be worth it," Westly muttered as he dipped both hands into the water, bringing it up to his face so he could drown himself. As the water slipped between his fingers, the warmth spread across his skin like a salve. Bringing up another handful, the blood began to wash away and the pain lost its edge. Inhaling, Westly brought the water up a third time and clenched his jaw. As the water slipped away, he found the broken pieces under his fingers. With a thought and a prayer, he straightened his hands and forced the bones to set properly.

Tears sprang to his eyes as he doubled over the basin, one hand supporting him and the other dipping back into the water as it took everything he had not to cry out. As he drowned himself, the energy surged to meet him and when he took away his hand for good, he scraped away the excess and shook it back into the basin.

Looking up, he could finally breathe, but his vision had somehow shifted into the riot of light and colors that was his secondsight. As he stood there trying and failing to shift them back to normal, he panicked when he heard a voice right beside him.

"You alright, Wes?"

Westly's heart was in his throat as he turned. Unfortunately, all he could see was the dark uniform and a shock of blonde hair on the crown of his head. The rest was lost to the overabundance of light. His voice was familiar, though, Westly realized when he spoke again.

"Sorry, man. I didn't mean to startle you."

It was Tyrsten, who was a member of Nichi's House.

Tyrsten, who was the leader of Rylan and Micah's squad.

Tyrsten, who was the Primarch of the eighty-strong century of tyros.

Tyrsten who—

"Are you all right?" Tyrsten asked, setting a hand on his wing to steady him.

Cared, Westly realized, the shock of the contact bringing him back to his senses. Cared about him and not about the magic.

"Y-Yeah," Westly stammered, so relieved he didn't know what to say.

"What in the winds happened in here?" Tyrsten asked quietly. "I saw Nichi storming out of here and the way that you look now... Everyone in the House knows that his brood is stubborn about their health, Wes. We knew someone was going to knock some sense into Nichi eventually, so it's better that it was a chiron rather than one of the tyros," Tyrsten said, and then added: "Better that it was you."

"What?" Westly asked, taking the towel Tyrsten offered. "What do you mean, better it was me?"

"Ah, I've said too much," Tyrsten said, hesitating. "Nichi is supposed to be the one to talk to you," Tyrsten sighed, realizing he was talking in circles. "He's only a House prince when it suits him, you know. But it's not my place to go spreading House gossip, even if it's true."

"You are so helpful," Westly complained, which made Tyrsten laugh.

"Glad to be of service," he replied, and made a mock bow. "Just know that it's a good thing and that you have our respect."

"I'll keep that in mind," Westly said, still confused.

"So you'll be all right?" Tyrsten asked. "I heard Mike say something about Mother?"

"That part wasn't about Nichi," Westly said, reassuring House Windover that there wouldn't be an issue with their prince. "But I do need to make certain Micah doesn't give Nichi too much of a piece of his mind."

"You need backup?" Tyrsten asked, even if he was a bit hesitant. "I mean, I still have to go find Rylan, but if you need help..."

"He's in the Great Mess," Westly said. "He hates that they made him Bevy Primarch as much as you hate that it's him, Tyr. Probably more than you do, but he needs your help."

"I know that," Tyrsten scoffed, though there was a weary laugh in it as well. "I also know he's going to make me cadre, so I've been up all night. I just need to make sure he hasn't messed up what I already planned for units. I'd be surprised if he even knows the squad rosters."

Westly just shook his head. Of course Tyrsten would think he had to pick up the slack as Rylan took care of 'more important things'. Again.

"I'll handle Micah and Nichi, you take Rylan?" Westly asked.

"My brother Ren is with the chirons in the Armory already to help set up, but he'll help me grab Rylan if he starts sulking," Tyrsten said, giving him a casual salute. "Catch you there at the ninth mark? That's where we're doing first formation. I came in here to let everyone know."

"Of course," Westly said, returning it with his thanks.

No one watched him as he left, or at least they didn't once they realized that it still looked like Westly had a moderately broken nose. Thanks to Vinicia's lesson the night before, Westly had repaired the bones, but left his skin bruised for now.

Exiting the washroom, Westly went back to rubbing at his eyes to clear them. He had thought trying to focus on Tyrsten would have dissipated the haze, but it still felt like he was staring through a fog. If Tyrsten hadn't mentioned it, though, then his secondsight was hindered since his eyes usually went opaque.

After a few moments standing half-blind in the hall, he just gave up. It was more important to figure out where Nichi had gone than to get his eyes working. Closing them completely, he reached out with his mind, feeling for Micah among the melee of energy in the barracks. After a moment, he found him in the middle of the wing and realized that Micah had followed him down to Nichi's private room.

I can make it that far.

As Westly started down the hall, his worry got the better of him. Why had he sent Micah ahead of him? Micah was unstable enough without a target for his anger. He didn't need a righteous reason to take that anger out on someone, especially someone he had come so close to over the past two cycles.

On the Streets, friends were one thing, but your crew brothers were another. For all his easy time among the younger court, Micah was still not one of them even if being with them was one of the last things that Westly could keep Micah focused on. Without that distraction, Micah would flounder just like Westly had when they first arrived and Micah was far more self-destructive without Sera around.

Unfortunately, the closer he got to Nichi's room, the better he and anyone listening could hear Micah's tirade.

"What in the winds was that?" Micah demanded.

"I don't know, all right!" Nichi returned. "I didn't mean to, but he just—Mike, he started it!"

"*You* started it," Micah insisted. "You put hands on a Palace Chiurgeon and he had every right to knock some sense into you. Tyr and I both saw you messing with your wings last night, and you *are* molting."

"It's just an itch!" Nichi swore, throwing up his hands only to grip at the back of his neck with frustration. "Gods, I'm supposed to ask him about helping my father, not me. What in the winds am I going to do now?"

As their voices lowered, Westly made it the rest of the way down the hall. He almost had his hand on the door when Micah began to speak again, sighing in exasperation.

"Dammit, Nichi," Micah said, and the hesitation in his voice made Westly stop as well.

Keeping as quiet as he could manage, Westly stepped to where he could just see his crew-brother and the taller Windover standing together at the far end of the room. "Last night you said you actually liked him and then you go and do this? What has gotten into you?"

He did what? Westly thought in surprise, watching as Nichi's normally pale skin flushed with red. Nichi, at least, he could see through the fog.

"I do like him," Nichi defended, not meeting Micah's eyes as he cradled his fist. "I like him so much that the first time I hit on him I broke my blicing hand."

"Let me see, you idiot," Micah insisted, moving to stop him from worrying at his bloody knuckles.

"This is why I knew I couldn't talk to him," Nichi insisted, flinching as Micah shifted his hand. "Every time I even think about getting close to him I go crazy."

"You were fine last night," Micah said, shaking his head. "Let me go get him. I'm sure he can fix this after you apologize."

"Apologize?" Nichi balked. "For what?"

"For being an idiot," Micah swore, giving up Nichi's hand. "For threatening to sic your brother on him? He's a Palace Chiurgeon, Nichi, not some court idiot. His reputation is bigger than yours."

"Ugh, don't remind me," Nichi groaned, cradling his hand again. "Gods, what was I thinking?"

"You weren't," Micah said, looking back towards the door only to see Westly standing there, eavesdropping. "But Westly was," he went on. "And if he thinks that there's something wrong with you, then there probably is."

"I don't have time for something to be wrong," Nichi muttered, readjusting his wings with his nerves as Micah gave him a subtle wave to come inside. "And I certainly don't have time to explain how sorry I am. I just—Mike, it's dangerous for him if I talk to him in front of people. I couldn't live with myself if I put a target on his back."

"I've had a target on me since I was born," Westly said, pushing into the room at last. "Nothing you do is going to change that."

Nichi's head snapped up to hear Westly's voice at the door, his face going pale as he fell back a step. At the same time, Westly watched Micah's head snack up as he lurched away from the two of them, hands to his temples as he swore in surprise.

"Holy gods," Micah growled. "Will the two of you stop?"

Westly knew Micah could read people, but this was different. With his altered vision, Westly watched as Micah's energy began to fracture under the tension in the room. Unsteady as his bardic magic been the past few turns, it was starting to go wild. Under the circumstances, he couldn't wait anymore.

"Nichi you need to look at me," Westly said, blinking into his healer's sight as he closed the door. "At me, not him."

"What—What's going on?" Nichi stammered, worried as Micah backed away from them. Of all the things he and Micah had figured out about his empathic gift, they knew for certain that having someone's attention on him directly could be incredibly, physically painful. Without Sera to balance him, all he could do was shift the attention away.

"Look at me," Westly snapped, redirecting his attention with a wave of his hand.

Nichi looked, though when he saw Westly stalking towards him, he was the one backing away. He wasn't screaming, though, and he wasn't bracing himself for another fight. He looked absolutely terrified and yet fascinated at the same time. Hoping to catch him in the fascination, Westly flared his wings as he put himself between the two soldier tyros.

"The past few turns Micah has come to me more often than he used to because of his Gift," he said, speaking low and soft. "His warbard Gift. Do you understand what I'm saying?"

Nichi's throat bobbed as he nodded. "Kait said he might have one. I mean he caught the attention of a Preem last night. Last night at the revel."

"And now he has a backlash headache," Westly said, shifting so that Nichi could look through him. "That makes him even more sensitive, especially to the emotions of people he cares about."

"You mean us?" Nichi asked, only to swear as he realized it for himself, watching Micah collapse on the far side of the room. "Wes, I'm sorry. I didn't—"

"I don't care," Westly said, cutting him off. "I just need you to calm down. He needs you to. Can you do that?"

Nichi swallowed around the knot in his throat again. "Mike said he smoked the last of his terra last night," he said, moving further away from Micah in the small room. Only when his wings were up against his locker did he stop, though his terror had faded to panic. "My brother said Lord Seventh used to smoke terra for his warbard headaches, too. Maybe that would help? Gods, it certainly knocked me out last night..."

"You've had my terra?" Westly said, surprised. "The stuff I give Micah?"

"Only a drag here and there," Nichi answered, uncomfortable. Tyros weren't supposed to have any terra, but Mother knew what Westly had been doing so she didn't mind. No one else should have had it, though. Not his terra.

"How much have you had?" Westly balked, pulling Nichi's attention away completely. "How often?"

Westly's heart was in his throat. "Nichi, terra is poison at the strength I can grow it," he insisted. "Gods of my ancestors, you're lucky it's only your feathers falling out."

Nichi was about to say something, but whatever it was, it caught in his throat. As Westly got his vision to shift fully into his secondsight, his eyes filmed over with the opaque haze and Nichi went rigid. Pressing on for Micah's sake, Westly put his hands on Nichi's temples and saw that Nichi looked very much like Micah had this morning: a soft sapphire aura with threads of the terra. Even if Nichi was telling the truth, without the antidote, the toxins building in his system matched almost as much terra as Micah had consumed over the course of the past few moonturns.

"Nichi, you are not okay," Westly said quietly. "But I can help you. The faster I can help you, the faster I can help Micah. Okay?"

Nichi nodded once, still white with fear, and Westly grounded himself as best as he could this far from his garden. His only chance at helping Nichi was using himself to filter it out all at once.

Since he was immune to the plant's effects it might just work or it would kill him since he had only seen Vinicia do it the once. Either way, he was the only one in the Palace who had a chance at saving Nichi from himself and he was bound to try.

Once the circle was complete, Westly opened himself and reached into the wealth of power that lay before him as Nichi's distinct energy. At first all he could sense was the numbing feel of the terra, but there was something deeper and far more lethal lurking behind it.

Westly pulled harder, stripping away the coating of terra, only to have the energy of Nichi's core burn like he had stuck his hand inside a furnace. Before Westly could do anything to stop it, the sensation swept down his left arm and across his chest, burned like fire through his center, and then swept into his right arm and back to its source. As the trail of it left him decimated, his secondsight exploded with pain.

Not being a complete idiot, Nichi realized the panic Westly was in and grabbed at his shoulders to keep him on his feet, completing the circle between them once again with intention. After everything he had just felt, the surge of power was simply too much.

The next thing Westly remembered was the sound of Micah screaming his name and shaking him so hard Micah must have thought he was dead. "Westly!"

"I'm... I'm fine," Westly said as the world swam back into focus. He could see again, but Micah was terrified. "I'm fine. I'm okay. I..."

"Stop!" Nichi finally said, coming out of nowhere to free Westly from Micah's death grip. "Mike, he's awake!"

As Micah finally let him go, he turned on Nichi.

"What did you do to him?" Micah demanded, shoving Nichi back as his wings flared.

"What did I do to him?" Nichi defended. "Mike, what did he do to me?"

Westly finally found his feet and put a hand on Micah's wing. Unlike Sera, Westly couldn't ground the energy Micah had raised in his panic, but he could still it, at least momentarily. Micah swore, but when he turned to pull himself free, Westly caught him with both hands and matched him gaze for gaze.

"Micah!" Westly snapped and Micah reeled as he looked back at him. "Calm down!" He said, projecting the calmness he felt inside his garden. "I'm fine. I promise. You need to rest."

Micah considered him blankly for a moment and then nodded. "Rest," he repeated, and exhaustion swept over him as he started to believe it.

"Why don't you sit down?" Westly suggested and then stared daggers at Nichi until he pulled the pile of his things off his lounge so Micah could collapse onto it.

"Okay," Micah said, dropping his head in his hands.

Westly looked at Nichi and gestured for him to move away from Micah. Westly wanted to collapse as well, but if this was the first time Nichi had seen true magic worked, the Alexandrian would likely run off and raise a panic if Westly didn't stay calm.

Surprisingly, all traces of Nichi's fear was gone, exchanged for the quick thinking of the officer he was training to be. *It's about blicing time*, Westly thought, sagging with relief.

"Westly?" Nichi asked, sounding more calm than he had ever heard the man before. "Westly are you all right?"

"I think so," Westly said and had to take a deep breath as he felt bile rising. Whatever had been hiding in Nichi's blood had been more than terra. Whatever this was burned like a nightshade. "And so should you. Mike is just... he's exhausted."

"Are you okay?" Nichi asked, peering into his eyes. "Your eyes are still in your secondsight."

"I think so?" Westly said, squinting as he had to shield his face from Nichi's sapphire glow.

"What can you see?" Nichi asked, curious but trying not to pry. "I mean, what does it look like?"

Westly frowned, not sure how to explain the phenomenon and not wanting to try right now. Worse, it wasn't like Micah or Rylan had ever asked, so he didn't know what to say. "Usually it just turns people into blobs of color. Both you and Micah are normally blue—"

"You've looked at me with your sight before?" Nichi asked, surprised.

Now it was Westly's turn to be embarrassed. "I do it without thinking most of the time," he confessed. "It doesn't do anything to you. It's just another layer to things I see. It can't hurt you, I promise."

"I—" Nichi started to say, only to swallow his defensiveness. "I'm sorry, man," he said, if awkwardly. "Gods, I'm so sorry. I'm not an idiot. I know about kindred. I know way too much about kindred, to be honest, and I just—"

The way he stopped himself, the way he looked so absolutely mortified, made Westly realize Nichi's apology was for more than the past half a candlemark.

"What?" Westly asked.

"I'm sorry," Nichi said again, looking away. "Kaitlyn is my near-sister. Her family... Well, it's only her and my uncle, now. They've lived with us since before I can remember. Anything she knows about magic or dryads and anything fae, she told me about a hundred times. She told me because I wanted to know if I ever met...."

"Oh," Westly said, realizing Nichi was gesturing to him.

"Gods, I'm such an idiot," Nichi said, raking his left hand through his hair. "I never wanted to be such an ass to you, but I just... I couldn't help myself. It was the only thing I could think of doing to keep away from you, but Mike is your brother. I should have just told him what was going on. I should have told you. But you backed me into a corner this dawning and I just came out swinging. I don't know what came over me."

As Micah groaned from his place on the lounge, Westly waved at him to keep his voice down. "Your training," he said. "Same as mine. I see a stubborn patient, so I throw my weight around. You see someone squaring off with you, so you fight back. It's what we're supposed to do."

"Yeah, but I'm not supposed to attack my best mate's brother," he said and reached his good hand to pull at the back of his neck. "You're something else, man."

"So are you," Westly replied and squinted as he tried to look at Nichi again. "Yesterday you were just a big blue blob in my mind, but when you grabbed me, my whole head shattered. Now you're about ten shades of blue and twenty other colors besides, and I can see every one of them in painful, vivid detail. It's..." Westly said, and covered his eyes again. "It burns like I tried looking into the day star."

"I'm sorry?" Nichi said, closing his wings tightly behind him. Westly breathed a little easier without all the white and then Nichi went on. "I mean, I feel better than I have in a cycle because of whatever you did. I can never repay you for that, but maybe I can make it up to you?"

"You should thank him for not destroying you in that fight," Micah muttered, interrupting them.

"Thank him?" Nichi said, surprised. "But I—"

"Do you think you could take Rylan in a fight?" Micah cut in, not about to listen to any of Nichi's boasting.

"What's that got to do with anything?" Nichi asked, which was clearly a 'No'.

"I taught Rylan how to fight," Westly said, not sorry for the way Nichi's mouth dropped open in surprise. As he shifted with his nerves, Westly flinched as he got a better line of sight on Micah and it was like looking into the day star all over again. Unlike Nichi, though, Micah shone with an inner light that made Nichi's sapphire glow look pale by comparison. Micah had far too much power for his frame, if Nichi was any measure of a normal windwalker. Not that Westly had any idea how to handle that.

"Micah," Westly said, shielding his eyes. "I think I need to find Mother. Can you—?"

"The Barracks Mother?" Nichi repeated. "What would she know?"

"She's dealt with kindred before," Micah answered vaguely, coming back to his feet. "Can I what, Wes?"

"Can you get him to breakfast?" Westly asked as Micah rose to join them. "I can't see. I mean, I can, but... I can't in the normal way."

Westly flinched as Micah pulled down the arm protecting his eyes.

"If I didn't know you were kin, I'd say they were godseyes," Micah said, and Westly could feel Nichi peering at him as well. As much as Micah accepted his talents, the sight usually unsettled him. Given the circumstances, Westly agreed with his hesitation. "Can you even find her like this? I'm sure we can help."

"She's in her office," Westly assured him. "I just need you to make sure Nichi actually breaks his fast."

"We'll go right by her office on the way to the Mess if we take the lame man's stairs," Nichi said, genuinely concerned. "You shouldn't be flying if you can't see. Let us help you."

Let me help you.

Westly felt his heart starting to race again as he looked back to Nichi, trying to steady his nerves for Micah's sake. "I think you've done enough for one morning," he said, trying to keep his tone even as he watched the words cut at Nichi's earnest concern. "And if you don't take care of yourself, you'll be worse off than before I healed you."

"What are you talking about?" Nichi asked.

"Have you ever been so sick you couldn't eat for a sennite and then once you felt better, you couldn't stop eating for days?" Westly asked, serious. "Because that's about to happen to you and the faster you get something in your system, the easier of a time you will have."

"So we'll get you some food," Micah said, though his look for Westly was hard as well. "I need to eat for the same blicing reason. It doesn't mean we can't help you get downstairs, though. Don't be an idiot just because he was one," he insisted. "I cannot handle this from both of you."

Westly tried not to grimace as he looked back to Nichi to see the princeling hesitant smile. If not for the whiplash of them having just tried to kill each other, if not for the two cycles of torment knowing how hated he had been, he still would have refused. But if Nichi was fascinated by kindred, if he had thought to push Westly away rather than risk being his friend... Well he was an idiot, but Westly didn't have to hold it against him.

"Fine," Westly said, sighing. "But we need to hurry. I can skip formations, but you two can't. Not this one. You know Rylan's going to make you cadre."

"He's going to make you cadre, too," Nichi grinned, his words a hope that made Westly's heart ache. Ever since meeting the Windover prince he had wanted that smile turned on him, but to see it now? To know they'd be working together and Nichi wouldn't hate his very existence the whole time? That he never had?

Westly's cheeks heated as Nichi turned from them both to grab a shirt that wasn't covered in blood. Micah watched them both, just shaking his head.

"If I didn't know you could wipe the floor with him, he'd be dead by now," he muttered, his voice low enough that only Westly caught it. When Nichi looked back to them from the neck of his clean shirt, he added: "Don't you even think of being an idiot again while I'm gone," Micah said. Unlike the two of them, he was still in just his towel. "I'll be right back."

"Course not," Nichi said, hands going up in surrender as Micah left the room. When the door was closed behind him, Nichi began to tuck his shirt into his high-waisted uniform pants. As he worked, Westly turned to look at anything other than the hard bodied princeling of Windover, praying his face wasn't red.

Nichi was back into his whole uniform a few moments later, though when Westly turned to see him, he found the princeling watching him. "I guess I didn't do as much damage to your face as I thought," Nichi greeted, hips resting back against the platform for his nest as he crossed his arms over his chest. Well, one of them. He was cradling his right hand in the corner of his left.

Westly matched him, resting back against the desk even if he had to splay his wings to do so. "Is that an apology?" he replied, though he regretted the bite in his words the moment they left his lips.

Nichi had the gall to look affronted, but seemed to remember himself before answering. "I'm sorry. I... Apparently I can't do anything right this dawning."

"Whatever it is, Tyrsten says it runs in your family," Westly said, which made Nichi laugh.

"He's probably right," Nichi admitted, looking away. "Still, it's not an excuse."

"I wasn't exactly fair to you, either," Westly admitted. "That's basically the first rule of being a chiurgeon: don't attack your patients, especially the stubborn ones."

Nichi exhaled a laugh, looking down at his fist as he spoke. "So, how did you, ah..." he started to ask, only to bite his lip to stop himself. "Never mind."

I am not so different from you, Westly thought. This was what he hated the most. The more that people danced around his bloodline the more awkward he felt, which was absurd. He was proud of what he was.

"The same way you would fix a broken nose," Westly said. "I put it back in place and wiped the blood off. What did you think I did?"

Nichi looked up at him, focused on his bruised face for a few moments, and then looked away flushing. He couldn't even say it.

"Well, you're not wrong," Westly said. "Though the last time I healed myself when people knew I was that hurt I was nearly killed for it."

"I heard about that," Nichi said, shifting uncomfortably. "When you first got here, I mean."

"That's why I moved into the garden," Westly said, which seemed to ease the tension between them. "But I am glad that chirons are not taught to fight. I only survived because I knew how to defend myself."

"Hah," Nichi laughed, finally looking up. "That's an understatement. Who taught you?"

"Taught me what?" Westly asked, confused.

"How to fight," Nichi repeated. "If you taught Rylan, who taught you?"

"Oh." Now it was Westly's turn to laugh. "It's an Ehkeski style I learned as a fledgling in Kelsineah. I grew up wingbound on the Boar Flats, so my caretakers wanted me to be able to defend myself. It's pretty easy, actually," he went on, only to look up and see Nichi's horrified face.

"You grew up what?" He asked.

Westly just shrugged. "Wingbound. It's not uncommon with kindred," he said quietly. "The Clans don't have the nets and lines and cages that a Kosaran family would have to keep a windwalker fledgling from flying off, so they wingbind us. It didn't hurt. Honestly I didn't know there was a difference until I was old enough to be out in the city when the Legions pass through in the spring. Then I just thought it was a thing they did to keep us safe."

"Westly that wasn't right," Nichi insisted. "They should have given you to a windwalker family when you started to fledge. Someone who would have known how to care for you. Who wouldn't have—"

"Killed me?" he interrupted as Nichi groped for what he thought should have been done. "For having a dryad for a mother? Because one day I might be able to talk to plants? Might be able to bind creatures with air and earth? Might be able to rip someone's soul from their body on a whim?"

Nichi's face had gone grey.

"I can do all but the last of that, Nichi," he said, not about to lie. "But I do touch a person's spirit to heal them and that is close enough for most."

Nichi's hand flexed as he matched eyes with him. "It also wasn't evil," he defended. "You're not evil."

Given the heat of his stare, Westly didn't argue any further. It was nice to know Nichi felt that way when so many other people had told him differently most of his life. When the Second Counsel Lord insisted on it, only staying his hand because Lord Seventh outranked him more than twice over.

"So that's why they taught me to fight with my hands," Westly said, trying to salvage the conversation. "So I wouldn't resort to magic in a panic."

"Whatever the reason, you're blicing good at it," he said. "I never had a chance, did I?"

"Micah tried to warn you," Westly said. "But it's really easy. You just get your hands up in front of your face and if you can keep the space between yourself and the other person guarded, you'll be fine. If they rush you, just let them pass and do what you can to help them along. It's all natural movements."

"That's how you got me on the ground, isn't it?" Nichi realized, thinking back. "I tried to punch you but you just knocked it out of the way and the next thing I knew I was soaring past you."

"Well, I needed to get on top of you," Westly said, though he immediately regretted the phrase as he saw Nichi smirk. "To look at your eyes, I mean," he corrected, hating the hot flush in his cheeks as he looked away. "I just—I could tell if it was the terra if I saw it in your eyes. Windows to the soul and all that."

"Oh," Nichi replied, looking back with the same flustered tension. "Well, whatever you did, I feel better than I have in moonturns."

"You should," Westly said, glad for the change of subject. "I'm not sure what happened, but I do know that it helped restore what you'd lost."

Nichi glanced up as Westly trailed off, holding his gaze for so long that Westly almost took it for an invitation. Almost.

This is not fair, Westly mourned, dropping his eyes as Nichi shifted uncomfortably again. *He's too damn beautiful to be angry at and he knows it.*

As he flexed his hand, Westly's eye caught on the heavy gold signet ring he wore. It looked a little worse for wear after so many cycles as a tyro, which was to be expected. That was the reason their uniforms were dyed with indigo after all. The color had nothing on the way he felt seeing the curve of Nichi's muscled arms through his wool jacket or the set of his shoulders as he supported his wings without any effort at all. Honestly, just being close to Nichi was enough to make him forget about everything else in the world.

This is so not fair...

Westly bit on the inside of his lip as his mind reeled back through their fight. No matter the intention, all the places they had made contact burned with the intensity of Nichi's spirit. When Westly looked up again, he found Nichi watching him with a sort of incredulous, half-amused smile.

"What?" Westly asked, suddenly self-conscious.

"Your hair, man," Nichi said, and finally did laugh. "It's so long."

Westly flushed with the observation, grabbing his hat from his pocket to cover it again. "I'm only a chiurgeon. I don't have to wear a warcrest if I don't want to."

"It would look good on you," Nichi said, glancing away as he ran his hand through his own hair, only to hiss with pain.

Westly winced as he watched Nichi try to clench his fist again.

"Can I take a look?" He asked, relieved when Nichi seemed to swallow his pride as he nodded. Pushing off the desk, he moved through the small room, tucking his wings behind him as Nichi took a seat on the platform in front of his nest.

"I think something's out of joint," Nichi said, trying not to flinch as Westly spread out his fingers to see what he had done. After a moment of considering, he blinked into his second sight and then frowned to see the tiny fractures in the bones of his first two knuckles.

"This is going to need a lot of rest," Westly said, blinking out of his secondsight before looking up again. "Or I can tend it now before it gets any worse."

Nichi paled a little with the offer. "How long would it take if I was easy on it?"

"A fortnight at least," Westly said, honest. "Probably more. You wouldn't want to use it much, either."

"Well, it's not like I have anything important to do in the next turn," Nichi said, miserable.

"I can heal it," Westly shrugged. "That would just make it go away."

"All of it?" Nichi asked, surprised. "Just like that?"

"This is nothing compared to your wings," Westly reminded him. "I could do it here or I can bandage it and take care of it later if you wanted to come back to the Garden with me. Then I could at least pretend to be a normal chiurgeon."

"You're not, though," Nichi said, wavering as he looked down to his hand. "And I'd rather show you I trust you. Maybe then you can forgive me for being such an ass earlier."

"For the past candlemark or the past two cycles?" Westly said, arching an eyebrow.

Nichi actually laughed at that. "I'll start with the past candlemark," he said. "If you'd let me make up for the rest, I'd be glad to. You have no idea how much I wanted to talk to you before," he said, wincing as Westly shifted his hand between them. "I just... I didn't want to get you involved in House politics like Micah. Maybe after I have my commission I can come help you in the Garden, though. I'd love to know what it is you do in there. Tyrren and Raleigh never stop talking about how incredible it is."

"They what?" Westly said, pausing as he slid his left hand beneath Nichi's before covering it with his right.

"Tyrren," Nichi said. "You know, Tyrsten's near-brother? He hangs out with the chirons and Raleigh all the time and they keep trying to explain to everyone how you added a fifth element to the chiurgeon's garden. No one believes them. Well, no one but me but I keep out of it."

"People talk about me?" Westly said, still surprised. "About what I've done?"

"You have no idea how incredible you are, do you?" Nichi said, risking a smile. "Westly, people like you. They're fascinated by you. They're..." Westly's heart ached as Nichi had to look away. "They trust your talents a lot more than you know."

"Oh," Westly said, blinking back into his secondsight as he closed the circle of power through Nichi's hand, shivering shivering to feel the deep font of azure energy. Nichi must have felt it too, because he sucked in a breath as Westly's energy began to pass through him.

"Holy gods," Nichi said, his hand flexing to take hold of Westly's with strength. "That feels..."

Westly closed his eyes as Nichi braced against the power. As the princeling sucked in air to steady himself, Nichi's other hand covered his own, keeping their hands pressed hard together. When he was finally done, Westly looked up to see Nichi staring at him with a desire so obvious it made his heart stagger.

"Does it always feel like that?" Nichi managed, as breathless as if he had flown ten laps around the Palace.

Westly nodded, just barely, at Nichi's amazement. "Yeah," he said quietly. "But the first few times are the most intense."

"There is no getting used to that," Nichi protested. "Blood and ice, man," he went on, shaking his head as he laughed. "I envy the man that takes you to nest if that is what happens under your fleeting attention."

Westly turned scarlet as Nichi smiled. Seeing him color, the sireling shifted his own hand out of Westly's, taking hold of his right with both of his own. As Westly watched, Nichi lifted his knuckles to his lips, sharing the same kiss of greeting Westly so often saw between the lovers who thought to stroll through his Garden, not realizing he was there. As Westly saw the intent from Nichi was the same, he recognized the invitation for what it was and Nichi's smoldering look gave Westly whiplash all over again.

"You two wingmates yet," said a voice at the door. "Or are you still trying to kill each other?"

Westly nearly jumped out of his skin.

"What? No, I mean—" Westly stammered, yanking his hand back.

"You ready to go?" Nichi asked, ignoring Micah's jab as he came to his feet.

"Are you?" Micah asked, looking to Nichi's hand as Westly stepped back.

"I will be after I eat," Nichi shrugged, casual as ever.

"Everyone else is at meal already," Micah said. "Wes, you feeling okay now?"

Westly blinked in surprise, only now realizing he had been focusing so hard on working with Nichi that he hadn't noticed the power balancing between them. Whatever Nichi had done, whatever Westly had done to him, the fog over his eyes was gone.

"Yeah," he said, trying not to sound surprised. "I should probably still talk to Mother, though," he added. "Just to be sure."

As Micah nodded, turning to clear the doorway for them, Westly stole one last glance at the Windover prince. Nichi was watching him, the offer still plainly there, and the strength of Nichi's focus on him was amazing. Trying to calm his racing heart, Westly forced himself to exhale and look back at Micah in the hallway only to see Tyrsten and his near-brother Tyrren hailing them all.

As Westly and Nichi moved, Tyrren looked between the three of them with interest.

"Hey, Wes," Ren greeted, oblivious to Westly's own flustered reaction. "Raleigh said to let you know he'd meet you in the Armory. I left him as the point man for issuing out gear, so you just need to check in with him once we're done with cadre stuff."

"Ah, thanks," Westly said.

"Speaking of which," Tyrsten said as they all started to follow him. "Rylan is in the Armory with food for all of us now. Everyone will be there in half a mark."

"You so eager to get demoted that you're gonna hurry through breakfast, Primarch?" Micah called, amused as they moved down the hall.

"Gods no," Tyrsten said with a laugh. "But the sooner we get our gear and finish the briefing, the sooner I can get back into my nest and sleep off this hangover."

"Glory to that," Ren laughed, moving ahead of them to hit the flight path first. Tyrsten followed just after him, heading down with a lazy speed, and it was Micah next until he stopped at the threshold to the flight corridor.

"Did you actually ask him your question?" Micah reminded, looking at Nichi.

"Oh, shit," Nichi said, eyes wide as he looked to Westly. "No, I got distracted."

"Course you did," Micah said, rolling his eyes. "Well, ask him now. We're not going to have time later."

"Ask me what?" Westly said, confused.

"House Windover would like to formally request your services as a Palace Chiurgeon, Westly," Nichi said with a formality that startled him. "My Sire will be in our apartments tomorrow and our own chiurgeons have no idea what is wrong with him. If you would extend the use of your talents, we would be in your debt."

Westly blinked a few times, realizing what he meant.

"You want me to heal your father?" he asked, cutting through the Court-crafted words.

"If you can heal me, perhaps you can heal him," Nichi said. "I would forever be in your debt."

"Well?" Micah prompted.

"It would be my honor," Westly said, holding his hand out to mark their agreement. Nichi took it, though Westly's heart started to race as he lifted it to his lips in thanks.

Seeing the touch between them a second time, Micah's snort of laughter pulled them out of the moment. "Are you two going to fuck or can we get on with this? I'm starving."

As Westly started to stammer an excuse, Nichi took his hand back so he could shove Micah into the flight corridor. When he was gone, when it was just the two of them, Nichi's look was smoldering.

"He's just jealous I won't be chasing his tail feathers anymore," Nichi explained, adding a wolfish grin as Westly realized what he meant.

"Oh," he managed, shifting back only to feel his wings hit the wall.

Nichi's look didn't change as he moved to follow him, stepping toe to toe with him like he had done during their fight. His hand came up the same as well, though Westly froze as he set just his fingertips against Westly's chest, holding him in place.

"I mean," Nichi said, leaning in close enough to whisper in his ear. "If that's all right with you."

"I..." Westly breathed, heart thundering in his chest as he felt Nichi's breath along his neck. Westly had seen lovers doing this before, trading whispered moments in dark shadows, but he hadn't expected to feel so dizzy as a result. No matter the lightness of Nichi's touch, there was still power sparking between them and Westly was staggered by the feeling of something inside of himself blossoming open to take it in.

Holy Matron, Westly swore, shuddering as Nichi's hand pressed flat on his chest. *What is happening to me?*

As the pressure of the touch intensified, so too did the power suddenly pouring into him, the power Nichi was pouring into him without even trying. Just as Nichi's hand slid up from his chest to his jaw, holding him steady as Nichi pressed his lips against Westly's neck, Westly was drowning in the torrent of bliss. As his eyes rolled back into his head, it was all Westly could do to remain standing.

Westly wasn't sure when Nichi realized something odd was happening, but when he did finally draw back, Westly was staggered with the sudden loss. Coming back to himself, Westly opened his eyes to find Nichi was still hovering close, apparently ready to catch him if need be.

"You all right?" Nichi asked as Westly took a shuddering breath. "You went all still and I don't—"

"I'm okay," Westly managed, strangling back a sudden ravenous desire. Kindred dryads could devour the souls of windwalkers and Westly suspected he had just found out why. One touch, one taste of that power and it was all Westly could focus on. If this was the energy at the core of a windwalker, he had been starving all his life.

Knowing this existed, could he survive on anything less?

"You sure?" Nichi asked, exhaling a nervous laugh.

Hands flexing at his side, Westly shrugged his wings together to push him back onto his feet. "I'm sure," he insisted.

As Nichi's worry flowed back into a hesitant smile, Westly heard Micah calling after them both to 'stop fucking around already'.

"Good," Nichi said, eagerness lighting up a dazzling smile. "Because I would really like to, well…" He winced as Micah called a third time, using his warbard's strength in case they had been ignoring him. "I'd like to get to know you better, Westly. If you wouldn't mind the company."

"No, I wouldn't mind," Westly confirmed, blushing furiously as Nichi stepped back to make a proper courtier's bow. Hands to his heart, he bent over one well-turned leg as he flared his wings ever so slightly, demure but determined. That kind of overt, courting display Westly had most definitely seen before between lovers, and it took all Westly's strength to not swoon against the wall.

Nichi Windover knew who he was.

Nichi Windover didn't care he was kindred.

Nichi Windover liked him, clearly, to preen like that.

Gods give me strength, Westly prayed as Nichi turned and yelled back down to Micah to go fuck himself instead of bothering them. Laughing in an echo of Micah's own amusement, Nichi tossed Westly one last look before launching into the open space.

When he was gone, Westly collapsed against the wall. If this is what it meant to come into your power—if this is what it felt like to be able to feel the true energy inside a windwalker—then he had to be very careful.

If he could manage it, though…?

Micah was going to be so jealous.

CHAPTER 11: MICAH

Thursday, 12:30

Five candlemarks later, arms full of issued gear, Micah was still shaking his head about everything that had happened that dawning. "I am *not* jealous," Micah insisted, glowering as Nichi lingered in the hallway to wait for Westly. What did he care if his best mate and his crew-brother were getting on so well? He was glad for it!

"That's what you get when you knock people's heads together," Tyrsten said, stalling as Ren got the door to the lecture hall. "Sometimes they sort themselves out."

"Wait, did you do that on purpose?" Micah accused, realizing that Westly *had* said Tyrsten had told him to come into the washroom instead of waiting. "Tyr!"

"So what if I did," he said, smirking. "You're not the only person in our century who is headed for the cantullus corps. I can get a pretty good read on folks myself, even without a lute."

Micah's scoff didn't even phase him.

"Damn it, Tyr," he went on, glowering. "Nichi threw a proper fit last night thinking that he was going to get Westly killed by drawing attention to him. He even said that he thinks Lord Seventh means to, well..."

Micah cut himself off as they passed into the room. Westly and Nichi were still trailing behind them, with Nichi still trying to bend over backwards to make up for the past two cycles of idiocy. Whatever he was doing, it did seem to be helping the chiurgeon tyros work with him, especially Raleigh.

"Means to what?" Tyrsten asked as the door closed behind the three of them. They had a whole five beats to get their gear set before Red Bevy was going to file in after mid-meal.

"Name Heir Kreychi as Counselheir," Micah said, unsure how either of them would react. Of all things, though, he had not expected sputtering laughter.

"Kreychi?!" Tyrsten balked, dropping his gear next to the back wall. "Gods, and you believed him? You really were drunk last night. Kreychi isn't even in the Host anymore."

Micah just sighed as he looked between them. "Fine," he said, dropping his own gear next to Tyrsten's. "So why was he such an ass to Westly all these cycles?"

"Well, that is because of Kreychi," Ren said, joining them. "But they look at me and Tyr the same way, so what does it matter? Any sireling who can inherit gets shit for taking a man to nest if it's not on the Plains. It's all mind games from the Daughters. I thought you would have picked up on that by now, Mike. They want to catch, so they'll give a House prince ten times the grief to make sure he gives them a chance at catching from him. That's all it is."

"Nichi is such an idiot," Tyrsten said, rolling his eyes. "But if he's stupid for your crew brother, then fine. Wes is great and I've always said it. A little stand offish—"

"Because Nichi has been an ass," Ren cut in.

"—But great all the same. I'm kind of excited he's in our cadre for the Bevy," Tyrsten said, with a look to his brother. "Not that Raleigh wouldn't have been great, but if it's Rylan in charge..."

"I know," Ren said, waving off Tyrsten's apology. "It's fine. Raleigh likes Westly, too. He's the only one Wes can stand, so it's good they can work together. Maybe he'll actually have a friend in Kelsineah when we all get drafted after the tourni."

"Unless they're just going to keep him in the Garden," Tyrsten said, frowning as he looked to Micah for an answer. "Has anyone said?"

"I know Mother was looking into it, but that's all. Westly would know better," he said, only to turn as there was noise at the rear of the lecture hall.

"Speak of the demons and they appear," Tyrsten said, raising a hand to hail Westly and Nichi as they moved into the room. Nichi was carrying both sets of their gear as Westly got the door, though it made more sense when they saw Rylan coming in behind them.

Westly, Raleigh, and Rylan had spent all of mid-meal going over the chiurgeon assignments, Westly to learn the men themselves and Raleigh to make sure they would work with the tasks they had to take on. Each squad got at least one chiurgeon flying with them, though what Rylan was doing to the squads themselves still confused Micah. He had said it would all make sense after the briefing so the rest of them had given up asking about it.

Realizing Nichi was struggling with the two heavy bags, Micah moved to help him, only to have to stand back as the other two came into the room. Once they had passed, Nichi gave up one of the duffle bags for Micah to carry. When he didn't release the strap, though, Micah's interest piqued.

"You two are getting along now," he observed, watching Nichi as he watched after Westly.

"I told you this would happen," he said, even as his eyes went soft to see Westly glancing back at the two of them. "Gods, I just—He's blicing brilliant. After he sees to my father, I said I'd show him around the suite. He said he liked the idea."

"Show him around the suite?" Micah repeated, laughing. "Isn't that the line you used on me?"

"It worked, didn't it?" Nichi threw back, chewing his lower lip to keep the smile from spreading across his face. He failed miserably. "But this is different. It feels like I'm hunting rabbits with a war bow. Anytime I was helping him, he couldn't stop staring when he thought I wasn't looking, but if I tried to get close to him, he just backed off. I tried to kiss him when we were in the lower levels of the armory grabbing a few more of the crank crossbows for your guys, but he pulled back so fast I started second guessing myself. Then he set me to task and let Raleigh steal him away for a whole candlemark. I only got next to him again at mid-meal, but then Rylan had to sit down and take over the whole blicing table with his notes. At this point I have no idea what to do. You have to help me!"

"Breathe, man, or you'll be cursed with hands like the tide," Micah said, quoting his mother's favorite saying. "All the court stuff isn't going to work on him, Nichi. He's probably terrified of you. He's still a bowen."

"What do you mean a bowen?" Nichi repeated, gawking as he lowered his voice. "How! How is he still a bowen? There's no way! With that face?"

"He is," Micah insisted. "So slow down. He doesn't think like a sireling and he isn't interested in taking anyone to nest that isn't his friend. So be his friend first, all right?"

For the first time in his life Micah saw Nichi Windover blush.

"You think he'd be my friend?" He asked, eyes wide as he looked back to Micah. It was like the thought had never occurred to him. "Like, actually my friend? Gods, I want to show him the Estate back home. All the woods and wild places where I grew up. I mean there are gryphons around, sure, but we just have to chase off the little ones who still think they can eat our cattle. There's moose and the fishing and—"

"That sounds great, Nichi," Micah said, trying not to laugh. "You take him there after we get done with graduation, okay? As for getting in his nest," he said as Nichi finally tore his eyes away. "If you manage to apologize for being an ass all these cycles, I'm pretty sure you'll be set."

As Nichi just stood there moon-eyed at the idea, Micah pulled the duffle bag against his side with his wing moved into the room. Westly's gear, Rylan's, and Nichi's all went in a line on the back wall with the others.

Once they were set aside, the two of them moved to join the others of their cadre squad as they looked at the map that Rylan had spread out over the table in the front of the lecture hall. At first glance it looked like a basic map of Delton, but then Rylan pulled out a second, thinner sheet of paper that was nearly translucent. Seeing the strange lines and the markings for territories, Micah's eyes went wide as both he and Westly realized that Rylan had sketched out the territories for the streets as they related to the events, rather than using the districts as they had been drawn on the map.

"You wanted to know what I've been doing for the past day," Rylan said, spreading out the map that was curled after so long in the red leather script. "Well, here it is. This is also how I'm going to stay hidden, from Fionn or anyone else who thinks they're going to grab me during this fight," he said, looking up to Micah. "So we're going to set up groups that can run through spaces like this. I figure if we cover that ground like crews, not like the Host, we'll have our edge. You and Wes and I know how to do that, so that's easy," he said, hands braced on the table. "But it's only going to work if you two are on board," he said, bringing Tyrsten and Ren into the huddle they were starting to make. "And if you can tell me exactly what you think Fionn is going to do, since he plays by the rules."

"Because you never do," Tyrsten laughed, clearly loving this idea.

"I have never had the luxury of being able to do anything the way people expect," Rylan said, correcting his friend with the subtle intensity of the words. "My honor is in survival. My glory will be making that bastard of a Lord Seventh rue the day he ever thought to conscript me into this Host."

Standing directly across from him, Tyrsten took his time setting his hands on the table to face Rylan. "So you're in it to win?"

"There is no winning or losing, Tyr," Rylan said. "There is life and death, and I mean to tear this tournament apart from the inside out. Are you with me?"

"Oh I'm with you," Tyrsten said, grinning. "How about you, brother?"

"For Honor and Glory," Tyrren said, equally eager. "Let's get suited up."

By the time Red Bevy had finished with mid-meal and made it into the lecture hall, all five of them had sorted through their gear and put on the white leather cadre jackets they had been issued. They were padded against the cold and armored just enough to keep them safe from the blunted projectiles used for the tournament events, but the cut and style of them was classic. Fitted to their torso and arms, their left arms had the red shadow of a Praetor's pauldron to mark their rank while Rylan's held the full red shoulder of the bevy Primarch. While four of them had the buttons of the front done up securely, Rylan had left the split front of his doublet open. He was still at work, still pouring over the map with the cuffs of his sleeves pushed back over his forearms as he worked.

After two cycles of not trying at all, Rylan had given his word to Mother and now he would.

Micah took a breath as the room saw him stepping apart from the others. Everyone in the bevy knew he was the strongest warbard among them, and more than a few had heard the rumor of his getting the attention of Lord Seventh's Cantullus Preem the night before. Now, watching him chew his lip as he stepped out to call them to attention, he didn't need his Gift to feel the intense energy of the moment.

Feet set together at a hard right angle, Micah came to braced attention to give the command that would start the briefing.

"Wings up!" He ordered. All forty men of the bevy, came to their feet.

Now Rylan came to braced attention, raising his fist to the red leather of his left shoulder as he acknowledged them.

"Easy On," he said, letting the tyros take their ease on the stools again as Tyrsten launched into logistics.

"None of this should be new to you," he began, moving to the front of the lecture hall as Rylan's attention went back to his maps. "We will be taking on five types of challenges over the city, with two challenges for each soldier specialization: Lead, Signal, Weapons, Overwatch, and Chiron," he said. "Once we get the squads assigned to tasks, it will be up to you to take the position by beating out your rival squad from Green Bevy for the objective. You will have four candlemarks from the start to take and hold the position. Once complete, it will be held for a half candlemark before being reset, at which point the challenge can be taken again. Each challenge should take no more than fifteen beats to complete, so it is more than likely that you will have to run the challenge multiple times, with time for reassignments from us," he said. "Any questions so far?"

When there were none, Tyrsten moved on.

"Of the five challenges, the breakdown is as follows: the two Lead challenges will focus on strategy and tactics for deploying the appropriate soldier into the role best suited for them. This cycle, Lord Sixth has taken veteran volunteers to act as elite units that will need to be outwitted appropriately."

With more than half of the men nodding their understanding, Micah watched as the room glanced back to see what Rylan was doing. Their entire bevy had expected Tyrsten to be the one who would lead and more than a few of them had lost coin when Rylan was thrust into the role. All of them were waiting to see what he actually meant to do, or if he was really going to let Tyrsten do it all as some of them feared.

"The Signal challenges," Tyrsten went on, recognizing the shifting attention as well. "Will rely on cryptics and clear communication. We have reports that Lord Fifth has had his Blackwings come up with the message challenges, so you can expect to encounter anything from our own Kosaran writing to Lan'lieanan or even Ehkeski script," he said, pausing just long enough to find Westly in the room. "Chiurgeon Westly is our resident language expert," he said. "If you have questions, go to him."

"Hoi," Westly said, acknowledging the assignment.

That said, Tyrsten shifted his weight as he continued with their information. "Three of these challenges will be the standard four we have seen in previous cycles. There will be a flight through an extensive ring path, various target runs for speed and accuracy, and a path of ground targets and aerial obstacles for the heavy crossbowmen. However, it has been confirmed that they are combining the high-flyers run and the drop and catch for the speed divers this cycle. It seems the game you idiots made of trying to catch bolts coming from higher mates will be its own event this cycle," he added, giving the tyros in the room the permission to gawk or cheer at the prospect.

When the excited chatter had worn itself out, Tyrsten shifted to give his attention to Rylan. As annoyed as Rylan had first been at being placed in charge of their Bevy, Micah knew that his ego had gotten the better of him at some point last night. Rylan might not care about winning, but he hated to lose and that would make him focus whether he liked it or not. How would he go about it, though?

Micah's own curiosity was caught as Tyrsten stepped aside, giving the center of the lecture hall to Rylan for his part of their briefing. Given his hesitant look, this must have been one of the things they had been arguing about. Since Rylan was the Bevy Primarch, they were clearly going with his plan.

When Rylan began, he gave up the check on his sour mood. "Before we hand out these unit assignments, let me make two things clear," he said, scanning the crowd for the few tyros he knew hated him. "If you have a problem with me, you need to leave. You can go join Fionn's men or wait at the end for the shelf for the Winds run, I really don't care. What I do care about is if you are going to follow the orders you're given from my cadre."

Rylan waited until the echo of his words faded before going on. All they needed to do to earn their individual rank-pauldrons was to fly the Ice Winds and they all knew it. As a result, if they didn't agree with Rylan's plan, they could just go to the end of the shelf and wait until noon when the Ice Winds run would begin. The only reason to participate in the war game, other than the Honor and Glory of doing so, was the chance it gave them to impress a Praetor or Primarch that intended to select a new apprentice while in Delton.

This war game was your only opportunity to be seen as more than a report on parchment and it could make or break a career. Refusing to participate for reasons other than a chiurgeon's guidance would look terrible, but Rylan wasn't about to stop them from cutting their own wings off. Instead, he was giving them the knife to do it.

Fortunately no one was that stupid.

"If you all can manage that," Rylan went on. "Then the second thing is that if you have a problem with fighting this as if your lives depended on it, you need to leave. If you only mean to participate to show the proctors that you can outwit their individual challenges, then I don't want you. That is not my objective and it will not be yours if you are under my command. Anyone got a problem with that?"

Rylan let the silence hang in the room longer this time and was rewarded when he saw one of the tyros on the second tier, Cormac, come to an uneasy attention. "Permission to speak?"

"Primarch," Tyrsten said, prompting the honorific.

"Primarch," Cormac added begrudgingly.

"Go on," Rylan said, rolling his eyes.

"What is your objective?" He said, his tone as even as he could manage. "We all know you were in the High Cells last night and you still look like shit. Are you going to dick out on us again mid-tournament?"

"Am I going to—?" Rylan began to repeat and then flared his wings with such a snap that Cormac actually stepped back. "The Tournament is a blicing farce," he said. "The whole point for me—the whole point for all of us—is to demonstrate how the War Plains are too large for any military force to hold. It's the same reason they pit us against Delton itself. All eight centuries of the Tyro Legion couldn't hold this much ground, even if we were all veterans. Because of that, because of how ridiculous it is to even think we could do it, our actual task is simple. We find Fionn and take him out. Him and his entire cadre. Cut the head off the snake and you win."

Cormac actually looked shocked to hear his response, though he did stand up straighter as he realized that yes, Rylan did know what he was blicing talking about.

"And if you think for a second that going onto the Plains will be about air battles and territory possession, you're a fool. There is an entire nation of Ehkeski that will gut you if you so much as set down in the wrong place. As for graduation," he went on. "I grew up in the Houses on this shelf long before I lived on its streets. I know what kind of coin gets handed out to encourage folks to mess with the tyros, even if you don't. For that matter, I know what the veterans do for fun to try and break officer-tyros like us. What makes you think that anything we do to cover ground or take airspace wins us anything other than more moments to find Fionn and his boys?"

Cormac obviously didn't think Rylan expected him to answer, which was well enough because he didn't.

"Exactly," Rylan said, gesturing at him. "Now if you are quite satisfied, you can sit your ass back down and I can finish."

"Hoi, Primarch," Cormac said, saluting before taking his seat.

"Now," Rylan said, looking around the room. He most definitely had Red Bevy's attention. "All of you get on your feet again and go sit with whoever it is you take meals with or would if your schedules allowed it. None of this sitting with your assigned squad nonsense. Sit with the people you pull the best pranks with or study with, whatever it is. Just go."

There was a moment of confusion, but then the tyros got to their feet as he and the command cadre watched. After a good five beats, the groupings started to look more familiar and everyone in them looked far more relaxed. Unsurprisingly, a few of the new squad units were a bit bigger than the others, a few smaller, but overall they still had a decent ratio. Micah, Nichi, Westly, and Ren had all remained where they were. They were cadre, after all.

"Okay," Rylan went on, catching their attention once again. "Now point at the man in your squad who you trust to tell Mother that one of your mates was in trouble. Real trouble." After some confused faces, there seemed to be a consensus among each of the groups. "That man's your new Lead," Rylan said. "Leads, you report to Tyrsten."

A few eyes went wide as they realized what Rylan had just done, but no one objected.

"As for the Heavies, Mike, you're going to need to pick someone you trust to handle them. As of right now, you're my Preem and I want you rested," Rylan said. "We are going to scour this city, and I am not wasting men as warbards when you'll serve well enough."

Micah was about to protest until he saw the fire in Rylan's look, though his brother waited until he nodded before moving on.

"The rest of you unsorted folk, you're my Weapons, high or low. You report to Nichi and Ren for your assignments. Tyr has it from here," he said. "Now I need to get some fucking sleep."

Micah came to braced attention while Rylan grabbed his gear. Once he had his things together, Micah called for "Wings up!" Bringing the bevy to its feet as Rylan stalked out of the room with the red leather script in his hands.

"I knew he'd make me his Canto," Micah said into the stunned silence of the room. "But I'm not a Preem. I can't send orders to the whole bevy at once when we're scattered over the city…"

Nichi's look was incredulous.

Tyrsten, however, seemed to expect this. "Show of hands, brothers. How many of you heard Micah playing for the Windover revel last night?" he said, raising his hand once again. "I don't care if you were drunk or fucking or halfway across the city in your Estates visiting family, how many of you heard him?"

As everyone in the room raised their hands, Micah felt the floor drop out from beneath him.

"As much shit as you give Rylan about the Lord Seventh's supposed sorcery," Tyrsten said, looking to Micah. "All Seventh's men eventually become warbards because we work under the Preems who pass on Lord Seventh's Orders, but the Preems can only do that because the Lord Seventh passes on Founder Noventrio's blessing. Cousin Kait says his Seventh's Gift is mind-speech whether we want to admit it or not, and I didn't until my own father explained how Kiernan su'Illiandria has caused there to be more Preems in his seven cycles than Kosar has seen in living memory."

Micah didn't know what to say.

"As for Rylan," Nichi said, glancing to their fellow tyros as if to better explain. "Canto Primarch Decius made it clear he wants you as his apprentice this winter and Rylan knows it. Rylan also knows that his House, defunct or not, was the House that gave birth to the line of Sevenths. So if you're working for him, if you're passing on his orders for this wargame, he believes you will be able to reach us all."

"You just have to give a shit for once and stop coasting like you do in class," Tyrren added, though the laugh in his voice softened the blow. "You are so much stronger than you think you are, Mike. Don't you remember how much talent it takes to be a preem? What it means when you are able to be silent and still call orders over the wind? We spent three whole moonturns listening to lectures about it our first cycle here."

Micah just shook his head. "I only got conscripted two years ago. I never… What do you mean Preems are silent on purpose?"

"They don't use their voices because they don't have to anymore," Tyrsten explained, though the whole room looked shocked to realize Micah's confusion was genuine. "That's how strong their Warbard Gift is because of how closely they work with Lord Seventh, but they still have a chain of command it runs through. Decius said your lute was a crutch, but that's only because his Cantos can't judge the extent of your skill in class. We've all heard you play, Micah, and it's the only time you let down your guard. Even if you're drunk and high, the raw power you can wield when is incredible."

Micah wasn't sure what to say.

"Last night you let your guard down with the whole of the Cantullus Corps in the city heard it," Nichi went on. "Everyone heard you projecting nothing but music in the middle of a revel. Preems do that, Mike, and you're going to be one. That's why Primarch Decius wants you as his apprentice. There's no use hiding your abilities anymore, and that's why Rylan wants to use you for the wargame."

"But I wasn't hiding," Micah objected, terrified. "And the music and smoke, it's the only thing that keeps the Warhost out of my head. It's the only thing that lets me hear myself think anymore. Nichi..." He said, his voice dropping to a whisper as Nichi flared his wings to give Micah space to breathe. "I don't know what's going on. My mother said Sera's gift was supposed to balance mine, but if they take me any further from her—"

As Micah bit his lip to stop himself from speaking, Nichi pulled him into an embrace.

"Micah, it's okay," his friend said. "Canto Xavier can help. Do you want to go find him?"

"No," Micah murmured, shaking his head as the room began to fill with the sound of rustling wings and tyros shifting in their places. A moment later, Micah saw Westly stepping around Nichi's wings, concern radiating from both of them. From everyone, actually...

Oh Gods, I'm going to be sick...

"Decius said if I wanted to be his apprentice, I had to call to him during the Tourni," Micah remembered, pulling out of the embrace. "But if I don't, then he won't, right? If I'm not high... If I'm not drunk, Gods trying to call with that much strength will make my ears bleed. I'm not going to do that for him," he said, angry now. "And I'm not going to do it for Rylan, either. Not just so he can get revenge on Lord Seventh."

"This isn't about revenge," Nichi said, serious no matter his friend's anger. "This is about Honor and Glory, remember?"

Whose, though? Micah thought. *Blood on my ashes, Rylan is right. There is no Honor in seeking the Glory of a Lord fucking Seventh going on Envoy.*

"I need to get out of here," he said aloud, backing away from Nichi. "I need to get somewhere quiet. I don't think all the terra in the world could save me now."

"Kait is in the House suite," Nichi offered, pulling in his wings as Micah dodged Westly's concerned look. "It's just her while the rest of the family moves to the Estate in the Lower City. I'm sure—"

It was all he needed to hear. A heartbeat later, Micah turned and fled.

CHAPTER 12: KIERNAN

Thursday, 13:00

"It isn't pointless," Kiernan argued, bringing the last of the twist to his lips. "Terra has a point, at least for me."

"And that is?" Kreychi said, curious as he came to the threshold between Kiernan's sleeping quarters and his office. Kiernan breathed in the azure smoke as he glanced at the man, only to have his heart race to see Kreychi leaning against the frame. Even if Kreychi wasn't as hard bodied as he had been on the plains, the softness that now covered the muscle was still incredibly attractive. The fact that he was letting the silken comforts slip down his legs as Kiernan watched didn't hurt, either. Kreychi had traded a veteran's body for a courtier's calculated game of seduction, and he loved both equally.

As Kreychi began to prowl towards him, black silk sheet still concealing the man's arousal, Kiernan exhaled the last of his terra in a halo over his head. "I can hear myself think again," he said, relaxing into the tall back of his chair. "Thanks to you."

Kreychi's smoldering look as he came to a stop in front of Kiernan was impressive. "You can thank me again now that you're done with that twist," he said, letting the silk pool at his feet at last. "How does that sound?"

"Again?" Kiernan asked, exhaling a laugh as Kreychi put one hand along Kiernan's collarbone to hold him in place. The other wasn't nearly as kind, clawing open the front of his robe for the man's true intent.

"Yes, again," Kreychi murmured, lips so very close to Kiernan's own as he dragged a hand up the inside of Kiernan's thigh. "If that is all you do for the next three days it still wouldn't be enough."

"Gods, Kreya," Kiernan breathed, bracing against the chair as Kreychi took hold of him with strength. After not having taken a partner for almost a cycle, suddenly Kiernan couldn't get rid of him. Not that he wanted to. Not anymore.

Alive, Kiernan thought, groaning as Kreychi shifted to come down onto his knees before the chair. *Gods, he makes me feel so alive.*

Kreychi's hands were still on him as he set himself, lips and tongue not far behind. A moment more and Kiernan's head fell against the high back of his chair, hands digging into the unbound length of Kreychi's platinum hair as he was swallowed whole.

No matter his vanished hawkeye or the work Kiernan still had to do before he left, Kreychi had come back to his suite after the mid-meal with a case of icewine and more terra than Kiernan had thought existed on the Palace shelf. He had only requested one thing in exchange and Kiernan had been more than happy to make that trade. So as soon as the azure smoke had clouded out the voices in his mind, they had done their best to reenact their first glorious summer together on the Plains.

The only reason they had stopped was because Kiernan had fallen asleep in Kreychi's arms, exhausted and spent, but that had left the terra wear off entirely. Now that he was back in that haze again...

Kiernan's breath caught as his wingmate stilled around him, threatening to give up his affection until Kiernan's grip tightened in his hair. Kreychi had always done this, always brought him to the edge of pleasure before backing off to make Kiernan chase after him. To make him pin him in a nest or to this oaken desk, all of it to drive him insane until Kreychi was the one putting Kiernan on his knees, overwhelming him with the pleasure of being made to submit to someone else's will.

Kiernan didn't mean to let that happen right now. Powerless as he felt in his life, when his wingmate started to pull off, Kiernan's hands locked him in place. Kreychi's grip on his thigh acknowledged the request until Kreychi's subtle, gagging struggle brought Kiernan to the edge of a different kind of—

"Are you fucking serious?" Hest'lre swore from the doorway, recoiling from a sight he had clearly not expected. They hadn't even heard him open the door. "Blood on my ashes, Kiernan, I cannot believe you! Both of you!"

Kiernan released his wingmate at once, though as Kreychi backed off, the hand dragging across the back of his mouth covered more than just a swallowed curse.

Gods, but they should have locked the door.

"Hest'lre—" Kiernan started to say, only to bite his lip to see Hest'lre's hand blocking the sight he had found.

"He is not part of the Host!" Hest'lre swore and Kiernan's heart ached as Kreychi fled into Kiernan's personal quarters. "He cannot be your wingmate, Kiernan. Fuck!"

He never stopped, Kiernan wanted to say, knowing the truth of it now. *I never let him stop.*

When Kreychi had finally fled back to his sleeping quarters, all he said was: "He's gone, Hest'lre."

"We will be too," Hest'lre said, glaring fury as Kiernan came to his feet. "So get dressed and get your pauldron. We're going to Aaron's."

"My pauldron?" Kiernan balked. "Why?"

"Because with the amount of terra you smoked, the whole blicing Warhost knows you got laid," Hest'lre said, shooting him a dark look. "Or did you also forget you're the most powerful fucking warbard in Kosar?"

As Kiernan's mouth fell open to realize just what that meant, Hest'lre pressed on.

"And Lenae is going to be furious," he added. "So if I leave you with him, she'll tan both our hides. She told you not to fuck him cycles ago."

"But what about my eyes? My hair?" Kiernan said. "They've both gone silver."

"Just get dressed," Hest'lre said, turning to leave.

Sighing, Kiernan came to his feet, dragging the robe around his body to fight off the cold. It wasn't like this was the first time he and Kreychi had ever been interrupted, but it still gave him whiplash to lose the intensity of the moment. To think that he had possibly broadcast any of the past half a day... Kiernan could feel Kreychi's own mortification like a physical pain. His wingmate had been so breathtakingly happy one moment and now, realizing everyone would know what they'd done?

Stepping inside the smaller room, he found Kreychi already back into the leather breeches that Kiernan had stripped off him candlemarks before. He had apparently stopped to gather Kiernan's own uniform and kama, hearing how Kiernan needed to leave.

Kiernan didn't say a word as Kreychi moved towards him, eyes on the floor. Instead, Kiernan just took the pieces he was handed and got back into them. Socks and fitted pants went beneath his soft flight boots and then the silk undershirt, wool over shirt, and tailored leather jacket. That done, Kreychi helped him into the draping tunic of the kama and Kiernan tied that around his wings and waist as Kreychi went back for the voluminous pants. After so many candlemarks spent in only his flesh and feathers, the layers felt like a prison rather than the prestige of his Seat.

The last piece was his sculpted quicksilver pauldron and though it fit like second-skin, Kreychi was meticulous in the lay of the leather over the brocade of his left sleeve. Once Kreychi had it buckled around his arm, he brought the leather straps around Kiernan's wings, fastening it across his chest. When he was finished, Kiernan ducked his head, letting Kreychi press down the sides of his warcrest to set that back to rights.

"Thank you, Kreya," Kiernan said softly. "For everything."

"All I ever wanted to do was take care of you," Kreychi said, fragile in the moment.

"I know," Kiernan assured him, embracing the man before he could pull away. "Gods, I know. Please don't regret this. You mean the world to me, Kreya. You always have."

"He's right, though," Kreychi whispered, hating the truth of it. "Kiernan, I never should have asked, but I can't let go of you. I don't even want to. Iskander save me, what is wrong with me?"

"Nothing is wrong with you," Kiernan swore, letting out a low growl of frustration as he shifted his hold on the man. "Nothing you have ever done has been wrong. I am the one hurting you and I am sorry. Truly."

There was pain in Kreychi's eyes as he looked up at last.

"And I promise you," Kiernan insisted, touching the man's cheek. "I will always cherish the time we shared, but this is not our end. I am going back to War, true, but once you are Patriarch of your House, you will be as well. The House of Lords is as much a battle ground as any we ever faced and you will be brilliant there, I know it," he insisted. "Find your Glory there, Kreya. Honor me by making it possible to come home with peace. Can you do that?" he pleaded. "For me?"

Kreychi's eyes were brimming with tears and even though Kiernan could hear Hest'lre calling down the hall, he still closed the distance between them. Tender as the moment was, Kreychi stood with him in strength until the kiss they shared came to an end.

"I will seek the Glory of the House of Windover," Kiernan insisted, his voice rough and low for all the emotion he strangled back. "Say it."

"I will seek the Glory of the House of Windover," Kreychi repeated. "So long as the Gods are with you."

Realizing the goodbye for what it was, Kiernan steeled himself as he stepped away. As he turned to leave, he saw Kreychi washing his hands over his face to collect himself, accepting the break between them. As Kiernan moved back into his office, he was scrubbing at his own eyes as he found the glass of ice wine still on his desk and downed it to steady his nerves. That done, he went for the door, picking up one of the new bottles and tucking it under his arm before moving into the receiving room for the greater apartments.

Counsel Lord Hest'lre was waiting for him at the balcony exit.

"This came for you," Hest'lre said, holding the small parchment as Kiernan belted on his over-cloak. "Not that you noticed. Henrick said your suite has reeked of terra for candlemarks."

"Better to have my head in a cloud than be trapped inside the Warhost," Kiernan said, handing him the ice wine to hold. "I should be good for the few candlemarks we need to be down there."

When Kiernan had his flight cloak secure, Hest'lre waved the letter in his face again to make certain he took it. Hoping it wasn't from the Canto Primarch he had rebuffed earlier, Kiernan's hope began to rise as he saw the sealing wax. It was his dragon seal, which meant it was from Counsel Lord Eirik. After skimming the chicken-scratch writing, Kiernan nodded to himself.

"Good news?" Hest'lre asked, taking a moment to adjust his own pauldron under his cloak. Unlike Kiernan's which was thin enough to wrap softly around his arm, Hest'lre's gryphon was mounted on the bands of hardened leather the rest of the Warhost wore. On top of that, the neck of the pauldron was built up into a half-gorget, which had fought with the lay of his cloak his entire time as Sixth.

"Let's get going," Kiernan said, tucking the paper away as Hest'lre finished.

"Is that about your choice of an heir?" Hest'lre asked. "Because whenever you finally name him, then I can name mine and focus on training with Shayan. This Envoy isn't all about you. You know that right?"

"I'll tell you after Winter Court," Kiernan returned, and Hest'lre took it for the cut that it was. If both he and Kreychi weren't going to tell him whatever it was that Lenae was keeping from him, then Kiernan wasn't going to tell them either.

"You're an ass," Hest'lre said, and meant it. A moment later he let out a deep breath and the laugh he had been trying to suppress.

"Like calls to like," Kiernan returned, ducking as Hest'lre took a half-hearted swing at him. His friend would forgive him eventually, but Kiernan was glad to see any sign of it right now. "Which way?"

Directly across from them was the jagged slope of the rest of the mountain, but to their right was a field between the Sires' Wing and Soldier Tyros' Wing where graduation would occur. At the head of that space was the Armory tower, connected to the Soldier Tyros' Wing by a thin covered walkway. The gap between the two buildings was their target tonight and Kiernan let Hest'lre lead the way. They would leave Kiernan's Shadow Guard here and with it, his official presence.

Once they made the trip between the gap, they were able to land in the small salle that was reserved for tyros training for the kind of skills that would be needed if they had to work with men of Fifth Counsel Lord Roder's Vanguard. As opposed to the Delton Tyro Legion, the recruits for Roder's Blackwing Fumentari all came out of the Warhost and dealt with the Ehkeski more of the cycle. As a result, this area had enough height for an aerial fight but it was also filled with balconies, awnings, and an assortment of marketplace furniture and makeshift weapons. It wasn't quite an Ehkeski marketplace, but for an orientation into the difference in special operations tactics, it served well enough.

As far as most were concerned, it was a garbage dump for the tyros. The tyros themselves would never fight in these conditions, just needed to know what it would look like, so it wasn't actually used. Kiernan had no official opinion, leaving the whole issue to Headmaster-Counsel Lord Aaron and his subordinates who made that call. All Kiernan truly wanted were powerful warbards to move his commands through the Host.

Leaving the salle behind them, it was a short walk to reach the rear door to Counsel Lord Aaron's suite. At least, it would have been had the way not been barred by the nine men Kiernan absolutely did not want to see. All of them were dressed in the silver-blue of Kiernan's Primarchs, complete with rank pauldrons and formal kama.

"Did you organize this?" Kiernan asked quietly, slowing his steps as he realized the men were also wearing their wingblades. If they were in full ceremonial kit, they were not here to talk. There were here to kill him.

Hest'lre shook his head, coming to a stop beside Kiernan. "Blood and ice," he swore. "Is this really happening?"

Kiernan took a breath, steadying his nerves as Decius, Kiernan's Cantullus Preem, took a step towards them. In addition to the heavy Primarch's pauldron covering his left chest and shoulder, Decius also wore the matching right-sided pauldron that marked him as the most powerful warbard of the Nine Legions. Clearly the man meant to be heard, even if it meant bringing Kiernan to his knees with his ears bleeding.

"Is there something I can do for you, Preem?" Kiernan asked, even as his heart raced.

::"There is,":: Decius said evenly, and Kiernan flinched as the two words rang with a keening intensity that sent Hest'lre beside him reeling.

"And what is that?" Kiernan replied, grunting under the force of the man's words. For all he had studied under Founder Noventrio to expand his Gifts, Kiernan could easily out-warbard a Preem. Given that his head was full of terra, though, all he had the strength to do was stand next to his Sixth.

"Tell me," Decius said, stalling as the other Primarchs fanned out around Kiernan's position. "Did you enjoy the terra?"

Kiernan's gut clenched, realizing the betrayal. Even if Kreychi had been discrete about asking for the terra, he would have been seen coming into Kiernan's suite with it earlier. That much would have gotten an entire Legion high, but there was only one man who might need that much himself.

"We wondered how long it might take for you to come out of that cloud, but then your Partner here so rudely interrupted you," he said, glancing at Hest'lre. "You really should learn to keep your thoughts to yourself, Lord Sixth."

Hest'lre blanched as the Preem looked between them.

::"As for you, Ser,":: Decius went on, moving a step closer to Kiernan as the others flared their wings. "I'd ask you again if you're going on Envoy, but it seems rather obvious now. Your eyes have gone grey."

Kiernan grit his teeth as the man's words rattled around the inside of his skull. He kept his stare on Decius, though, even as the man to Kiernan's right set the edge of his wingblade on Kiernan's throat.

"The Hawkeye is gone, Preem," Primarch Treybon confirmed, unimpressed.

::"Who did you give it to, Kiernan?":: Decius asked, this time with all the force of a gale. ::"Who have you named your Counselheir?"::

"No one, yet," Kiernan managed, hoping to everything holy that his voice didn't waver. "I mean to name him after the Graduation tournament. You will know soon enough."

"We will know now, Ser," Treybon insisted and Kiernan swallowed hard against the press of the blade. "Or choose one ourselves."

"Not if he's given away the hawkeye," Decius said, sucking air through his teeth with the thought. It was the only tell the man had, and only when he was rethinking a plan. Brilliant as he was, it didn't happen often.

Gods above, Kiernan swore, feeling the pressure of Decius' bardic gift ebbing with his sudden unease. If he had his hawkeye with him, Kiernan's men would have just cut it off and named their own Seventh. But since he didn't they were at a loss.

As silence hung heavy in the courtyard, Kiernan took his chance. Closing his eyes, he reached to feel who of his nearby soldiers could possibly come to his aid. When nothing came back, not even a guard on the eastern side of the Palace compound, Kiernan realized just how thorough his men had been in clearing the path for their betrayal.

"What now?" Treybon asked.

Still holding Decius' stare, Kiernan tried to ignore the blood he could feel seeping down his neck. What they would do seemed entirely up to him.

At least, it did until Kiernan's attention was drawn by a flutter of movement just over the man's right shoulder. Decius didn't have a chance to move before the man behind him had stolen his second wingblade. A heartbeat later, Kiernan's sharp intake of breath was the only sound in the courtyard as Decius collapsed. As blood poured out of the man's throat, the figure taking his place was the one man in the world he would never have expected to see coming to his rescue: Fifth Counsel Lord Roder.

As Treybon drew back in surprise, Kiernan felt the weight of Decius' gift disappear. Gathering himself in the moment, Kiernan turned the full force of his own Gift on the men that remained, sending a silent, penetrating call into the minds of his remaining Primarchs. Fear, it seemed, could overcome any amount of terra without Decius demanding his attention.

::Stand! Down!::

Now it was Roder's turn to blink in surprise, as the men who had been moments away from ending Kiernan's life dropped their weapons in unison. As Kiernan leaned into the message, flaring his wings to shove the men away, he felt the sharp, exquisite agony of their deaths surging back along his Gift. For the first and only time in his life, he also reveled in the relief of knowing that nine dead Kosarans meant one more chance at freedom for him.

"You alive, Hest'lre?" Roder called, unfazed by the carnage. As the Fifth Counsel Lord, Kiernan's Gift couldn't touch him for all his own Seat Founder protected him. Hest'lre, however...

"Barely," Hest'lre said, dazed as he took the help of one of Roder's men to get back to his feet. "Blood and ice, Kiernan."

"Get inside, both of you," Roder said, dropping Decius' wing blade beside the dead man. When he was done, he raised a hand in the air, circling it overhead twice before turning for the door. "Now."

Kiernan didn't argue, though he did have to steel himself as he heard the wings of at least five men backwinging behind them. They were obviously Roder's, especially if Kiernan hadn't been able to feel them with his search. Then again, the men wouldn't have wanted to give his position away as he came in to help. Roder might be pushing six decades, but he had no qualms about putting down men who needed it.

Kiernan pounded on the door to Aaron's suite a few times until they could hear someone shouting for patience, and then the door opened to let light stream into the dark.

"I thought I heard something," Aaron said, indifferent until he realized the massacre outside his door. "Gods, what happened out there?"

"I told my cadre I'm going on Envoy," Kiernan muttered, stepping past Aaron as the other men stepped around the circle of bodies.

Behind him, Kiernan heard Roder telling his men to clear the area and then set up a guard. That much Kiernan had expected, especially since Roder had been setting Blackwings to stalk him for the past fortnight. Annoyed as he had wanted to be about the guard, he couldn't deny that Roder had just saved his life.

As his eyes adjusted to the dim, Kiernan was surprised to see Fourth Counsel Lord Blake sitting at Aaron's dicing table wearing his elaborate rank-pauldron and Eighth Counsel Lord Lucien in his law-speaker's half cloak and cords. At this rate, the only three missing were First Counsel Lord Terrance who oversaw the House of Lords, Second Counsel Lord and Chiurgeon Headmaster Gallen, and Ninth Counsel Lord Shayan, a man at least thirty winters their senior who had once been Eirik's Sixth.

All three would have reacted badly to his missing hawkeye.

"Help yourself," Lord Fourth greeted, gesturing to the cask that was just off to their left. As stout as the man was strong, Blake wore the expertly hammered metal rank-pauldron like it weighed no more than Kiernan's own. Like as not he didn't notice, since the man was a metallurgist and had worn the weight of the piece longer than Kiernan had been alive.

With that age also came Blake's tendency to forget that Kiernan had a limited pallet for alcohol. Lord Fourth would drink anything and everything, all with the aim to improve his own brews. Research and development of any kind, military or otherwise, just ran in the man's blood.

"I'm good," Kiernan said, declining with a wave of his own bottle.

"That your ice wine?" Blake guessed. "What's the occasion?"

"I didn't want to take it with me when I leave," Kiernan shrugged. As he moved to set the wine on the table so he could take off his cloak, he realized Roder was eyeing him a little too closely.

"So that's why your men hadn't killed you when I showed up," he said, finally looking Kiernan in the eye. "You're not wearing your hawkeye so they couldn't take it from you. Was that intentional?"

Kiernan ignored him and the jab for information. He and Roder had never gotten along, if only because Roder had taken it as a personal insult that someone as young and inexperienced as Kiernan had been given the Seventh's Seat after the Fall of Kirath. The only reason Roder had accepted him at all was the fact that Kiernan had been a pivotal part in driving off the Lan'lieanan women from Kirath. Kiernan had been one of the few of Hewn's men with the strength of will to rally the scattered forces to the city's defense as Roder's Blackwings went to defend the Fifth Seat-Founder's temple.

Seeing him now set Kiernan on edge, especially with how rarely Roder deigned to actually wear his rank-pauldron. It was worse to wear under cloaks than Hest'lre's, given how the shoulder cap flared with three individually sculpted feather splays, one enameled in each color of the fumentari under his control in the Vanguard. Like as not, Roder could probably impale someone with it if he wanted.

Roder was on a warpath when he wore the thing to Counsel meetings. The man absolutely loathed being in the high mountains any longer than he had to. His fight was on the Plains and his Citadel in the foothills of Kirath.

"I got your quorum," Hest'lre said. "Get on with it."

As Hest'lre took a seat on Roder's right, Roder gave Hest'lre the same, unimpressed stare he had first leveled at Kiernan.

Kiernan stepped away to toss his cloak on a lounge to give himself something to do while he ignored their stares. When he came back for his wine, he was glad he had thought to grab a new bottle for as long as this was going to take.

"Sit down, Hawkeye," Roder said, calling him back to the table.

"Am I being fêted?" Kiernan asked, refusing to sit, even if it was petty. The attempt on his life had cleared his mind for a while, but he was still too high to care. "Or do you save me just for the pleasure of being able to kill me yourself?"

"That's up to you, Hawkeye," Roder said, which Kiernan again ignored in favor of reopening his wine. "Are you going to tell us the name of your Counselheir?"

Kiernan rolled his eyes as he took his seat, landing on Hest'lre with anger. "Is this the only reason you dragged me down here?"

"One of them," Lucien said, speaking as Hest'lre scowled. "I got a note last night that Tyro Rylan was in the High Cells," he said, unimpressed. "Did you set that up just so you could speak with Roder's loralae?"

"His loralae?" Kiernan balked. "I brought her here."

"After refusing to hand her over to my Vanguard," Roder reminded. Was he never going to let that go? "How you ever survived her, I have no idea. That woman could kill with a look if she truly wanted."

"She certainly tries every time I go down there," Kiernan said, starting after his icewine again. "Not that I have in cycles. The only reason I went down last night was to see Tyro Rylan."

"Why?" Lucien demanded. "All it did was confirm that the boy was brought into the Cells when I would have preferred to release him without your meddling. Or his," he added, with a sharp look to Hest'lre.

"I wasn't about to go down until that woman of yours came after me for how the Guard treated him during the transfer," Hest'lre defended. "You'd think Rylan was a chick out of her own body for how furious she was. The idiot brought that on himself and I am not about to stop my men from taking their pound of flesh after two cycles of Aaron's woman being unable to control him."

"What do you mean woman?" Kiernan repeated, ignoring Hest'lre's jab in favor of Aaron's information. "What woman?"

"The Barracks Mother," Hest'lre answered when Aaron would only glare. "Did you know we had a Barracks Mother? I didn't until last night."

"You have thirty Primarchs and I can't have one person to help with my tyros?" Aaron spat.

"You have the entire Cantullus Corps, Aaron," he shot back. "They handle discipline in the barracks."

"They work for you, Kiernan," Aaron said. "And your leaving on Envoy takes priority for them over my graduation tournament, you know that. This woman is one blicing secretary."

"Whoever she is, she is better informed than all three of you," Lucien interrupted as Blake refused to be pulled into the argument. "She is the alleged mastermind behind this petition I have to stay the sale of the House Northern Estate on behalf of your Tyro Rylan. It has brought my entire civil court to a halt since the patent of nobility for House Kirath requires an Estate to house them. Do you know how ridiculous it is to have to bend to the will of a woman that isn't part of Lenae's Court? They, at least, are known for interfering on her behalf, but I've never even heard of a Barracks Mother? What even is she?"

"She's a pain in my ass," Hest'lre said, rolling his eyes. "And she knows Shayan, apparently. That's why she can quote from lawspeakers who died before you were ever born."

"Will you two be quiet!" Aaron bristled. " The Gods alone know what Eirik will do if he finds out you mentioned her in front of him," he said, meaning Kiernan.

Hest'lre just shrugged. "I'm not scared of a man who hasn't left his roost in cycles," he said, unimpressed. "Besides, as soon as Kiernan leaves the shelf, both Rylan and Eirik will answer to me."

"*She* won't," Aaron said, still irate. "And I will still be responsible for her meddling. The whole reason she was put in place was to give me more space to breathe, not less."

It took Kiernan actually slamming his hand on the table to get their attention. "What is going on?" He demanded. "Who are you talking about?"

After one last nasty look to Hest'lre, it was Aaron who answered. "She is a servant in the tyro barracks," he said, and Kiernan gave him an incredulous look as Aaron tried and failed to remain calm. Obviously if this woman could infuriate the Eighth Counsel Lord and get away with it, she was not 'some servant'. "She assists me with day-to-day personnel issues and reports on their progress for the four cycles they are here. She has written most of the reports you read for the graduating tyros—"

"That's your blicing job, Aaron," Kiernan balked. "You can't just delegate that review to some—some woman!"

Surprisingly it was Blake who came to her defense. "Oh, shut it, Kiernan," the elder weapons-master barked, as annoyed as if Kiernan had tried to fire the wrong end of a crossbow. "She did the same for Hewn before you and a better job besides."

With as much as they were suddenly telling him, Kiernan wasn't sure what to say. When he looked back to Lucien, the man seemed pleased at Aaron's discomfort. This woman must have made quite the disturbance to make revealing the secret of her position to Kiernan an equal play.

"Just what makes this woman think she has any right to speak to the Courts?" Kiernan asked. "Whose Daughter is she that she has been trained in the law?"

"She is not trained in the law," Aaron insisted, though from his tone, that might have been a technicality.

"Then who is she?" Kiernan said again. "Do you even know? How in the world do you trust this woman if you don't know her background?"

"Kiernan," Blake snapped, getting his attention off Aaron. "It was Eirik who put her in place. If you have a problem, take it up with him. She has kept to herself in the barracks for over ten cycles, so of course she has learned a thing or two. That's only to be expected."

"I don't care if Eirik is her blicing father," Kiernan said, starting to see red. "She stays away from my tyros. Especially Rylan."

"Damn it, Kiernan," Aaron swore, and then glared at Hest'lre. "This is why I have been trying to keep them at opposite ends of the Palace until he left. But, no. You had to bring her up."

Kiernan's grip on his icewine was so hard his knuckles had turned white. Was this why it had taken so much to get Rylan to hate him? Had he been working with an ally this entire time? If Rylan thought he could rely on anyone, if he thought he did not have to find the strength to overcome from within…

"Kiernan, I had no idea she even existed until last night," Hest'lre said, as if to placate him. "She wasn't part of the Barracks when we were tyros, but she is now and she has forced all of our hands. All but Lucien's, and that is only because of his position as Eighth."

"It is not," Lucien insisted. "I have absolutely no reason to hear an argument of the law from a woman I didn't know existed until this morning. What she is attempting to do is beyond ridiculous, which I suppose makes sense as it was your idea," Lucien said, turning his anger on Kiernan. "You blicing Illiandrians allowing women to hold title in trust. Do you realize how complicated that is? How much of an insult it is to have to delay auctioning an Estate because of a woman? They will kill her to clear the title just as fast as they will kill you for being Hewn's heir and seeking to stop them."

"Stop them from what?" Kiernan demanded, suddenly cursing himself for not reading Rylan's letters with the attention they deserved. Kreychi had seen something in them, even if all he had seen was nonsense. "What are you talking about?"

"From taking ownership of the Estate," Lucien said, though the words were hard. "The unlanded nobility of Kirath that were displaced during the Fall of the Citadel are requesting a patent of nobility from King Braeden. Hewn evacuated every noble house from the city when the Lan'lieanans attacked, but you are the one who has occupied what is left of their Houses with the Warhost for a decade. If you refuse to make them whole again by returning their lands, what recourse do they have but to seek a new patent through the Courts?"

"But I never made them leave!" Kiernan scoffed. He had gone through this fight with Lucien since the Fall for all the man was Kirathy born, not that the man's position had ever wavered. "All I told them was that we needed to make certain it was safe for them to return, and we did. As Seventh I pushed the front back a thousand leagues, but still they're furious with me. It has been their choice to remain scattered throughout the range, not my insistence. The only reason they blame me is because I am Hewn's Counselheir and their city fell when Hewn was on the Seat and you know that."

But Lucien didn't care. He never did, so Kiernan wasn't sure why he cared as well. Why he cared at all for anyone in the Kingdom, if the people he had helped the most now loved him the least.

Surprisingly, it was Roder who spoke into the heady silence. "He's not wrong, Lucien," the man said, eyes narrowed. "You know I want the Houses restored for all they served the Warhost before, but it is Yellowings running my Citadel right now. I have better things for them to do than serve meals and issue gear."

Lucien just rolled his eyes, though when his look landed on Hest'lre, Kiernan held his breath. For as angry as his friend had been over the past few dawnings, would he stand up to Lucien for once?

"You know I don't have the manpower from the shelves to have people living in the Legion fortresses all cycle," he said, matter of fact. "Every Legatus I have throughout the range wants the Kirathy nobility to return, but they refuse. Landed or not, they have no wish to leave their new homes."

"What they want," Blake added, his voice dangerously soft in the moment. "Is a seat of power inside Delton. They blame Kiernan for every hangnail at this point, but they do it only because you are willing to hand them what they want. You are becoming their pawn, Lucien, and if you refuse to see that, you are either complicit or a blicing fool."

Lucien's eyes were full of fury, though as he looked around the circular table, it was clear how the other Counsel Lords saw the matter. Warlords that they all were, when Lucien looked to Aaron for support, the man just dropped his eyes.

"The point remains," Lucien said into their silence. "Whoever this Barracks Mother is, if she actually shows her face for the hearing about the patent, they will kill her in the halls. Warn her if you wish, but she is marked just as much as this one is," he said, focusing on Kiernan once again.

"Blood and ice," Kiernan swore, feeling his patience snap. Was this really all they were going to argue about? None of it even mattered! He was leaving in three dawnings and once he was gone, this Barracks Mother wouldn't matter at all. "Stay the proceeding, Lucien," he went on, matching the man's stare. "Stay all of it until Graduation is done. That's an Order."

"An Order?" Lucien scoffed. "You're as good as dead if you step outside this room and anyone from Kirath can line up a shot on you."

"Is that a threat?" Kiernan repeated, eyes hard as he braced his hands on the table. Lucien's entire family was from Kirath, or had been before the fall. He hadn't lived on the shelf in decades, but that didn't mean his loyalties had shifted. If he wanted this House Kirath formed, for all he was a Counsel Lord, he would find a way.

"Would you like it to be?" Lucien asked, his laughter tinged with violence. "I outrank you. You idiot."

"Rylan is the last son of House Northern," Kiernan said, wings flaring in the tight space for all he could feel his Founder's focus burning in him with the words. "The House belongs to him."

"Rylan may be the last, but he is not the only one," Lucien countered, eyes narrowing with Kiernan's challenge. "And if you mean to allow him to stand in the way of my family returning to their rightful place, then they are right to want to see you dead. You and Hewn and Eirik, for all the fool still lives. You are the reason our Shelf burned and I mean to see that legacy ended. The title to that Estate is only the first step towards reparations for all you and the Sevenths before you have done. If you think that you can stand in my way then you have clearly lost your mind."

They were both on their feet now, staring across the table. None of the other Counsel Lord's moved. No one could. Without Shayan present, Lucien outranked them all.

"You can't kill everyone who disagrees with you, Hawkeye," Roder said, leaning back in his chair as he sighed. "It gives people ideas of what could be done to you, instead."

Kiernan clenched his teeth as the threat of violence burned through the room. Swallowing down his anger, Kiernan could see that the men watching him were not above killing him. Roder especially. The Gods knew other Counsel Lords had done it before.

What they didn't know was that Kiernan was prepared for this. From the ancestor Sevenths in the Library, he knew there was always a line the Seventh had to cross, some point of no return, even if he didn't know when or where it would happen. In his arrogance, Kiernan had just crossed it and there was no going back.

Reaching into his pocket for the note from Counsel Lord Eirik, Kiernan threw it like an ante in the center of the table. Hest'lre looked at him and then took up the note, reading the words before looking back at Kiernan in horror.

"Stay the proceeding, Lucien," he warned.

Lucien grabbed the piece of paper from Hest'lre's hand, only to have his pallor turn to ash. One by one, the Counsel Lords passed the note and then looked to Kiernan as if he had grown a third wing before their eyes.

But Counsel Lord Eirik agreed with him. The Ancestor Sevenths supported him. Upon his completion of the graduation tournament, Tyro Rylan would be named the Seventh Counsel Lord and Kiernan would leave on Envoy.

He was so certain of his choice that Rylan's wings might begin the show the seven dark wing-bars that would proclaim him once Kiernan was truly gone from the shelf. Even without the hawkeye to hand over, if Noventrio wanted Rylan as a Seventh, there was nothing that could prevent Rylan from taking up the Seat.

"I thought you were untested when they raised you, but this is madness," Roder said, his voice a dark hollow of rage. "Stark, raving madness."

"But if Kiernan returns from Envoy alive," Hest'lre said, covering his eyes with a hand. "The boy will be perfect."

Rylan, who hated Kiernan more than words could describe, would take up the mantle of Seventh and refuse to do anything at all. Not because he hated Kiernan, but because he hated the war and everything it had ever done to him at home. He would refuse to lead them, refuse to order anyone to their deaths, and Kiernan would have the chaos of his appointment to negotiate a cease fire. An armistice. A parlay, however tenuous, that lasted long enough for him to make peace with the women of Lan'lieana.

More importantly, once Rylan was the Seventh, he would be allowed to request title to any Estate on the Delton shelf, especially one that had belonged to his own family. It would be the first command out of his lips, the first vindication after a lifetime of wrongs, and he would have to accept being Counsel Lord in order to do it.

"There is always a method to madness," Kiernan said, coming to his feet no matter how lightheaded he was from the wine and adrenaline.

His secret finally out, Kiernan left the table and started back for the door when his hand went to his neck, only to feel the dried blood he had forgotten in the moment. The other Counsel Lords began to move as well. As they were gathering their things, Kiernan was trying to figure out how he was going to get back to the safety of his suite. Not only was it too dangerous for him to fly in his drunken state, but for as much power as he had taken in to defend himself against his Primarchs, his vision was starting to cloud over again.

Swearing at himself, Kiernan moved his flight cloak and sat heavily on the lounge near the door they had entered from. Head in his hands, he tried to stop himself from shaking. As the other Counsel Lords left out the front of the suite, he had never felt so alone in his life. Even as they railed against Kiernan's ability to cause a disaster and walk away unscathed, Kiernan envied their ability to remain and build a life. To fight for something other than survival. All that was left for him was the relief of having survived yet another dawning and the terror of knowing he had to do it all over again tomorrow. For the first time in his life, the hope of going home with Lenae beside him was not enough, not when he had destroyed every other part of himself in the process.

Listening to the noise of the Counsel Lords abandoning him, Kiernan wanted to weep for the man he had become and for the lives he had destroyed to get this far.

Rylan, I am so sorry, Kiernan thought, his eyes burning as he felt his soon-to-be Counselheir's thoughts swelling back into his mind. *But I am going to end this and the peace you must want is at home. That is the War you have lived through and you hate it as much as the rest of us hate the Plains. When I rip our Kingdom apart, you at least will want to rebuild.*

A long time passed before Kiernan heard Hest'lre's heavy footfalls nearing him. Kiernan winced as he slowed to a stop and the uneasiness in his friend's voice made him sick with grief all over again.

"I'm heading back up," Hest'lre said quietly. "Aaron doesn't mind if you stay the night to dry out. Roder is taking over your guard. I will have Henrick and Lyonel on your suite, but I cannot do more than that."

"I understand," he managed, even if he couldn't bear to look up. "Hest'lre, I'm sorry. For all of this."

"So am I," Hest'lre said and the resignation in his friend's voice broke him all over again. "All I have ever wanted to do was help you, brother, but I can't save you from yourself."

When Kiernan woke next, it was to the taste of rancid fermentation and a lifetime of terrible decisions. Determined to go back to sleep, Kiernan tensed to shift his wing to a more comfortable position, but even that small movement sent his stomach rioting.

Putting a hand out to steady himself, Kiernan meant to shift just a touch, but he grabbed at naught but air and slid to the stone floor unsupported. Tears sprang to his eyes as his left wing caught on the lounge and the strain wrenched more than a few muscles in his back. Flailing, Kiernan twisted to press his head to the stone floor as the world collapsed on top of him. Again. But just as he forced himself to his feet, he opened his eyes to realize that he was completely blind.

Kiernan's heart started thundering in his chest as he reached out with his hands and wings, orienting himself back towards the doorway. There was only one way to find out if the darkness was in his mind or just the pitch of this room and given the bile waiting to rise with the sway of his step, he didn't have long.

Aaron would never forgive me, Kiernan thought in a panic.

As his stomach roiled in protest, Kiernan grabbed up his cloak and made it back to the salle door with singular determination. Somehow he managed the lock, found the side of the building, and lost the contents of his stomach in the icy morning air.

When his nausea had passed, he backed away from the wall and the mess, spitting to clear his mouth as best he could. Already mortified, he used his wings for shelter as he pulled on the cloak and promised himself he would never drink again. Death couldn't hurt more than this tyro's stunt.

"Good dawning, Lord Seventh."

Kiernan grimaced as he remembered that Roder had left a guard of Blackwings at Aaron's suite for him. If he was going to walk around the Palace as a Seventh on Envoy, then he would take the guard he deserved. It was the last thing Roder had said to him. Deserved, because the Lord Fifth's true duty with respect to a Seventh Counsel Lord on Envoy was to make certain that the man left the city before he could kill every living soul inside.

For a hundred generations, the Fifth's Seat Founder, Great Matron Idalia, had granted a special protection to the men of the Blackwing Fumentari, keeping them safe from the bardic gift of the Seventh Counsel Lord. As a result, they were the only men who could ignore a Seventh's commands and, in effect, the only ones who could put him out of his misery if he had truly lost himself to the minds of the Warhost.

Hearing him now, especially with the fog of his godseyes clouding his sight, made Kiernan's skin crawl.

"Ser, are you all right?" The man said as Kiernan covered his eyes with a hand as he held his aching head.

What a loaded question...

"My head is still inside a bottle, I fear," Kiernan said, waving off the man's concern.

"We are to escort you back to your suite, Ser," the man went on, keeping his distance. "Do you think you can manage?"

"Honestly, no," Kiernan said, coming unsteadily to his feet with the assistance of the Soldier Tyros' Wing. "But I can make it to Lord Fourth's Armory, ah...?" He said, only to realize he hadn't gotten the man's name. From what he could see through the fog, he was at least a praetor.

"Praetor Iven, Lord Seventh," the man supplied, saluting.

"Praetor, I mean to speak with Lord Fourth this dawning," Kiernan said, standing a little taller. "If you and your boys want to see me to the Armory, fine, but feel free to shift out of this cold and take a meal."

"With the tyros, My Lord Seventh?" Iven said, almost amused. "I think we can manage our own way if it comes to that. We'll stay posted on the lower doors and the armory roof until you're ready to return to your suite. Lord Fifth has another couple of squads on rotation around the Palace in case you find an alternate exit."

"Of course he does," Kiernan said, trying not to sigh. It wasn't a half-bad idea after last night when he had killed his Cadre Primarchs. Kiernan had no idea at all why Roder had let him live past that point, though he suspected because he hadn't named his Counselheir.

As Kiernan sighed and pulled himself together, Praetor Iven raised a hand to rally his men. Kiernan gave them the moment to organize and then started for the end of the Soldier Tyros' Wing, one hand covering his eyes while he kept his wing brushing along the building to orient himself. After a few hundred spans, Kiernan steeled himself as he lost the wall, glad for the change in color to the dirt and stone at his feet that let him find the walkway to the armory proper. How he was going to get out of this place, he had no idea. Counsel Lord Eirik was just as blind and he hadn't seen the man since he had moved into the suite on the roof of the Armory seven cycles ago.

"This is far enough, Praetor," Kiernan said, waving off the man's attempt to get the door for him into the Armory. "I'll be in with Lord Fourth for the foreseeable future."

Once inside he had three options, Fourth Counsel Lord Blake's suite to his left, the Armory proper through the forward doors, and the latrine on his right that reeked of sweat and exhausted tyros. Choosing the latrine, Kiernan used his hands to find the doorway and managed to get to the slow flow of water at the sinks. After drowning himself in the icy water, Kiernan still felt drunk, but he didn't have to taste it anymore.

Once his face was washed and he had water in his stomach, he gave up the latrine and went back into the main foyer, only to stop in the center of the room and close his eyes.

The only difference the gesture made was to dim the light in his mind. Everything else was just a grey haze as the chaos of the Warhost began to swell into his consciousness. Swearing at himself, Kiernan dug into the pocket of his uniform beneath the layers of the indigo kama. He still had a bit of the terra Kreychi had said to keep for emergencies. It was something chiurgeons apparently used for healing on the Plains.

Finding it, Kiernan shoved the piece of sugar and herb into his mouth, letting it dissolve under his tongue as he threw himself towards the door that would take him deeper into the armory. Finding it with his hands, Kiernan pulled open the heavy door and moved himself into the vaulted space as his mind lurched halfway across the known world to the heart of the Plains.

"It's coming again, Ser!"

"I see it, Prefect," Kiernan called back, hands gripping around the heavy dragon pole. At three paces long, the ironwood staff was as wide as his wingspan and he needed every bit of it to keep the mad woman outside of the one hard-walled building of the small Ehkeski village. It was the community center for the wingless men and women who served the nearby Legion operations, helping them transport goods to a fortress near the front. Now, this squat adobe building was the only thing that stood between them and the Lan'lieanan monster searching for her next kill.

They had all thought the woman had died when Kiernan put an arrow in her chest not a candlemark ago. Their last arrow. Now, seeing the fire-haired woman ready to run on their position, wings dropped low for all the gore that coated them, all they could do was pray. All Kiernan could do was regrip the long pole, hoping he wouldn't fall like so many of their brothers before him.

Kiernan set himself as the woman started her sprint, arms trailing behind her as the magic she wielded crackled in her hands. It was almost like white lightning, skittering along her skin as she reached the end of his dragon pole. As she grabbed hold of it, incredibly fast and impossibly strong, Kiernan closed his eyes. In a heartbeat, that lighting would be up the pole, shattering his grip and his sanity as it had the rest of his men.

How did you fight a monster like this?

How could you do anything other than flee?

Kiernan gasped as he came back to himself, hands on his head as lightning seared along his veins. He was feeling the man's soul being ripped from his body, torn free by a power not of their Gods but one rooted in the blood magic all loralae wielded. Be it earth, wood, water, metal, or stone, they commanded elemental magic for their slaughter. As they sought out and killed every living creature in their path, they bent the natural world to their will and Kiernan, attached to every officer in his Legions by his Seventh Counsel Lord's gift, could only scream as he felt the man's soul get ripped from the mountains. Heart thundering in his chest, it was all he could do to try and open his eyes, to try and find the true world before he was sucked back into that mire and chaos.

He wasn't fast enough.

As screams echoed behind him, Kiernan watched in horror as his Prefect was dragged from the safety of the community center and out into the dawning light. Dead before he hit the ground, the Loralae used her nails like claws to rip into his skin. Blood gushed from gaping wounds as she covered her hands with it, a crazed light in her eye. Worse than that, he could see the runes along the woman's skin glowing bright despite the filth that covered her. Her short hair was matted with it, what chest armor and rough pants she had close to shredded, but her skin was on fire with bright, red light.

Kiernan turned to look at the mass of terrified Ehkeski behind him, knowing what he had to do. "When I go out there, close the door," he said, knowing they could understand him. "Hoi?"

The boy immediately behind him nodded, gripping at his young sister to keep her back. There were so many people in here, all of them trapped.

"For Honor and Glory," Kiernan prayed, pulling his wings in tight as he moved to take the place where his Prefect had been. Everyone else was dead. It was up to him.

Knowing the loralae was distracted for the moment, Kiernan picked up the staff in his hands. All he had to do was pull her attention and the rest of them could live. They could, he kept telling himself, even if it was a lie. If he couldn't kill this thing, she would break down that door and kill everyone inside.

As unobtrusively as he could, Kiernan managed the three paces it took to pick up the staff where it had fallen and then launched himself at the loralae.

VOLUME 2: THE WOMEN OF KOSAR

A man with a dream needs a woman with a vision.

Chapter 13: Soldier Tyro Barracks Mother

Vinicia keh'Tresha du'Kirath

Friday, 05:00

Vinicia cursed the day she ever let Lord Fourth talk her into wearing a piece of Lan'lieanan armor to use while sparring with her family. Sure it had helped him understand how the wrapped leather worked and what weakness it had, but now?

Vinicia panicked at the sight of a Kosaran man dressed in the most formal kama she had ever seen launching himself from the Armory door. Swearing, she clawed her way back into the heights, tucking in among the blackness of the crossbeams in the dim room as the man took a defensive position between herself and her uncle. She hadn't meant to land the blow to Shayan's head, but he had been just as startled as her to realize someone was coming into the Armory. When she hadn't been able to pull her swing in time, he had taken the full force of it, collapsing nearly on the spot. She had been down beside him immediately, trying to see if he needed healing only to be run off by this man who probably thought she had been trying to kill the Ninth Counsel Lord.

"Who sent you?" The man demanded in Lan'lieanan, coming into the soft light at the center of the Armory. As the man flared his wings, meaning to defend her uncle's lifeless body, her jaw fell open. It was the Seventh Counsel Lord.

"Ser, this isn't what you think," she insisted.

"I said who sent you!" Kiernan demanded, threatening her with his staff even if it barely reached the beam she was standing on. Dragon poles were only so long. "Fight me, loralae, and let this be ended!"

"Loralae?" Vinicia repeated, confused. She was a kindred dryad, not an Ehkeski river demon.

"That's what you are, isn't it?" Kiernan said, shoving the end of the dragon pole at her feet. "Sorceress! Mad woman! You may have killed all of my brothers, but you will not kill the Ehkeski I am sworn to protect. This ends now, hear me? Come out of the sky at once!"

Vinicia had no idea what to say to him. He probably didn't even know what he was saying.

"If I come down, will you let me surrender?" she asked, raising her hands for peace.

"Surrender? After you murdered my brothers?" Kiernan spat, jabbing at her shin once again. "Never!"

"I thought the Seventh Counsel Lord was on a mission for peace," Vinicia scoffed. "Not mindless slaughter."

Kiernan froze with the words, eyes closing as his whole body seemed to twitch. A heartbeat later, the dragon pole dropped from his hands and Kiernan collapsed forward onto his knees, hands going to his head.

"No, not again," he pleaded, panting like he was flying a gale. "Gods, not again."

Vinicia's eyes went wide as she recognized the panic. She had seen it in Counsel Lord Hewn after the Fall of Kirath when he had realized what had happened to his men. Hewn hadn't even been close to going on Envoy and the strain on his spirit to feel so many people die at once had broken him.

Vinicia dropped from the safety of her beam, approaching him with her hands raised for peace. This close, she could tell that the man's hair wasn't the dirty blond she had always seen before, but a bright, silver-white of a Seventh on Envoy.

He had taken off his hawkeye, then, but why was he still in the city? Why was he so close to so many men of the Host when it was clearly driving him mad?

Kiernan's scream of rage had Vinicia backwinging away, taking a knee next to her uncle, who was still on his wings.

"I said get away from him!" Kiernan swore, eyes focused on her now, even if they were clouded over with white. In losing one sense, it seemed he was grasping out with all the others. Daughter of a Seventh that she was, he could feel her and her uncle's presence before him.

"Kiernan, you are not yourself," Vinicia pleaded, flinging out a hand to call the dragon pole away from him. He flung his hand out as well, catching it with more strength of will than Vinicia realized another sorcerer could have, and the sight of it left her gaping. The Sevenths weren't sorcerers. Her father, sure, but not Kiernan!

And yet he is as strong as I am right now, Vinicia swore, reaching a hand behind her to where her uncle's dragon pole had been cast aside.

Just as she got the staff in her hands, Kiernan rushed her. Meaning to take out his feet, she swung the pole deep and low, but Kiernan leapt into the air to avoid the strike. As she brought herself out of the crouch, her staff followed him up in an arc and caught him square in the back before he could get to height.

Kiernan cried out in surprise but managed to maintain his climb, only to realize she had launched as well and was gaining fast. When he stalled three stories up, she overtook him and sent his staff plummeting with two calculated strikes.

As Kiernan scrambled to retrieve the staff, she landed and twisted to follow him. When Kiernan set himself to face her, she was swearing at him.

"Blood and ice, Kiernan," - he leapt as she swung at his ankles, then crouched as she swung over him - "Will you just," - she doubled back too fast for him to react and he lost control from one hand - "Focus," - she feinted to swing and Kiernan saw it too late, instead throwing himself onto the butt of her staff - "For one blicing moment!"

Kiernan backed away, gasping for air, and as he fought to parry, she gave chase. He paused when he saw an opening to attack and then she dropped out of his vision. When he realized she was on her knees, it was too late.

Kiernan screamed as her staff powered through his legs with one violent sweep. As pain ripped through his right knee, the sound of bone breaking seemed to tear a hole through the madness that had overwhelmed his mind. As he collapsed, his staff skittering off to the side, he brought his hands up to cover his face.

"Mercy!" He cried. "Sweet gods, mercy!"

Vinicia clenched her hands around her staff, stopping herself. There were tears streaming down his face as she loomed over him, but she could tell that the terror was more pure, more focused on this place rather than the violent panic he had been in before. He was back with them, back from wherever his Seventh Counsellor's Gift had taken him on the Plains, and Vinicia threw her staff aside as she shook with the adrenaline of the moment.

It is Hewn all over again, she thought, terrified. Hewn had spent two cycles struggling to regain control of the Warhost after the Fall of Kirath, losing himself to fits like this more often than not. Now Kiernan was riding that edge and she had almost killed him. She had stopped herself, but she could have killed him.

"No, no, no," she swore, dropping to her knees beside Kiernan. Her hands were shaking as she stared at the dark pool of blood on the man's silken kama. "Gods, no. I didn't mean to hurt you. I just—I had to stop you. You weren't yourself..."

"Vinicia, he will be all right," said a voice from behind her. Her uncle Shayan as he set a hand on her wing. "It's just his leg. You healed your Tyro Rylan from worse than this last night, did you not?"

"Barely," she said, her voice a whisper in the silence of the Armory. "Uncle, I was too exhausted to heal him completely. I lied to Westly, telling him to leave the bruising. I just... I didn't have the strength. I knew I could mend the rest, but that last bit. It takes finesse and I am so blicing tired."

"Dig deep, girl," he said, confident despite her fears. "Blake warned me he is being followed by Blackwings now. If you mean for this one to live, he needs your help."

Vinicia nodded, steadying herself in the moment. If they saw him like this—if they asked why she had defended herself—either she would die for assaulting a Seventh or he would for losing himself to his Gift. That was what the Blackwings did in the mountains. It was why Lord Fifth was here at all. Lord Fifth's men had put Hewn down when he had lost himself to the Warhost in the Sires' Wing just after Court had let out.

"Vinicia?" her uncle prompted, stepping so that she could see him.

Vinicia's head snapped up, mind frozen with panic.

"Be quick," he said. "Take off your hawkeye if you need to."

"Hoi, Uncle," she said, turning her mind towards the wounded Seventh.

Terrified by her lack of options, Vinicia touched the armored leather vest she had worn for their practice. Hidden beneath was the one token she had from her dryad mother, a blue-black pendant that was the same type of hawkeye stone her father had worn, if from a source beyond the Counsel Lord's Library. It was a rare thing that she took it off, since it hid both the bright red-gold of her hair and green of her eyes, but if Kiernan was truly injured...

After a moment prying the metal king chain from where it had become swaddled by her hair, she set the stone a pace away from her. She imagined that freeing herself from the stone was like the relief a court daughter must feel unlacing a bodice, strange as that seemed. Instead of being able to relax, though, all of her senses came more alive. Sounds once muffled by the Armory walls chittered on the edge of her perception and smells of the morning meal swept in with the draft from outside. Even if most of her soldier tyros had left, she still had eighty preparing to graduate, her chirugeon tyros, and the law-speaker tyros specializing in military law over the winter break. Once they were gone, the Mess would be turned over in full to serve the Lord Seventh's men who would occupy not only the Sires' Wing but the barracks as well.

Shifting into her secondsight, Vinicia swore as Kiernan lit up in her mind's eye like the daystar on Summer Solstice. If Counsel Lord Hewn had been a spark, Kiernan was an inferno. With the taste of spiced honey catching in the back of her throat, she had to close her eyes to focus through the intensity of it. She had never met anyone in her life who radiated such pure, raw power.

As tempting as it was to drown herself in it, she knew her ability to manipulate that power was tied closely to her emotional state. The more love she felt for a person, maternal or otherwise, the more powerful her workings could be.

The reality of her sorcery was that the same was true of hate or fear. So while her talents were a blessing for her rough-and-tumble tyros, she knew full dryads could devour the souls of creatures who trespassed into their groves. Standing before Kiernan, unguarded and unshielded, she could feel why. As much as she had feared coming into contact with the man after Hewn's death, that only heightened the draw to the power that existed at his core.

Vinicia exhaled roughly and rubbed her hands together, igniting the latent energy between them. As she took a knee beside him, she was relieved to find he had passed out from his pain, which meant that this working would go a lot faster. Fighting a mind that didn't want to be healed was much more difficult than healing a mind that couldn't comprehend what was happening.

When she was settled, Vinicia reached out to touch her hands to Kiernan's skin, only to realize that his energy was sparking off her own. As her mouth fell open in shock, she saw their energy raging in opposition, sending heat and light into true manifestation around her.

How does he even know who I am? she gaped. *He shouldn't know of me at all, especially not while unconscious.*

With her eyes burning under the strain, she gave up the mental shields she had thought to keep and let herself be caught up in him completely.

As she did, she felt her ancestral guardian blossoming in her thoughts, unbidden and unkind. This was not the first time the spirit had come calling when Vinicia had attempted to heal a badly injured windwalker and Vinicia doubted it would be of any help this time, given who it was.

::Why risk yourself and your power on a fool?::

::Because he is my father's Counselheir,:: Vinicia answered weakly.

::He is not worthy of the title,:: the ancestor objected, full of the hate it had for the man. ::He has tortured your fledglings, disgraced your father, and has shown your uncle nothing but disrespect. If his mind is gone, there is no sense in healing him.::

::He isn't gone, he just needs to leave on his Envoy,:: she said, knowing and hating that it was true. ::After all I could not do for Hewn, I will help Kiernan now. I will not be the reason the Blackwings take another Seventh's life.::

::Heal him then,:: the ancestor said with disgust. ::If that is your choice.::

As the ancestor's mental touch vanished, Vinicia set to her task. With a roll of her right wrist, she gestured to the barracks and the energy snapped to attention like so many tyros. It might not be much with only eighty young men in residence, but it had worked for Rylan the night before. As she pulled, though, she was surprised to feel the latent energy of the Seventh Counsel Lord's Library stirring as well. Heart racing with hope, she realized that with Kiernan so thoroughly on this side of the veil, the power she needed to heal him might come from the tree itself.

If Kiernan was tied to it, wasn't it also tied to him?

Vinicia rolled her wrist again, not about to question the feeling any further. Once she had the energy gathered towards the crown of Kiernan's head. She flexed her right hand flat to steady it and, with her left held softly over Kiernan's abdomen, started to draw power out of his core. As soon as their energy merged, she heard her uncle swearing for her to hurry and opened her eyes to see that there were crackling wisps of white power manifesting all around them like fireflies in the night. Wil-o-wisps were forming from the power now radiating off the two of them from her draw out of the Library.

Looking back to Kiernan, Vinicia's vision focused through the amber. With his energy looping from her left hand through her core and to her right, she could see the angry red streaks that were his wounds and found where she needed to act. Kiernan groaned as she fed the raw energy through him, allowing his body to take what it needed to heal itself. Unfortunately, her limited experience wielding so much power at once made her task that much harder. Just as she thought she was managing, the over-eager rush snagged and Kiernan screamed as his eyes snapped open.

"Gods be good," Vinicia swore, fighting to bring him under control. To help, she slid her right hand down over his eyes and the gesture seemed to give him peace. As Kiernan relaxed, so did she, and the energy between them flowed smoothly once again.

With her mind firmly inside the flow of Kiernan's power, she connected the pieces of him back together, reminding them what it was like to be whole. As energy poured into him, wrapping him in light, he groaned like a lover as his body burned away the excess. With her steady control, she managed to turn the dark red cloud of pain into the softened maple leaves in fall that, very much like their kin, eventually shriveled and dropped away.

With his knee healed and the high of power and purpose still driving her, Vinicia explored through the rest of him, seeking out and clearing the other ailments she knew she would find: the torment of stress, old sprains nagging with the weather, and all the things that would be deadly if they flared in the Eihwaz while he was on Envoy.

When at last Kiernan's body was a pure amber-gold, she allowed herself to breathe easy again. There was no fear in him now, no doubt or anxiety, and as her working ended, she realized that the stench of wine had left him and the pool of blood at his feet had vanished. Bones mended, wounds healed...

And chicks dig scars, she thought, finishing the tyro's rhyme.

Her work complete, Vinicia drew her right hand away from his forehead and her left away from his core. With some effort, she gave the youthful tyro-energy back into the barracks. Kiernan's own energy she held a moment longer, lost in the warmth of it as that lonely, starving part of her wept with relief. In one man, in one touch, she could feel the strength of her Tyro Legion once again. She could probably feel the entire Warhost in him if she tried, but for the moment, just being in his presence was enough.

Some day long ago, mother must have seen father this way, she thought. *Drawn to his spirit like a moth to a flame.*

In her own life, Seventh Counsel Lord Hewn had been this kind of flame to her, though for as many times as she had been around Hewn, his spirit had never sung in her like Kiernan's did now. No, Kiernan was a bonfire by comparison and as she soaked in the warmth and life he radiated, the world began to regain its luster. She could likely kneel here all day and never...

"I think that is enough, love."

Vinicia's eyes came open with a start as she felt her uncle's hand on her wing.

"Yes," Vinicia said, relinquishing the connection in an embarrassed rush. "Of course."

"I don't think I've ever seen you work with so much at once," Shayan said, though it was almost a question. She had told him of how badly Rylan had been beaten, but Rylan didn't have ten cycles of lingering injuries from war dragging at him in addition to wine, stress, and everything else.

"I don't think I have either," Vinicia said, flexing her hands as the energy pulsed under her skin. "Not since I... Well, not since Hewn," she admitted, forcing herself into the memory of grief if only to draw back from Kiernan's light.

"All the stories say that the more a kindred touches, the more they want to touch it. I never quite believed it until now."

"You do well to keep your talents hidden, I think," he said, and squeezed the crest of her wing with affection. "I would hate to lose you to the Green like your young friend when you enjoy your tyros so much."

"I don't think the chiurgeons would appreciate my talents any more than Westly's," she said with a weak laugh, sighing as she looked back to Kiernan. "I take it the Blackwings are gone?"

"No," her Uncle sighed. "But they know to stay outside. These wingbars are still good for something, thankfully. You will have to put on your coat before you leave, however," he added, looking to the Lan'lieanan armor she still wore.

"At least I'm not in a kurta," she said. "I don't care what Blake says, why a woman would ever wear a knee-length, open backed dress to fight in is beyond me. Give me a good set of Kosaran flying leathers any day."

Her uncle just sighed as he shook his head. They had been through this argument countless times before, and he agreed with her, at least on that point.

"Uncle, he is so strong in his Gift," she said, looking back down to Kiernan with a sigh. "Stronger than Hewn or even Weylan before him. He might even be stronger than Father if Noventrio has taught him how to work the Seventh's Gift."

"Given how he handled himself last night, he has more talent than even your father imagined," Shayan answered, and seemed about to say more when they both realized Kiernan was coming awake again.

::You are still a fool,:: her ancestor tsked. ::Healing your enemy.::

::He is not my enemy,:: Vinicia replied and then drew up her own mental shields to keep the meddling spirit away. ::He is just an asshole.::

Granted, Kiernan hadn't even been that when he had been a tyro, but as she had said to Rylan the night before, war changed men and usually for the worse. But as much as she disliked what he had become, he was still a Seventh and the Seventh was a peacemaker. Maybe if she had given him a piece of her mind long before this, he would not have been such a problem, but her father had been right.

For all Kiernan had been studying dryads to prepare for his Envoy, he might realize exactly who and what she was if he ever saw her. At this point, trying to pretend like she hadn't just healed him would raise more questions than it would answer.

"Do you think you can walk him back to his quarters?" Her uncle asked.

"Can't the Blackwings do that?" Vinicia objected, shifting back.

"I don't know any Blackwings who can woodwalk, love," Shayan laughed, shaking his head as he looked towards the door to the Armory.

"Oh, that kind of walk," Vinicia realized, setting her hands on her hips. "I know I can move you through the Palace because you aren't a sorcerer, but I could end up stepping out into the Halls of Justice with him for all I know. I have irritated Lord Eighth enough for a lifetime."

"Lucien will be fine," he said, dismissing her concern. "Eirik has said that your mother could walk with him through the Eihwaz, so I would think you could at least get him back to his suite."

"Mother could woodwalk with Father while in her grove, sure," Vinicia argued. "But all I have is deadwood and stone."

"Eirik has also said that you have made the shelf your grove," Shayan added more gently. "The people, if not the place itself."

Vinicia couldn't argue with that. Not really. From what she had learned of plant networks from Westly, she had made a grove of people, strange as that was. Being with her tyros, cultivating their minds, she might as well have been passing her energy through a hearth tree as her mother would.

"Besides, look at his warcrest," Shayan said, shaking his head. "Eirik was right. He has taken off his hawkeye."

"Do you think he gave it to his Counselheir?" Vinicia asked, frowning after her uncle.

"I don't think he's that much of an idiot," Shayan said, only to bite his tongue with the sharp look Vinicia was giving him. "If he did just take it off, then you know where it went."

"I knew where it went when Father took his off," she deflected, looking away.

"And you don't think it's in the same place?" he argued. "For exactly the same reason?" Seeing the wounded look on her face, though, Shayan set a hand on her wing. "Oh, love. Just... Just give Kiernan yours for now and get him back to his suite," he said gently. "If he hasn't handed it off to his Counselheir, then you know where it is and you are the only one who can retrieve it for him."

"Father said I wasn't to go inside the Library proper after Hewn passed," Vinicia said, accepting her heavy chain and hawkeye back from her uncle. "It was Kiernan's now."

"I also know how much you listen to your father," Shayan warned, even if it was gentle. "Think of this as a favor to me. I need him to name his Counselheir so that I can retire and Kiernan can't do that without the stone. So unless you want to give your stone up instead of going fully inside the Library..."

"You know I can't do that," Vinicia said, close to sulking.

"Go on, girl," Shayan said, knowing he was right. "I need to check in with Eirik. He's going to have felt your workings and he will want answers."

"So you're just going to leave me with Kiernan?" Vinicia scoffed. "You don't want to explain who I am when he wakes up, so he doesn't panic?"

"I think you can do that well enough," Shayan said. "You did fine with Hewn when you first met."

"I also hadn't just put him on his wings for attacking me," Vinicia balked, watching as he stepped back for space. "Do you really not care what Kiernan thinks of me, dressed like this?"

"You'll be fine," Shayan assured her, unfolding his wings.

"I cannot believe you, uncle," Vinicia muttered. "You really want to see what he can do to ruin my life in two dawnings?"

"No," he admitted. "But I would like to see what you can do to his."

"Some help you are," Vinicia swore, watching her uncle throw himself into the air of the Armory. Even at almost seventy cycles old, he could and did regularly put her on her wings.

Speaking of ancestors, Vinicia closed her eyes as she felt her own returning, a soft, confident murmur despite her racing thoughts. ::I told you that you should have let him die.::

::No,:: Vinicia said in return.

::Think of all the things you could have done with the time you are now about to waste with him,:: the voice went on, even as Vinicia looked back to Kiernan. ::You could have gone into the Lower City. Maybe done some shopping.::

::You know I would have just helped Aaron prepare for the tournament,:: Vinicia said, sighing.

Her Ancestor was unimpressed. ::With your brains, I would think you would want to do more than play at being a secretary,:: it insisted. ::You will never grow into your strength if all you do is clean up after men.::

::I have strength enough as it is,:: Vinicia said, turning her focus inwards so she could set her visual shielding without the hawkeye's help. They were still there, thankfully, but maintaining the constant change to her green eyes and otherwise red-gold hair took more effort than she realized. Once she was set, she squatted down by the Counsel Lord to set the kingchain over his head. ::Though I pray it will be enough to handle him.::

::You are more than enough to handle one idiot man, sweetness,:: the ancestor said, its presence shifting into the background as Vinicia waited for the man to come awake.

"What?" Kiernan said, struggling to come back to his senses. "Where am I?"

"My Armory," Vinicia greeted, letting her no-nonsense Barracks Mother attitude raise like a second shield. Men of the Host were always easier to deal with if you fought them, so for as hesitant as she had been before, she had to find her strength once again. He didn't know her like this, hadn't met her while she was in her power in this place, and so she would have to lean on it hard. If he recognized her for the tyro he had gone through the Delton Academy with, she had no idea what she would do.

"Who...?" Kiernan said, rubbing at his head with a hand.

Vinicia waited for his eyes to focus. One of the things she had done while healing him was rebalance the power at his core, drawing away the blindness from the Host for at least the moment. She had done the same for her own Father for cycles until he had refused her help, choosing to be trapped in his prison of a room if only to live through the minds he could access with his Gift.

"Will you please stop glowing?" Kiernan insisted, as if it was her fault.

"I am not," she said, calm despite his annoyance. "You are using your secondsight."

"My what?" Kiernan asked, confused.

Vinicia sighed and came to her feet so she could flick a finger between his eyes. He probably wasn't used to how powerful his godseyes could become without the weight of a hawkeye, though it seemed like her own was having a hard time trying to keep up with his strength.

"Oww," Kiernan said, rubbing at his forehead as the godseyes focused and vanished.

"Better?" She asked, offering her hand to help him up.

"Yes," he said, still unsure of himself. "That has never happened before."

When his focus changed from her to the surrounding room, to the fact that he was lying on his wings, he seemed to realize that there was a strange woman in armor standing over him.

"You!" He yelped, eyes going wide. "You tried to kill me!"

"Excuse me?" She said, her offered hand pulling back to turn into a knife-handed accusation. "You were the one who attacked me."

"You were trying to kill me!" Kiernan insisted, his voice rising in volume. "I was going to see Lord Fourth and you... There was a loralae, and I tried to stop it, but then you were here..." He said, shaking his head with the jumble of memories. "Just who are you, woman?" He demanded. "Who hired you?"

"No one would have to hire me to beat some sense into you, Seventh," Vinicia scoffed, raising her hands to throw up a shield to dampen the sound of their argument. "But if those Blackwings had found you, if you had attacked them instead of me, you would be dead right now."

"Damn it, woman," Kiernan insisted, struggling to get to his feet. "Just tell me who you are."

Vinicia ground her teeth and looked away as she gestured with a hand, pulling the air inside the Armory towards her into a surge that brought him upright at last. Without her hawkeye to soften the effect, she would fill the room with wil-o-wisps if she didn't do something with the power sparking between them.

::You know,:: her ancestor said as Kiernan fought to find his balance. ::I have been meaning to teach you how to transfix someone. I just didn't think your tyros would be a suitable subject. Quick as you need to learn, you'd want to start with someone who didn't respect you so you could bring them into your influence. Feel like trying now? He is staggered enough to let you set the hook and if you can overwhelm him somehow, he'll be yours.::

::Oh, I can manage that,:: Vinicia sent back, exhaling to stop herself from laughing at the terrified look on Kiernan's face. He was afraid of a little wind? He should have been afraid of her.

"Who are you?" He demanded, arms spread as he found his feet at last.

"Vinicia keh'Tresha du'Kirath," she answered, crossing her arms under her chest.

"Keh..." He repeated, and she reveled in the way the blood drained from his face as she came to her full height. Given her mother's bloodline, she was almost half-a-hand taller than the man himself.

::There's the hook,:: her ancestor said, shifting in her mind as if to get a better look. ::Now reel him in.::

"My mother is Heatherwood keh'Tresha," she clarified, Keh'Tresha being the southern conclave of the Eihwaz Forest where she had been born. He should know it, given what he had studied about dryads. "And you are?" She prompted, leaning into the question as she tugged at the confusion in his mind.

"Kiernan," he replied, and in saying it, he started to remember. "Su'Illiandria."

"And here I thought you were something more," she argued, standing taller. Names had power and his name was well known among windwalkers. The first time she had met Hewn, the same exchange had nearly transfixed him just with her knowledge of his full title. "I thought you were Kiernan su'Illiandria, High Wing Commander at War, Sovereign of the Seventh Seat, Dedicate of His Majesty, King Braeden, Heir to the Throne of the Windwalkers, Avatar of the Gods of our Ancestors, Blessed be his reign," she said, smirking. It wasn't every day she could use her father's formal title on his Counselheir.

Kiernan tried to pick his jaw off the floor and failed.

::Got him!:: Her ancestor laughed. ::Oh you are good, sapling. Now see what you can get from him before he realizes the trap.::

Her introduction done, Vinicia moved to offer her hand again, which Kiernan was rightfully hesitant to take. He looked as if he was about to faint until she gripped his forearm, drawing him even tighter into her control.

"I am the daughter of Seventh Counsel Lord Eirik," she said, so self-possessed that it looked like he believed her. "And as you are his Counselheir, I meant you no harm."

Though she couldn't read his mind, his reaction was clear enough: no, he wasn't dreaming. Yes, he had been attacked by a woman. Yes, he had been healed by a kin. She was both that woman and that kin. She had not been trying to kill him. She had been trying to protect herself.

When Kiernan's death-grip relaxed, she almost pitied him.

"I'm sorry," he said, obviously overwhelmed. "What was your name?"

"Vinicia," she repeated. "The tyros call me Mother. I'm their Barracks Mother."

"Kiernan," he replied, though when he raised her hand to his lips to offer his kiss of greeting, sparks flew between them in a riot of colors.

"Can you see it?" She asked as he paused. "In your secondsight."

"Second? Oh, you mean...?" As his eyes washed over with white, he stared down at their hands. All at once, the colors focused to a prism and streaked around them as if through a sun-catcher in a matron's bower.

"You're not half bad when you have a hawkeye on," Vinicia admitted, flexing her hand in his grip.

It took a moment, but eventually Kiernan heard what she had said and his hand went to his neck to find her hawkeye on its thick silver kingchain. With that much magic surging between them, it had likely turned to ice against his chest.

"That isn't yours, by the way," she said as he let go of her hand to pick up the stone. "That is the one my mother gave me. Where is yours?"

"There's more than one?" Kiernan asked, surprised. "Are you sure this isn't mine?"

"Does that chain look like yours?" She asked, giving him a flat stare.

She rolled her eyes as Kiernan tucked his chin, staring at the thick rope of intricate silver that made up the chain and the two dragon-headed terminations. The mouths of the dragons were holding a silver ring between them and on that was the same silver spiral that held the stone Kiernan would have been familiar with. The rest had come from Lord Fourth as a gift when she had first started working in the Armory over ten cycles ago.

"Well, no," Kiernan admitted, looking back at her. "But why do you need one?"

Because I am a thirty-eight cycle old dryad kin, you idiot, she wanted to say. Instead, she merely smiled and let her guise drop. The hook sank deeper as she staggered him a second time.

"Do you think I would have a job taking care of your soldier tyros if I walked around the Palace looking like a loralae?" She asked, gesturing to her hair.

"Probably not," he said and Vinicia saw the fear in him she had wondered about. Many of the ancestor Sevenths had hated her for being one of Them—a dryad, even if only by half—while the others had been nothing but curious about her. Kiernan, it seemed, was the curious sort, although that might have just been her hook in his mind, suppressing his genuine reaction.

"That stone is how I keep hidden," she went on, flaring her wings as she resettled into the guise again. "The fact that I can do it without the stone is a temporary thing, so answer my question. Where did you put your hawkeye?"

"I, uh..." Kiernan started to say, only to take a step back as she loomed over him. "I lost it?"

::Don't lean too hard, girl, or you'll lose him,:: her ancestor warned.

"So you took it off," she said, to which he nodded. "What in the ever-loving winds possessed you to do that? Your Gift rivals my own father's for strength and yet you'll be just fine in Kosar without your stone? Have you seen him recently?" She said, gesturing into the heights of the Armory. "No, because he can't fly any more. He is blind, Kiernan, and there is nothing even I can do to clear his sight. Unlike you," she added, threatening to flick his forehead once again. "Do you want to end up like him?"

Kiernan's jaw was hanging open, though he managed to shake his head.

::Better,:: her ancestor said, though the confidence was wavering.

"Where did you put it when you took it off?" She asked, trying to be patient. Either she had to toss the man's room for him like an idiot tyro who had lost a piece of issued gear or she had to go into the Seventh Counsel Lord's Library to retrieve it like her father's. The first would be much easier.

"I, ah, threw it against the wall in my suite with the daggers that got put on me two nights ago," he said. "But I've looked for it. I've looked everywhere for it and I can't find it. Kreychi even looked before he—Before we..." Kiernan shook himself as Vinicia felt the hook waver. "Wait, why am I telling you this?"

Vinicia looked away, crossing her arms under her chest as she felt the man's mental shields returning. Her hawkeye or not, he could protect himself once again and it was good that he had remembered to try.

::You got some information from him, though,:: her ancestor consoled.

"What did you do to me?" He demanded, flaring his wings as he pulled completely free of her influence.

"Nothing compared to what a true dryad would do to you for storming into her grove with your head up your ass," she said, flaring her wings to match. "Be glad I am only dryad by half."

As Kiernan's face scrunched up with affront, Vinicia barreled on. "Where is your hawkeye, Seventh?" She asked for the third time.

"I don't know," he shot back. "It should be in my rooms, but it isn't. I've looked everywhere."

"It's in the Library, then," she swore, rolling her eyes as she realized just what kind of trouble this was going to be. "I can get it from the Library."

"Not without a hawkeye, you can't," he said, hand going to the one around his throat. "Wait, does this...?"

"Of course it does," she said, as if it should have been obvious. "But if you have marks on you, I am not about to let some assassin pinpoint your location. Not with two days before you leave. Just come with me for now. I can't walk around the Palace like this," she said, gesturing to her armor. "I need to change first."

"I have a guard, you know," he scoffed, following her to where she had left her water skin and heavy coat. "Well, a Blackwing guard."

"Those men would rather you were dead so they can get on with their lives," she said, ignoring him as she got her things together. The coat would at least cover her practice armor and with the last Winter Court happening tomorrow, it wasn't like anyone would be up early this dawning. Not after the revel the night before.

"I told them to stay outside and they did," he scoffed, stepping back as she flared her wings to settle her coat. "I just needed time to sort myself out."

"You needed a miracle, Seventh. Be glad you found one," she growled in return, picking up her waterskin. "Now come on. You can stay in my office until I retrieve your hawkeye. Then, at least, you won't have to risk being seen on Envoy any longer," she said, gesturing to his silvered hair and eyes.

"But you can't just walk into the Library," he protested. "Someone will see you. The Sires' Wing is never empty this time of the cycle."

"I'm not going in through the Sires' Wing," she said.

"What are you going to do, then? Woodwalk?" He scoffed, only to balk as he realized that was exactly what she meant to do. "You can't woodwalk in Delton. There aren't any trees!"

"There is quite a large tree in the Library," she corrected, stopping to pull open the door. "Or did you not know that? You have been inside, haven't you?"

Kiernan opened his mouth to argue and then closed it as he realized that her knowing about the Great Tree meant she had indeed been inside.

That was one of the many secrets no Seventh ever told the outside world. Something must have gone horribly wrong in the distant past for the Founders to have built a shelter for the war god's ancient temple tree, not that Noventrio ever deigned to talk about it.

"That doesn't mean I'll just let you in," he said, scrambling for authority as he shoved the door closed to stop her from walking out.

"Do you really think you can stop me?" She asked, drawing herself up to her full height as he flared his wings in front of the door.

Kiernan's weight shifted, bracing himself as if he meant to fight her. When his intention was clear, she decided to show him just how powerless he was.

With a breath to gather her strength, Vinicia grabbed onto the straps of the Counsel Lord's pauldron over his kama and then willed them both into the splinter of space between the material world and the fae lines she walked on the Palace shelf. Considering the Armory had been a home to her for cycles, dead wood or not, she was able to Step them both back into the open area at the center where she had healed him. The movement completed, she brought them both out of the space and threw Kiernan on his wings in an undignified sprawl.

::Show off,:: her ancestor laughed and Vinicia smirked to hear approval in the tone. Usually, Vinicia didn't have the power to Step like she just had under the weight of her hawkeye, but she felt as if she could do anything right now and it was rapidly going to her head.

To his credit, Kiernan managed to roll onto his feet, even if he looked like he wanted to be sick. As he realized just how far they had moved in the space of a heartbeat, she gloried in the angry look in his eyes.

"You're right out of a fae tale, you know that?" He accused, still braced on his hands and knees.

"You have no idea what I could do to you, so stand down and shut it for once in your life."

Kiernan's eyes narrowed with her words and even if she hadn't meant it for a challenge, it clearly was.

"Excuse me?" He demanded. "You want me to stand down? You're the one assaulting a Counsel Lord. I could have you arrested for that alone!"

"Assault?" She balked. "You literally came at me with a dragon pole!"

"Which you handled with no problem at all," he threw back, coming to his feet. "Who taught you how to fight? Was it Counsel Lord Shayan?"

"For your information, it was Counsel Lord Blake," Vinicia said. "And I have been training with it and every other weapon in this entire building twice as long as you've been at war."

"Blood on my Ancestors," Kiernan swore, looking past her towards Lord Fourth's apartments. "You are literally a walking case of treason."

Vinicia ground her teeth, wings flaring as her anger spiked. All her life she had supported the Sevenths, had helped her father and all his Counselheirs in the Library and this man— this idiot — had the gall to call her work treason. He wouldn't have done half as well at war if she hadn't been guiding his new officers towards skills and strength. She was speechless with rage.

::Remind me why you saved his life?:: Her ancestor asked, and Vinicia was glad she had spent most of the past four cycles keeping a straight face despite the mental comments.

::Not now, please,:: Vinicia sent, hoping the ancestor would just listen for once. ::I am trying to be nice.::

::This is nice?:: Her ancestor laughed. ::Remind me never to piss you off.::

"You were a tyro, weren't you?" Kiernan accused, seeming to realize it as he spoke. "Like Lenae. Eirik put you through the system. I've heard rumors that kindred can pass as either gender before they come into their power and you..."

As Kiernan's vision shifted into his secondsight once again, Vinicia swore. He was looking straight through her shields. He was looking at the core of her power rather than the form she wore, and it would have been a violation if she hadn't realized he was recognizing her for who she truly was. Who she had been, when she was in the tyro system with him. In his very squad.

"Kehvin?" Kiernan gaped, his anger shattering into confusion and awe. "Holy shit."

Vinicia's heart was racing as he closed his wings behind him. She didn't know what to do as he gaped, surprise replacing his hatred from a moment before. Clearly, beating the snot out of him again was out of the question, what with the grin suddenly splitting his face.

"We called you Kehvin," he repeated, absolutely beside himself as he saw her. "Kehvin su'Kirath. You were Shayan's nephew. That's why you could be the chiurgeon for our squad. That's why they trusted you to be with Lenae. Gods of my Ancestors, you were a woman this whole time?"

"Yes, this whole time," Vinicia defended, her anger lost to awkwardness. "I was—I mean—It's only the gender of true dryads that can be fluid like people think. I just, I was—No one even looks at a chiurgeon who can pull his weight. When you three graduated, I started working for Hewn full time and he... He's the one who set me up as Barracks Mother. Him and my father."

"You worked for Hewn?" Kiernan said, hand coming to his mouth as he blinked into his normal vision. "Just here or in Kirath too?"

"Only here," she said, shifting under the weight of his stare. "I've never even left this shelf except to come up from the Eihwaz with my father, but he knew the way back. He'd already done it once before," she said, taking a step back as Kiernan stepped forward. "What matters now is that when he brought me back to the Palace, the other Sevenths immediately stole his hawkeye. I was the one who found it and brought it back to him. He swore I had saved his life, but then it vanished after a few marks more. I was too young to realize that woodwalking through the deadwood between his suite and the Library wasn't supposed to have been a game."

"Wait, what?" Kiernan said, turning to follow her as she started for the door, just to get away from his gaping stare. "How old are you?"

"That's none of your business," she answered, knowing she didn't look a day over three and twenty. "All you need to know is that I have lived in the Barracks most of my life."

Kiernan's hand on the door out of the Armory stopped her from pulling it open. Vinicia refused to look at him, squirming on the inside for all the awkwardness of admitting a secret she had only told Hewn before.

"I know dryad-kin age slowly, Kehvin, but that's an incredible time to be at the Palace with no one knowing you were here. Where were you before that?"

"They kept me in the Seventh's Suite as a fledgling," she confessed, stepping back from him as he blocked the door. If Kiernan was going to keep asking questions, she couldn't exactly answer them anywhere else. "Consort Telessa arranged for my care," she added, stalling his pressure.

"But since they built the Library around one of the Founder's Great Trees, I stayed in there when I started to fly."

"What about before that?" Kiernan asked, a touch of wonder in his voice. "Do you remember living in the Eihwaz?"

Skittish as she was, he had dropped his wings low to set her at ease.

"No," Vinicia said, crossing her arms beneath her chest for all her awkwardness. "My first memories are in the Library. As far as I remember, I've never even left the Palace shelf. Well," she corrected. "I have been to the Lower City a handful of times, but that's still Delton."

"What did you do?" He asked. "All those cycles?"

"I, ah... Read everything I could get my hands on, which was pretty much everything," she said, glancing up to see him, only to find his head tilted in wonder. "What?"

"I never had time to do that," Kiernan said, finally taking his hand off the door. "I never had time to do anything other than grab books on dryads and learn what I could between the war seasons."

"Well, I'm not about to let you study me," Vinicia said, looking at him fully. "You're leaving, aren't you? On Envoy."

"I am," Kiernan said, and the sadness that flashed in his eyes made her hesitate. "But only the Gods know how I will survive it."

Vinicia tried to will herself to find her anger again. She had tried for so long to forget the curious tyro he had been while she had trained with him. The fool in love with his Consort, who would do anything for anyone if they asked. The compassionate, empathic, kind-hearted boy who had died on the War Plains if his work as a Seventh was any show of it. But if he hadn't truly died, if he was still in there somewhere, didn't she have a duty to bring that back out? She had done the same for Rylan, hadn't she, and he was only her tyro?

"Which ones were your favorite?" He asked. "Which books?"

"The, ah," she hesitated to say. "The stories of Lan'lieanans," she confessed, quiet but honest. "The adventures about sailing are fascinating. All those ships and the ocean they sail and as much of their culture as you would expect to find in a looted bit of Val'Corps entertainment."

"And I didn't even know they were in there," he admitted and Vinicia had the terrifying realization that he wasn't talking about the books. He was talking about her. He hadn't known she was in there.

Well, I wasn't, she knew. *I was staying away from you, for my father's sake. For my own sake, curious as you are.*

"Hewn didn't have time for them either," Vinicia defended, looking through the door he still blocked. "But I could tell him whatever he needed or I could look it up for him if he really wanted to know. I started writing his tyro reports, too, and when my father found out he got Aaron to agree that I could manage a better report than he ever could. Since he oversees the education of more than just the Delton tyros, he never has enough time," she said, hesitating again.

"And here I threw a fit last night when I found out," Kiernan said, amazed. "But if what you say is true, I would have accomplished nothing as a Seventh without you."

As he watched her, Vinicia flushed with embarrassment. She hadn't felt so acknowledged since she had worked for Hewn. It was an uncomfortable feeling either way and she had no idea what to say in response. Seeing her uneasiness, Kiernan swallowed his pride.

"Vinicia, I fear I am in debt to you more than I ever realized," he said, the formality of it startling her. "Would you please assist me in retrieving my hawkeye? It is not an easy thing I ask, knowing that you worked for Hewn as I did."

The words hung heavy between them. If she meant to go into the Library to retrieve his hawkeye, then she might encounter the man's shade. Of all the men on the shelf, Kiernan had been one of his cadre primarchs, for however briefly he had managed.

"Of course," she said, nodding. "Like I said, just come with me. You can wait in my office while I search for it. That way we can keep the Blacks off your wingtips."

"I should like that," Kiernan said, looking over his shoulder as if he could see through the walls. "After what happened with my cadre last night..."

"My uncle told me," she said as his words failed him. "Warned me, at least, in case any of my tyros asked about it."

Kiernan just nodded. "I didn't know I had strength enough to do that," he said.

"If it makes you feel any better," Vinicia said. "I can do worse. On your behalf, though," she added when he looked up. "That is to say, if you would feel safer just staying with me for a while, I would allow it."

Kiernan considered her offer for a long moment before nodding. "I think I would like that, Kehvin."

"It's just Vin now," she said, risking a smile as he moved to open the door for her. "But maybe if you have time, I can find you one of my books about Lan'lieanan ships before you go. I hope you will need that information one day."

"I do as well," Kiernan agreed, following her out into the cold. "I mean to come back."

"For Lenae," Vinicia nodded. "I know."

Chapter 14: Consort Lenae du'Illiandria

Friday, 06:00

Lenae picked at the lace that covered the backs of her hands, tugging the tiny thread left in the seam between her thumb and finger. The seam would split if she kept after it, and it frustrated her. What good was a glove if it couldn't withstand a little worrying? Beautiful or not, if it failed in its one purpose, it had no worth it all.

Much to the dismay of her entourage, Lenae had long since done away with the fingertips. But the tragedy she effected on a simple set of gloves that cobbled her sense of touch had set fire to the fashion that ruled the Court. Now her worrying filled the coffers of the women who designed the lace and challenged their good-natured competitors to improve on the style. The talk was endless. Why remove only the tips of the glove when you could do away with the fingers all together? Why stop at the wrist when the arm could be closed in wool, cashmere, or even luxurious kivet?

All she had wanted was the ability to write her family without the vexation of seams across her fingertips. What she had begun was a revolution of practicality which, as pointless as that seemed, was a revolution nonetheless. It had confirmed her continuing influence in some part and had filled her suite with baskets full of styles.

Each new gift came with love notes from Matrons and Daughters who wished to emulate her innovative spirit. They claimed she must be an inspiration to Braeden and his Counsel Lords, especially to First Counsel Lord Terrance. Surely, they must all see and cherish her worth.

Lord First was the Master of Coin, true, but he put no value on a woman's talents. Only a woman could see how the volume of their thread, needles, and lace moved wealth among the Houses. All he saw was money spent on trinkets, but she knew better. She and Kiernan knew better. His apprenticeship and skill with rasha as a fledgling had moved money among so many Houses that Kiernan's name had been more well-known than Lenae's that first winter at Court.

And I was the new Consort! She thought with a huff.

With one last tug at the stray thread, the glove on her hand pulled halfway off, only to catch on her royal signet ring, and she sighed. The stitch was strong and her will to destroy it was not. Understanding Kiernan more closely than she preferred, Lenae removed the glove entirely. She then removed its mate, stood, and threw the gloves against the wall behind the desk.

"Well, at least I know where Kiernan gets it from," her Sixth Counsel Lord observed, turning his attention to her. "What did those gloves ever do to you?"

"More than you care to know," Lenae said. "We should have found it by now. It can't have just disappeared."

"Unfortunately," Hest'lre said. "That's exactly what it's done."

It was something both he and Kiernan were doing far too often these days: agreeing that all was lost. There was more to life than meticulous plans and seeing them through, though if Hest'lre truly felt that way, he had been cooped up with Kiernan too long.

Some might argue that Hest'lre was the better half of their duo. When Kiernan's counselheir was named, Hest'lre would be promoted to Ninth Counsel Lord and set to choosing a counselheir to hold the Sixth Seat that would complement Kiernan's choice. He wouldn't abandon the kingdom to court their enemy into peace; he would move to serve a higher purpose. Given the breath of his life, it was just another dawning for Hest'lre and Lenae gloried in the good he could do in the Seat once he took it.

All of his humility and grace came from the fact that Hest'lre's life had started out harder than just about anyone she had ever known. With his father a veteran that had been grounded by a wing injury during the war, there weren't many opportunities available to him—in life or in love. At some point, his father had met his mother, a wingless Ehkeski woman living in Alexandria, and Hest'lre had been born in one of the slope-side gondola villages. He was lucky, though. Despite an Ehkeski parent, he had at least been born with wings, unlike his younger sister Honoria that Lenae had met and adored.

It had been Hest'lre's intimacy with his mother's Ehkeski culture and traditions that had drawn him into the Sixth Counsel Lord's workings as a young man. To that end, Hest'lre had also made a name for himself by the time he earned the honor of being sent to train as an officer tyro in Delton by the Alexandrian Legion. Given his late arrival and strange duties with the Sixth's men at the time, Hest'lre had been sent into a flight squad with Lenae, Kiernan, and a tyro chirurgeon named Kehvin who had apparently been the nephew of the then Sixth Counsel Lord.

Still, of the number of people she had trained with, it had always come back to the three of them. That intimacy between them, especially Kiernan and Hest'lre, had made all the difference when they were raised to Counsel Lords together after only four cycles on the Plains. The youth and promise they brought to the Seats were a blessing and a boon, and together they had turned the tide of war. The longer they were paired, the more the kingdom saw what Lenae had known all along; the balance between Kiernan's unrelenting idealism and Hest'lre's limitless practicality was exactly what Kosar needed. That tension between them, that fire of purpose, it had always worked out into a stunningly effective compromise.

At least, it had until now...

As far as Lenae was concerned, neither one of her closest friends was succeeding at their tasks. Kiernan couldn't trust the web he had woven in the past seven cycles and Hest'lre couldn't trust his soldiers to give Kiernan the space to survive. Worse, Hest'lre was also Kiernan's best mate, which meant that both he and Lenae were losing a lifelong friend.

As she watched Hest'lre look over Kiernan's room, she could see the struggle he was trying to hide. It was difficult to let Kiernan go, no matter how hard he was making Hest'lre's life at the moment. But friendships were a work in progress, as were their duties to their Seats. While they never expected the responsibilities to be easy, there was a distinct difference between this impasse and the truly impossible.

"When we were fledglings," Lenae said aloud. "Kiernan would love to eat grapes when he was working. When he was careless with them, he would end up staining the rasha reeds for his projects red and his father would be furious. Eventually, I learned to watch out for him. I could find even a white grape skin in a bucket of wet rasha reeds, not because I wanted to, but because I had to. Kiernan was worth it," she said. "And he still is."

"I know, Lenae," Hest'lre sighed, turning to retrieve her gloves from behind Kiernan's desk. "But I just—" As he bent down, however, he started swearing. "By Earth and Sky..."

"What?" Lenae asked, as he leaned further down. After a moment, she heard metal scraping against the hard stone floor. "What is it?"

As he stood, Hest'lre was stunned. "You're not going to believe this."

Lenae gasped as Hest'lre turned to her. In one hand he had gathered three daggers, each of varying metalwork, and in the other...

"Is that—?" she gasped, understanding his shock. The leather was cut, the expertly crafted silver spiral holding the stone was intact, but the stone itself...

"Where is the stone?" She demanded.

No matter the copper hue to his skin, Hest'lre blanched.

"I thought he said he threw the stone!" Lenae insisted. "Hest'lre, he didn't take it out, did he? Take it out and throw it? Did someone else take it? Gods, who could do such a thing? Hest'lre, you have to help him!"

"Kiernan is fine, Lenae," Hest'lre assured her. "I saw him only a few candlemarks ago. He is with Aaron and surrounded by Blackwings. He's drunk, not dead."

"But how can you be sure?" She demanded. "You know he can slip from his guards when he truly wants. Oh Gods, why did you ever leave him by himself? How could you let this happen?"

"Lenae, please," Hest'lre begged, setting the three knives on the desk. "You can't lose yourself to this. You have to calm down."

As Hest'lre took her hands, her mind swam with all the terrible, horrible things that could have happened to him. She fought to breathe as her throat closed with worry and her tears brimmed so fast that she lost her sight.

"Lenae, I left him with Aaron because he wanted to be alone," he said softly. "He is safe, I am sure of it. I will send Henrick and Lyonel to go find him just as soon as you compose yourself."

"You have to stay with him," she pleaded. "I can't lose him. I won't make it. I can't do this by myself."

"You're not alone, Lenae," Hest'lre soothed, and pulled her into the embrace she desperately needed. This was not the first time she had fallen apart with him and it wouldn't be the last. Not if Kiernan was truly leaving. "I will always be here for you. You know that, right?"

Lenae wanted to trust him, wanted to believe every kind word Hest'lre said, but they were wrong. As she stood staring at the face of one of the few friends she had made at Court, she was miserable. For as much as she loved her Hest'lre, she was only the Consort. She was no companion to them and the company they kept was far beyond her. Worse, she had no allies to reach out to, no woman other than the few who served as her entourage and they hated her for being Consort in their place. Even if she owed her loyalty to Braeden, Kiernan was her everything and they all knew it.

As Hest'lre made small circles in the space between her wings, Lenae fought to reclaim herself. She swallowed huge gulps of air, fighting back her tears until she found her calm once again. When she finally pulled away, Hest'lre looked as shaken as she was.

"I'm sorry," she said. "I trust you. I believe you. I just..."

"Please, Lenae," Hest'lre said, refusing her apology. "There is a reason the Sixth Counsel Lord becomes the Ninth. At the end of the day, this transition wounds us both. Though I may not have known him as long as you, he is like a brother to me. I promise you, I will do everything in my power to get him safely back to Illiandria this winter."

"I know you will," she admitted. "I just...I can't handle much more of this."

"We are not out of the fog just yet," Hest'lre sighed, stepping back from her.

"You don't think someone took it, do you?" Lenae wondered aloud, watching as Hest'lre fanned out the three daggers. As he picked at something stuck in a dent on one of the blades, she went on guessing. "Just came into his room and took it from the spiral while you were gone?"

"The only person who could have come in here is Kreychi," Hest'lre said, shaking his head. "So, no."

"But what if the stone was already gone from the spiral?"

"No, it hit the wall as well," Hest'lre said, and turned to point. "If the spiral was empty, it would have bounced. Or at least, it would have bounced farther than it did."

"Then what does this mean?" she insisted. "What does any of it mean?"

Hest'lre set two of the daggers back, considering the third one with a blacksmith's eye. It was barely more than a silver spike with a small, unremarkable handle. There was a ring where a pommel stone could have been inserted, and the four rough sides came to a stiletto point. Hest'lre pushed the pad of his thumb along the small blade, frowning, and then took the thing with two hands and tested the strength of the blade itself. Much to Lenae's surprise, it bent, the silver enamel giving way easily to reveal a soft pewter core.

"Talk to me, Hest'lre," Lenae said, wary of the dark look on her friend's face. "What does it mean?"

"More than you likely want to know," he said and then looked up at her.

"I wouldn't have asked if I didn't want to know," she insisted.

Hest'lre shrugged and explained.

"This is very soft metal," he began. "Metal that is strong is difficult to make. It takes skill to make the alloy and an eye for the craft to make it hold an edge."

"And that..." She prompted, gesturing as Hest'lre bent the blade back into shape.

"Is cored with pewter," he said with disdain. "You can boil down the metal over a cook fire, cast it in a mold, and write whatever you want with a harder metal on the side. Whoever had this commissioned meant it as an insult. It is beautiful on the outside, but with a rotten core."

"So they think Kiernan is weak," Lenae guessed.

"And they don't care if we know it, either." Hest'lre sighed and set the first of the three blades on the table. "That, or they've done it as a stunt. Show off a fine blade, mock your intent, and get it on Kiernan while others are watching."

"A low ante, with a large payoff."

"Hoi," Hest'lre agreed. "A pretty talking point and not much more, unless you want to think that even the Lower Court would—"

Lenae's raised hand stopped him from saying more. Both of them knew what it meant and she didn't need to hear it spoken aloud to be sure of it.

"What of the other two?" She prompted.

Hest'lre set the bent pewter spike on the desk and focused on the second blade as Lenae leaned in to get a better look. This one was different, more ornate but still a functional piece. The handle was wrapped in leather with a twisted copper wire to keep it in place, and the oil from someone's hand had worked into it well. It had obviously been someone's personal dagger long before it made it into Kiernan's pocket.

Hest'lre turned it over in his hand, testing the weight of it, and then flipped it so that he caught it by the blade. He gave Lenae a look that asked her permission and Lenae leaned back. When she was safe, he brought his arm up and snapped it forward, sending the blade flipping into the far wall.

Much to her surprise, it hit flat and dropped solidly to the floor. Hest'lre, who could pick an apple off the top of a cat's head, failed to put the blade into the wall.

"What does that mean?" Lenae asked again.

"That is an eating dagger," Hest'lre said with such certainty that she didn't see a point in arguing. "It's not quality enough steel to be useful for much else," he said, retrieving the dagger for further inspection.

"So someone decided on an impulse to take whatever blade they were carrying and place it on Kiernan?"

"More than that," Hest'lre said, scratching at the writing on the blade. "But not much more. The writing on this one is scrawled. They had better tools, but didn't want to waste them on the gesture. This was done with anger."

"Anger at what?" Lenae demanded. "Kiernan has done nothing but help them, all of them, for cycles—and this is how they repay him?"

"This is how our kingdom has always repaid the Seventh," Hest'lre reminded, setting the second blade on the table. "It's why they think they can do it. It's why there's an entire culture of marking someone for an assassination, Seventh or not. It is a gesture that means something."

Lenae sighed, crossing her arms against his logic once again.

"Have you never seen the daggers hidden in the portrait frames of the past Seventh Counsel Lords? It's how they all died, or at least the ones that never left the Palace…"

"Yes, Hest'lre, I have," Lenae snapped, and he let the thought trail away at her irate look. He picked up the third blade with just a hint of hesitation.

"Now this one," Hest'lre began, presenting it to her with respect. "The gesture is the entire purpose of this blade."

Lenae nodded. "But that is… What do they call it? Living steel?"

"It is." Hest'lre was impressed.

"Braedon's ancestral sword is made of this," Lenae explained. "It hangs in his chambers."

"And that blade is older than these mountains," Hest'lre said, and Lenae watched as the blacksmith's son came through his reserved exterior. "At my father's forge, we would take commissions for a living steel dagger maybe once a cycle. The process to make it requires almost two moonturns of adding carbon to the mix. The result is a steel that is resilient and extremely flexible, like a newborn chick. This made the mark on the wall, although I'm not sure Kiernan knew what he was throwing. No one throws a blade this precious."

I would, Lenae thought with venom. *Right off the Palace shelf while whoever commissioned it was watching.*

She kept the thought to herself as Hest'lre admired the craftsmanship. More important was the fact that someone had spent a fortune crafting this blade and was about to spend another fortune to have someone retrieve it from Kiernan's corpse.

"What more can we do to protect him?" Lenae asked. "You know he's a target."

"Sevenths are always a target," he answered. "At this point, there are only so many men I trust to stand with him, and those men have already been foiled. Now that he has Blackwings following him, he'll become even more of a target."

"And what if he just keeps company with the other Counsel Lords?" Lenae asked.

"We tried that last night," he answered. "And he ended up throwing his weight around and angering what few friends he had left."

"What if he stayed with me?" She asked. "No one would dare attack him in my presence."

"It's been done before," Hest'lre said, shaking his head. "Granted, it was nearly a hundred cycles ago, but it has been tried. You are the only woman who could hope to defend him and you're in no position to be fighting. And as for your ladies," he went on. "There is no telling who of your Court has been placed there in case that exact situation arose. Perhaps if you had let me vet them..."

Lenae sighed and looked down at the silver spiral she held. Seeing how worn it was, how empty and delicate it was, she could see only herself. How she would be the moment he left, realizing that everything that had ever happened to her beloved Kier'n had been her fault.

If she had just let him leave to become a tyro...

If she hadn't demanded the Gods themselves come to her aid to keep them together...

"Lenae?" Hest'lre asked, growing concerned as her hand closed into a fist.

None of this would have happened. She would never have been chosen Consort, never have been betrothed to Braeden, and never had to watch Kiernan convince himself that he wasn't about to leave her forever on a suicide mission.

"Lenae, you have to breathe."

Four cycles at Delton and then four at War and he would have retired as a veteran. Eight cycles and then her partner for life. They could have united their guilds and lived happily ever after, but no—she couldn't wait. She had convinced Kiernan that they had to take their promise papers to Great Matron Celenae's temple themselves before he left. They had to make sure the Goddess knew just how much they wanted to be together. How much she wanted to be with him.

"Lenae, please. Breathe."

As Hest'lre pulled her into an embrace again, she finally let herself dissolve.

"Everything that ever happened to him has been my fault," she sobbed, gasping for breath around one of the few secrets neither she nor Kiernan had ever shared with their friend. "I raged at the Gods to let me follow him here and gave myself to Founder Kerowyn willingly. When Kier'n went to war, I told Hewn about our betrothal. I asked him to take care of him for me. I knew we would never be married, but Kiernan refused to go home without me. And then when the Fall happened and Hewn died... Hest'lre, he wanted a chance to save me from a fate I chose, but he will die because of it. Hest'lre, he's going to die. He's going to die because of me. Because I didn't think I could live without him. And now? Now, I am killing him."

Hest'lre didn't say a word, but in truth he didn't have to. Lenae could feel the man's own tears as they fell into her hair. Even if they had known it ever since Kiernan had taken up the Seat, they felt it now. They were losing him, losing a beloved and a brother, and it killed them both.

"There has to be something," Lenae whispered, even if she knew it was a lie. "We have to do something. Anything..."

"He will be safe from all of this if we send him home," Hest'lre said, finally pulling back to reveal the red of tears around his slanted eyes. "Once the tournament is over, we will get him to Illiandria. His guild will keep him safer than any guard I could ever muster."

"I should be able to protect him here," she insisted, stubborn if only by habit. "There has to be something I can do."

"You have already done a great deal, Lenae," Hest'lre reminded. "His gear is halfway to Illiandria because of you. Until then, there is nothing more we can do."

Hest'lre offered his hand to her and she slid off the desk, considering her options. "You say he's down in Aaron's quarters?"

"Sleeping off the wine," Hest'lre confirmed. "I'd be surprised if we see him before mid-meal at the rate he was drinking last night. No one but the other Counsel Lords and a few Blackwings know he's there."

"Do you think we could get him a nest in the Library?" She asked and moved to leave the room. "At least that way we know he is the only one who can enter."

"Only if we find the hawkeye," Hest'lre said, following her down the hallway. "But if it's true that the spirits of the other Sevenths are in there, that is the last place he'd want to be. They'd be worse than the Sires at telling him what to do."

Lenae didn't press the issue, but the thought of poor Kiernan dealing with the ancestor spirits made her uneasy. Kiernan had never been fond of the guild ancestors or their priests, and he had very little love for the men who had held his Seat before him.

As she and Hest'lre emerged into the main seating area, her entourage rose to greet her. Hest'lre thanked her for her visit and then excused himself and continued towards his own chambers.

"Morning audiences begin in two marks, Your Grace," Dame Elissa greeted. "Would you like to return to the Royal Suite?"

Lenae chewed her lower lip, looking out the large window at the rear of the room. As the daystar continued its steady climb, she could see the outline of the Armory through the mist. The only person she had not consulted was Kiernan's predecessor, who was tucked out of sight and out of mind in the Armory. It was not a place she had visited often since her cycles as a tyro emeritus, but the gravity of the situation warranted it.

"No," Lenae replied, which made her honor guards uncomfortable. "We should have enough time for one last stop."

"Where is that, Your Grace?" The younger of the two asked.

His name was Hunter, which was appropriate since he had grown up hunting ore in Yaltana with his family. Standing next to him, his elder brother Laerin was more reserved. He knew this appointment and the coin that came with it depended on his ability to keep the Consort from putting herself in danger. That made him something of a spoil-sport for impromptu sorties, but under the circumstances, he would have to acquiesce.

"The Armory," she said. "I believe it is long past time I visited Counsel Lord Eirik."

"That may not be wise, Your Grace," Laerin advised, watching as she walked towards the window. "The weather is bitter cold and flying can't be good for you in your condition."

The last bit made her laugh. "Youngling, women have been in 'my condition' since the ages began. If we couldn't fly like this, why were we born with wings?"

As he tried to stammer a response, Lenae opened the latch on the window and stepped out onto the balcony. Elissa was quick to follow her and Hunter as well, which left Laerin to close the latch and catch up as the three of them took off towards the Armory.

"Just who are we going to see, Your Grace?" Laerin asked, when they backwinged at the entrance to the Armory.

"You are going to stay with Counsel Lord Blake," Lenae said, inclining her head as the group of Blackwings standing at the Armory doors came to attention. "I am going to see Ser Eirik. Good dawning, Praetor."

"Good dawning, Your Grace," the man replied, hand flat over his left chest as she approached. "I am Praetor Iven."

"Are you the detail assigned to my Seventh?" She asked. Given their black uniforms and flared enameled pauldron, they were certainly Blackwings. Kiernan absolutely hated Blackwings. They were one of the few men he couldn't find in his Seventh's Gift.

"Part of it, Your Grace," the Praetor replied. "Lord Fifth has another few squads in rotation on the shelf. Lord Seventh went into the Wing with the Barracks Mother a few moments ago."

The what?

"Then why are you out here?" Lenae asked.

"Lord Ninth ordered us to remain here rather than bother the tyros in the Armory or in the Wing, Your Grace," Praetor Iven said, and for once Lenae was glad to realize the man was serious about his duty protecting Kiernan. "There is another squad waiting for him on the roof and a third at the exit to the Soldier Tyros' Wing should he leave in that direction. He is secure, Your Grace."

"So it seems," Lenae said, allowing herself a small smile. "Thank you for your work, Ser."

"Glory to Serve, Your Grace," Praetor Iven said, giving her a second salute before gesturing for the man behind him to get the door.

"Thank you, Praetor," Lenae said, nodding once again before moving to enter the Armory.

Given the cold, Lenae was glad that their trip between the Sires' Wing and the Armory had been so short. Now, as Laerin shut the door of the foyer firmly behind them, they shook off the cold from their wings and hurried into the much warmer inner room.

Hearing the unexpected commotion, the voice of Counsel Lord Blake greeted them. "The Armory is closed, boys," he said and Lenae could tell he was moving to stand.

She had them wait in silence as he came out of his office, not willing to spoil the surprise.

After a long moment, the elder Counsel Lord appeared just to the left of the entrance. "Well, I'll be!" he said, pleasantly surprised. "Lenae! What are you doing here?"

As he opened his muscular arms to her, she marveled at how little he had changed from the man who had welcomed her into her unusual life as a tyro so long ago. His hair had turned to salt and pepper over the cycles, but his jaw was still hard set and his affectionate scowl was just as unfailing.

"Where in the winds did you come from?" He asked, embracing her. "You're near frozen, girl."

Lenae couldn't stop herself from smiling as she caught a glimpse of the look on Laerin's face. Only a few men in the Kingdom could address the Consort so informally, but three of them lived here in the Armory.

"I was speaking with Hest'lre in his suite before," she explained as he released her. "And it was so much faster to fly..."

"Well, make certain you walk back through the Tyros' Wing," he warned. "I don't want you catching your death."

"Of course," she assured him. "But first I must speak with Eirik. Do you know the marks he keeps these days?"

Blake looked unsure. "The only man who knows that would be Shayan," he answered. "He was gone by the time I came back from breaking my fast, but he is likely in the suite with Eirik. Are you sure this can't wait until after your audiences? I'm certain I can find out by then and have him come meet you here or back in the Royal Wing."

"Unfortunately, the matter is urgent," she confessed. "I will simply have to try my luck."

"If you insist," Blake said and then looked to the three that followed her like shadows. "You all are welcome to the hearth in my office until she returns. This is the only door into or out of the Armory at the moment. The rest have been sealed against the Ice Winds."

They immediately turned to her for direction. Despite their duty, there was only so much she could ask from them. Counsel Lord Eirik was more than a bit disturbing to those who had not known him before the madness of his dryad curse.

"Stay," she insisted. "I should not be long."

Relieved, Laerin and his young brother assured her they would stand guard at the inner doors. That would ensure her safety and privacy if the Blackwings waiting for Kiernan could not.

"I assume you remember your way?" Blake said, offering her the opportunity for an escort.

"I do," she said, politely refusing. "It will be nice to stretch my wings."

"It has been far too long," Blake agreed. "I always say you should visit me more often. I would be happy to put you through your paces whenever you are free."

"Perhaps in the spring," she laughed and then turned to enter the towering expanse that was the Armory proper. Young Laerin insisted on opening the door for her, but after that she was on her on.

Twilight and silence closed in around her as he shut the door and she breathed a sigh of relief. This place was one of the few that truly felt like home and with so much turmoil in her life, it was a peace she hadn't known she missed. She had spent so much of her youth within these walls, striving to master skills that they still thought she would be better off without.

But for all the adversity, she had loved it. It was the one place in the world that she truly felt alive. With the thrill of the fight at hand, nothing could distract her from her cause. No stray worry could surmount the adrenaline as she winged her way to and fro, diving and climbing and struggling for victory with crossbow, staff, and the occasional wooden sword.

It took more than courage to master the skill of weapons work, and she had that spark. She had shown a dedication to the craft that few Consorts before her had known and it had given her the first chance at leverage in this new place. Because of her skill, she hadn't simply been taken through the motions, she had demanded and received a full tyro's education. Her graduation had been cause for a grand celebration and though she had never flown the Ice Winds, every cycle she still envied those who could take that flight.

The vaulted training space was abandoned now, but in her mind she could recall the sounds and smells of the bustling armory. While it had certainly seen better days, it was still polished to perfection. The building towered up nine stories overall, one for each Seat on Braeden's High Counsel, with one set into the earth of the Palace shelf for storage and six rising high in the air for the tyro's practice in a nod to the Sixth Counsel Lord. The Seventh and final story, though, had a different purpose altogether.

Looking up to the far left-hand corner of the ceiling, she saw the small landing and tight set of staircases that were her destination. Gathering her courage and her cloak about her, she opened her wings and took a few running steps to begin the climb.

Of all the places on the Palace grounds that she had explored—and she had indeed explored them all—there were only three that had been constructed to prevent easy access. The first were the Cells built into the bedrock beneath the

Palace, for obvious reasons. The second was the tightly sealed door of the Counsel Lord's Library at the top level of the Sires' Wing.

That she had entered with Kiernan when he was first named to the Seat, but even if she was only a priestess to Founder Kerowyn, the amount of ancestral power inside the place had given her quite a headache. The third was this place, with its small door and tiny winding stairs. At one time it had been used as quarters for the Weapons Master Counsel Lord, with access given only through the Armory itself. Three and ten cycles past, though, Blake had vacated when the first Seventh Counsel Lord in living memory had returned from his Envoy, blinded and half-mad from the journey.

Ever since that day, the Armory quarters had been the home of Seventh Counsel Lord Eirik and his brother, who had been promoted from Sixth to Ninth in his absence. These days, Eirik was an enigma to both the Court and the veterans, with Shayan his only true keeper. Thankfully, after passing his duties to Weylan, Hewn, and later to Kiernan, Eirik was left well enough alone to his tower and very few seemed to remember his presence.

Even she had forgotten, until desperation had drawn her mind out to him. Whatever the reason, her ancestors had guided her this far in her life, and she did not mind another nudge in the right direction. Not that she was sure what good it would do talking to Eirik, but he was her first Seventh and had always been like a father to her. She knew in her heart that if there was ever to be an end to this war, it would involve Eirik as much as it involved Kiernan. Why else would he have lived?

Lenae exhaled in relief as she reached the top of the twisting set of wooden steps. She took a moment to calm her breathing and then approached the ornate wooden door where a huge heavy ring waited to be knocked. She reached for it with a sense of trepidation and an icy shiver ran down between her wings as she dropped the weight to announce herself. When nothing happened and there seemed to be no movement inside, she reach to touch the ring again only to have the door click and slide open.

When she could see inside, her heart was racing. No hand had moved the door and there was no gear-driven contraption to move it either. Like a tale of the fae, it had just opened by itself, for no reason other than her knock.

"Come in, love," came a voice from deeper within the chambers. "I've been expecting you."

Lenae came up to sharp attention, hearing the asking in the ancient Counsel Lord's voice. For as much as she may have forgotten about him, it seemed the man had not forgotten her.

Lenae smoothed out the front of her embroidered bodice, stalling without truly realizing it. Mustering her nerves, she put a hand up to the threshold and let it pass through the barrier that she knew was there. It was the same kind of barrier that protected the Counsel Lord's Library, but for whatever reason this one would allow her in. Now it protected the rest of the Palace from Eirik, or Eirik from them, depending on how one viewed sorcery.

Even though she didn't need to, Lenae held her breath as she passed through and was almost a little surprised when she didn't feel a change.

I'm only here to ask for his assistance, she reminded herself. But as the door slid back into place without her prompting, she still felt trapped.

Lenae distracted herself from her fear by looking about the room, focusing on the perfectly ordinary map of the War Plains, even if it was the biggest one she had ever seen. The canvas stretched from floor to ceiling across nearly ten spans of stone wall. There were scratches and scrawls across the entire length, but from this distance she couldn't make out the writing.

Patient, but only just, she moved into the room so she could get a closer look at the map. Unfortunately, even when she was right up next to it, the markings were nothing more than scrawls. She frowned, touching the map to identify one of the larger markings, and then heard the unmistakable, chirring cry of the gryphling that Eirik had brought back with him from the Eihwaz.

Moments later, the creature appeared from beneath a lounge, every part the copy of its larger gryphon cousins that lived among the mountains of the Kihara range. The only difference was the fact that the gryphling looked more like a cross between a grey house cat and a peregrine falcon, rather than one of the enormous plains cats and a white-headed eagle. The other difference was in the creature's bright emerald eyes, which glinted with an intelligence that outstripped the body it wore.

"Sal'weh, Aevi," Lenae greeted, squatting down as it prowled around her heels to demand affection. After a moment, the gryphling head-butted her hand to return the greeting and then jumped up onto her shoulder with a little help from her wings.

Once she was settled, Lenae looked over at her curiously and the emerald-eyed gryphling stretched out her neck to let her smooth down the feathers under its chin. Lenae gave her a bit more love before looking back at the map.

Surprisingly, that was when the gryphling churred again and tilted her head to the side, trying to nudge Lenae's head over in the process. Lenae was confused until she realized the gryphling was also looking at the map.

Is she squinting?

Knowing the creature was far more clever than she appeared, Lenae also squinted at the map, but the scratches remained unintelligible. Stubborn and curious, she squinted harder, which still did nothing. She then attempted to relax her eyes as if she was in flight, and then the map came to life.

Lenae gaped as the letters all seemed to stand at attention for her, stretching out their secret code along the leagues of canvas. The gryphling chirred again and nuzzled her cheek, apparently glad this windwalker had picked up on her hint.

Not long after, Lenae yelped when she felt a hand tap her right shoulder and the gryphling shifted, gathered her weight, and leapt away. Lenae turned to see who it was who had joined her, only to realize that all she could focus on was the immensely magnified image of a white beard. Squeezing her eyes shut again, she rubbed at them until the flight lenses reset and she could see.

Waiting for her was the sunken image of the Seventh Counsel Lord she had known in her youth, weighed down by time and travel. If it wasn't for the seven ash-black markings on his wings and the fact that he looked like the oldest living soul in her kingdom, she would have thought he was an ancestor taking corporeal form. His eyes, washed over with the opalescent film of his dryad's curse, only added to the effect.

But as he stared through her, waiting for little Aevi to re-settle herself on the modified rank-pauldron Eirik wore to support her weight, Lenae wasn't convinced of the man's blindness. More likely, Lenae suspected that his clouded eyes were very much like the twin godseyes Kiernan had been fighting, which meant he could see, just not what everyone else saw.

Maybe it is Aevi who does all the normal seeing for him, she realized, watching the gryphling follow her movements.

"I have so few visitors these days," Eirik began, extending his hand for hers. Lenae took it without hesitation, clasping it in both of her own. "It is wonderful to see your beautiful face."

When Lenae started to correct him, Eirik chuckled in the way that old men do when they have a secret. She looked back at the gryphling and it winked a green eye.

"It is a wonder to see you, Sire," she returned as he kissed her hand.

"Sire, eh? So I've been found out," he sighed. "Bless, it's only been forty-odd cycles."

"Excuse me?" She asked, not sure she understood.

"Being a sire. Tell me, how did you figure—" he said, as the gryphling studied her confusion. "Oh, so you haven't! Well, we won't talk about it then," he said, changing the subject by pointing at her own abdomen. "How are you coming along, eh?"

"But I haven't even told—" she said, and then swallowed the confession. "How can you tell?"

They were even now.

"I guessed and you were simply being polite," he answered. "But the Consort rarely consults a Seventh on parenting advice, so how may I be of assistance?"

Lenae led them both to the lounges in the room, given that the great window was the only place with true sunlight in this tower. Once Eirik had moved to the Armory, Counsel Lord Shayan had followed and soon insisted on building a balcony so that he would not have to cut through classes every time he wished to return to his own business.

When they were seated, Lenae answered. "Why don't you tell me?" She offered.

"I think you want something from me," he answered. "The Ice Winds are too close for you to be out in the cold, otherwise."

"I think you're correct," she echoed, watching as the gryphling alighted from Eirik's shoulder to his knee for a scritch.

"So is this for yourself or for Kiernan?" He began.

"Both?" She guessed, which amused him.

"Women always want the world, don't they?" Eirik asked the gryphling, who bobbed sympathetically. "Unfortunately, I can only help with one."

"You don't even know what the problem is," Lenae objected.

"Ah, but I do. You are not the first Consort worried about the Seventh's Envoy to the Plains. The answer is simple," he declared. "Let things play themselves out as I've crafted and the world will be fine."

"But things are not fine," Lenae argued. "Without help, Kiernan may not survive to leave the shelf, much less start out on his Envoy. I only want to ensure that he is sound in body and mind so he can."

"As do I," Eirik agreed. "Being whole of neither is rather vexing."

Lenae took his dark humor in stride. "Please," she said. "You are the only Seventh to have ever made it back from your Envoy alive. You must know some secret..."

"There's no secret to my survival," Eirik said, confused. "And I haven't done anything for Kiernan. He wasn't the one I was supposed to be helping, anyway."

"But you just said to let things develop as you crafted," Lenae pressed. "What do you mean?"

"Yes, well, I only had a small part in the crafting," Eirik laughed. "As all men are want to do."

"Well, if you haven't done anything more, then who has?" Lenae demanded, perhaps with more force than was called for. *Senile old fool...*

"Heatherwood," he explained with pride.

"Heather-who?" Now he was making absolutely no sense and his gryphling was dancing from foot to foot, beak gaping in a suspicious grin.

"My dryad," Eirik answered, enjoying this game.

"Is she the one who took your eyes?" Lenae asked, truly at a loss.

"Oh, no," he smiled, and it was the most genuine expression she had ever seen on him. "She is the one who opened them."

Lenae looked to the gryphling resting happily across Erik's knees and sighed. While she did not mind trading wits with anyone, this was not the time nor the place for games with Kiernan's life on the line. The gryphling just shrugged her wings and resettled, and Eirik let out a long breath.

"And my brother Shayan, I suppose," he said. "He's done quite a bit of crafting himself, but not in a woman's way."

"So will he assist me with Kiernan?" Lenae asked, pressing the obvious.

"Oh goodness no," Eirik chuckled, which made the gryphling dance and flap to keep her place. "He has enough to worry about at the moment training Hest'lre to take his place."

"And if I asked you to come to Court, just for the next fortnight, you would...?"

"Refuse," he said, apologetic. "I am sorry, love, but my appearance will only reinforce that another Seventh can be chosen."

That, at least, was a valid point. Hest'lre had said the same thing.

"Then how shall I protect him?" She said, hoping the senile Counsel Lord would take her opening and reveal whatever tricks he had lain out for Kiernan.

"I told you," he said, digging through the pockets of his robe. "I have already taken care of it."

Lenae did her best not to look cross, but as she grasped for another argument, Shayan came to her rescue from deeper within the suite.

"You're too late, you old fool," Shayan said to his brother as he worked to absorb water out of his long warcrest with a towel. As he did so, Lenae had to bring up a hand to hide from the physique of the shirtless, elder Counsel Lord. Despite being older than Eirik by five cycles and nearly twice her own age, Shayan looked as hard bodied as any of the Blackwings who had been set to guard Kiernan himself. "I told you what happened with Kiernan when I came in. Or have you already forgotten?"

"Blast!" Eirik exclaimed, only to remember himself. "Well, what happened? Where are they?"

"The fool lost his hawk—" Shayan began, finishing with his warcrest to realize Lenae's presence. As he bowed slightly, dropping the towel down to cover himself for propriety's sake, she finished for him.

"His hawkeye, I know," Lenae said. "That was another thing I wanted to ask you about."

"Well, this changes everything!" Eirik said. "Why didn't you say anything, youngling?"

"I was trying to," Lenae insisted.

"I bet I can find it if I try," Eirik said, closing his eyes, but his brother had a hand on his wing before he started.

"Please don't," Shayan insisted, breaking his concentration. "It's being handled."

"But Hest'lre and I looked everywhere," Lenae said, pulling out the silver spiral from a pocket in her cloak. "This is all we found."

"So they have taken it," Eirik swore as his brother inspected the jewelry. "Those meddling old birds!"

"They?" Lenae pressed. "Who would take it from him?"

"The ancestor Sevenths," Shayan answered. "They did it several times when Eirik came back."

"Damn, I thought he was leaving for Envoy," Eirik swore, slapping his chair. Unimpressed, the little gryphling moved to join Lenae once again. "I was certain of it."

"But he is," Lenae insisted as she gathered up the creature.

"Oh, good!" Eirik said, opening his eyes. The gryphling's stare went back and forth between her and Eirik as he thought. "Then she can still be persuaded. It can all still work out."

"She?" Lenae asked. "Is this what you meant? You know someone who I can send with him to Court?"

"My daughter," Eirik answered with a beam of pride. "I know she has plans for turning House Northern into an auxiliary Seventh's Library, but she is more duty-bound to the Seat than she thinks."

"But how do you know that?" Shayan insisted as Lenae gaped. Eirik had a daughter? "How can you be sure she will go along? With any of this? No one wants to be the Seventh Counsel Lord."

"You think I don't know that?" Eirik said, and his look was wicked. "This is why she has been wearing the Seventh's hawkeye since the day I gave one to her."

As Counsel Lord Shayan's eyes went wide, Lenae covered her open mouth with her hands. To put someone under a gaesh without their knowing... It was almost too terrible to think.

"And Kiernan?" Shayan asked, his voice hard as he stared at his brother. No, as he stared at his former Seventh and partner. "What has he been wearing?"

"The one meant for Vinicia," Eirik explained and had the audacity to laugh. "Why else do you think his Gift has grown so strong? I will admit he has become a bit more self-centered than I imagined, but if you're compelled to assist the Seventh Counsel Lord at his task and happen to also be that Seventh, you turn into a self-centered prick," he said, amused as he looked back to Lenae.

"I knew he had changed, but everyone kept telling me it was the Warhost in him. In my heart, I knew something was wrong. I knew that was not my Kier'n," she said, her quiet building into fury. "Eirik, what have you done?"

"Vinicia is already setting it right," he said. "She has given him her hawkeye, which by all accounts is his. When she retrieves the other one... If Counsel Lord Hewn's shade does not tell her," he said, and then looked back to his brother. "Then I will."

"Be my guest," Eirik said, raising his hands before him in surrender. "She will need her mother's hawkeye now if she means to leave the shelf. As I said before, things will work out as they should and Kiernan will have his escort through the Eihwaz as we have been planning."

"We?" Lenae repeated, curious even if she was still upset.

"My predecessors and I," Eirik explained with a wink. "We mean to pull one over on our warmongering Seat-Founder."

"But it will only work if Vinicia agrees to assist him," Shayan said, sighing. "Eirik, she almost killed him this morning. She is not just going to—" Shayan stopped short as he realized what he had just said and looked back to Lenae with an apology. "A figure of speech, of course," he insisted, remembering both her position and her entire reason for being here. "This morning he came upon us sparring in the armory and thought to help."

"However," Eirik said. "If she can best him at staves, she will be an even better escort for him in the Eihwaz. You see, Vinicia has studied the Seventh's lore all her life. I meant for her to be a knowledgeable companion, but Shayan refused to let her go into the woods without being able to defend herself the old-fashioned way," Eirik said, looking at Shayan with a beam of pride. "She will realize all of this soon. Honestly, she almost realized it with Hewn, which is why I forbade her from speaking with Kiernan. She needed to find strength and purpose in her own life before trying to help anyone else with theirs, especially someone who knew her before she came into her power. I did not mean to make the same mistake I made letting her work with Hewn and tie herself to his purpose. She has her own now and is stronger for it."

"But you know how stubborn she is," Shayan sighed. "For as often as Kiernan has demanded to have his way in all things, do you honestly think he will let you insist he take someone on what is meant to be his solitary Envoy? He will hate you for it as much as she will for making her fear even speaking with the man before this."

"They can hate me all they like! I haven't had a good row in ages," Eirik said, balling up his fists as if to fight.

"But they will not hate me," Lenae interjected, thinking aloud as her mind raced with the possibility.

For as long as Kiernan had followed her with an unwavering devotion, it had never occurred to her that Kiernan might thrive with a woman at his side. It had to be the right woman, of course, as Shayan was correct. Kiernan would never trust anyone new this close to his Envoy, but if this idea came from her...

"What was that, my dear?" Shayan asked and the attention of both men was suddenly on her.

"It has to come from me," Lenae said, this time with more certainty. "I came to speak with you this dawning because of the boon that is owed to the position of Consort by your family," she said, and then looked directly at her Ninth Counsel Lord. "Consider this the request for my boon. You will determine how I can create a Court of Consorts like Braeden has a High Counsel by tomorrow morning so that I can introduce it with the first Winter Court," she said, growing bolder as her confidence in this plan grew. "I shall make Vinicia Kiernan's consort and I have the day to figure out pairings for the rest."

"A Court of Consorts?" Shayan repeated, now watching her with as much trepidation as he used for his brother. "But what will that make you?" He asked as she stood to leave.

"High Consort," she said, though she honestly didn't care. "Can you do what I ask in that time?"

"Yes, I believe so," Shayan said, standing straighter as he started to think through what work was ahead of him.

"Whatever it is, you have my blessing," Eirik added and held out his hand to her. She took it and kissed his ancient knuckles in thanks. "As long as you get those two working together, I'll be happy."

"If I can do it this way, I have no doubt it will work," she said and turned back towards the door to the Armory. "But now I must return to the Royal Wing if I am going to see this through. Where should I send her missive when the time comes?"

"She has an office in the Soldier Tyros' Wing," Shayan said, but Lenae was watching Eirik as he closed his eyes. When he opened them again, he was grinning.

"She just got to her office," he said with confidence. "But she should be with him for a while yet.

Chapter 15: Vinicia

Friday, 0630

"Welcome to my office," Vinicia said, letting the Counsel Lord into the small room that was stuffed with reports, books, and miscellaneous bits of issued gear that tyros always seemed to lose. "I don't get many visitors, but this is all work for you or Aaron, so feel free to entertain yourself. I'll be back in a moment."

"So you really are going to woodwalk?" Kiernan asked, glancing around the room as she closed the door.

"I do it all the time," she said.

When all the man could do was watch, curious, Vinicia moved to stand beside him at the desk. As Kiernan's gaze lingered on her, she set her hand on the space that was clear of bookshelves in the back of her office.

"I'll be right back," she said.

Considering how unsettling her talk with Kiernan had been, Vinicia decided her first stop would be to step into her windowless room within the Great Tree itself before she braved the Library. This way, she could at least change out of her armor and gather her nerve before she had to ruin the rest of her morning. When she opened her eyes, the ball of glass she had suspended from the ceiling began to glow with power. Many cycles ago, Vinicia had trained the excess energy she radiated to pool in that one place, and that its final purpose was to give off the light she needed. With her unguarded presence, she was lucky the glass didn't shatter as she entered.

As the safety of her room settled her nerves, she stripped free of her armor and underclothes, dropping them in a pile near enough to her wardrobe that she would remember to clean them later. That done, she moved over to the small corner she had lined with ceramic tiles for a quick shower when she realized that, without her hawkeye, she could just…

Vinicia shivered as she pulled just enough water out of the air to get herself wet and then shook herself dry as she sent the water away. *Oh that is nice,* she laughed, growing light-headed as she gave herself the chance to indulge in her magic. Like a daughter craving sweet-cakes, she couldn't really stop at just one trick.

Clean now, Vinicia went to her wardrobe and found her favorite indigo-died silk shirt. That over her head, she tied the back and side pieces around her wings and started searching for her nicer pair of leather breeches and flight boots. Then she picked up the fitted wool doublet she had for the rare occasions she would leave the barracks, also died the soldier tyros' indigo. The only real difference was that the front of her doublet was one piece, which was more proper for a woman than the split-front man's version that could be opened from the neck to the waist. If she intended to stay in any sort of anonymity, she couldn't exactly cross-dress around courtiers.

When she finally had it all on, she exhaled in a rush to see herself. *I'm going to look like I'm in charge of something one of these days.*

::You are in charge of something,:: her ancestor chimed in, all love and affection now that Kiernan was away from her.

::I'm in charge of making sure nothing goes wrong from the shadows,:: Vinicia argued, pulling at the shirt so it would lie flat beneath the square neck of the doublet. ::That makes me responsible for everything, but in charge of nothing.::

::Behind every great man is a woman worth twice his weight in salt,:: her ancestor agreed, not that it made any sense.

::Whatever you say,:: Vinicia said and caught up the long silk ties that attached to the back panel of the doublet. Once those were threaded through the loops at her natural waist, she tightened it against her sides and wrapped the ties around again before knotting it behind her.

With the piece secure, she took a steadying breath, glancing to the side room in her little suite of apartments that she had kept dark despite her entrance. She wasn't alone in this place, but for all the quiet that was needed, she hadn't said a word aloud yet.

::How is she?:: Her ancestor asked, worry tinging the sending.

::Terrible,:: Vinicia sighed, raising a hand to alert the young Windover Dame that she was coming inside the room. Kaitlyn looked up from the book she had been reading beside the nest she watched over, her exhaustion showing clearly in the candlelight. The young woman in the nest looked even worse, pale olive skin gone grey and taught with pain, but she was alive.

"She stirred a little when you were gone," Kaitlyn whispered. "I think I may have dozed, but I found one of your books and the candle, so I'm okay now. I'll stay as long as you need me to stay, Mother."

"You have stayed through the worst of it," Vinicia assured her, amused to see the woman was halfway through the Lan'lieanan high seas adventure she had wanted to find for Kiernan. "And I have regained more strength than I believed. I can take you back to your suite now. I need you to send word if Micah can feel what has happened to her. Close as they are, I am not sure how he will react."

"Of course," Kaitlyn said, closing her book. "But if you need me, please..."

"I will ask," Vinicia assured her, coming into the room at last.

As Kaitlyn gathered her things, Vinicia stalled at the edge of the small nest, leaning over to place a gentle hand on the young woman's head to check for fever. New as the girl was inside Vinicia's own influence, she didn't have to make contact to check on her, but the touch seemed to soothe the pain from the woman's face. Brutally as she had been beaten, it made Rylan's wounds look like horse play.

The only reason Seraleia had survived was because Vinicia had Walked her out of that place; walked her from the Lower City and back to the Palace shelf while using the very last of her strength to do it. That was why she hadn't been able to heal Rylan as she should have. She had used all her strength saving this girl's life. If Kaitlyn hadn't been there to help her get the woman sorted, to bring them both food and water to make sure Sera survived that healing, no questions asked...

Kaitlyn was a goddess, and that was all there was to it. She had already suspected Vinicia was kindred and had taken all the terrible news in stride. After losing so much of her own family to war and worrying over the politics of her House, she knew how important it was to make sure Sera was taken care of. Sera was the one thing holding all three of her precious tyros together and if anything happened to her, the world would burn.

"When are you going to tell the boys?" Kaitlyn asked as she came to her feet.

"When I am sure she will survive," Vinicia sent back. "It is good that she is stirring, but she needs her rest. My strength in this place will heal her more than Westly's herbs ever could."

::You could be stronger,:: her ancestor added in the back of her mind. ::As much as I despise that Seventh, his power was good for you.::

::I thought you said I don't need a greenman,:: Vinicia returned, giving Kaitlyn a small smile as she moved to follow Vinicia out of the room.

::With you and the other kindred on the shelf, you need a greater source of power while your tyros are gone,:: her ancestor said, if begrudgingly. ::So use the Seventh if you must. Salt water heals all wounds; it only kills you if it is all you have to drink.::

Vinicia let out a slow breath as she waved for Kaitlyn to follow her towards the great mural of tree-knots that she had constructed on the wall of her room. Shortly after she had discovered that she could woodwalk through the Palace, she had taken it upon herself to gather a knot from each of the floors and arrange them here. That way, she could move through the Palace freely without ever getting in anyone's way. Her uncle Shayan obviously knew of her ability, though he was always wary of her using it. The thought of stepping out a wall with some unknown someone walking past to see her terrified him more than the act of woodwalking itself.

Kaitlyn, however, trusted her completely.

"The closest I can get you is the stairwell next to the Seventh's Library," she warned.

"That is near enough to my own suites," Kaitlyn assured her. "Mother, I can always watch over her at the Delton Estate if she needs more care. My family is moving after graduation, but we will have a place for her."

"I will keep it in mind," Vinicia said, giving a small smile despite the overwhelming gloom. "Thank you, Kaitlyn."

"Of course, Mother," she said, returning the smile.

"Be well," she said, extending her left hand as she set her right on the knot she would use to move Kaitlyn through the palace. Kaitlyn's smile never faltered as Vinicia gathered power around her, slipping the woman through the network of fae lines she had over the palace to deposit her a world away in the Sires' Wing.

That done, Vinicia took a slow breath and shifted her hand on the mural. Considering how long she had gone to and from the Library as a chick, the one she wanted now was the heart-piece to the mural that she had pried out of the Great Tree itself. As she stepped up to it, though, she had to steady her nerves. It had been an honest age since she had attempted to Walk fully inside the Library and for as much as the men would likely understand, it didn't make it any easier. They were all dead, but this was the first time she had known one of them while he had been alive.

With her intention set, Vinicia reached towards the center knot and felt a tendril of energy surge to meet her. As it connected, the wall in front of her flashed with white and melded into one enormous knot—much like the door to the library itself—except this one sat on hinges of light. There was a handle as well, a circle of thick ivy growing from the center of the knot-door-thing and her will to move was transferred into an urge to open the door.

::Ancestor?:: Vinicia called, realizing her hands were shaking as she lost the will to move forward.

::Yes, love?::

::I don't want to do this,:: she said, hesitating. ::I don't want to see him again. I am the reason he died. If I had just been public with who I was, what I could do...::

::Things would have played out very differently,:: the ancestor replied.

::He could have lived?:: Vinicia said, wanting it to be the truth so much that it hurt.

::No, you would have died with him,:: her ancestor corrected and the gentleness of the words was almost worse than her own fear. ::You are lucky you have this hearth tree to stand in for all your strength, but if you had used it to save him, you would not have survived. You know that.::

Vinicia's eyes were burning to feel the love emanating through the bond between them. It would be the same with Hewn, she knew. All ancestors and shades could touch the living world that much, but the Ancestor Sevenths still bore the wounds that had sent them across the veil.

Hewn would still have his and worse than the others. His spirit had been so strong before he had died and he just...

Gathering her courage, Vinicia pressed on the door to open it and stood in wonder as she looked into the vast, empty darkness. She forced herself to cross the threshold and swore as several glass globes very much like the one in her own room came alight with her presence.

::Beloved, it will be all right,:: her ancestor said, giving her strength to move into the abandoned library.

::Seven cycles,:: Vinicia sent back, covering her eyes with a hand. ::Seven cycles I have put this off. I don't want to do this.::

As her ancestor sent a pulse of love to guide her steps, Vinicia looked back through the open doorway. ::The fact that you do shows how much you Honor his memory,:: the spirit sent. ::The fact that you still serve the Seat brings him Glory as well. He knows that as well as I do.::

::Honor and Glory,:: Vinicia sighed, scrubbing the tears from her eyes as she tried to find strength in the words. ::Gods, but I do not have to like it.::

::No, you do not,:: her ancestor agreed. ::But I will be with you either way. Have courage, love, and the things you fear can never control you.::

Feeling the presence fade, Vinicia let out a long, slow sigh as she refocused her attention, only to frown at something drifting in the air in front of her. She held still to see what it was and then winced when she saw the entire floor of the Library was covered in dust.

Seven cycles of neglect, she realized as the dust swirled around her in the stale air. Vinicia steeled herself and took a knee within the soft, shifting substance so she could put her hand on the ancient earthen floor. Closing her eyes, she let her senses expand with the touch, tracing along the lines of the Library in her mind to see if anything had shifted since she had last been here. Other than a few items on the very top floor that Kiernan had moved, the rest was just as she and Hewn had left it.

When she was certain what parts of it were only dust, Vinicia flexed her hands against the floor and reached with her mind to the energy of the Kir below the Palace in its hidden tunnels. With the rush of it in her ears, she scooped up a handful of the dust and then pressed her hands together with a technique she credited to young Westly. Unlike his growth, however, Vinicia separated the combined elements back into their component parts and send what remained down through the earth to be carried away by the Kir itself.

When she opened her eyes, all the dust was gone, and she felt as if she had done some of the penance she deserved for letting the place get so out of sorts.

"Vinicia!" The surrounding stacks greeted. "Brothers, she has returned!"

Vinicia did her best to remain neutral as she blinked into her secondsight so she could see the shades taking form around her. After a moment, the air was electric with the presence of the ancestors and then one of them finally appeared in a bright shimmer of silver-blue.

"I was wondering how long it would take for you to return," Counsel Lord Weylan greeted, still as short and stalky as he had been in life. Weylan had been her father's immediate predecessor and the one who had made it possible for her to remain at the Palace with the previous Consort. To that end, Weylan and one of his predecessors, Counsel Lord Broc, were the closest thing she had ever known to grandsires.

"Was there a pool going?" Vinicia asked, trying to find humor in his excitement.

"We have little to wager with, sapling," Weylan chuckled, looking back to the door. "However, you picked a good time to come by. The past day Noventrio has been hand-holding the young Seventh, though now he is distracted by seeing just how far he can get himself from the Library."

"You mean he couldn't leave before?" She asked, confused. "I saw him in Father's suite plenty of times."

"Not in corporeal form," Weylan added, though the whole topic didn't seem to interest him. "We've never seen the Dragon so animated, to be honest. Not even the elder Sevenths remember him like this."

Outside of the Library, 'The Dragon' was what the world called the living Seventh considering all the heraldry he wore that showed the creatures, but inside the Library it only referred to the Delton shelf Founder Noventrio. If she never saw that ancestor again, it would be a cycle too soon. He had been furious at her father when he had returned alive, not only because he had returned, but because he meant to sully the Library with her presence. Thus, the fight over the hawkeye.

"So if Noventrio is gone, who stole the hawkeye?" Vinicia insisted. "They must have known that I would get involved."

"Oh, well," Weylan said, suddenly wary. "Hewn is the one who took it. "He is waiting for you in the canopy," he added, making a soft gesture towards the barren branches of the Great Tree.

"I'll meet you up there," Vinicia said, watching as the shade vanished back into the dim.

Resolved to not become overly emotional, Vinicia stepped towards the tree and closed the strange door. It vanished when it was flush with the tree once again, and all that remained was a small knot of wood where the door handle had been.

That done, Vinicia set her hand just to the side of the knot and willed herself into the ancient energy of the tree. When she opened her eyes again, she was standing in the small alcove that she had loved to nap in as a fledgling. Surprisingly, the silken leaves she had crafted were still here, if lifeless from the lack of wind.

To say she was expected was an understatement. As she moved towards the work area she used to share with Hewn, the energy in the Library began to hum with the presence of the silver-blue shades. They were all men of forty to fifty cycles, standing pressed together as if they were waiting for a bard's performance at the height of a midsummer's fair. Unlike the excitement for a bard, though, the faces staring back at her were a mix of anger and irritation. The disapproving vanished after a few moments, but not before murmuring their disgust.

"Mortals," one of them added, sighing tragically as he appeared next to her. "They never write, they never come calling..."

The ancestor crossed his arms, scowling as best he could, and Vinicia recognized him as Counsel Lord Broc. Broc was the first ancestor who had taken a liking to her when she was a fledgling, and he had been her closest ally before Hewn had been chosen. Broc would always tell her where her father had hidden the texts he thought she shouldn't be reading, not that it changed Broc's betrayal in the end. Broc had been the one who had kept her from Hewn until it was too late to do anything, even with her power, to save his life.

"Sal'weh, Broc," she greeted, watching as his shade radiated pleasure despite his attempt at the opposite. Even in death, the man's soft features were not ones to hold anger long.

"It is so good to see you, my love," Broc said, all anger vanishing. "Your presence has been missed."

"I speak to more ancestors than you Sevenths," Vinicia said, as if to admonish him. "With their help, I have done well enough."

"And yet you have left this place to ruin," Broc said, his irritation returning. "Just like your father and the fledgling he put in charge of our War."

"I am here now," she said. "And I suspect you know why Kiernan is not."

Knowing her true purpose, many of the shades who had been watching the spectacle shimmered and faded until it was only Weylan and Broc before her. As the silence stretched out, Vinicia thought they might refuse her request for the stone until a new voice rose to join them.

"I will take it from here," Counsel Lord Hewn said softly.

As the two elder shades faded out, in their place stood the image of Hewn su'Greying, just as tall and quietly handsome as the day he had crossed the veil. Unlike the other shades, Hewn's youth better preserved his memory in the Library, and that fact showed in the heavy opacity of his spirit. It also preserved the memory of his murder and the sight of the blood at his neck nearly broke her.

"It is good to see you, Vinicia," Hewn said as grief closed in around her.

For all the things she had agonized about telling him for so long, all she could manage was a small nod.

"I had a good reason for taking this," he went on as he looked to the hawkeye that warped the image of his hands. Incorporeal or not, the Sevenths always seemed to be able to touch the stone that controlled so much of their lives.

"Oh?" She managed and shamed herself as the tears she had been fighting gave way with the word.

"This stone is actually yours," Hewn said, looking back up to her. "From your mother, I mean. I know now that Eirik gave me the one meant for you when I began my term, trying to help me be a stronger Seventh. My empathic gift was never very strong, so I never noticed, but when it was passed to Kiernan..." He said, hesitating. "We have all seen what it did to his potential. By the time I realized how much it was allowing Noventrio to corrupt his spirit, I could not reach you."

Vinicia wasn't sure what to think. She hadn't even known her mother had sent her back with a hawkeye until she had started to come into her power and that was while Hewn was alive. "What do you mean, corrupt his spirit?"

"When he was given this stone, he should have gained skill with the Seventh's Gift, but that isn't what happened," Hewn said, rolling the ancient stone in his hands with regret. "Instead, Kiernan became a channel for Noventrio's wrath on the War Plains. He doesn't have the bloodline to allow him to be the Founder's avatar, but he has been warped by that power all the same. He is a true sorcerer now and stronger than even Eirik was before him, and your father was trained by dryads."

Vinicia needed no explanation of the man's strength of Gift after the morning she had been through. Even if he had no idea how to use the power overwhelming his spirit, she certainly did. Even if she was only a kindred dryad, her very nature made her want to seek out that kind of power and put it to purpose. To find it in one person, though, was still incredible. If the Seventh's Founder had been using him for the past seven cycles, it was no wonder his mind had collapsed into the rage of the Warhost after losing the hawkeye. That would have been the only shield he had ever been given against it.

Hewn sighed, as unsettled as she was. "In raw talent alone, Kiernan may be as strong as the last Seventh who was a true sorcerer among us, and that man was an avatar," he said, offering her the stone at last.

"An avatar?" Vinicia asked, her hands shaking as she took it.

"A man born of the Great House of the Northern Lights," he said. "He was apparently strong enough to keep from being drawn back into the Library when he died, like the rest of us, which is why so few know of him," Hewn explained. "So if you ever wondered why House Northern lost favor with their Founder..."

Vinicia couldn't help it. Her jaw went a little slack just to think of the implications. Just how jealous was Founder Noventrio to doom a House to spite one descendant?

"So, you will understand when I say that Noventrio was furious with me for taking Kiernan's stone after he threw it away," Hewn said, exhaling. "But only because he had to manage the monster he had created instead of focusing his attention on bringing the Counselheir to our line. To be honest, I do not think even the Founder knew the stones were switched or that Kiernan's strength grew as a result. Noventrio does not know quite a few things as it turns out, thanks to the last few of us."

"Is there truly a difference between them?" She asked. "My stone and the Sevenths? I thought they were just void-stones to sink power."

"The one meant for the Seventh compels the wearer to work towards an end to the War, no matter the cost," Hewn said. "I believe Eirik meant for you to wear that one on purpose. He meant for you to be of service to me and other Sevenths as they passed through this place."

"I would not need a compulsion for that," Vinicia said, surprised. "I would have helped you, regardless."

Now it was Hewn's turn at hollow amusement. "Me, yes, but what of my Counselheir?" He said, and Vinicia scowled when she realized he meant Kiernan.

That might have taken a compulsion, she knew.

"But what of yours on me?" She asked, looking to the stone in her hand as she tried to change the subject.

"I think Eirik gave you the Seventh's stone to keep you safe," he answered. "Under its greater shielding, you have not had to take in nearly as much power as a kindred half your age. You must know that, for all you work with young Westly."

"I know I have done well enough," she said and reached out with her awareness as the new hawkeye settled over her senses. "But if Kiernan has become a sorcerer, what will happen when he is under stronger shields?"

"Honestly?" Hewn laughed. "I hope he will stop being a self-centered prick. He is all cunning and guile now, without the empathy to know when what he asks of his men is too much. Or he was until he threw away the stone. I must say, the past day has been agonizing for him, realizing all he has done."

"You will forgive me if I don't pity him," Vinicia said, glad to know that Hewn could also see just how much of a wretch Kiernan was.

"But it is not all on him, Vinicia," Hewn said, reigning in his annoyance. "You know as well as I do that he inherited a Warhost in chaos. I am only glad that Eirik could set him in the Seat at all, as I intended."

Vinicia didn't bother to hide her surprise. "You actually meant him to be your Counselheir?"

"He was the first I considered," Hewn said with a touch of pride. "I realized his bardic talent before the fall of Kirath, but the way he rallied the Warhost during that fight was truly courageous. He is a good man in his heart, both intelligent and compassionate."

"I have yet to see any of that," she scoffed. "He has been nothing but a terror to the fledglings I guard."

"Vinicia, please remember yourself," Hewn said, matching her easy anger with disapproval. "I know you are fond of throwing your weight around, but Kiernan was one of my cadre before he was a Counsel Lord. It wounds me to know that you have been so at odds with a man you valued as a friend during your time as a tyro. A man you worked with, even in your obfuscation. I had hoped that in speaking with him again that you of all people would have some compassion for what happened to him. You alone can know what it is he is facing and the terror that holds. He deserves your respect for the Seat, if not your admiration for surviving the torture Noventrio has put him through these last seven cycles."

As the weight of his admonishment settled over her, Vinicia flushed with shame. Here Hewn was speaking about the man he meant to be his Counselheir for true, and she had dismissed even the idea without a second thought. It was a direct dishonor to Hewn to take nothing he said with the weight it deserved, and she hated herself for acting a fledgling. This man had been her first true, living friend despite her sheltered life and he still meant the world to her.

When she looked up again, she was humbled. "Hewn, I am sorry," she managed, swallowing her pride as he watched. "Knowing you meant him for the Seat does mean a great deal to me. When I see him next, I will greet him with the respect he deserves as your heir and as a Seventh in the face of his Envoy. I give you my word I will help him in whatever way I can."

"You cannot know what joy that brings me," Hewn said and as his smile returned, she breathed a little easier. She did not mean to gather the courage to return to this place, only to insult the man she loved most within its walls. If Hewn had seen something in Kiernan, then something was there. She might have to dig around to find it, but she would. She owed Hewn that much.

In the awkward silence that followed, Vinicia looked to the hawkeye in her hands, turning it over as she searched for the shield the void-stone could generate. For as wingbound as the other stone has kept her, swallowing up any excess power back into itself, this one felt like having no limits at all. Just the thought of having to find enough power to fill that space and manage what had been so simple before was beyond disheartening. If her tyros had been in session she might have been able to manage it, but the only reason she had felt up to doing any of this today was because of Kiernan himself. After all he had been through this morning, she couldn't exactly ask him to let her consume more of his soul just so she could hide her hair and eyes.

Sighing to herself, Vinicia looked up to the door at the formal entrance of the Library, knowing she had to return.

"Before you go," Hewn said, having left her to her thoughts. "There is another matter we must speak on."

Vinicia looked back to him and was surprised to find his palm extended to her with a third piece of hawkeye. Unlike her own or Kiernan's, this one was suspended from a hempen cord and tiny net that looked as if it had grown over the stone. She took it by the cord, wary of the strange resonance it gave off.

"This one was brought up by a tuuka last dawning," he said, confused himself. "Or what was once a tuuka? I am sorry to report that the little tree squirrel perished after making the delivery."

"A what?" Vinicia asked, confused.

"A tuuka," Hewn repeated. "It's a woodland creature out of the Northern Eihwaz. Broc was the one that found it, so perhaps..."

Hearing his name, the elder Counsel Lord materialized at Hewn's left, curious despite himself.

"A tuuka is a rodent that lives in the hearth trees of dryads in the Northern Conclave," he explained. "They're a bit like pets, but they will steal anything small and round that you do not have secured in your things. They are especially fond of hawkeyes, which is why we know of them," he finished, frowning at her. "I thought you had read the Travel Journals."

"Twenty cycles ago, maybe," she admitted. "My first time through, I just wanted to know more about my mother."

"Well, the tuuka are messengers from dryads in Kelsineah," Broc added. "So there is that. The only message this one had for me was to say 'for the leaf blown west of the Kir' before it fell from the tower. I was able to bring the hawkeye through the crystal, but I have no idea what the message meant."

"Leaf blown west of the Kir?" She repeated, thinking aloud. "Could that mean West Leaf? Or Westly?" Vinicia asked, knowing a small measure of the dryad naming convention. Westly wasn't exactly a Kosaran name, but if that was the case, then any dryad-kin born on the Ehkeski plains could have been named Westly since most came out of the woods by way of Kelsineah. Truthfully, most died after a few moonturns, so the name itself was still rare.

She was different only because she had been raised on the east side of the Kir, so her name reflected her father's purpose and not the location of her birth. Vinicia was 'venture to the sea' or close enough. To her knowledge, she was the first of her namesake.

"Perhaps," Broc shrugged. "I assume this was sent here for the same reason your mother gave yours to Eirik. If your protégé has come into his power, he may need this as you did."

"You know about him?" Vinicia asked, surprised.

"We know everything having to do with energy moving on the Delton shelf," Broc explained, shrugging. His part over, Vinicia watched him begin to shimmer and fade as he turned to stroll further into the Library.

"Westly hasn't come into his full power," Hewn went on. "Or at least, he has come into his power about as much as you ever came into yours."

"Huh?" Vinicia said, only to realize Hewn was attempting to sidestep a subject she might not want to discuss. The caution was warranted, given the chaos that she had gone through when she had first tried. Touching a person's spirit was an intense emotional experience. Most kindred had that first moment as part of an intimate physical experience as well, though she most definitely hadn't. Hewn had been decades older than her, but even the idea of having a friend—a real, living friend she could touch—had been incredibly intimate for someone so sheltered.

"So Westly has met someone," Vinicia said, forcing them past the awkwardness. "And is raising enough power to scare himself?"

"Yes," Hewn confirmed. "And as he has deep roots in several people, he is not letting it disperse. Therein lies the problem, since he has not held on to so much power before this. Instead, he has always grounded that energy, but his garden can only handle so much. That excess has to go somewhere."

"Or into someone," Vinicia realized aloud. "Oh, Gods."

Folding her hand around the stone, Vinicia knew why Westly would be so desperate to hold it back. Just like Vinicia had reached into Kiernan to heal him, Westly had done the same thing to his crew-mates on multiple occasions. But where she used the energy left in the barracks, Westly only had the garden. If Westly came into his power as much as she had, the excess pushed into his two crew-brothers would manifest as wild magic. It would most certainly explain Rylan's impulsive anxiety and Micah's incredible strength as a warbard.

Hewn could read the worry across her face. "The stone will help," he assured her. "It will pull the excess off of him and from those who he has unwittingly used to slow his strength."

"How long have you known this was happening?" Vinicia asked.

"We've only known these past few candlemarks," he assured her. "Someone is fueling him and he is resisting, but he is running out of options. He knows not to set excess inside of a windwalker, but there is no telling how much he can hold without it slipping out of his control. If you could deliver this to him…"

"Of course," Vinicia said, though from the look he was giving her, it seemed like he was considering something. "Was there anything else?"

"There is one more thing," he admitted, shifting uneasily. "As far as we know, full dryads cannot live as close to one another as you and Westly do now. Though you are both kindred, you have also survived longer than most other kin we have heard tales of in Kosar. The problem we fear now is that, well..."

Vinicia didn't like the look in his eyes as he watched her, weighing whatever words he meant to use against her capacity to handle them.

"While it is true you were set up in this space long before the boy arrived, he is far stronger than you have allowed yourself to become," he said, holding a hand up to stall her objection. "That is to say, he has accepted that he must move energy through himself to balance his power, where you have all but refused to do the same. Because of that, if and when he does take on this partner, the energy they raise may serve to sever you from the fragile roots you have on this shelf."

Vinicia stared back at Hewn in utter disbelief.

"Vinicia," Hewn began again, as gentle as he could manage. "Love, even when I was alive you only ever took in enough to survive," he went on, raising a hand as if to touch her cheek. "Every cycle you collapse into this wasting sickness when your tyros leave the shelf, and it brings you closer to joining us here than you know. For all the power you could hold, for all the power you have refused for so long, when Westly's strength grows beyond what his Garden and his stone can handle..."

I will have nothing, she realized, pulling back from his hand as the truth of what he suggested settled over her. *I will have nothing because I have claimed nothing, because I am nothing.*

And then she remembered.

"The House Northern Estate is on the lower shelf," she said, her heart racing with relief. "Once the title is taken, I can move from this shelf and try from that place. This hawkeye will let me hold much more than I could before. Perhaps under this I can remain hidden still—"

"No sanctuary is ever guaranteed, Vinicia," Hewn said, speaking over her as she tried to calm her panic. "And even if you do gain it, what if you are too late? What happens if he accepts this partner and comes into his power fully before you can leave?"

"Then I... I..." She said, groping for an answer even when she knew she didn't have one. "Gods, I don't know."

"Then I beg of you, Vinicia. Please do not fight this stone," he said, holding his hands out for peace. "Find the edge of whatever shield it creates for you and fill yourself with the life that thrives all around you. Fill yourself to bursting however you can and live."

Terrified, it was all Vinicia could do to nod. She would have to, wouldn't she? Somehow?

"In the meanwhile," he went on. "Give Westly his own hawkeye and slow his progress. Spend time with Kiernan and help him to leave on his Envoy. The man needs a friend right now more than anyone in this place, save perhaps yourself."

Vinicia forced herself to take a few deep, calming breaths.

"I can do that," she agreed. "I can do all of that."

"Of course you can," Hewn said. "And for all you may be in a panic now, I am glad for the chance to speak again. I had hoped to not have to force it, but—"

"But I am a coward," she said, cutting him off as her insides flailed with panic. "I just—"

"A coward would have let my Counselheir die, Vinicia," Hewn said, stalling her protest. "You have lived with courage every moment you have spent in these mountains, even if it was in the shadow of the Sevenths," he went on, and she shivered to feel the chill of his shade against her cheek as he reached for her again. "Believe in yourself, Vinicia. You deserve to live, and for as long as you can manage."

"I will live long enough for both of us," she assured him, her voice shaking to sense the love he offered with that look. Vinicia wasn't sure whether shades could weep as the living did, but the look on Hewn's face would have broken her heart if she hadn't known it for hope.

"For Honor and Glory, beloved," he said, watching her own tears finally slip down her cheek. "I will always be here for you if you have need of me."

"I know," she managed, closing her eyes as he began to shimmer and fade.

Steeling herself, Vinicia took three slow breaths before opening her eyes and finding herself very much alone. Her heart still fluttering through panic and sorrow, she started towards the Great Tree once again, trying not to flee. It was one thing to hold on to one hawkeye that wouldn't restrict her power, but Westly's stone a massive weight against her spirit. It also seemed to have a dissonance with her own, which was making her light-headed.

Somehow, she managed the short flight to the bottom level of the Library and reentered her rooms, allowing the portal she had made to close behind her. As the knot work on the wall reappeared, Vinicia took another steadying breath and then reached for the knot that would take her back to Kiernan and her office. Hopefully, he was still there.

As she rematerialized, she was impressed to see the man only glance up from the cup of caffea he lingered over. There were plates on a tray from the morning meal and a second covered tray as well, clearly meant for her. It was a surprising courtesy after ten cycles of eating alone.

"Last night, Hest'lre told me I needed to review the commissioning packets for the tyros, but I got distracted. Then I saw these on your desk," he said, lifting the papers from his lap. "This is the raw information Aaron uses to make his final recommendations, I take it?"

Vinicia swallowed around the knot in her throat. Hewn had meant this man to be his Counselheir, and he was reading her reports as Hewn once had. Reports she had given to Aaron, sure, but Aaron had always made his own additions. As she watched Kiernan sip his caffea, she knew he held her entire life in his hands. Her entire world, for all that had ever been allowed to her, and as much as she hated it, her ego was on a knife's edge to know what he thought. To know what Hewn's Counselheir had thought of her work—of her—and she just...

"I remember getting these briefings from Hewn when I was a member of his cadre after the Fall," Kiernan said into her silence. "The observations always got to the heart of a new officer's ability to command, not just their ability to be taught how to excel. This is what we all used on the War Plains to further their assignments—what I wanted to use as Seventh—but no one ever knew who Hewn got them from. It was you this entire time, wasn't it?"

Vinicia's heart was thundering in her chest as she remembered to breathe. She hated how much she suddenly craved this man's approval. How much she needed it and had grieved the loss of it with Hewn. How much he could likely see it in her eyes and in the white-knuckled grip she had on the thin back of the chair at her desk...

"Yes," she said, ducking her head as he attempted to smile at her. "Lord Fourth gave my reports to Aaron after Hewn was slain. I could always tell if a tyro was going to be an exceptionally gifted warbard because of what I am. I was told Aaron incorporated the information into his own reports, but I never saw the final product."

"Nothing Aaron gave me was ever this good," Kiernan said, clearly impressed.

"You Honor me with the complement," she said, forcing herself to release the chair so she could sit. As she did so, the stones she had almost forgotten clacked in her hands and she sucked in a breath in surprise. She had thought just holding the second one was making her light-headed, but now that she was in the room with three of the stones—now that she was in the room with his radiant presence of purpose—she wasn't sure how she was on her feet.

"I take it you found..." Kiernan began, only to hesitate as she set the two stones before her on the desk as she took a seat. "You found two of them?"

She nodded, even if it sent the world into vertigo.

"Why two?" He prompted, eyeing the hawkeye with the hempen cord.

"Hewn said..." She began, only to have to clear her throat. "He said the stone you are wearing now, the one I have been wearing, that was actually the Seventh's stone. The one you have been wearing was the one my mother meant for me."

"Excuse me?" Kiernan said, surprised.

"My hawkeye allows for a person to wield much stronger magic beneath it," she explained. "But when Hewn took up my seat with such a weak empathic Gift and I was struggling to contain my own, my father switched them. He only meant to protect me as I came into my power, but it did nothing for Hewn. When you were given my hawkeye and have a truly powerful Gift to start... Well..."

"He wasn't about to stop me from using that kind of advantage at War," Kiernan said, nodding. "I can't say I blame him. I have done some incredible things with a Gift so strong."

"It is worse than that," Vinicia hesitated to say. "By this point, you know there is a gaesh, a sort of compulsion set on the Seventh's hawkeye to work towards an end to the War, but the one that is on mine compels the person wearing it to serve the Seventh's Seat."

Kiernan frowned as she waited for him to grasp what that would mean. "It was meant to make you help us?" he said, confused.

"Correct," Vinicia confirmed. "But if you *are* the working Seventh, that means you have been compelled to serve yourself and your own goals, without compromise."

"With a strength of Gift no man in living memory has seen," he said as the realization struck.

"War can change a man, but I hated the monster it created of you," she said, watching him go pale with the knowledge. "You were exactly what the Host needed after Kirath, however," she allowed. "For all that happened, they needed that strength."

"Yes, but I did not need to bludgeon the world with it," he said, a hand covering his mouth as he looked back down to the stack of papers he had been reading.

Vinicia took a steadying breath, only to have her mouth water as she remembered the food on her desk. Seeing her hesitation, he gestured to the covered platter.

"I didn't bring it to taunt you," he said. "Please."

Vinicia chewed her lip, caught between the hunger in her belly and the ease she felt just existing in the room with him. She was ravenous for both, dangerous as that was. Setting both her shields and the cover for the meal aside, she pulled it in front of her to eat. When she finished a few moments later, she looked up to find Kiernan trying to hide how he had been watching her.

"What?" She asked, taking a breath as he poured her a cup of caffea from the glass carafe.

"You eat like a tyro," he said, even if his smile was fleeting.

"I do not have the luxury of time to enjoy a meal," she said, closing the tray and stacking it on top of his to clear the space. Seeing him still enjoying his caffea, she took up the cup he had poured for her, forcing herself to slow down, if only a little.

"I have nothing but time at the moment," Kiernan said, picking up the tyro reports he had been reading before. "Not until this is done."

"Two days and a wake up," she said, risking a smile as he looked back at her.

"Do they still say that?" He asked, amused. "Gods, but I always counted sleeps. How many more nights did I have to manage until I could be gone? Until I was one step closer to coming home."

"Until you made this place your home," Vinicia said, looking to the pauldron he wore. "Well, until my father did."

"I can't say I ever wanted to be a Counsel Lord," Kiernan said, looking up from the page he held. "But the moment your father offered me the Seat, I knew I would take it. If Lenae meant to take her fate in her own hands, then I would take mine as well and make a world where we could be together."

"You might not have meant to be a Seventh," Vinicia said, considering him. "But did you know Hewn meant for you to be his Counselheir?"

"I can't say that I did," Kiernan said, though it was clear he was honored with the knowledge. "Even after all Eirik told me, I still thought it was done for Lenae."

"It did appear that way," Vinicia said. "I was rather angry at Father for choosing you as well, if only because it meant my own time helping the Sevenths was done. For all I have been able to obfuscate my presence in the barracks, you knew me within a few moments of meeting me. Knew who I really was, I mean."

"Kehvin," Kiernan said, smiling with the name. "I still can't believe it, even if I see it in every part of you now. I always thought he was, well *you* were, a little standoffish and shy. Those things are more common with chiurgeons, but as Lord Sixth, Shayan had such a powerful personality and it didn't make sense that you were so reserved. Most of the other tyros didn't say anything, but I always thought you were hiding something."

"And now you know you were right," she said, finishing the last of her caffea. "I suppose that means my father was also right to tell me to stay far from you. Lenae has become rather jealous, I hear."

"Focused is perhaps the better word," Kiernan said, looking into what remained of his own cup. "She wants me to remain focused on the War so that we can both be free of it. Whenever I let myself become distracted, things do not go well."

"Distracted?" She asked, confused. "You're one of the most dedicated Sevenths I have ever seen, if only by reputation."

Kiernan chewed his lip before answering, which was a significant tell as his thoughts turned inwards. "Did you hear about the Val'Kyr woman I brought up from the Plains?" He asked. "The one I keep in the High Cells?"

When Vinicia's eyes narrowed in confusion, he exhaled a laugh. "You would have, if you had been working for me. Gods, maybe she would have even spoken to you if I had been able to use you as a resource. She was a rabid loralae when we met, though she seems to have calmed down without her focus stone. A little like myself, if I'm honest," he said, looking to the hawkeye around his neck.

"What does this have to do with Lenae?" Vinicia asked, confused.

"Lenae thought the woman was a distraction," he explained, shifting so he could split the last of the caffea between their cups. "She has wanted me to hand the woman over to Lord Fifth ever since she was brought to Delton, but I had thought it would be a way to understand Lan'lieanan women better. If I could talk with her, perhaps I could talk with all of them."

"I take it the effort did not go well?" She asked.

"It has angered Lenae well enough that I had to make peace with her instead," he said, exhaling a weary laugh. "But once I leave, the Loralae will be handed over to Roder's Blackwings and that will be the end of it."

"But not the end of everything," Vinicia said, eyeing him. "Speaking of leaving, who is it you mean to name as your Counselheir?"

Kiernan's eyes cut towards her with surprise. If he hadn't told the world of it, fine, but she would be one of the few in a position to help whoever he would name. When his hesitation lasted longer than she thought was reasonable, she asked again.

"Kiernan," she pressed, using the voice she had perfected on her often-petulant tyros. "Who are you naming as your Counselheir?"

"I have only told the Counsel Lords who I mean to name as my Heir," he said, shifting under her intense focus.

When Vinicia's hard look didn't waver, Kiernan's resolve did. All he did was hand her the report that he had been staring at as she ate. "You wrote the recommendation, Mother," he said quietly.

Vinicia felt her blood running cold as she read the name at the top of the report. "Rylan?" She asked. "You mean to name Tyro Rylan as your Counselheir?" Kiernan didn't even flinch as she recoiled from him.

"Are you out of your mind?" She demanded, refusing to take the report.

"Hewn was the one who told me of him," Kiernan explained, as if that would help calm her sudden anger. "And Noventrio told Hewn of the boy when he first tested to enter the Academy."

"He was meant to be a Seventh, sure, but not as a fledgling," Vinicia balked. "Let him come to know the Host; come to understand it. Let him serve because he wants to find peace, not because he has no other option."

"As it stands, Kosar has no other option," Kiernan countered. "And Rylan does not need to go to the War Plains to know he hates it. He knows our histories and his own, has watched his House fall into ruin and still—" he said, cutting himself off as realization dawned in him. "You are the one who is supporting him in this bid for the Estate, aren't you? You put the idea into his head that if he served, he could rebuild his House."

Vinicia was shameless. "It is the only reason he has to graduate," she said. "The War holds nothing for him, Kiernan, and he will not send anyone to fight it. There is no honor in that kind of glory, which is why—" Vinicia said, though as she spoke the words, Kiernan looked up with such agreement that the rest of her screed caught in her throat.

Was that exactly what the man had intended?

"There shouldn't be, after the life he has led," Kiernan said. "That life made him into the man Kosar will need as a Seventh when the war is over. When the fighting will be within our own borders, someone will have to care about what it means to value hearth, home, and family above all else. When the end of the War with Lan'lieana tears us apart, he will know how to rebuild. He has done it before and he will do it again. I may give my life for peace, but I refuse to leave Kosar in the hands of another warmonger. Instead I will leave it in the hands of a man I think has the strength to surpass me. Rylan is a man of his own honor and he will make his own glory in time. He may be the last son of the Great House of the Northern Lights, but he will be the first in a new line of Sevenths."

It was a vaulted argument, meant to sacrifice Rylan's innocence for the greater good, and she hated it because of how it might break her precious tyro. Kiernan's plan would make him either rise to the challenge or die trying, but it was a choice every Seventh had to face: whose life they would ruin next? Who could they count on to pick up where they had left off? Who would they sacrifice for the mission they themselves would die trying to complete?

"He is not the only man with his own sense of honor," Vinicia said, though the words were soft in the heavy silence between them. Kiernan looked up at that, more than a little flushed to realize she did, in fact, understand.

"Have you chosen his Sixth as well?" Vinicia asked, cautious with the question. "Rylan is uncommonly stubborn for a Delton officer."

"Everyone I know comes out of House blicing Windover," Kiernan said, his free hand pressing back the long length of his warcrest in a rare show of stress. "Kreychi may hate me for it, but I believe Tyro Tyrsten will work well in the position. Rylan has already selected him as part of his cadre for the war game, and if they win, they may prove themselves before they are named."

"Tyrsten?" Vinicia repeated, confused. "Kiernan, if you name anyone as Sixth it would have to be Micah. Rylan wouldn't trust anyone else as far as he could throw them, even if he was on his tyro squad."

"It can't be Micah," Kiernan said, looking up with a grim certainty. "Once that boy gets out into the sun on the Plains it will be far too obvious. Vinicia, he has to be warborn. His height, his hair... That is what Lan'lieanan men look like. Hest'lre had a hard enough time as Sixth and he is only half-Ehkeski. I think my men would hunt me through the Eihwaz if I even thought about naming a man with a Lan'lieanan parent to a Counsel Lord's Seat."

"And you think they won't after you pull this stunt?" Vinicia asked, having to trust Kiernan's guess. She had never seen a Lan'lieanan herself, man or woman. "Why did you let Micah into the Delton program at all if you thought he was warborn?"

"Because of Rylan," Kiernan said. "Rylan cleared the tyro trials before House Northern fell, but once he was cast out of the House, he wasn't allowed in. When I looked into the reason, I realized there had been a rumor of his having a talent for fire-starting. Since Noventrio needs a Seventh to have the spark of sorcery to become a Counsel Lord, when he showed up to request a boon from the Palace, Micah was the least of my problems. It was Westly they refused, and I had to force the chiurgeons to take on a dryad-kin just so I could have Rylan."

"Two cycles you have known this," Vinicia said, realizing it as she looked to the report on Rylan sitting between them on her desk. "You said Noventrio wanted him as well?"

"He was the one who told Hewn," Kiernan acknowledged. "Something about the boy being strong enough to be an avatar for the Founder's power. If that is the case, then all my efforts at war will seem a chick's game when his own Gift is fully fledged."

"He is not the only one with a powerful Gifts," Vinicia said, setting her hand on the hawkeye Kiernan had worn for so long. "Tyro Micah and Chiurgeon Westly both have their own strengths, though it has taken all of my efforts to keep them in balance. Given this," she said, gesturing to the third hawkeye as the thought of picking it up again made her stomach turn. "This is intended for Westly. It will help him in ways I cannot, though for the life of me I do not want to touch it again. Would you mind taking a walk with me?"

"You did say I could stay on your wing tips," he reminded. "And something tells me Hest'lre would prefer I spend the day with you rather than repeating the day I spent with Kreychi."

As Vinicia raised an eyebrow, Kiernan almost flushed.

"There was a lot of terra involved," he said, waving a hand to dismiss her interest.

"Then take the stone," she said, slipping her own in the small pocket on the front of her doublet. "And we can add that to the list of places we will visit."

"Where else did you have in mind?" He hesitated to ask.

"I need to check in on Tyro Micah," she said, matching eyes with him. "His Gift as a warbard is beyond incredible and it has been hurting him the past few moonturns. I believe his missing sister may be the key to helping him, however the girl is terrified to come onto the Palace shelf."

"If she looks anything like her brother, it may be the soldiers she fears," Kiernan said. "If you do mean to bring her into the Palace, I could make arrangements for her to be taken care of. House Windover owes me a boon and she would be safe with that family for a noble sponsor."

"True," Vinicia said, considering him. "But I need them together to balance their magic and Windover is moving off the shelf after graduation."

"Not necessarily," Kiernan said. "If she will stay with Windover until the tournament, then when I name Rylan as Counselheir, she can stay with him in the suites. There is certainly space enough for her and Micah there. I know how inseparable they are. It is why I held her hostage for so long, knowing it would make Rylan hate me."

Vinicia sniffed, not wanting to comment on what she could see was an act he clearly regretted now. "I suppose if it is only two more days, it will not matter."

"Where is she now?" Kiernan asked, shifting as Vinicia pulled in her wings to come to standing.

"I brought her into my personal suites," Vinicia said, finally showing her hand. "It is a long story, but Rylan's brother is being used by this new House Kirath to challenge Rylan's claim to the House Northern estate. Unfortunately, Rylan went out into the Lower City last night and found out the hard way," she said, knowing he was aware of that much. "His brother then realized Sera had been spying on them for me and nearly killed her for it. If I hadn't managed to get to her when I did, she would have been dead."

Kiernan blanched as he came to his feet. "You got to her in time, then?"

"Barely," Vinicia said. "But she will be fine. She is recovering."

"Alone?" Kiernan pressed. "Shouldn't Westly be watching over her?"

"I am the one who taught Westly how to heal blood and bone," Vinicia said, risking a smile. "What she needs now is rest and steady meals, so if you can find her a home in Windover, she will get better that much faster. Then we can stop by Westly's Garden, give him the hawkeye, and get you back somewhere safe so I can return to my actual duties."

"Of course," he said, pulling in his wings as she rounded the desk. As she picked up their trays, the profound sense of appreciation for all she had done from the shadows was like a palpable thing between them. It was strange to be acknowledged, but then again so was the sense of eagerness she could feel in him to stay near to her. Heady as the sensation was, as she stepped back to let him open the door, she wondered if he could feel it as well.

"Vinicia, I am sorry about earlier," Kiernan said, hand stalling on the handle.

"You caught me at rock bottom this dawning and I'm not sure I would have minded dying just then. You may be the only person on this shelf other than Eirik or perhaps Shayan who wouldn't have killed me and I... I owe you my life. Thank you."

"You're welcome," Vinicia said, her lip twisting into a smile as he opened the door to let her be rid of the trays.

"My Lord Seventh?" Called a voice in the hall, half panicked and wholly relieved. "Oh, thank the Gods. Have you been here this entire time?"

Vinicia winced to hear the alarm in the voice, but when she turned to see who was moving down the hall, Vinicia's smile betrayed her.

"Sal'weh, Lyonel. Henrick," she acknowledged, easing his worry as two of her former tyros closed the distance between them with speed. "My apologies for spiriting him away this morning," she said, with a sideways look to the Blackwings she could see lingering near the end of the hall. "I found him in my Armory and figured I would sort him out myself before Green Bevy came in to set up their gear."

Seeing their Barracks Mother scowling at their Counsel Lord's rather imposing guard, her former tyros failed to hide their amusement. They both knew that it didn't matter who you were to her, if she found out you were acting an idiot, she was going to set you straight.

"She's really not one to mess with, Lord Seventh," Lyonel said, more candid than Vinicia expected as he came to a stop beside Henrick before her. "She threw Henrick here in a linen closet during his third cycle when he lost a fight with a bottle of mead and made a mess of the washroom."

When his Primarch didn't argue, Kiernan looked to her for an explanation.

"It's not like they'll give me my own cells," she said, shrugging. "The closets work just fine and I have two on every level."

"Noted," Kiernan said, amused. "Are you the only ones on duty this dawning, or is there anyone else waiting to stalk me?"

"We were going to be stuck on the door until Lord Sixth sent us looking for you," Lyonel explained. "Lord Fifth's men told us to shove off, but I suspected they didn't know about Mother. Or," he said, looking to her again. "Perhaps they do and knew to leave you well enough alone?"

Vinicia just smirked. A woman in power never revealed her secrets.

As Henrick let out a laugh, Kiernan gave an innocent shrug. "I told Lord Fifth ages ago that his men wouldn't be able to keep up."

"Well if they can't, rest assured I can," Vinicia said. "I can keep track of anyone."

"Are you sure about that, Mother?" Kiernan asked, doubtful as he raised an eyebrow. "If you could keep track of everyone, how did Tyro Rylan get out all these cycles?"

"I let him," Vinicia scoffed. "No one goes in or out of those barracks without my knowing."

"You let him?" Kiernan said, honestly surprised. "Against my order?"

"It was a stupid order," Vinicia scoffed. "More than that, Lord Third agreed with me. Rylan had every right to visit his family and it is a good thing he did last night, as you well know."

"Well it isn't like I can do anything about it now," Kiernan said, shaking his head in disbelief as he turned his attention to the Blackwings now braving the hallway towards them. "We are heading back to the Sires' Wing, Praetor Iven. Care to join us?"

"Is she coming with you, Lord Seventh?" The Praetor asked, looking at Vinicia as if she was as likely as anyone else to cut Kiernan down if given the chance.

"Yes. She is my guest," Kiernan explained as Vinicia inclined her head.

"Understood," the Praetor said and then tossed his chin at the others. "Set up a perimeter."

Vinicia glanced over at Kiernan and found him with his eyes closed, counting to ten as they worked to make him a prisoner instead of a Warlord. When he looked up, she had her hand out to him in escort and the thanks in his eyes was genuine. She would make a finer escort than two squads of Blackwings any day and a better guard besides.

"We are on our way to the Windover apartments," Kiernan said to no one in particular, starting towards the southern exit to the Soldier Tyros' Wing that would lead them back to the Long Hall and Sires' Wing beyond.

CHAPTER 16: DAME KAITLYN DU'ALEXANDRIA, HOUSE WINDOVER

Friday, 09:00

Kaitlyn stifled a yawn as she shifted on her kneeler, trying and failing to focus on giving proper honor to her House's Founder, Iskander. She had gone into the family's shrine to be out of the way of the veterans moving her family's luggage to the Delton Estate, but if she was here, she might as well pray. The shrine itself wasn't much, just marble shelves in an ancient room that allowed the House's Ancestors to be viewed for worship, but that didn't bother her. Given her love of books and stories, she had always seen the room as a Library of ancestors and any time she was here, the fledglings of the House always wanted to hear her stories.

Fortunately, telling those stories was part of her duties to the House and for as much as she also enjoyed tales of fae, the best House legends held a touch of magic as well. What was a warbard's gift to whisper into another man's mind, if not magic? What was the ability to see the spirits of their ancestors with a left eye gone silver-white, if not magic?

The family priests called both proof that a person had been touched or blessed by the ancestors, but Kaitlyn knew in her heart they were holding back the truth.

All they said was to keep praying for the Founder's blessing and, if she was worthy, she would be marked as blessed herself and then the truth would be made clear to her. And so Kaitlyn continued to serve the shrine here in Delton without complaint. As the only Dame of the ruling Windover branch present at Court most of the cycle, she was the woman charged with caring for the altar itself, replacing candles, incense, and offerings as needed to appease her ancestors.

Occasionally that caring also meant defending it, though the only true defense it needed was running off couples who tried to use the dark corners it provided for trysts in the middle of revels. Amusingly, half the time those amorous couples she found invited her to join them rather than be put out. She never did take them up on that offer, knowing that Micahleia alone held her heart. More importantly, Kaitlyn knew that while she was free to choose her partners, any chicks she bore would mean she could be married out of the House and she wasn't ready for that yet. If she was honest with herself she might never be ready.

Stifling another yawn, Kaitlyn shook herself and resettled her wings, refocusing on the mosaic of Founder Iskander before her. Depicted as a tall man with a splay of six brilliant white wings behind him, his golden hair matched Kaitlyn's own for all the glory he wore as a halo around his face.

Guardian that he was over the Alexandrian mountain, it was by his might, along with that of the lesser Houses on the shelf, that the wild woods of the Kihara range had been tamed. His favored house in Windover tamed it still, charged to guard the shelves from the gryphons that still prowled the pillars and foothill surrounding it by Iskander himself a thousand cycles ago. Charged the men, at least.

For Kaitlyn, her charge as a Dame was to keep the customs and courtesies of the House while the other women worked to turn all parts of the beasts raised by the House into goods to be shared among the peak. *He who guarded, guided*, the saying went.

Smiling, Kaitlyn shivered with the knowledge of purpose that still gave her. As Dame of the House, she guarded fledglings and courtiers alike, especially in Delton, though all she seemed to be guarding today was her own thoughts and prayers as she waited for the veterans to finish their work.

"Wings up!"

Kaitlyn froze as the sounds behind her suddenly stopped. Twisting from her position on the kneeler, she came fully awake as she realized the veterans who had been moving gear were all standing at attention, wings tightly behind them as a number of Blackwings moved into the suite. A few moments later, two others moved inside and Kaitlyn came to her feet as she realized it was Counsel Lord Kiernan and Barracks Mother Vinicia. With everyone having gone elsewhere to stay clear of the veterans, she was the only Dame of the House available to greet them.

Smoothing down her bodice and silks, Kaitlyn tried to not seem startled as the five Blackwing guards who had entered the suite turned towards her. It was one thing to know that the Seventh Counsel Lord often had to worry about the threat of assassination, but to see his guard strengthened so close to his possible Envoy was unsettling. Still, she pressed her palms together before her and bowed slightly, offering her greeting as she came to the threshold of the temple.

"You honor us, Counsel Lord. Dame Vinicia," she said, calling his attention towards the shrine. "May the blessing of Founder Iskander find you well this day."

"Glory to the House of Windover," Kiernan returned, matching the hands she held in prayer.

"To what do we owe the Honor?" She asked, moving towards the two of them once the Blackwings had allowed her to pass.

"I am here to ask after a boon," Kiernan said as she joined them. "I understand your Patriarch is arriving soon or will arrive soon? If he is not in, I would know when to return."

"Patron Gaius has arrived," Kaitlyn said, inclining her head. "However, Heir Kreychi is speaking with my father in the rear receiving room, now. I am certain he will see you."

"And while you are speaking to him, I can check on Tyro Micah," Vinicia said and Kaitlyn was surprised to realize that Vinicia was searching for a way to not go with them.

"Won't you join me to speak with Heir Kreychi, Mother?" Kiernan asked and Kaitlyn was a little surprised to see her hesitate. "You said your first cycle in the barracks was his last, yes?"

Vinicia shifted her weight, which was as much a show of nerves as Kaitlyn had ever seen her give. Why she was so uneasy about speaking to her near-brother, though, Kaitlyn had no idea. Hoping to give her the moment to breathe, Kaitlyn spoke into the uneasy silence.

"Micah is still sleeping, Mother," Kaitlyn answered, hoping she had been wrong about Sera's own illness being what was truly affecting Micah. "The quiet of my rooms has eased the headache he seems to have given himself since he called to the Preem two nights ago. He will not notice a delay if you waited to check on him."

Wincing with the news, Vinicia looked to Kiernan at last. "I suppose I do not want to wake him if he is resting," she said, finding her confidence once again. "And it would be better to wake him with good news, would it not? Kaitlyn," she said, shifting her attention as Kiernan smiled at her. "You had said it would be possible to host Seraleia in your House's estate, but I would host her here if possible."

"Of course," Kaitlyn said immediately, eyes going wide. "For how long?"

"Just as long as it takes for her brother to earn his pauldron," Kiernan said, as Kaitlyn's hope began to rise. "If we can speak with Heir Kreychi about the matter, I believe that would settle the boon between the House and the Seat."

"And if he recognizes me, you will do the explaining," Vinicia added, though the words were low and meant for Kiernan alone.

Leaving them to their quiet conversation, Kaitlyn turned to guide them into the suite with hope in her heart. The House had requested a boon of the Counsel Lord, so it was only fitting that he would ask a boon from them in return. To think they would take in Micah's twin for the duration of the war... She had never had a sister, but Sera was so precious to her friends that she was certain the two of them would be close as well if given the chance.

Kaitlyn's path through the Windover apartments was a blur, though she knew the two were following along given the soft click of their leather heels on the marble walkway. As they neared the receiving room, Kaitlyn could see the afternoon light coming through the windows at the far end of the suites, and then the sound of her father speaking with Kreychi grew to more than a subtle murmur.

When their conversation came to a natural lull, she set a gentle knock against the door before opening it for the three of them.

"Sire, Heir," she began, giving a small courtesy. "Counsel Lord Kiernan and Barracks Mother Vinicia have come to request an audience."

When Kreychi looked up to see Kiernan within the suite, there was true happiness in his smile. For all their elders begrudged the man's presence, Counsel Lord Kiernan had given a great deal of Glory to the House with Kreychi's appointment as Primarch of his Shadow Guard, even if the honor of his more intimate affections was less desirable. Seeing her father's suspicious curiosity, Kaitlyn dropped her eyes as she deflected the attention away from herself. This could be seen as going over both their heads to have her way about taking in Micah's sister and she had only asked them to consider it a few candlemarks ago...

"My Lord Seventh," Kreychi called, his easy smile lighting up the room as Kiernan and Vinicia moved to join them. "What a pleasure it is to see you again so soon."

"The pleasure is mine, truly," Kiernan returned. Vinicia moved into the room as well, all of her hesitancy gone as she walked up to the two men as if they were no more than the boys she oversaw in the Soldier Tyros' Wing. Much to Kaitlyn's surprise, Vinicia gestured for her to join them as well. Kaitlyn went, smiling to see the approval on her father's face as she did so. Her Illiandrian mother had been so bold, he often said.

"I had meant to invite you to the suite this day, Ser, though I cannot say I expected the company," Kreychi said, releasing Kiernan's handshake. "To what do we owe this honor?"

"To this lovely Dame," Kiernan began, gesturing to Kaitlyn. "And to my Barracks Mother, who has brought an interesting set of circumstances to my attention."

"Greetings Mother," Kreychi said, extending his hand to her as well. "I dare say your reputation precedes you. From what I hear from my cousins, I was lucky to have escaped before you found your way into overseeing nest checks."

Vinicia smiled as she clasped hands with Kreychi. "That all depends on how you kept your rooms," she said. "If you are anything like your brother Nichi, you would have been fine. Tyrsten however..."

"Cousin Tyrsten was quite taken with her when he was first a tyro," Kreychi explained when Kiernan seemed confused. "He stills sings her praises, I believe."

"Only because he knows I'm untouchable," Vinicia explained and Kaitlyn had to stop herself from giggling.

"Hopefully that is all he has been noted for, Counsel Lord," her father said. "I can assure you both that the other matter has been resolved."

"As I knew it would be, Lord Marius," Kiernan answered. "No, this request actually concerns Tyro Micah, who I know to be a favored guest in your suite."

"Ah yes, Micah," Kreychi confirmed. "Given the three of you, I should have guessed. I must say Kaitlyn's friends fly far higher than I would have expected."

The last he added with a laugh, which took away the sting of going outside of the House for an answer to her personal insistences. Then again, she had shown nothing more than concern for the circumstances Sera would find herself in when they were gone, a feeling she knew was echoed by Vinicia. If Vinicia had turned Counsel Lord Kiernan's ear on her behalf, so be it.

"How can I be of assistance?" Kreychi prompted.

"I have determined how best to settle the boon between us, new though it might be," Kiernan said, reaching into his pocket for the token Kreychi would have given him when he asked for the favor. "For the past few cycles, I have been housing Tyro Micah's twin sister in a veteran's tavern while he was a part of the Delton Academy. I would like it very much if your House would see to her care for the duration of his military service."

Kaitlyn held her breath, watching as Kreychi and her father traded looks.

"Of course," Kreychi answered, almost too quickly for Kaitlyn to believe. "It had been our plan to offer Micah a permanent place in our House after the War, but we were waiting to confirm the offer with Patron Gaius upon his arrival. However, given the missive I have just received…"

"News?" Kiernan questioned.

"It seems I am to become inducted into the House of Lords for Windover with the start of Winter Court," Kreychi said, his voice solemn for all it meant. "My father has made it clear that while he will be joining us, it will not be as Patriarch."

"So, the decision is yours?" Kiernan asked, though the answer was clear.

"Hoi," Kreychi confirmed and glanced at Kaitlyn. "And I am happy to add both him and his sister to our House permanently. I am well aware of the friend he is to Nichi, and it is long past time for the House to take in new blood."

Kaitlyn's excited gasp started them all to laughter.

"Have you seen my brother, Kaitlyn?" Kreychi asked. "I wish to give Micah the news, but I thought Nichi might like to do the honors."

"I believe Nichi is in the barracks," she said, unsure. "Micah is still in the suite, given how poorly he was feeling."

"If you think it might lift his spirits," Kreychi amended. "Then you could be the one to let him know. Would you like the honors?"

"I most certainly would!" Kaitlyn beamed.

"I will leave it to you, then, sweet sister," Kreychi said, and then looked to Kiernan. "Given the boon between us, I am inclined to make Micah a blood-brother to the House. He has certainly earned the right."

As Kaitlyn's hands came up to hide her surprise, Kreychi's look turned back to her with a smile. It was her own father who spoke, though.

"I have not missed how you wear your ring for him, daughter," Marius said with pride. "And he has my blessing."

"And mine," Kreychi added with a wink.

Kaitlyn was speechless as the focus of the room turned to her. After her brothers had fallen on the plains and her mother had died so shortly after her own birth, the fate of the branch House had been in doubt as she had grown. There was simply no way to keep Aerie alive with only her to lead it, but if Windover itself was taking in Micah, it would elevate the Branch back into the ruling House. Her father would lose his seat in the House of Lords, but given how he had been acting as Patriarch for cycles as Kreychi trained to replace him, it would be a welcome relief.

"It may be the end of my Aerie," her father said, confirming her suspicions. "But it will strengthen the House to see you two ringed. As a blood-brother to Nichi, he will be a fine match for your heart and hearth." Seeing the tears brimming in her eyes, her father opened his arms with the last. "Daughter, you know all I want in this world is your happiness."

Kaitlyn fled into his embrace with the words and she couldn't care less if she looked a fledgling among them. As the room darkened inside her father's wings, she heard him speaking softly into her hair.

"I know that Katharina would have loved Micah, too," he said, invoking her mother's name like some sort of secret between them. "Killiam would have honored his strength, and both Leaon and Liam would have sung up the stars with him every solstice. We two may be the last of the branch, but we are not alone. They are with us both; always in our hearts."

By the time his hug ended, her tears of grief and joy were a true waterfall of relief. Embarrassed as she was by her own display, she was glad no one in the room seemed to hold it against her.

"My apologies for dropping in only to fly once again," Kiernan said, speaking to Kreychi as he extended his hand to press the boon token back into his palm. "But Mother and I have continuing business."

"Of course," Kreychi replied, his grip lingering for all the affection still between them. "Do not let us keep you."

"I should go tell Micah," Kaitlyn said, collecting herself as her father refolded his wings. After a moment to scrub at her eyes, she turned back to Kreychi and their guests as Vinicia started to speak.

"Thank you for this," Vinicia said, extending her hand to Kreychi. "It means more than you know."

Kreychi took it, pleased as well. "If it means as much to these tyros as it does to my sweet sister, then I know well enough," he said, and Vinicia was inclined to agree.

Kaitlyn flushed under their attention, but there was no hiding her joy.

"And my thanks to you," Kiernan added, looking to Kaitlyn with a smile. "It seems you have impeccable timing."

"The pleasure was all mine," she replied, curtsying deeply. "For both of you, Mother."

"You do Micah and his brothers a great service," Vinicia returned as Kiernan moved back to her side. "Now go spread the good news. I do not want to spoil the surprise, so I will delay checking on him for a moment. Hopefully this good news is all he needs to feel whole again."

"Of course," Kaitlyn beamed, moving back enough so she could give a quick courtesy to the room. "I will only be a few moments."

"Take your time, love," Vinicia chuckled.

"Yes, Mother," Kaitlyn said, and then grinned as Vinicia motioned for her to be on her way.

Once Kaitlyn was clear, she hurried to the main receiving room and then took off running as fast as she could manage. By the time she reached the door to her suite, her heart felt as if it was going to burst, but she managed to calm herself. Charging into the room would do little to help Micah's head; the news would work its own magic.

Entering the small receiving area, she found no one else had risen, so she hurried past the platter of bread, fruit, and cheeses on a sideboard and walked down the short hallway to her suite. With a controlled and gentle touch, she opened the door and slipped inside. No matter her quiet, Micah came awake at once.

"Kait?" He called, startled and groggy as he fought the blankets trapping him. "What's going on? Why is everyone so loud?"

Thinking back to the silent rooms she had just passed, Kaitlyn's worry grew that much stronger. The veterans had been moving gear, true, but that was in the front of the suite. Here in the back, most were still in their nests as Micah was.

"I have good news," she said, picking up the grimoire she had left on the stool beside the nest so she could take a seat.

Micah pulled the blanket down from his face, relieved as the cold air hit his skin. Concerned, Kaitlyn set the inside of her wrist to his forehead as she had been doing every candlemark or so. He was still burning up and his normally warm olive complexion was ashen and pale.

"What?" He managed, flinching away from her touch.

What is the best way to put this? Kaitlyn thought to herself. *There is so much to say, but he'll only want what matters to him.*

"Just say it," Micah grumbled, closing his eyes again. "I'll want to know it all eventually."

Kaitlyn smiled. Micah knew her so well it was like he knew what she was thinking.

"Heir Kreychi has just agreed to adopt you and your sister as blood-relations to House Windover. That means that Sera will be with me while you are away at War," she said, trying to calm her excitement. "It was Counsel Lord Kiernan's request."

That got his attention.

"Lord Seventh would never agree to that," he muttered, looking at her with irritation.

"But he did," she insisted. "He said so himself, to my face. I could barely believe it!"

"When do you ever speak with Lord Seventh?" Micah scoffed.

"He came to the suite with Mother," she explained. "They are still—"

"Mother hates Lord Seventh almost as much as Rylan does," Micah said, cutting her off. "She would never be seen with him."

"I'm only telling you what I saw," Kaitlyn insisted, confused. *I would never lie to you...*

"Of course you would," Micah scowled. "You're just like the rest of them. You would lie to me to serve your own purposes, even if it was just a half-truth."

Kaitlyn paused, not quite sure what to say. Micah could certainly read people, but she had not said a word about lying to him. Not out loud.

Micah groaned and began to push himself out of her nest, swearing at the comforts.

"Micah?" She asked hesitantly. "Are you feeling all right?"

"What do you think?" He shot back, free of the blankets but still trapped in the nest. " I have the shelf's worse hangover and from what? Nothing. I haven't touched anything since that blicing revel."

"I don't think this is the ale, love."

"The terra then?" He snapped. "I know what you think about that."

I think it helps, but not enough, Kaitlyn mourned, watching him sit up in the nest.

"No, it doesn't," Micah agreed, washing a hand over his face. "It just makes everything a blur."

Kaitlyn's jaw dropped. *What is going on!*

"What?" Micah swore. "Nothing is going on."

"But I didn't say anything," she stammered. "I mean, not then..."

"You're always saying things," Micah said, squeezing his eyes shut. "Dawning, midday, and night. You never stop."

As he put his hands to his temples, Kaitlyn felt the pit of her stomach drop. She had always suspected that Micah could wield bardic magic, what with his success as a warbard and the way his music could make people dance, but this? This was something different.

Kaitlyn looked down to the grimoire in her lap, one of the largest of her collection that she had brought with her from Alexandria. Dona Avitam: The Gifts of the Ancestors. She had almost given up on her studies as a fledgling's fancy when Micah had appeared in her life, but when she realized Westly was his crew brother, she had begun to read again in earnest. Now the possibility that it could all be real was as terrifying as it had once been thrilling. But if it was real, then all her studies might have not been in vain.

"Micah," Kaitlyn said finally. "Please, look at me."

When he turned, Kaitlyn bit onto her lower lip and thought at him as hard as she could. If that was even possible.

Can you hear me?

The blood drained out of Micah's face. He knew exactly what she had said. She could see it in his eyes.

"You heard me, didn't you?" Kaitlyn insisted.

"Of-of course I didn't. That's ins-sane," Micah stammered, now shoving himself up and out of the nest. "I can't hear what you're thinking."

Kaitlyn didn't know what to say. Didn't know what to think. Well, didn't know what to think except that he could hear her, that much she had proven. He had a Gift. As she stared him down, knowing the truth, Micah finally caved.

"Fine!" He swore, exasperated as he found his clothes in the pile where he had left them. "Yes. Yes, I can hear you. Congratulations."

"But why didn't you tell me?" She asked, clutching her book to her chest as he picked his uniform breeches off the floor.

"With what you read?" He said, looking to the grimoire. "You might have actually enjoyed knowing. Sharing that knowledge. Being part of some Society of Secret Keepers?"

Kaitlyn flushed and he knew he was right.

"But it's a Gift," Kaitlyn insisted. "A Gift of the Ancestors. It's—"

"It's a blicing curse," Micah snapped, trying to dress himself even as he came apart at the seams. "Did you ever think what the Court would do to a warbard who can hear people outside of the Host? If anyone finds out, they'll kill me. They'll just straight-up kill me rather than risk their plotting. Gods, there was a reason I was always drunk or smoking around you people, but now I can't even do that. Apparently it's making everyone inside my head louder!"

You people? Kaitlyn thought, clutching her book like a shield. *He can't mean that.*

He was hurt. In pain. Women giving birth screamed such insanities that made their ringed lords blush, but they were all love and laughter with a chick in their arms. This must be something like that. Words of pain and anger, not of venom.

Micah's tirade paused as he fought to lace his shirt around his wings. When he was done, he still refused to look at her and the silence hung brittle between them.

"I should have gone to Westly."

"But, Micah," she started. "It can't be safe for you out—"

"Nowhere is safe for me," he threw back. "I can always hear them. It's just never.... Never been this loud. Gods, why am I even telling you this?"

"Micah, you could hurt yourself," she said, her heart breaking for him. "You were barely able to walk yesterday when you crashed through my door."

"Kaitlyn, stop trying to help. Stop trying to make it right," he said, putting his hands to his temples again.

"I'm not trying to," she pleaded. "But there is nothing wrong with you. Micah— "

"Everything is wrong," he threw back. "My mother died before she taught me how to control my magic and I haven't seen Sera in cycles.

And now Westly is going out of his bloody mind about Nichi and I'm starting to hear the whole blicing Warhost like a true Preem. Worst of all," Micah said, his look turning dark. "Worst of all, you keep trying to take her place."

"Whose place?" Kaitlyn asked, trembling.

"Sera's!" Micah snapped, his voice rising with anger. "But you don't have her gift, so you can't make it right. You can't keep them out. So just... just stop!"

As Micah glared at her, Kaitlyn felt her whole body freeze. She tried to swallow, tried to move, but for the life of her, she couldn't. She was literally stopped in place and time.

Is this what happens when you lose control? She panicked, unable to even breathe.

Micah's jaw dropped as he realized what had happened; what he had done. His anger vanished as he rushed towards her and his hand on her shoulders melted whatever paralysis he had caused. There was terror in his voice as he tried to apologize.

"I'm sorry, Kait! I didn't mean it. I—I can't control it." He was shaking, crushing her against him as if she could make him stop. "Gods, I'm so sorry. I don't want to hurt you."

"I want to help you," she said, hugging him back. "Micah, I have read about this kind of Gift before—Whispering—and if I can't help then Westly can. You said so yourself."

"Westly," he repeated, releasing her. He staggered as he put a hand to his head, trying to think through the melee of both their racing thoughts. "I'm sorry," he repeated a third time and then turned and fled.

Kaitlyn threw the grimoire back into her nest to follow him out her doorway, but Micah was faster than she'd imagined. Just as she reached the receiving chamber in the main suite, he was already out the door. There was only one place he would go in this state and as long as she stayed with him, he would be safe. Westly would know what to do. He had to. Kindred dryads always knew what to do in her stories.

But before she could grab a cloak from the pegs next to the door, she heard a woman call out her name. *Dame Vinicia!* Kaitlyn turned just as the woman reached her, Counsel Lord Kiernan in tow.

"Was that Micah?" Vinicia asked, her concern obvious.

Kaitlyn wanted to tell her everything at once and so quickly that all she could do was nod and swallow around the knot in her throat. Kiernan fanned his massive, marked wings to shield them from the Blackwing guard in the room.

"What happened?" Vinicia asked, giving her a look that reminded her of Micah when he performed. As an unnatural calm settled over her, Kaitlyn found her voice.

"It's his Gift as a warbard," she managed. "I think he's lost control of it. Mother, he's so scared."

"Is he going to Westly?" Vinicia asked, and when Kaitlyn nodded, she lowered her voice and spoke with Kiernan. "I have to deal with this, Kiernan," she said, even as she looked past him to where the Blackwings were spoiling for a fight. "Alone. Can you do anything?"

"I can block him from the Host, at least temporarily. The Blackwings can take me to the Library as well, and then I'll be shielded. All of it should help," the Counsel Lord assured her, though his hand went to his pocket again. "What about the stone?"

Vinicia's eyes cut back to Kaitlyn. Confused, Kaitlyn looked to the man, only to realize he was handing her what looked like a pendant on a hempen cord. Only his serious look kept her from gasping in surprise, though her hands shook as she realized it was a hawkeye.

"When we find Westly, you go straight to him and give him that stone," Vinicia said quietly. "I will handle Micah."

Kaitlyn wrapped up the hempen cord around her palm before gripping the stone tightly in her hand. She was not about to drop this mid-flight, no matter her nerves. "Yes, Mother."

Their plan set, Kiernan re-folded his wings as she and Vinicia moved for the door. When they were through, Kaitlyn led them both down into the Sires' Wing and then Vinicia took the lead as they turned to the right to travel down the Long Hall. There, just beyond the mass of courtiers preparing for morning audiences, they caught a glimpse of Micah before he disappeared into the Chiurgeon Tyros' Wing.

They followed faster than Kaitlyn thought possible, but it was not fast enough; one person fleeing made far better time than two in pursuit. Sure, Micah had carved a path for them, and seeing Dame Vinicia in a hurry got many moving, but still more were put to insult as they rushed past.

When they finally broke through into the long, vaulted hallway of the Chirons' Wing, Kaitlyn almost forgot why they were in such a rush. Instead, she was left gawking as Vinicia took four steps down the hall and then launched into the air with a veteran's ease. When she didn't look as if she would slow at all, Kaitlyn gasped and watched her twist to run a few more steps on the right wall before spiraling into the open doors of the Glass Garden.

Kaitlyn sprinted to catch up to her, but when she rounded the doorway she screamed to see Micah had collapsed with his arms wrapped around his head just beyond the threshold.

"Close the door!" Vinicia commanded and the sharpness of her tone brought Kaitlyn out of her stupor. Once she had pushed the heavy wooden door back into place, she turned to see Vinicia with her hands resting gingerly on Micah's temples. As Vinicia tilted his head, Kaitlyn felt faint. There was blood coming out of his nose, and enough that it had pooled under him, smearing down the side of his face.

"He's okay," Vinicia explained. "He must have tripped when he came in. I'm sure he's done that more than once from too much mead, eh?"

She's trying to comfort me, Kaitlyn realized and then remembered to breathe. She nodded, shakily, and then winced as pain blossomed behind her right eye. As she pressed her fingers against her temple, a third voice suddenly joined theirs.

"Hey! Who's there?" The voice was muffled, struggling. "Whoever you are, come and help me!"

"Nichi?" Kaitlyn realized at once.

"Kait? Kait! Come help me, will you?" He begged. "Westly fell on top of me. My wings are pinned."

Kaitlyn was torn, looking back to Micah and Vinicia.

"I have him," Vinicia reassured her. "I need you to take that stone to Westly. Just put it on him, okay? It is from his mother."

His mother the dryad? There was a dryad here in Kosar? In Delton?! Kaitlyn's head spun with questions that Vinicia could see all over her face.

"It will help with—"

"He's coming into his power. I know," Kaitlyn supplied, coming to her feet even as she felt a stab of pain behind her eyes. She swore as she pressed her palm to her forehead, demanding that the pain go away, and then looked back to Vinicia who was now worried about her.

"Kait!" Nichi called out again, struggling. "Come on!"

"You can do this, love," Vinicia said. "Just put the stone on him. I will take Micah to my rooms and then send Sera to yours the same way I did with you this dawning."

Kaitlyn's mind was spinning so fast she was getting dizzy. If she stood here much longer, she might actually faint.

"Yes, Mother," Kaitlyn said, clutching the hawkeye to her chest as she found her courage.

"Give me half a candlemark," Vinicia said, her mission set. "And have a message sent to Rylan. Tell him Sera is joining the House and you need him in the Suite."

"Yes, Mother," Kaitlyn said again, watching her prepare to leave. "I'll do as you ask."

Vinicia nodded as if she had expected nothing else.

Determined, Kaitlyn finally moved from Micah, powering up and over the labyrinth until she saw where Nichi was pinned under Westly. When she landed, the relief on Nichi's face was evident.

"I swear this isn't what it looks like," Nichi began to babble. He was flushed, though if that was from embarrassment or the weight of Westly crushing him, she wasn't sure. "He just fell on me when Micah came into the Garden."

"I don't care what it looks like," Kaitlyn said, kneeling next to them both so she could get the pendant over Westly's head. Once she let it go, she gasped as the air around them began to shimmer and then a sudden blinding light flashed in the Garden. Kaitlyn looked over the herbs, but all she saw was the echo of the image of Vinicia with Micah's arm around her neck as it vanished.

When she looked back to Nichi, it was if she was staring into the daystar. Forced back on her heels, she cursed as the stabbing sensation in her eyes surfaced once again. The whole world was swimming in a silver mire so bad she thought she might lose her stomach until all at once a strange double-image began to appear over both men.

"Kait!" Nichi demanded, panicked once again. "What is going on?"

"Wil-o-wisps," Kaitlyn gasped, realizing she could see them with more clarity if she let her vision soft-focus. To her extreme pleasure, the longer she held her eyes that way, the easier it was to see them. It was almost like looking at water. She couldn't see the water itself, but she could see how it moved in relation to everything else around it.

When she looked back to Nichi, she almost swore—there was light coming out of him, too! Not only that, but the energy was moving towards the three of them with startling urgency.

As Nichi continued to struggle, Kaitlyn remembered that she had come over here to help him. After a moment to find somewhere to take hold of Westly, she pulled with all her might but the dead weight was too much for her alone. It was almost as if he was physically stuck.

As Kaitlyn fought the inexplicable pull between her brother and the kindred, the wisps that hung in the air around them suddenly began to move. In the span of a heartbeat, they were surrounded as the things were sucked in by the force of the hawkeye.

Kaitlyn wouldn't have believed it unless she had felt it, but the faster the light streaked, the lighter Westly became. After long enough, Westly relaxed and she was able to slide an arm around his chest. With more force that she thought she could muster, she planted a foot next to Nichi on the floor and lifted Westly bodily. The kindred came away with her like a newborn chick, his head lolling on her shoulder as Nichi righted himself.

"By all the Gods," Nichi swore.

The two of them stood apart from Nichi, surrounded by light, but Nichi wasn't its only source. As she turned her head to check on her brother, she realized that light was streaking out of the Garden as well. More, it seemed, than was coming from Nichi. She hoped that was a good thing.

"Kait...?" Westly breathed, disoriented.

"I've got you," she said, reaffirming her grip. "Don't you worry."

"But Micah..." He said with more urgency.

"Mother took him," she answered as he picked his head up off her shoulder.

"What's going on?" He asked, staring back at Nichi. "I've never seen anything like this before."

Kaitlyn kept an arm on him as he came under his own power. When he turned back to look at her, his eyes had changed from their vibrant emerald green to what Kaitlyn would have sworn were two godseyes.

"They're wil-o-wisps" she explained. "Creatures born of pure Wellspring energy. A manifestation of it."

Westly shook his head and she was glad he seemed to be coming back to himself.

"But where are they going?" He asked, since she seemed to know.

"Into that hawkeye," Kaitlyn said and touched the pendant around his neck. All at once her vision of the wisps was gone and as the world collapsed from its riot of color and vibrancy, she had to shake herself. "Vinicia gave it to me to give to you. She said it was from your mother."

Westly looked down at the pendant and his eyes went wide. "And Micah?" He asked.

"She took Micah away," Kaitlyn said. "Do you think she can heal him?"

"I don't doubt it," Westly said. "Vinicia taught me everything I know."

Nichi looked between the two of them, trying and failing to be staggered by the revelation that his Barracks Mother was a kindred dryad.Worse, when he settled on Kaitlyn, she winced to see the hurt in his eyes.

"Why didn't you tell me?" he asked. "Kait, how long have you known?"

"It wasn't my secret to tell," she defended. "And I've only known for certain since last night when she needed my help with Sera..."

CHAPTER 17: SERALEIA DU'DELTON

Friday, 13:30

Wings pressed against the walls of the strange, pitch-black room she had found herself in, Sera fought to make her eyes focus through her tears. She had searched every crevice of this place, every wall and bookshelf and desk, and there was no way out. Absolutely no way out. At least in death she could have been free, but she knew she was still very much alive. For one thing, she was ravenously hungry, thirsty like she had never been in her life, and all her other senses were straining to orient herself in the surreal, otherworldly intensity.

Heart racing, breath rasping, she had fought so hard to see in this horrible place that either she had gone mad or her eyes had finally started to cooperate. Instead of light, however, all the edges of the world had become inverted in their colors, streaking through her mind with violet, amber, and azure power. It was as if the world was filled with bio-luminescence only she could see and anything living throbbed in her sight. The bracelet from her mother's life before they were born had burned on her wrist, igniting some sort of latent talent within her, and as she panted through her panic, she knew that the walls of this place were alive.

Now she just had to find a way out. She *would* find a way out. She would claw her way out of whatever dragon had thought to devour her and rip it apart one bloody scale at a time to reclaim her brother. She didn't care where he was anymore; Palace or War Plains or beyond the veil, she would drag him screaming back from that place so they could be together once again. He was her responsibility and she had let him try to survive without her for too long.

All her life, her mother had told her to stay close to him. That it was important. That they were special. But her mother had said nothing about what would happen if they were apart. The night before Rylan had appeared, for the first time in a decade she had tried to rip open her mother's old book for answers, but whatever force of magic kept the chains in place refused to unlock for her, no matter her need. Her mother had said the stone that was attached to her mother's bracelet had been the book's key, but it had shattered the day they'd been born. That book was gone now, left in the hiding space of House Northern despite the rest of her things being in a pile next to the nest she had woken in, but none of it meant anything without Micah in this prison.

Her mother had told them they'd been born with a Gift, their mother's Gift, though it had passed down to them in halves with their birth. For her part, Sera had the ability to catch a person's mind with her own—to Transfix them—so that Micah could work his Suggestive magic. More importantly, she could also act as Micah's shield, transfixing him alone to close his thoughts off from the world. During their long separation, Sera had been terrified of what would happen to him with no shields at all. Now she knew. She was so close to him and he was hurting so much. Hurting and she had just let him suffer, thinking it was easier to push through instead of doing what she knew she must.

Sera sat back on her heels as she let the last of her mental protections collapse, groping after the feel of him. As she did so, the vibrancy of the strange, blackwater sight came into focus. The wooden walls of this place were rough against her wings and the hunger inside of her was gnawing at her backbone. She could smell the leather clothing on the floor, the sweat of exertion, and the dust of this place as if it was spread over her skin. It overwhelmed her, made her stomach riot, and yet the idea that she was trapped here made her blood boil.

She would get out. She would be free. She would—

Sera froze as the center of the large room began to crackle with light. Ducking her head behind her hand, she braced herself for a fight, preparing to launch as a strange creature of blinding crimson stepped through. As the creature took a knee, wings flaring in the space, Sera let her eyes adjust and found the auburn-haired kindred she had met at the Live Oak holding her brother in her arms.

Shaming herself, Sera burst into tears as she came to her feet, rushing over to help the woman manage Micah's weight as the room flooded with true light. Vinicia's thanks were obvious as she pulled her wings back to let Sera get Micah's arm over her neck, lifting him as Vinicia looked towards the room where Sera had initially come from.

Once they had him in the nest, Vinicia took a knee again, dizzy with the effort it had taken to get them both into this place. This kindred place, Sera realized. She wasn't in a prison. She was probably in the safest place in the world if this woman was involved.

"Vinicia?" She said as the woman wavered. "Vinicia, what's going on? Is he okay? Are you okay?"

"He is not okay," Vinicia said, steadying herself on the edge of the freestanding nest. "But I can help him in this place. This is my home," she said, as if to answer Sera's unspoken question. "I did not mean to leave you here alone, but so much is happening so fast. Sera, he needs you more than I can explain."

"No, I know. I know," Sera assured her, pushing up onto her feet again. "Oh Goddess, he hurts so much."

"He is shielded now," Vinicia said, setting a hand on her wing to stall her from climbing into the nest with him. "And more strongly than you or I could manage alone."

Sera's heart skipped as she watched the woman drag herself to her feet. "But?" She asked.

"But if you are awake, I must take you out of this place," she said, and Sera could tell it was news she did not want to deliver. "You need to eat far more than I can manage and I must continue my work as he rests. I have arranged for you to stay with Kaitlyn if you will come with me while he sleeps."

Violence flashed through her as she stepped away from the woman, wings flaring. She absolutely would not be separated from her brother again.

"I give you my word I will bring him to you as soon as your presence alone will be enough," Vinicia said, raising her hands for peace. "But until then, would you not like to be reunited with Rylan?"

Sera's heart fluttered at Rylan's name.

"With Westly?"

As her anger gave way to wavering, Vinicia's hesitant smile almost had her in tears again. If she was close to them, it meant she was on the Palace shelf. Her mother had made her promise she would never come to this place...

"I can't," she said. For as badly as she had been beaten, and she had memories of that, she hadn't come to this place in anything more than the torn satin shirt and thin hose she had been wearing before. The bodice was gone, stripped from her for all the blood Vinicia had found on it since Sera had given worse than she had gotten in that fight.

"Kaitlyn has an entire wardrobe for you, if you will meet with her," Vinicia said. "The Windovers have offered you a place as a Daughter of their House, Sera, and their colors are black and gold. You will fit right in, I promise."

Sera's hand went to the long length of black hair draped over her shoulder, surprised.

"I... I am hungry," she lied. She was starving, but the panic of not knowing where her brother was had driven it out of her mind. Now, realizing this sanctuary, it was all flooding back.

"Take my hand?" Vinicia offered.

Sera closed her eyes, releasing the grip on her brother's wing. A moment later, she felt a gut-wrenching shift and heard a gasp of surprise.

"Iskander be praised," someone greeted with a touch of awe. "You really are his twin!"

Opening her eyes, Sera found herself standing in someone's private nesting quarters, her haversack of things at her feet and two people standing before her. Rylan was one, but the other was a birch-pale woman of about her own age. The woman was dressed in a black, fitted court bodice and tight leather breeches, though the waist of the jacket flared out prettily about her hips. All the black was trimmed in bright gold, matching the tight, golden curls that fell in spirals past her shoulders.

"She is at that," Rylan said, stepping to the side as the two women sized each other up. "Sera this is..."

"Kaitlyn," the woman said, smiling as she stepped up closer. "But please call me Kait."

Sera had expected to shake hands with the woman or curtsy, but she froze when Kaitlyn kept moving closer. She only stopped when she set her hands lightly on Sera's shoulders and kissed the air on either side of her cheeks.

"It is bad luck among the Court to not share the Kiss of Greeting," Kaitlyn said, a little embarrassed as she stepped back. "But it becomes part of the Court dance soon enough, I promise. I'm—I'm sorry. I should have explained," she added, looking to Rylan. "I just assumed..."

"Not everyone on the streets is from a House, Kait," Rylan teased. "Some people are born there."

Sera exhaled the breath she hadn't realized she was holding. She hadn't been sure if it was her own gift out of control or something else. Clearly, it was something else.

"It's okay. Really," Sera insisted. "I'm just not used to folks wanting to be so close to me," she said, which was mostly true. If they came that close without her asking, she would usually put them on their wings like her mother had taught her. "Now that I know, I won't be so startled. I promise. I'm a quick study."

Kaitlyn had her hands clasped at her waist as she smiled, which Sera took for her, trying to compose herself again. "If you are anything like Micah, I do believe it," she said, easing away from the awkwardness.

"Well, it's good to know we still look alike," Sera said, smiling back at her as she returned to Kaitlyn's initial reaction. "I'd hate to think he went and dyed his hair a funny color like this one does," she added, stepping to the side to include Rylan in their little circle.

"Micah's got a bit more muscle than you," Rylan said, and Sera narrowed her eyes at him. Not to be outdone, she stepped back to give her best impression of a Court bow, which was to say she shifted her weight onto her back leg and folded over her extended right with a dancer's flat back and flourish.

"I think she got all the grace," Kaitlyn observed, watching her with obvious approval. "Micah told me you are a marvelous dancer."

"Don't let him fool you, he is too," Sera chuckled. "Though he hides behind his lute so much you'd never know it."

"You're kidding!" Kaitlyn gasped and then looked to Rylan who had his hands up and was backing away. "Rylan, is that true?"

"I know nothing," he defended, turning away from them to go towards a sideboard where bundles of vegetables and meat were wrapped up in a thin piece of flat bread.

Sera couldn't help but grin and when she looked back to Kaitlyn she found the woman giggling. "Ask Micah to show you what an *uumi* is," Sera suggested. "But don't tell him I told you. His eyes will fall out of his head and it will serve him right."

"I shall have to do that," Kaitlyn agreed, laughing as Sera lost her hesitancy and hurried forward, joining Rylan at his enormous plate.

"Mother said she healed you," Rylan said around a mouth full of food. "She didn't say why."

"Don't tell me I look like you do," Sera said, picking up one of the bundles of meat and bread.

"Hey," he scoffed, waterglass halfway to his mouth. "Westly healed me, too."

"Oh, so that's just your face," Sera teased, lifting the water pitcher to toast him before taking a drink herself. Glass be damned, she was thirsty. "Who was it that got you?"

"Dylan's boys," he said, rolling his eyes. "And he traded my sorry ass for fifty crowns."

"They tried to kill me," Sera said, nudging him with a wing. "Good thing I learned how to fight from my mother instead of Westly, eh?"

"You fuck them up?" Rylan said, laughing as he watched her put away the second wrap of food to pick up a third before he was halfway through his first.

"I always give worse than I get," Sera said, and her smirk was smoldering as she looked over at him, one eyebrow raised. Bowen that he was, now that she knew just how he felt about her, she meant to change that right after... Right after she had more of whatever this food was. She wasn't even tasting it, but by the Gods if she wasn't about to eat all of it. Or maybe they already had?

Rylan actually took her hand as she realized she was sucking crumbs off her fingers, looking around for more to eat.

"I think that's enough," he laughed. "Kait needs to get you dressed."

Sera blinked a few times, watching as he folded her hand over his own to kiss her knuckles. Street-raised or not, he still had some manners and she smiled to see the love in his look. When he finally gave up her hand, Kaitlyn was still waiting, patient and clearly amused.

"I thought you might want to freshen up before you changed into your Blacks," she said. "We are close enough in size that it shouldn't be too hard to find you something to wear."

"Blacks?" Sera repeated, only to realize that Kaitlyn was gesturing to the outfit she was wearing.

"Black and gold are the House colors," she said. "So if you are a member of House Windover in Alexandria, you wear this to let people know. I should take some measurements, though, so I can pick out things while you get cleaned up."

Rylan gave Kaitlyn a small salute, this one with his hand flat against his chest, though he flushed to realize Sera meant to strip free of the garb she had worn while at House Northern.

"What are these colors for?" Kaitlyn asked as Rylan gathered the violet and crimson to throw it out as Sera stood before her in her small clothes.

"Some attempt at a 'House Kirath', apparently, not that any of the crews cared. New clothes are new clothes, and if they're finely made all the better. I just took these to blend in among them and stay warm," Sera said. "Some of my things are still hidden in the House. Do you think someone could go with me to get them? I mean, they're hidden pretty well, but it's really important I get them."

"Anything you need, we can provide you," Kaitlyn said, surprised by her urgency. "I promise."

"Not this," Sera said, trying to explain as Kaitlyn gestured towards the small bathing chamber. "It was my mother's and one of the only things we have left from her. It's a book—"

Sera stopped as she saw the woman's eyes go wide. Rich girls always had something they loved and from all the bookshelves she had seen as she had stuffed her face, Sera had guessed that might be it.

"This one would kill a man for a book," Rylan laughed, rejoining them with an amused grin. "But you don't need to, Kait. I'll make sure we grab it during the tournament. Dylan's boys have nothing on a forty-strong bevy of soldier tyros. Eighty," he added with emphasis. "If you'll tell the century what they did to you. They'll follow me that far into trouble to do you honor."

From the hard look in his eyes, Sera could tell how serious Rylan was. He knew how important that book was to her and the thought of him turning the Delton Tyro Legion on that House just to get it back? It was fucking romantic.

"All books are priceless," Kaitlyn assured her, missing the hungry look between them. "I'm sure we can send someone down there to get your things, I promise. But let's get you dressed first. Okay?"

Sera let out a rough breath before nodding and followed her into the bathing chamber.

"Fortunately, the Blacks will suit you, given your coloring," Kaitlyn said, shaking her head. "Not that you'll be able to see them under the winter garb. Rylan was saying you hate the cold, so I will find every bit of warm gear we have so you will never have to worry about that again."

As she closed the door behind them for privacy, Sera began to relax. Not only was the room warm and humid, but there was a hot stream of water pouring down like rain through a metal sieve in the otherwise tile-covered room.

What a marvelous looking contraption.

Before Sera could free herself of her small clothes, though, Kaitlyn had her measurements to take.

"Arms up," she said, smiling as Sera put her hands together and set them on top of her head and out of the way. Kaitlyn moved in and reached around her with a thin line of rope, and then dropped the slack down around the widest part of her hips before pulling it taught. After marking the position with a knot, she dropped one of the ends, made another knot, and then looped it around the smallest part of Sera's waist to mark the placement for a third. The last measurement Kaitlyn took brought them face to face again, as the rope looped from the base of her wings and then traveled up and over her breasts...

Kaitlyn flushed and quickly marked the place, tying the final knot before setting the rope around her neck for safe keeping. When Kaitlyn looked back up, she seemed to be caught in the full sight of her.

Stupid gift, Sera swore, realizing now what the difference between that Kiss of Greeting and her gift would be as she dropped her arms down to cover herself. *Stupid, stupid gift. She is for Micah, not for me. I don't even like girls! Gods, just stop it, you stupid thing,* she insisted, turning around to free the woman from her spell.

"Could you send Rylan in after you?" She asked, honest and innocent as she pretended she had turned around for some reason other than hiding herself. "My wings haven't been properly oiled in cycles and I wouldn't mind some help," she added and then risked looking back over a wing.

Kaitlyn came back to herself in a rush as the spell was broken. "Of course," she said, stepping back as she rubbed at her eyes. "But as Rylan likely doesn't know lady's soaps from healer's salves, the body soap is just over there," Kaitlyn said, pointing to a small shelf on the wall behind the fall of hot rain. "The violet colored one will clean and soften your hair and the wing-oil is actually suspended in the white liquid."

Sera laughed, happily. "I'll try them all, I promise."

"Then I will send him right in," Kaitlyn said and took her leave.

When the door closed, Sera slipped out of the remaining scraps of her clothing and tossed them at what looked like a rubbish bin. That done, she moved towards the strange water spray, tested it, and found it to be quite pleasant. How these folks had worked that particular trick she couldn't imagine, but she knew that money could do just about anything.

As she turned around to pick up one of the soaps from its little shelf, Rylan let himself in and closed the door behind him.

"Think you can help...?" Sera started to ask, but her words fell away as she watched him slip out of his flight boots and stockings.

When he looked up, watching her as he unlaced the indigo tunic he wore, he seemed to realize she was speechless. Her heart was racing as he pulled the tunic over his head, revealing the whipcord and muscle beneath. He still had all the scars he had ever earned on the street, but the strength inside of him was radiant. He was so self-possessed as he stood before her, so clear about his focus on her alone, that she had to put a hand up to hide her smile as he started after the laces at his hip. She had seen him undress before, right down to his flesh and feathers, but this was the first time she had known what she meant to him or him to her. It was different somehow and the fact that he didn't have to but chose to simply because she had asked was magical.

As he stripped free of the last of his uniform, standing again with his head ducked to hide his smile, Sera's heart was racing. No matter all the cycles on the streets she had turned pleasure into coin, nothing had ever felt like this. Her mother had even said there would be one, but she had never thought it would be him. Rylan was all fire and fury, all no nonsense and take command, but now he stopped at the edge of the tile before her, unsure.

"You skin shy now, soldier boy?" She teased as his attention worked over her curves through the curtain of his platinum tyro crest. She was surprised, then, when she realized what he was looking at were the dark purple welts mottling her skin.

"Sera, I'm going to kill him," he said, his voice rough with his frustration. "The next time I see Dylan, I'm just going to slit his throat and end this. He can torture me, fine, but you? If he hurt you thinking he could get to me, that's it. If he tries it again, if he even breathes the same air as you, I'll kill him."

"You'll do no such thing," Sera insisted, holding out her hand to him. "Will you come here, please?"

Rylan looked away as he did so, moving forward a step. Arms crossed over his chest, it took her finding his hand and peeling it away before he took that final step towards her. As he dropped his forehead against the crown of her head, frustrated and anxious in the moment, she squeezed his hand.

"This isn't like you, sweetness," she said. Strong as he was, he was always softness with her when they were alone. "What's going on?"

"Nothing?" He began, glancing back to her with such pain in his look that it broke her heart. "Everything? Gods, Sera, he hurt you because of me. Because I didn't listen to you and came after you. Because I didn't listen to Micah or Mother when they told me to not go. Because I just *had* to see you when it could have ruined everything."

Sera cupped a hand on his cheek as the words came pouring out.

"Why do I have to do everything on my own again?" He went on, though she was glad to feel his hands on her waist as he held onto her. "I hate this stupid tournament and I hate being in charge and I just want to hide in here with you, but I can't. Instead I have to make an ass out of myself trying to lead idiots to war just so some Prefect or Praetor can use me for their Legion while I leave you here alone. Sera, I can't do that. I can't abandon you, not when that's exactly what he—"

Sera's hand on his jaw slipped forward, stopping him from saying more as she set a finger over his lips.

"You are not your brother," she insisted, and firmly. "And going to war is not you abandoning me, it's doing your duty. As for last night, I was deep in their crew so it was only a matter of time. Given what day it was, I should have known you might come to find me. I hadn't gotten a letter from you in as long as you hadn't gotten one from me, but that's over now," she insisted. "And both of us are whole again. Meanwhile, your asshole of a brother is nursing a split lip for just trying to touch me. He won't be able to hide from that and you know how vain he is."

Rylan's weak snort of laughter was a good sign.

"You split his lip?" He asked, and Sera smiled to feel his hands at her waist gripping her more firmly. If she had thought him sending his bevy to retrieve her book was romantic, marring his brother's pretty face was clearly the same sort of gesture for him.

"Consider it your graduation present," she said, moving her hand around the back of his neck as he pulled her close. "Besides, you know what my mother always said about men who need killing."

"Never give a man an easy death when suffering is owed," Rylan said, a smile on his lips as she snaked her other arm around his neck.

"That's right," she said, chasing after his kiss only to laugh as he pulled back. "So how about my reward?"

"Reward?" He scoffed. "For what?"

"Cycles of self-control," she said, dragging him down to her level again with her hands laced in his tyro crest. "I'd like it now, if we're done talking about your idiot brother."

When Rylan dodged her kiss a second time, Sera wasn't sure if he was teasing her on purpose or if it was something else. Given the look on his face, she suspected the latter.

"Ry," she asked as she found him chewing his lip. "Why are you playing kestrel?"

"I'm not," he defended, and she saw his face had gone scarlet with embarrassment. "Sera, I just—"

"You're acting like a bowen," she teased, only to pause as he flinched at the term. Utterly surprised, Sera touched a finger to his chin, turning his attention back to her. "Rylan, are you a bowen?"

When he ducked his head, pulling out of her arms, it was all she could do to catch his hand.

"Of course I am," he said, clearly ashamed of it. "But I've never felt this way about anyone before. I didn't even realize I was in love with you until Tyrsten pointed it out. But now that I know, I don't know what to do about it. All I know is I want to rip you to pieces because I can't get close enough to you, but I don't want to touch you because I could hurt you. Because you are hurt and it's my fault. And the way you look at me? I know what you want, but I've never... I don't know how to do that stuff. I know you do, but I can't do that for you. I mean, I don't think I can," he said, the words stalling as he looked her in the eye. "Can I?"

Sera was speechless. Every trick she had learned to draw a person into her nest, every defense she had learned to not fall in love, it was nothing against the innocence in his asking. He was desperate to make her happy, that much was clear, but he just didn't know how. He might not want it for himself, but he wanted it for her. Or at least, he knew she wanted it, but even the idea of it was foreign to him. Worst of all...

"And what if I do it wrong?" He asked, terrified. "Will you even want me?"

Sera's smile was all love and softness as she beamed back at him.

Her mother had always said Love came in many forms, but the way it was expressed was as varied as the stars. Some love was physical, sure, but it could also be time spent in stillness together. It could be a thousand little gifts over a lifetime of companionship, candlemarks spent talking over absolutely nothing, and acts of devoted service that showed just how far one person would go for another.

Rylan was that last sort, all loyalty and devotion, and Sera wanted more from him than he knew how to give. It was the gift of himself, in service to her needs. It was exactly what her mother had said was the mark of a good man.

"I know enough for the both of us, Rylan," she soothed, pulling him back into the water one reluctant step at a time. "If you will consent to be taught, I can show you as well."

"I just want to make you happy," he said, dropping his head to shield his eyes from the water as he joined her at last. "Sera, that's all I've ever wanted."

"I know, sweetness," Sera said, falling in love with him all over again. "But I don't want to make you upset with the trying. Whatever we do, it should make both of us happy. I promise it feels good," she added with a chuckle. "So good you may never get enough."

"If it makes you happy," he whispered. "I may never want to stop."

There was hesitancy in his eyes as he set his hands on her waist, relenting at last to her gentle insistence to close the distance between them. He was ready to join with her, that much was physically obvious, but the kiss they shared was breathtakingly slow. Rylan, who had always been sharp looks and hard reason, was suddenly focusing all of that intensity on her, and it made her swoon. When Rylan gave something his all, no one in the world could match him.

As that first, slow kiss came to an end, Sera found his hands with her own and guided them up from her hips. Rylan shifted to study what she was doing, encouraged when she gave a soft gasp of pleasure with the calluses of his hand over her chest. His lips were on her own as he gave up one hand to catch the small of her back, holding her steady as he tested just what kind of touch and grip she preferred. Surprised but also melting into his embrace, she slipped her arms around his neck to keep herself on her feet. As her own breath began to quicken, he chased after her kiss, stealing her breath fully as heat and longing flushed through her.

When they came up for air, Rylan tossing his head back into the water spray to sort his tyro crest, Sera's wings were on the wall for support as she panted. Once he had smoothed his hair out of his eyes, he set them back on her and the gold fire inside the chestnut made her knees go weak.

"You learn quick," she managed, shivering with the feel of his lips on her neck.

"I like being this close to you," he whispered, and her heart skipped as he pulled her against him. "Gods, Sera, but I've missed you so much."

"Do you want to get closer?" She murmured, encouraged as she felt one of his hands sliding down her curves. Before he could come up again, she gave him a wicked smile and caught his hand, keeping it low.

"Closer than this?" he asked, curious as she drew his hand down her torso to stop at the bend of her hip.

Realizing what they were about to do was enough to set her heart thundering, but Rylan didn't move from where she had placed him. One delicate hand over his own, holding him against her, Sera reached towards him with the other. His breath caught to feel her taking hold of him, and Sera's smile broadened with the breath he exhaled through his teeth to keep standing.

"Don't tell me you've never found your own pleasure," she teased.

"I don't see how that's releva... Oh," Rylan swore, his free hand leaving her waist as he braced himself against the wall between her wings. "Oh, you're really..."

"I am," Sera smirked. "And I mean to find your tail feathers here and now."

The look of promise in her eyes must have swayed him, even as he swore an oath about the sorcery of slender hands.

"What do you say, soldier boy?" She asked, looking up at him with a wicked smile. "Think you can pick me up?"

"Does that mean you'll stop touching me?" Rylan gasped as she took a firmer grip.

"Only for a moment," she promised, laughing as he gave up his hold on her. Something had snapped in him with all her teasing and as he reached for her hips, she slid her arms around his neck, kissing him fiercely. When his grip firmed, she pressed her wings against the wall to help him lift her into his arms. Rylan caught her easily enough, hands sliding down to support the back of her thighs as she wrapped her legs around him.

"Holy gods," he growled into her shoulder, absolutely lost to the moment. "This is..."

"This is only the beginning," Sera whispered, though the heady promise was almost lost as the strength of him filled her with joy. Petite as she was and strong as Rylan had become, he supported her weight like she was nothing at all. With the water pouring down around them, with him desperate to bring them even closer, she lost herself in the pleasure she had wanted with him for so long.

A whole candlemark later, finally clean and pleasantly exhausted, Sera realized she was starting to sense Micah's presence in her mind. She couldn't make contact for all that he was unconscious, but if she could feel him it meant Vinicia had moved him out from behind the incredible shields that obfuscated her personal apartments.

So after Rylan found his way back into his uniform, Sera traded his affection for a new set of silk and lace small clothes and joined Kaitlyn to see what she had 'found lying around' that Sera could wear as she devoured another platter of food all by herself.

"Are these all for me?" Sera asked, looking back to Kaitlyn.

It was almost obscene how many offhand clothes the girl had set before her. The pile was likely worth more money than Sera could remember seeing in her lifetime.

"Only if you want them," Kaitlyn answered, sheepish. "Now that I have your measure, we can get garb made to your true figure once the festivities are over. I hope you don't mind these for now."

"Mind?" With her hair and body still wrapped in an impossibly soft towel, she stepped up to the display of silks, leather, and whisper-thin linen with wonder. "Blood on my ancestors, if you only knew..."

Kaitlyn seemed a little startled by her language, but Rylan just chuckled from where he had settled into what was meant to be Sera's nest and tucked himself in to watch.

He has earned himself a nice long nap, Sera smirked, not missing his heavy lids. She wouldn't mind one herself after all of their exertions, but she soldiered on. She was warm right down to her core and she meant to stay that way.

"Start with this," Kaitlyn said, touching the soft linen pile. "That is the base layer."

Sera picked up the set dutifully, but was confused to see two pieces. "What is this for?" She asked, holding up what looked to be the length of fitted half-shirt, with a tie to cinch the bottom.

"That's a middler," she said. "It's to support your chest. It's quite comfortable. I would have brought you a corset, but I hate the things so I don't have one," she said, shrugging.

"They always look like they would make it hard to fly," Sera agreed, thinking of the way her mother's garb had always had something like this, though hers had just been a sash of silk draped behind her neck and crossing over her chest. "This is perfect. Thank you."

Kaitlyn preened under the praise and then stood so she could better gesture from the other side of the heap. "The women of our House generally prefer a good pair of fleece-lined leather breeches, tall boots, and a silk-lined doublet, jacket, or bodice. The men's tops tend to be close fitted and longer in the torso, but the women's, well..." Kaitlyn gestured to the outfit she was wearing.

Like the second and third-hand bodices Sera had seen on the streets, Kaitlyn's was all one piece in the front, with a square neck she had snuck her head through before getting into the sleeves. After that it looked like the top of the back panel had been artfully embroidered with the Windover House's golden gryphon while the middle had a thick waist belt with buckles that closed at the front. Unlike the fitted men's doublet, all of the panels were tight down to Kaitlyn's natural waist and then flared out with an excess of fabric, giving her quite a striking figure.

"I like the ruffles on the back," Kaitlyn added, spinning to show how the long, trailing peplum would flutter out as she moved.

"It's nice," Sera smiled, close to giggling like Kaitlyn for all the simple joy of the moment. "I think it balances out the tightness."

"The lower tier daughters laugh at us about having bird tails," Kaitlyn explained. "But they look like dolls standing in the middle of a cream cake given the volume of their skirts, so it's an even trade."

"Well, I'd rather be a bird and eat a cake, so that's easy," Sera said, picking up a set of black leather breeches with a long stripe of gold down the outside of the legs. Kaitlyn helped her find the matching jacket for the piece, and then gestured to a pile of silk shirts to choose from. The shirts themselves were of varying colors of blue, green, or purple, but all of them had the gold running through. Red was completely missing.

"Oh, the colors," Kaitlyn said, almost sighing. "I have a whole book on the colors that I will show you when we have time. But for now, just know that black is the Alexandrian shelf color for every House, so if you see someone in Black at court, they are from Alexandria. It is the piping or trim they wear will distinguish what House they are from. We are the ruling house in Alexandria, so we have gold. I have the other shirt colors just because I love them and everyone knows who I am, anyway."

"Can I wear the blue for the tyros?" Sera asked, picking up a sapphire shirt with a critical eye. This one had a high, stiff collar that was embroidered with little sparrow hawks, which seemed cute enough.

"You most certainly can," Kaitlyn said. "That is not uncommon at all."

"You just want to set off your eyes," Rylan added, though his voice was muffled by the comforts he had pulled over himself. "Bad as Micah."

"No one asked you," Sera called back as Kaitlyn giggled to hear the exchange. "Go back to sleep, soldier boy."

"This is for you as well," Kaitlyn said, standing from her seat next to the chest so she could pick up a long rectangle of fabric and hand it to her. "This is called kivet. It is some of the finest wool that comes out of our House's heard of muskox in Greying," Kaitlyn explained as Sera touched the incredibly soft fabric. "And that little bit is worth about a crown. However," she added, as Sera's eyes went wide. "Since it is both the warmest and softest fabric you will ever come across, I am giving you my set. You already said you get cold easily and I will not stand for you to be cold on my watch," she said, adding a matching set of fingerless gloves, thick stockings, and wool-lined sleeves to the lid of the chest. "So please, this is my gift to you."

"But won't you be cold?" Sera objected, even as her hands shook to realize she was holding twenty crowns worth of fabric. "I just couldn't—"

"I insist," Kaitlyn said, and Sera looked up to see the woman's happiness as she made the gift. "If it makes you feel any better, I haven't had the chance to wear these in at least a cycle because they are actually too warm. I usually wear cashmere or silk most days."

"I need to put all of this on right now," Sera exclaimed, accepting the gift as Kaitlyn smiled at her.

"Start with the stockings," Kaitlyn said, and then reached for a pair of the breeches. "Then these, the shirt, the jacket, sleeves, and then gloves."

Sera scooped up the pile Kaitlyn had made and then scurried off behind the tall room-divider. After making quick work of twisting her wet hair onto her head without the towel, Sera happily worked her way into every impossibly soft layer that Kaitlyn insisted on her wearing. Next, she stepped into the fleece-lined breeches and tied up the laces at her hips before ducking into the sapphire blue shirt. Once she had her arms in the sleeves and the back panel between her wings, she wrapped the sides around her middle and made it lie flat with a clever tuck that Kaitlyn showed her. The thick wool stockings were next, doubling over at the knee to make the gently used leather flight-boots fit perfectly. That done, she ducked her head into the neck-opening of the jacket and wrapped the sides around to the front and then had to let Kaitlyn do the rest of the puzzle.

"The front of this one is just a little stiff since I didn't get the chance to wear it much," she explained, taking the side pieces in hand so she could make a few minor adjustments. "And then the left side actually threads through a hole in the right one..." She went on, joining the pieces together. "And then both wrap around you a second time, slip through this loop in the back and then join here in the front again," she said, working so fast that Sera had no idea what was actually going on.

When she was done, Sera knew that the piece was fitted comfortably, if snugly around her middle and was sure that none of it would leave her exposed while she was flying. That was what really mattered, anyway.

"Don't worry. You'll be able to do it for yourself in no time," Kaitlyn assured her, stepping back to admire the full effect. "And Micah certainly knows how mine comes off, so I'm sure that he can figure out how to get you into one if I'm not around. What I wouldn't give to be able to wear one of the men's, though! That just laces up the front like a reasonable piece of clothing," she said, sighing. "Instead, we get flared collars and a neckline that puts our chest on display."

"Yeah, I... I'm not sure about that," Sera said, hesitating. "It's a bit cold to be this open, even with the shirt."

"That's what this is for," Kaitlyn said, and picked up the last rectangle of kivet. "One side tucks into the bodice front, goes around your neck, and then crosses itself and tucks into the other side," she explained, pointing at the golden silk version she had on.

"Oh!" Sera said, fascinated as she snuck the scarf she held beneath her hair. "How clever! I thought that was just part of your shirt."

Warmth and modesty, Sera thought, crossing the piece like Kaitlyn's before tucking it in. *My blicing magic is good enough to make a mess of things. I don't need clothes that help!*

Kaitlyn looked immensely pleased. "I'm so glad everything fits!" She cheered. "Oh, and there are pockets built into that peplum," she added with a wink.

"I don't know what I'd do without them, but we can get you a thigh-bag if you want, too. I'm not sure what you like to keep at hand."

"Snacks," Sera said immediately and Kaitlyn grinned as she looked to the empty sideboard in the room. "But there is one thing that I still need, she went on, pulling the long length of her hair over a shoulder. "Before she died, I promised my mother I would cover my hair when I went outside. Is there anything you have that, well..."

"Oh," Kaitlyn said, surprised to see Sera's hesitancy. "Oh, hair coverings haven't been in fashion for quite a few cycles, but... No, I'm sure we can find something. Just a moment."

Sera swallowed around her uneasiness as she followed Kaitlyn out from behind the changing screen, though her fear was abruptly distracted as she heard Rylan's reaction to her garb.

"Oh, wow," he breathed, finally seeing her.

"I don't look terrible?" Sera asked, flushing as Rylan came to his feet.

"You look awesome," he insisted, and the look in his eyes reignited the memory of their shared shower. "Micah's gonna loose his mind."

"I found it!" Kaitlyn declared, coming to her feet again from where she had been sifting through a pile of accessories in her own chest of clothing. "I knew I still had one. It never looked right on me, but on your hair..."

Both Sera and Rylan turned their attention to her as she moved to rejoin them. In her hand was a woven net of gold cloth. It wasn't much, but then again...

"What is that?" Sera asked as Kaitlyn expanded the net to show her.

"It's called a snood," she said. "You can fold up all of your hair close to your head and then slip this on and it settles into the net. They're quite comfortable, but with so many people in the house having curly hair, we could never get them to sit right. And then with the way Consort Lenae's braids became popular, we just gave up. But on you," Kaitlyn said, grinning as Sera took it. "It will look glorious on you."

"Black and gold are their house colors," Rylan reminded. "They all have gold hair, but you have black. So what? It'll look great."

But if mother is right, I may still look Lan'lieanan, she thought, trying not to panic. "I may have too much hair for this. It may come right off."

Seeing her hesitancy, Kaitlyn turned back to her chest. Curious to see what else there was available, Sera followed her.

"What about this?" Kaitlyn said, pulling free a thick, golden hair pin. With the size of the thing, it would be able to secure her hair, but it would still all be exposed.

"Can I look?" She asked, remembering all of the trinkets, silks, and veils her mother used to have.

As Kaitlyn stepped back, Sera's heart leapt to see a hoard of both black and golden veils, hair caps, pins, and ribbons. It was everything she could ever need.

"This is perfect," Sera said with excitement, picking up a long golden ribbon. If she couldn't cover it without looking like a working woman, then she would disguise the color in the rest of the finery. Her mother had done as much whenever she had gone outside the brothel.

As Kaitlyn and Rylan watched, Sera selected two golden ribbons and set to work braiding them into her hair with two long, thick braids on either side of her head. That done, she picked up two of the pins and then wrapped the first braid so it covered her ear and then pinned it on top of her head. A moment more and she had the second braid pinned in the same way, and then the little black cap she had found went over all of it, securing the braids against her head and covering her hairline.

That done, she picked up the golden veil she had seen and tossed it over her hair, adjusting it so that it draped delicately around her face and shoulders. It was thin enough that even if it got in her face while she was flying, it wouldn't actually block her sight. Another few pins to keep that in place, and then she reached in for a braided bit of black and gold cord, tying it around her forehead so it would keep everything in place.

When she was done, she turned to look back at Kaitlyn and Rylan, only to see that Kaitlyn's mouth had fallen open in surprise.

"How...?" She said, looking to Rylan with disbelief. "How did she do that?"

"Sorcery," Rylan laughed, grinning like a fool. "She's a damn sorcerer about hair."

"I never had any idea," Kaitlyn exclaimed, finally laughing as she touched her own hair. "Gods, these were all my mothers, and I... I never knew what to do with any of that."

"I'll teach you everything I know," Sera promised, giving her best smile. "Cosmetics, too, if you have any. But for now," she said, turning back to the pile to pick up a bit of fancy black ribbon. "Right now I am dying to see my brother, so will this work?"

"Oh, Sera, you don't..." Kaitlyn said, trailing off as Sera placed the cord on Kaitlyn's brow and told her to hold it there. "You don't have to."

"Yes, I do," Sera insisted, slipping behind the girl's wings to take up one side of the cord. A few moments of work and she had tucked just enough of Kaitlyn's curls behind it to pull it all back from her face prettily. "Because you have every right to feel beautiful and if we're both fancy, fewer people will think mine is strange," she said, coming back around to pick up one of the circles of black silk in the pile.

Kaitlyn ducked her head as Sera tucked the silk behind the cord, covering just enough of her curls to be fancy. When she picked her head up again, Kaitlyn was beside herself.

"Micah gets all his cleverness from her," Rylan explained as Kaitlyn began to realize just what kind of woman they were bringing into the House.

"And I got mine from our mother," Sera said, grinning to see how Kaitlyn was flushing under all the attention.

"Anytime you want to fix my hair, please do," Kaitlyn insisted, embarrassed but eager all the same.

"I'd be happy to," Sera smiled. "Though right now, maybe we can go see Micah?"

"Micah!" Kaitlyn yelped, having completely forgotten. "Iskander forgive me, yes. I'm so sorry. We can go right now."

As they made their way, the most Sera could remember of the Palace they passed through was a writhing mass of court colors as they hurried from the Sires' Wing into the Soldier Tyros' Wing. Once they were inside, they started up some number of levels to reach the old wooden door of the room she had dreamed about for two cycles. When they finally reached it, Kaitlyn stepped aside as Rylan worked the nob, walking in first.

"Rylan?" Micah called, his voice weak with exhaustion. "Gods, Rylan, you won't believe what happened."

"It can wait," Rylan said, cutting him off.

Sera's heart was thundering in her chest as she followed him in.

When there was enough room, Rylan stepped aside and she saw Micah at last, leaning against the edge of a nest on the left side of the room. Though he had no doubt changed over the past two cycles, it didn't matter. He was still the other half of her heart.

"Micah!" She cried, rushing towards him. Her brother's eyes flew open at the sound of her voice and he caught her as she threw herself into his arms.

::I love you!:: He projected, crushing her against him.

::I love you, too!:: She echoed, bursting into tears.

Chapter 18: Kaitlyn

Friday, 17:00

Kaitlyn wasn't sure how she felt watching Micah sobbing in his twin's embrace. She had always known that she was just a placeholder for Sera in Micah's life, but watching herself being replaced cut deeper than she had expected. What would he think of her now? What did she mean to him? Even with her father's blessing, would Micah still need her the same way he had before? She honestly didn't know.

So as Micah and Sera lost themselves in each other, Kaitlyn looked to Rylan. There was love there as well. She could see it plainly as Rylan reached for the bend of her wing as he joined them. Love had called Rylan back to Sera despite the risk all these cycles, just as Sera's absence had driven Micah into Kaitlyn's arms. But did Micah know? He'd never spoken of it, but the anger and betrayal in Micah's depression could mean anything.

Love was a dangerous, delirious thing.

As Rylan neared Sera, it was Micah who pulled the three of them together. They were an honest crush of arms and wings with no lack of tears. No matter how happy she wanted to be for them, the sight tore at her until she had to close the door to keep from crying for an entirely different reason.

She had seen such love among the Houses, but ever since her brothers had died on the Plains, she had never known it. She never would know it, too, with all of them taken back into Founder Iskander's embrace.

Kaitlyn took a shuddering breath as she looked down the long hallway, torn between her loss for where to go and a complete lack of desire to go anywhere else. Her love was here as well as her passion, and though Sera had been a fast friend while a captive audience, she would undoubtedly like time with her family without a stranger involved.

Perhaps it wasn't that she was not wanted, but Kaitlyn knew that the polite thing to do was to step aside. It always had been, as far as House politics were concerned.

I have to think of something else, she thought desperately, fleeing the sounds of joy behind her. *I have to do something else. Be somewhere else.* But this place was her somewhere else, and replacing it would not be easy.

That was the reason she had offered her assistance to Barracks Mother Vinicia in watching over Micah, and she suspected Mother knew that Kaitlyn enjoyed spending so much time in the Tyros' Wing because it was a refuge from her duties to House and home. Unlike in the Windover suite, the young men of the Delton Tyro Legion worked towards a goal greater than themselves. They sought to better themselves for more than the personal satisfaction of besting a peer or for the glory of gold. They did it for the kingdom and for what that meant to everyone, abstract though it might seem.

She was not a fool, however. Not all tyros were as aspirational as she imagined, but those didn't fight for the chance to study in Delton and serve under the Seventh Counsel Lord. The boys here had the spark. Together in their brotherhood, they became more. Her time in the Palace had given her ample opportunity to see that, even if she had been unable to learn as a tyro herself.

Rather, her time here was a woman's. Since coming of age five cycles ago, she had lived in either the House's suite or the Delton Estate in order to learn the Way of Court. Since her own mother had not survived long after her birth, it was Matron Yulia who had instructed her in the Way of Keys so she might assist with governing House Windover's Aerie Branch with her father. With her subsequent elevation to Dame Kaitlyn then spent two more cycles at the right hand of her father, learning the Ways of Governance as he served as temporary Patriarch to the House at large.

This she needed in order to assist whomever she would ring, for she would not be able to rule of her own right. Such a thing wasn't done, even if some lower houses followed Consort Lenae's example.

If she was forced to speak the truth, Kaitlyn knew she preferred the company of men, tyros especially, as they were full of the intellectual curiosity that inspired her still. Courting, throwing fêtes, and preening over rings had never held much of a candle to the thought of the impact she may be able to make as a wife to a veteran, or as a matron if she could ever conceive a chick. Kaitlyn grimaced as she pressed the palms to her abdomen, feeling the strength of the muscles beneath.

Soon, she prayed. *If the Gods of our House are good, let it be soon.*

Even so, Kaitlyn still felt empty inside. She was as close as a woman could come to doing real good for her House, but there was an impenetrable wall between herself and her intended mate. With his sister at hand, would Micah stay and rule with her as the Elders had hoped or would he leave for war and never return? No ring could bind a man if he chose to forsake it and he hadn't even been told of the chance.

Finally far enough from the sounds of the crew's joy to slow her steps, Kaitlyn took her time making her way through the rest of the stone hallway, weaving herself among the tyros who were moving past and returning the greetings of those that hailed her. She was not a stranger to them and most knew of Micah's affection for her. An affection, she suspected, that Nichi shared with a certain dryad-kin.

Given the events of the morning, she knew Nichi had stayed with him in the Garden. However, since taking Westly to the suite would mean talking business with the Elders, Nichi would have invited Westly to his room here in the Tyros' Wing. In Nichi's absence, Sire Gaius and Matron Yulia had arrived on the Palace grounds and it was time that she collected him back to the suite. Not only that, but Westly would likely want to greet Sera as well.

Destination at hand, Kaitlyn slowed her steps as she neared Nichi's room near the center of the wing. She knocked when she arrived, and it took more than a few moments for them to investigate who was at the door.

"Sal'weh, Westly," Kaitlyn said, greeting the emerald eye that peered through the crack between the door and the threshold. His skin, muted and pale like the bark of a river-willow, blossomed to a rose's red at the sight of her.

"Sera's come home to roost," she said, disarming his worry. "I just wanted to let you know."

"Sera?" Westly repeated, though the way he closed his eyes made her suspect he could find Sera without her help. When he opened them there was a smile splitting his face. "So she has," he said, stepping back to let her enter. "Come in. Please."

Kaitlyn entered the room to find her shirtless near-brother resting his hips back against the platform that held his nest, a little cast iron tea pot on the shelf beside him. As she came into the room, he set down the cup he had been nursing as Westly closed the door.

"You're looking well," she greeted, only now realizing how wan and pale he had been the night before by comparison. Now he looked every bit the soldier tyro and though he wasn't as strong as Micah, what muscle he did have was on display with his shirt draped over the edge of his nest.

"All thanks to him," Nichi said, gesturing towards Westly as the kin moved to collect the script of herbs he had laid out on Nichi's desk. "Mother says I am to have him as my personal chiurgeon for the next fortnight."

Kaitlyn didn't miss the pleasure in his voice at the idea. "I am sure you will survive somehow," she said, letting her amusement show.

Nichi looked at Westly before dropping his eyes back into his heavy teacup, unable to hide his smile. Unsurprised by the pairing, Kaitlyn was glad to see him so at ease in his courting of the skittish dryad-kin. It had been quite a while since Nichi had been so caught up in someone, but to see him relaxed into the hunt was an even better sign. Nichi was relentless when he meant to court someone into his nest, but when he found someone worthy, he took his time to savor every moment. That was the only reason she had been able to steal away Micah that first night in the suite, not that Nichi had ever forgiven her for it.

"If you're done," Kaitlyn said as Westly slung his bag over his shoulder. "I need to collect him back to the suite. His sire and matron have arrived on the Palace grounds and would like to see him."

"Of course," Westly said, and his fluster was endearing. "He has what he needs, now. I'll come by later to check in," he said, glancing at Nichi. "If that's all right."

"You're welcome here any time," Nichi said, though it was obvious from his tone that the offer was for more than just another chiurgeon visit.

"Yes, as you said," Westly acknowledge, looking down at his hand on the strap of his shoulder bag.

The kindred's complete lack of composure was one of the most adorable things Kaitlyn had seen in quite a while. The innocence of it made her smile until she was struck with a sudden thought. Looking back to Nichi, she realized he might not know about the time it took for a kin to consider taking a lover at all.

"Westly, did Vinicia say you were coming into your power?" Kaitlyn asked, hoping that Westly knew that she knew that he may still be a bowen if the answer was yes. With Westly's mortified look, she knew she was correct.

As he started for the door, Nichi shot her an incredulous look, but it didn't last for long. Before Westly could move past her, Kaitlyn stepped into his path. Westly stopped just in front of her and she could tell that his hands were shaking. Nichi had made himself quite the temptation, which was fine for a windwalker, but kindred were different. Westly had survived twice as long as any other she had ever read about, save Vinicia. Whether Vinicia's guidance had helped or not, the only reason that was possible was because he had not taken a lover.

"If he tries anything foolish you just call out for me and I'll set him straight," Kaitlyn whispered and Westly looked up at her with such panic and relief that Kaitlyn was glad to have spoken up. "You have every right to deny him until you're ready and I will box his ears before he does anything you don't want him to."

"He couldn't force me into anything I didn't want," Westly said, suddenly amused. "I'm sorry, Kait, it's just—I don't want to hurt him any more than I already have," he confessed in a rush. "But he's so... It's so hard to stop myself. It's not him, I promise. I just don't know what I'm doing, but if Sera is here, I'll ask her. Thank you for letting me know," he said and then pressed on to pass her.

Kaitlyn stepped aside to let him go, concerned as she watched him leave. When the door was closed behind him, Kaitlyn saw Nichi was watching after the kin with a fragile expression.

"What is going on?" He asked, hoping to find answers from her since Westly had obviously not been able to explain.

"He hasn't come into his power yet," Kaitlyn said. "Which means he is a bowen."

"He has come into his power, healing me like he did yesterday," Nichi threw back and the defensiveness of his tone told her there was more to his fancy that perhaps Nichi himself realized.

"They have to touch the core of a windwalker and he did, but now he won't touch me at all. It's torture."

"Look at yourself, Nichi," she insisted. "You are torturing him, too. Worse, if you triggered the change in him, then he has a lot more than lovers marks and pleasure to consider."

"Like what?" Nichi asked, moving to pick up the indigo shirt he had shed. Given that she was only stealing him briefly, he would need to be in his uniform when he returned to the barracks.

"My books say that when kin are old enough, they are able to hold power in reserve," Kaitlyn said and for once Nichi wasn't giving her that overly annoyed look that she usually got when she tried to argue a point about fae stories with him.

"What's that got to do with me?" Nichi asked, standing to lace the shirt beneath his wings.

"If you triggered him, you are the first source of power he has ever realized he can hold," she said. "He will want to fill himself with it, but it would be like a man dying of thirst finding the River Kir. He could drown himself trying to drink too fast and he could kill you if he takes too much."

"Wes wouldn't kill me," Nichi scoffed.

"It's not about what he wants," Kaitlyn argued. "It's about what he needs. He knows he needs to take in more power, but he has to do it gradually and here you are wanting to tumble him into a nest. That is the ultimate expression of a friendship, Nichi, not the start."

Nichi flushed at that. True friends were rare among the Tyro Court; lovers, however, came and went with the winds.

"Be his friend, Nichi," Kaitlyn went on, watching as he picked up his uniform jacket from where he had dropped it beside his nest. "That alone can spark the wellspring in him if he truly does like you. And if you like him," she added, seeing how he was starting to guard his flustered reaction now that she had seen it. "You have every right to be happy with whoever you want. You are not a Prince right now, so don't let those idiot Daughters tell you that you can't take a man to nest. You will be a soldier in two days and then a veteran until you come back from War. Only then will you even have to think of getting ringed to any of the women you threw chicks on and none of that should stop you from taking a wingmate. Take five wingmates! So long as you're happy and focused and fighting for what matters."

As her lecture ended, Nichi smoothed down the front of his uniform and looked to her with a smirk. "What if I make Micah my wing while we're at War, hmm? How would you feel about that?"

"You better take care of him," Kaitlyn insisted, crossing her arms as she stared him down. "I want a happy man when he comes back to me, not someone who has forgotten what it's like to enjoy himself in a nest."

Nichi's grin nearly split the room as he laughed. "I just wanted to be sure, Kait," he insisted. "He really does love you and I don't want to hurt that."

Kaitlyn couldn't help herself, smiling as well. "I wish he would say that out loud if it's true," she confessed. "Father says we can be ringed if he'll ask. Same with Kreychi. It's a whole..." She stalled as Nichi's eyes went wide. "Gods, I didn't tell you. We're adopting Micah and Sera into the House because of the boon Kreychi gave to Counsel Lord Kiernan. That's why you need to go talk to them."

"Glory to the House of Windover!" Nichi laughed. "If Mike is my brother and you two get ringed, that brings you into the main branch, Kait. We'll really be first-sibs."

"Near-sibs by birth, siblings by law with the rings," Kaitlyn said, shrugging. "You're my brother, Nichi, and— Are you done?" She laughed, realizing they were just standing in his room. "Can we go, you peacock?"

"Speak for yourself," Nichi laughed, grabbing his cloak from where he had draped it across his lounge as they started for the door. "What's with the veil in your hair?"

"Sera did it for me," she preened, still ridiculously happy about that regardless of the rest of her emotions. "Gods, but you should see hers! She's so incredibly talented."

"Let's go then," Nichi said, joining her at the door. "I have to see what a female version of Mike looks like before she breaks hearts all over the barracks."

"Do you think that's wise after the way you just flustered Westly?" Kaitlyn reminded. "That's why I came to get you, anyway. I wanted to give them time together."

"Without us," Nichi said, disappointed but understanding. "I suppose there's always this evening."

"Two days and a wake up," Kaitlyn agreed with a laugh. "Gods it's almost one day and a wake up. Are you boys even ready?"

"We're almost there," he said, closing the door behind them. "What we really need to do is rest, so they're giving us that as well."

"And here I come dragging you to Court," Kaitlyn said, grimacing. "I'm sorry, Nichi."

"Don't be," he said, gesturing for her to lead him down the hall. "If I can help Mike or his sister, it's worth it. Come on, let's go."

By the time they reached the Windover House apartments, all the veterans that had been bustling through the suite had vanished. So, too, had all of the wardrobes and items that had been staged for removal down to the Delton Estate. Even the painted canvas was gone from the walls, stripped bare for space to hang maps and other military things that the Warhost officers needed while regrouping during the Winter season. With a new Seventh Counsel Lord expected to be named, everyone was preparing for an intense winter session.

Well, everyone except the Younger Court. Now that most of their elders were gone, they had flooded back into the suite to start after the excess of food and drink that wouldn't be taken with them from the Palace shelf. Instead it would feed them and any other roving band of courtiers as they celebrated the last two days before they all went home. As the saying went: Winter Court was for War Lords, not House Lords.

Given everyone's distractions, Kaitlyn had expected to follow her near-brother into the suite and back to the receiving room, but they were stopped almost at the door. Daughter Makayla, the dancer who often tried and failed to drag Micah into her nest any moment Kaitlyn took her eyes off him, was waiting for them. Kaitlyn kept her face neutral as they were formally addressed.

"Sire Marius will see you now, Heir Nichi," Makayla said, eyeing Kaitlyn's hair with a suspicious sort of approval. "Dame Kaitlyn, Matron Yulia has requested you attend to her," she added, as if Kaitlyn was in trouble. "They are both waiting in the receiving room."

"Thank you," Kaitlyn said, but Daughter Makayla was already walking away. Court them with kindness, her father always said and so she smiled despite her true feelings. Her hand still on Nichi's as escort, they followed the same path she had taken before with Counsel Lord Kiernan and Dame Vinicia to the receiving room at the heart of the Suite.

"Heir?" Nichi balked when they were out of earshot. "When did that happen!"

"Oh that," Kaitlyn said, wincing at Nichi's look. "That happened when they named Kreychi Patriarch this dawning. That makes you Heir now. It's just a formality..."

"But you just promised I could be a soldier," he said, shaking his head even if he was teasing. "I can't believe you, Kait. Going back on your word like that."

"You can," Kaitlyn laughed. "Just... Not right this moment. Gods, come on."

Nichi chuckled to himself as they made it the rest of the way down the hall. They separated from their escort when they reached the double doors, needing to push the one side open so they could enter.

"Andronicus," Matron Yulia greeted as they entered. "I see that your hand isn't broken."

Kaitlyn winced on Nichi's behalf as the silence of the room seemed to emphasize her use of Nichi's full name. As they watched, House Windover's Matron extended her left hand delicately towards her youngest son, who left Kaitlyn's side to take it.

"What gave you the cause for worry, Matron," Nichi replied, more formally than Kaitlyn would have expected. "This close to Graduation, you know they stop our letters."

Matron Yulia's sigh said she didn't believe a word of it. Beside her, Kaitlyn's own father just shook his head.

"He is my Son first, no matter what this place means to make of him, sending him to War," Yulia said as Nichi exchanged the Kiss of Greeting with her. "Kreychi found enough glory at war for any man, so I do not see why he must be here. For all the chicks he has thrown, he should be ringed and maintaining the Estates on Alexandria, not wasting his time in this place." As Marius closed his eyes, shaking his head with his refusal to argue, Yulia's attention turned back to Nichi. "You always loved the woods, my son. You do not have to accept this commission. If you return home, I will see you set up in the Ayrie Estate with the Daughter from Borean that she has given you a son."

Kaitlyn stood a little taler as she realized what Matron Yulia was trying to tempt him with. Nichi had fought so hard to be able to stay home, to not have to come to Court at all, but then their Sire had become sick and Kreychi had been recalled, and so he had gone to court to make certain the House was seen as serving the Host. He had been here four solar cycles now, was two days from graduating, and suddenly she wanted him to return home? This wasn't about what Nichi wanted at all, it was the fact that Kreychi didn't have a wife or fledglings because of his service at War. If the same thing happened to Nichi, they might have possible heirs, but none consecrated to the House. If Nichi died at war, the foundation of the House would be in jeopardy. Kaitlyn tried not to let her panic show as Matron Yulia's attention shifted ever so slightly to Kaitlyn herself.

Given how desperate her Matron was for an heir, if Kaitlyn was able to catch a chick from Micah, her Matron might make the argument that the two should trade rings before Micah even went to War. Scandal that it might be socially, Micah was not the Heir and Kaitlyn was already a Windover, so it would not be expressly forbidden. Worse, Kaitlyn had unintentionally made that possible by putting off all other suiters for the past few cycles. Micah held her heart, so any chick she caught would have to be from him. If there was an Heir and they were at least ringed, if not married, then even if Micah died at war the chick would be viable to inherit. A male chick, at least, but it would be worth the risk to her.

Taking a steadying breath, Kaitlyn made certain she returned her Matron's smile as the door to the receiving room clicked open once again. Turning to look, Kaitlyn saw her near-brother Kreychi stride into the room. There was no missing the new addition to his Windover Blacks, given how the wide, sapphire slash of color crossed his torso, anchored by the matching waist belt in the same blue satin. Even if Nichi was just now being told he was the Heir to Windover, Kreychi was returning from the Lower Shelf after having been inducted into the Kosaran House of Lords. Like the King's Counsel Lords, the House Lords worked to govern the city shelves and surrounding territories within the Kosaran Mountains.

"Heir Andronicus," Kreychi greeted, smirking as he brushed a hand along the satin of his new office. Nichi's face as Kreychi came to a stop in front of him nearly made Kaitlyn laugh.

"Krecentius," he returned, using his brother's full name as well. "You finally get your hair cut? Oh no, you just put it in a tail…"

"Asshole," Kreychi scoffed, moving to catch Nichi in a head lock before he could back out.

"Oh, the sash!" Nichi laughed, pretending to see it for the first time as Kreychi pressed his face against it. "Sorry, man. I didn't see it. It's just, all that black. It really doesn't show it off at all."

"Very funny, little brother," Kreychi said, releasing him from the hold. As they both resettled their wings, Kreychi put a hand up to smooth his long platinum hair. It was gathered in a low tail at the back of his head now, tidy but most definitely not a warcrest, and Kaitlyn wondered just what it would take for him to cut it short like he should have done four cycles ago when he had returned from the Plains.

Once they were presentable, Kaitlyn stepped up to make a proper line and then they all made their courtesies, Kaitlyn circling her right leg back as the other two bowed, hands over their hearts.

"Honor to the House," Kreychi said.

"Glory to the Ancestors," Sire Marius replied, releasing them from the formality. "Kaitlyn, I mean to speak with these two. Yuli, were you going to speak with Kaitlyn now or later?"

"Now," her Matron said, coming to her feet to let the heavy, high-low skirt she wore settle around her legs. "Walk with me, lovely."

Kaitlyn gave another small curtsy, falling into step with her House Matron as she passed. Moving from the center of the room to the sitting area some distance away, the elder woman was contemplative. Reserved as she normally appeared with her golden hair twisted up against the back of her head with pins and a soft, subtle veil, she looked on Kaitlyn's own change in appearance with approval.

"I heard a rumor that you had rediscovered your mother's trinkets," she observed, settling herself on one of the lounges in the sitting area. Kaitlyn followed her example, taking a seat on the nearby lounge and doing the same. She felt a little under dressed, given the peplum and her unbound hair, though everyone seemed so focused on the veil that Sera had added that she decided not to care.

"How has your time been at Court?" Matron Yulia began. "Do you find life here compelling?"

"More than compelling," Kaitlyn answered carefully, smoothing the black velvet of her leggings to try and settle her nerves. "Though it is not home."

"Home," her Matron said, considered their view out the nearby windows. In the spring it would show the Consort's gardens, but for now it was just the sleepy winter temple that would soon be covered in ice and snow; sparse, but not poor to look upon. "Home is not so much a physical place as it is where you desire to spend your efforts. To my estimation, that would place your home somewhere in the Tyros' Wing, yes?"

Kaitlyn flushed, but could not deny it. Even half the world away, her Matron knew her well.

"This Micah, he has become your home it seems," she went on, having confirmed her suspicion. "It is a blessing our new Patriarch has brought him and his sister into the House. Do you understand why?"

"Yes, Matron," Kaitlyn said, unable to miss how Yulia's right hand was touching the subtle golden signet ring on her left. When Matron Yulia had married into the main house from a lesser branch in Kelishe, it had been because Kreychi had proven such a strong fledgling in arms.

As her Matron considered her, however, she pulled her hands back, looking to Kaitlyn with a seriousness she had never seen before. "I do have cause to wonder, however," her Matron said, turning to look at her. "Given how he was raised, have you stopped yourself from catching? Has he?"

Kaitlyn absolutely did not want to talk about this.

Matron Yulia's barely patient look convinced her otherwise.

"At first I did, Matron," she said. "Though it was largely by Micah's own actions, not wanting to complicate our courtship. Where he was raised," she hesitated to add. "He knows far more of giving pleasure to a woman than any man I encountered before. More than even some women, I believe. When I meant to seek his pleasure, he always insisted on seeking mine first."

"And now?" She asked, taking it all in stride.

"Once I turned my ring for him last cycle, I didn't try quite as hard not to catch from him," she confessed. "But I have not caught, as far as I know."

"Does he still stop himself?" She asked.

"No, Matron," she answered, trying to keep an even face. "He will join with me without restraint and I have found his pleasure in him. In... In me, Matron, yes."

Kaitlyn was mortified.

Matron Yulia only nodded. "I was concerned you may have needed further education with so few female friends, but if you believe you can accomplish the task, I will trust you in that," Yulia said, considering her. "If you require assistance, I can have a companion brought in to join you, however. You understand why?"

"Yes, Matron," Kaitlyn said.

"And Nichi means to take him as a wingmate at war?" She asked. "I will not have either of them distracted from their duties to the House as Kreychi continues to be."

"If he is agreeable, yes," Kaitlyn said. "Which I believe he is. Nichi is rather cross with me that Micah will not take to nest with him while we are in the mountains."

"That is work well done, my love," Yulia said, which was more surprising than anything else.

"It is?" Kaitlyn asked.

"Windover has a son born into Borean because of your efforts," she said, a smile on her lips as she looked back from the garden to Kaitlyn herself. "If the Gods of our Ancestors cannot help you to catch before he leaves, then we will have our heir another way."

"Of course, Matron," Kaitlyn said.

"I would prefer you tie your own branch back to the main house, however," Yulia added. "Your own mother was House Borean, and I would not like for those men to have any ideas about stealing you away. I have trained you too well to see your efforts get waisted on that backwater mountain."

Kaitlyn's laughter was genuine as she saw the Matron's true affection shining through.

"You honor me, Matron," Kaitlyn said, bowing her head with the praise."

"Founder Iskander would curse us all to lose you as our House priestess, if I am honest," Yulia went on. "Pious as you are, I would have expected a godseye gifted to you by now."

"I ask our ancestors for nothing else every moment I am in prayer," Kaitlyn said, pressing her palms together. "I serve Iskander with my whole heart, Matron."

"Wonderful," Matron Yulia said, taking a breath as she glanced to where the three men were still standing, laughter coming out from their huddle more often than not. When she looked past them to the doorway, Kaitlyn realized her Matron would possibly want to return to Sire Gaius' side soon. As much as she had married for position and influence, she had come to love Kreychi and Nichi's father.

"Was that all, Matron?" Kaitlyn asked, not wanting to hold her longer than necessary.

"There is one other thing," Matron Yulia said, turning back to her. "What do you desire to do once this Micahleia is within our House? He will away to war and you will be...?"

"Awaiting his return," Kaitlyn answered immediately.

"As a wife?" Her Matron prompted.

"If he is agreeable," she answered, but from the look on her face it was not the right thing to say.

"Remember your place, Kaitlyn," she said, though there was no harshness to it. "You are the Dame of Ayrie. Your father has many cycles still to govern and perhaps take a second wife and birth a son, yes, but that is not the case at this time."

"You know my life is for the House," Kaitlyn answered. It was only proper.

"Your life is your own," Matron Yulia chided. "And a life lived for anyone other than yourself is no a life at all. You may desire to be a companion to another, but you must first guide yourself on your path. Only then will you know if this Micahleia is the mate to join you down it and only then can you guide others down their own paths. Such is the Way of Keys."

"Forgive me, Matron," Kaitlyn said. "I hear what you are saying, but I do not understand."

"I have a task for you," Matron Yulia began again. "As I understand, your scholarship in tales of both the gods and fae has grown during your time here."

Kaitlyn flushed. Yes, her fledgling interest had never waned and the books that filled her library were on a select topic indeed, convinced as she was that they were one in the same. "Yes, Matron."

"As a Dame of our House, you have the leisure of both time and study. We do not ask of you the same life as many Daughters, as you well know."

"This is true," she admitted, still unsure where she was being led.

"So what will you pursue for yourself?" She asked. "Will you return to the Alexandrian Estate as he gains his commission or would you be open to continuing to serve those who may have work for you here in Delton?"

Kaitlyn thought back to the revel the night before, of the women who danced and drank and nested among the tyros and other sirelings for sport. It had never been her calling, though she hadn't despised the entertainment. She loved to watch them, to watch their interactions, even if it meant not participating herself. On more than one occasion she had nudged now-ringed couples into each other's nests when they could not do it themselves.

But that isn't a life... That has never been my life.

"I am glad to know that you cannot make this answer quickly," Matron Yulia said at last, which was a relief. "It shows you have potential yet to rise."

"Thank you, Matron," Kaitlyn returned. As she did so, her Matron's tone changed to one of business.

"When do you judge that I may meet these twins?" Matron Yulia asked. "We do not have long before we must adjourn to the Delton Estate."

"Tomorrow morning may be the first opportunity," Kaitlyn replied. "I doubt they will be able to come out of their preparations for the tournament before then."

"Surely the space in that tyro room is insufficient for the three of them," her Matron said.

"Not necessarily," she replied, hiding her smile. "I am with Micahleia most nights. The Barracks Mother favors me and the nests are snug but not uncomfortably so."

Matron Yulia let out a soft laugh, understanding her meaning. "So be it." After a moment more, she put her hand to the purse at her side to pull out a folded piece of vellum. When she raised it between them, the next words were not a suggestion.

"This," she said simply. "Is for you."

Kaitlyn took the note, pausing as she saw the seal: a small, sharp winged falcon looking left, grasping a bundle of rasha. It was the Consort's seal.

"What is this?" Kaitlyn asked, looking up to her Matron.

"An opportunity few have received," her Matron said, a smile on her lips. "But it is one that I have raised you for."

Kaitlyn looked down to the note as she carefully broke the wax.

CHAPTER 19: VINICIA

Friday, 19:45

Greetings and Salutations to you, Lady Vinicia,
Daughter of Kirath, Daughter of Keh'Tresha,
Barracks Mother to tyros yet to War and
Friend to a chiurgeon of unique ability.
For you, these words have been written:
My dear sister-at-arms,
At dawning this day, I spoke with a man who had been Seventh Counsel Lord upon my coronation. He told me of many things, not the least of which was your most compelling life among these walls. To hear him speak, however, is a great sadness. He fears that your life, full and strange as it may seem to me, does not have the bounty he had hoped it would possess.

Given my station, I believe I may be of some assistance. While I appreciate that you have duties with respect to the upcoming tyro graduation, I must request the honor of your presence within the Royals' Wing come the twentieth 'mark this day. If you would be so kind as to collect my Seventh on your way, I would very much appreciate it. I believe we three have much to speak on.

By my troth,
Mistress Lenae du'Illiandria, Warrior Consort to King Braeden
Scribed by the hand of Kaitlyn du'Alexandria of House Windover
Consort to Third Counsel Lord Aaron su'Yaltana
Honored Dame of High Consort Lenae's Court

Vinicia looked up from the gilded script in disbelief. She turned over the thick vellum again to stare at the seal—the Consort's Seal—and then flipped it back to see her name in the wide, wild strokes of High Court calligraphy. Her full name, including the bit about the dryad conclave of Keh'Tresha.

As the sick sense of dread settled over her, Vinicia leaned on her wings against the door to her office. After everything she had been through this day, fighting with Kiernan, speaking with Hewn, putting the hawkeye on Westly and settling the affairs with his over-burdened companions, she couldn't even begin to unpack the court-crafted language. It had already taken her well into the afternoon before she started her duties as Barracks Mother, the first of which was figuring out what she could set aside for tomorrow.

After all of that, did the Consort really expect her to decipher this nonsense? The only thing that made sense was that she had to find her Seventh—was that Kiernan or her own father?—And report to the Royals' Wing in...

Less than half a candlemark, Vinicia groaned, looking at the gear-work contraption Counsel Lord Blake had fashioned for her to keep track of the candlemarks in an office stuffed with so many important parchments.

But before she could try to reach out to find the man with what little strength she still possessed, Vinicia felt her ancestor swelling into her thoughts.

::Love, if you do not take care of yourself you will collapse,:: her ancestor warned. ::You must take in energy to replace what you have used this day. You cannot expect to live in stagnation and have endless strength at your command.::

::I am not living in stagnation,:: Vinicia insisted, shrugging off the concern as the noise of her tyros at evening meal roared just beyond her door. ::This close to graduation they are all manic and mayhem. Perhaps I do need a little more food before I go searching for Kiernan, but I will be all right.::

::You will not be all right,:: her ancestor insisted and Vinicia could feel its agitation growing. ::You have been burning your own spirit most of the day and you are worse off than even last night.::

::I will be fine if I can just sleep,:: Vinicia insisted, shifting her wings against the door. She had gone through this argument with her ancestor before, but this was the first time the dangerous fatigue-to-come was actually dropping off notes. ::With some food and the energy of the tyros that remain, my body will recover and my reserves as well. I will be all right.::

::Your body may recover, but your spirit will remain just as weak,:: her ancestor persisted. ::Today you have done more with your magic than you have ever done in the past. It is only because you began the day by skimming life from that Seventh and your beloved tyros that you have not collapsed already. I had not thought you so cruel, Vinicia.::

::That is not what I did!:: Vinicia sent back, horrified by her ancestor's sudden change of tone. ::What energy a person or place has in abundance is what I draw from, nothing more. You know that.::

::I know that is what you think,:: her ancestor corrected. ::I have tried to tell you this a hundred times, but once you set power aside it stagnates and fades. The power of your tyros appears to remain only because the tyros themselves remain. I have seen you claim to be sick for cycles now when they leave for Winter Break, but you are not sick. You are starving yourself and that brings you near to death, girl. Every time!::

::I am not starving,:: Vinicia insisted. ::And I have plenty in reserve. Right now, I just need to sleep. That is all.::

::Sapling, either your head is under water or you are not listening to a word I say,:: her ancestor said and there was real bite to the sending. ::Any cache you think to make with that power will dissipate in the deadwood or stone you use to store it because it is living power. Once your influence is gone, it has no ability to maintain that structure. You are a dryad, not a greenman. Why can you not see that? Sense that?::

Vinicia took a slow breath as the ancestor's words echoed in her mind.

::If you doubt me,:: her ancestor challenged. ::If you have so much in reserve, then you should be able to gather all the power you have set aside right this instant and refresh yourself. The hawkeye you wear now will not stop you, that much is clear. If you can do that, I will stop bothering you.::

::Absolutely not,:: Vinicia sent, glowering as she opened her eyes, even if all she saw was the blank wall on the other side of her office.

::I have told you before. I do not mean to hold that amount of power in myself just because I can and I will not be tricked into doing so now to prove you wrong. If I have learned anything from the stories of other kin in Kosar, their descent into madness began when they held more power than they ever had use for. The more they held, the more their ability to hold power expanded and the more they were required to hold just to survive.::

::Nonsense!:: Her ancestor spat, angry now. ::Even if your feet never left the ground, you would still carry the burden of your wings and they would grow and molt and regrow the entire time. Your capacity to move energy as the daughter of a dryad is no different and it grows in you whether you believe it or not.::

Vinicia heard the note from the Consort crackle as her hands closed into fists.

::Would you let any one of your tyros go a day without eating?:: Her ancestor demanded. ::Would you let them fly the Ice Winds without proper sleep or water close at hand? That is what you are doing to yourself—starving yourself of what you need to survive—and for what? You are kindred, girl. Powerful and strong. If you would just embrace that you wouldn't feel so exhausted every day of your life.::

::I am just as Kosaran as I am kindred,:: Vinicia muttered, looking back at her timepiece. ::And I do not have time for this.::

::Vinicia, just *look* at what you accomplished today without even thinking,:: her ancestor challenged, heedless of her mortal concerns. ::The only reason you could do that is because you have the capacity to do so—the strength to do so, if not the will. But now you have drained yourself to nothing more than wishful thinking and if you do not do as I say, collapsing with exhaustion will be the least of your worries. For all your stubbornness, it is a dryad-kin who is starved for power that gives over to madness. I thought that is what you wanted to avoid, or have you now changed your mind?::

When Vinicia refused to dignify the insult with an answer, the feeling of the ancestor sharpened and was suddenly gone. For as much as she knew the spirit had been right about so many things, this was where Vinicia had drawn the line and she did not mean to cross it now. Just how much power she would hold was something she alone could decide. No amount of insults or hard words would ever convince her that the ancestor's insistence was anything more than the thing's own stubborn pride.

For so many cycles before the ancestral shade had appeared in her life, Vinicia had used the stories of fellow Kosaran dryad-kin to keep herself safe. With the benefit of her father's guidance in basic energy control and the safe space in the Library to experiment, she had mastered the art of only pulling as much energy as she needed through herself long before she had come into her power. Having done so well on her own, she clung to that discipline with pride, refusing the ancestor's insistence that it was dangerous for her to only replace as much as she thought she had used in her daily workings. It was only because she had such discipline that she had survived in the Palace at all.

Beneath the shield of the other hawkeye her methods had been perfectly fine, as she did not expend nearly as much energy as she took in by other natural means: food, drink, and the ambient energy of her robust tyros. All she maintained outside of emergencies were her shields and the obfuscations woven into them, hiding her red-gold hair and emerald eyes. It wasn't until just this moment, feeling the weight of today's workings dragging against her need to press on, that she had realized the ancestor might be right after all.

And for the life of me, I cannot back down from a blicing fight, Vinicia thought, slowly letting out the breath she held. With a stomach gnawing at her backbone and a mouth parched with thirst, she knew that no amount of gorging herself would fill that reserve. Food and drink only went so far when what she truly needed was the raw, living power around her that she was terrified to touch. The more she touched it, the more she knew anything else she did was just surviving on dried field rations.

She wants me to check, Vinicia thought, miserable. *Fine, I will check.*

Begrudgingly, Vinicia let go of the anger and reached out to find the caches of power that she maintained within the Palace... Only to come away with nothing. Worse, Hewn had been right about Westly's encroaching influence on the shelf.

"Oh, blood and ice," Vinicia swore, opening her eyes. "Why are ancestors always right?"

By her estimation, even if she took hold of all the power she could access in the Palace, she would only amass a bare third of the energy Westly was already moving in his Garden. Worse, if Hewn was right that Westly meant to take a lover, that would mean she needed to find and hold an amount equal to what he already controlled in that Garden. At the same time, she would have to find a way to outstrip his other gains, all so she could survive another few dawnings at most.

::So what am I supposed to do?:: Vinicia called, covering her eyes with a hand as she reached out for her ancestor. ::If he is so much stronger than me, how am I supposed to compete with that?::

::He is not stronger than you,:: her ancestor said, annoyed that Vinicia would think so little of herself. ::He simply has an active grove to draw from while you do not. You are far stronger than him and have ten cycles of greater experience.::

::But how am I supposed to start a grove in the middle of the tyro barracks?:: She asked, baffled. ::Even the House Northern Estate does not have space where I could put one to match the Palace Garden and that is ignoring the fact that I can't keep a plant alive to save my life. You were the one who taught me that power drawn from the blood of the grave allows me to kill things or keep them from dying, not actually give them bounty.::

::Lucky for you, sapling, not all kin-groves are made of plants,:: her ancestor said, obviously amused. ::And just because you wield Grave magic instead of Westly's Grove magic does not mean it cannot be cultivated. If you would pull the power of the tyros you skim into yourself and cycle it back to them constantly, you could fill your reserves and do more than survive. Are you willing to let me guide you, at last?::

Vinicia let go of a breath she hadn't realized she'd been holding. ::Yes?:: She said, half-relieved, but also still anxious.

::Well, don't sound so excited,:: her ancestor said in return. ::It will only keep you alive.::

With that jab, Vinicia finally laughed. ::Yes. Will you please show me? I would like the chance to live another few cycles.::

::Wonderful,:: the ancestor said and Vinicia shifted herself against the door so she was more settled. It wasn't the first lesson she had taken standing in the middle of her office when she had ten thousand other things to do, but it might prove to be the most important. ::Start by looking for one particular tyro.::

Vinicia nodded, even if the shade couldn't see her, and shivered as the crown of her head tingled with the expanding focus. Why it did that she had no idea, but whenever she reached for her tyros they were physically above her, so it followed that her tendrils of thought went upwards as well.

::Do you have it?:: Her ancestor asked. ::Is everyone accounted for?::

Vinicia chewed her lower lip as she searched for that answer. There were approximately eight hundred young men in the Delton Tyro Legion, but with the coming graduation most had already returned to their families.

As a result, only the Eighteenth Tyro Century was in the building and many of those were over in the Sires' Wing for the night, either taking part in a revel or preparing for the first Winter Court that would take place tomorrow mid-way between dawning and high sun. As for those who were left...

::Five and forty,:: she said, and then smiled as she found the knot of her favored tyros. It seemed that Sera had been reunited with Micah, Rylan, and Westly. That little cluster was sparkling with energy, but in a way that made her happy to see.

::Now that you have found them, what information can you pull back?:: Her ancestor asked. ::Are they all in good health? Is one or more of them hiding illness or too deep in their cups? Are there folks other than tyros scattered among those rooms?::

Vinicia focused on changing the outward reach into a pull that sent information streaming into her. Strangely, only about a third managed the energetic flip while the others fizzled out and died.

::Oh!:: Vinicia said, surprised. ::I lost them. I mean, I can pull information from some, but I lost the rest entirely.::

Her ancestor seemed to have expected this. ::The tyros you can pull information from will be the ones that you have a strong connection with already,:: she explained. ::Those that you have lost are ones who either have no strong opinion of you or a negative one. Those are the ones that will take work.::

::A personal connection?:: Vinicia supplied, feeling her ancestor's approval in return. ::So I need to get to know them better.::

::It is one thing to watch over a barracks full of young men, but quite another to have a relationship with them,:: her ancestor said. ::Would you believe me if I told you that Westly can do this kind of check-in with his plants? He may not speak to them with teeth and tongue, but they do whisper wisdom to him in their own way.::

:: I had not thought of it that way,:: Vinicia said. She knew Westly talked to his plants, but most gardeners did. She had thought it was because of the quiet company he kept, but it made sense if there was something to be learned.

::The easiest way to grow your connection with those you have lost from your search will be to keep that search in your mind when you are in the barracks,:: her ancestor went on, still lecturing. ::Then when you speak with a new tyro, you can loop them into your grove. Once they are included, it will be harder to lose them.::

::What happens if I let them all go?:: Vinicia asked, opening her eyes as she grew light-headed with the work. ::Will I have to start all over again?::

::Not necessarily,:: her ancestor said. ::But the longer you stay in that open mindset, the more power you will collect. It will be a trickle at first, as the task itself takes power to manage, but in time the expenditure will be more than adequately covered by the energy you generate when your reserves are full.::

::Something happens when my reserves are full?:: Vinicia asked, confused.

::Once you consistently draw that energy and information through you, the resonance will create the true Wellspring you need,:: her ancestor said and Vinicia could feel the wonder in her mental touch. ::The pure, honest joy of creation that bubbles up from inside every living creature. If you nurture their spark, if you are what makes them thrive, you will have your grove.::

::In time, though,:: Vinicia said as the feeling of the small grove slipped away. ::Thank you for the lesson, ancestor.::

::This is what I have been trying to explain to you,:: the spirit added, driving home the point while she had Vinicia's full attention. ::The 'power' that your kind can access when they 'come into their power' is that Wellspring because it is neither growth nor decay. It is both because living things are both growing and dying at the same time. This is the energy you use when you have emergencies, if only on a small scale, because of the panic it causes in you.::

::Speaking of panic,:: Vinicia repeated, trying to shift the subject away as she looked up at the time piece again. Five beats. ::I can start smaller than the full Tyro Legion, yes?:: She asked. ::I can start with one?::

::One century, one bevy, one...?:: Her ancestor asked.

::One tyro?:: She answered, sheepish.

::One tyro will not be enough,:: her ancestor said, disappointed. ::If you do not start by holding at least the minds that you can already feel, you may not survive to reach the rest.::

::But how am I supposed to hold them in my mind if I cannot get out of the hole I have dug myself into first?:: Vinicia thought, miserable. ::If you say that food and rest will not get me back to a place of strength, what option do I have? I cannot hide from a summons from the Consort.::

::You do not have to solve every minor problem in your life with magic, you realize?:: Her ancestor said and the concern in her mental touch felt like the hand Hewn had attempted to set against her cheek. ::There are those who love you and will lend you strength and aid by wholly mundane means. This woman called you sister-at-arms and spoke of your mother's conclave, did she not?::

Vinicia looked down to the note as she fingered it open. ::She does,:: Vinicia confirmed, sighing to herself.

::Then there is no reason to fight with your guise tonight. Take a scarf for your hair and let your smile distract the world,:: she said and Vinicia could feel her ancestor's encouragement shining through. ::Most of all, do not fear smudging the ink of a message that has long since dried because you do not have the strength to hide for the walk over there.::

::But this woman only knows of me because of father,:: Vinicia argued, forcing away the tension so she could let her head rest back against the door. ::And Kiernan himself said that I am a 'walking case of treason',:: she added, quoting what the Seventh had said earlier in his anger. ::I could not change the world, so I have changed myself. I became a happy, hiding shadow and yet you tell me I will die if I do not step into the light.::

::Beloved, you are not a shadow. You are *sha'doe*,:: her ancestor sent and though Vinicia did not know the strange word, the resonance of its importance to her ancestor struck a cord. ::And the first thing a *sha'doe* is ever taught is that the only way she will ever know love is to first find it in herself.::

For as nauseated as Vinicia's exhaustion was making her, the force of her ancestor's conviction was enough to set what little energy she did have into motion despite her darker thoughts. When her ancestor didn't say more, Vinicia realized the energy moving within her was not the only movement she could feel. Looking up, Vinicia's breath caught to see the space inside the room was shimmering with near-manifested power.

When her ancestor spoke again, Vinicia could feel the strain in the sending, but there was no regret in the words. ::The power of the Wellspring is the potential for life and death captured in one breathtaking moment. My love, if you would just take it into yourself, you would see how beautiful nature's balance can be.::

Vinicia's eyes were suddenly burning with tears as she realized the outpouring of power for what it was. Feeling the energy buffeting her like a true touch, all she could think of was what a tragedy it was to have so close a friend beyond the veil. Worse, she hated to realize that the sparks around her were from the opposition that love met. From a shield so reflexive and unconscious that it wasn't until this moment that she realized it came from her.

::I'm sorry,:: Vinicia managed, covering her eyes. She had no idea how to accept that kind of power and the strength of it terrified her. ::I don't know what's wrong with me. I want to accept it, I really do, but I can't. I don't know how. I can't—:: Vinicia's words fell off sharply as the ancestor's power vanished from one moment to the next.

::Great Mother of All, I cannot stand this,:: her ancestor swore and for the first time, Vinicia thought she felt the shade's true strength resonating in her sending. :: *Sha'doe*, I can come to you. I can, but I need — There is — So sick of these Cells! *Sha'doe*, just—::

::Ancestor?:: Vinicia called, realizing the spirit was fading from her thoughts. ::Ancestor! Where are you going? No, please! Please don't leave me!::

But for all the world, the presence that had been her rare and only comfort these past few cycles was suddenly gone. Vinicia's heart shattered as she tried calling out again, tried screaming into the void, but the only reply she got was silence. Her ancestor had pulled away in the past, but never like this, never because she could not accept love. Vinicia's hands came up to her face as her world crashed down around her.

Oh Gods, what have I done?

She didn't have more than a heartbeat to think when there was a knock against her oaken door. She had to bite her lip to keep from screaming in surprise and then swore at herself before calling out 'just a moment'. Vinicia gave herself the space of a long breath to hide her tears behind a heavy shield before she turned and set her hand on the knob.

"Can I help—?" she started to say, only to freeze when she saw who it was.

"Sal'weh, Mother," Counsel Lord Kiernan greeted, and though he continued speaking, she couldn't hear his words for the blinding wave of power crackling around him.

Vinicia took a step back as her vision was forced into her secondsight. With his amber glow swelling to fill her senses, she fell a second step back and he took it for her opening the door for him. As he moved into the office, Vinicia tore her eyes away, looking back in a panic as her wings hit the front of her desk. It didn't help. With how desperate she was for something to sustain her, the man's very presence was as cruel as it was incredible.

"Oh, you have gotten Lenae's note," Kiernan said, and she exhaled in a rush to hear the eagerness in his voice. "Are you ready, Kehvin?"

Vinicia flushed with embarrassment as he called her by her old name; the name of the person she had been with him here, in the barracks. The person she had been with Lenae. She wasn't that person anymore. She never could be that person walking so boldly in the light.

"Don't call me that," she swore, pulling her eyes away from him.

"Do the walls have ears now?" He asked, chuckling for the secret between them. "Or do you just not like that I remember the person you were as a tyro when you forgot you were supposed to be hiding?"

Vinicia didn't know whether to be furious or flustered. Choosing neither, she looked up to glare at him, only to have her vision dazzled a second time. His spirit was simply overflowing his mortal vessel, as if the Seventh's hawkeye couldn't contain the spiritual power inside of him. Worse, he seemed to offer it with his very presence. With all his jokes and coy smiles, he was so excited to be around her that it was a struggle to not flow with it. Like a sweet cake set before a starving tyro, she had to grip onto her desk to keep from reaching towards him. If she put both of her hands on him again, if she closed the circle of power between them, she would fill herself with his life and leave a corpse in exchange.

"Why are you here?" She demanded.

"Hest'lre said you'd been sent a note like we had, though you were supposed to collect me," Kiernan answered, oblivious to her discomfort. "I took evening meal in the Great Mess hoping to make things easier, but given the mark, I figured I would stop bothering the tyros and come to collect you instead," he explained, looking to the clock mounted on her wall just to their right. "We're already going to be a bit late."

"You were in the Great Mess?" Vinicia asked, growing lightheaded as he just stood there, mocking her with his strength.

"I was," he laughed. "Not that there were many tyros actually in attendance. Mother, are you feeling all right?"

No. No, I am not, she realized, and when he came a step closer, the strength of his spirit overwhelmed what shields she had been trying desperately to maintain. As she put a hand up to stop him, his warmth and life swelled in around her.

I cannot touch this, she thought desperately, closing her hand into a fist as her mouth watered. *He would not survive me.*

"Vinicia?" Kiernan asked quietly, nudging the door shut with a wing. "Vinicia, what's going on? What are these?"

These?

The word made her open her eyes and as she looked around the room in a panic, she realized her small office was filling with wil-o-wisps. But this wasn't her power. It was his, wasn't it? It had to be! And then she saw the heavy silver chain of her old hawkeye at his neck. It wasn't until Kiernan caught her hand in his own as she reached for the stone that she realized what he had done.

"Do you need this back?" he asked, moving to take it off. "I can give it back to you."

"No," she managed, struggling as his energy seeped into her palm. "But you—" She wanted it—wanted all of it—even if taking it would mean his life. "You can't—" As she fought against the surge he unwittingly offered, her resolve shredded. A heartbeat later, she shamed herself as her eyes rolled back into her head.

'It is only because you began the day by sucking the life out of your beloved tyros that you have not collapsed already', her ancestor had warned.

"Vinicia?" Kiernan asked, speaking quietly but with urgency. "Vinicia, are you all right?"

"Huh?" She asked, realizing as she came back to consciousness that the only reason she was standing was because Kiernan had managed to get his arms around her. Her forehead was resting on his shoulder, but the rest of the room was a nauseating wobble.

"I think we may have asked more of you than we had a right to this day," Kiernan said, guilt in his voice as he readjusted his embrace. "Here, I think I can help. Just hold on."

"What?" Vinicia murmured, closing her eyes as she felt his palms shifting to set against her waist.

A moment more and she gasped in surprise, her head coming off his shoulder as he cycled power through her core. Her hands met his on her waist as he continued, and she had to bite her lower lip to keep from crying out with the pure, unbridled pleasure of it. As her mind raged against the violation, a deep-seated part of her was sobbing with relief. Finally, finally there was something that could fill the gaping void in her. Kiernan had just saved her life, though she had no idea how he had saved himself from her as he pulled his hands away.

"I think," he said, his own breathing ragged. "I think it worked?"

When he took a step back, Vinicia was both sagging with relief and completely, utterly pissed off. Kiernan had no idea what was happening as her right arm pulled back, but after she sent his head spinning to the left, he knew he had done something wrong.

"ASK!" She screamed.

Kiernan was horrified as his hand came up to cover his cheek. "I'm sorry," he stammered. "I thought—"

"No! You didn't!" She hissed and fled from him until her wings hit her desk again. As the world swelled back into brilliant color, she felt more alive now than she had since they had first met in the Armory, but that was not an excuse. The ends did not justify the means.

"Do you just go around forcing yourself on women all the time?" She demanded more quietly, seeing that her door had not closed completely behind him.

Kiernan's jaw fell open as he realized what she meant, stepping back as the color drained from his face. For all the force of her swing, it made the red mark that much uglier. "Gods, no. I didn't mean—"

"Blood and ice, Seventh!" She said, closing her eyes as she tried to calm down. This was no way to walk Kiernan over to see the Consort, who she knew was his very close and personal friend. She had to calm down. Furious as she was, she had to calm down.

"I didn't mean—I mean, you collapsed," he said, panicked. "You look like you had fallen down the face of the mountain, Vinicia. I knew how radiant you had been this morning and when I saw you now... I just—I just wanted to help. I thought I could help."

"You did help," she said, if begrudgingly. "But dammit, you need to ask first. That is an incredibly intimate thing to do to a kindred," she finished, crossing her arms over her chest.

"I am so, so sorry," he said, pressing his palms together before raising them to his forehead and bowing in what space was allowed. "Please, I did not mean to offend."

"Gods, stop it," Vinicia said, waving for him to stop praying for her forgiveness like she was some Founder. "Just ask next time."

Why am I assuming there will be a next time? She wondered, even as that other part of herself, now awake and ravenous, watched him like a harpy eagle. *Why am I not making him do that again right now? Right blicing now? Devour him and I could bring the world to its knees.*

As Kiernan stood tall once again, wary but still concerned, she strangled the second voice back to silence.

"Is this because we switched hawkeyes?" He asked.

Half terrified he would see the hunger still in her, she looked down to the spare cage and dragon-headed kingchain she had gotten from her father for her mother's hawkeye. "Probably," she admitted. "Every little thing I have done all my life is suddenly twice as hard to maintain, but it is also twice as easy to do. I have done more today than I have in my life," she said, hating the echo of her ancestor's words. "Until you came in, I wasn't sure how I was going to make it to the Royals' Wing."

"You certainly would have caught some attention with hair like a loralae," he said and her eyes went wide as she realized her hair must have reverted to the red-gold she always hid. "But when I touched your hand, it felt like ice. I've been burning up since I lost my hawkeye, so I thought... Well, I had hoped to warm you up. I'm not a sorcerer, or at least, I don't think I am. I might be, given what I did to my Primarchs, but... Gods, am I making any sense at all?"

"You are," she said, looking away from him as she built up her shields. Once her hair and eyes were muted properly, she sighed. "The Seventh's Gift isn't limited to mental magic in me, so there is no reason it should be limited in you, especially if my father has been meddling. My mother made him something of a greenman because he taught me almost everything I know about power. I am," she said, hesitating. "I am glad that you tried to help. Your instincts are good and I needed the help, as you obviously saw."

"To be honest, the fact that you were so angry with me made me feel better," he said with a hint of a laugh. "It meant you were feeling like yourself again."

Vinicia sniffed but couldn't disagree. "Yes, well," she admitted. "I am the Barracks Mother in these halls, not Kehvin any longer. I haven't been the person you think I am for a decade," she insisted.

"I'm not so sure about that," he said, letting his amusement show. "The Kehvin I remember could wipe the floor with me, out-argue me in lecture, and always acted first and apologized later. That still seems pretty true, even if you present as female now."

Vinicia scowled, if only to hide her embarrassment. Why did he have to continue to be right?

"My name is not Kehvin," she insisted.

"Vin, then," he countered. "Will that suffice?"

"Whatever," she sighed, rolling her eyes. "You'll be gone in two days, so what do I care? This isn't even why you're here. You meant to escort me?"

"I did," Kiernan said, wincing to realize they were going to be even later at this rate.

As she collected her indigo cloak and barracks keys, he turned to reopen the door and the two of them stepped out into the unusually quiet hallway. Unfortunately, given Kiernan's long presence in the Wing, they had something of an audience.

"Everything all right, My Lord Seventh?" The Blackwing Praetor asked, scratching his left cheek conspicuously. Despite her uncle Shayan's warning, Ivan and his men had apparently come into the hallway after hearing her scream.

"Yes," Kiernan said, massaging the cheek she had slapped with ease. "Here's some wisdom for you boys," he said, glancing to where more than a few tyros were watching. "Never try to take keys from the Barracks Mother."

Vinicia almost laughed at the way the boys' mouths dropped open to see her stepping out of the room behind him, but she smiled all the same. "All you need to do is ask," she added, taking the hand he offered in escort.

With that, the Blackwings started them off down the hallway and the two of them kept their peace until they were out of earshot. When they reached the Long Hall, Kiernan stalled to let the Blackwings get the door.

"Do you mind if I read your missive?" he said, and with the way he looked at her, she knew he had been chewing on a number of thoughts.

"I don't see why not," she said. "All that I could figure out was I needed to report."

She dug out the note from her cloak and let him have it as Kiernan's Blackwing guard cleared their path through the Long Hall. It only took him a moment to scan over the words, but he seemed no more confident about it than she had been.

"I had this bit about Kaitlyn Windover, too," Kiernan said. "Kaitlyn works with you in the barracks, does she not?"

"Kaitlyn has helped me with a few projects," Vinicia said, confused. She hadn't remembered seeing anything about the Windover Dame. "What is there about her in the note?"

"She was the scribe," Kiernan said, pointing to the signature. "What's strange is that Lenae doesn't have a High Court and I didn't think that there could be a 'Consort' other than her, but there's no denying that Kaitlyn is now on this 'High Court' and has been made a 'Consort' to Counsel Lord Aaron. That signature was deliberate."

Vinicia's brow furrowed as she took back the note to read it for herself. "Am I being replaced?"

"Maybe?" Kiernan hazarded and looked pleased to realize they had reached the Sires' Wing. "Though I'm not sure what else it would be. You're too much like Lenae for your own good, I'm afraid. Shall we see?"

"Lead the way," Vinicia said, and followed him once again. It wasn't until they had crossed the threshold into the Royals Wing and the Blackwings agreed to stay posted at the entrance that she spoke to him again. "Anything I should know?" She asked, unnerved as she realized the hallway was full of life-sized portraits.

"Lenae can rival your father for cunning," Kiernan laughed.

"That's supposed to comfort me?" Vinicia scoffed.

"You asked what you should know," he reminded. "Not what might be interesting to know."

"Fair enough," she conceded, and then resolved herself to the silence of the hallway as they approached the two guards posted at the formal entrance. Unsurprisingly, the circular receiving room was bustling with activity.

As they stepped inside, Vinicia found she knew several of the women who were running about, if only because of her extensive time in the Palace. Chief among them was young Kaitlyn, who looked happy to see them. For the first time Vinicia could remember, though, she was not wearing some combination of her black and gold House colors.

Now she wore a bodice and pants of fitted dark-purple leather, with a cascade of cloth-of-silver bustling that created the high front, low backed skirts that had recently become the dress of the Royal Court. There was also, Vinicia realized, a copy of the Consort's sigil cast in silver and pinned to her left shoulder. The only change was the fact that the falcon was carrying a tome in its talons instead of the Consort's rasha.

"And now we only need Counsel Lord Hest'lre," Kaitlyn said, happily marking off a parchment with the piece of graphite in her hand. "Welcome to both of you. The High Consort will see you in her sitting room."

"Any idea what's going on?" Vinicia asked, but Kaitlyn's smile betrayed nothing.

"We'll know soon enough," Kiernan replied, and then gestured to the second door on their left along the circular wall of the grand receiving room.

Vinicia followed him to the ornate double doors, but had to stop just after Kiernan pushed through the threshold.

"There you are, Kier'n!" a woman called fondly. "I was wondering where you were."

"We are not so late as that," he called back. "It is hard to steal this one away from her tyros, is all."

As he moved into the room to greet the Consort with startling familiarity, Vinicia could see two wing-marked men she recognized, her father and uncle, looking anxious for all they tried not to show it.

Her father's gryphling was also with him and at seeing Vinicia, Aevi immediately scrambled down from his shoulder. After a few running steps, Aevi leapt into the air and then backwinged in front of her so Vinicia could collect her.

Aevi's claws weren't quite full falcon talons, but they were certainly more than those of a mere house cat. Usually that didn't matter, as the right shoulder of her work jackets were reinforced. Unfortunately, since Vinicia had tried to look a little nicer as she ran around Delton today, Aevi would have to settle for her lap.

Once Vinicia had Aevi settled, she looked up to find that she was the center of attention.

"And our guest of honor," said a woman who looked strikingly similar to Kiernan. Dressed in a court bodice with a high-low skirt over storm-grey velvet leggings, her bright golden hair and hourglass figure made it clear she was an Illiandrian-born Guildswomen. Something was weighing heavily on her to dim the famed silver of her eyes, though as she looked Vinicia over, there was a good measure of relief as well.

Just what does she want from me? Vinicia wondered, suddenly glad for the gryphling in her arms. After what felt like an eternity, the woman clasped her hands before her and tensed all over with an extremely feminine sort of excitement. "Oh, Eirik has told me everything about you!"

"I suppose that is what I'm worried about, Your Grace," Vinicia replied awkwardly and then realized that Aevi was going to make any kind of obeisance difficult.

"Oh, please don't bother," the Consort insisted, waving for her to come deeper into the room. "I can't thank you enough for coming, Kehvin."

Vinicia flushed, surprised to realize the woman must have been told of her secret to address her so informally. As her mouth went dry, looking to her father, Kiernan came to her rescue.

"It's just Vin now, Lenae," he said, offering the gentle correction as he moved them towards the semi-circle of padded benches facing an enormous hearth. Vinicia looked at a rather ornate silver chair and then decided it too closely matched the Consort's silver and resigned herself to a seat next to Kiernan.

"I must say it is a surprise to see you both here," Kiernan said, greeting the two men they joined.

"Family business," Eirik greeted, squinting at his Counselheir as Aevi twisted to get a better look at Kiernan. "We are coming to repay a boon."

"And because of it," Lenae said, using the line to begin a rehearsed presentation. "I now have the means to keep you safe," she declared.

"Safe from what?" Kiernan asked, watching as she stood before them at the apex of the semi-circle. It was an honest question, given his Envoy.

As Kiernan tried to understand Lenae's enthusiasm, the door to the receiving room opened to let Counsel Lord Hest'lre inside.

"My apologies, Lenae," he said, closing the door behind him. "The veterans—"

"Just in time," Lenae assured him, waving off his excuse. She continued after he had found a seat as well. "Now," she began again. "This dawning I was speaking with Hest'lre about the three daggers we found in Kiernan's suite," she said, getting right to the point. "As well as how even this new Blackwing fumentari has been having issues staying in his shadow," she said and looked to Hest'lre, who took over.

"We now have one of the blade's origins settled and know that the second is likely a stunt, but we will take it seriously," Hest'lre said. "As for the third, I've just confirmed someone has been soliciting members of the Guard to be lax for their posting during the tournament itself. I've addressed as many as I could, but there isn't much to be said for how effective they were before we got involved."

Shayan spoke next, building on the point. "On Hest'lre's request, I have contacted those veterans I trust from my time as Sixth and they feel the same crosswind. They do not trust how close Kiernan is to you, Lenae. There is a real fear that Kiernan is not thinking clearly in his desperation to return and take you as his bride. The feelings are mixed as to what might happen because of that, but the result is the same: no one trusts his judgment."

About that time, Vinicia realized her uncle was actually speaking at her with this information. The rest of them would have known these things. Vinicia took a breath and looked down to come out from under their focus as she settled Aevi in her lap.

Why are they telling me all of this? She wondered, only to remember in a rush that she had so slighted her ancestor earlier that the spirit had fled her thoughts. Aevi didn't seem to mind her anxious hands, though, nuzzling into them for a scritch all the same.

"Under the circumstances," Lenae went on, putting a hand up to stall Kiernan's intent to defend himself. "I am taking what actions I can. After some discussion with Lucien, I have determined that I am within my rights as Consort to organize a court of women for my personal edification. This Court, in compliment to Braeden's, will be made exclusively of women to whom I can speak regarding matters throughout this kingdom. Women who are known for both their own personal intelligence and their dedication to the Counsel Lords whom they will serve. They will be given the title 'Consort' as well, and with it, certain immunities that allow them to act as steward for any matters their Counsel Lord may allow."

As Lenae paused for breath, Vinicia looked up again. "The note you sent me," she said, catching everyone's attention. "It was signed Dame Kaitlyn, Consort to Counsel Lord Aaron. If she is a member of your Court, am I being replaced?"

"You are," Lenae answered, unapologetic. "But because of it, I have been able to give the position the express legal authority to have a say in the demands, expectations, and quality of life of the tyros that will be under her care. I understand this to be exactly what brought you to Counsel Lord Lucien's attention yesterday, is it not?"

"It is," Vinicia admitted and Aevi's continued nuzzling seemed to be an attempt to set her at ease. "But what is to become of me? What exactly have they told you?"

Lenae's smile was a league wide. "They have told me you were trained as a tyro for a purpose beyond this shelf," she said. "One I mean to see fulfilled."

"What purpose?" Vinicia asked, and her look went from Lenae to her father. "What is she talking about?"

"You can't honestly believe I would have had you train all these cycles for nothing," her father said, his tone thick with his own self-importance. "It took a boon to allow you to live safely in the Palace and it is a boon we must repay."

"Boon?" Vinicia repeated, though she lost her voice as she realized her uncle was rubbing at his temples with the precursors to one of his stress headaches. That was never good.

"Vinicia, you were born to be a resource for a Seventh Counsel Lord going into the Eihwaz," Eirik said, matter-of-fact. "When Counsel Lord Broc took me with him, I thought it was to learn what I could to survive, but after all my cycles, I am now certain of his intention. His and your mother's, when he sent me into her hearth. My love, this Envoy is your birthright as much as any gift you have and it is well past time you set out to claim it."

Vinicia's eyes nearly came out of her head as her father looked to Lenae with pride. Beside Lenae, Kiernan and Hest'lre's jaws were as slack as her own. The only one not reeling was little Aevi, and she was flexing her talons against Vinicia's leg to get her to breathe again.

"The day your father brought you to the Palace, my predecessor, Consort Telessa, asked a boon of him to keep your secret," Lenae explained and gestured to the silver circle that sat on the short table they had gathered around. In her ignorance, Vinicia had thought the table had a silver top. "I called on that boon this morning, not knowing what it was. All I knew was that there had to be a way to protect Kiernan, but Gods above," she said with relief. "To think that a woman—a kindred—had been trained to act as a companion to the Seventh Counsel Lord in the same way I was trained to be Consort to Braeden... It is utterly perfect."

Vinicia felt the pit of her stomach drop as the gryphling's churring grew louder. Old as she was, she had never thought to leave the shelf. She honestly didn't think she could, but if she didn't have a grove and Westly was about to push her out of this space... This could be her way out. She almost breathed easier until she looked to her father and saw the smugness that, like Kiernan had said of Lenae, reeked of manipulation.

"You were meant to go with Hewn," Eirik confessed under her suspicion. "Honestly, girl. Your abilities were growing strong enough when you two were first introduced that I was holding my breath you would last his term. But when he could not go..."

"You gave me the Seventh Counsel Lord's hawkeye instead of the one my mother meant for me," she supplied flatly. "Hewn told me this morning when he gave me back my stone. He had stolen it from Kiernan."

As Lenae and Hest'lre exchanged surprised looks, her father nodded as if that had been part of his plan all along.

"Why would you take that from me?" She demanded, not caring if she aired their family's problems in public. "Why would you give him the one my mother meant for me?"

"To make it possible for you to remain on the shelf," Eirik answered. "With the one meant for the Seventh, your Gift was stalled, but the one meant for you allowed Kiernan's ability to channel power from Noventrio to grow great enough to support you. To my great delight, it seems I have made him a proper channel for you, the same as I was made for your mother."

"I'm a what?" Kiernan balked. "What are you talking about?"

"A channel," Eirik repeated. "You may be a priest for Founder Noventrio, but he made you a sorcerer long ago. Or did you not realize you are the first Seventh who has reached into the eyes of a first-rotation soldier in over two hundred cycles?"

"Likely not," Vinicia said, unable to stop herself. "He has barely been in the Library for all the dust I found."

"Yes, well," Kiernan said, shrinking under their attention.

"You being a sorcerer would explain you ability to kill nine Primarchs with your strength as a warbard," Hest'lre said, with a significant look to Kiernan. "And your ability to move anywhere you damn well please, despite both my and Roder's best men hounding you."

"That last bit is on her," Kiernan defended, pointing the blame at Vinicia. "She... Well," he said, hesitating to admit just what she could do. "She is the sorcerer, not me."

As Vinicia tried not to roll her eyes, her father called them back to the reason they were gathered.

"But a boon is a boon," he said. "And our repayment will be your service to her Seventh on his Envoy. He will serve you as well, if in a different way."

Vinicia didn't answer, but the look she shared with her father made it clear he knew just how she could use the strength of Kiernan's Gift for her own purposes. Just being in the man's presence was intense, but now she knew that wasn't by accident. If her father meant for her to work with Kiernan and for him to support her, then he had meant to make her desperate to be with him. All this after being made to swear she would have nothing to do with the man.

It was absolutely infuriating.

Never in her life had she been able to have a true, living friend, and now one was shoved at her? She had befriended shades, sure. Counsel Lords, certainly. But a peer? A person who knew all of who she was and what she had been through? Never.

For a decade she had consoled herself with the companionship of her tyros, all mothering and tough love, and she lived through them. Now her father meant to force her from all of it. He had brought her to the edge of sanity just as blindly as the Ancestor Sevenths had done to Kiernan, taking his hawkeye before he was ready to leave. Both of them were standing on a knife edge, staring at one another as a last, desperate hope. This would either work or they would both fail.

"You always wanted your chance to fight for peace, love," her uncle Shayan added, undercutting their silent fight with his patient logic. "Here is your commission."

Vinicia's heart staggered. After all the things her uncle had done to protect her from her father's maddening plans, if he supported this...

"Why?" Vinicia demanded, trying to strangle back the anger that was so useless now. "Why didn't you introduce us before this? I was a tyro in their squad, but you told me to keep to myself. I worked with Hewn for cycles, but I had to stay in the Library. When Kiernan was raised, I wasn't to go anywhere near him. I wasn't to help him at all. I just had to sit here and watch him become a monster when I could have helped. Father, I could have done something! I could have done something for Hewn as well if you had just—"

Vinicia wasn't sure when she had come to her feet, but Aevi was swirling at her ankles, churring fiercely as her words cut off. Hand to her mouth, her eyes burned with tears as she remembered the last time she had seen Hewn alive. He had been struggling with his madness and she had begged him to stay with her, but he had gone to Court anyway. She had felt it when he had lost himself, when the Blackwings had cut him down, and then she had been told to wait in the Library with only dead men to console her. For days she had waited, only to realize that the reason Shayan had let her out was because Hewn was now trapped inside.

That had all changed this dawning when Kiernan had thrown himself into her life, desperate for help, and she had met the Seventh her father had always said to avoid. The Seventh who had taken Hewn's place. The one who had made her go back to face Hewn after all this time...

"I can't do this," she whispered, closing her eyes as her tears slipped free. "How can I protect a man I do not know when I couldn't even protect the one I loved?"

"Vinicia," her uncle said, arms circling around her as the room grew silent.

"Hewn could not have you with him after Kirath fell to the Lan'lieanans," he said as Vinicia shook with strangled sobs. "Not with what you are. The Lord Fifth would have seen you as a loralae that had gotten close to his Lord Seventh and we could not have saved you. We had to hide you, beloved, for your own sake."

Vinicia gasped for a breath, head buried against her uncle's shoulder.

"Kiernan was with him, though," Shayan went on. "When he returned to Delton, he was one of Hewn's Primarchs. If you had known him then, you would have hated him for taking Hewn's place. He was not Hewn and he never could be, no matter what you wanted."

"That," her father said, speaking into the heavy silence. "And the man you had known as a tyro became quite full of himself the moment I gave him your stone. From all I read, Noventrio's vicious streak comes through if a Seventh can truly channel his power. But," he added, shifting to speak to Kiernan as Vinicia composed herself. "I take it you are feeling more level-headed now? Under the Seventh's hawkeye, you should feel like a peacemaker again."

Kiernan just nodded, which seemed to pale against the audacity of the information.

Vinicia exhaled slowly, coming out of her uncle's embrace. As she looked to take her seat again, though, she saw Kiernan watching her with heart-wrenching sympathy. She tried to look away, only to find that Consort Lenae had moved to stand before her as she hesitated.

Seeing the woman wrapped up in vulnerability, Vinicia's anger truly fled. Knowing all Vinicia herself had lost in Hewn, she could see how terrified Lenae felt at just the idea of losing Kiernan. She knew that pain and where Vinicia's family had kept her from Hewn, here this woman was trying to offer her the chance to do what she had always wanted—to protect the Seventh, no matter what the rest of the kingdom planned for him. To use her Gifts to protect the fragile hope of peace that Kiernan held as Hewn's Counselheir.

"All our lives we are told that our sons, brothers, and fathers go to war for us," Lenae said quietly. "They work to win with battle and cunning, and then they sacrifice the only man who truly wants to end it. This time we can protect him through the Eihwaz. This time we can get him to the sea. With you at his side, peace will have a fighting chance. And if I am honest," she added, as if it was a secret between the two of them. "I doubt any man could change their mind. It will take a woman's voice or none at all."

That thought had occurred to Vinicia before and Lenae saw the realization for what it was. What was it her ancestor had said? Behind every great man was a woman worth twice his weight in salt?

"I swear to you by the Founder of my Consort's Seat," Lenae went on. "I would not have come to collect this boon unless it was my very last resort, but there is absolutely no one else I can trust with his life. So I will ask you the same thing Founder Kerowyn asked of me when she changed my eyes and my fate: will you serve?"

Vinicia risked a look at Kiernan, fearing his anger at having someone thrust into his most sacred duty, only to find him staring back with such desperate hope that her heart started to thunder in her chest.

"Of course," she said. "Your will is my own, Consort," she added, touching her right hand to her left shoulder in salute.

"Then I charge you with this task, Vinicia," Lenae said, standing taller in the moment. "Through the power vested in me by the Founder of my sacred Seat, you are named Consort to the Seventh Counsel Lord. You will accompany him on his Envoy to make peace with Lan'lieana and return him to me once the task is done."

"I will," Vinicia agreed, matching the woman's silvered eyes with her own.

"You will go with me?" Kiernan asked, coming to his feet as if to make certain he had heard her right. "All the way to Lan'lieana?"

"That is what her name means," Eirik said proudly, drawing everyone's attention as he stood. "Venture to the sea. Dryads are named for the place they will go to set down their roots."

"All this time," Vinicia said, suddenly confused. "All this time, I thought it was because of what you were doing when I was born."

"You never give yourself enough credit, girl," her father said, shaking his head. "However, if you allow this one to help you, you will see just how far you can go. Come speak with me before you leave and I will tell you the rest of what you need to know."

With that, Eirik set a hand on Shayan's wing and then the two of them disappeared in a flash of light. He had Stepped, just as she could, though Vinicia did not know how he had ever found the strength.

Superstitious as the man was, Counsel Lord Hest'lre just gaped at the disappearance. "Can you do that?" He accused, looking to Kiernan. "Can all Sevenths?!"

"She can," Kiernan returned, no matter his own shock. "I found out about it this morning. I'll, ah, tell you about it later."

"Blood on my ancestors," Hest'lre said, shaking his head with disbelief. "My men never had a chance."

As the tension in the room loosened, Lenae opened her hand to reveal the silver brooch she hoped Vinicia would take. As the Consort set it on her palm, Vinicia saw the silver token was a quicksilver dragon in miniature, held by the falcon that was her symbol.

"This is for you," Lenae said, watching as Vinicia turned the broach over in her hand.

"What do you need me to do before he leaves?" She asked, feeling like an imposter despite everything they had said. "I have never been to Court in my life. I will look like a fool—"

She stopped as Lenae raised her hand.

"You and the other eight Consorts will be given your formal titles with the start of Winter Court tomorrow," Lenae answered and Vinicia did not miss the way the woman eyed the elevated tyro blues she wore. "That will give you the official title and rank-rights associated with my new Court. I should be able to dress you as I am dressing the others in my purple and silver, but I daresay you have more strength of body than perhaps even Kiernan does."

As Kiernan scoffed, Hest'lre just laughed aloud. "I told you that you were getting soft," he commented, looking towards the door.

"Let me take your measure at least and I will see what my women can manage," Lenae said, stepping back so Vinicia could do so.

"As for when you two mean to leave," Hest'lre said, taking up the topic as Lenae walked off to fetch a bit of string. "The ice storms look ready to start the day after next. Shayan told me a bit of the day you have had, but... You didn't happen to get those commission packets done, did you Vinicia?" He asked hopefully.

"They are in my office," Vinicia said, much to his relief. "You can grab them if you like. Aaron can let you in."

"Thank you," Hest'lre said, pressing his palms together in a most expressive prayer. "I will see you both come dawning," he added, seeing himself out as Lenae rejoined them with her tailor's string.

"I was planning to leave immediately after graduation," Kiernan said, watching as Lenae motioned for Vinicia to stand and be measured. "I have a sortie planned between the shelves, but the rations I've set up should support the two of us well enough for the fortnight it should take us to get there," he said.

"Until then," Lenae said, cutting in before they could get distracted by logistics. "Your father mentioned that you have quarters in the Soldier Tyros' Wing that only you can access?"

"I do," Vinicia admitted, watching as Lenae looped the knotted cord around her neck for safe keeping.

"Then I expect you can sequester him there," she said, with a significant look to Kiernan. "This guardian I will not have you ghosting. From what Eirik says, she can find you anywhere and at any time, so you will do exactly what she says. Yes?"

Kiernan's only response was to nod as he stepped past Vinicia to embrace Lenae. Seeing them about to kiss, Vinicia looked away so she wouldn't have to watch the full exchange.

When they separated, one of Kiernan's arm still around her waist, Lenae held her hand out to Vinicia. "I take it you understand the gravity of the situation between Kier'n and I," she asked, and it was clear she meant to take Vinicia into as much confidence as she held Kiernan.

In a gesture of good will, Vinicia offered her hand to the woman, who squeezed it with affection. "I think I do," Vinicia said with some hesitancy.

"If this Envoy succeeds, we can be together. Openly," Lenae added and stepped out of the circle of Kiernan's arm to take his hand instead. "In all of this, what I fear most is losing him to the whim of some slighted dryad before his journey has even begun. This is the true reason I ask this of you," Lenae said and Vinicia saw a vulnerability that she didn't realize could exist in the powerful woman. "Dame Kaitlyn has told me many things of dryads and their kin this evening, and I understand it is possible for them to transfix the men they share intimacy with. On this Envoy, you must realize that only a woman of your birth could hope to stand between him and that forest. If you believe that taking him to nest will help either of you in any way, then I ask you to act as his wingmate until you return him to me."

Vinicia had never turned so scarlet so fast in her entire life. Her father clearly meant for her to use the overabundant power Kiernan gave off for her own purposes, but that did not have to include physical intimacy. Lenae, however, meant exactly that.

"And woman to woman," Lenae added, doubling down on her offer with a wicked smile. "I have made certain he knows his way around a woman's pleasure. I assure you he will not disappoint."

When Kiernan said nothing in response, Vinicia looked to him fearing the worst, only to see he was just as red-faced as she was.

"Lenae, a woman cannot be a wingmate. That's not how it works," Kiernan hesitated to say, only to have the Consort turn to him with fierce determination.

"I do not care that the term is used for men, she is going to War with you," she said, not giving him a moment to argue. "Call her your goddess for all I care, but she is clearly more of a warfighter than you are if she can put you on your wings at first meeting. She now has my permission to sit on you to make certain you do not act an idiot. Speaking of which," Lenae went on, poking his chest with a finger to make her point. "I swear to Great Matron Celenae, if you ever think to take Kreychi Windover to nest again while I live and breathe, I will skin you alive. He is Patriarch of their House now. He needs to take a wife, Kier'n, not cling to the desperate hope that he can somehow become yours."

As Kiernan ducked his head from her fury, he turned to see Vinicia's shadowed look staring back at him. Vinicia knew as much as either of them that Kreychi had been in love with him for cycles, even as tyros. What neither knew was just how much she had needed to deal with Kreychi's own weeping as Barracks Mother the cycle Kiernan had left. There was no hiding the truth of what Kreychi wanted with Kiernan from her. Taboo as it was, men did not trade rings with other men in the mountains.

As Kiernan let out a rough breath, closing his eyes, all the love Lenae had for him showed again as she dragged his face back towards her own. "If you ever loved him," she said quietly. "Let him go, Kier'n. Please. You are hurting him by letting him cling to you so tightly."

"It won't happen again," Kiernan breathed, opening his eyes at the sound of the pleading in her voice.

As Lenae moved in to kiss him, Vinicia was in awe of the moment, never having realized what kind of power such a pure emotion could generate. If this love was power, the spark between the two of them was bright enough to blind her. Simply standing in their presence, she could feel the Wellspring spiraling out from them, surging into her whether she liked it or not.

"Vinicia," the Consort said and Vinicia came back to herself in a rush as the woman tapped her shoulder. "You will take care of him for me, won't you? You will be his wingmate?"

"Your will is my own, Your Grace," Vinicia said, even if Kiernan was unable to match eyes with her. For as pulled inside of himself as the man was, she wasn't surprised. She had known the way Lenae had been able to take him by the downy as tyros and nothing seemed to have changed at all. Then again, they were both people who wielded incredible power, so throwing their weight around at one another was to be expected. The fact that Lenae always seemed to win, though, was strange.

"Wonderful," Lenae said, stepping back so they could turn to leave. "Then I leave him in your most capable hands. Please take him wherever it is you mean to keep him sequestered for the night. I have work to do that does not involve the two of you."

With that, Consort Lenae waved them off before closing the door firmly behind them.

Kiernan let out a slow, even breath as he stared at the door, listening to Lenae's footfalls walking away. He looked about as shocked as she felt, resigned to a fate that neither could fight alone. Not and survive. Together, however, it seemed like the people who loved them the most hoped they would stand a chance.

"Do you ever stand up to her?" Vinicia asked, for lack of anything else to say.

Kiernan's exhaled laughter caught her off guard. "Of course I do," he said. "But I know when to pick my battles. Kreychi... He isn't one of them. We have been trying to find him a wife ever since he left the Host, but yesterday he saved my life. I was losing myself to my Gift and he brought me the terra I needed to hear myself think again. Lenae just didn't like what I said I'd do for him in return."

"Which was taking him to nest?" Vinicia prompted, wincing.

"From about mid-meal until Hest'lre grabbed me to go down to Aaron's, yeah," he said, waving at her to join him as they moved towards the exit of the Royal's Wing. "Hest'lre walked in on us, so he must have told her."

"Hest'lre doesn't like Kreychi?" Vinicia asked.

"Hest'lre is terrified of upsetting Lenae," Kiernan laughed. "He always has been. But you should know that," he said, nudging her with a wing. "Very little about the three of us has changed. You, however..."

Vinicia made a face at him, refusing to be baited. "I am the same person I was in the barracks."

"You absolutely are not," he laughed. "You are so much more than that and don't you ever think otherwise."

Vinicia glowered at the words he clearly meant for a compliment, defensive even if she had no idea why. She also had no idea how she would survive the next cycle at this man's side, but she had given her word twice now. Once to Hewn because he was the man's intended Counselheir and once to Lenae just now. Sighing, Vinicia spoke again, hoping to change the subject.

"Do you need to get anything from your rooms before we turn in?" She asked. He was still in that ridiculously formal kama.

"That depends on where we're going," he said in return. "Lenae mentioned that you have quarters in the Tyro's Wing, but I can't exactly go through that wall."

"I live in The Library," she said, answering his lingering question. "My room is inside the Great Tree."

"You mean the canopy or do you...?" He said, trailing off as he realized she meant she lived inside the tree. "Oh, you have got to be kidding me. Really?"

"Yes, really," Vinicia said. "There is a nest I used to use in the canopy, however. I'm sure you can make do with that or the lounges on the highest level."

"I can't go into your rooms with you?" Kiernan asked, crestfallen.

"Do you need to?" She countered.

"Well, there isn't a latrine in the Library," he said, about to laugh before he realized there might not be one inside the Great Tree either. "Is there... Well, what exactly is in your rooms?"

"Everything I need," she defended, latrine included. "I have an entire suite of apartments, an office, a nest, a wardrobe. I even have my own library, though it is only made up of the books from the House Northern Estate that I bought as the House was collapsing."

Kiernan's mouth fell open as he came to a stop in the middle of the hallway. "*You* bought those?" He said, incredulous. "I tried to have them donated to the Seventh's Collection and they refused!"

"Of course they refused," Vinicia scoffed, stopping as well. "The Gods take charity, but windwalkers need to eat."

Kiernan just shook his head. "At least someone has them," he said, starting down the hallway again. "I would like to see them, though. They should be a part of the Seventh's Library."

"They are," Vinicia insisted, moving with him.

"Not if they're inside the Great Tree where only you can access them," he argued.

"Well, you took the Counsel Lord travel journals," she shot back.

"I did not — No, I did," he said, surprised to realize it. "Gods, that was cycles ago. How do you know about that?"

"They were next to all the books that have to do with dryads, which were also missing when I checked this dawning," she said, letting her irritation show. "I had them all collected on the top floor, so you must have moved them."

"Because you need them so much," he scoffed. "You're kindred."

"And those books are the only guidance I had on how to survive," she said, grabbing the wide sleeve of his kama to stop him once again. "You took them from me when you took them out of the Library."

"Vinicia, I didn't know you existed," Kiernan defended. "I took them to study so I knew what I was going into, but now you are here beside me and I hope," he said, pausing as she released him. "I hope we can work together without tearing each other's heads off."

Vinicia wanted to be angry with him, wanted to see the man she had thought he had become, but as they stood there in the hallway, the tyro she had once loved was staring back at her instead. Wearing her hawkeye really had changed him that much. Every moment they were together, though, he was more and more like his old self.

"I may have become a Counsel Lord in time," he went on. "But you have served the Seat your entire life. If we can help one another, then that is what I want to do. We do not have time to fight over what actions we may have taken if we had known of one another before. It is all in the past."

Vinicia couldn't argue with that. She also didn't want to, though it was a surprise to realize the overwhelming energy Kiernan was radiating was part of the reason. He was oozing with calm and though he was a powerful warbard, it looked like he had no idea how to handle the empathic gift at the core of it. Instead of being a bard playing an instrument, now that the hate and warmongering were gone, his words simply reached out and touched her soul. It was incredible. Almost as incredible as the hook and interrogation her own ancestor had taught her that dawning, if inverted to a greater purpose.

"You're right, of course," Vinicia said, resettling her wings as they stood facing one another in the hallway. "And of course you can come into my apartments. My home is your own until we leave."

"Thank you," he said, risking a smile. "Do you mind if we make one stop before we end up there, however?" he said, a look of sudden realization overtaking him. "There is someone you need to meet before we leave and it is late enough that we can manage it."

"Someone else?" She asked. "Haven't I met enough people today?"

"This is different," he said, looking to where his guard of Blackwings was waiting. "Remember the Val'Kyr woman I spoke about before? The Loralae I have in the high cells?" When Vinicia nodded, he went on. "I have always offered her the chance to come with me on this Envoy, though she has refused me out of spite. Knowing who you are, though, she may speak to you. You speak the Old Tongue, yes?"

"Yes," Vinicia said, hesitant. "But I thought you said she was to be handed over to Lord Fifth when you left."

"She will be, if she does not agree to come with me," he said. "But I think the two of you may actually get on, given your fire. Assassin or not, ff she can respect the strength in you, perhaps she will at least consider my offer. Our offer," he amended. "Since it is the two of us going on Envoy. If nothing else, we can test this theory of Lenae's that the Vals will only negotiate with a woman."

"I thought the songs said that you had tamed her with your silver tongue," Vinicia said. "If that is the case, why will she no longer speak with you?"

"Because I didn't stop her from killing me that night," Kiernan said, lifting a hand to gesture to the heavy kingchain she wore. "Your hawkeye did."

VOLUME 3: THE ICE WINDS

And the winds will rise,
And many men all will die,
And all the world will bow down,
To the Loralae...

CHAPTER 20: THE LORALAE

Friday, 22:00

*I*t's that bloody hawkeye again, Lora thought, seething as she paced the length of her cell. *It saved that idiot Dragon Lord from my balefire and now it is hiding her from me. Great Good Goddess, I will kill him with my bare hands this time, just as soon as I get out of this place. He took my entire life, but he will not take my sha'doe. Vinicia is mine.*

Lora set her hands on the threshold that barred her way, gathering her anger and calling to mind the destructive force she had once been when she dominated the Plains.

I was not just some Ehkeski river demon, she thought. *I was The Loralae. The only one that mattered. The only one they truly feared. The one who fought and was captured, but could not be killed. Now,* she thought, looking up with focus. *Now, I will not be caged.*

Determined, she hit her palm against the wall and the force that rebounded was an insult to her true strength.

Great Mother of All, Lora swore, turning to pace the ten lengths that made up her prison. *I do not want to have to kill someone to get out of here, but if I have no other choice...*

As she reached the end of her cell, Lora moved to the small hole that let in fresh air and sunlight this deep into the mountain. By some trick of engineering, the Kosarans had tunneled through their bedrock and set polished stones at angles to let in light to the deep cells during the day. For her benefit, it also let in fresh air that carried the hint of rain.

Or ice, she realized, forcing herself to let the irritability of having to manage this escape in winter flare inside of her. The Ice Winds the Kosarans were so afraid of were nothing more than the straight-line winds hitting the mountains, but they seemed to worship them. It wasn't a half bad idea since it meant each of their men had the wing strength of any four women in the Vals, but if the ice fell mid-tournament then many of those same men might die flying.

What the storm meant for her was that she was at her strongest, as far as her natural affinity for water went. Even before she had been abducted by dryads, Lora had known she had a gift with water magic. The dryad who had claimed her had taken credit for that strength, folding it into a greater gift for blood magic. Lora had a massive pool of magic nearby thanks to the Kir raging around the Palace, though she hadn't made use of it for all she lacked the will to fight after twenty cycles at war. Unfortunately, she would need to use blood magic for her escape to work, which meant luring one of the Kosaran guards to his death so she could take his face.

Closing her eyes, Lora wet her thumb on her lip and then cupped her hands together as she worked to expand the slip of wetness into a manifestation of power. As she focused, she felt the energy sliding from her thumb and into her palms as it took on the shape of a large drop in her mind. Once it was steady, she let the surface tension solidify into an almost-tangible ball and, with a little push, she had it set. Opening her eyes, she threw the ball from one hand to the other and the hard, wet slap it made was more than satisfying. The fact that it was still invisible to the naked eye was perfection.

I've still got it, she congratulated herself, moving to take a seat within full view of the door. With the ball gripped in her right hand, she drew her arm back to throw it, looked at the wall on the other side of her cell and let it fly. After a moment, it hit the floor and then the far wall with a wet *ka'thunk* before she pulled it back into her hand.

Toss. Ka'thunk. Catch.

Toss. Ka'thunk. Catch.

Toss. Ka'thunk. Catch.

The movement was almost meditative until the guard in the hall took notice and stopped with a hand on the bars of her cell.

"What are you doing?" He demanded in Kosaran. It was Johan.

Sweet Mother of All, she thought, thrilled. *You do remember your daughter.*

Lora ignored him and continued to throw her energy ball against the wall. One of the last things her dryad had done before releasing her across the Kir was to trap her speech within the Old Tongue, so unless they could also speak it, she really had nothing to say. It drove them mad, which she rather enjoyed.

"Oh, come on," Johan insisted. "I know you can understand me, lana."

That last bit made her angry. Lana was the term these idiots used for every one of her people. What they didn't know was that Lan'a, when pronounced correctly, was the slur for a woman in exile who could call no island home: 'Lan' meaning island and 'a' meaning without. Having been born the daughter of a Tor Mother, it was more than an insult. Just how much her mother had fallen or what Lora chose to call herself now was a different matter, but it irritated her that she was responding to 'lana' at all.

Lora glared at him and then returned to throwing her ball of energy against the wall.

This one's broken, Johan thought to himself, looking at her so intently that Lora couldn't not hear his thoughts. *It's so pathetic... Maybe I should just give her a real blicing ball. Then it wouldn't look so creepy.*

After a moment staring at what he could only see as an imaginary game of catch, he vanished from the bars of her cell. They always did. She knew the guards had a running pool on who would finally get her to talk, but she had never had a reason to rouse their excitement. Today was different.

Toss. Ka'thunk. Catch.

Toss. Ka'thunk. Catch.

Lora only stopped when she heard the guard returning. This time, he had an actual leather ball, which she assumed they used to amuse themselves. As he showed it to her through the bars, she looked between it and the guard's dark brown eyes. Dark, because all Kosarans were full of shit.

"Interested?"

She didn't look away, which for him was as good as a yes.

Johan raised an eyebrow as he dropped it inside. This wasn't the only time a guard had tried to give her something. The first time, cycles ago, she had found out the hard way just how fond Kosarans were of contact poison. She had been lucky it was one of the few she had built a tolerance for as a kyree. Not that it hadn't made her ill, but she had still had the strength to fight off the three men that had attempted to make use of her that night.

As the guards rotated with the seasons, some new recruit would try the same trick again, but she was prepared. After that first time, she had begun to study the Kosaran energy so she could protect herself from their natural toxins. Fortunately, in doing so, she had also found the River Kir that sustained her, even if touching it came with a price.

A slip in sanity was a small sum against the likes of those vile men, especially this one. If she remembered correctly, this was the one who had bragged about how badly he had taken after Vinicia's beloved tyro Rylan when he had first been brought into the cells.

Vinicia couldn't possibly mind if I killed this one, she thought and pushed herself onto her feet. She walked the few paces it took to reach the ball and ignored it, looking to the guard instead.

"Just what did you do in Lan'lieana?" he asked. "Before the war, I mean. We all know what kyree do."

Lora considered him, considered the lines on his face, and the shift in his weight as he studied her through the bars. If she was going to mimic him, she would need to make certain she did it perfectly.

::I fished,:: she answered, speaking into his mind while she made her mouth move appropriately. The dryad's gift allowed such things, which made it possible for her to speak to almost anyone if they were alone. Mind-to-mind, all thoughts were energy. ::You?::

The guard's jaw hung open for a moment and then he glanced down the hallway towards his post.

::They won't believe you if you tell them,:: she whispered into his subconscious.

"I am a Son of new-founded House Kirath," he answered, apparently agreeing with her Suggestion. "I trained for the Guard, since there was more money to be made."

::I thought Kirath was one of your city-shelves,:: Lora commented innocently, knowing full well her sister-kyree had set it aflame. If she could get his blood boiling before she made her move, the magic would be much more potent.

"It was," he admitted, his look turning dark as he remembered just what kind of Lan'lieanan Lora was. "Were you part of that attack?"

::No,:: she sent, rolling her eyes before she could stop herself. Not everyone in the whole bloody Vals was there, no matter how Kosarans insisted they all looked the same. ::Why? Were you?::

The young man's glower deepened. "I was too young to fight when the city fell, but not too young to remember having to evacuate. All the nobility that survived, we're forming our own House now and it's about blicing time."

::If you say so,:: she mouthed and then straightened, fanning her wings to get his full attention. When he smirked to see the slim figure she made, Lora caught his eyes and set her hook in his mind. Now she would see just what she could do to stretch her influence with her quiet interrogation. ::What's your name?::

"Johan su'Kirath of House Kirath," he answered, easily transfixed.

::A good name,:: she said, disarming him with a smile that her own *sha'dara* had never been able to resist. ::What's your measure?::

"Five hands and four," he said, though he wasn't proud of it. By her reckoning, he was rather short for a Kosaran. Young Rylan had been a head taller than that, easily.

::That's not so bad,:: she assured him.

"They said you were the kyree that tried to kill Lord Seventh," Johan said, looking her over. "But you're nothing special."

::I am a sorceress,:: she answered, since it didn't matter anyway. He wasn't long for this world. ::The Vals trained me to use it to find your Dragon Lord. Did you know is a sorcerer, too?::

"Wavewalkers wielding fae magic are just stories told to keep fledglings in line," Johan scoffed. "But the Seventh is gifted at being an ass, I'll give you that."

Lora laughed, openly now. ::You amuse me, Johan.::

"I can be more than amusing," he said, his smirk dissolving into an open leer.

As he did so, Lora stepped back a pace and his attention was caught. She bit her lower lip as he watched and in a few fluid motions, shed the sad excuse for clothing she wore with an unhurried grace. Disrobed, she stepped away from the pile, away from him, until her wings were flared invitingly against the back wall of her cell. Hands pressed against the slick stone, she drew power from the water magic she had stored there and compelled him to open the door.

::Come and get me,:: she called, pulling on the hook in his mind.

It only took a heartbeat for the man to fit the key into the lock and two more for him to step inside. When his body was pressed against hers, Lora wrapped the liquid energy around him like a lover's embrace. She allowed him one attempt at her lips and used that moment to catch the water she had fed in around him, pulling it through his core. When she finally gave him the taste he wanted, she bit his lip hard enough to draw blood and he began to choke with no idea why. As water poured from his mouth, Lora shoved his face to the side and let the man fall to the floor with his hands at his throat, drowning in the torrent of the River Kir.

Only when he was still did she call the water back from his body, and for the first time in ages, pull it and the power that lay dormant in the room directly into her reserves. As it flared to life in her control, she used the first part of it to reclaim the strong shields she had once worn on the Plains. This simple protection felt more like armor than any metal or cloth she had ever worn, and she reveled in the feel of it returning.

Truly alive for the first time in an age, Lora looked to her open cell door. As her body screamed for her to run, only her discipline kept her in place to finish the job. She started by stripping the guard of his possessions and then clothed him with the rags that she had worn. In exchange, she put on his boots, his breeches, and his guard's doublet as she, too, measured five hands and four.

When she was done, she kicked the ball he had brought her next to his hand and staged the scene. ::Poor lana,:: she said, tasting the man's accent. ::The herb was too much for her.::

Satisfied, she knelt and connected the circle of power between them. With one a hand on his bloodied lip and another on his core, she latched onto the lingering vitality of his corpse. Closing her eyes, she propelled her will through the image of the man in her mind and the image of herself as they saw her. From the Gods to the Sea to us, from us to the Sea to the Gods... She finished her spell by streaking the man's blood under her eyes, and then it was done.

::Idiot lana,:: she repeated, now looking down at the image of the woman she would have been if she had lost her fight against the dryad's curse.

When she was sure the switched images would stay, Lora picked up the keys to her cell and took her freedom. As she neared the guard's station at the end of the hallway, the other man on shift called to her in surprise.

"Who were you talking to?" He asked, confused.

::The idiot lana,:: she replied, hiding her mouth as she neared. ::The herb was too much for her.::

The guard's eyes went wide as he lurched to his feet.

"You're kidding!"

::See for yourself,:: she sent, continuing past him.

"Where are you going?" He demanded, stopping her with a shove she was too physically weak to defend against. Given a choice between her shields and her physical strength, she would always choose her shielding. "You can't leave. This is all on you!"

::No,:: she corrected, catching his wrist. As the man glared at her, she pushed a different thought under his skin. ::This is on you,:: she insisted as his eyes glazed over. ::You gave her the ball. You gave her the herbs. You killed her.::

"I killed her," he repeated, dazed.

Lora shoved the man away and moved into the room beyond the cells. If she was lucky, there would be some sort of place that would have her possessions still locked inside. What she found looked promising, as one side of the guard room was filled with cubbies from floor to ceiling. Most of them were empty, but a few near the floor were larger and largely forgotten.

One in particular looked as if someone had been unsuccessfully trying to pick the lock for moonturns, or in her case, cycles...

Kneeling next to the abused door, Lora picked up the lock in her hand, brought up the image of waves crashing against the rocks at sea and drove that image through the pins holding the catch secure. As expected, the metal fell away in pieces, dripping with water. When the door swung open, though, the only thing waiting in the cubby was a note, yellow and faded, with one word in the flowing Kosaran calligraphy: *Kiernan's.*

Rage dropped over her as she crumbled the fragile parchment. Of course he would have her things. They were his trophies as much as her life continued to be.

Lora stood with purpose, gathered the haversack that was obviously this dead guard's, and moved up the stairs. After a short climb that tested her prison-weary legs, she passed a man that recognized the face she wore.

"You're off duty, already?" The man asked, more friendly than Lora cared to deal with. "No, I bet you have the honor of working in the Hall for the Announcement, eh? What I wouldn't give for the rank-right to be on that third tier."

::We use what we're given,:: Lora sent, still looking away from him and then pushed past the man without another word.

Lora hadn't gone more than two flights before she realized she was out of breath again. Swearing at herself, she stopped on the next landing and doubled over with her hand to her side, sucking in air. Apparently being trapped in a cell had affected her more than she realized, but there was no going back now. She could either use her energy for the magic she would need to remain hidden or use it to heal herself from the cycles of atrophy. Only one of those would guarantee her success.

After long enough, Lora could finally stand up without the stitch. Before moving on, she glanced back down the stairs and could feel the panic of the men below. *I need to get out of here and out of this face before anyone else he knows comes across him.*

Just as she turned to head up the stairs, she heard two more people coming down. Quiet as they had been in their flight boots, Lora hadn't realized their presence until she looked up to see Counsel Lord Kiernan with her beautiful *sha'doe* following at his heels.

Lora snapped to attention, mimicking the Kosaran salute with her right fist to her left breast as Kiernan joined her on the landing. With her eyes to the ground, she prayed to any ancestor that would listen that neither one of them could sense the magic covering her. Worse, no matter her skill, there was no hiding the blue of her eyes. Not even her dryad had been able to change that.

"Do you really think this is wise?" Vinicia was asking, stopping short as she realized Kiernan had needed to tighten his wings to pass by a guard mid-salute.

"It is worth letting you speak with her, at least," Kiernan said, returning the salute as he passed. "If she will not speak with even you, then she will be Roder's prisoner when I am gone."

Lora's heart was racing as Kiernan continued, knowing they were speaking about her, but when Vinicia passed, her heart spasmed. The woman was tall for a Kosaran, taller than Kiernan in fact, but she was full of grace for all her mother's blood. She was a dream moving through this wretched place and Lora could hear the smile in her voice as she spoke.

"Please excuse us," Vinicia said, pulling her wings in as she slipped past to follow.

Lora wanted to scream. She couldn't say a word aloud without giving herself away. Worse, Vinicia stalled as she moved past her, almost recognizing her, impossible as that seemed.

"Do I know you?" she asked, hesitating as Lora felt the shields around her fluctuating under the press of Vinicia's intense curiosity. Powerful as she was in her own right, she was not used to seeing power in others, but she knew something was wrong. Heart in her throat, Lora shook her head, saluting once again before she turned and fled up the stairs.

Lora was halfway to the next landing when she heard Kiernan calling for her. "Vinicia? Did I lose you?"

"No, I'm coming," Vinicia called, remembering herself as she moved deeper into the cells.

By the time Lora reached the second to last landing at the top of the stairs, she had to stop and find her wind again. Now, in addition to the sheer exhaustion of having run up more stairs than she could handle, she was absolutely furious with herself for acting so rashly.

Why am I always so bloody impulsive? She thought and slammed her palm against the wall just to distract herself with the pain. *Fire and fates, that hurt! Why do I always hit stone!*

Hating herself even more, Lora took the moment to grab at her stinging palm, folding down to sit on her heels as she clutched it to her core. As she did, she realized to her great shame that her eyes were stinging with tears she couldn't shed. Not with this face, at least. Not if she meant to keep the blood magic active while she figured out what in the world she was going to do.

Why didn't I just stay with her? She thought, digging her hands into her hair to distract herself further. *I knew she was going to speak with the Consort about her birthright. What else would she have needed to talk about with the Consort but the bloody Dragon Lord? The man was going through the Eihwaz, wasn't he? And that's where Vinicia was born! Gods, Loraleia, are you ever not dense?*

The sound of surprise and chaos echoing up the stairwell brought her attention back into the moment, though it was the rush of men swarming onto the stairs that had her back on her feet.

This is not over, she thought, her mind snapping into the same discipline that had saved her when she had been close to dying on the Plains. *I just need food, a change of clothes, and another face and I can talk with her. I can explain. Just— not right now.*

From where she stood, she only had two options: a huddle of irritated Blackwings and a hallway that went deeper into the Palace. From what Vinicia had said about all the highborn families moving out of the Sires' Wing in order to let the military take up residence for the winter, Lora figured she should be able to blend in without a problem with this man for a guise. For now, preferring to move her illusion away from those who might actually know him, going deeper into the Palace was her best option. That, and it would leave the Dragon Lord and her *sha'doe* far behind her.

When she pushed through the double doors at the end of the hallway, Lora realized it connected to the Palace. There were a few members of the guard standing around the entrance to one area, so she looked to her left, and—

Great Mothers!

Lora exhaled in a rush as she stared at the space beyond the wood paneling. Rising above her on the vaulted stone, the area had been painted with images of war. As the door sealed behind her, she was overcome by a panic she hadn't felt since before her capture. Groping for the wall behind her, she dropped her wings low and, for an instant she inhaled against the tight embrace of armor she hadn't felt in cycles. Her head was spinning as she forced herself to see the fresco for what it was; to see how little these men had allowed their artisans to depict her own people slaughtered. How much they focused on themselves, on a triumphant return some hundred fighting-seasons back.

Because we haven't lost ground to you since then. Not until Kiernan.

Lora shook herself from the paintings as she heard a door opening far to her left. Glancing down the hallway, she caught sight of a young, platinum haired man in Warhost indigo coming to his feet. He had been watching her until whoever he was waiting for had come through the doors. Strangely, his friend was carrying a thin plank of wood nearly as tall as himself...

"What's with the board, Micah?" the young man greeted with a laugh.

Lora's heart nearly stopped to see the man who called back. He was short for a Kosaran, but he had the broad shoulders and muscled build of any Lan'lieanan man she had ever seen. His skin was the same, soft olive as well, and though his hair was shaved on either side of his head to leave only the strip that would start the Kosaran warcrest, there was no denying the sea in him. Not to her.

"He wants me to take it to the barracks," Micah said as his friend fell in beside him. "And yes, I apologized to him for the way you acted today. He's not used to so much attention and it spooked him, but it should be okay now. Oh, and he gave me more of the detox tea for the both of us. We should get some sleep, though."

"Tomorrow's our rest day," the first scoffed, and Lora stepped back to let the two men pass. "I'd rather stay up with you if you'd let me."

"You would like that," Micah laughed, shoving him away with his wing.

Time slowed as the two passed in front of her, and Lora held her breath as the man glanced her way. His blue-grey eyes were round like her own, cunning and quick as he looked over Lora's disguise, though he couldn't see through it. His presence alone made her swallow hard around the knot in her throat.

"What's up with that guy?" Micah asked, glancing back at Lora once they had passed.

"No idea," his friend said, which was Lora's cue to move. She wouldn't have much time to hide herself again since Johan's body had been found so quickly. Just as she started to go, though, she heard the guards posted in the hallway call *'Wings up!'* with purpose.

Lora hesitated half a heartbeat before following the example of the two young men, coming into a braced attention as Blackwings flooded into the hallway. Given the events in the Cells, Lora grimaced as she watched the Counsel Lord and her *sha'doe* appear amid the crowd, though they were moving with purpose towards the hall Lora had been about to flee into.

After they had passed into the hall with their Blackwing shadows, the guard in the hall gave them an *'As you were!'* and everyone who had been stopped shifted back into their ease. Since this might be her only chance to follow the two of them, Lora put her head down and moved as if she had every right to be going that way. Somehow, blessedly, no one stopped her.

Unfortunately, she made it inside the wing with just enough time to watch as the Counsel Lord and his entourage took to the sky, powering their way to the highest level of the towering building with an ease that made her wings ache.

Eighteen stories into the air through a path I cannot take, Lora knew, sighing as she moved to see what door they were heading for. It wasn't just her lack of strength that kept her out of those heights, but the memory of sharp reeds against the soles of her feet the one time she had thought to fly instead of walk in the Lan'lieanan Court. You only had to suffer an Auntie's wrath once to learn never to fly indoors.

So as the Dragon Lord and her *sha'doe* landed on the highest level to enter what she assumed was his set of suites, Lora searched for the stairs. By the time she had walked all the way to the other side of the Wing, though, she had to stop to catch her breath. She was not in the kind of shape a man like Johan should be in as a member of the Guard and it showed. Worse, she could feel her connection to the man waning the farther she moved from his corpse. She would need a new guise, and soon. As soon as Johan's actual body had been found, the power it had taken for her to pass as Johan had redoubled. Once one of those Blackwings got ahold of it... Well, they would never believe she was dead.

And so it was that she made her way, determined if dreading it, to the dark corridor where she could see a set of steps leading into a dim spiral. When she reached them, Lora put her head down and made her way up, her mind spinning with thoughts.

I just have to get close enough, she reasoned to herself. *If I do not have the distance between us, I should be able to speak to her no matter the hawkeye she wears. If I can speak to her, explain myself to her, then maybe she can get him to give me back my falconstone and I will not have to leave a trail of bodies in this place to maintain a stupid guise.*

No, with her stone she could fill both her reserves of blood magic and water magic and they would last for a moonturn with no effort at all.

Goddess, the things I do for love...

An agonizing number of risers later, Lora realized she had lost track of how high she had climbed. When she finally reached the landing at the top, she put her hands on top of her head, leaning her wings against the wall so she wouldn't crush her lungs with their weight. At this point, she would have to go out onto the balcony to reorient herself, but... Later.

Now I need to breathe.

Lora closed her eyes, inhaling and exhaling with purpose. When she opened them again, she found she was not alone. Instead, she saw the ghost of a man staring back at her from an arm's length away and would have screamed if she had the breath left in her.

"I heard a rumor you were dead," the spirit said, speaking the Old Tongue as he hovered before her. "Loralae, is it?"

"I—I, ah," Lora stammered. Of the many things she had seen in her lifetime, dryads, dragons, and elemental spirits... the shade of an ancestor was not one of them.

"What an interesting guise you wear," he said, waving his hand in front of his face. "Blood magic?" he said, tsking. "How crude."

He is not of this plane, Lora reminded herself. *He can do no harm to me.*

"What else would you have me use?" she challenged. "Four cycles of captivity left me no other choice."

"I would like to know who taught you that trick," he answered, floating closer to peer at her face. Lora leaned back as he neared, but it only made him more curious. "How long does it last?"

Lora swallowed around the knot in her throat. "Until the body is cremated," she answered. "Until then, I can wear his mask."

"And what will you do when he comes to us?" He pressed.

"Why?" Lora challenged. "What is it to you?"

"It might be relevant," he said and moved close enough that he would have been able to touch her if he yet lived.

Lora started as she felt the skin on her cheeks tingling. The blood that had cooled with her magic was suddenly burning like a pepper salve. Cursing the Kosarans for their quick funeral pyres, Lora used the sleeve of the stolen tunic to wipe off as much of the dried blood as she could manage.

"What now?" The shade cackled as the spell released.

"If you were alive, I would kill you and take your place the same way I did his," she answered.

"I've been dead a little long for that," he laughed. "Try again."

"I need to find my things," she said, exasperated. It wasn't like the shade could stop her. "That bastard Dragon Lord took them from me when he threw me in that cell."

"And what's so special about a pair of eating sticks and a haversack full of armor?" The shade asked.

"They are mine," Lora insisted, angry, desperate, and powerless all at once. "Four cycles I have staved off madness in this horrible place, with little thanks to you or your kind. I am a wavewalker, not a windwalker like you fools, and the magic of your mountains has been trying to devour me since I was brought here. Even you must know that."

"So there is something in that sack you want?" He asked, drawing out the question with painful ignorance.

"My falconstone," she said, angry to be arguing with a shadow of a man she would have otherwise killed. "It is a focus for my magic made by those who cursed me. Do you have it?"

"I do," the spirit said, glancing to the wall beyond her. "Well, we do."

"We?" Lora repeated, cautious.

"I am Broc su'Delton," he explained, nonchalant. "My kinsmen and I, all Sevenths past, reside just beyond that wall."

Lora paled, which seemed to please the shade.

"Are you up for a trade, little loralae?" He said, reaching out his hand to her.

"What trade?"

"Why exactly did the dryads teach you blood magic?" He asked, curious.

"To seek, to find, to lure, and to bind," Lora answered immediately, though it pained her to repeat the words. "And if we cannot bind, we kill."

"Kill what?" Broc asked, considering her. "Did the dryads mean for you to come after the Sevenths?"

"The dryads and the Great Tor Mothers both sent me to kill your kind," Lora answered with spite. "Although trying to survive your High Cells without my falconstone has taken me halfway to being a bloody meriad."

"Better half-fish than full harpy," Broc said and shrugged. "For you can still be of some use to us. As you are no-doubt aware, we have two dryad-kin with us on the shelf. One is the half-blooded daughter of a Seventh, the other a sapling born on the Plains. Not two nights back, a messenger from his mother paid us a visit with a hawkeye. He wears it now, but still his power grows. Do you believe you can bind him, as you were taught to do?"

"If he needs such a stone, he is beyond my ability to bind," Lora answered. "I would sooner kill him."

"No," the shade snapped. "He must be bound."

"I never said I wouldn't try," Lora snapped back. "But to do that I need my stone. Too much power bleeds energy, bleeds light, and this will require great power to do. I cannot do this just to be discovered. I assume you do not want Vinicia finding out or you would have asked her yourself?"

"Indeed you cannot," the shade said, somewhat surprised to realize she might know who Vinicia was. "Will you come with me?"

"Do I have a choice?" She scoffed.

"No," he answered and set a hand on her wing. "Not really."

As she felt the magic begin to pull her from the stairwell, she closed her eyes. Of all the things in the world, she hated this twisting sensation the most. Spiraling out of control and then back in to focus, Lora came back to herself on her knees in a dark and silent room. When she opened her eyes she was surrounded by shades.

As the Dragon Lord she had been speaking with moved away, a younger, less transparent shade moved in to replace him. This one she recognized from her time on the Plains. It was Seventh Counsel Lord Hewn.

"I was wondering how you died," she said, seeing the bloody wound the shade still carried at his neck.

The Counsel Lord ignored her. "And you are?" he asked.

"Loralae," she answered, giving him the twisting of her true-name she had preferred while locked away in their cells. The woman she had been on the islands had died over two decades ago.

"I asked who you are, not what you are," Hewn corrected. "Do you want the stone or not?"

"Who I am is irrelevant," Lora said, sighing. "I am from the House of the Omega." Last because of her bastard birth, not that it mattered. She was already either presumed dead or exiled to her fate as a loralae. Her dryad had made certain she knew that before sending her back over the River Kir to begin her work.

"Truly? Your father was one of us?" Hewn said, extending his hand to her. Settled on his palm was the leather wrist cuff that hid her falconstone. When she went to take it, however, he pulled it back. "You will bind the sapling's power?"

"Yes," she said, furious that the shade would play such a fledgling trick. "If it is possible, I will do it."

"If it is possible?" He repeated.

"It is not an easy thing you ask," Lora insisted. "Kindred can be bound when they are young, but once they come into their power it is difficult. Even if I don't kill them, they will kill themselves because they prefer suicide to slow starvation."

Hewn considered her and then looked to where the shade of Counsel Lord Broc hovered suspiciously. "And if he is wearing a hawkeye?"

"If it is anything like my stone, then he has grounded the excess of his power," Lora lied. If it was anything like Vinicia's stone, then it was grounding him. Lora's own stone only amplified what energy she could access, either from blood magic or her natural affinity for water. "It siphons excess power, since too much would drive him mad. Too much power has already driven me half-mad as it is," she repeated angrily. "Now. Give. Me. My. Stone."

"You heard the woman," Broc said.

Lora reached out again and then Hewn and his companions vanished. The stone and leather strap dropped onto her palm a heartbeat later, bitter cold from the shade's touch. Relieved, she checked the wire wrapping that kept the flat stone bound to the leather and then half-panicked as she saw the stone was near to breaking. Not sure what that meant, she pressed the wrap against her wrist and wound the thick strap around her arm. That secure, she looped the strap against itself and slipped the tail underneath to hold it all firmly in place.

Once it was set, a calm washed over her and her knees buckled. The torture, the imprisonment, and the desperation that had ruled her for so long was forgotten as the world righted itself. She laughed, near hysterical as she reclaimed the weave of shields protecting her mind, weak as they were. With her hands pressed to her temples, she purged herself of the vile Kosaran energy and the sick feeling that came with it. When she finally looked up, her vision had turned to water. The raw power of the River Kir flowing through and around the Palace surged into her senses and for a moment she could taste the salty sea air at its termination.

"No matter how different we are," Hewn said, shocking her back to the present. "Creature comforts never fail."

As she looked up to reply, her rage overcame her fear of being surrounded by so many ancestors. But as she had no idea where she was, other than what she guessed was some proximity to the risers she had climbed, she had to humble herself. Raging against them would do little in this place.

As she finally relaxed, she looked around and her jaw went slack. There were tomes lining the walls of this chamber that enclosed an enormous barren tree and shelves upon shelves of literature beyond where she stood. Her hands flexed around the memory of the tome she had handed over to her *sha'dara* to aid her in breaking free of the dryad's curse. MiaSera had needed it far more than she had, so she had let it go. It, and the last of her instruction on just how to work her falconstone. What she knew now was only trial, error, and memory.

But that tree...

Lora's hand came up to her mouth to cover her surprise as she realized just where she was. Moving to the edge of the canopy that rose in the vaulted upper story, she blinked into her darkwater secondsight as she marveled at the true majesty of it. She had known her *sha'doe* lived in one of the great Kosaran temple trees, but she had not realized that the tree itself was alive only because of her efforts. The power in the one before her was like cold molasses, stagnant and rotten for all the dead men it contained. The only reason the power in the tree moved at all was because of Vinicia's constant presence within it.

Lora's heart sank as her knees turned to water, realizing where her *sha'doe* likely was. For all her sorcery, she could not contact her in this place, not surrounded by so many ancestral guardians. Worse, for all the time she had spent tracking Dragon Lords on the Plains, she could see that Kiernan was with her as well.

He was a bright spark of life beside her, part of the power of the tree and yet different because he still lived.

Floating beside her, Counsel Lord Hewn seemed to understand.

"Vinicia said she talked to spirits other than ourselves," the shade said. "Have you been the one she speaks with? Teaching her, when we could not?"

Lora nodded numbly.

"You do not mean to kill her."

It was more a statement than a question.

"I love her," Lora breathed.

Hewn considered her as she scrubbed a hand over her face. "You might as well stay here for the night," he said. "It is late and you will do your work better with a proper night's sleep."

Lora nodded again, watching the two bright points of light dancing around one another in the tree as if to spite her.

"Do you have my haversack?" She asked, her voice rough with emotion. They had found her stone, which meant they must have the rest of her things.

Hewn pointed to an overstuffed nest near the war-beaten tomes. Coming to her feet, Lora found what it was she sought: a rough leather bag that held her woven armor, a spare kurta and pants that had somehow survived the cycles, her personal grooming effects, and the oilskin cloth that had once held the chain-bound book she had given to MiaSera. After trading her stolen clothes for her armor, pants, and kurta, she tossed the bulk of the haversack onto the floor before throwing herself into the nest.

With all she had done, with all she had been through this day, she was nearly asleep when she realized the shade was still hovering nearby.

"One last question," Hewn began. "You are not the first dryad-trained sorceress to make it to Delton. There was another like you that we could feel in the city, but the winds took her a decade past."

"Many women have reached this city," she answered vaguely, drawing her wing over her to act as a comfort. She had never liked nests, preferring the hammocks used by the Vals when they had barracks inside one of the Tors.

Hewn raised an eyebrow at her, calling her bluff. "The Sevenths felt it when she died, I just did not know what she was. I feel that same sensation now, just as I feel the touch of her energy in you. Are there other loralae in the city?"

"You think I'd know after being in the Cells for four cycles?" Lora scoffed, her heart aching again to think MiaSera had possibly made it into the heart of Delton. That had been her compulsion, after all. "I was made to hunt creatures over-balanced with power, not my own sisters. What you feel is probably a powerfully gifted windwalker," she said, drawing an arm up over her head pointedly. "The Gods know you all seem to gather in this place."

It didn't help.

"What do you mean, gifted?" Hewn insisted, the light of his spirit glowing in her eyes despite. "This power I feel is out of control."

"Look, shade," she said, angry now. "I was made to kill things with gifts, yourself included. Now I understand it is your Dragon Lord who has used his gift to turn the tide of War against us. The more soldiers he has, the stronger he is. The stronger he is, the more power he can raise. The more power he can raise, the more the gifts appear in your soldiers. Your existence," she said, pointing a finger at him. "Is only because you cling to the power you raised when you were alive. The more you focus on something, or someone, the more power you give them. So if you think someone has too much power, look to your Dragon Lord. If it is not him, it is his fault."

With that, Lora shifted to set her right hand on her left, closing the circle with the falconstone. After a few murmured words, she brought up the shield of water magic she had been taught to let her pass through the world unseen. Wretched as she felt, she lost herself in the memory of hot summer sands and the salted sea. She would find neither in this place given the icy wind and rains to come, but for the moment she could escape her fate in her dreams.

CHAPTER 21: SERA

Saturday, 06:00

While her presence within the Soldier Tyros' Wing still felt like a dream come true, the howl of icy wind was more than unsettling. Sera shivered as she pulled aside the heavy curtain to reassure herself it was only the wind, but the sight of the dawn struggling to break through the fast-moving clouds over the Palace courtyard made it seem as if dawn was fighting for its life. As tendrils of cold worked their way through the thick glass, her terror grew, and deep in her heart she knew there was no way to stop it.

The Ice Winds were coming.

Sera stepped back from the balcony window with a shiver, pulling Micah's heavy uniform tunic around her shoulders as she turned back into the room. Small and sterile as it was with a stone floor and wooden furniture, it served Micah and Rylan well enough. There were lockers for their gear flanking the balcony exit, two cushioned nests supported in platform boxes she suspected were filled with downy and two desks near the door that led into the barracks. The nests themselves were free of comforts, given how they had piled everything in the middle of the room to make a floor nest to share, but only Micah was in it.

Rylan had been at his desk for the past candlemark, using the light of a dim lantern to stare at whatever parchment he had been working with. As much as he wanted to sleep, he had said something about their bardic gifts making his pin feathers stand on end, so he had left them alone. As a result, he had worked through most of the night.

Folded up in the safety of Sera's arms, Micah had slept through most of the afternoon as Sera brought her brother's half of their shared empathic gift under control. Though Micah had started as a shell of himself, drained and hollow, the strength of her love and her ability to shield him had made a world of difference. Sometime in the middle of the night, she had brought their full gift into balance by drawing the overwhelming emotion he could feel into her own reserves instead.

Amusingly, once Micah had felt better, he had realized the attraction between her and Rylan so clearly that it had made him laugh.

"I suppose you haven't been a bowen for a while then, if you've been going to see her," he had said, eyeing them both.

"Why?" Rylan had scoffed, radiating a frustration so strong that she couldn't tell if it was magic or single-minded devotion. "Gods, it wasn't until Tyrsten said something that I realized I felt like this and I only told her last night. Why does no one blicing believe me?"

"It's a rare thing to feel love before every other physical affection," Sera had said, placating him as Micah rolled his eyes. "He understands it well enough for how devoted he is to his Kaitlyn," she had teased and had been immediately rewarded as she got to see Micah's ears turn bright red for the first time in forever. Reminded of her, though, and of her noble cousin, Micah had said something about needing to talk to Westly and had taken himself off to the chiurgeon's garden, giving her and Rylan time to lose themselves in one another.

That was all last night, though. Now that the sun was rising, she couldn't force herself back to sleep if she had tried.

Looking to entertain herself, Sera shifted towards Rylan's locker and opened the door to reveal the ordered collection of gear. Unlike any home they had ever made in the Streets, all his things were either hung or neatly folded away on the shelves. Rylan had said most of what they'd used the past two cycles had already been returned to the Armory, but they still had their crossbows and practice bolts, things covered in dense cloth that stung but wouldn't kill you because of the light pull on the crossbow itself.

They also had a set of enormous white coverings with red left arms meant to be worn during the tournament, which she had seen other tyros wearing before. Saying they were white was generous, too, since they were clearly ancient pieces of equipment. The most impressive piece in Rylan's collection, though, was the brand-new indigo leather jacket that was hanging in the locker.

This was his first piece of true Warhost gear, meant to identify him on the Plains as an officer under the Seventh Counsel Lord, and it was probably more expensive than anything Kaitlyn had thought to show her the night before. From the quality of the leather to the cut and finish of the seams, this one jacket might serve him for twenty cycles if he cared for it well. It was meant for a lifetime of service, given how the left chest, shoulder, and arm were covered with suede where even a Primarch's pauldron might sit one day.

He is going to do so well as the Tyro Primarch, Sera thought, stealing a glance towards Rylan only to realize he had caught her poking around again. Chin on his hand and wings drooping with exhaustion, he still had enough energy to give her the easy, adoring smile that twisted her heart into knots.

"I really don't understand what you see in there," he said, one eyebrow raised.

"The moment I saw you in this," she said, dragging out just the sleeve of the Warhost jacket so he could see it. "I wanted to tear it off you. It's so blicing sexy I can't even stand it."

Rylan just exhaled a laugh. Sure, he might not feel the same impromptu physical attraction, but he had certainly enjoyed the results of her attraction to him. After candle marks spent finding one another's pleasure, he had also promised that anytime she wanted to 'clear her head' like that again, he would definitely help. It *was* fun, just like she'd said, even if it would never occur to him to do it unless she asked.

As she stood there giving him her best smile, need fluttering in her chest as he gazed at her, she wondered for a moment if he could see how much she wanted him. After long enough, he looked back to his maps and she actually laughed out loud.

"What?" He asked, only to see her amused annoyance.

"You have absolutely no idea what you do to me, do you soldier boy?" She asked, moving past where Micah was curled up in the remnants of their floor nest to join him at his desk.

"Oh, I know," he said, shifting in his chair as she came up behind him. "But it's fun to tease you, since you clearly want something you can't have right now."

Rylan was absolutely not about to take her to nest if Micah was in it with them. Sera's sniff of annoyance only made his grin deepen.

"It's a good thing you're cute," she sulked, moving between his wings. After she set a kiss on the long length of his dirty platinum tyro's crest, she slid her hands across his shoulders, reaching down his chest as she trailed kisses along his neck.

Rylan shivered with the feel of it, bringing his hands up to hold her own as he pulled his wings together in an embrace. When he relaxed again, he let out a slow, heavy breath as he rested his head against her torso and closed his eyes.

"You're still working on your map?" She asked softly.

Rylan nodded as Sera looked over the sections he had been trying to sketch out. He had broken the city into street crew territories, but the areas were old and vague. Given how well he had always done on the streets predicting the movements of the other crew leaders, this war game was infuriating him. Rylan was a brilliant tactician, but he had clearly hoped for something more during their graduation tournament. War was brutal, bloody, violent chaos but this war game was too predictable to engage him at all.

Peace was elusive as a plan, even under the best circumstances.

"There really is no winning, is there?" She said as he shifted his head and set his lips against her cheek.

"No, there isn't," he confirmed, resting his head against hers. "We either exhaust ourselves by trying to win the challenges and risk not being able to fly the Ice Winds, or risk looking like a fool and save ourselves for the final flight. All the while, we have every chance to fail. Fail our team, fail our trials, fail ourselves... If either Fionn or I get caught by the other team? Failure."

"Well, you're not going to get caught," she scoffed. "You know the Streets. No one will find you there."

"Can I even go there?" Rylan asked, and she could hear the edge in his voice. "They crews know I'm going into the city for the war game, and even I know it's obvious that I'll go into hiding down there. If Dylan sends people hunting for me, they won't stop at kicking my teeth in this time."

"And that's different from two days ago, how?" Sera asked, standing once again. "The Streets are your strength, sweetness, and you should be able to use that."

Rylan just shrugged, shifting as she moved to step around his wings.

"Ignoring your brother," she said, moving him past the point. "What about Fionn? Is he any good at hiding?"

"I barely know the guy," Rylan said, shrugging. "Tyr says he's dangerously clever, but so am I. So is Micah, in his own way," he said, glancing past her. "It's what they make us into in this place. It's nothing special."

"Well, if I was Fionn," Sera said, meaning to be clever herself. "I would set up a trap for you since you like to break the rules. You could do the same to him if you know what would tempt him while he's off the Palace shelf."

"Tempt him with what?" Rylan asked, confused. "All any of us want right now is our pauldrons."

"All *you* want is your pauldron," Sera corrected. "The other tyros want their first shot at Honor and Glory, remember?"

Rylan's scoff was unforgiving. "There is no glory in this fight," he said, shaking his head. "You can't win. You can only not lose more than the other person is not losing. The whole blicing thing is a metaphor for the War and everyone knows you can't win that either."

"So what if you can't win the war?" Sera said again. "Fionn wants to win a battle. This one," she insisted, pointing at his map. "If you tempt him, he might actually go for it. That's all I'm saying."

"I hear you," Rylan said, shoving a fist in front of his face as he stifled a yawn.

"Soldier boy, I think you need a nap," Sera admonished. "When did you actually have to be up today?"

"Today is our rest day," he said, sighing. "We don't have to be anywhere until noon when they're feeding us in the Armory. It's our first Warhost feast, since on the Plains they'll feast everyone the night before a big fight. That way, everyone has enough energy for the day ahead."

"If that's the case," Sera said, shifting to step out of his embrace. "Then it's time for you to get back in that nest."

"Will you be there?" He asked, anything but innocent.

"In a few," she laughed, pulling him up onto his feet. "I want to get a look at your maps one more time. Maybe I can be clever where you cannot, hmm?"

"Now that," Rylan murmured, following her as she led him to the nest. "That is sexy. That head on your shoulders..."

"Sure thing, soldier boy," she laughed, sending him onto his knees in the nest. "But about that nap."

Micah grunted to feel the comforts shifting, but Rylan was down next to him soon enough, flexing his wings into the softness to hollow out a space for himself. Exhausted as he was, he curled up into Micah's searching embrace just as he would do if Sera had been in the nest. After a bit of fussing to get the comforts over them both, Sera was able to plant a kiss on each of their temples as they snuggled in together.

That done, she moved to the map and chewed her lip, ready to work. Rylan had all the streets and challenges marked out, but he wasn't seeing how they interacted with the city itself. Instead, it was all overlay and theory, and she knew he was leaving out a huge chunk of his own knowledge of the city.

He had grown up here. He had lived and fought here, right alongside her. What he hadn't grown up with, though, was Sera's mother. Even if it wasn't street fights and territory battles, her mother had held the brothel she ran like her own little Warhost. The territory they had fought over wasn't property but patronage, and the souls they brought in turned over coin instead of glory, but still. Her mother had taught her everything she knew about a woman's war and she could help Rylan in this, she just knew it.

Now, even when he couldn't see the forest for the trees, if she could just show him the way this war game matched how they had fought on the streets she knew he would sink his teeth into it at last. Even better, as much as Dylan was an issue for Rylan, if they won this war game with time to spare, then he really could take the whole tyro century to House Northern to get her book, Dylan and his stupid crew be damned.

Shuffling through the stack of parchment, Sera found the bit of graphite he had been using and began to create a new overlay for his map. She knew the current territories and where they were in relation to the challenges he had sketched out. If she could make the space mean something, it would change his entire approach to the war game. Head down and mind focused, Sera knew she would only have so much time to finish before Rylan woke up and distracted her.

Two candle marks later, her eyes were as crossed as Rylan's had been, but she had made her adjustments. Now Rylan's map held the crew territories as they currently were and the real enemy he would fight, all those collections of discarded sons and daughters roughed out like the squads of an opposing tyro century. She was a little worried that Rylan and Micah would be upset to realize she had been keeping track of them so closely, but it had been much easier to avoid everyone if she just knew where they were. Now Rylan could use it to protect himself, since he was going into the city one way or another.

Unfortunately, all that work had left her hand covered in black ink and silver lead, so before too many of the boys found their way out of their nests, Sera slipped out into the silent hallway. Since the last time she had looked outside, someone had come through with more oil to brighten the pitch, but the clouds outside the Palace kept the place dark and foreboding.

Sera closed the door behind her and almost jumped when she saw a familiar figure moving through the hallway.

"Kaitlyn!" Sera called, trying to sound more delighted than startled.

"Good dawning, Sera," the noble woman greeted, raising her hand as she came fully into the light.

"Oh, Kaitlyn" Sera replied, trying not to gawk at the silver and purple Court garments she was wearing. "Can you stand guard on the door to the washroom for me? I need to clean my hands."

"Of course," Kaitlyn said, looking down the hallway to where the washroom door was at the very end. "Did you manage the night well enough?"

"When they were both snuggled up with me, yes," Sera laughed, following Kaitlyn's lead. "I cannot believe how absolutely freezing it is in this place."

"Unfortunately, yes," Kaitlyn agreed. "You'd think they'd keep it warmer, but they want the boys to get acclimated to the Ice Winds for the tournament. The Sires' Wing is much better."

"Anything is better than this," Sera said. "I mean, they kept me warm, but I've never had the same tolerance for the cold. Not since, well…"

Kaitlyn was kind enough to let the thought remain incomplete.

"Lucky for you, I was hard at work last night searching my things," she said, smiling. "If you come back with me to the Sires' Wing while the boys do their work, I will gift you all the warmest things I own."

"I will happily give anything warm a new home," Sera said, grateful as they approached the end of the hallway.

"Just be quick," she said. "The water that comes in from the aquifer brings in the cold as well."

Determined, Sera slipped into the room and washed up as quick as possible. Not only did the room have absolutely no heat, but the water felt like ice.

"You weren't kidding!" Sera swore, returning to the hall with a shiver. "You're sure the Sires' Wing is warmer?"

"I promise," Kaitlyn said as they hurried back to the boys' room.

Sera closed the door behind them, leaving Kaitlyn to gasp in surprise as she found Micah and Rylan cuddling together on the floor nest in the middle of the room. Even if they fought when they were awake, especially over anything having to do with her, they would die for one another just as easily. Rebalancing Micah's gift had done an incredible amount at reconciling them to one another, and it was beyond comforting to see them so close once again. Given Kaitlyn's amazed reaction, she had never seen them like this at all.

"Are they all right?" She whispered, looking to Sera with wide eyes. "What happened?"

"This is how we slept for cycles," she said, grinning as she stepped into the nest so she could settle in between them. "It's the warmest spot in the whole kingdom."

Feeling the movement, Rylan woke and butted heads with her as she got situated. Micah, on the other hand, rolled onto his wings as he grumbled at having to tuck Sera's out of his way. As Sera got settled, Micah looked up and realized that Kaitlyn was standing over them.

"Sal'weh, gorgeous," he greeted, extending his hand up to her. In all the cycles she had known him, Kaitlyn had probably never seen him this happy.

"Good dawning, sleepy," Kaitlyn returned, taking his hand to assist him in standing. "You're looking worlds better."

As he gripped it, though, he tugged Kaitlyn down to join them instead. Kaitlyn tried to catch herself, but Micah pulled her on top of him with a grin.

Sera wriggled again, making space for Kaitlyn to fit down against her, using a blanket to keep their wings from getting tangled. Micah was the gentleman and covered them both, wings and all, with his own blanket.

"You realize that I'm dressed for Court," Kaitlyn laughed, trapped in his embrace.

"You're always dressed for Court," Micah replied, kissing her quiet.

Sera grinned as Rylan nuzzled closer. "Besides," he added with a yawn. "We have very important crew business to attend to before anything else this dawning."

Sera felt Kaitlyn shift and looked over her shoulder. "More important than Court?"

"Family is always more important than Court," Sera added, and winked.

"If the two of us are going to be part of your family," Micah said, drawing her attention. "You should be a part of ours. Rylan, you start."

Sera rolled onto her wings as Rylan took Kaitlyn's hand. He was quiet as he spoke, but his sincerity was obvious. Blood oaths always were.

"I owe you my life, Kaitlyn," he began. "I don't know how I could have done this without you watching out for us. I was a horrible friend at times and a terrible brother to Micah and Westly, but I've come out the other side because you never gave up on us. It means more to me than I can say. Kaitlyn, sister, if you ever need anything, I am at your call."

"Of course," Kaitlyn answered, touched if still a little confused.

"Your go," Rylan said, turning to Sera.

With great effort, Sera shifted in the soft floor nest. She matched eyes with the woman who had come to so love her brother and smiled. "I owe you my life, Kaitlyn," she began, much the same as Rylan. "I don't know how I could have managed living so far from Micah without you beside him. I couldn't reach him, but I dreamed I could hear him calling to me. He was desperate and alone, suffering until he came to know you. You've been such a gift to him and I can never thank you enough. Kaitlyn, sister, if you ever need anything, anything at all, I am at your call."

"I—I will," Kaitlyn answered, becoming overwhelmed.

When she looked back to Micah, though, there were tears in her eyes. Micah's hand around her waist pulsed in a gentle hug as he moved the hand in her hair to her cheek. "I owe you my life, Kaitlyn," he said simply. "I would not have survived without you. So far from my kin, so divided from my brothers, I have not been myself. I want to make it up to you. Anything you ask of me, I will do."

Kaitlyn kissed him, her cheeks wet with tears, and Sera shifted back to look at Rylan as the warmth of their exchange melted her heart. As she smiled, Rylan nuzzled close to her again.

"And now if you two are quite finished," Rylan said after long enough. "Will you please take this girl into the Sires' Wing where it's warm? I have more to do to get ready and her chattering teeth are going to keep us both distracted."

"If you insist," Kaitlyn laughed, wiping her eyes despite her beaming smile.

"Yes!" Sera agreed. "I'm tired of freezing like a soldier. I want to be warm like you."

"We know," Micah laughed, nudging Sera through the blanket. "You won't stop talking about it."

"All agreed?" Rylan asked, looking at Kaitlyn.

"You'll have to come with me to the Sires' Wing," she answered. "If you twins are going to be part of my House, my *warm* House, then I need to get you presentable for Court. Do you think you can get out of this nest for some winter garb?"

"I do enjoy a bribe made of fleece," Sera cheered and the four of them began the slow process of extracting themselves from the pile. Sera was first and Rylan followed her. When there was room, Kaitlyn finally slid off of Micah and they both got to their feet.

"Fleece and wool and silk, " Kaitlyn grinned as the three of them found warmer clothes.

Once Sera gave Micah his jacket back, trading it for the tyro's uniform over-cloak that Rylan offered, Micah turned back to her only to hesitate as he truly saw Kaitlyn for the first time.

"Kait, where is your black and gold?" He asked. "Did something happen in Windover?"

Sera looked at them both, surprised by the sheepish yet proud smile Kaitlyn wore. "I've been invited to join the Consort's Court. Matron Yulia said it was an incredible opportunity and I just couldn't—"

"Like a handmaiden?" Sera interrupted excitedly. "To the Consort?"

"More than a handmaiden," Kaitlyn confessed. "It's part of the Announcement today. She's making a High Court of Consorts and I've... Well," she said, flushing. "I've been asked to become the new Barracks Mother. I hope that's all right," she finished, suddenly worried as Micah moved towards her.

"Why wouldn't it be?" He said, a grin spreading over his face as he embraced her. "You've been helping Mother for cycles. Kait, this is incredible! When do you start?"

Finally seeing Micah happy, Sera knew it was okay to let herself squeal with excitement. She wasn't sure what was going on, but Kaitlyn looked ecstatic to see his approval and radiated pleasure as Micah kissed her with his congratulations.

"What's happening to Vinicia?" Rylan asked, watching as they parted. "Did they find out she's kin or something?"

"Yes and no," Kaitlyn replied, and Sera knew her tone for a woman hiding secrets. "It will all be announced shortly. I mean, I'm not even supposed to tell you three as much as I have, but, well..."

"It is rather obvious you've gone and done something outside of Windover," Micah said, stepping back to wave off Rylan's budding anger. "No need to jump to conclusions, Ry. If something bad had happened to Mother, Westly would have known last night."

"Yeah, I guess," Rylan muttered, crossing his arms over his chest. "I don't like it, though. Her being replaced. Not that you aren't suited to do what she's been doing, Kait, but—"

"She is moving on to bigger things," Kaitlyn said and smiled. "This is a promotion, even if it was a surprise to everyone who has been asked to be part of the new Court. It will all make sense soon enough, I promise. Until then," she said, pushing on. "Where is Westly, by the way? I wanted to see if he would come as well..."

Micah had an answer for that one, looking mischievous as he gestured to an oak wall-panel leaning in the corner of the room. "See that board over there?" he said. The board was one hand wide and newly slit from another piece from the looks of it. "I brought it back last night. It's from Westly's room in the Garden. He's figured out a new trick. Ry, see if you can call on him again. He always answers when you knock."

As Micah adjusted his own indigo over-cloak, Rylan uncrossed his arms and moved to the panel, knocking on the wood like he would a proper door.

When nothing happened, Micah frowned. "Try it again."

Rylan knocked a second time and they heard laughter in the distance. Not in the hallway, per se, but closer... And then the image of Westly's head and shoulders appeared like a ghost from the panel. Sera grinned to see Kaitlyn hide her gasp behind a hand as Westly spoke, much like she had done when Westly had first showed them the trick of it late last night.

"Yes? Can I help you?" Westly asked, flushing as he shoved aside whatever it was he had been dealing with to speak with them.

"Are we interrupting, brother?" Micah asked, hopeful.

"I wish!" Came a loud, exasperated reply and Sera smirked to realize it was Nichi's voice she heard. According to Micah, nothing had happened between their crew brother and Micah's best mate, but after their talk about the Soft Arts last night, Westly was better prepared for what to do when he did feel ready.

It's about time he found someone to help tend his garden, she thought as Westly rolled his eyes for the group of them to see.

"G'dawning, Kaitlyn," he said, inclining his head to her. "I thought you might like to see this. I think I've figured out the trick of it."

"Are you woodwalking?" she asked, fascinated as she moved closer to see the shimmer of magic over the board.

"Something like that," he said, grinning. "After everything that happened yesterday, Mother told me to find creative ways to burn off excess power, so I have been trying to woodwalk like she does through deadwood."

"You aren't wrong," Kaitlyn said. "Though I am afraid I do not have too much time to be curious this dawning. Court is in less than a mark and I need to get going. Will you be coming to the suite after the armory feast to see to Sire Gaius?"

"Yes, of course," Westly promised, glancing back into the garden. A moment more and the sounds vanished, Westly and Nichi with them.

"So..." Sera asked, directing the question at Kaitlyn. "Any idea how he can do that?"

As long as their crew had been together, Westly had never done anything quite that spectacular. From what Micah said, Kaitlyn might actually know what was going on.

"I think it's a form of woodwalking," Kaitlyn answered, still a bit beside herself to see it. "Dryads are tree spirits, so they can merge with trees, or in this case, with wood. Usually a dryad will move into one tree and out the other in some part of their grove, but those are thought to be connected by roots. I suppose they could send a part of themselves or their presence without moving entirely."

"Oh, he came all the way through last night," Sera said. "He couldn't bring Nichi, though we could hear him. The companion plank is in the Garden."

"If it's the same tree that he's moving between, that would work," Kaitlyn said, honestly puzzled. "And the Garden is the safest place to try it since no one wants to bother him. Most of the courtiers are scared of him."

"But it's Westly!" Sera protested. "He wouldn't hurt anyone."

"He might not," Kaitlyn agreed. "But if anyone knew Westly could listen through the walls, they might prefer to see him dead than risk their plotting. He really should ask Mother before doing too much more like that."

"Of course," Micah said, looking to the plank with a laugh. "It is a pretty wild trick, though, yeh?"

"As long as it doesn't become a revel trick, then yes," Kaitlyn warned and then seemed to realize something as she looked over the three of them. "Is there anything else I should know? I mean, if something ever goes wrong, I should be able to explain a few things away."

From the shadowed looks on their faces, the answer was yes.

"Well," Micah said. "I've always been able to hear Sera like a Preem, which made the warbard training easy enough. Hearing people beyond the host is a new addition, though," he said, looking to Sera. "As for the two of us..."

"His Gift is supposed to work with my Gift," Sera added. "Normally, mine is a curse since it causes people to have a much greater reaction to me. I get their attention with a dance, Micah reads them as he plays, I draw out their interest, and he nudges them in a direction we want. When there are too many people around, I can also shield him by overwhelming his senses with myself. We've always been able to talk thought-to-thought, though."

"Which is how they've kept in contact the past few cycles," Rylan said. "But he lost track of her a few moonturns ago. That's why I left the shelf the other night. I had to make sure something hadn't happened to her."

"It doesn't work over very long distances," Micah agreed, catching up Sera's hand as if even that gap was too much. "When I fled your rooms, it was because I was hearing voices all over the Palace. Hundreds of them, all at once. I could barely hear myself think until Mother brought Sera back."

"So not to be pedantic," Kaitlyn said, wincing. "But not everything that has to do with magic is a Gift. Some things are actually Talents. 'Gifts'," she said, hesitating to explain. "The way my books talk about them, they are things that come from the Ancestors. Godseyes, visions, the warbards ability to call orders over the winds... That is a Gift from Founder Noventrio, passed onto the men who work for the Seventh Counsel Lord."

"But that's not what I do," Micah said, confused. "I mean, I can, but I've always been able to do it. I was born with it."

"You were born with a 'Talent' for Whispering," Kaitlyn explained. "Talents are things you're born with or things you develop if you happen to have an affinity for an element. Like kindred dryads have an affinity for the magic of the Wood. It's not their mother's fae magic, which is an ability to generate Grove or Grave magic to create Wellspring, but... Oh, I've lost you haven't I? Gods, I'm so embarrassed..."

Sera didn't know what to say as Kaitlyn flushed, hand to her mouth to stop herself. Micah, though, just smiled.

"You are talking over our heads, but I'll hear it," he said, smiling at her. "So I've got a Talent for something, not a Gift. That's it? Why does it matter?"

Kaitlyn gave a hesitant smile in return. "Well, Talents are usually what most Kosarans call sorcery. Since it doesn't come from the Gods or Ancestors, that means it's dangerous. Too much power pooled in one person is unsafe, be it magical, political, or otherwise. It's why we were founded with a House of Lords and why the king, strong as he is in ancestral power, is really just a priest. An important one, granted, but Kosar is guided by the King's Counsel Lords and ruled by the House of Lords..."

"Makes sense," Micah said, looking to Rylan and Sera. "So Westly is a kindred sorcerer, the two of us have bardic magic, and Rylan... What did you say your family had a Talent for?"

"I didn't," Rylan said, suddenly uncomfortable.

"He has a Talent for firestarting," Sera said, not willing to let him lie to Kaitlyn when the two of them had been so honest. "Usually it's only when he's frustrated or angry, though."

As Rylan shot her a devastated look, Sera gave him a flat 'I told you I would tell her' in return. A heartbeat later, he looked away again. He hated having any kind of sorcerous ability, but hating it had never made it go away. If anyone was going to cause a problem Kait might have to deal with, it would likely be him.

"Are you sure?" Kaitlyn said, and Sera didn't miss the touch of awe. "If you really think there is more to it than luck... Rylan, fire-starting is very rare."

"My family hates me because of it," Rylan muttered. "Not that it matters now. Other than the kindling for our crew, I never tried to use it. Around Sera I could barely use it at all."

Kaitlyn nodded and from the look of it, was thinking rapidly. "It is possible that Sera's Talent could dampen all kinds of abilities, not just Micah's," she reasoned. "The stronger the magic, the stronger Sera's ability to suppress it would be. Westly might know, but then again, Sera might be able to dampen Westly's Talents as well. We really should ask Mother. I can talk to her when I see her at Court?"

As the boys shrugged, Sera suddenly recalled the name of the book her mother had given her. "Vocivae!" She exclaimed, as they all turned to her. "Micah, I bet your Barracks Mother could open our book if we asked."

"A book?" Kaitlyn repeated, both excited and confused as Micah considered the suggestion. "What book?"

"The one that got left at House Northern," Sera reminded, crestfallen even as Rylan relaxed with the change of subject. "Our Mother said it had all sorts of answers inside of it about magic. The only problem is that it's locked and the key is broken," she said, pushing up her sleeve to reveal the leather wrist wrap and the shattered stone that was mounted on it.

But Kaitlyn wasn't looking at the key. Instead, she had lost herself in the sorrow of knowing there was a book on magic somewhere in the world that was lost.

"I told you," Rylan said. "I'm sure we can get it during the tournament."

"After we finish the war game, though," Micah interjected. "On the way to the Ice Winds run. We can send it back with the chirons."

"If you can even find it," Sera scoffed. "Mother got all of my other things except that book when she came to get me. I hid it well."

"I think we can figure all of this out later," Micah insisted. "But Kait, didn't you have to get to Court?"

Sera almost laughed as she felt the wave of jealousy radiating from her brother. ::Really? You're jealous of a book?::

::I'd be jealous of *you* if she felt about you the way she does for a book she's never even seen,:: Micah threw back. ::Okay, maybe not jealous, but I would be put out if you kept her from my nest for marks on end.:: "But first things first," he went on aloud. "You said you had something warm Sera could wear?"

As Sera let him refocus the conversation, the burst of thanks and chagrin from Micah made her smile even more.

"Yes!" Sera cheered. "Something warm. Let's get to it!"

CHAPTER 22: KAITLYN

Saturday, 07:00

Acacophony greeted them as they pushed through the double doors of the Windover suite. All at once, her House was packing to move back to the Alexandrian shelf, preparing to celebrate their graduating tyros, and curious to see what their new Patriarch's rule would bring. As much as Kaitlyn loved the challenge of such complex planning, for once she was glad to simply be present among them.

Instead of adjourning to the Delton Estate for the winter, she would move into the Royals' Wing to attend Consort Lenae as part of the newly formed High Court. From her brief meeting with the Consort, Kaitlyn's first duty was to assist Counsel Lord Aaron as needed for the Graduation Tournament. Once that was done, she was to return for a special assignment from the Consort herself. Apparently, Counsel Lord Aaron spent most of the winter in his native Yaltana and would not require her assistance over the tyro break.

For now, Kaitlyn would make sure her new family was ready for Court and then present to the Royals' Wing again to be gifted the official title of Barracks Mother. Until then, she could busy herself with enjoying Micah in his happiness at long last.

But first things first, she had promised Sera her old winter garb. As the flock of them filed into Kaitlyn's half-packed room, Micah turned up the wick on the oil-lamp and Rylan set to lighting the others. Sera stared at the three large trunks that had been moved into the center of Kaitlyn's room, honestly confused.

"I've never seen so much stuff for one person," Sera said, just as wide-eyed as Kaitlyn had been at the prospect of a new book.

"As the only daughter born to my House, my Sire spared no expense on my garb. Anything you want is yours."

Sera squealed, turning to Kaitlyn with obvious joy. Before she moved, though, she kissed Kaitlyn on both cheeks and then dove into the trunks with glee. Beside her, Micah laughed as he watched Sera disappear. Rylan was grinning as well, following Sera to gather her selections in his arms. When she was ready, Rylan followed her behind the divider to help her change.

"I haven't known her for more than a few marks and I already love her," Kaitlyn whispered, resettling her wings as she put her hands to where Sera had kissed her cheeks. "She will be a blessing in this family."

"Oh, she's a curse as well," Micah laughed, picking up the bag of Sera's belongings from where it had been set aside in the room.

"What do you mean?"

As he reached into the bag, Kaitlyn recognized the soft shuffle of a coin-belt, though when he brought out a corner of the blue silken garment, it was her turn to gawk.

But you're from the streets! She thought, trying her best to keep it to herself.

Micah heard her anyway and winked. "You forget, it was my mother who taught us to turn our gifts into gold. These are just some of her possessions, though. The rest we had to trade for room and board after some girls from our mother's brothel started complaining how Lan'lieanan Sera looked," he said, digging into the depths of the bag. "My mother they didn't care about, but Sera?" Micah rolled his eyes. "Gods, where is this thing? Somewhere in here there is a pouch with a great deal of jewelry. There are even some shells from the ocean I wanted to show you..."

"Your mother really was from the southern War Plains, then?" Kaitlyn said, surprised. "Is that why you know how to play the instrument that goes with the dances? She taught you?"

"She never told us just how far south, but yeah," Micah said, looking up. "The oude is a southern Ehkeski instrument. I thought I had told you that."

"Not in so many words," Kaitlyn replied, realizing she probably should have figured that out by now. "I just saw how happy the music made you."

"That is what counts, I suppose," Micah said, finally giving up his search. "Speaking of which, do you think the two of us could entertain tonight?"

"Once you accept your rings at Court, you may do whatever you like," she answered and then remembered what Sera had said when they had first met. "By the way, do you know what an uumi is?" she asked, all innocence.

Micah's face for cards was impressive. "A what?" he said, only to turn and glare at his sister as she stepped from behind the divider.

"Hot damn, do I look good," Sera laughed, striking a pose for the room.

With the back of one hand on her forehead and the other hand draped along the curve of her hip, Sera's shifting weight drew Kaitlyn's attention up the long lines of her curves. The set was one of Kaitlyn's favorites, a pair of fleece-lined, fitted breeches and peplumed bodice, but all of Sera's curves were that of muscle, not softness. The gold piping along the seams made it clear just how hard-bodied she was, and Kaitlyn wondered for a moment if she should have just gotten her a set of the men's breeches for all her strength. The leggings she wore now stretched like a second skin.

Kaitlyn flushed as she got caught up in Sera's bright, blue-eyed stare and cursed the olive skin the woman shared with her twin. They were both too gorgeous for their own good, even if Sera continued to insist on covering her heavy waves of black hair with another incredible creation of cap and golden veil.

"Okay, you showed them," Rylan said, taking up her hips from behind to pull her against him. "Now you can try on the other ones, right?"

"What, so you can pretend like we can't hear you because of that screen?" Micah asked, and Kaitlyn laughed to see how quickly Rylan took his hands off Sera. "Yeah, that's what I thought."

"You think I can't be quiet?" Sera smirked, leveling a challenge at Micah across the room as Rylan looked anywhere but his crew-brother.

"Today is our rest day," Micah threw back. "He needs to rest."

"Fine," she scoffed, rolling her eyes as she started towards them. Ignoring Micah further, Sera's smoldering look turned on Kaitlyn. "Thank you so much, sister," she said. "I love all of it."

Kaitlyn could only nod, lost in the shift of the woman's step. She was just so incredibly gorgeous...

"Sera," Micah warned, reaching out to put a hand on Kaitlyn's wing. "Watch yourself."

Kaitlyn sucked in a breath as Micah's hand on her wing freed her from the weight of Sera's bardic gift. Surprisingly, Sera's eyes went wide as she realized what had happened. A moment later she looked over at Rylan, confused.

"Why doesn't it work on you?" She insisted, as if Rylan had an answer for why Kaitlyn had so easily fallen under her spell.

"Because he's as dense as bedrock," Micah said, rolling his eyes. "Be glad for it," he added as Sera and Rylan circled up with them.

"You three are incredible," Kaitlyn said, massaging at her temples as a sharp twinge of pain shot through her eyes. All her life she had hoped to have a sign that the magic she believed in was real, and here were three friends with sorcerous abilities standing before her.

Iskander be praised, she thought as her eyes burned. It was more than she had ever asked for.

"If you are set," she said. "I really should be on my way to assist with preparations at Court. Can you finish getting dressed without me, Micah?"

"I'll get us all there on time," Micah assured her, stealing a kiss before giving her over to Sera for a hug.

"Tell me you love your hair," Sera said, kissing her cheeks before drawing back.

"I love it," Kaitlyn assured her, raising a hand to the twisted coronet of golden curls Micah had made of her hair while they had waited on Sera to change. There were ribbons as well, which was the one touch of Windover Black she needed to feel like herself again.

When Sera was finally convinced, Kaitlyn pulled back to see Rylan looking at her awkwardly and so she caught him up in an embrace as well.

"Congratulations," he said before pulling away. "I can't think of anyone else who could even come close to Mother in the barracks." Coming from him, it was a high compliment.

Just as she was about to reply, Kaitlyn heard the door to the room click open and saw Nichi coming in with Westly on his heels.

"Better late than never," Nichi greeted, doing a double take at the twins standing with their arms around each other. "Good gods!" He laughed. "You weren't kidding about being nearly identical."

"The spitting image," Micah grinned, kissing the top of Sera's head. As short as Micah was compared to Nichi or Westly, he was still taller than his own sister. "I will never let this woman out of my sight again. Ever."

"Wait, Nichi?" Sera greeted, bouncing with her happiness. "Oh shit. It's great to finally meet you!"

"Same to you," Nichi said, grinning as he held out his hand. Sera ignored it and grabbed him up in a hug, nearly lifting him off the ground.

"Woah!" Nichi laughed, his eyes going wide with surprise. "Blood and ice, man! She's as strong as you are!"

As Micah started to joke about strong blood in their family, Kaitlyn took the chance to squeeze by them so she could get to the door. She had been about to slip by Westly as well when she saw the serious look he was trying to hide from the others.

"I got a note from Lord Seventh asking about greenmen," Westly said quietly. "He said he wanted to talk to me, but I don't know anything about greenmen. I just know about kindred. Do you know anything?"

"Only what I've read," Kaitlyn said. "I can speak with him when I get to Court if you'd like and if he still needs to talk to you, I can let you know?"

Westly seemed satisfied with the arrangement, so Kaitlyn moved in to embrace him to complete the round of hugs she had given out, much to his surprise.

"No more being overly formal," she chided, kissing his cheek before she pulled away. "I'm part of your crew now."

Westly was confused for a moment before his eyes went wide as he looked to Micah and Rylan. "When did they—?"

"This dawning," she smiled. "Just before we saw you through the board you left in the room."

"I told them to wait," he grumbled, though he did not look displeased. "But someone was trying to distract me," he said, glancing back to Nichi.

"He can be quite persistent when he sets his mind to something," Kaitlyn said and smiled. "Or someone. He's gotten everything he has ever wanted his whole life."

"That explains a few things," Westly laughed.

"If he gets to be a pest, just let me know," Kaitlyn said. "I'll drag him to his matron if he can't be reasoned with."

"I think I can handle him," Westly said, looking to Nichi as he talked with the twins.

When all three of them realized she was making to leave, Kaitlyn waved. "I will meet you all in the armory after Court, yes? That is at midday?"

"Until sundown," Nichi confirmed. "Then we're supposed to be in our nests, but you know Windover is throwing us a revel. If you don't find us, we'll be back here tonight."

"Of course you will," Kaitlyn chuckled, taking in the sight of all five of them. Her family.

"Good luck!" Sera called, and she waved before turning into the hallway.

Kaitlyn was beaming. For as long as she had been a part of this House without a mother or siblings, it was glorious to know she had a flock to call her own within the Palace now. Before she could celebrate, though, she had her duty to attend to.

Down on the ground floor, Kaitlyn's new garb and identity were already known to the guards posted at the entrance to the Royals' Wing. She was welcomed to pass, and after a short walk down a long hallway, she found herself in a large receiving room that was bustling with activity.

Many of the women she didn't recognize, but the men she knew. Each one had a conspicuous number of wing-bars marking their Seat in King Braeden's Counsel of Nine. When fully open, the markings were varied and indistinguishable, excellent for camouflaging their true rank, but when closed the black lines were heavy and imposing. Given that all nine of them were assembled here, imposing was an understatement.

For those women in the room, Consort Lenae was doing something incredible. In much the same way that her humble upbringing tempered the ancestral lineage of the King, Lenae had gathered a flock of women who would accompany the Counsel Lords. While at first it seemed as if Lenae was diluting her title of Consort, Kaitlyn saw now that she was doing it with a purpose. She was balancing the Court with the education, perspective, and influence that many of the women wielded in their personal lives. It was a bold risk, but her timing was brilliant.

As Kaitlyn glanced around the room, she recognized a few of Lenae's choices from the Court. Dame Phaedra of House Tailsa in Illiandria was a gorgeous singer before being chosen to act as Consort to Fourth Counsel Lord Blake, the Weapons Master.

Her powerful operatic voice had been a weapon at Court and a boon to the Counsel Lord's warbards, more than a few of whom she was already tutoring. With this new title and authority, there was talk she would serve as a voice coach for the warbards officially, acting as Counsel Lord Blake's right hand.

The next woman Kaitlyn recognized was Dame Cassidy from the Kelishe Peak, but she did not know the woman's Guild. What she did know is that she was masterful at figures and she had been chosen to accompany First Counsel Lord Terrance, the Coin Master. Her knowledge had brought more than one House back from the brink of collapse and mainly through the workings of women's crafting between the Houses. With direct access to Lenae, Cassidy would be able to move Court stylings to the other peaks, and coin along with the crafts.

The other woman Kaitlyn recognized was Dame Elissa, who was also from a guild, but from the Greying Peak. The only thing Kaitlyn knew of Greying was that Second Counsel Lord Gallen, the Chiurgeon Headmaster, and Fifth Counsel Lord Roder were both from the mountain. From her own personal interests, Kaitlyn knew that both Elissa and Gallen held dryad-kin in extremely low esteem.

As for the Fifth Counsel Lord's opinion, from what her brothers had said the few times they had come home from War, Counsel Lord Roder was the most suspicious man they had ever met, but suspicious was different than superstitious. Her own Alexandrian peak held the more superstitious citizens of Kosar, though why that was the case she wasn't sure. In her deepest heart, she knew that the stories of fae she loved so dearly were just as magical as the gifts from the Ancestors, no matter how the family priests had admonished her.

Sighing, Kaitlyn kept scanning the room to see what other women had been gathered. From their somewhat nervous bearing, it looked like Kaitlyn was not alone in being raised from relative obscurity. She was the daughter of a noble House, sure, but she did not have the doe-eyed stare of the slender young woman that looked absolutely lost. Just as Kaitlyn moved to say sal'weh, though, a voice she recognized called out to her.

"Good dawning, Kaitlyn," Vinicia greeted and Kaitlyn couldn't decide which she was more surprised to see: the Barracks Mother dressed in the colors of Court or how what she wore looked like a copy of true Warhost flying leathers. It even had the split front!

"Good dawning, Mother," Kaitlyn said automatically, only to flush at the reproach in Vinicia's look. "Consort," she amended.

"You are the Barracks Mother as of this dawning," she said, smiling once again. "My father has said I am not allowed to work for Aaron any longer, given my duties egg-sitting his Counselheir," she said, looking over her shoulder. "So, my apologies if you find my office in a mess."

His Counselheir? Kaitlyn wondered, only to realize she meant Kiernan, who was trailing behind her. *Gods be good, her father is Seventh Counsel Lord Eirik! That would be the only way a woman would be put in charge of tyros. No one else could tell him no.*

"I hear Vinicia has trained you well, Kaitlyn," Counsel Lord Kiernan greeted, and Vinicia stepped to the side to make room for him.

"I will have enormous shoes to fill, Ser," Kaitlyn demurred.

"I would stay and train you more, but this one needs someone on his arm for his sister's ringing," Vinicia said, and Kaitlyn did not fail to see Kiernan's hand lingering on her wing as they pulled in to let people pass behind them. They were stunning together, a matched pair like the others, but there was also something more. It was almost as if there was a resonance between them, something that reminded her of Westly and Nichi...

"Ring Ceremonies are dangerous things," he said, completely serious. "My sisters are going to throttle me for staying away too long as it is, but if you mean to stand with me, then I should survive."

She is his bodyguard, Kaitlyn realized all at once. If the Seventh Counsel Lord was a sorcerer as her books claimed, then having a dryad-kin at his side was a perfect companion, not only in Kosar, but through the Eihwaz as well.

Kaitlyn's head was spinning as she looked between the two of them, over-awed as she realized just what would have had to happen to bring her and Kiernan together in time for his Envoy.

I need to write this down, she realized. *There is a true Kosaran tale of fae standing right in front of me and if I am not the one to write it down, no one will ever know!*

"They'd be in the right," Vinicia said and then looked to Kaitlyn.

"You're going with him, aren't you?" She asked, trying to speak softly. "Into the Eihwaz."

"He will take me to his home and I will take him to mine," Vinicia replied, gesturing for them to move to the open lounges in the receiving area.

"But have you ever traveled between the shelves?" Kaitlyn asked, even as she gawked. "After you came up, of course..."

When Vinicia didn't immediately answer, Kaitlyn realized she had touched on something very important.

"Westly has moved between the shelves," Vinicia said as they settled onto the lounges. "But it wouldn't hurt to speak with him before we head out. I don't expect there to be a problem, though," she said, glancing at Kiernan as he stepped between her wings to take up less space as he remained standing. "My father made some... Arrangements."

"You wouldn't happen to know of windwalkers being turned into greenmen, would you?" Kiernan said, a strange sort of laughter in his words as Kaitlyn watched Vinicia close her eyes. Exhausted as the woman had been ever since the great wealth of her tyros had left the Barracks, she looked as if she had gotten the first good night's sleep in ages. With Kiernan behind her, she also looked more physically at ease than Kaitlyn had ever seen her, even if she was anxious for other reasons.

"I can't say that I have read any story like that in particular," Kaitlyn answered, considering them both. "But in general, greenmen offer their strength to dryads whose natural environment cannot support them, for whatever reason," she said, her heart racing as she realized they were both hanging on her words. "They collect it from the woods and bring it to the dryad, like... Like one person collecting a meal for another when they cannot step away from a meeting."

And the more intimate the exchange, the more power that is transferred, Kaitlyn knew, not that she wanted to speak about that in such a public place. Worse, windwalkers and kindred were different. A windwalker's own personal strength was not a thing that could be refreshed as far as she knew and kindred, once they had a taste for that kind of power, had the potential to devour a person's soul. That was why so many kindred were killed long before they ever came into their power.

"Before we leave for Illiandria, though," Vinicia said, changing subjects as she saw the worry in Kaitlyn's features. "Is there anything I can help you with? I tried to write down as much as I could of the tyro's schedule last night, but it is largely run by the Cantullus Corps. What I did was always in concert with them, and Lord Fourth has assured me his armorers will work with you in the same way."

"That is good to know," Kaitlyn admitted. "Though, if you could show me around your office, I would appreciate it. I believe Lord Third means for me to take up your record keeping duties as well."

He would expect that," Vinicia said, looking past Kaitlyn's wings with a knowing eye. "Wouldn't you, Aaron?"

As the older, short-statured man took a seat next to Kaitlyn on the lounges, Kaitlyn tried to sit up a little straighter. He must have been in his early fifties and he wore every cycle of it upon his face this close to graduation.

"You're not upset with me, are you, girl?" Aaron asked of Vinicia.

"For what?" Vinicia replied. "I think Lenae has made a fine match for you in Kaitlyn."

"Oh good," Aaron said, and bent his head towards Kaitlyn in greeting. "I've never had a Court Dame so interested in my tyros as anything other than sport, so you can imagine my surprise. I can certainly use your youth, however."

"I am more than happy to assist in any way I can," Kaitlyn assured him. "I've been accused of having energy for a fortnight, despite managing our tyro court."

Aaron was happy to hear that. "Consort Lenae also said that she has a project for your spare time?"

While Kaitlyn wasn't sure why Consort Lenae had been so interested in her studies of fae and magic, it was what her Matron had said would be her most valued asset. If the Consort agreed, then so be it.

"Yes, Counsel Lord—" Kaitlyn replied.

"Please, just Aaron," he interrupted. "Formalities are fine for the Court, but we have far too many tyros to wrangle through this Graduation to use them behind closed doors. Is that acceptable?"

"Only if you call me Kait," she said, smiling. "Consort Lenae's task is something of a research project, so it shouldn't take too much time. I like to have my nose in a book every night as it is."

"Perfect," Aaron agreed. "I'm sure that we could open the tyros' library to you for Lenae's purposes and perhaps the law-speakers' as well, though you'll likely need to go in with a guide. It really is nothing more than a pile of scrolls."

Before Kaitlyn could exclaim her thanks, the double doors near the back of the room opened and everyone came to attention. Standing in the doorway to the Consort's chamber was a woman dressed very differently than the day before. Rather than her leather and lace, Lenae was dressed in soft silks and flowing cloth-of-silver fabric that cinched in just under her breasts.

Kaitlyn's jaw fell open as she realized the only thing the change could mean: the Consort was carrying the King's heir. *That was her announcement for Winter Court?!*

Beside her, Vinicia excused herself as the Royal Court gave their congratulations, moving to stand with Kiernan. With Hest'lre at his side and Vinicia's wings flared to cut off his sight of Lenae, Kaitlyn recognized the look of strangled anguish. What little she knew of the Consort's relationship with Counsel Lord Kiernan was that they had once been betrothed, but there was nothing he could do to stop that. Nothing, that was, except end the war.

Then, and only then, could the marriage between the Ancestral descendants of the two Kingdoms release the Consort from her duty to Kosar. It was for this very reason that noble Houses forbid relations between fledglings until after they had seen eighteen cycles. It was also why the guilds withheld betrothals until after their sons had returned from War. But if the rumors were true, Kiernan and Lenae had been wrapped up in each other since the day they became guild apprentices. When Lenae was chosen, they remained close throughout her training, and then through Kiernan's time at war.

Counsel Lord Eirik was said to have bent to the will of Lenae's broken heart and named Kiernan her Counsel Lord out of pity when Hewn had been killed. But now, watching as Vinicia broke through Kiernan's shock, Kaitlyn realized what Lenae was attempting. In Vinicia she had found a woman who was as much a tyro as herself. Given Vinicia's family, she was also a woman who was not struck by Kiernan's station. Vinicia would likely strong-arm the man into leaving for Envoy when he would want nothing more than to stay and protect the chick that he felt should have been of his own body. Vinicia could make him leave and given what Kaitlyn had seen of the dryad-kin's power, she may actually be able to escort him home from Lan'lieana, too.

It was desperate, but it was also right out of the pages of one of her romances, and the whole of it made her swoon.

"Thank you, everyone," Consort Lenae greeted, clasping her hands as the congratulations came to an end. "Hopefully this will show why I have gathered my own High Court. As you are all no doubt aware, I have asked each of the women who stand among you now to act as my emissary for your needs. They, like myself, are consorts to your cause and their appointment will help me assist King Braeden with my own duties."

"But I already have a wife," Counsel Lord Terrance noted, which was met with laughter and a patient smile from Lenae.

"A Consort is not a wife," Lenae reminded, which was more than poignant given her own status. "We are subordinate to and have companion duties for your office. For the King, the Consort bears his heir. For you, the women I have chosen will provide the finesse and attention only a woman can grant. But for now—"

"And if I refuse?" a voice asked, cutting off the Consort's speech. As the anger and annoyance in the Fifth Counsel Lord's voice cut through the room, Katelyn saw the terrified young woman she had seen before standing meekly in the man's shadow. "A soft woman is the exact opposite of what I need in the service of my Seat."

"The woman is for Lenae's benefit," Kiernan said, speaking for the first time since the announcement. "Not for your use."

"Then give me a woman who has flown the Plains," Roder threw back, and the crowd in the room parted as the two men stared each other down. "I will have your kyree trophy for this abomination, or none at all. Even a warborn in chains will be of more use to me than any Kosaran woman."

"The Loralae is dead," Kiernan said flatly. "I saw her corpse myself last night."

In the heavy silence that followed, Kaitlyn watched as Roder's look shifted to take in Vinicia standing beside him. Suspicious did not begin to describe the hatred he showed at the sight of the woman. Rather than saying more, Roder merely closed his eyes and inhaled, visibly controlling himself. No matter his own ire, Kiernan still outranked him and so he held his tongue as his smoldering look went back to the High Consort.

"Let us be quick," Lenae said, as if nothing at all had been spoken.

With that, the Counsel Lords moved to give their congratulations to the otherwise aloof King entering on the far side of the room with his entourage of priests. By contrast, Consort Lenae moved towards the door leading into the Sires' Wing. With a gesture, she called together the nine women who now made up her High Court.

"I will enter the Great Hall on the first level with my entourage," Lenae explained, looking around the circle with forced excitement. "Once the Counsel Lords have processed, you nine will flank them, standing on the left hand of their seats. Once His Grace enters, he will call for me from the throne. I will come in from the ground floor and rise to stand with him and Court will begin."

Kaitlyn and the other ladies nodded their understanding. Lenae was nothing if not unconventional, which was a refreshing change from the daughters she had grown up with in the House. Still, the tension in the room weighed on her heavily. She had known there would be issues with High Court of Consorts, and it would not have surprised Kaitlyn if the woman had put together the entire idea simply to shield Vinicia's true nature as a bodyguard to the man she loved.

For all their sakes, Kaitlyn hoped that fact was not as obvious to the rest of the kingdom as it was to her.

"Ready?" Lenae asked, and with her Court in agreement, they processed to their positions.

CHAPTER 23: MICAH

Saturday, 09:00

"Of course you're ready for this," Nichi said, grinning like a fool as they waited to process into the Great Hall with the other third tier families.

"Are you sure?" Micah asked again, still tugging at his new set of Windover Blacks. As uncomfortable as Micah was in the new clothes, he couldn't help but look forward to the look in Kaitlyn's eyes when she first saw him in it. The idea of her seeing him dressed like a proper House member only to have to wait candle marks before she could tear it off of him made him laugh out loud every time he remembered.

"You're going to ruin that if you keep tugging at it," Sera chided, doing her best to douse him with restraint through their bond. As she adjusted the doublet ties at his wings, she added ::And those breeches are far too tight for you to be so excited about seeing Kaitlyn again.::

Micah sent back an apology and his embarrassed thanks. The back piece fit much better with her adjustments, even if it still felt awkward. He couldn't remember a time when he had ever worn clothing this fitted, but he had to admit that the black silk shirt was excessively comfortable.

"He looks fine," Rylan assured her, having missed the real conversation, and then drew Sera back against him once again. They made quite an attractive pair as Rylan snaked his arms around her waist from behind, though the face she made when he set his chin on her head was still funny. Unlike the rest of them, Rylan was still in his tyro uniform, though he had at least let Sera clean it up before they had left the Windover suite.

Micah just thanked him, amused to find Westly standing awkwardly as Nichi fiddled with the same errant back piece that Sera had just fixed for him. With nothing formal enough for court to wear himself, Nichi had found him a set of Windover Blacks that fit well enough, saying it would work for the day. As far as Westly was concerned, it might as well have been Winter Solstice for how happy he was, just because he had Nichi's attention.

Westly exhaled a laugh when he saw Micah watching, but just shrugged as Nichi finished. Westly had the opposite problem with the outfit, it seemed. Where the tyros were muscular and strong, Westly was thin and willowy, not to mention significantly taller. To get it to fit properly, Nichi had needed to overlap the under-wing grommets in the back on both sides of the wing-panel to get it laced tight enough. Once Nichi had the leather finally in place, Westly cut a striking figure as his emerald street-crest seemed to glow compared to the black leather.

"Are you ready?" Micah asked, looking to Nichi as he finished with Westly's doublet.

"I'm more than ready," Nichi said. "It's about blicing time my brother took on his duties as Patriarch."

"Speaking of brothers," Micah said, watching as the House Windover's newly raised Patriarch approached them with a hand smoothing down the new addition of the blue satin across his doublet.

Micah raised a hand as Kreychi hailed them and the grin on his face nearly split the hall. "Nichi!" he called, closing the distance for a rough embrace. "Thank you for getting them ready for Court," he continued, looking to Micah as he roughed up the tyro-crest Nichi had so meticulously combed through with wax earlier. "Once this is done, though, I expect you to rest."

"Right after the Armory revel," Micah said, watching Nichi glower as he smoothed his hair back once again.

"And the House revel, yes," Kreychi said, moving on to clasp forearms with Micah. "I will be with the family at the Delton estate, but I expect to hear good stories after you graduate."

Releasing Micah's hand, Kreychi's attention turned to the guards as they began to open the immense doors to the Great Hall so that the Upper Court could progress. The Middle and Lower Courts had been allowed to enter earlier, giving them time to collect on their respective middle balcony and ground floor.

Given Sire Gaius's weakened condition, he had remained in the Windover suite, but Matron Yulia and her entourage of Daughters had taken the formal stairs to make their slow ascent to the highest level. The rest of the House, Micah and his reunited crew included, would process with Kreychi and Nichi.

As the doors swung open to the fanfare of trumpets, Micah watched the swarm of courtiers turn to see them. Unlike themselves, folks were a stark contrast to the black of the Alexandrian Houses and the cacophony of colors made Micah's eyes water.

Apparently, every Alexandrian House of the Upper Court wore the same black base, while the other shelves distinguished themselves with a differing color. The Illiandrian houses were in deep indigo, given their great mountain pool, the Yaltanan houses in white like their snowy peak, the Greying houses wore grey like the fog that covered the high shelf, and the Kelsineahan houses were in green, since they took up most of the land rolling down the mountain hills into the Plains. Kelishe was a burnt orange for their closeness to the deserts on the far west side of the range and the last, Kirath, had been red, but few wore those colors any longer. All the Delton houses, including the Palace, wore a midnight-purple.

The only difference for the Royals was that the gold and silver accent colors in Delton were reserved for them. The King and his entourage were gold and the accents for his Consort were silver. Shelves other than Delton could use the color, but the tradition had long held that the most influential House, like the Windovers, wore the gold accent while the most influential Guild wore the silver. Every other House would wear whatever color coordinated to the shelf their main House was from, which for Windover meant black.

As much as that seemed to make sense to Nichi, Micah still had a hard time understanding how the Middle Court, which was largely made up of guilds and a few lesser houses, used the city's crest color as their accent and shared the base colors or patterns by guild type. So while it made sense that the most influential guild should have silver, the way it truly worked was that the most influential collection of guilds would share the silver.

Counsel Lord Kiernan's family's Guild, having a son as a Counsel Lord, wore deep indigo clothing with silver woven into flowing rasha patterns as accents everywhere, almost as if they were a gaudy royal House of the Illiandrian shelf Micah put a hand to his head to stop himself from sorting out the intricacies of the noble houses, only to laugh as he realized Sera's eyes were as wide as the moon.

Instead of being overwhelmed, she was complementing a flock of Lower Court daughters on the fabric of their dresses as they passed with Nichi's House. Unlike the Middle or Upper Courts, these women tried to make light of their position on the ground floor by wearing voluminous hooped skirts. The flightless volume of fabric and layers, not to mention their heavy jeweled adornments and the masterfully crafted if eccentric clothing was its own statement. Micah wasn't sure what kind of statement Sera thought it was, but to him it was clear: stay away!

As the crowd parted to allow them to reach the flight circle at the center of the Lower Court with its elaborate ramp and launch point, Micah looked to Nichi and his brother for guidance. He made a note to himself that there were smaller flight circles along the perimeter of the octagonal Court with the same tall ramps, but it seemed as if those were used by people moving to the Middle Court on the first balcony. This larger landing circle and guided ramp seemed reserved for the Upper Court's transition.

"Get used to this, you three," Kreychi said, looking back one last time as he stepped into the flight circle. "The eyes of Kosar are upon you. And as for you, little brother, mark this the last time you catch my wind. You'll be at my side when next we ascend. Brothers in arms at last."

And then, much to Micah's surprise, Kreychi leapt up into the air without so much as a step to set him off. Apparently not knowing if you were a veteran or a courtier ran in the family...

As Kreychi caught wind, Nichi gave his brother room enough for rank, but his brother backwinged as they reached the highest balcony, touching down with him in unison.

"They are certainly fond of showing off," Rylan observed.

"Nothing we can't overcome," Sera reminded as she pulled them up beside her at the edge of the ramp. They too took flight in unison and aimed for the platform directly opposite the Royals.

As they landed, Nichi moved to be with his family and Micah took a moment to search for Kaitlyn. Only Sera's hand on his arm pulled him away, turning him back towards their own business since it was obvious Kaitlyn was not in the Great Hall yet.

Westly and Rylan were already waiting, as was most of the House as the procession continued. There were some members of the House still missing, but those would be folks directing their veteran kin where the various chests needed to be moved while everyone else was out of the way.

That, and Nichi's near-cousin Tyrsten who had specifically been told to stay put in the Soldier Tyro barracks for all he had crossed the Lord Seventh the day before.

By the time Micah joined his crew-brothers, Kreychi had taken a seat on a large, decorated lounge next to his Matron who seemed to have recovered from the exertion of the stairs. Micah stepped forward and bent a knee respectfully before rising and offering his hand to Matron Yulia. She took it, thanking him for his attendance while Micah touched his lips to the back of her hand. Sera stepped into his place when he was done, curtsying deeply before exchanging the kiss of greeting with the Matron, one kiss in the air near each cheek, and then stepping back.

When they were both standing before the House elders, Kreychi spoke loud enough for the entire House to hear.

"Tyro Micahleia," he began, addressing him directly as he was the best known to the House. "As is the tradition within Windover, the lead family may choose to adopt individuals who have proven themselves worthy of becoming a part of the brood. This practice allows for a renewal of the blood within the ruling family, as well as the ability to strengthen the trunk of the House with the talents of those from outside."

As Micah and Sera gave their best smiles, Kreychi reached for something he had in the pocket of his doublet just under the sapphire sash he wore as a House of Lords. Once it was in hand, he looked to them with a solemnity that surprised them both.

"For your dedication to my first-brother and with my near-sister's most eloquent insistence, I ask if you would be adopted into House Windover in Alexandria," he said. "If that is agreeable to you, we would be honored to embrace you as one of our own."

Kreychi then opened his hand to reveal two rings: one heavy golden signet ring bearing the rampant gryphon crest of House Windover and a delicate gold band with an onyx teardrop of the ebony stone from the House's foundation in Alexandria. Micah reached for Sera's hand as Kreychi spoke again.

"Micahleia su'Delton, will you be reborn as a Son of the House of Windover in Alexandria?"

"I will," Micah replied formally, finding his voice.

"Then come and take your fate," Kreychi said, offering the ring to him.

Micah released Sera's hand as he stepped forward to take the heavy ring. Once it was on his right hand, Kreychi clasped forearms with him, thanking him for the friendship and loyalty he had always shown to Nichi. He then passed Micah on to Matron Yulia, who embraced him with a love that startled him. In his mind, he saw the memory of his own mother when he had been young, holding him just as close, and it took his breath away.

Micah pieced himself back together in time to see Sera making the same pledge, though, once she had the ring on her hand, she was passed off to Matron Yulia in tears.

"Thank you," Micah could hear her say. "Thank you so much. I don't know what I would have done without you and your family."

"Bold as you are with cap and veil, you will do this family proud, Daughter," Matron Yulia said, holding Sera long enough for her to collect herself.

Giving them the moment, Kreychi turned his attention to address the crowd at large to give a rousing call.

"Twins are born unto the House of Windover!" He declared. "They are named Micahleia and Seraleia! They shall now and forever be known as true and honored members of the House of Windover in Alexandria!"

As if on cue, the nearby Windovers filled the Hall with their roaring approval. As they did, Nichi extended his forearm to Micah.

"Thank you," Micah said simply. "I owe you my life, brother. Anything you ask of me, I will do."

"We will do," Sera echoed and then embraced Nichi as only a first-sister could in such a public place.

"Oh, I bet you will—" Micah began, but "Oh we're just getting started," Nichi answered, pointing them both back to where Kreychi had stepped to stand with Westly in the obfuscated moment. "Look."

Micah had just enough time to find his crew-brother in the crowd before he saw a second, heavy golden signet ring glistening in Kreychi's hands. Matron Yulia was standing with him as well, and Kaitlyn's father, Sire Marius, was calling out to the House members for their attention.

"Chiurgeon Westly su'Kelsineah," Kreychi said, solemn in the moment. "What we ask of you is not an easy thing, but I want it know here and now that whatever happens, whatever you are able to do or not to help my father, you will have the strength of the House in Alexandria to back you. For all the faith I have in My Lord Seventh and all the good we have seen you work on the shelf, it would be our honor to accept you into the brood. Kindred that you are, would you consent to becoming kin to us as well? A true and honored Son of the House of Windover?"

Westly was speechless.

Seeing his hesitation, Nichi cut him off, guilty as Westly heard his name and turned to them.

"moved away from the huddle that he, Micah, and Sera had become. "If you would live with us, we," he said, and Micah realized his friend was speaking as the Heir to Windover now, rather than Westly's friend. "We could build you your own Garden," Nichi said, answering the question in Westly's look. "Though you'll never be rid of the Daughters if you grow flowers cycle round.". Whatever happens, we are forever in your debt."

 Isn't that the truth, Westly ducked his head, looking to the ring as he gathered himself. "You mean to protect me?" he said, almost too softly for Micah to hear. "No matter what happens."

"No matter what happens," Kreychi promised, and the look from the remaining members of the ruling House were rock-solid in their confidence. "My grandsire's wingmate was a chiurgeon like yourself and your unique ability can be honored for the glory it will bring to this house. Those who guard, guide."

When Westly took the ring from Kreychi's hand, the House of Windover exploded into cheers once again. Micah and Sera just gaped to see Westly shaking hands with the house members as Rylan beside them grinned.

"I thought they were going to do something like this," he said, as if that should have explained everything. "There was no other reason for Nichi to insist on Westly getting into those Blacks otherwise..."

"You could have told us," Micah said, shoving Rylan with a wing. "I thought you wanted us all to be in House Northern once you revived it."

"Never wait for what may be when you can seize an opportunity right in front of you," Rylan said, though it sounded as if he was quoting something. "Besides, I'll tie Windover to House Northern soon enough. If she'll have me..."

The last he said for only Micah to hear, though his eyes and his heart were clearly on his twin. Missing the moment, when Sera turned to share her joy, Rylan looked away as his cheeks burned red.

I think she might, Micah thought, looking around at the members of his new family. Even without his bardic talents, Micah knew that there was only one thing on their minds: tonight's revel would be without peer.

As Micah looked back to his crew, Westly and Nichi moved to rejoin them, the sound of the hushing courtiers nearly drowned out his thoughts.

"Are things about to get started?" Sera asked, noticing as well. "Should we move towards the railing? I want to see!"

"We should," Nichi said, and pointed to a clearing that had yet to be filled. "That should work."

"Do you know if they're starting the revel in the Armory right after this?," Micah asked.

"They'll probably start without us," Nichi laughed, and then turned to lead the group through a small opening of courtiers to the balcony railing. Once they began to move, the rest of the younger Court followed their lead, pressing in just comfortably enough so that everyone could have a proper view of the empty Hawk and Falcon thrones.

Micah was standing amid the splay of Sera's wings, arms encircling her as he flexed the muscles around his eyes into the flight-lenses that would sharpen the distant image for him. Nichi stepped beside them, his wing adjusting to lie over Westly's as he moved to stand closer together. As Micah turned to survey the lower Courts, the herald standing to the left of the thrones flared his wings and the warbards posted throughout the Great Hall picked up their trumpets.

When they were ready, the voice of the Royal Herald rang out, and his great "Hail" brought stillness to the Courtiers. When they were silent, he called out again. "Give hail good Courtiers! Hail to the Warlords of Kosar! Hail the Counsel of Nine!"

As the Court minstrels answered him with fanfare, nine men emerged from the darkness behind the thrones. Wings half flared, the dominance of the black wing-bars of their Counsel Seats was unmistakable as they formed an open semi-circle around the massive gold and silver thrones. The Counsel Lord Seats looked like ebony pedestals beside them, given the towering splay of seven carved and gilded wings making up the back of the thrones. Seven, because when King Braeden and Consort Lenae were seated, their two wings would show the true spiritual power of the nine-winged Founders they served.

Counsel Lord Kiernan was the first to come into view, standing just before his own Seat with the splay of five black wings to match his seven wingbars. Behind him was Sixth Counsel Lord Hest'lre, Third Counsel Lord Aaron, and Fourth Counsel Lord Blake, all taking their places amid their own displays, even if they were smaller by comparison to the first two. To the left of the King, the procession was led by Ninth Counsel Lord Shayan, who took his position between the two thrones, First Counsel Lord Terrance, Second Counsel Lord Gallen, Fifth Counsel Lord Roder, and Eighth Counsel Lord Lucien.

Once they were in position, the Counsel Lords brought their wings behind them, diminishing the great spread of their combined markings. After a breath of silence for the crowd to pay respects to the men's Seat Founders, the Royal Herald called out once again.

"For a moonturn, Consort Lenae has given word of a great Announcement!" He began, and the crowd stirred with excitement. "This news comes in two parts, the first of which is the creation of a High Court of Consorts. With the blessing of King Braeden and Justicar Counsel Lord Lucien, I ask that you give hail to the great Ladies of Kosar! Hail to High Consort Lenae's Royal Court!"

As the crowd stared in anticipation and focus, nine women emerged from behind the thrones. Like the High Consort's own fashion, they were garbed in the dark purple leather they had seen on Kaitlyn earlier and Micah had to admit, his Barracks Mother looked impressive in the courtier's style.

"I'm not surprised she's paired with Lord Seventh," Rylan observed. "She's probably the only one on the shelf who can keep him in line."

Sera let out a soft laugh, looking to Micah as Rylan gripped onto Sera's hand with the words. Counsel Lord Kiernan wasn't the only man in Delton in need of such a woman.

As the clamor of the Court finally died down to see the new Consorts moving to take their places, Micah wondered how many Matrons would try to politic their own Daughters into these new positions. If there was about to be a new Sixth and Seventh Counsel Lord, there would be two new women to be raised with them as well...

When the Royal Herald began naming the women who had appeared, silence reigned once again, except for the small bursts of cheer for each of the women from varying parts of the crowd. Micah was pleased as the tyros present reacted with equal fervor to Kaitlyn and Vinicia, though there was a good deal of surprise when it was revealed that Vinicia was a Dame of the Kirathy shelf. For as much grumbling as Micah had heard about the Kirathy nobles not having a place at Court after the Fall of Kirath, the fact that one of their own had taken a position in support of Lord Seventh was a shock.

When the fanfare for the Royal Herald called for quiet once again, the Court obliged. While Micah had no idea what would follow, so many other minds were attempting to guess that Micah found even their silence disorienting. Realizing his unease, Sera laid her free hand on top of his and her gift quieted his mind.

"Give hail, Patrons!" The Royal Herald called. "Give hail, Guildsmen and Sires! Hail the true son of the Founders, Avatar of the Ancestors, and Patriarch of all Kosar, King Braeden!"

"Long live the King!" The Court echoed, as the white and gold clad king entered with his entourage of priests who stepped to the left of the circle of Counsel Lords. Young as he was, even at this distance there was no mistaking the slim build, aquiline nose, and snow-white hair that made the king look more like an ancestor than a mere mortal like the rest of the kingdom. This man was an avatar of the founders, and while Westly might say the power of the Founders radiated from Rylan or Nichi because of their birth, it was nothing compared to their monarch.

"Long live the memory of the Gods of our Ancestors," King Braeden acknowledged, and then remained standing. With a nod from the King, the Royal Herald continued.

"Give hail all you fledglings of Kosar. Give hail, all you who have Sired, all you who have nursed veterans and guild masters and the great Lords of Court. You stand as fledglings still in the shadow of Lenae du'Illiandria, Priestess of Great Matron Kerowyn. Veterans! Courtiers! Counsel Lords, give hail!"

You could have heard a feather falling in the silence of the Hall. After a moment, a startled cry went up from the Lower Court and the roar of rustling wings threatened to drown out the moment. Standing in the threshold where the Upper Court had begun its procession was the King's Consort. Barefoot and unguarded, she walked among them towards the flight circle at the center of the Lower Court. Those members who had been present for more than two decades knew the meaning of such an entrance.

As Lenae spread her wings to fly, the herald made one last call.

"Hail and welcome the ascension of the yet unborn Heir of Kosar!"

Now the Court came to life. Fanfare out of star-struck trumpeters began, elder Matrons whispered what was soon to come and the many Daughters cried out in joy. She was no longer simply their Consort, she was soon to be a Matron, and more than one person sent a prayer to the Ancestors that she would live with the Heir instead of dying before he had fledged like the Consort before her.

It took mere moments for her to ascend, setting one bare foot on the top level of Court before King Braeden moved to meet her. Beside them, Micah watched as Counsel Lord Kiernan, long known for his affections for the Consort, stood silent and outwardly respectful. When Consort Lenae took her place at Braeden's side, Kiernan applauded, but he did not have the same enthusiasm as the rest of Court.

As the congratulatory cheers morphed into chatter, the Royal Herald made one final call.

"Hail, all graduating Tyros. Let it be known that your first true revel has begun. We will see you all tomorrow at dawn as your war games commence. For Honor and Glory!"

As the cheers of 'Honor and Glory' roared up around them, Micah laughed to see the nearby tyros moving towards the balcony. Nichi was the first to clamber on top of the railing, flaring his wings as his far-cousins followed him down to the flight circle in the Lower Court. They landed hard, that much Micah could see, and as other tyros swarmed to meet them, Rylan grabbed up Sera's hand. Micah cast one last look at Kaitlyn across the great chasm of the Hall, and she waved back at him.

Go! I'll see you soon, she projected, knowing that he could hear her.

And then Vinicia was at her side, distracting her with a hand on her wing. They would have their own procession back through the safety of the Royals' Wing with their Counsel Lords close at hand.

Chapter 24: The Loralae

Saturday, 11:00

Lora sucked her teeth as she paced along the glass double doors she had been standing behind to watch her *sha'doe* and the idiot Dragon Lord as they sat through the Kosaran Court. Annoyingly, she hadn't been able to see much, given how the upper level of the Court itself was a huge balcony. When she had been inside the full room earlier, she had seen the two other stories below, one huge platform and then the ground floor, but the entire hall made her claustrophobic. Masters of stonework or not, she did not trust the eerily delicate buttressing that held the crystal ceiling aloft. The fact that almost every massive indoor space in this Palace was capped with the stuff was enough to set her teeth on edge, worrying if it would fall.

Muttering to herself, it was with some relief when she saw the Counsel Lords and their new Consorts processing out of the hall. For all her hesitancy to be a part of this moment, Vinicia seemed to be stalling to let the others go before them, which served Lora well enough. The fewer people she had to dodge, the less likely her cover would be blown. The sheer amount of magic she had needed to use to keep up the shield of water that refracted light around her was exhausting!

Finally, though, it seemed as if her *sha'doe* and the Dragon Lord were searching for an escape beyond the exit this place allowed. Lora froze as she saw the Kosaran looking her way. In addition to the double doors of stained glass she stood behind, there was a second set that let out into the gardens beyond. She had been hoping they would come this way, if only to make her standing out in this bloody cold worth the wait. She took it as a sign from the Great Mothers, then, when the roar of the court ebbed and she was able to hear the two of them speaking.

"So," Kiernan mused, catching Vinicia's attention away from the bustle of the Court before them. "I suppose this means it's really happening."

"In for a copper, in for a crown," Vinicia replied. "Although you may have to fight to keep me awake if the rest of your duties are this tedious."

"If the naming of an heir and the creation of a new Court aren't exciting enough for you, you would never make it through a formal audience," Kiernan laughed. "This was all shock and awe, with hardly anything else needing to be said. Honestly, it will take more time to leave Court than it took to hold it. That's why they told the tyros to go first."

"Good Gods," Vinicia scoffed, turning to him fully. "The idea of an audience sounds like cleaning up other people's quarrels," she said. "I spend enough time doing that in the barracks."

Isn't that the truth, Lora thought. She had done her own service as a mentor to the women on the Val'Corps training islands, and even her two cycles had been too long. The Val'Kyr women she had helped her *sha'dara* train had been much more entertaining, if only because they were twenty when they made their attempt. After two cycles at war, they knew what they wanted and were rising to a genuine challenge.

"So that's what I get to look forward to?" A young woman said, smiling politely as she inserted herself beside Vinicia and her Dragon Lord. Lora was fairly certain this one's name was Kaitlyn. She was highborn and soft, not a fighter at all, but even in Lan'lieana, the highborn tended to carry more weight than their warriors. When you had to fly on the wind at speed, you wanted the weight to be muscle.

"Unfortunately, yes," Vinicia said, opening their circle so she could join them. "Though you may look less of a mess doing it."

"I doubt that," Kaitlyn confessed. "I've kept up with enough fledglings that I already have a wardrobe of working leathers. I am quite convinced that chicks are made of snot and spit until they fledge."

"Tyros are not much better," Vinicia laughed. "Though, though I have dealt with my share of bloody noses as well."

Lora smirked to see the Dragon Lord between them wincing. Having been one of those who caused such messes, he was wise to keep his mouth shut. Unfortunately, he was rescued when one of the other Counsel Lords came over to speak with them.

"Vinicia, I have been told your presence is requested in the Armory," Lord Third greeted, and Lora was interested to put a face to the man Vinicia herself worked for. "If the two of you do not have further planning to take care of."

"Nothing that can't wait the mark," Kiernan said before she could answer. "Who made the request?"

"The Eighteenth Century," Aaron said, apparently amused. "For all she has been a part of their lives, they mean to see her graduated into this Court in their own way."

Vinicia didn't know what to say, though she couldn't help but smile. Lora grinned as well. It was about time those young men honored her for the warrior she was, especially after a lifetime of cleaning up after them. Perhaps Rylan was not the only decent man among them.

"You have impacted more than my own life, it seems," Kiernan added, smiling to ease her fears. "As long as they don't mind a few Blackwings around them, I don't see why not."

"Perhaps the revel will contain itself with your guard playing chaperone," Vinicia mused as the other Counsel Lords had moved out of the Royal's Wing. Lora, however, was startled to realize they had come so close to her position. After four cycles of talking with the woman, she could truly lose herself taking in the sight of her. Unfortunately, if those Blackwings realized Lora's presence, she might also lose her freedom again, and she didn't have time for that.

Shifting her weight against the chill in the room, Lora watched as Aaron and Kaitlyn moved to leave. As they did, the Kosaran Gryphon Lord moved to take his place with his own Consort. Lora grinned to see the full figured, dark haired woman with him. This woman knew how to wield her will, and for as much as Hest'lre might be their Warhost's Counsel Lord, the way he moved in response to the woman's caress made the dominant personality in their relationship clear.

This woman was worth twice his weight in salt, indeed.

"Truce, Kehvin?" Hest'lre asked.

Vinicia took his hand without issue. "Of course," she said. "And it's just Vin now."

"As you say," Hest'lre acknowledged.

"Hest'lre explained the confusion," the woman beside him said, which earned a laugh from Kiernan. "It will be good to stand with him as you do, Vinicia. I have worked this one's hide from the shadows of the Lower City too long to let him serve as Lord Ninth without a little guidance."

Vinicia's smile was brilliant as the Gryphon Lord rolled his eyes, but Lora nodded with approval as the woman set her hand on his wing. Maybe as their Lord Ninth, he could do more for the Ehkeski than he had as Sixth. That was the man's one saving grace as far as Lora was concerned. With his heritage split between the mountains and the War Plains, the Kosarans had worked much better with the Ehkeski with him in command. She had seen it first-hand being hidden among those Ehkeski so often as a recovering loralae.

"I wish you all the best, Livia," Vinicia said as the two men spoke among themselves.

It was good to see her *sha'doe* speaking with such ease in this new place. It was a pity she could not wield power among them since she meant to leave with the Dragon Lord, but Lora could forgive it. At least if she made it home she could report the High Consort wielded the power of a Great Matriarch while she was heavy with chick.

As the Gryphon Lord and his Consort excused themselves, Vinicia and her Dragon were left on the topmost floor alone, if surrounded by Blackwings. "Gods, but I have always hated crowds," she said, shifting in place uneasily. "It is why I Step so often rather than walk the halls."

"I suppose you could Step us," Kiernan said, glancing to where the Blackwing Praetor was studying her. Given all the things Lora knew, the Lord Fifth had been asking what loralae could do, having so many of his own men around Kiernan was for more than the man's safety. They probably meant to watch Vinicia just as much as they had ever watched Lora herself.

"I don't think your friends would appreciate that," Vinicia said, sighing. "But I also don't appreciate having to wait a candlemark just to get out of this place."

"Stepping would make for an easier trip," Kiernan said, not minding if the men overheard. "However, there is an exit to the outside through this door," he said, and Lora panicked as she realized the man was pointing towards the door she was hiding behind.

It had been sealed against the winter winds, but not so terribly that she hadn't been able to slip inside. "Would you prefer to go this way?"

Blood on my ashes, Lora swore, tucking herself into the shadows of the walkway as the group started for the doors. From what little Lora could see in hiding, once Vinicia nodded, their Blackwing shadows shifted to free the door. With that open, Vinicia passed through the walkway with Kiernan at her side and then the Blackwings followed them through a second set of double doors and into the biting wind.

"The Armory, Lord Seventh?" Praetor Ivan asked, waiting for the Dragon Lord to secure the sleeves of his heavy kama for the flight. When Kiernan was ready, he flared his wings alongside Vinicia and then all twelve of them were on the wind.

Lora swore as she took off after them a beat later, hating every moment she had to be outside.

Once they had flown the length of the Sires' Wing, they rounded what Lora suspected was the Seventh Counsel Lord's Library before turning to their right and aiming for the lower entrance to a vaulted stone building. As they neared, Lora muttered to herself, cutting to the right so she could set down on the eastern side of another enormous hall that reeked of men's sweat and tears.

As the Dragon Lord and her *sha'doe* continued forward, Lora touched the falconstone on her left wrist, making certain her shield of water magic was still in place.

And the Great Mothers save me if I need to do more with my magic than this, she thought, hating how she was already halfway through her reserves with all this skulking about. Vinicia was worth it, though. She just had to keep reminding herself of that.

And one of these marks she is going to leave that man's side so I can speak with her for a blicing moment.

Muttering at her own accursed luck, she checked around the edge of the building, only to find that the Blackwings were stalling at the door.

"Do you know how long you will be, Ser?" Praetor Iven asked as his men spread out around the entrance.

"No," Vinicia answered for him, already moving for the door. "But you are free to wait here if you do not mean to mingle with my tyros. I was not lying when I said my boys could use a few chaperones."

Praetor Ivan's brows rose at that, leaving Kiernan to follow Vinicia towards the doors to the front of the Armory.

Blackwings liked confined, busy spaces about as much as any Val'Kyr, which was to say not at all. However much they hated that, though, they were at least dressed for the winds. Lora was not, so she would need to find her own way inside or thread the needle and attempt to sneak past them when a group of tyros went in.

As she stood scowling at her lack of options, a few of the Blackwings stepped away from the entrance to the Armory. As their Praetor pulled out a pipe, Lora made a face. *Terra,* she sniffed. *Don't they know it tastes better fermented?*

"Ser, we should probably go inside," the man said as Iven worked to light the pipe with an iron striker despite the wind. "I told you my cousin is graduating next cycle, but he found out from one of his mates what they mean to do for the Consort."

"And that's something we should see, Brayan?" Iven said, finally getting his pipe lit.

"It is, Prae," the man confirmed. "Dragon Lady that she is, they mean to challenge her. Sure, it's only staves and dragon poles, but don't you want to see if the woman can fight?"

Praetor Ivan let out a long breath of azure smoke, eyes narrowed at the young man.

"I know you do, Prae," he laughed. "Think of it. A Rock girl up this far north and Kosaran born? I already put money down that it doesn't take Lord Seventh more than a night to nest with her. You know Lord Seventh took his Loralae to task as well, soon as he had her safely hidden in those Cells."

Lora wasn't sure who rolled their eyes harder, the Praetor or Lora herself. "Lord Seventh did fuck the Loralae," he said. "And his Consort can put any of those tyros in there on their wings. They're book-smart, not actual warfighters. Do you really want to see how soft they are?"

"Yes, I do," he said, undeterred. "I also want to grab something to eat in the next five candlemarks. And—"

Brayan's words stopped as the Praetor's attention shifted from him with a start, catching sight of a group of three more Blackwings coming into the area. Lora winced to see the ranking man among them was the Raven Lord's Blackwing Cadre Primarch, Fabian, who she was intimately familiar with. That was the one man on the entire shelf she absolutely didn't want to run into. The Raven Lord was a close second, but Fabian? He had honestly tried to kill her a couple of times in that cell.

"Wings Up!" Praetor Ivan called.

As the Blackwings came to attention, the Praetor called for the men lingering around the door to fall in to hear whatever the Primarch meant to share. Lora, knowing better than to let this opportunity go to waste, bolted for the door.

Before she had managed to slip inside, however, she caught one snippet of conversation. Whoever was taking aim at the Dragon Lord was likely inside that Armory, dressed in House colors of violet and crimson. They had just driven out three young men prowling through the Soldier Tyro barracks in the same colors, and though they didn't have cause to charge them with anything, they were exactly the sort to try it.

Noted, Lora thought, touching her wrist to guise herself as one of the chiurgeon she had seen walking around earlier. *A tyro in uniform it is, then.*

By the time Lora had slipped inside the Armory, she didn't have to worry about hiding at all. Instead, she grinned to realize all eyes were on her *sha'doe* and the Lord Seventh as they spoke to a tyro Lora was intrigued to finally see. For all Vinicia had described the young man in charge of the Tyro Century, his adoration was clear as he walked towards her with a mug in hand. Brilliant as his smile was, Vinicia's laughter rang in the room as Tyrsten waxed poetic about the past four cycles that she had overseen their care.

As he spoke, Lora slipped inside, passing a table near to overflowing with food and drink beside the door. Most of it was meat and cheese, but there were some vegetables as well, apples and other fruits she could recognize, and mugs meant to be filled out of a tapped keg. After filling one mug with foodstuffs, she filled a second with the sweet liquid and took to wing to settle onto a low crossbeam to watch the spectacle. She wasn't the only soul who had come up a few stories into this place, though as she found her perch, she was amused to realize that most up this high were not looking at her at all. Rather, each of the couples were talking in quiet, amorous whispers inside the curl of their partner's wings.

If the rumors were true of Kosaran encampments on the Plains, this sort of feasting and fucking the night before a mission was common in the Warhost. Lan'lieanan women might take after one another to clear their head before a fight, but these men were just giving themselves hangovers as if it would help them during their fights. How they fought at all the next day still baffled her, since it just made them easier targets on the wind.

Turning her attention back to the sight of her *sha'doe*, Lora brought a foot up onto her perch, resting her chin on her knee as she watched the woman flowing through the room. It was just so bloody sexy to see how she dominated the space, demanding these idiots give her the recognition she so rightly deserved. As the young men gave her space to breathe, Tyrsten came closer with his own quiet question.

Reaching with a trick of her own, Lora could hear the words he spoke as if she was standing next to them.

"Mother," Tyrsten said with exasperation. "How many times have you told us all that members of the Tyro Legion aren't supposed to get involved with Court politics?"

"Those are the rules I set," Vinicia returned, unable to hide her smile as she took the mug he offered. "However, having one wing in the Legion and one in Court is not what I have done, unlike a certain someone I know."

"Yes, well," Tyrsten defended, glancing sideways at the Dragon Lord. "I have made amends for that situation. You, however—"

"Consort Vinicia has been Honored, Tyro," Kiernan said, flaring his wings ever so slightly. "At my request, might I add."

Your request? Lora scoffed. *Your mate arranged this entirely. No one but a woman could make certain you kept your wings attached to your body, you idiot man.*

"A well-deserved promotion, My Lord Seventh, and one we mean to celebrate," Tyrsten agreed, gesturing to the tyros and young courtiers that watched them. "With your blessing, of course."

"By all means," Kiernan said, giving up his looming as Vinicia hid her amusement in her mug. Seeing her drink, Kiernan glanced to where the ale had come from. As he stepped away, Tyrsten wiped his brow in relief and Vinicia finally did laugh.

No matter the moment, as soon as Kiernan was out of earshot, Tyrsten's exasperation was obvious. "Mother," he insisted. "Why did Rylan get named to lead the bevy? Have I not done enough these past four cycles? Gods, there isn't anything else I could have done for you—for them! I just—"

"You have already proven that you can command, Tyrsten," Vinicia answered, her pride in him obvious. "What they want to see is how well you can take orders. I believe that is the correct assessment," she added as the Dragon Lord returned.

"Indeed," he said, and Tyrsten stood taller as Kiernan spoke. "There are veterans on the Plains that need good subordinates, but the more you can show that you're able to reign in someone with a chip on their shoulder, the easier it will be to place you where you can make an impact."

Now Tyrsten could see the compliment for what it was. "Hoi, My Lord Seventh," he said, saluting again. That done, Lora picked up her mug, toasting Vinicia as she took a sip from the spiced, if thin ale.

Her sip taken, Lora was surprised to see Tyrsten still holding his salute, but it made more sense as a new man walked into the open area of the Armory to join the Dragon Lord and his new Consort. This was the famed Lord Forth, or the Forge Lord as her Val'Corps sisters called the man. The Val'Tara women, especially, since they were so obsessed getting their hands on the spring-steel he had made commonplace for his men on the War Plains.

"Sal'weh, Blake," the Dragon Lord hailed as he came out of his own apartments to investigate the commotion. Once inside the Armory proper, though, Blake had eyes only for her *sha'doe*. For as much as Lora knew, this man had been the only one of Vinicia's keepers who had welcomed her tyro training without a second thought. As a result, she had spent more time with him talking tactics, weapons, and practical body mechanics than she ever spent with her other professors. For that alone, Lora forgave him for being Kosaran.

As he approached, the dark haired and leathered skinned man embraced Vinicia like his own daughter.

"My strongest and best," he said quietly. "Is this your will?"

"It is," she said as Blake looked to Kiernan with bemused suspicion. "Though father has made it clear I have no other choice."

"He would say that," Blake agreed, releasing her to grip the Dragon Lord's extended arm. "Both of you are welcome," he said. "Though once the tyros realized there was a changing of the guard, they started making plans. What they have in store for you may set your Court afire with scandal, but it is no surprise to me."

"Truly?" Kiernan asked, intrigued as Blake smirked.

"Hawkeye, I had tyros in this armory mere moments after Winter Court was finished, all buzzing with intentions. Look about you, love," he said as Vinicia surveyed the tyros waiting for her to be done with their Counsel Lords.

They weren't alone, either. Vinicia seemed amused to realize there were a good number of courtiers here as well, men and women she had always been hastening from the barracks.

"These are your strongest and best," he said with pride. "And they wish to challenge you. Formally, of course," he said, his voice traveling to those around them with intent. "Because you are too well known for putting even the worst of them in their place, they wish to test themselves on your skill."

Lora sat up straighter at that, as eager as anyone gathered to see Vinicia rising to the challenge.

"One condition," her *sha'doe* said, looking from Blake to Kiernan. "If you stand with him, I will not have abandoned my duty and I shall meet their challenge."

"I am happy to do that," Blake agreed, though he did glance back to the entrance of the Armory as a swirl of chill wind entered. "But we will have Roder's men as well for chaperons, I think."

"So we will," Vinicia acknowledged.

As Kiernan tried not to react, the Forge Lord spoke one last time. "When I got wind of the tyros' planning, I sent word to your uncle. He had a set of your armor sent down and I can stall them if you wish to change."

"Save that for the Tourni," Vinicia said, turning to view the tyros waiting for their little war to begin. They were dressed as she was in weighted cloth or leather meant to stall against the heavy weather and it was clear she meant to match them fairly. "Let them see what strength I have as a Consort."

As the room erupted in cheers to see her toasting them, Lora adjusted herself, settling in against the crossbeam and pillar while Vinicia loosened the fit of her court garments with quick efficiency. Once she had her cloth-of-silver sleeves rolled to just past her elbows, she stepped from the company of the Counsel Lords.

"May you always have the right to challenge those above you," Vinicia called. "I am honored to bruise the wings of the very best of fools in service to the Falcon Throne."

The gathered masses hailed her challenge as she held her mug up to them. She would give them the opportunity to spar fairly, in their right minds and ready condition, knowing she was coming, and she welcomed them all. Lora took a drink of her own mug to honor her, heart racing once again just to be in the presence of the woman who had affected her so deeply over the past cycles.

As Vinicia handed her empty mug back to Kiernan, she turned to find Tyrsten standing before her with a broom in hand.

"Tyrsten," she acknowledged, watching as he dislodged the head from the pole and tossed it aside. The long, hardwood handle he dropped before her and she put one booted foot on it as it settled, watching as he too rolled up his sleeves.

"Until the war game starts, I am still the Century Primarch," he explained with a grin. "So I still the right to be the first in this, at least."

"If you insist," Vinicia laughed, rolling the bar onto the top of her foot to launch it into the air. As Tyrsten was already armed, she picked the pole out of its ascent and spun it out alongside her in salutation. Half for Court, half for their well-trained Warhost, Lora's heart sang to see Vinicia realize that this was the belated beginning of her own graduation as well.

Standing before her, Tyrsten squared off to Vinicia on the ground with equal flare, training crossbow and blunted bolts in hand. They saluted one another with their right fist to right shoulder for the duel and Vinicia projected her voice loud enough for the room to hear: "The goal is to land a torso shot that steals the person's wind or three torso shots at distance regardless of the hit's strength."

"Agreed," Tyrsten answered and then stepped one leg back into a crouch.

"On my mark," the Dragon Lord called. He waited three breaths, inhaled, and then his "Go!" Resounded around the room with his warbard's strength.

Tyrsten took to wing immediately, but Vinicia remained on the ground, mimicking the Lan'lieanan tactics she had trained. Vinicia wasn't nearly as heavily armored as a Val'Corps woman, but in return, she had the finesse, speed, and point control to keep the blunted ammunition from contacting her. Clearly she would have been a Val'Kyr like Lora herself had she been born in the sea.

As Vinicia paused, letting her awareness expand to follow his movements, Lora felt the woman reaching out with her sorcery. In addition to her sight, she knew Vinicia felt the pulse of the earth beneath her feet, breathed in the dry chill of the air, and Lora laughed to realize Vinicia might be checking to see if she could thin or thicken the little humidity it held against the lift on Tyrsten's wings. The heat of her passion for combat sang in every fiber of Vinicia's being, waiting to heat the metal of his crossbow or to bring the wood in his hands back to life around him.

Lora had talked with her many times about how she had tested all those things on her uncle and while he had never discouraged her, he made certain she focused on martial skill in addition to her sorcery.

Tyrsten steeled himself as he reached the height of Lora's own position and turned to drop straight back, wings tucked flat and sharp for speed. His weapon was already loaded on his wrist and she could see five other bolts in his hand, waiting to go. The first shot he sent wide, testing to see if she would stand her ground. He loaded the second halfway into his fall, taking his first true shot before he watched her swat the bolt aside with precision.

Clearly Vinicia had more point control in her staff than he could overcome with simple direct hits. Two stories from the ground, Tyrsten pulled up sharply, swung his legs underneath him, and landed hard on one of the horizontal supports. Once his third shot went off, he only had two bolts left, and as he reached for them, Vinicia took the initiative. With her staff braced along the length of her arm, she leapt into the air. As Tyrsten realized she meant to rush him, he gave up reloading and ran down the support, launching back into the air just before she reached him.

She followed, doggedly, until Tyrsten crested halfway to the roof and fired in an arc that, if she hadn't been so wing-strong, would have hit her squarely. As it was, she powered higher and Tyrsten cursed, diving towards the balcony as several weapons were held aloft for him to choose from. Vinicia backwinged in her decent, hovering for just an instant to see which weapon and new angle he chose, and then banked so she would land just after he did.

Holy Mothers, she is sexy...

Tyrsten landed hard, nearly coming to his knees from the speed of his dive, but he remained standing. He had been a fool to only arm himself with projectiles, but Lora laughed aloud to see his choice of the wooden sword. Now he was at an even greater disadvantage, as he would have to get inside the arc of her staff before he could touch her at all. It was as if he had forgotten he was fighting her in front of two Kosaran Warlords. That, or he was extremely sure of himself.

Vinicia landed with a dangerous flourish, watching his arms stiffen as he kept his death grip on his sword. When his foot twisted for grip on the floor and his wings flared back to propel himself, Vinicia knew his intent. He wanted to attack the staff, to wrench it out of her hands.

It might have worked under other circumstances, but instead of meeting his blow, Vinicia yielded with the impact, stalling his blade in its swing, and then twisted and flung both him and his force straight past her.

So fucking sexy...

The young courtiers who had snuck in with the graduating tyros gasped, but Lora heard the hum of quiet conversation explaining what had just happened. Vinicia glanced at Kiernan, winked, and then brought up the tip of her pole between herself and Tyrsten to keep him at a distance.

"Care to try again?" She asked.

Tyrsten was on his feet, drawing up his weapon with a grin.

This time, Tyrsten rushed forward, feinting with the sword to get a hand on her staff. Vinicia let him have it, though when his sword arm came forward to strike her, she stepped her back foot out into a deep lunge, dropping her center of gravity, and then recovered backwards to snap the staff out of his grip and avoid the sword entirely. Before Tyrsten realized what had happened, Vinicia set the staff against his knee, took a step to compress her angle, and then swept Tyrsten completely off his feet.

Lora kept silent with her own mocking laughter while the crowd winced and groaned, as even the uninitiated could hear how hard he had landed. If Vinicia had done any more than throw him, if she had wound up for that shot, Tyrsten would have been out of the War, not just this fight. Still, Tyrsten was also doing well enough despite his bruising, pushing back on his feet with the sword still in his hand. More than a few tyros were impressed, though if they were cheering for her or Tyrsten, she couldn't be sure.

Once Tyrsten had recovered, Vinicia engaged him once again, thrusting with the tip of the staff when she was in range. This time, with both hands on his sword, Tyrsten stopped her swing, though his wings flared for balance as he fought the heavy weight. As Vinicia added pressure against the block, Tyrsten found his footing and snapped his wings in so he could duck beneath the staff, letting the momentum of her pressure move over him.

Finally within range, Tyrsten lunged to bring the sword down across her chest and the crowd roared. With both hands on her staff, it seemed there was very little Vinicia could do to protect herself. However, as Tyrsten swung the sword, Vinicia stepped to the side, and reversed the staff from a long guard with the tip high to a high guard with the tip low and stopped his blow. Tyrsten staggered with the unexpected reversal, only to watch her reverse it again to slam the butt end into his solar plexus.

Tyrsten doubled over as it connected, and the crowd gasped as his sword went flying. Vinicia panicked for an instant, thinking she hadn't pulled the blow quite enough, but he looked up at her grinning.

"I submit! I submit!" Tyrsten gasped, laughing. Relieved, Vinicia knew it was his pride she had shattered, and not his sternum.

"Well done," Vinicia grinned, and offered her hand to assist him in standing.

Seeing that he was okay, the crowd roared their approval. Lora nearly lost her mind, clenching her jaw as she struggled to keep the trilling Val'Kyr cry just behind her teeth. This was her *sha'doe*. Her beautiful, brilliant, deadly *sha'doe* and Lora couldn't have been prouder of her. A woman after her own heart, Vinicia had fire in her soul and kindness in every fiber of her being. It made her want to weep to think she was so close and yet still so far away.

"As I said before, first of fools," Tyrsten declared, and as they released hands, Vinicia's pride in him was obvious. "But I'm glad you're on our side," he added, laughing as he looked to his squad standing in the distance. "I do not want to think what would happen if we lost you to Lan'lieana."

CHAPTER 25: WESTLY

Saturday, 15:00

As Tyrsten limped back to their group, Westly watched Vinicia with pride. He was impressed that the woman hadn't used her dryad talents in that fight, but she had said she would be fair and had remained true to her word. Still, he had felt her reaching for the elements as she moved, and it gave him more than a few ideas of what he might be able to do if he ever had the need. Then again, for all the grief Westly had been given about his ability to heal with herbs by the chiurgeons, her demonstrated skill as a warrior had Kiernan's Blackwing guard on edge. It might not be worth the risk.

No matter Westly's own hesitation, though, Vinicia missed it all. Instead, she was caught up in the moment, exclaiming her pride in the graduating tyros to the Counsel Lords before her. Tyrsten, by contrast, looked glad just to have survived the encounter. As he took the ale Micah offered, downing it like water, Westly was curious to see how he would defend his loss.

Once Lord Seventh took the mug back from her, he returned to stand with Lord Fourth and a second tyro presented himself. This one was defending himself with two smaller staves meant for aerial dueling and tossed a matching set at her feet. Vinicia seemed intrigued and took his challenge.

Tyrsten was just glad to take the mead that Micah offered.

"She's all strength, that one," Tyrsten said between panted gulps. "All strength and damn fast."

"I told you," Rylan reminded, watching as Vinicia's next challenger, Fionn from Green Bevy, presented her with a set of short fighting staves. He had a similar pair, which meant he intended their sparring to include an aerial duel.

"Hey now," Tyrsten laughed, finally taking a breath as he found the bottom of his mug. "I've never been under her ire before. How was I supposed to know?"

"You could have trusted me," Rylan said, his attention more on the fight than Tyrsten's complaint.

"I'm not about to trust you to give me advice on women," Tyrsten said, rolling his eyes, only to land on Sera coming towards them with six mugs of ale in her hands. "Look how long it took you to realize what a treasure this one is. Sal'weh, gorgeous. Can I help?"

Sera flashed him a brilliant smile, not to be outdone for charm. Tyrsten was already transfixed, though, hypnotized by the lines of gold piping that highlighted the sway of her hips. As a shiver went down Westly's spine, Micah's snicker confirmed that Sera had called up her bardic gift in the moment. Whether it was to call Tyrsten's attention to her rather than grousing at Rylan, Westly couldn't tell, but the man was caught up in the sight of her all the same.

"I spent two cycles serving in a tavern," Sera laughed, offering Tyrsten the first of the mugs. "I think I can handle it."

"I bet you can," he agreed, taking a sip only to keep watching her over the rim. "Given the company you keep, you can do anything you want. Or make them do it for you," he added, looking to Rylan, Micah, and Westly.

Micah exhaled a laugh, thanking Sera for the drink as she came near. "Never underestimate a woman who works for her living, Mother included," he said, and Westly shivered to feel Micah redirecting Tyrsten's attention further. "Mother has kept nearly a thousand men in line over her ten cycles here, and now she's bodyguard to a Counsel Lord. What did you honestly think was going to happen in that fight?",

"She's a Consort to a Counsel Lord," Tyrsten argued, though as the sound of the dueling staves filled the Armory, he winced. "Okay, so she's probably his bodyguard, too," he conceded, his tone turning curious as he watched Sera. "Speaking of which, Ry said you got into a scrap before Mother brought you here. Did Wes teach you how to fight, too?"

Sera laughed as she handed Nichi his ale and Westly his water. "My Mother taught me how to fight," she said, turning to look at him. "But the first thing she taught me was to never fight a caretaker. They're sweet as candy until you cross them, and then..."

As she made a cutting motion across her throat, Nichi actually laughed.

"Can confirm," he said, though the smile he flashed at Westly made it clear he hadn't minded the lesson at all.

"How would you have beaten Mother, then?" Tyrsten said, wings flaring slightly as she looked to Rylan. For all Tyrsten's training, Westly was impressed to see the way he was flexing into his warbard's strength to keep her attention. More than that, it also seemed like his courtier's skill was focusing that strength more than any guidance from their Cantos. Seventh's man that he was meant to be, his talent with the Gift that came from the Seventh Counsel Lord was incredibly strong. Unfortunately, Sera's own strength put his to shame. She was a natural, and no training could overcome that kind of inherent talent.

"A crossbow and my wings," Sera said, innocent no matter the heavy blow to Tyrsten's pride. As Micah, Westly, and Nichi burst out laughing at Tyrsten's affront, Rylan glanced back with a wicked smile.

"I am slain!" Tyrsten crowed, hand to his heart as he staggered back a step. "Great Matron Celenae, may I rest in your mercy!"

"I knew I loved you for a reason," Rylan said, trading a kiss for the mug she offered.

Sera's bardic gift skittered and released as she laughed, buckling under the true joy in Tyrsten's own.

"Need me to kiss it and make it better?" Sera cooed, batting her eyelashes at his performance.

Tyrsten recovered in an instant, eyes alight with just the thought.

"I wouldn't say no," he purred, only to see the sharp look from Rylan. New as Rylan was to Sera's affection, the thought of Sera leaving his side was not welcome. "I don't need to say yes, either," he added, resettling his wings. "Though I am honored by the compliment of the offer."

Sera's smile was easy as she raised her glass, though she made a point to turn to Rylan at the end of the exchange. When Rylan just looked at her, she took him by the uniform collar and folded her wings around them.

Tyrsten's grin to see it nearly split the room. "I did that," he mouthed, pointing at them.

"Yes, I know. We all know," Micah said, groaning good-naturedly as he sought after something to distract them from the amorous exchange. "If I had to pick anything to use against Mother, I think I'd want my old set of wingblades. That, or a sword and shield. Either way, you have to get inside the arc of that staff to do anything against it, but all you'll get is one hit."

"Shields are for women," Tyrsten scoffed. "And they're too blicing heavy to fly with."

"And single swords are for Ehkeski," Micah said in return. "That's why the crossbow really is the best weapon. All of Kosar uses it for a reason."

"You try hitting her, then," Tyrsten said, but his remark was almost lost to the cries that surged up around them.

Looking to Vinicia, Westly was unsurprised to find her second challenger already on his knees. His aerial intention had been thwarted as she forced him to submit with his own weapons at his throat.

"Yield?" She questioned, and the tyro agreed.

Westly turned as he heard laughter from the balcony, watching as coins passed between several well-dressed sirelings.

"Ry, are you going to challenge her?" Micah asked, and Westly could see the maths the man was doing in his head.

Rylan just shrugged, keeping Sera against him with an arm around her waist. "Why would I?"

Micah pointed to the balcony. "I think it's already ten to one against for her."

"What?" Rylan asked, confused.

"No one thinks you can win," Nichi explained. "You haven't been paying attention at all, have you?"

Rylan looked up, confused until he realized there were quite a few people staring expectantly at him. "I am not some pawn to be bought," he informed them.

Tyrsten sighed. "Two cycles ago, Vinicia made a fool of you when she thew you in that linen closet," he said. "And now you're not going to redeem the face you lost?"

"I hadn't realized I'd lost any," Rylan countered, and his look traveled to those around him. "And I have nothing to prove to the likes of you."

"What about him?" Micah said and pointed across the Armory to where Lord Seventh was standing. "The Gods know you've bitched about what he thinks of you."

As Rylan looked to Vinicia, Westly knew that his crew-brother would never fight the woman. Vinicia had done too much for them for too long, and he thought of her as part of their family as much as Kaitlyn. It was as simple as that.

"I'll show him tomorrow," Rylan said, his grip hard around his wooden mug. "Right now, all I want is more food." Given the tone he used, no one asked him anything more.

As Sera set a hand on his wing to ease his growing frustration, Westly knew his friend would be all right. Given how much magic had been pushed through all of his friends recently, it was no wonder Rylan was on edge. Allowing himself to be soothed, Rylan followed Sera's pull towards the feast once again. As Micah moved to join them, Tyrsten was left looking between Westly and Nichi.

"Didn't you have to go check on your sire, Heir?" he asked, and the use of the honorific made Nichi stand up a little straighter.

"I was supposed to bring Westly by when we were done here," Nichi said, glancing to where Lord Fourth stood near the doorway. "But I thought we'd have to wait until we were released..."

"You don't have to wait if you're with me," Westly said, glad for the excuse to leave. Vinicia might enjoy the chaos of war, but for all he loved his quiet garden, it just gave him a headache. "Even without my bloodcloak, Counsel Lord Kiernan knows what we're about," he said. " He won't mind if we leave now."

Nichi's relief was palpable as he set down his empty mug. As they went for their flight cloaks, Westly saw the Counsel Lord raising his mug in salutation before glancing towards the door. At a small nod from Westly, Kiernan went back to watching Vinicia chase yet another tyro around the Armory. When they neared the door, the only thing he said was: "Give your mother my best, Nichi."

"I will, Lord Seventh," Nichi said, tapping his left shoulder with a salute as he followed Westly out of the Armory.

When they arrived in the Windover suite, Nichi led them through the barren entrance towards a curtained entrance to the far right. Though Westly had never been in the suite before, Micah had explained what the Windover's entertainment suite looked like. Now, though, it was overflowing with excess. The wet bar in the corner was stacked nearly to the ceiling with half-started cases of mead, more than a few kegs of ale, and the side tables were piled with food left over from the House's feast that afternoon.

From the look on the faces of the young courtiers lounging in the room, though, they were doing their best to show restraint. Only once the tyros were let out of their feast would the true revelry begin.

"What's going on?" Westly asked, slowing as she looked around.

"The Younger Court and graduating tyros will have the run of the place tonight," Nichi explained as they came inside. "For now, we just want to stay out of everyone's way."

"Nichi!" One of the women in the room greeted, turning to the newcomers with relief. "How was the Armory?"

"A riot, Roslyn," Nichi said, and Westly matched the voice to a woman about Kaitlyn's age, dressed in Illiandrian blue. The difference was the black trim on her collar and cuffs, and the rampant gryphon of Windover stitched on the flat front of her bodice. "You'll regret missing it," he went on. "The tyros are having a go at Consort Vinicia before she leaves her post as Barracks Mother. Your brother was the first to challenge her and has a flattened crest to show for it."

"Beaten by a woman?" Roslyn tsked, and as she stood the flock of Illiandrian-born cousins began to move towards them. "I bet he says that he let her win."

"Mother let *him* lose with dignity," Nichi said, laughing.

As the group moved near, Westly was startled to realize just how many of them looked kin to Tyrsten. All Westly had ever known was Tyrsten's near-brother Ren. The rest were apparently women, all here to try their luck at catching a chick for the glory of the Borean Branch in Illiandria.

Westly relaxed as the reality of what his adoption into Windover truly meant. No matter the stories, it seemed like these Alexandrians were not as superstitious as he had been led to believe. But just as he began to let his guard down, Westly panicked to see the flock of Court Daughters headed straight for him. The one thing Westly knew was that Micah had talked him up as the source of most of his court information and they would be happy to take him for what he was worth: a vault of gossip.

"Rose, I need to go check in with my Matron," Nichi said. "Can you stay with Wes until I return? It shouldn't be long."

"Of course, Heir," Roselyn said, ducking her head.

Nichi just shook his own in return, clearly not used to the title. "I'll just be a few moments. Be nice, Rose."

"Of course," she echoed, bending her knees in a brief courtesy as Nichi turned to leave down one of the long halls. Steeling himself, Westly turned his attention to the woman who stood before him.

"So you're the kin we've heard so much about," Roselyn said with open curiosity as the five other girls filled in a circle around him. "Where are you from, exactly?"

"Kelsineah," Westly answered, happy to talk about something other than rumors. "My father died when I was very young, so I was raised by the Eastwatch Clan of Ehkeski until I was about twenty."

"Oh, how horrible!" One girl gasped. "How did you ever learn to fly?"

"Obviously there are windwalkers in Kelsineah," Roselyn said, waving off her vapors. "It's our city, after all."

Westly smiled weakly. Sure, there were windwalkers in Kelsineah, but it wasn't like the men who raised him had ever let him go up into the Kosaran part of the city. Instead, he had remained wingbound in the Ehkeski flats until they had taken him back across the River Kir to return to his mother's grove. Or that had been the plan until he snuck off and scrambled up the towering cliffs that bordered the edge of the Eihwaz Forest to get into Kosar. His entire life, Eastwatch had been insistent he return to the Eihwaz to help them reclaim the igapo that had overtaken their dryad's grove, but Westly knew that he had been meant to live beyond the Eihwaz, not return to it. Why else would he have been born with wings?

Even with as much as Eastwatch had been insistent he return to his mother's grove, Westly knew that his mother had meant for him to live beyond the Kir. Why else would he have been born with wings? Not that these women would care...

"How did you manage after that?" Roselyn asked, moving the cousins past the point.

"The kindness of strangers has always seen me through," he answered vaguely. "That, and the Long Road that winds through the base of the mountains was easy enough to follow. I learned a lot about the herbs and berries along the mountain paths, too, not that they're very well kept..." As they didn't seem interested in his evaluation of the foothills, Westly moved on. "I eventually found my way to Delton and met Seraleia who introduced me to their crew."

"Sera, you mean?" Roselyn repeated.

"Micah's sister," Westly confirmed.

"Oh, she is quite lovely," Roselyn agreed, and Westly was glad to see it was a sentiment shared among the other girls. "I heard a rumor that she knows the Plains dance. Is that true?"

"She does," Westly confirmed. "I think she is planning on dancing at the revel tonight. Micah has been talking about it all day."

"He's been telling us for cycles that she's better than Makayla," one of the girls standing with Roselyn said. "So she will have big shoes to fill."

"I think she dances barefoot," Westly said, confused until he realized the women hadn't literally meant shoes to dance in. As he flushed, Roselyn raised a hand to stop the girls' giggling.

"So what brings you here to us?" She asked, moving them past the point. "There was talk of a boon with Counsel Lord Kiernan, but no one has a story that makes sense. Especially since we know it had something to do with Sera having to see the Palace chiurgeons. If you have such a great gift, why ask for help?"

Westly swallowed around the knot in his throat. They weren't asking about Sera; they were asking why he thought he could heal their former Patriarch where so many others had failed. "I didn't have the skill or the resources where we were living at the time," he answered.

"Could you not ask for assistance from an apothecary?" Another girl asked. "There must be resources where to members of the Lower City for something so common as cold."

These people have no idea what it's like to be out in the Ice Winds unprotected.

Westly exhaled, thinking of how to answer. Almost losing Sera had changed his relationship to his healing magic on a fundamental level. Instead of hiding and using just enough to get by, he had forced himself to grow his skills. Access to the Chiurgeons' Garden had given him far more resources than he ever would have managed on the streets, and with Vinicia's guidance, he understood how his magic worked and why. In two cycles he had more than redoubled his strength.

"Apothecaries don't appreciate someone with my talents, I'm afraid," Westly said, raising a nervous hand to smooth back his mess of dark emerald hair. He had learned that the hard way long before he had met Rylan, Micah, and Sera, but here in Delton just asking for help had gotten him run out of the shop. The chiurgeon bias against fae healing within the Palace walls clearly extended throughout the city.

"I did the best I could with what I had available," he explained. "It was only when there was no other recourse that we had to bring her here and request a boon; two cycles of training and four cycles at War for her life."

As the women paled to realize the expense, Westly gave a weak smile. "Men with the skill of a true chiurgeon are precious on the streets," he explained, trying to soften the blow. "I was lucky to do as much as I could with what we had, and we are honored to find such a silver lining to the story."

"You will bring Glory to the House of Windover, Westly," Roselyn agreed, smiling with encouragement. "We know."

Westly ducked his head with the praise, humbled by their trust.

Before any of the other girls could ask a question, she went on, working to lighten the mood. "My near-cousin Lyndal was a chiurgeon long before you appeared," she mused. "He says the way the Garden was rearranged was proof of your natural talent. He's not quite comfortable calling you a Palace Chiurgeon, but he also doesn't hold it against you. You make his work easier with such an abundant supply of materials."

"Oh," Westly replied, a little startled. "Well, give him my thanks. If he wants a tour of the new arrangement before I leave, I'd be happy to give him one. I'm giving one to Chiron Raleigh tomorrow, as it turns out."

"What he really wants is a tour of your nest," Roselyn laughed. "But I'll tell him all the same."

Fortunately, before Westly could do more than blush, Nichi came striding into the entertainment suite.

"Chiurgeon Westly," he said formally, which caught everyone's attention. "If you would please come with me. Sire Gaius will see you now."

"Of course," Westly answered, making his excuses.

Nichi fell into step with him as they left, though as they entered the smaller hallway, he was quick to point out the thick branch of gold inlay that they walked over. "That is meant for me after I'm done at War, though a First Praetor will make use of it over the winter," he said, and Westly followed to where the thick branch split off into a nearby room. "And that is my brother's suite, which he shares with a Primarch," he said, pointing to the door on their left.

"There isn't much room for subtly with sires or the Host, is there?" Westly said.

"No," Nichi agreed, amused.

At the end of the hallway, the room opened into a formal receiving area for the House filled with lounges, portraits, and other artistic flourishes, but the hearth in the room was cold. Westly realized why when he saw the door in the rear of the room was slightly cracked, letting out the whispered murmurings of folks gathered inside.

Nichi stalled as they reached the threshold, tugging on the back of his neck to calm his nerves.

"Nichi?" Westly asked, suddenly anxious. "What is it?"

"I just... I want to warn you," Nichi said. "While I can promise that my House has requested this because they trust your skill, I can't speak for every elder. That won't bother anything, will it? Their negativity?"

"It shouldn't," Westly said, doing his best to sound reassuring. "The world is full of all sorts of energy that we build up with our actions, but your family wants to see him healed. That's all that matters."

As Nichi reached for Westly's hand, the warmth they had shared in the barracks flared to life again. Chewing his lip to steady his nerves, Nichi finally let out the breath he held and then raised Westly's hand to his lips in the same gesture he would have used to show respect to his elders. "Thank you," he said, and then stepped out of the privacy of the moment.

Westly nodded, resolved to his purpose as he realized Nichi's concern had soothed his own frazzled nerves. He would need every ounce of power he could manage going into this, along with his courage, and it was a relief to have someone standing beside him that believed in the goodness of his talents.

After a few moments alone to collect himself, Nichi pushed open the door and released the familiar scent of burning herbs and humid heat of the Chiurgeons' Wing. Nichi's sire was resting on a large platform in the center of the room, and Westly could see from here that the man was gaunt and pale. The mattress he was resting on looked soft, however, and it was covered with pillows that could be moved to support his wings in whatever comfortable position he could manage.

There was also a fire roaring on the hearth for the exterior wall and food laid out on a side table for those family members in attendance. No one was speaking, though there were probably eight healthy men present.

The heads of the Windover branch Houses, Westly realized. *They're here to make certain he isn't going to die, or if he does, that they can blame it on me.*

Westly stopped as Nichi did and waited to be formally announced. "Give hail, respected elders, to Palace Chiurgeon Westly su'Kelsineah of House Windover in Alexandria."

"Is he now?" An elder man scoffed. "Counsel Lord Gallen was forced to grant this kindred a bloodrobe and now you have made him a Son of your House? How absolutely—"

"Lord Second's bigotry is none of our concern, Malkan," Sire Marius snapped, and Westly was startled to hear Kaitlyn's father speaking with enough anger to silence the chiurgeon.

This was the reaction Westly had expected from every member of House Windover, and it gave him whiplash to realize the fight they had clearly been having before he entered the room. Unsure what to do in the moment, he hesitated only to realize Nichi had shifted to stand closer to him in a show of support.

Sire Malkan huffed, but it was the last he said.

"You Honor us with your presence, Westly," he said, his tone soft with the welcome as he raised his hands in prayer. "I pray that Iskander finds you well   ."

"Glory to the House of Windover," Westly said, mimicking the gesture as he gave the formal reply. "I am glad I can be of service, Sire."

As the tension in the room eased a hair, Westly breathed in the heady scent of mint and clove that was meant to soothe everyone inside. As for the people, in addition to Sire Gaius, the walls were lined with men Westly had never seen before. Given the varied colors of their court clothing, rank robes, and pauldrons, it was a relief when Matron Yulia greeted him as well.

"Thank you for coming, Westly," she said. "I was worried they would not let you free for candlemarks yet."

"Counsel Lord Kiernan was present in the Armory," Westly explained. "He knew why we needed to leave."

"Indeed he does, if he has been speaking to Kreychi," Yulia acknowledged, exhaling a soft sigh. "Well, now that you are here, please…"

As she shifted to look at Sire Gaius, Nichi flared his wing subtly against Westly's.

"Do you need me to hold the… You know?" he whispered.

"Oh," Westly realized, and touched the hawkeye at his chest. While he had certainly raised power with it around his neck, he had not had to expend any under its burden. He knew Vinicia managed it, but he was not quite so strong. So lest he castrate his own talents, Westly made quick work of slipping it over his head as he removed the borrowed Windover flight-cloak. He handed both to Nichi with his thanks.

Once freed of the hawkeye, Westly bowed respectfully to the other Sires as Matron Yulia introduced them. The first was Sire Lorcan from the Aurae Branch in Delton. He was not the Patron of the Delton House, but rather the lead chiurgeon, as was evident from the yoke of burnt orange silk that trimmed the bloodrobe he wore atop his Windover blacks. In addition, he also had a crossed-poppy medallion on a heavy golden chain, declaring his specialty as a true surgeon. As he toyed with it, Westly couldn't decide what the man thought of Westly's own skill at healing blood and bone.

Looking past the man for all his hard stare, Westly was next introduced to Sire Willem of Branch Skyron in Kelsineah. This man wore a base of emerald leather with black piping that Westly was familiar with, having grown up in the low-lying city. Unlike Lorcan, Sire Willem wore a Primarch's pauldron over his court clothing. Given his rank, the man's crossed-poppy medallion was cast onto a silver concho and secured to the leather covering his left breast. This man's entire career must have been served in command of medicos at the Chiurgeon Citadel in Kelsineah if he had forsaken his bloodrobe entirely.

Nodding to the man, Westly turned his attention to the three sires seated on the lounges near the roaring hearth. These men weren't wearing bloodrobes either, though that made sense when Westly realized they were wearing law-speakers' cloaks instead. Unlike the bloodrobes, these were only half as long, pinned to the right shoulder and then dropped so the left side of the cloak was actually slung beneath their wings. As a result, the front of the cloak was held in place by the cords crossing each of the men's chest, one for each branch of law they studied: civilian, military, and religious. The trio included Sires Tyrian of the Borean Branch of Illiandria, Traver of Branch Kaikas of Yaltana, and Leslie of Branch Meses of Greying.

After greeting the three men, Westly looked back to Matron Yulia and Sire Marius, only now realizing that the Patriarch of Windover, Kreychi, was noticeably absent.

"How is it that you effect your healing, Westly?" Matron Yulia asked, beckoning him to approach.

Westly smiled and kissed her extended hand. "The best way to explain it is to liken it to singers. Bards have the ability to read music, to project their voices and to harmonize with others. My talents let me see the notes that exists within the body. When I find a flat or a sharp chord in another person, I can shift the energy into harmony. If there is something there that shouldn't be, I can escort the player out of the room. If there is something that should be there that isn't, I can remove it from the chorus. Once the body can sing, then it can heal itself."

"And if there is something that should be there and he wants you dead, he can remove it without a trace," Sire Malkan added, only to be hushed by the glare from Marius.

"Thank you, Westly," Matron Yulia said. "I have not heard it put so simply, or so elegantly. Please," she said, and gestured for Westly to replace her at Sire Gaius's head.

Westly took the position graciously and touched the man's temple, letting his vision shift to his secondsight. After a moment, he was able to make out the dark sapphire aura of pain that surrounded Gaius like a double image. Westly glanced back at Nichi for comparison and found the sireling lit up like a summer sky, all crystal blue and full of life. With the perspective in mind, he looked back to Gaius and stretched the spectrum of his sight so that he could see the layered colors beneath the darkness.

"What were his initial symptoms?" Westly asked to no one in particular.

There was a rustle of feathers behind him and heavy footsteps moved to join him at the nest. Sire Willem answered as Matron Yulia moved to stand with her younger son.

"The worst of it started with indigestion almost five cycles ago," he said. "The House Chiurgeons tried to assist him in purging the foods from his system, which led to a fortnight of vomiting, and then every other treatment you can imagine since that time to settle him. Though the nausea has largely abated, in the past cycle he has had swelling of his wrists and ankles and all but lost his appetite. He is down nearly two stones in weight and does not wear this wasting sickness well."

"What remedies were tried?" Westly asked.

It was Matron Yulia who answered.

"The House chiurgeons have tried lighter foods and liquids, as well as leeching to encourage his body to reduce the swelling. The only lasting effect has been to his vision. He swears the world glows a sickly yellow for him now, though there is no way for our chiurgeons to check. He could be hallucinating for all we know."

"Has anything remained constant?" Westly went on. "Anything the chiurgeons haven't changed."

Sire Willem spoke again. "There are a number of herbal teas that the House has tried, traditional concoctions to restore vitality and life. Since the purging was affecting him so poorly, I believe one of the chiurgeons included a papa flower tea for him. The papaver seemed to help and I understand it is close to the terra which you study," he added. "The tea masks the pain so that he may rest, but that is all. I don't believe the tea was brought with us to the shelf, so he hasn't had it in almost a fortnight."

"That...may be part of the problem," Westly said, and returned his look to Sire Gaius. With some perspective, Westly touched his other hand to the Sire's temple, closing the circle so he could pass the man's energy through himself. As good as it was to hear from your patient's caretakers what the symptoms were, dryad-kin had an immeasurable advantage being able to experience them on some small level.

For this, Sire Willem stepped back to give him room.

At first, Westly's senses were affronted by the similar sickly taste that papaver shared with terra, but much like Nichi, it was only the first layer of the problem. For as much as Westly studied terra, its use was warranted for medicating illness, but too much too soon, or in Sire Gaius's case, too little for too long, could throw the body into shock. Where Nichi had over-done himself in his abandon, Sire Gaius was struggling through withdrawal.

Right now, Westly was weaning Nichi from the terra with the same papaver tea that Sire Gaius had likely been given. Fortunately, he had made another round for Nichi this morning, and stored it in his cloak so they wouldn't have to return to the Garden.

"Nichi?" He called, and the sireling appeared beside him in a heartbeat. "There should be a few of your teas folded into the pockets of my cloak. Can you brew one for me? That should help with his immediate symptoms."

"Of course," Nichi said. Fortunately, there were mugs on the table to the side of the room with the array of food and he could gather one quickly. As he moved to the hearth to pull the steaming kettle from its place over the fire, Sire Willem had another question.

"What's in the tea?" He asked.

"The same papaver that I suspect your House chiurgeons gave him in Alexandria and two other herbs: clove to settle the stomach and a touch of toasted caffea for vitality. Whoever thought he should have been cut off from the papaver so quickly was misguided," Westly added. "You have to come off of it slowly, especially after sustained use, or you'll do more harm than good."

Matron Yulia's demeanor hardened, and she looked over her shoulder to Sire Malkan. "Did you know of this complication?"

"If you intend to act on the words of this sorcerer, then you no longer require my services," Sire Malkan answered and stood with a huff. "My Branch has never suffered this wasting as Gaius does now. The fault lies with his bloodline, not with my skill as a chiurgeon."

"Malkan, it is time for you to leave," Sire Marius insisted, though the man was already halfway there.

As the door slammed shut, Nichi returned to Westly's side with the tea and a thick cloth. Westly had heard of these so-called 'secret' House teas, but he had always thought it was a mixture of herbs and caffea. To think of so many people using something as potent as papaver without the respect it deserved...

"What else is in the House tea?" he asked. "Is that a secret, or widely known?"

"The base is a black tea," Sire Willem answered. "But what is in the mix varies from House to House, even branch to branch."

"So you have no idea," Westly repeated.

Sire Willem exhaled roughly. "Some Houses add trace amounts of poison to their teas to inoculate their kin. If they thought Gaius was under duress, they may have added any number of things to assist him. It is a dangerous practice and one that they wouldn't want even the other Branches to know about. If you know what is in one House's blend, then you can counter with another that is not commonly used."

Westly blinked a few times in disbelief. When he looked at Nichi, his friend just shrugged. "It has saved more lives than it's claimed," he said, handing Westly the tea. "But if you think it is a bad idea, as Heir to the House, I can make them stop."

Westly nodded, and with a look from Nichi to Willem, the matter was settled.

"For now, if the dosing has been so irregular and guarded, then we must work with what he has been given in the past few dawnings. Sire Willem, is there any chance that he could have been given purpurea for the swelling at any point?"

"Foxglove?" The Sire repeated, frowning. "I believe so. Patron Gaius has a long history of disconcerting heartbeats."

Westly did his best not to exhale his frustration, but looking at Matron Yulia, he could see that she had suspected treachery. This had gone on far too long for any reasonable illness known to the Houses.

"Then there is your cause," Westly explained. "Purpurea is lethal in strong doses. Papaver is also lethal, but more so when not weaned out of the system. As for poisoning agents, I cannot fathom if someone attempted to alter the contents to tip the balance of his health, but he suffers more from his treatments than whatever started this."

Sire Willem's look went to Matron Yulia, who had gone pale with rage.

"Kirath," she said coldly. "This all started with the Fall of Kirath. The moment we heard that the Estate had burned in the Fall, I knew something like this would happen. I knew and still—"

As the woman cut herself off to take visible control of herself, Westly looked to Nichi. He was cowed by just the threat of his Matron's anger released. They all were.

This is why I am here, Westly realized. *They had to have it confirmed. Someone has poisoned their Patron and they cannot bring him back to health. I am their last resort.*

"Is there anything you can do that we cannot?" Matron Yulia asked when she had composed herself. "Anything."

"Yes," Westly answered, and he saw in her look the permission he needed to use the full expanse of his talents. With a firm grip of confidence on his newfound reserves of power, Westly turned to Sire Gaius with purpose.

Letting go of the decorum of formality, Westly opened his senses and what he found on the other side was as gruesome as it was fascinating. In windwalker bodies, there was one trait shared by all, dryad-kin or no. Once exposed to a disease, a toxin, or an allergen, the body would adapt and become stronger. In a healthy body, that was all that was needed to retain the balance of energies. In a body weakened by pain or age, that resistance was not enough. In a body weakened by treason, that resistance was suppressed, causing hyper-sensitivity to any change in health. For Sire Gaius that would mean inflammation, nausea, weight loss... All things he had been through.

At this point, a Palace trained chiurgeon would apply all sorts of tools to balance the body's natural energies again. These tools affected the raw energy of earth, metal, fire, and water moving through them. What they left out was the energy of life that moved through all people: the energy of The Wood. Being kindred made that obvious, allowing him to see the Wood's effect upon the other elements with ease. The fact that he could correct an imbalance with raw power is what made him repulsive to the chiurgeons. For the House that needed him, though, he was a lifeline.

Armed with the information on the poison, on the edema and foxglove treatments, he knew Sire Gaius was days away from death. There was simply too much going on in the man's system and anything a chiurgeon would do now would throw him further out of balance. It would look like utter incompetence had killed their Sire, even when they knew that wasn't the truth. Now it was up to Westly to use his magic to cleanse Gaius's energy completely, much like he had done to Nichi.

Here's hoping I don't pass out...

Westly settled himself next to Sire Gaius anew and placed his hands on the man's temples. With a thought, Westly caught onto the raw power of the flame in the hearth, gathering its cleansing properties into his hands to increase his workings. After a few moments, he drew the man's sickly energy out through his left hand, passed it through the tempering furnace of his concentration, and then allowed it to flow slowly back into his patient.

As it moved through the circle, Westly could taste every herb, poison, and poppy running rampant in the man's weakened body. Once he had sifted out the chaff, he projected it towards the hearth, in exchange for the pure, potent energy that thrived within it. Given the man's slight frame, it did not take long for him to complete the process.

When Westly finished, he opened his eyes and the hearth in front of him flared before suddenly banking of its own accord. Matron Yulia gasped, startled by the sudden darkness, but her fear didn't last for long.

"Gods of my ancestors," Gaius gasped, waking as if from a nightmare.

"Sal'weh, Sire," Westly said, removing his hands from the man's temples as the oil lamps in the room were brightened.

"You!" The elder man roared. "You are a gift from Iskander himself."

"It has been my honor to serve," Westly said.

From the excitement in the surrounding elders, this is exactly what they had been hoping to hear. As Matron Yulia embraced her partner with near-hysterical relief, Sire Willem stepped up to take any parting instructions. He could see how pale Westly had gone with the working and did not mean to keep him long. "I would suggest he eat his fill, but in small meals so that he doesn't overindulge," he said, bowing respectfully. "However, if you have no further need of my services, I would be happy to make a clean version of the Papa Tea while Windover remains in residence at the Palace. I can include a recipe as well, so you know what it is I use."

"That would be much appreciated," Sire Willem agreed, thanking him even as Sire Gaius called him away.

"I will just need to return to the Garden to prepare them," Westly said, speaking to Nichi as he came near, cloak and hawkeye in hand.

"Thank you, Wes," he said, over-awed by the sight of his father's sudden vigor. "Windover is truly in your debt."

"There is no debt between family," Westly said, bowing. "It has been my great honor to serve. I will be happy to do so again if needed, Heir."

"Hopefully it won't be," Nichi said, surprised by the title, but not about to correct him. Instead, he just handed over his burdens. With the blessings of Nichi's Matron and a final parting, they took their leave.

"That was brilliant," Nichi whispered as they hurried down the hallway to freedom.

"Just a moment," Westly said, remembering what Nichi had said about a room off to the side being meant for his use. "Is there a water closet in here?"

Nichi stalled as Westly moved inside. "Yeah, right through there," he said, following him in. "That door..."

It only took a few steps before Nichi realized why Westly was so urgently heading towards the room. Thankfully, Westly managed to keep his stomach until he found the cold tile in the corner.

"Are you okay, Wes?" Nichi asked, terrified as he came up behind him. It wasn't every day that anyone saw black bile and the person losing it live to see their next dawning.

Westly pushed back on his heels as the intense feeling of nausea left him, glad to be rid of it. A moment later, Nichi handed him a wooden cup filled with water.

Westly thanked him with a nod and then used the water to clean his mouth of the poisons that he had pulled from Nichi's father.

"I'll be okay," he said, trying to sound reassuring as he climbed back to his feet. As Nichi took a moment to clear the mess down the drains, Westly went and refilled the cup from the pitcher Nichi had used, actually taking a drink this time. It was miraculous how much better he felt without a hard knot of slime in his belly.

"Was that what I think it was?" Nichi asked, handing Westly a licorice twig. "Was that poison?"

"I never said being kindred was glamorous," Westly said, taking the twig with relief. The stick would clear the foul taste far more than the water. "Purging toxins is something I can do with my greater strength. You weren't nearly so bad, so I just got a little nauseated, but your father..."

As he shivered with disgust, Nichi set a hand on his wing and Westly could see the honest thanks staring back at him. "It's over now, though," he said. "And he's got the tea. Why don't we get you back into your garden so you can rest?"

"And so I can make more doses," Westly added. "Gods, this is going to take forever."

"Why don't you head over there now," Nichi said. "I still have to do some work for my teams, but I can just grab it from the barracks and let Tyrsten know I'll be with you. How does that sound?"

"I think that's probably for the best," Westly said, sighing. After a moment to collect himself, Westly let Nichi take his hand, leading him out of the greater part of the Windover Suite and out of the Sires' Wing.

A short while later, Westly made it back to his Garden a great deal more winded than he expected. Instead of taking to wing and flying to his workstation, he took his time walking through the room, gathering strength from the fire and herbs he passed as he breathed in the humidity. All he needed was some time in here alone to reset himself and then he should be fine.

He flinched, then, when he saw a chiurgeon standing at his desk, flipping through the notebook Westly had been drafting for Raleigh about the inner workings of the garden.

Gods, but I don't have the strength for this...

"Can I help you?" Westly said anyway, his steps slowing as he reached the chiurgeon.

"This is good work," the man said, though Westly frowned at the strange buzzing inside his head as if the chiron was warbard trained. "You do this all yourself?"

"I did," Westly said as the pit of his stomach dropped. No chiurgeon had ever gone into his personal room as far as he knew. Why had this one—

"How long did it take you?" The chiron asked.

"Cycles," Westly returned, vaguely. He didn't have time for this. He needed his nest before he fell on his face after working with that much power. "Did you need something, Chiron?" He asked again. "I have a patient that needs one of my teas, if you don't mind."

"I don't mind," the man said, moving from Westly's workstation with a casual grace. "Though are you sure you should be working? You seem exhausted. Maybe you should take a seat."

That did sound like a good idea, even if he wanted his nest. If this man was going to be here for long, he might as well.

"I am tired," he said, taking the place where the chiurgeon had been. "I just got done with a patient."

If the man wasn't going to look at him, Westly wasn't about to force him. Many chiurgeons couldn't quite meet his eyes, knowing what kind of strength he had.

"You shouldn't strain yourself over much, you know," the chiron said as Westly turned his attention to the journal the man had left open on the workstation. He had been reading about the theory Westly had made with woodworking, though it seemed as if someone had made a correction. Quite a few corrections, he realized, skimming back through the page.

When Westly twisted to address the man, however, his mouth fell open to see the face of a woman standing over him. Despite the image he had seen before, she stood maybe as tall as Sera with fire-red hair, sapphire blue eyes, and a sadness Westly couldn't quite place.

"For how strong you are in your sorcery," the woman said, trapping him inside her stare. "It would be better for everyone if you rested now. Take the fortnight to center yourself, seedling," she went on, her voice a soft, lulling song as she bade him turn towards the workstation. "Let the snows slow your growth. Let the ice chill the strength in your veins. Strong as you are, it will be safer for her if you rest a little while before digging your roots any further into this shelf."

Westly shivered with the feel of the woman's soft touch between his wings, though for all her strangeness, the words were a balm to the tension over his soul. Nichi might be able to spark a fire in him, but he did not need to grow that strength. He could enjoy the slow burn of it filling his core instead. Touch the Wellspring, but not take it in.

Until she is gone, sapling, said a voice in his mind. *I swore to myself I would never kill your kind again, but you will kill her if you do not give her the chance to flee. For all she means to me, I cannot allow that.*

CHAPTER 26: SOLDIER TYRO ANDRONICUS SU'ALEXANDRIA HOUSE WINDOVER

Saturday, 16:00

Given his concern for Westly, Nichi made quick work of gathering his things from the barracks. He also let Tyrsten know he was heading to the Garden, but that they'd meet everyone in Windover for the revel soon. Almost a candlemark later, he was finally making his way through the Chiurgeon Tyros' Wing and to the safety of Westly's Garden.

As he entered, he was greeted by silence and a heat that put his father's healing room to shame. Though Westly hadn't believed it this dawning, Nichi had never actually been in a glass garden before. Instead, he had spent his time as a fledgling flying around the outskirts of Alexandria, forsaking Court for season-long treks spent hunting and fishing around the valleys at the edge of his family's land.

This glass garden at the Palace was different, though. Given Westly's presence within the enormous, crystal room, the whole place was bursting with greenery, making him feel like he was stepping back into his favored wilderness, rather than the sort of sculpted, academic intensity.

After coming to Delton at nine and ten, Nichi had spent the four cycles since indoors and in study, save the field training exercises that took them to long-used plots of land on the backside of Mount Delton. Those he had reveled in, especially when they were required to live off the land instead of hauling out their own supplies. Rylan and Micah had hated it, but Nichi had taken care of them well enough with Tyrsten and Ren for help.

Turning the corner to come along the edge of the plants, Nichi was unsurprised to find Westly draped over his chiurgeon journal, dead asleep. Given how Westly had pushed through more than a few nights trying to prepare the Garden to be taken over by chiurgeon tyros again, Nichi couldn't say he blamed him.

Approaching the kindred on silent feet, Nichi wondered if he could help. Westly still had the empty jars from making the detox tea last night in front of him, but it looked like he needed to refill them first. Fortunately, each jar was labeled with the herb's name, season, and remedial qualities so he could at least identify them.

Realizing what he could do to help, Nichi plucked the chiurgeon's journal from the circle of Westly's arms and carefully gathered the empty jars at the far edge of the massive wooden workbench. With the journal for a guide, he could probably figure out where the supplies were without making too much noise.

Wait, hadn't Westly been writing all of that down for Raleigh?

Chewing his lip, Nichi opened the journal to the index of herbs at the back. All those names seemed to have one of five colors associated with them along with a number, and looking up to the bookshelves it was clear that Westly had made a grid system among the towering storage. All Nichi had to do was find what he needed, where it was, and then he would be in business...

It took him the better part of half a candlemark, but eventually he had the jars topped off and rearranged back in front of Westly. There was one herb he couldn't get, papaver, and some amount of caffea as well, but he assumed that was because Westly had them both hidden somewhere. When he was done, Nichi set the chiurgeon journal back in its place and turned his attention to Westly.

With a gentle hand set on his wing, Nichi was about to say his name when he felt Westly flinch, and then suddenly Nichi couldn't move at all. Heart racing with panic, he tried to pull away, but it was like he was trapped within his own skin. He could breathe, just barely, and his panic was matched by the wild look in Westly's eyes.

Hands out to defend himself, Westly was on his feet and a full pace away. Seeing Nichi frozen beside him, realizing the workspace and hutch and everything else hadn't moved, his eyes lost his terror and he realized what he had done.

"Gods, Nichi. It's just you," he breathed, hand to his heart. "How long—?"

You were out when I came back from the Tyros' Wing, Nichi tried to send, hating how weak his warbard's gift was, but hoping Westly could still hear him. There was a reason Kreychi had been assigned as a bodyguard to Lord Seventh, rather than training as a canto. *It's okay. I've been here the whole time.*

Westly had to resettle his wings, pulling in on himself as he washed his hands over his face. "I haven't done that in ages," he said, clearly shaken. "I can't do that. I can't..."

Wes, it's all right, Nichi sent again, flooding the thoughts with calm. Emotions he could manage, but words were much harder. It was a miracle Westly could even hear him. *You're okay. I won't let anyone hurt you.*

Westly took a breath, wanting desperately to believe him. After a long, fragile moment, the prison of air around him relaxed. Catching himself on the desk, Nichi gave a quiet grunt of relief. No matter his own panic, he refused to let it show. If Westly's first reaction was to defend himself with magic, clearly he had been attacked in his sleep before. It was the only explanation.

I found your list of herbs while you were asleep," Nichi went on, trying to act as if nothing out of the ordinary had happened. "I got what you needed from your supplies. I just couldn't find the papaver or the caffea."

"I have the papaver locked away and Rylan drank the last of my caffea," Westly said, surprised as he looked at the jars Nichi had arranged on the workbench. "Does your House drink caffea?" he asked, still hesitant. "If that's the case, they can just steep the tea in it and that will work."

"My Sire loves caffea, but our chiurgeons wouldn't let him have it with his stomach troubles," he said. "I'm sure he will be happy to hear he can have it once again."

Westly smiled in return, though he couldn't match eyes with him for long. "I can get the teas put together and then you can take it back up. I still need to finish the notes for Raleigh."

"I thought you said you were finished," Nichi said, surprised. "I had everything I needed to find the herbs. I'm sure they can piece together what's left while you sleep a few candlemarks more. Unless you didn't mean to go to the House revel..."

Westly looked like he was about to say that was exactly what he meant to do until he saw the asking in Nichi's eyes.

"It might work better if you gave Raleigh that journal now," Nichi added. "That way, he can let you know if it actually he needs more notes. The way he gushes when he hangs out with Ren, I know he'll find all of it fascinating. He loves the idea of your five-element system, but that book has nothing about the theory in it. I know he'll want to know," he said, risking a smile. "I mean, I want to know. It must be why everything in this place is so gorgeous."

Westly flushed, and Nichi hoped it was because the compliment was meant for both the garden and Westly himself.

"I have no idea how the chiurgeons kept this place alive before I came," Westly said, about to let the topic drop until he saw he had Nichi's rapt attention. "The, ah, four-element system just puts everything into a neat box, but it's not natural. If you force it into four alignments, you will only ever go so far. It is why the chiurgeon's so-called 'herb theory' makes no sense. Plants grow together because of how they work together, and that isn't a theory. It's fact."

"And a five-element system takes that into consideration?" Nichi prompted. He honestly wanted to know, and given how Westly had lit up to talk about it, now he couldn't wait to hear. Micah had been right. Courtier's nonsense would never work with Westly. He had to be the kindred's friend first, and the gods alone knew just how badly Nichi had wanted that from the first moment they had met.

"It's not about the number," Westly said, looking to the garden. "What matters is whether or not life can thrive. A five-element theory acknowledges the circle of power. There is no exact opposite, only transformation and change. Growth and decay."

"If you're not living, you're dying," Nichi said, catching on to Westly's meaning.

Westly's smile in return held far more than amusement. "I don't understand you, Andronicus," he said, shaking his head. "Two cycles you've kept me at arm's length and in the span of a day, you show that you understand me more than Rylan, Micah, or Sera ever could."

Nichi ducked his head to hide his smile, one hand pulling at the back of his neck. "And here I feel like I've known you all my life," he confessed.

"Do you know that you're the first person I've ever met who isn't afraid of me," Westly said. "I heal you with a strength that scares even me and you just shake it off. I heal your father and vomit black bile and all you do is hand me water. I bind you with air and you just…"

Westly's words fell away as Nichi looked up again. "I won't apologize for not being surprised that you do exactly what makes you wonderful," he said. "And I will not make you apologize for defending yourself, now or yesterday. After all you've been through, I should have known better. I should have offered to help rather than think I could just not make it worse. I'm sorry, Westly. I truly am."

Westly's eyes were emerald on fire, realizing how deeply Nichi cared. Hands spread for peace and heart on his sleeve, he meant every word and, of all things, it seemed to terrify the kindred.

"You shouldn't be," Westly said, drawing back into himself. "Anytime people try to help me, it never works. Chiron Raleigh, he… Well, he has been trying to help me the whole time I've been here. I just don't know what to do with people like that, so I end up shoving them away."

"What about Mike and Ry?" Nichi asked. "They help you."

"I helped them," Westly corrected, crossing his arms over his chest. "And this is where it got me."

Nichi followed his look towards the massive garden. "Would you rather be somewhere else?"

"Anywhere else," Westly said. "This forced cultivation is bringing me into my power, but I have nothing to do with it. Mother is afraid they're going to send me to Kelsineah to make me heal the Warhost. That's all Grave magic down there, which is her specialty—healing blood and bone. I need a grove. I need life and living things, but this…?"

As he let out a long sigh, Nichi wasn't sure what to say. They were all of them going to War and every soldier, chiurgeon or not, would stare death in the face.

"That is why we earn 'bloodcloaks', since we'll be covered in blood soon enough and we might as well match," Westly said into the silence. "Redwing Chiurgeons serving the Warhost under Lord Sixth are reminded all the time that we are no different that other soldiers, Palace trained or not. Our motto isn't 'For Honor and Glory', though. It's Pro Vitae. For Life," he said, though the tone he used was bitter. "It should be Memento Mori. Remember death."

Nichi didn't know what to say, though when he reached out to set a hand on Westly's wing, the kindred didn't flinch. It was good to be reminded that you were alive, and Westly said every time they touched, he could feel the spark of Founder Iskander radiating through him. All of that raw, spiritual energy that supported the Alexandrian Mountain. That had been why Westly had found him so attractive at first, that power, though the way Nichi had been so relentlessly loyal to Micah for the past two cycles had cemented that opinion.

After a long, quiet moment, Westly composed himself once again. "I learned a few things from Mother that were good, though," he said, forcing a laugh to ease the tension. "She can't keep a plant alive to save her life, but she's very good with deadwood. I can show you something she showed me, if you're interested."

"You could show me a pile of rocks and I'd probably like it," Nichi grinned, waving at him to go on as Westly turned for his room. A few moments later, the kindred reappeared with a small, heavy block of wood and set it on the workbench between them. It was ancient from the look of it and though it had handles on the sides, there was no hinge at all.

"What's this?" Nichi asked.

Instead of answering, Westly set a hand on the box and Nichi heard the sound of wood scraping on wood. When the sound stopped, Westly lifted his hand and the top came off like a lid.

"Impressive," Nichi exclaimed as the sickly sweet scent of terra, papaver, and a few other potent herbs rose from the container. "How did you make that?"

"Mother had it for ages and gave it to me to practice with deadwood," Westly shrugged. "I got the idea to use it for the more toxic herbs when I started living in here. There really is only one way to open a box like this."

"Have you tried making one?" Nichi asked, picking up the lid only to realize it was just a square of wood. Westly had literally unfused it with his magic to open the box. "What is it even made of?"

"Mother said it was wood from a hearth tree," Westly said. "I don't know where she got it from, but it means only she and I can manipulate it."

"Hearthwood?" Nichi repeated, eyes going wide as Westly took the lid back so she could secure it once again. "That is really hearthwood? Where did it come from?"

"She wouldn't say," Westly said. "She has more secrets than any person I've ever met in the mountains."

"Apparently," Nichi said, watching as Westly picked up the clever box. When he moved to secure it back in his room, Nichi was left to linger next to the desk. That, at least, was something he was used to. You didn't barge into someone's personal roost; you got invited in no matter how much you wanted them.

"I'd love for you to tell me more about how you set this place up," Nichi said as Westly reemerged, moving to join him at the workbench. "You can do that and bag the tea at the same time, right?"

"I suppose," Westly said, moving to rejoin him at the workbench. "Why do you want to know?"

"Because I want to know everything about you," Nichi laughed, as if it should have been obvious. "And if some stupid soldier tyro can understand it, maybe the other chirons can come off their high perches and listen to me. They'll be at the revel later, you know."

"Yeah, I know," Westly said, looking over his shoulder towards the labyrinth. "That's why I hadn't planned on going before, but..."

"But what?" Nichi asked, shifting to rest his hip against the workbench as Westly watched.

"Before you," he said simply, breaking eye contact almost as fast as he had made it.

Nichi smiled as Westly's attention turned to the ingredients before him. He wanted to give the kindred space enough to work, but he also didn't feel like being too far away, either. No matter his own nerves, Westly exuded an aura of calm that reminded Nichi of his fledgling days in the Alexandrian wilderness and it was incredible to feel that again.

The fact that Westly was also fascinating and breathtakingly beautiful made him that much more attractive. Just standing here and talking to the kindred made him weak in the knees, and as Westly looked back to his herbs, Nichi ran a hand through his platinum tyro crest to hide how his face was heating.

Had Micah been right? Could they be wingmates? Would Westly even want to? If Westly was still a bowen at this age, maybe he didn't feel that kind of attraction at all. It was only the stories that said kindred preferred their own kind and greenmen, men like Westly, they always cared for their dryads and dryads were female.

I would be his greenman, though, Nichi thought, risking a look at the kindred as he shifted with his work. *I would find a place to build you a grove back home. I would find every tree and flowering thing and lay it at your feet, just to see that smile.*

Westly glanced up as Nichi tore his eyes away, overwhelmed by just the possibility of that kind of happiness. They only had to serve a few cycles at war, and then they could run away together. If his brother wasn't the Counselheir—if Nichi himself didn't have to rule—they could take over his uncle Marius' estate at the Aerie House and be together, just the two of them. Sure, Nichi would have to marry one of the Daughters who had given the House a son, but she would run the House and he and Westly could manage the estate. That was what his great-grandsire had done, wasn't it? A wife and a kindred partner...

Nichi's head was spinning as Westly began to speak again.

"When I first came to this garden," he said. "The chiurgeons had set it up so that the four corners were dedicated to individual elements: earth here, fire by the hearth you passed coming in, air directly across the room from us, and water by the fountain to our left. The herbs associated with those elements were then placed near those corners, since some elder chiurgeon believed it would strengthen the herbs as they grew."

"So arbitrarily, you mean?" Nichi guessed, sensing the annoyance in Westly's tone.

"Worse than arbitrary," Westly confirmed. "Because no two chiurgeons could ever agree on what properties any individual herb had, the garden was constantly moving around. There is just no way for a windwalker to know for certain, so the plants never had a chance to thrive."

"But you can know for certain?" Nichi guessed. "You can see it when your eyes do that thing?"

"When I use my secondsight," Westly supplied.

"Well, that's descriptive," Nichi chuckled. "Is that just what you call it, or do other kin use that term?"

"I got the term from Mother," Westly said, shrugging. "What else would you call it?"

"That depends on what you see," Nichi said as Westly looked over to him. When he flushed to realize Nichi had given him his full, undivided attention, it made him grin that much more.

"Have you, ah... Have you ever seen sunlight broken into different colors by a piece of crystal?" Westly asked. "That's what it looks like to me all the time. Or at least when I am looking at it that way."

"What are you actually looking at, though?" Nichi pressed, honestly curious.

"Energy," Westly said, though it seemed an under-whelming answer. "I really don't think of it much. It's just another way I see things, like you when you shift into your flight lenses."

"Flight lenses are natural. Your second sight is because you're kindred, so natural for you is pure fae magic to me," Nichi said. "What about this? Since you're half-dryad and you're seeing something, why not dry-sight?" He suggested. "That even sounds like eyesight."

"That sounds like you mashed two words together in order to sound clever," Westly laughed, amused but incredulous. "Nice try."

"Fine," Nichi grinned, glad that Westly was enjoying himself as he prepared the tea packets. "You were saying that since you can see these colors..."

"Since I can see the energy, I can also see how they interact. When I tried to explain to the Palace chiurgeons that there was a second layer to their theory, that there was a transformative nature of the elements into one another, I was laughed out of the Green. They were so certain they had it all figured out, but I thought if I could just show them, they would see I was right. Taking over this place was my last resort and by all accounts I have proven my theory, not that anyone has acknowledged it."

That's not what Tyrren and Raleigh say, Nichi knew, but kept it to himself. He didn't want to put Westly on the defensive.

"How is the Garden different, now?" He asked, shifting to look past Westly's wings.

"Two things," Westly said, grabbing up the final tea bag, much to Nichi's delight. "For starters, the corner across from us is no longer aligned with 'Air'. Instead, it is what I call ore or metal. It represents things that affect the quality of your blood."

Nichi certainly couldn't argue with that. "If you bite your tongue and it bleeds, it certainly tastes like old metal smells, that's for sure," he said, picking up one of the tea bags to tie it off. He was happy to help and even happier that Westly trusted him to be able to manage it. Most chirons just ran you off.

As Westly went on, Nichi could tell he was encouraged by the observation. "The second change is a fifth element," he said. "Any guess what that would be?"

Glancing around the Garden, Nichi was at a loss until he remembered the shelving. Looking to where he had gathered herbs, he realized many of the towering sections were relatively new, making it so the garden was encircled by them on three of the four sides. Only the side with Fire and Metal had a wall of stone from the Palace...

"Wood?" He guessed, and Westly was ecstatic.

"Yes!" He said. "Gods, Raleigh was the only other person who even came close to figuring that out. Any guess at why?"

"Kait thinks that dryads live in trees. Well, she says they're a spirit that lives in a tree. Or is it through trees?" Nichi said, trying to remember. "You know, like you did this morning, looking through the wood to get to Rylan and Micah's room."

"Close enough," Westly said, happily. "Wood is living, but solid at the same time. It is a base element, but also an actual thing. When a dryad gathers and condenses enough Wellspring inside her to produce a seed, a new dryad can be born. The element of wood makes us whole, keeps us together. It is what we are."

Nichi smiled as Westly waxed poetic. Westly saw it as he handed him the last of the teas, but this time the kindred didn't look away. Instead, he just smiled in return and Nichi's heart melted to realized Westly was truly happy in the moment.

"And what about air?" Nichi asked, done with his work. As much as it was fascinating to think of Westly or his mother having some strange quality to their spirit, it was still a little awkward to think that windwalkers were made of wood. On an abstract level he supposed it made sense, but he preferred to be flesh and feathers. Dryad and their kindred could be whatever fantastical fae creatures they wanted to be.

"Air and Spirit are just names for the same thing, but in a different context," Westly said, taking the moment to gather the teas into a box for transport. "We know that the force exists because we can see the effects of both, even if we can't see the power itself. 'Spirit' is the easier idea to understand, since the godseye a priest develops allows them to see the ancestors. With one normal eye and one shifted to see energy, they can see how their ancestor's spirit is stuck half-manifested in a world otherwise full of movement."

"So that's how that works," Nichi said, and almost laughed. "Is that what you can do?"

"Almost," he said, encouraged. "Since I have two godseyes, I can see how the elements act upon one another. I can see their movement and stagnation, though it has taken me three decades to sort them into the colors they present as. Does that make sense?"

"I suppose that would make the prism make more sense," Nichi agreed.

"Think of it this way," Westly began again, setting the box aside. "When I first came into the garden, the herbs were arranged by type. When I changed the garden, I put them into positions that arranged them by transformative process. In doing that, I created a path for the energy to flow like it would in the wild and the whole place came to life. If that's not enough proof that their herb theory is nonsense..."

As Westly looked away, Nichi realized they had touched on Westly's frustrations with the other chiurgeons. Nichi could hear the pain in his voice, see it in how Westly stared through the hutch in frustration, and it took reaching to the kindred to call him back from the dark spiral of thought. Given the confidences they now shared, Nichi was able to take up his hand, turning Westly towards him as he sighed.

"I am the only person who is necessary to manage the Garden now, but they're still not happy," he said softly. "As far as they're concerned, I just got lucky. I mean, they get lucky when they try new techniques, but they have no idea what they're doing at all. To them, healing is just trying new ways to suppress symptoms or pain. But I'm talking right past you now, aren't I?" Westly asked, somewhat embarrassed as he realize Nichi was massaging his one hand with both of his own to calm his nerves.

"I appreciate your enthusiasm," Nichi admitted, raising Westly's hands to his lips for a courtier's kiss. "I never thought there was much to being a chiron other than memorizing ailments and treatments."

"Most chiurgeons work that way," Westly said, flexing his hand as he took it back. "Good chiurgeons try to understand the functions of the body. They intuitively discover the associations of energy that I can just see. They attempt to reason out where that intuition comes from, but I don't see the point. It would be like trying to explain to an Ehkeski what it's like to fly. The elders argue we shouldn't be able to given our physical shape, but we do it anyway. So the study of herbal theory is fascinating, but I can't appreciate it nearly as much as I should, given my talents. It's the same reason I don't understand why your House chiurgeons would try to build up a tolerance to specific poisons. One wrong dose and you'll be dead of your own accord. One disgruntled chiurgeon and you're all at risk."

"It's just the way it's done," Nichi said, shrugging. "Do you not do things like that on the street?"

"Not at all," Westly said. "We just beat the snot out of each other and end it with weapons. A slow death, a subtle death like poison brings on, it's not worth it."

"But aren't those expensive?" Nichi asked. "Weapons?"

Westly stalled for a moment, having to stifle a massive yawn with a fist.

"Do you want to go lay down?" Nichi asked as Westly recovered. "You said you've pulled two all-nighters and if you mean to come to the House revel..."

"I'm not that kind of tired," Westly defended. "I just need to sit down for a little while. You could come in my room with me if you'd like..."

"I would like that," Nichi said, letting his curiosity show as Westly stood and led them towards the vines that covered the doorway. There was a bit of fabric there as well, though Nichi laughed as he realized he was pushing past Westly's bloodcloak.

Once they were inside, Nichi had to shake himself as he looked around. Everything in this room was a master-crafted sculpture of living material, putting the small hearthwood box Westly had pulled out to shame.

The nest of rasha in the corner was a work of art, and beside that there was another desk and hutch covered in Westly's personal affects. The bookshelves were more rasha weavings and vines growing artfully alongside of it. Even the simple stool he offered to Nichi was a study in carving no true master could ever hope to replicate. Not only was Westly a chiurgeon, he was an artist. The entire room was incredible and...

"I'm sorry," Westly said, his voice suddenly tinged with worry. "If it's too much, you don't have to come inside. I made it to keep people out. We can sit in the garden if—"

"Keep people out?" Nichi said, hand to his mouth to hide his gawking. "Westly, how can you ever leave this place?"

Westly flushed as Nichi pulled his wings inside, letting the vines drop behind him.

"Gods, I may never leave this place," he admitted, exhaling a laugh as he tried to look at everything at once. "This is you? All you?"

Westly shied back from Nichi's excitement, embarrassed by the reaction. "Mother helped move the bookshelves so I could work," he defended. "But, yeah. She also warned me about people who are fascinated with kindred," he added, and the heady tone he used stopped Nichi's gawking cold. "We draw people in because of our nature, but it's all shock and awe. It's hard to know if someone cares about you or about what you can do for them. To them," he added, no matter the embarrassment now. "You felt my magic before."

"Westly," Nichi said, so earnest it seemed to startle him. "If there is anyone on this entire mountain who can understand that, it's me. I am the Heir to the greatest House in Alexandria. No one looks at me for who I am, only what I can do for them. What fledglings I can give them if they chase after me hard enough. I have three now and one of them is at court to make certain I want to marry her mother rather than someone else. All the while, I just want to do right by my family. I want to serve and then go home and hide in the wilderness they ripped me from, but here you are just... Just being yourself and I might never want to leave."

Nichi's heart was thundering in his chest as he watched Westly make the connection Nichi had made himself the first few dawnings he had known of the kindred. For so long he had tried to ignore it, tried to refuse to acknowledge just how isolated Westly might feel because Westly might actually understand him and give him that escape from his duty.

Westly was the woods come to life—Nichi's dream of a perfect companion suddenly appearing in the place that he had hated for so long—and he had fallen so hard so fast that it had killed him to keep the kindred at arm's length. But after two entire solar cycles coming to know him as a squad mate, hearing stories of him from Micah and Rylan when Westly wasn't around, Nichi could honestly say this wasn't some sort of romanticized fantasy.

"Westly, all I want is to be your friend," Nichi said, walking back the intensity of his words as he tried to collect himself. "You can understand me in a way no one but Micah has managed before, but you are also everything I gave up to be in this place. If I could help you in any way, if I could pay you back for that, all you would have to do is ask."

Westly's eyes went wide with the tension between them and Nichi was terrified he had said something wrong. When the kindred had to look away, flustered beyond belief, Nichi had to know.

"Was it something I said?" He prodded, bringing his wings in tight. If Westly wanted him to leave...

"I love you," Westly said in return, whisper soft and completely serious. "On the streets, the words you said... They mean I love you."

As the moment hung heavy between them, Nichi dared to hope. When Westly refused to look away, Nichi recognized the tension between them wasn't the fear he had expected, but the intensity of realizing Westly had confirmed their shared affection.

"All I want to do is take care of you," Nichi said, cheeks suddenly on fire as Westly settled into the moment. "If you would let me."

"Micah is going to be pretty upset if he thinks I've stolen his wingmate," Westly said, and so softly that Nichi almost missed it.

"Wingmate?" Nichi repeated, just to make sure.

"If you'll have me," Westly confirmed.

"Has anyone talked to you about where you'll be assigned for the next fighting season?" Nichi asked. "I know most chiurgeons go to Kelsineah, but you're different. You're always different."

"Only Lord Seventh knows," Westly said, shrugging. "But the Kelsin Legion is technically under Lord Sixth with the assistance of Lord Second, so it depends on who the next Lord Sixth is. I could be out if the Warhost entirely if whoever it is doesn't want to deal with Lord Second."

"My brother still has influence," Nichi said, meaning it. "Westly, wherever you go, I want to be with you. You shouldn't be alone, not in the Host."

"And you shouldn't ruin your career just because you think I can't take care of myself," Westly reminded.

"Oh, you can take care of yourself," Nichi said, shaking his head with a laugh as he took a step closer. "If you can put me on my wings, you can put anyone. It's the Host I'll move out of your way so you can keep using your incredible Gifts to make the world a better place."

Westly's fluster was genuine as Nichi came to a stop in front of him. "Westly su'Kelsineah keh'Vala," Nichi said, taking up his hand again with both of his own. "Will you be my wingmate?"

"I thought you just wanted to be my friend," Westly defended.

"I'd be lying if I said I didn't want to strip you down to your flesh and feathers and give you the kind of strength I know you need," Nichi confessed, raising Westly's knuckles to his lips once again. "Kindred that you are, you would never have to eat or sleep again if I shared a nest with you. Can you touch the Wellspring in a person yet?" He asked. "Have you come into your power?"

"I think I touched it in you yesterday," Westly breathed, seeing the asking in Nichi's eyes. "But I've never felt this kind of connection with anyone before, so I don't know. Gods, Nichi, it is terrifying and so absolutely incredible. I've watched you from afar for cycles and now you're suddenly here. What am I supposed to do with that? What am I supposed to do with you? Half the time, I don't believe this is real."

"Well, I am," Nichi said, squeezing Westly's hand with affection. "And as long as you're okay with me being here, we can do whatever you want. I've waited cycles just to talk to you properly and I can wait a lifetime if that's all you want to do. Just being near you makes me happy."

Westly's answer was to chew his lip, which was as endearing as it was so very attractive. Nichi smiled in return and then moved to set their heads together, glad they were of a close enough height that it wasn't an awkward gesture. After a long moment, Nichi felt Westly's hand coming up between them and realized Westly was pulling something over his head and dropping it over his. It was the hawkeye Kaitlyn had put on him, a token from his dryad Mother that was supposed to ease the transition of coming into his power. Void stone that all hawkeyes were, it could syphon off excess from a kindred, but it protected a windwalker. It was the reason that the Seventh Counsel Lords wore the stone, needing protection from the Host as they used the Gift granted to them by Founder Noventrio.

"I don't want to hurt you," Westly said. "I almost killed you by accident and I couldn't live with myself if I did it again."

"The terra was my own stupidity," Nichi corrected, reaching up to run his fingers through Westly's mess of emerald hair. "You managed to save me, remember?"

"I know," Westly said, exhaling in a rush. "If you know about kin coming into their power, then you know I'm dangerous," he added, the words a whisper as Nichi set his lips on his cheek. "If I lose focus..."

"I'll help you focus," Nichi promised, hands slipping down to hold Westly's jaw as the kindred's eyes closed. Just the feel of Westly's lips set Nichi's head spinning, but he had the most experience between them. Bowen that Westly was, he had the only experience.

"I could touch your energy again," he said, words failing as Nichi kissed him a second time, lingering in the heady madness sparking between them. Westly's hands were on Nichi's waist now, holding himself upright as Nichi pulled back.

"You can touch any part of me you want," Nichi murmured, almost dizzy with the incredible feel of Westly's magic. The whole world had collapsed down to the two of them, on Westly's bright emerald eyes and birch-white skin that was suddenly flushing, not with embarrassment, but with true strength. No, with heat—and enough that Nichi realized his own skin was going ice cold.

"But you can't touch me," Westly said, panting for a breath as Nichi worked to strip him of his doublet. "You keep closing the circle between us. You are giving me power and I have only just figured out how to hold it. I can't do anything with it, not yet. Nichi," he said, and the iron grip on his wrists made him hesitate. "Nichi, you have to stop."

Nichi had never wanted anything more in his life, but Westly had told him to stop and he did.

"You can't," Westly pleaded. "You won't survive me."

"What can I do, then?" Nichi asked, searching the kindred's panic for an answer. "Gods, anything you ask of me, I will do."

Westly's eyes were emerald on fire again as his grip released. Westly didn't want to stop either, but from the way he was searching the room, he had an idea.

"I need you to trust me," he finally said. Commanded, really, for all the intent the words held. "Can you do that?"

Nichi nodded, once.

"Do you know what a Suggestion is?" Westly asked.

Nichi nodded again. It was one of the sorcerous talents that dryads used to protect themselves from trespassers in their groves. Some stories told of men being bound with air as Westly had done before, but other stories talked of dryads needling into your mind, telling you to stay away or come closer. Whatever they made you do, it was to protect themselves. Half the time that Suggestion ended with the creatures in the story dead, but Westly had said to trust him. Given that he might not have lived through the Ice Winds without Westly's help, Nichi's life was already in his hands.

The energy in the room intensified as Westly came to his full height. Heart quickening with the tension between them, Nichi waited to see what it was Westly would ask.

"Sit down, Andronicus," Westly commanded, and the snap in his voice held a knife-edge of intent. A warbard had nothing on Westly's raw talent. Not even Micah's.

"Where?" He asked, using every bit of training the Delton academy had given him to resist. If Westly was going to use his strength, Nichi wanted to make sure he knew how to use it well.

::"In the nest,":: Westly said, leaning into the command.

Nichi's breath caught as he staggered a few steps, doing exactly as Westly asked. When he looked back, he did a double take to see the mossy wall behind the kin had turned bright purple with the tiny flowers that had grown in the wake of Westly's own interest.

I thought only female dryads grew plants with excess, Nichi thought, even as he smiled. Whatever the case, it was obvious that Westly was doing something with the power he had access to in the moment.

"Sit back," Westly said, the intensity softening as he said the words. Nichi did as Westly asked, relaxing his wings against the curve of the massive bowl of comforts. As he did, Nichi saw the look of hesitation in the kindred melting away to the hunger Nichi had known was underneath. "I have an idea."

"As you wish," Nichi said, lacing his fingers behind his head as he waited for Westly to speak again.

Westly just closed his eyes, arms crossed over his chest as he concentrated. A moment later, Nichi jumped as he heard the rasha nest shifting beneath him, snaking through his pillows until they had wrapped around his wrists. Now he really wouldn't be able to move.

"Do you mind?" Westly asked, not quite sure what to make of the look on Nichi's face as he tested the bonds.

"Mind?" Nichi managed, fighting for a moment with all his strength. It was one thing to have a wingmate who didn't care who your sire was, but it was quite another to feel so breathtakingly powerless. "No," he said. "Gods, no. You go right on ahead."

As Westly looked him over, eyes white as snow with his secondsight, Nichi's own eyes raked down the body before him. Chiurgeon that he was, or perhaps kindred that he was, Westly didn't have the same muscled frame as the rest of their graduating class. Instead he had a slim, largely androgynous figure that was strong without being hard, handsome without being masculine, and willowy without the feminine curves that usually caught Nichi's eye. He was just...

Perfect.

Nichi's lips parted as his heart truly started to race, pressing back into the bowl of the nest as Westly moved to join him. Knees set to either side of Nichi's hips, Westly hovered over him with more courage than Nichi would ever have been able to muster. Westly had said he was terrified, but instead of fleeing, the absolute trust between them shone through.

::You will not touch me until I say you can,":: he said, eyes locked on Nichi's own.

Nichi's breathing went ragged as he nodded, watch Westly strip out of the rest of his doublet, though the black silk shirt remained. When he turned back, he set a tentative finger against the soft leather of the doublet Nichi still wore, curious and considering as power sparked between them. Realizing the effect it was having, Westly pressed his hand flat against Nichi's chest, soothing the burn into a warmth that spread with an intoxicating heat.

"Better?" He whispered, looking up to meet Nichi's eyes.

Nichi nodded, speechless for all he was trying not to groan for the pleasure of it. "What about...?"

Nichi's eyes rolled back in his head as Westly pressed his other palm on the side of his chest. Westly had closed the circle of power through him, leaving him in control of everything it seemed. With two hands, he drew out as much as he returned until Nichi's mind went pure white with the ecstasy of it.

"Too much?" Westly asked, drawing back in a rush.

Nichi tried to shake his head as he panted for breath. He was sweating now, fighting the restraints that held his wrists only to stop as he felt Westly shifting over his hips. No matter his hands, Westly was still touching him in so many other places. It was their fight in the Soldier Tyros' Wing all over again and he absolutely did not want to win.

"Don't," he finally managed. "Don't stop."

Westly's smile was as embarrassed as it was eager.

"As you wish," he said, shifting again to slide his palms up Nichi's chest. Nichi groaned with the feel of it, a wave of relaxation and heady affection flowing up his body with the touch. When he shifted again, carrying the momentum to his shoulders and along his arms, Nichi's wings flexed into the nest, pressing them together as he arched under the exquisite strain.

Knees tightening around his hips for balance, Westly's touch continued upwards until he held Nichi's jaw in his hands. As he hesitated, sending life and light into him with whatever magic he wielded, Nichi opened his eyes.

"Please," he begged, breathless in the moment. "Westly, please."

The smile on his wingmate's lips was the last thing Nichi saw as he shifted forward, closing the distance between them. As the whole of Nichi's world became the incredible warmth pouring into him, he was delirious with the feel of it. If this was all the kindred could manage in sharing a nest, Nichi could have died happy. What else Westly meant to do, he didn't care. He had found a way inside the crest of Westly's wings and he meant to enjoy the overwhelming chaos for as long as it lasted.

Chapter 27: Kaitlyn

Saturday, 19:00

"Blood and ice, Sera. How long are you going to be?" Rylan groaned, his head lolling on the rim of the nest. "It can't take this long to put on next to nothing."

Kaitlyn giggled as Micah shot him a nasty look from around the changing screen. "She'll take as long as she needs," he said in return. "And shouldn't you be working, anyway?"

"I'm done," Rylan said, glowering in return. "I was done a candlemark ago."

"I'm done, too!" Sera echoed, laughing at their bickering. A moment later, she stepped from behind the screen a few steps to strike a dramatic dancer's pose that sent the whole of her costume swirling. "What do you think?"

Kaitlyn wasn't sure what to say. After cycles spent loathing the Plains costumes with their gaudy trappings and coins, she felt like a hypocrite. Then again, she had never seen a costume quite like the one Sera wore and it was different in almost every way.

When Sera had first taken the outfit from her haversack, it looked more like a wad of ruined silk than a dress. As she laid it out, though, there had been a ritual to the way she carefully untangled all of the cords and thin silver chain that held the pieces together. Like an act of devotion to their fallen mother, it was clear that Sera and Micah viewed the process of preparing the garment with the same reverence that Kaitlyn viewed tending the Windover House shrine.

Realizing that, honoring that, she had stood in respectful silence as Sera removed each of the eight small net bags from the collection of silk. As she heard the soft whisper of metal jewelry singing with the freedom to once again move in the world, Kaitlyn had sent a prayer to Founder Kerowyn that this dancer might honor all Matrons in such a place.

Once the bags had been separated from the garment itself, Sera had thanked each one with a kiss before setting them in a line. It was only then that she had picked up the fitted top that was made of just enough sapphire silk to cover her chest. Those attached to straps that crossed between her wings and tied at her back, displaying her ample chest amid a brocade swirl of silver feathers. With the top found in good repair, Sera had set it aside and unfolded another piece of the skirt. Here, she had withdrawn a heavier belt made of more swirling brocade that had a both long panel that would hang at the front of her hips and two drapes of tattered lace netting for the sides.

Where at first Kaitlyn thought the belt must be ruined, Sera had explained that the effect was intentional. The netting actually attached under a panel that sat between her hip bones so that the other fabric could drape at her hips. While that was clever enough, what amazed her were the thin strings of shells that had come all the way from the shores of Lan'lieana.

When Sera had finally spread out the skirt to check the seams, it had become obvious that the performance tonight would be so much more than some simple dance. Kaitlyn had never known the costumes could have such meaning, or that they could be as ornate as the Consort's own coronation gown.

Later Sera had said this piece was not only her mother's favorite garment to dance in, but the only one they had been able to save after their mother had died. The rest had been stolen from them, along with the small fortune their mother had amassed as the brothel's overseeing matron. With nowhere else to go and Sera's promise to not trade in flesh and feathers until she had started her monthly cycles, the debt they had racked up against Wenda's good graces had made them no better than slaves to the brothel for over two cycles. Once they had both begun to work, the pressure had eased, but there was no recovering the costumes or other keepsakes that Wenda had seized from them. The only reason they even had this costume or her mother's book was because her mother had hidden them from everyone's knowledge. Everyone, save Micah and Sera...

Now, seeing the costume given new life within the safety of House Windover, Kaitlyn was speechless. As Sera stepped away from the room divider, even Rylan came out of the nest, love-struck all over again at the sight of the woman he adored.

Even in this light, Sera's pale olive skin made the bright blue and silver come alive. The fitted sapphire silk swam around her lower legs like the tail of a meriad and the netting at her hips framed the place where the fabric had been cut away to reveal the outside of her thigh. Now, as Sera walked to join her, Kaitlyn was caught up in her spell. It was as if the only part of her that moved were her hips, floating like a leaf on a current in the Kir.

Sera smirked as she came to a stop in front of Kaitlyn and then looked to where Micah was picking through the tones of his instrument. "I think she likes it."

"I think you transfixed her again," Micah countered, nudging Kaitlyn with a wing. "And she hates the Plains dances and the dresses they wear at Court. Maybe your gift really has gotten stronger."

"Maybe?" Sera scoffed. "My gift is just as strong as yours and I didn't need some warbard training to do it, either."

As Micah rolled his eyes, Kaitlyn was glad the distraction of their bickering had broken the spell.

"I have always wanted to dance in this, but I never had the chance," Sera said, and handed the last piece of the silver and shell drape to Micah so he pin it in her hair. The drape itself was a collection of pearls, shells, and crystal pieces strung on thin cords, suspending them in shimmering lines through her waist-length waves of black hair. For once, in this piece and in the safety of the entertainment suite, she felt safe enough to wear it down.

"It fits you so well," Micah complimented, as Sera made final adjustments, tugging at the tie of an armband so that it would sit tighter. On her wrists and fingers were jewelry from the same craftsman, but most surprising was the piece that hung across Sera's bare midsection. While even Makayla would cover the strength she showed, Sera had adorned it with an expertly crafted silver shell.

When she was finished, Micah picked up his fretless lute again, strumming dramatically as Sera posed with such a flourish that Kaitlyn lost her words again.

"Too bad we can't play them for fools," Rylan added, not nearly so distracted by Sera's costume. "I wouldn't mind a heavier purse going into winter."

"We'll have our stipend soon," Micah said, and not for the first time. "We need no more coin than that."

Rylan shrugged uncomfortably and Kaitlyn saw for one vulnerable moment the young princeling he had been. He would always want for coin since his own House had gone bankrupt, of that she was sure.

"If we're done here," Micah said, turning the instrument around his body so the belly of it was tucked up between his wings. "I'm ready."

"Let me be certain the stage is set," Kaitlyn said, rising to her feet. "Nichi is back now and should have things in order out there... Micah, why don't you come with me? When we're ready to start, you can begin to play and Sera can have her entrance. Rylan knows where she should stand until then."

"It won't be a surprise if you continue to plan an entrance, love," Micah reminded her, though she didn't much care. While it was true he had learned a great deal of Court during the House revels, he was still a foreigner to the level of production that went into moments like these. Considering that she wanted to affirm a place for them in the memory of the House before they went to war, she would continue to plan whether or not he thought it was helpful.

With a wave to Rylan and Sera, they slipped out of the room quietly. Kaitlyn smiled as Micah came up beside her, though she slowed as he caught up her hand.

"I missed you last night," he said, pulling her towards him with hunger in his look. "Rylan said you came with him to drop off Sera, but then you were gone..."

"I thought you would want to be with her," Kaitlyn confessed as his hands gripped at her waist.

"I did," he laughed, glancing back towards the room they had just left. "But soon enough I knew exactly what had happened between them and how much *they* wanted to be alone together. I never thought I would want to be so far away from her again in my life, but when I went to find you," he murmured, searching for the ticklish spot just below her peplum. "No one knew where you had gone. I had to spend half the evening coaching my crew-brother through Nichi's courting, and then the other half fending off Nichi himself. Enjoyable as that torture can be, he was not the Windover I was aching for..."

Kaitlyn gasped with laughter as he found the place she had been trying to defend and no amount of protesting would make him stop. "I didn't know I would be gone so long, I promise!" she defended, tugging him in close to distract him from his torture. "But with Vinicia relieved of duty and the Ice Winds coming in such a rush, there were a lot of details to sort through. It appears the High Consort told Lord Third how proficient I am with such things, and he needs my help."

"You do have an exquisite attention to detail," Micah agreed, his hands sliding behind her as he set their heads together. "Have you been conscripted tonight as well, hmm?"

Kaitlyn was about to answer that she hadn't when she realized she actually didn't know. "I, well..." She managed. "I may be, love."

When he looked back up at her, blue-grey eyes full of longing, she was suddenly overwhelmed by a sharp pain behind her eyes. Closing her eyes to catch her breath, though, Micah kissed took it all away. Whatever magic he wove with his touch and attention set her heart on fire, leaving her desperate for him before his long sortie tomorrow.

Encouraged by her response, Micah lowered himself for an instant and picked up one of her legs at the knee. When he lifted her with his soldier's strength, Kaitlyn's wings flared for balance and she gasped to feel the drive of his hips holding her against the wall. As he tore away the modest fabric at her neck to reach the skin beneath, her mind raced until she realized the room just to their right was empty. Gloriously empty.

"Micah?" Kaitlyn breathed, flushing as he tore at her laces in the center of the hallway. "Micah!"

When he finally looked up, she turned and pointed to the door to the empty suite. Micah's smirk had never been more thrilling.

Kaitlyn groaned as he let her down from the wall, weak kneed but still able to walk the few paces to the doorway. She lifted the handle, bounced it against the lock to flip it free, and then Micah shouted: "Give us a moment!" Down the hallway before scooping her up into his arms to toss her into the room.

As he closed the door behind him, Kaitlyn laughed to hear Sera demanding he better be taking a lot longer than 'just a moment' with her new sister or she'd come and show him how it was done.

"Gods, she can be such a bitch," Micah laughed, closing the distance between them as his hands went to the last of her laces.

His lips were on her own as he walked them back towards the nest in the middle of the suite, dropping the bodice as they moved. By the time her knees hit the low entrance to the bowl of the massive nest, Micah had freed the laces that tied up her leggings and when he let her come up for air, it was only so he could take a knee before her. With a few expert tugs, Kaitlyn's flight boots came off as easily as the sculpted velvet leggings.

"Micahleia," Kaitlyn said, dragging a hand through his sable tyro's crest as he nuzzled the soft flesh before him.

"Yes, sweetness," he purred, looking up at her insistence.

"I will never bear your chicks if you only ever seek to please me," she said, even as she flushed with embarrassment. This was beyond forward, but it was the truth. Her matron hadn't been wrong.

"Is that what you want?" He asked, realizing the seriousness in her tone. For the first time in her life, she wanted nothing more than to join with him. That alone would give her the joy she was after, pleasure be damned.

"You are a true and honored Son of the House of Windover," she declared. "But it is not enough for me. Not if you are going to War."

As the grip on her hips changed with an intensity she'd never seen before, she gave up the hold on his hair. Coming to his feet, Kaitlyn flushed to see the seriousness in him that spoke to his true nature as a warrior.

"You think I am not already at war?" he asked, his words slow as he stripped free of his own clothing. "That I haven't been struggling to hold myself back since you turned your ring for me?"

Kaitlyn's heart was racing as his hand brushed her cheek. The only thing they wore now were their signets and she might have burst for the desire she saw reflected in his eyes.

"My mother always insisted that chicks are best caught at the height of pleasure," he whispered. "That is why I make certain you find your pleasure, sweetness," he went on, heart bared. "You will always be first in my life. Your pleasure will always come first."

"This dawning you made me a promise," she said as his other hand dropped down her torso. "And I want," she tried again, breathless as she gripped onto his wrist to stall him. "Micah, I want to carry your chicks. Only your chicks."

That was love in the Houses, as sacred as the promise he had made to her this morning in the pile with his crew. They had showed that they loved her like a sister, but she loved him like a wife. Selfish as that was, the thought of losing him at war was enough to break her heart. If she caught his chick, at least their love would have wings of its own. It was all any Kosaran woman could hope for: a chance to channel the power of a pleasured moment into the extension of an ancestral line.

"How could I ever say no when you ask so sweetly?," Micah breathed, drawing her up against him.

"If you will bring Glory to the House of Windover," Kaitlyn said, her heart full to bursting. "I will Honor you with sons all the days of my life."

Two candlemarks later, Kaitlyn opened her eyes to find her dark-haired, brooding, beloved Micahleia just couldn't stop smiling. She had never known a man to take such pleasure in partner, but she had asked and he had given his word. She might be sore for a fortnight as well, but there was love in his look as he watched her. Having given his word, he was not about to stop finding his pleasure in her until the Legions tore him from her arms. Even then, with how clever he was, he might steal back into her nest for one final chance to let her catch.

Seeing him smiling now, Kaitlyn couldn't help but smile back. Nichi had mentioned earlier that Micah seemed to be a changed man with Sera around. He had noticed that there was something different about him, but Kaitlyn hadn't had the chance to see it for herself. As she lay curled up with him in their shared nest, though, wings splayed over the sides as the sweat on their bodies cooled, she finally had to ask: "What?"

Micah smiled as he readjusted in the nest, coming onto one elbow before he answered. Kaitlyn tucked her wings in tighter, rolling back into the hollow as he brushed a damp strand of hair from her cheek.

"Do you know how loud it can get in the Sires' Wing right after Court?" He asked. When she nodded, he went on: "That is what the inside of my head sounds like when Sera isn't around. Everyone else's thoughts and emotions in a riot of sound until I can no longer think. The longer she was away, the louder it got unless I was inside a bottle."

"So it's quiet now," Kaitlyn surmised. "And that's why you're happy?"

"Well, that helps," Micah said, glancing down at his hands. "But it also means that I can get into my own thoughts and since I don't think I'll have a better chance to tell you this..."

Kaitlyn laughed as he looked back to her, beaming.

"Yes?" she asked as Micah fidgeted.

When he ducked his head, there was a secret to his smile she had only seen in him a rare few times before. When she smiled back, he looked down at his hand, and she saw he had slipped off his House signet ring. "I have wanted to turn this for you since it was given to me," he confessed, tapping her on the nose with the ring. "But I don't know how it's done."

"That's because I'm the one who does it," Kaitlyn answered, and her hand shook as she took the ring from him. After a steadying breath, she turned it and went to put it back on his right hand when she realized he was only offering his left.

Kaitlyn's heart skipped a beat as she stared at him, hope surging into what had been such an easy moment.

"You said you wanted to carry my chicks alone," Micah said with a secret smile.

"I know what that means in the Houses, Kait, and you Honor me with the asking. If you will have me for a husband, then I accept."

Kaitlyn's hands were shaking as she turned his ring once again, pointing the tip of the crest away from his fingers before sliding it home. *Betrothed,* her heart sang. After a lifetime of playing matchmaker, she would be ringed into the main Windover House.

"Do I get to do it for you?" He asked, hopeful.

"Of course," Kaitlyn flushed and then worked to free it for him. He took over when it was past her first knuckle, slipping the delicate gold and onyx ring from her right hand. She, in turn, offered him her left and he slid the ring home with the point of the teardrop facing away from her fingers. When they were truly wed, they would turn the rings one final time to point the crest towards their hands and signal their joining.

Kaitlyn couldn't stop the waterfall of joy spilling down her cheeks as he looked back to her. As she laced his left in hers, he leaned forward to seal the moment with the gentlest kiss Kaitlyn had ever experienced. And then they just lay there, heads together, with her sobbing like a chick and him smiling like a fool as he stared at their hands.

When Kaitlyn had recovered at least some of her composure, they heard a gentle knock on the door and a cautious voice inquired as to their state of dress.

"Just a moment," Kaitlyn answered and then blessed the thoughtful soul who had set up this boudoir. They were presentable in short order and when Micah pulled the door open, they found Rylan and Sera standing together, grinning like mad.

"Did you ask her?" Rylan whispered, or at least tried to whisper, and Micah's grin back at them could have split the room.

"Of course he did!" Sera exclaimed happily, bounding through the door to fling her arms around Kaitlyn. Kaitlyn embraced her back, thankful for the opaque overdress Sera now wore to protect the complicated dancing outfit.

"She asked me, actually," Micah answered. "That's what took so long. I had to, well..."

"Worship her," Sera finished for him, kissing the air on either side of Kaitlyn's cheeks. "I had to take Rylan to nest again just to block out how happy you both were. Not that he minded," Sera said as Kaitlyn flushed. "Did you?"

"Anytime you want to clear your head, that's fine with me," Rylan said, smirking until he saw Micah's look to realize what they'd done. "Gods, Mike. You're going to be a Preem. half the Palace probably heard you taking her to nest. Forgive me for trying to drown you out by making your sister sing as well."

Kaitlyn just laughed as Sera beside her smirked. She understood the intent, however. There was a reason Kaitlyn had left Nichi and Micah alone two nights ago when they'd had their heads in a bottle. Nichi was as smitten with Micah as Kaitlyn was, but if they were going to take after one another before they got to the Plains, she didn't exactly want to watch. Nichi was still her brother. Now that he was distracted by Westly, however, it seemed Micah was hers, alone.

"So what happens next," Rylan asked, picking up Micah's double-stringed lute where he had discarded it halfway to the nest. As he handed it back, there seemed to be a truce between them again.

"It is time for us to set the stage," Kaitlyn said, looking to the door that led out of the room.

"Lead the way," Micah said, releasing her from the escort to walk just behind her. Rylan and Sera remained, though Kaitlyn still caught her whispered cheer.

"She loves him so much!" Sera said to Rylan in her loud whisper. "I can *feel* it! Do you know how amazing that is?!"

After conquering the hallway, Kaitlyn and Micah entered the main suite to find the revelry had long since begun. Here, everyone from the younger court was dressed in their absolute best, as if they had known how amazing her day was going to be and had come ready for the occasion.

Fortunately for her, she was set apart not only because of her broach of office in the High Court, but also by her joy. As she passed through the celebratory crowd, most hailed her with congratulations for her station and a clever few squealed as they saw her signet had switched hands. The fact that she couldn't let go of Micah made their intimacy even more apparent.

And I might become a true Matron, now, she thought, only to glance at Micah before realizing what she'd done.

Micah raised an eyebrow at her, smirking. ::I have been hoping you would catch from me for longer than just today,:: he sent and his affection blossomed alongside his words in her mind. ::I know you have wanted one of your own ever since we met, but I didn't want to presume.::

Kaitlyn flushed at their silent exchange and poured her love for him back through the bond between them. They were linked now, or perhaps they had been for quite some time, and as excited as she was about having her ring moved to her left hand, it was just icing on the sweet-cake.

::And for as much as my mother helped other women not catch,:: he went on, still whispering to her as they moved through the room. ::She also played midwife to women who were trying. She had excellent luck with it as well, so I know what might help to see it done.::

As the words in Micah's whispered thoughts were replaced with the memory of the two of them in that nest, him driving into her more deeply than she had ever joined with another partner, she nearly missed a step. Those memories held emotion as well, his emotion, and he had taken his pleasure in her as she had asked. The smoldering look he gave her as he continued to walk was almost her undoing.

::I made a vow and I mean to keep it,:: he said, lifting her hand to his lips with a kiss. ::After Sera dances, I mean to drag you back into that nest and pick up where I left off. You really seemed to like...::

Kaitlyn's cheeks were absolutely on fire with the images he flooded into her mind.

Then again, she wasn't sure if she was more embarrassed or excited by the prospect of losing herself in him. Still trying to walk, Kaitlyn fanned her hand in front of her face, which only flashed the turned signet ring for others to see. Everyone would know what they were up to now and given the match, more than a few might offer to 'help' as Sera had threatened before. If it took more than one lover to assist, then so be it. People would come out of the woodwork to make certain a couple with a genuine love match would catch. Kaitlyn had every confidence that Micah could handle her just fine, though, so she fought to recover her composure as they walked.

Finally reaching the entertainment suite, Micah extended his arm so she would pass into the entertaining suite in front of him. When they entered, Kaitlyn saw Nichi and Westly sitting close together, her brother's eyes closed to enjoy the feel of Westly's hand trailing through his platinum tyro crest. Given his intoxicated smile, Kaitlyn was certain Nichi was as happy being under the kindred's affection as she had been under Micah's.

Truly, for all her time at Court, she had never seen him so content and it warmed her heart. For once, it seemed like he could enjoy being with someone without having to worry what it was the person wanted from him. Considering Westly's own life, it looked like the kindred was at ease enough with the affection to not worry about the simple touch. He also looked more self-possessed than Kaitlyn had ever seen him, which made her suspect he was truly coming into his power. Clearly, anything Westly asked of him, Nichi would do.

When they were finally close enough to be seen by the pair, Kaitlyn waved to them, only to have the nagging pain behind her eyes flare as they turned to look at her. Kaitlyn let Micah lead her a few steps so she could clear the blurry sensation and then firmly dismissed the feeling in favor of the otherwise amazing revel in progress.

At the moment, the Younger Court was being entertained by three Daughters known for their fondness for story-telling. In the middle of them was one of the graduating warbards, singing with a tenor so vibrant that she would have sworn he had a bardic Talent like Micah. Kaitlyn had heard this tale performed many times, something about an Illiandrian yak herder in the mountains who had attempted to court three women at once. Each of the Daughters sung the words of one of the women being courted and when they sang their story, one overlapping the other, the ruse of the poor man was revealed.

As the performance came to an end with the three women deciding to share the fellow, Nichi waved for her to join them. When the applause circled the room for the singers, she took her opportunity to pass politely through the edge of the circle. Micah followed her and was asked if he knew where Makayla and her troupe were, and if he was about to play for them.

"I think they're dancing on the ground floor somewhere," Micah answered, drawing his instrument in front of him as he emerged from the crowd. "Tonight, I play for my sister."

That piqued some interest.

"Everyone refill your cups!" Micah called, looking at Nichi with a grin. "And mine. Your sister gave me quite a workout earlier. It seems she wants to catch my chick."

Nichi's eyes lit up as he looked to Kaitlyn who was searching for the glass of honey wine with her left hand. "Glory to the House of Windover!" he cheered, and Kaitlyn's smile was a league wide as she toasted his praise. Realizing her thirst, Kaitlyn finished the drink as if it was water and then raised it for the tyro that was coming around to refill any upheld cups. Tonight of all nights she could certainly indulge.

"Drummers, On Perch!" Micah called, gathering the room's attention at last.

Soon enough, the circle had shifted to allow the three drummers to take their places, settling into position as the room filled with chatter of folks resettling themselves.

"Let me check if anyone else in the area wants to see," Kaitlyn said, taking the moment to cross over the empty performance area and back to the entrance. That was her 'cue' to get Sera ready. Once she came back in, Micah would start playing. Until then, the drummers entertained themselves with their lively warm up.

When she reached the threshold to the main receiving room, Kaitlyn called out. "For those who may be interested, we have a special performance to begin in a few moments. If you care to join us, please do so quickly."

That caught the looks of some folks, not the least of which was her far-cousin Tyrsten who was being fed small bits of fruit by several Daughters. Well, they were throwing it at his face and he was trying to catch it, but it produced the same amount of flirtatious giggling.

"Tyrsten," she called after him. "I know you are enjoying yourself, but I promise you'll want to see this."

"See what?" Tyrsten replied, only to follow Kaitlyn's gesture to where Sera was waiting with Rylan in the shadows of the far hallway.

That certainly got his attention, and both he and his flock of daughters moved inside. Kaitlyn held the heavy curtain open for them as they passed and then waved for Sera and Rylan to come join her. Just as they began to move, however, another group came to a stop at the open doors of the main suite.

"Would you look at that," a woman laughed, and Kaitlyn's hackles rose as she recognized the voice.

Kariin! She thought in a panic. *What is she doing here?*

Kaitlyn's mouth went dry as the tall, blond-haired woman and her entourage moved past the threshold. Sera was caught halfway to the entertaining suite with Rylan hanging back in the hallway. It was a good thing, too, since the entire group seemed to be a canvas of violet cloth and crimson piping.

Kirathy colors, Kaitlyn realized, and wanted to swear. *So the rumors of a new noble House were true.*

After Kariin's attempt to get Nichi to promise to ring her had failed, Kaitlyn had heard whisperings of a House being made to take in the now-landless Kirathy nobility. Kirath's colors had always been a deep maroon, but the crimson they wore now reeked of the massacre that had been The Fall of Kirath.

Sera kept on her way towards Kaitlyn as the group of them entered, spreading out in a way that made Kaitlyn think Kariin had brought bodyguards rather than an entourage.

"Look at what?" Asked a second voice and the crowd opened enough to let Kaitlyn see a woman likely ten cycles her senior joining Kariin.

Unlike the former Windover, this woman had dark brown hair up into a street crest: all of its length pulled into five ponytails down the center of her head and puffed out and pinned into an incredible volume. It must have been twice as tall as any veteran's braided crest.

"That girl's hair is black as pitch," Kariin said, gesturing to Sera as she came to a stop beside Kaitlyn. "Have you ever seen something so ugly?"

Sera bristled at the description and from her look, likely hated the woman as much as Kaitlyn hated Kariin.

"I have," she said with a laugh. "She used to be one of my whores. Her and her brother. That black hair fetched a crown for half a candlemark."

"Truly?" Kariin said, both surprised and amused as she looked over at what they could see of Sera's dancing outfit. "Well, I suppose the rest of her doesn't seem so terrible."

Kaitlyn wanted to scream. *They come into my House and insult my sister without even acknowledging that we are standing right here.*

"Kariin," Kaitlyn snapped, demanding their attention. "You are not welcome in this suite. You or your kith," she added, not sure what else to call the thugs that surrounded them.

"It is Dame Kariin to you," the woman corrected, shifting her eyes from their appraisal of Sera to Kaitlyn herself. "My ladies and I are making the rounds to confirm the rumor of our new House and make the necessary introductions. I thought you knew that much of Court protocol."

"What ladies?" Kaitlyn asked, gesturing to the men surrounding them. "All you have brought are brutes."

"And street trash," Sera added, her voice biting and cold.

"Speak for yourself, chickie," Wenda said, unimpressed. "We're the ones forming a House."

"Over my dead body you will," Rylan growled, stepping out from the shadow of the hallway. As he did, the man standing just to Wenda's left set his hand underneath his cloak.

"If you insist," the man said, and Kaitlyn panicked as Rylan's wings flared to ready himself.

"Knock it off, Oren," Wenda snapped, flaring a wing out in front of the man. "Dylan, get your ass in here."

A moment later, the last person in the Kirath party stepped into the doorway and Kaitlyn knew at once that something was wrong when the pain behind her eyes flared. Beside her, Sera threw her wing out as Wenda had done, stopping Rylan with a look that made even Kaitlyn shiver. She had never seen a Suggestion at work before, but from her stories she knew it could stop a person in their tracks, no matter their intent.

"Kaitlyn," Kariin said, drawing her attention back. "Since your new sibs seem to know who this is, I hate to leave you out. This is my fiancé, Dylan su'Delton of the Great House of the Northern Lights."

Kaitlyn didn't know what to say. From what little Sera had time to tell her about the feud between the brothers, Rylan and Dylan had hated one another since they had been thrown out of House Northern. Then again, from what she had heard from Kreychi, there was something about House Kirath's claim to the House Northern estate that meant Dylan could also inherit it. It was a whole fight with the justicars now, hinging on some technicality he couldn't explain.

"You look well, little brother," Dylan said, making his way into the room. "Think you'll be able to fly the Ice Winds?"

Rylan was speechless with rage, watching as Dylan came to a stop beside Kariin, chewing on his split lip. "Let's get out of here, woman," he said, loud enough for them all to hear. "I mean to put a chick in you on every floor of this Wing."

Kariin rolled her eyes. "I've already caught your chick, honey," she said, peeling away from him as the flock snickered among themselves to see Rylan's reaction.

"Just to be clear, Ry," Wenda said. "Once that chick is born, any claim you make after you return from War alive will have to go up against a rightful heir."

Still speechless, Rylan looked over at Sera. It was obvious he was seething, but he was also smart enough to know not to kill his brother in open Court. Instead, he simply turned around, muttering about how he should have just stayed in the barracks.

"Rylan!" Sera called, only to watch Rylan disappear into the dark hallway.

"But enough about our new House," Kariin said, calling the attention back to herself. "I simply must know about these new blood-sibs that have been adopted into yours. Desperate as your House is for any grasp at power, you really must be barren. The Gods alone know Kreychi only ever got a promotion by letting the Lord Seventh fuck him. Is that how you got your promotion, Consort? Did you let the Lord Seventh fuck Nichi as well?"

If Kaitlyn's eyes were daggers, Kariin would have been dead.

For a moment there was silence in the suite and then the two women shared a laugh that made Kaitlyn that much angrier. She was half a heartbeat away from going into the entertainment suite to ask her cousins to throw them out when she felt Sera's hand squeeze her wing.

"Kariin, was it?" Sera asked, and Kaitlyn felt a shiver of ice slide down her spine as Sera's voice took on a haunting, sultry quality. "Won't you come see my performance," she went on. "I would love to dance for you to celebrate your new kith."

"Don't listen to her Kariin," Wenda tried to cut in. "She's a blicing sorceress."

"I have been called a talented dancer," Sera agreed, and Kaitlyn felt the shiver of ice again with her words. "I can promise you it will be a night you will never forget."

"I... Think that sounds... Good," Kariin replied, dazed as Sera took her hand from Kaitlyn's wing. "Wenda?"

"We go where you go," the older crew woman replied, looking about as dazed as Kariin did.

"Please," Sera said, and Kaitlyn could hear the intended venom in her voice as she beckoned them closer. "Join us."

"If you insist," Kariin said, still blinking to clear her thoughts.

"I do," Sera said, looking back to Kaitlyn with a wink. "We do."

Kaitlyn was gaping as she watched Kariin incline her head with respect, leading the crew and its noble entourage towards the entertainment suite. "Consort."

Kaitlyn stepped aside as they passed, speechless at the sudden change in them.

"What was that?" She asked when they were through the curtain. "Did you do something to Kariin?"

"I didn't need Micah's gift to know that woman gets off on causing you pain," Sera said, and Kaitlyn saw the obvious disgust, even as she freed herself from the cover-up for her costume. "Are you all right? Who is she?"

"That was Kariin," Kaitlyn answered. "She is the one Micah foiled in her attempt to ring Nichi, but that doesn't mean we don't have to deal with her. She is a viper."

"The woman that was with her," Sera explained, handing her the silk robe for safe keeping. "Wenda is one of my vipers, but Micah and I will change their tune. I have a hook in them now, all I need is his strength to set them straight."

"But how?" Kaitlyn asked, only to hear Micah picking out the song she was meant to dance to. A moment more, and Sera flared her wings to match the sultry, wandering notes and began her entrance into the suite.

By the time Kaitlyn found her seat next to Micah, Nichi, and Westly, Sera had traveled into the center of the performance platform and was posing gently as she waited, wrists crossed to frame her face. Beneath the day-star lanterns' muted glow, Sera's costuming shimmered and reflected like water. She was a statue dripping with silver and shells until the sound of Micah's trilling on the fretless lute brought her to life.

With her wings held tightly behind her, the entire room could see her as she moved. She started by dropping her right hand with a soft sweep, and then stepped and curtsied with her left leg bent beneath her. When Micah played the trill again, Sera dropped her left hand with a sweep, and then curtsied with her right leg beneath her.

Moving into the full introduction of the song, Sera raised her arms slowly above her head. When the backs of her hands faced each other to make a pleasant frame, Micah gave the signal for the drummers to start and the room came alive with the swirling sound. When Sera began to move, it was as if all her flesh and feathers had turned to water. Though her wings remained completely still, her chest rose forward and then dropped backwards, creating a cascade of muscle that rippled down to her hips. Skirts swaying, jewelry shimmering, she created a spectacle of the focused light until she took a step forward and the undulation involved her full body.

The entire room went silent, and Kaitlyn wasn't the only one with her jaw on the floor. This bare introduction had so outpaced the other daughters' attempts that Kaitlyn would have sworn she had never seen a Plains dance before this moment. Micah caught Kaitlyn's look and winked as he silenced the strings of the lute. As the percussion of the drums overwhelmed the space, Micah used his signet ring to tap out the change of pace he wanted, and they followed along.

Sera acknowledged him as well, dropping her hands from above her head to reach out beside her, palms down. Now, Sera planted her feet beneath her and let the weight of her wings roll her shoulders back, transforming the body waves into an almost serpentine sway that used only her arms and chest. As the shells and pearls of her jewelry shifted, Kaitlyn was hypnotized. She had never known a body could move like that.

When Micah stopped his slow tapping, the change caught Sera's attention. The drums followed Micah's lead, transforming into the heavy heartbeat he preferred as Sera's posture became deadly serious. The look she exchanged with her brother was more of a challenge than a cue, and Micah nodded as Sera slunk towards him. Micah reached out to her as Sera neared, but when their hands touched, Kaitlyn felt a rush of heat and she half-fainted against Nichi to her right.

"Kait!" Westly whispered from behind him, helping her sit up with a hand on her wing. "Kait, are you all right?"

Kaitlyn opened her eyes and was about to speak when she lost her words. Looking to Sera she saw five, no... Ten balls of light orbiting her slight frame as Sera walked around the circle.

"You don't see that?" Kaitlyn whispered, trying to point.

"See what?" Nichi asked, obviously watching her and nothing else.

"The wil-o-wisps," she insisted, realizing what they were. As she turned to look at Nichi, he swore.

"Your eyes!" He said, still in a whisper.

"What?" She demanded, trying to keep the panic out of her voice.

Those around them shushed her and Kaitlyn was forced to look back to the dance in silence.

Sera was smiling as she rode the rhythm in the room, matching the drums four-on-four beat. As she stepped past each reveler, she touched their outstretched hand with a smile just for them, and as she moved on, she connected the next reveler to the last with a thin, bright line of energy that led directly back to Micah. When she had made it halfway around the room, Sera took the hand of the new Kirath courtiers as if there was nothing different about them at all. Surprisingly, Sera managed to touch hands with Kariin, who was amused by the gesture, and Wenda, who took part only at Kariin's insistence.

Sera kept up this coy game around the rest of the circle until she reached Kaitlyn herself. Sera's eyes widened as she saw her and Kaitlyn felt the compulsion to reach out to take Sera's hand. Westly stopped her, though, and Sera nodded before spinning away from them both to return to her place before Micah. Here, she inclined her head and Micah put his hands back to the strings in a solo that outstripped the beat of the drums. As he did, Sera travelled to the center of the room, matching his flourishes with her own. Finally, when Micah's head went down over his instrument, Sera dropped her arms into a frame that highlighted her waist and hips.

Micah's pace was even and steady for a moment, and then the fingering he worked on the strings began to draw bursts of light from his hands. He closed his eyes, his focus completely on the music he made, and Kaitlyn was awed by the power surging through the thin line connecting the room.

In the center of it, Sera continued her dance, matching the movement of his playing with the sway of her hips. As Micah picked up speed, so did Sera, until the sway became a step and pop that kicked her skirts out with a flourish. When Micah built into a crescendo, Sera's movements tightened into the subtle, vibrating undulations that had just enough energy to push the silver and shells over her costume into disarray.

They're raising power... Kaitlyn realized, watching as Sera slowly lifted her arms above her head. As she did so, the power Micah had pushed around the circle drew up as well. All at once, Sera turned her head down and to the side and clapped in a dramatic end to the song.

As the crowd roared their approval, Kaitlyn's vision danced with the explosion of light. But as she felt herself growing faint again, Nichi put a hand on her arm to steady her. Beside her, Micah reached out as well and between the two of them she began to even out.

"You may have a Gift after all, sweetness," Micah said, tucking the lute against his body to give Kaitlyn his full attention. Meanwhile, Nichi and Westly shifted so that Westly could set his wrist on her forehead.

"You feeling all right, Kait?" The kindred asked.

"I am so hungry," she said, suddenly feeling as if she hadn't eaten for a fortnight.

"There should still be food in the other room," Nichi offered.

"Can you two help her out?" Micah said. "She might need a hand and I need to stay with Sera."

"Yes," Kaitlyn agreed, still a little dazed. "I'd like that."

"Come on, Kait," Nichi said, moving so he could help her to her feet.

"Just watch out for Kariin," Kaitlyn said. "I don't know why she's here, but she knows that she's not welcome."

When Micah looked over to where Kariin was standing with her entourage, he didn't seem too worried. Then again, if they were truly working magic, she might not be able to see the effects as easily as she had seen their working of it. As much as she wanted to stay, it was probably safer to get out of the influence of the twin's magic.

Sera noticed as they stood to leave, taking their place as she fanned her wings to create a breeze.

"You were incredible," Kaitlyn said to her, awestruck as Nichi drew her away.

CHAPTER 28: SERA

Saturday 19:00

With Kaitlyn disappearing into the crowd, Sera turned to Micah with excitement. "You were the incredible one," she declared. "How in the world did you get the other tyros to play with you?"

"They already knew how to play, I just taught them the patterns," Micah said, laughing to himself as he came to his feet. "Gods, Sera. You have no idea how many times I wanted you to be here, doing this with me... It just wasn't right without you."

"There are other women who dance here?" Sera asked, excited as she moved towards him. "Where are they? I would love to dance with them."

"And they would hate to dance with you," Micah laughed, handing her back her cover up. "You make them look like jesters trying to get a laugh in open court, especially in mother's costuming."

As Sera laughed, he helped her get the cover up settled between her wings.

::She would be so proud of you, though,:: he added, stepping back as she secured the silk around her waist. ::You know how competitive she was.::

::I do,:: she said, sighing. ::I just wish I had people to compete with. You only get better when you are challenged, not when you are the biggest fish in the pond.::

Micah's chuckling, while amusing, was little consolation. "I'm going to take a break," he said, picking up the ale at his feet. "Did you need something?"

"Space," she laughed, shoving him back onto his lounge. "It's so warm in here!"

"Keep complaining and I'll have them open one of the balcony doors to let in a breeze," he teased, leaning back to avoid her wings. Sighing, Sera turned from him to soak in the energy of the room that was buzzing around her. Micah just put his nose in his ale, enjoying himself as well.

As Sera looked around, she was surprised when she came across a woman far older than anyone else in the suite who, like Micah, seemed to have been unaffected by the spirited dancing. True, she wasn't the only older person in the suite and she might have simply poked her head in to see what the commotion was about, but something felt different about her.

Noticing she had been spotted, the woman raised an eyebrow. As the crowd threatened to swallow up the sight of her, Sera saw the woman blink once and then look over her right shoulder before looking back with an unblinking stare. It was her mother's old signal to come to her.

Sera's heart skipped a beat when the woman turned over her right shoulder and moved towards the exit to the room.

::Micah,:: Sera sent mind-to-mind, already following after the woman. ::I'll be right back.::

::Everything okay?:: He called, concerned as he saw her moving with purpose.

::Yeh, just—I'll be right back,:: she sent, tucking her wings in close. Fortunately, her long strides and radiating presence made the crowd open up before her.

When Sera reached the corner where the woman had gone, she didn't know what to make of the sight. The woman was of a height with her, with soft copper skin and eyes of the most brilliant sapphire Sera had ever seen. If it hadn't been for her fire-red hair, Sera would have cried for how closely the woman resembled her own mother.

::You can shake the salt from the sea,:: the woman prompted.

::But not from your wings,:: Sera answered immediately, hearing a voice echoing in her mind. It was a call and response her mother had taught her.

::Whose daughter are you that you weave such moonlight?:: the woman said, asking the second part of the prompt.

::I am a daughter of the sacred singers,:: she answered, not that she knew what it meant. ::Born to dance with hands and heart and feet for the Mother of All.::

Sera's heart began to race as the woman looked over her right shoulder again. The answer had earned her more than a small measure of trust.

::How do you know those words?:: Sera asked hesitantly.

The woman's eyes were flat as she stared back and Sera knew it for a mask. Her only true answer was to deliberately fold her arms under her chest to expose a worn leather cuff. It was twin to the one Sera herself wore in memory of her mother.

::How did you get this?:: The woman asked, meaning Sera's own bracelet.

Sera almost couldn't answer, surprised as she was to see the matching jewelry. ::It was my mother's,:: she managed, though as the woman reached for her wrist, Sera had to fight to hold on to even the thought of moving. As she struggled, she heard Micah's voice in her mind, panicked.

::Sera?:: He asked, his voice unusually loud in her thoughts. ::What's going on? Who is that with you?::

::Hold still,:: the woman ordered and Sera gasped to feel the overwhelming force of the Suggestion behind the command. Frozen in place, Sera could only watch as the woman unlaced the cover of the cuff to reveal the shattered red stone beneath.

::This is broken,:: the woman said, releasing the bracelet and the Suggestion with a strange look of relief. ::Where did it come from?::

Sera brought the bracelet against her chest, covering it with her other hand protectively. ::It was my mother's,:: she defended.

::And where is your mother now?::

Sera clenched her jaw, but the woman's icy stare held just as much power as her Whispered word. She was trapped again in an instant and the compulsion she felt to answer made the Suggestion she and Micah had just managed seem like a toy for chicks.

"Dead," she confessed, her mind racing too quickly to think straight. "Ten cycles, now."

That was not what the woman wanted to hear.

"Did you know her?" Sera asked, too afraid to know better, "Did you know my mother?"

The woman's composure cracked another hair and Sera could see the pain as plain as if she had been weeping.

::I thought you were her,:: the woman confessed awkwardly. ::But I've been underwater so long any woman with the sea in her would look like blood of my *sha'dara*.::

The last she muttered to herself before looking to the exit. Realizing the woman meant to leave, Sera reached out to catch her arm.

::Did you know my mother?:: she insisted. ::You must know something, or you would not have called me over.::

::The last I knew of my *sha'dara*, she had become so heavy with chick she could not fly,:: the woman answered, agony in her sending. ::I had thought—::

::But my mother was Ehkeski,:: Sera interrupted, releasing the woman's arm for all her surprise. ::She could never fly.::

Now the woman looked back to her, only to put a hand to her bracelet in a rush. A moment later, Sera gaped as the woman's wrist-cuff shimmered with power and then Sera watched the woman transform into a young chiurgeon tyro. Powerful as the spell was, the tyro looked so absolutely average Sera would have been at a loss to describe him.

"This guy bothering you?" Micah asked, taking her hand as he came to stand beside her.

With their power linked, Sera tried to see through the guise the woman wore, but there was nothing she could do. Whatever the woman had done, it was beyond her strength.

"No," she admitted. ::Two moments ago, the person before me was a woman. She has one of mother's stones like I do. She did something to mask herself, and I cannot unsee it.::

Micah frowned and she felt him add his power to her own as he laced their hands together. He believed her, even if he couldn't see anything different himself. The woman-turned-tyro just stared between the two of them, her pain redoubling.

"Sera?" She heard Westly ask, suddenly pushing through the curtain to re-enter the entertainment suite. "Micah? Is everything all right?"

::Just a bit of confusion,:: the woman-tyro projected, greeting Westly with familiarity even as she bowed to hide the fact that she wasn't actually speaking.

"If there is a chiurgeon needed, I can manage," Westly said, offering to trade places as the woman-tyro moved to leave.

::I'll be off, then,:: the woman-tyro sent, walking walked out of the suite without another word.

Sera wanted to scream at her to stay, wanted to plead with her to answer her questions, but the further away she moved, the harder it was to cling to the memory of her at all. When she was finally gone, Sera felt dizzy and lightheaded all at once, but Micah was there to support her.

"Why were you over here?" He asked, looking at the empty corner of the room.

Sera blinked at him in confusion, not sure herself.

"I don't know," Sera said. "I must have overheated. It is cooler over here."

"That happens all the time in this place," Micah assured her. "And it has been a while since you've danced."

That seemed to make sense.

"Why don't you step out and get something to drink," Westly suggested, realizing he was holding the curtain open already.

"There you are," Nichi declared, coming up behind the kindred. "You done talking to that chiron?"

"I finished talking to him a while ago," Westly said, and Sera smiled to see the way Westly's eyes lit up to be with Nichi again.

"We're just going to get some air," Micah said as the two men made moon eyes at one another. Even without her gift, Sera could tell that he wanted nothing more than to drag the sireling into a nest.

"Westly, your eyes are brown," Nichi said in surprise. "What does that...?"

Westly's grin was wicked. Sera actually gasped in excitement as she watched Westly—shy, introverted Westly—take hold of the open front of Nichi's doublet and kiss him for all he was worth.

"Vin's eyes are brown and she's come into her power," Micah explained as the two went hands-all-over. "I guess this means he has come into his power."

Sera couldn't help but cheer as Westly pulled back from the exchange. He looked dizzy at first and then flushed scarlet as he realized the folks inside the entertaining suite were cheering them on.

"Get a room, you two!" Micah laughed. Both men took it as a lifeline and fled out of the suite, nearly tripping over one another as they raced towards the nearby hallway.

"Have fun!" Sera called after them, full of giggles as she turned back to Micah. "It's about time! Nichi has been clawing at Wes's wings every time I've seen him."

"Better Westly's than mine," Micah laughed, and Sera giggled again as she found a big mug to fill with water on a sideboard. Hungry as she still was because of Vinicia's healing magic, she was twice as thirsty after raising so much power with her dance.

When they were back inside, Sera was startled to realize that Wenda was waving at her to join them. Trusting her talents, she decided to see just how persuasive her dance had been.

When she joined them, the praise from what had once been a violent crew was unsettling. The same man who had beaten her nearly to death two days before was now leering, and his brother Ulyn was chivalrously telling him to knock it off. Their crew leader, Wenda, made even less sense. It was as if the violence the night before had simply been some joke between friends.

"You are so full of surprises, Sera," Wenda laughed, genuinely amused. "I knew you had talent in a nest, but I had no idea you could do anything while standing on your feet."

"Thanks?" Sera answered, not quite sure that was a compliment.

Wenda toasted her, regardless.

::Are you hearing this?:: Sera sent, looking over her shoulder at Micah. They noticed where she was looking, though, and called to him with equal enthusiasm.

"Micah!" Wenda said, waving emphatically to her brother. "Come join us!"

"I also can't believe your luck," Wenda went on. "To think that the Windover House would adopt you after all you've done on the Streets."

"And you, with House Kirath," Sera replied. "Have they adopted you as well?"

"Better," she said, truly gossiping now. "We are to be part of the new House Kirath as they adopt all the unlanded nobility into their new House. Until then, we will be the force that holds the Estate while the issues with the title get sorted."

"Is that so?" Micah asked, taking Ulyn's extended hand in greeting. Oren was next, and he placed his free hand over the grip he had with Micah, insistent with his praise. Micah thanked him and stole his hand back, looking over at Sera with disbelief. ::I know we're good, but...::

::We've never gotten this kind of response before,:: Sera agreed, unsettled. ::At least, not with such a wild swing from hatred to this.::

::Mother did say that the better we could perform, the better the result could be, and this is the best hall we've ever performed in,:: Micah sent. ::The room is shaped for sound, the floor polished for dancing, and lit for theatre. Maybe this is too much of a good thing?::

Sera just shrugged. Whatever it was, it was creepy.

"So how did you two end up in House Windover?" Wenda asked, honestly curious. "I didn't realize that you had been adopted until Dame Kariin said that we should crash the revel."

"That was my doing," Micah said, his pride obvious. "I made friends with a Son of the main House when we first arrived. Nichi."

"Right," Wenda said, as if she had heard that news before. "Dylan said that Nichi had agreed to ring Kariin, but the arrangement fell through. She couldn't get him to have the ceremony until after his commission was over for some reason."

"That's how it works for the Houses," Micah explained. "Even a prince has to survive on the War Plains before they can commit to politics."

"Oh, obviously," Wenda laughed, making eyes at Micah the same way Oren continued to make them at Sera. "You've always been so clever, Micah," she said, laying a hand on his arm. "If you had stayed with me, I may have just kept you for myself."

Despite being a little startled, Micah played along. Persuasive magic always worked in strange ways. "Ah, but you know we are loyal to Rylan," he said, apologetic.

"Yes. Yes, of course," Wenda said, though she was pained by that fact. Micah consoled her with an arm around her shoulders and she swooned against him.

::Your turn,:: he said, smirking a challenge at her as Sera turned her focus to the leering Oren. The brute perked up with her attention and sidled over. Sera extended her jeweled hand for him to take and dipped under his arm, mirroring the position Micah had with Wenda.

"So what is this business with Kirath all about?" Micah asked and Sera was glad for his watchful gaze. That, at least, seemed to keep Oren's hands where she could see them. She would murder the man if he so much as set a bead of her costume out of the place.

"You mean you haven't been told what Dylan's plan is, yet?" Wenda said, surprised.

"No, I can't say we have." Sera had to bite her tongue to keep from laughing as Micah looked down to her. "But I would love for you to tell me so we can help out."

::Gods, she's making moon eyes at you!:: Sera blurted out, unable to stop her mental laughter. She about died when, watching Wenda's lip quiver with a response, Micah actually kissed her. ::Oh, that's so gross!::

"O-of course," Wenda said, breathless.

::In for a copper, in for a crown,:: he sent, amused. "So what are you flock doing here, hmm?"

"Following the Daughter around, mostly," Wenda complained. "Dylan was looking for Rylan, but he won't go after him in the suite. I think he's off to those tyro barracks to look around again."

Micah's eyes narrowed at that, though from the far-away look he got, Sera wasn't sure if she could reach him Rylan alone. Micah had apparently been taught to target people with his warbard's training, but it was something he had actively refused to train since it had reminded him so much of speaking to Sera. Now that he didn't mind trying, he could possibly send Rylan a warning, but everyone on the shelf might hear him given the power they had raised to fuel their bardic magic.

"Why does he need to look around there?" Sera asked, recalling her attention as Micah focused.

He came back to himself a moment later when he scowled to see Oren's hand tugging at the high slit of her skirt. With Sera's murderous look, Micah caught Oren with a stare until his hand was back around Sera's waist instead.

::Thank you,:: Sera sent.

"Why does anyone need to check out hide sites?" Oren said, shrugging. "If we're going to line up a shot, he wants to make sure we're one and done."

"Why do you need a hide site?" Sera prompted, turning inside his encroaching embrace.

"Because one dagger is worth ten thousand gold, honey," he said, hand dropping to her hip once again as he pulled her against him.

Sera grunted, hand braced against Oren's chest to keep him away just enough. He was lucky she didn't put her knee in his groin.

"Dagger?" Micah repeated, looking to Wenda.

"Don't play coy, Micah," Wenda said and winked. "There is only one man on the shelf whose head on a platter is worth ten thousand crowns. Other than Rylan, at least."

::Sweet ancestors,:: Sera swore, though she forced herself to continue the farce. "That is a task fit for someone brave like Dylan," Sera agreed. "He has the skill, the practice..."

"I'm the one who gets to do it," Oren said, as if to earn back her affection. "And there's a bonus if we can take out the next one as well. Dylan's just doing recon."

"But since everyone knows the Seventh will name his Counselheir during the graduation, we need to be set up," she said. "Half the officers for the Host will be there, so if it's coming from them..."

As Sera stood staring at Micah in horror, their spell seemed to shake. Another member of Wenda's crew who had been eavesdropping appeared at her side, mentioning some fanciful thing that they could do with all that blood money. The absolute lack of concern for two lives sickened her.

In an effort to extract themselves, Sera looked from Micah to the door and he nodded, equally ready to be done with this game.

"Wenda, love," Micah said, catching her attention. "I promise I will return, but for now I must beg my leave."

"Oh, but why?" She sulked as he slipped free.

"I must rest if I am to be of any use for the tourni," he said and kissed her knuckles. As he pulled back, Wenda blinked a few times and Micah extracted himself from the enchantment.

"I will see you to your nest, brother," Sera added, thanking Oren for his 'kindness'.

"There's more where that came from," he said, before releasing her. "You will always have a place in my nest if you join us in Kirath."

Sera forced a coy smile and then turned to Micah to stalk, discretely, away from the crew.

::We have to tell someone, right?:: She asked, following Micah out of the entertainment suite.

::We have to tell Kreychi,:: Micah said. ::He'll know who needs to know beyond that.::

::But what about Vinicia?:: Sera insisted. ::She's his Consort.::

::Both she and Lord Seventh are surrounded by Blackwings,:: Micah said, shaking his head. ::If they can't stop someone, no one can. No, Kreychi will be able to help us more than Mother. We just have to find out where he is tonight.::

Sera exhaled roughly and looked around the gathered crowd. The other woman who had come with them, Kariin, was nowhere to be found. It was possible Kariin had followed Kaitlyn into the main area, trailing after her with the same strange affection they had just escaped from. As for everyone else, Sera looked around the circle and was glad to see simple smiles on the faces of the folk who had gathered for the performance. Having had no opinion of her or her brother before, they were allies now, but that was it.

"Sera?" Micah said, stumbling as he reached for her. "I think I may have overextended myself."

"Oh!" She said, turning to see him wiping blood from his nose. "Oh Gods, Micah."

Rylan had told her about Micah's headaches while she had been away. She also knew that Westly had been trying to help Micah use his magic without her to balance the flow, but it had hurt him more than once. She had hoped that the issue would go away with her close by, but with as much influence as they had apparently had, she wasn't sure.

As the crowd fell to silence, Micah led the way to the heavy curtain and Sera lifted it for them both to pass. His relief was evident as they entered the almost vacant chamber beyond. Once he saw Kaitlyn, what little spirit he could muster was lifted once again.

::She is so good for you,:: Sera noted, as they moved to join Kaitlyn at the table still overflowing with food and drink.

::I knew you would like her,:: Micah returned, even if his smile was marred by the blood at his lip.

As they approached, Sera saw the same look of concern in Kaitlyn at seeing Micah's distress.

"I'll be fine," Micah assured them both with a tone that said he had told her the same lie many times before.

"You sit," Sera told him, and left him on a lounge with a kerchief with Kaitlyn.

"Eat," Kaitlyn ordered, handing him the rest of the cheese she had on her plate. "Before I finish everything myself. What happened in there?"

"Just a little nudge in the right direction," Sera said as she tore the center out of a heel of bread left on the table. As she stuffed it full of meat for Micah, Kaitlyn went on.

"Was it a Suggestion?" Kaitlyn said, as if to confirm the name of the particular talent Sera was referencing.

"My Transfixion, Micha's Suggestion," Sera said, handing the heel to her brother. "It will last at least until the sun comes up."

"At least?" Kaitlyn repeated.

"That's how long it has lasted before," Sera said, gathering food for herself. "But this time, we raised so much power. It could last longer than that."

"But how do you know?" Kaitlyn wondered. "I thought the effect wasn't supposed to be obvious."

"Obvious?" Micah scoffed. "After you left, Wenda and Oren were falling over themselves to impress us with what they were doing for House Kirath. Kait, do you know where to find Kreychi at this 'mark? They've just told us that, well..."

Micah's look went to Kaitlyn, and as he raised an eyebrow at her, Sera knew he was speaking mind-to-mind. As Kaitlyn's mouth fell open in surprise, Micah looked up to see Tyrsten and his near-brother coming over to join them. Late as it was, they looked ready to head back to the barracks for tomorrow's early morning.

"Hey, have you flock seen Rylan?" He asked, clearly concerned.

"He's not with you?" Micah said, surprised.

"He said he never should have left barracks," Sera said, only to realize just what that meant. If Dylan had been going to the barracks and Rylan was there as well...

"Fuck," Micah swore, coming to his feet.

"What is it?" Tyrsten said, bracing for the bad news he had feared when he had walked up to them.

Instead of answering, Sera's mouth fell open at the strength of sending coming out of her brother. It was strange compared to their own speaking, a curl of targeted power and purpose where they usually worked in subtle bursts, but the strength of it left her seeing stars.

::Red bevy!:: Micah called with his warbard's strength. ::Back to barracks! Time now!::

"Damn, Mike," Tyrsten swore, eyes closed as he staggered back a step. "You really will be a Preem."

"I know, I know," he muttered, taking the lute back to hand to Sera as she recovered. "Stay here until I say it's safe, Sera. Kaitlyn, I'll see you tomorrow. Okay?"

"I'm going to get Vinicia," Sera said instead. "She can help, too."

"Sera—" Micah began, only to stop himself with the sharp look she gave him. "At least change first," he muttered.

As the boys turned to leave, Kaitlyn reached out for her arm. "Sera, we can check upstairs to see if she's with Counsel Lord Kiernan," she said. "She will be there if anywhere. Kreychi didn't come back from Court with me, so he is probably at the Delton Estate to get Sire Gaius settled."

Their plans set, Sera and Kaitlyn left the main area, though as they started down the hallway to Kaitlyn's suite, the door to their left suddenly opened as they passed. Looking back, they found Nichi standing in his flesh and feathers, gawking.

"Was that Micah?" He asked, realizing Sera and Kaitlyn were nearby. "Kait, what's going on?"

"I told you it was Micah," Westly said, coming up behind him. Westly didn't have a stitch on either, but given the worry, they clearly didn't care. "Come on, Nichi. We have to go."

"Dylan is in the Palace," Sera said, letting her fear finally show.

As Westly pulled Nichi back into their room to explain, Kaitlyn and Sera hurried down the hall. She was changed back into her Windover Blacks in no time, though all the tyros were gone when they made it to the front of the suite again.

"Do you really think she's just upstairs?" Sera asked as they moved onto the balcony. The front entrance was abandoned, which didn't make sense if Kiernan was supposed to be guarded by Blackwings. Then again, it was always easier to defend a door like that from the inside, so they could very well just be in his suite.

Sera watched as Kaitlyn came out onto the balcony behind her, rubbing at her eyes for all she was having a hard time seeing. Worried, Sera offered what Kaitlyn really needed: a hand. "Why don't we take the stairs?" She said, looking to the left where the dark, twisting staircase was hiding.

"Yes, please," Kaitlyn agreed, stepping back from the railing with relief. As she turned to join her, Sera caught up her hand and tucked it against the crook of her arm. In just the time it had taken to change and get to this place, the brown of Kaitlyn's eyes had clouded over completely with an eerie white film.

Hopefully, Vinicia can help with that as well...

They made their way down the long balcony to the stairs at the corner of the hall and then up to the next level. Sera stopped at the top riser, unsure where to go. "So, ah..." She began. "We can go back the way we came, or to the left."

"Left," Kaitlyn said, stumbling a bit as they turned. "It should be directly across from the Windover suite."

Sera patted Kaitlyn's hand on her arm and then started walking them forward. As they reached the center of the balcony, though, Kaitlyn winced.

"What is that?" She asked, reflexively covering her eyes.

"There is a big wooden door next to us and a small blue-black statute of a hawk sitting on a stack of books," Sera said, though when Kaitlyn went to look, she immediately flinched away.

"That's the Hawk," Kaitlyn explained, wistful no matter her pain. "Legend has it that Counsel Lord Kiernan's hawkeye came from this statue ages ago."

"You can't be serious," Sera laughed, but as they got close to it, she saw Kaitlyn was right. "It is literally the eye of a hawk?"

And then suddenly, Sera felt her wrist-cuff begin to warm. Looking down at it, a knot of fear grew in her belly. If this reacted to the Library as well, then was it something like a hawkeye? Her mother had said that the stone had opened the book that she held so dear, but once the pieces shattered, it had refused to work. That was when her mother had the pieces reassembled with gold to fill the cracks and mounted on the wrist cuff for safe keeping. Broken or not, she had continued to wear it until the day she died. Sera had worn it as well to honor her memory, but in ten cycles it had never been more than jewelry...

"Is something wrong?" Kaitlyn asked, as Sera stalled before the statue.

"No," Sera confessed, peering at the locking mechanism for the door. "I just wonder..."

Sera chewed her underlip. *If it would not work on the book, would it work on this door?*

Sera edged closer to the door as she thought, her wrist cuff continuing to warm against her arm, until suddenly she could move no further. *Odd.* Thinking back to the lessons her mother had taught her, she concentrated, focused her intention, and swept her arm forward as she would during the dance.

Shoulder, elbow, wrist...

As her fingers touched the door, Sera felt a power greater than herself swell in defense. Sera tried to draw her hand back, only to be caught by something she could not see.

"Did you honestly think a shattered falcon-stone would allow you into my domain?" a voice hissed, and Sera would have sworn it was in front of her.

"I... Ah..." Sera's heart was racing as she tried to pull her hand back. "I just..."

"What do you want, little loralae?" it demanded again, jerking her arm until she froze in place.

Just then, Sera saw Kaitlyn staring just in front of her and she looked furious.

"Let her go this instant!" Her friend commanded, absolutely unafraid.

The voice shifted towards Kaitlyn and was about to hiss once again when he suddenly looked concerned. A moment passed and Kaitlyn moved closer, trying to help Sera free her hand from whatever had grabbed her. Apparently, Kaitlyn could see it.

"Hewn! Get over here," it said, and Kaitlyn gasped as Sera felt a swell of magic passing through the wall, buffeting against the first.

"And you are?" The second voice asked, ignoring Sera for Kaitlyn.

Kaitlyn's face went white and Sera suddenly realized that Kaitlyn's eyes were focused, even though Sera couldn't tell what on. "Counsel Lord Hewn?" She gasped.

"Yes, fledgling," the second shade answered.

"Who are you to force entry to our realm with this sea-spawn?" The first sneered and Sera's arm was suddenly jarred for emphasis. "We already suffered one of you inside, and I will not stand for another."

"I am Dame Kaitlyn of House Aerie," Kaitlyn managed, finding her voice. "Consort to Third Counsel Lord Aaron." When that seemed to give both shades pause, she pressed on. "And we do not want into your Library. We want to leave. I demand that you release her this instant."

Sera was almost convinced they would listen until she heard the first shade burst into haunted laughter.

"And what does the Consort want with you?" Counsel Lord Hewn asked, confused.

"She, ah... She wants me to assist Counsel Lord Aaron," Kaitlyn answered, as if she was trying to keep a secret and failing. "To assist him in the Barracks. I am to replace Dame Vinicia in all things when she goes on Envoy with Counsel Lord Kiernan."

"I doubt you could replace her in *all* things," the first shade muttered, which only irritated Hewn.

"Do what she says," the Counsel Lord said. "If she knows about the Envoy, she is within Vinicia's confidences. you know where she is."

"Fine," the first shade huffed. "If she can see us, she has enough problems already."

And then all at once, Sera's arm was free and she went staggering into Kaitlyn beside her.

"Come inside," Counsel Lord Hewn said. "I do not wish to make a scene."

Kaitlyn's jaw was on the floor as the two of them felt a tremor in the air and then the heavy wooden door slid open to let them in. When it was big enough to get inside, Kaitlyn rushed in without a second thought. It was only Kaitlyn's grip on Sera's hand that kept her anywhere near the woman. Like or not, Sera wouldn't have gone inside on her own.

Sera jumped when she heard the door slide shut behind them and clung onto the cloak on her shoulders as Kaitlyn walked forward. As she moved, several glass globes blossom to life around them, revealing the otherwise hidden corners of what was most definitely a massive collection of books.

When Kaitlyn finally stopped to stare in wonder at the canopy of the tree, Sera scurried over to stand with her again.

"When did this start?" The first voice asked, and Kaitlyn's hand went to her temple. "You should not have the gift of Sight. It is not natural in you."

"Who are you to tell me I should not receive the blessing of Founder Iskander?" Kaitlyn challenged.

Meanwhile, Sera squinted until she had convinced herself she could just barely see the outline of a man standing just before them. Feeling the image shifting into place, she closed her eyes completely until the colors of the world inverted, letting her see the shades in trailing lines of power. It was something, at least.

"Sight this strong is not given by Iskander, fledgling," Hewn said, patient, but only just. "True secondsight comes from Aluvinor, Kerowyn, or Noventrio. For all your studies, you should know that much."

Kaitlyn blanched, realizing this man knew so much about her personal dealings. Then again, he was a Seventh, and as far as Sera was concerned, Sevenths knew far too much about everyone's personal dealings.

"It started just a few marks ago," Kaitlyn admitted. "I was watching, well..." She turned to look at Sera, revealing her from where she had been hiding behind Kaitlyn's wings.

"So this is your magic, little loralae?" The man asked, and Sera finally figured out how to see at the space where the ancestors shifted unnaturally in the otherwise stagnant room.

"It's a gift," she managed, rubbing at her eyes to see more clearly. "From my mother. She said she had magic once, but it passed on to my brother and I. It's just bardic magic, like you warbards..."

"You still wield far more power than you should, fledgling," Counsel Lord Hewn said, though his interest was certainly peaked. "And from the look of that hair, you are a long way from home. Very few of your kind have ever made it into our mountains."

"My mother was Ehkeski," Sera defended, glowering now that her vision seemed to have shifted more fully to let her see the ancestor spirits.

"Your mother was a loralae, to give you the darkwater sight you are using now," he scoffed, turning back to Kaitlyn. "And where were you during all of this?"

"I was watching her dance," Kaitlyn answered. "And then suddenly I could see it, see the magic. And, well, now I can't see at all."

"Indeed," Hewn agreed and then turned to call to another unseen shade in the Library. "Noventrio?" He said. "I believe you will want to see this."

"Noventrio," Kaitlyn gasped. "Founder Noventrio? The First Seventh Counsel Lord?"

After a few heartbeats, the one called Noventrio appeared as a disembodied head just next to Hewn. Unlike the Counsel Lord, though, Sera could see this one clearly. For all his power, this third shade was silver white with a slender face, a sharply hooked nose, and a long, thin mustache that trailed down where his chest would have been if he had cared to fully materialize.

As Noventrio stirred to speak, Sera heard the howl of the Ice Winds that had taken her mother in his voice. It was the same winds that had attempted to take her life only two cycles ago.

"This secondsight is from Kerowyn," the Founder said, with a tenor that chilled Sera's very soul. "But I can still use it," he decided, and then the rest of his body suddenly appeared before Kaitlyn. "Come here, fledgling."

Once revealed, Sera saw this shade was like no man she had ever seen. He was three paces tall, older than old, and dressed in an incredibly elaborate kama that hid most of his body. More importantly, as he stepped more fully into the space, his wings, all nine of them, glowed with white fire that threatened to blind her.

Before Kaitlyn could move, the Founder took her head in his hands, palms pressed over her eyes. Though there was no place for a draft this high in the Palace, Sera had to grab at her flight cloak to keep it from swirling in the wind the ancient being drew to himself.

Kaitlyn stood like a stone, her mouth open in awe. With her hands covering his on the sides of her face, Kaitlyn was caught up in his presence. Noventrio leaned into her, kissing Kaitlyn full on the mouth before drawing away. Kaitlyn inhaled, gasping, and Sera could see the silver magic linking the two of them together.

"Kerowyn was right to send you to me, though I thought we had agreed to wait until Spring," he said, frowning. "I suppose Vinicia will teach you the sight and the rest can wait until then," Noventrio went on, offering his hand. "Do not bother yourself with any temple other than mine. It is my work you will serve now, not my sister's."

When he was finished speaking, Kaitlyn looked down to the Founder's hand and gasped to see the small, blue-black stone he was offering.

"Is this...?" She asked, her hand shaking as she picked up the stone.

"Your way into my Library," the Founder answered. "Someone will need to tend to it when Vinicia is gone."

As he vanished, Counsel Lord Hewn let out a soft scoff of surprise.

"I do not believe he has ever done that," he observed, as struck by the events as they were.

"I can see," Kaitlyn said, coming back to herself. "I can see, and a Founder gave me a hawkeye. I—Oh, Gods..."

Sera swore as she realized what was happening, and it was all she could do to grab the woman before she fainted.

"Help!" Sera called, trying to keep Kaitlyn on her feet as Hewn looked on. "Anyone! Help!"

CHAPTER 29: RYLAN

Saturday, 21:00

"There's no one here to help you, little brother," Dylan said, spreading his wings to take up space in the doorway to Rylan's small room. Given the Tournament tomorrow, Rylan had been dimming his lantern when he'd heard a strange sound in the barracks. Someone was going through the hallway one room at a time, and for all he was used to hearing Mother's voice demanding they present themselves during a nest check, the silence that moved with this search had made his blood run cold. Fearing the worst, he'd managed to get out of his nest and grab Micah's heavy crossbow before the door to his own suite had swung open.

Rylan and his brother were in a stalemate now, with Dylan leering violence from the door while Rylan stood in his small clothes with his weapon drawn. Though the one bolt he had grabbed was tipped with warshot, contraband in training but deadly on the Plains, it was Rylan's only defense. If he loosed the shot and missed, Dylan would kill him with the wingblades he held pressed against the threshold. If he hit, however, Dylan would bleed out long before he found anyone to help him. The barracks were that empty.

"We could do this the easy way, you realize?" Dylan said, head tilting as Rylan pulled the crossbow harder against his shoulder. "You could just forfeit your rights to the Estate like the rest of the family."

"The House is mine, Dylan," Rylan swore, hating himself for how his hand was frozen on the side of the weapon. "You left, but I stayed. I'm the only one who hasn't given up on it, and I'm not going to do it just so you can get paid."

"Northern is dead, you idiot," Dylan scoffed. "It has been for cycles. The only thing of value is the Estate, and if I have to kill you to get it," he said, flexing his hands. "So be it."

Rylan took a breath to steady his nerves. Every time Dylan did something to ruin his life, Rylan swore he would kill him, but standing face to face like this... Dylan knew Rylan would never pull that trigger.

"Fuck you, Dylan," Rylan swore, hating how he had once worshiped his older brother.

As the seventh son of House Northern, Rylan had always known he would never earn his father's praise, but Dylan? Rylan had worshipped the ground he walked on while the rest of their brothers danced through Court. Dylan had loved every moment of it, too, eventually teaching Rylan to steal little things for him or using Rylan as a distraction while he snuck into the greater city. When Rylan was old enough, they became their own little House Northern Warhost, with Rylan playing at being the Seventh Counsel Lord and Dylan going on 'missions' into the Delton streets. It had all been in good fun for cycles, with Dylan bringing back treasure and stories of mischief, but when the House had started to fall...

Rylan's breath hitched as his mind flooded with memories.

When the House had arranged Dylan's marriage to a guild woman in Kelishe for an obscene amount of money, his brother had made a plan. While he had told Rylan it was just another game of Founder and Warhost, what Dylan had actually done was join a crew of men on the Streets. Realizing too late that their Son had fled, the family had turned on Rylan, demanding to know where Dylan had gone, but Rylan didn't know. Dylan had always come back from the 'War Plains', having promised not to leave him alone with the family that always ignored him. When Rylan was told that Dylan was dead, dead to the House at least, what Rylan had heard was that Dylan had died at war. Their own little 'war', sure, but Rylan had been seven cycles old. All he knew was that he had sent his brother out on mission and now he was never coming back.

Given the hysterical tantrum he had thrown over losing his brother, the family had locked Rylan in the House's unused library to calm down. With little time for a fledgling, his father had decided to drown him in Seventh's Lore so he might be sent to the Delton Academy as a tyro, no matter the rest of the family's failure. Rylan was told that the fate of the House depended on his learning everything he could about the Sevenths, but the terror of having killed his brother and being so utterly alone had eaten him alive. If he was going to be the Lord Seventh like he had promised in their Founder's temple, no one would ever die on his watch. Never again. He would end the War before he ever helped anyone fight it.

Cycles later when Rylan had found out Dylan was actually alive, he had nearly lost his mind. Suddenly the wild panic and grief he had smothered with academics roared to life again, manifesting not as a violent temper, but as a Gift for fire-starting that had nearly destroyed the Estate. Worse, when Rylan had fled that chaos to find his beloved brother on the Streets, Dylan had turned on him like the rest of the family.

Rylan was a fire-starter, a sorcerer, and an utter disgrace.

Rylan regripped the crossbow as his eyes burned.

You did this to me, he wanted to scream. *You lit this fire in me and now I can't put it out!*

Dylan's smirk to see Rylan's tears of rage almost did him in.

"Why do you want it, anyway?" Dylan asked, changing tactics as he shifted at the threshold of the room. "You promised our ancestors you would be a Lord Seventh, didn't you? Promised them you would bring Glory to the House of the Northern Lights."

His hail was a mockery of their vaulted lineage, and no matter how far it had fallen, Rylan stood his ground. Convinced as he still was of the Seventh's purpose to find peace on the War Plains, his Barracks Mother had shown him how serving as a Seventh's man could restore the Honor of his fallen House. Vinicia had given him a way to find the Glory at war that Kosar truly needed, and even if it wasn't what his House had demanded of him, it was what his ancestors had spoken of in the ancient texts. Kosar was founded to give peace to windwalkers, not to give them a place to rest while they planned for the next fight.

So no matter all Dylan had done to destroy him, Rylan meant to turn the violence of his youth into a true fire of purpose. If Kosar needed a Counsel Lord who fought for the kind of peace that would end a war, Rylan could be a part of that fight by rebuilding the Glory of Founder Noventrio's own noble House.

"You only want the Estate so you can sell it," Rylan said, his grip white-knuckle tight.

"What I want is your wings on my wall, " Dylan said, eyes narrowing with contempt. "You're the reason the House fell in the first place, and I'm the only one left to make you pay for it."

"What the fuck, Dylan?" Rylan swore. "I did everything they asked of me until our ancestors gave me this Gift, but now you want me dead? Why?"

"Because it wasn't a Gift, it was a curse, you fucking idiot," Dylan snapped, coming a step inside the room. "You were the Founder's pyre to what remained of our House and I should have killed you cycles ago. The Estate would be mine without a fight if I had," he said, though he seemed as angry with himself as he was with Rylan. "But, since I couldn't slit the throat of my fledgling brother, I waited until you were old enough to join the Legions. I almost had you until you got this fucking commission. Blood and ice, Rylan, you're such a pain in my ass."

"No more than you are in mine," Rylan shot back, moving his finger to the trigger at last. "But I have something worth fighting for, and that gives me an edge. Put the weapons down, Dylan, or I will end this."

Dylan's smirk was all the warning he had to realize someone had gotten on their belly behind his brother. Rylan had a heartbeat to register the crossbow being aimed between Dylan's legs before the shot snapped forward.

Fuck, Rylan thought, glad for every one of Mother's foxdrops as he threw himself to the floor. As the bolt shattered the window behind him, Rylan's warshot took out the man between Dylan's legs. The crewman screamed as Rylan caught himself on the ground, wings tight behind him as the Ice Winds ripped through the room. As Dylan rushed him, Rylan pushed off the ground, bringing the crossbow up in a wild swing.

Knowing it for Rylan's only move, Dylan stalled as he lunged, dodging the swing to step in and drive the point of the heavy, palm-wide wingblade into Rylan's neck. Or at least, he tried to when there was a sudden sound of steel-on-steel and another burst of wind shoved Rylan to the side. Pin feathers now standing on end, Rylan used the momentum to twist out of the way of his brother's blade, though both he and Dylan were gawking as an uncanny sliver of moonlight swirled out of the room.

"What the fuck was that?" Dylan demanded, as Rylan put a hand to his neck.

He should have been dead. He should have—

Rylan's heart was in his throat as he heard Tyrsten's voice booming through the hallway. Arrogant as the crewmen were, they were nothing compared to the sound of a forty-strong bevy swelling into the space. With only one exit open to them, the man Rylan had wounded threw himself towards Rylan's shattered window.

Swearing for all the commotion, Rylan scrambled onto the platform beside his nest, pressing his wings against the wall as the crew-men shot past. Dylan remained a moment longer, though Rylan's heart stopped when Dylan picked up the daystar lantern. The murderous rage in his look was the last thing Rylan saw before his world erupted in flames.

I'm going to die, he knew, twelve cycles old again as the lantern shattered just beside his head. Dropping onto his heels, Rylan screamed as oil coated his wings and flared to life. As he tried to call for help, acrid smoke burned his lungs, and what hadn't caught on him was roaring to life in the nest. Had his gift gone wild again or was it the lantern fire? Did it even matter? Either way he was going to die.

::"Rylan, get out of there!":: Tyrsten screamed, the command in his voice so powerful that it clawed through Rylan's panic. *::"Rylan!"::*

A moment later someone threw a blanket over his wings, dragging him onto the floor so others could smother the fire in the nest. As the roar of the flames transformed to stifling heat, Rylan knew what would come next. The only thing left for him was agony.

"Westly! Someone get Westly!"

Rylan's consciousness floated outside of his body as he dissolved into screaming chaos. The fire was out now, but as they pulled the blankets off of him, his flesh and feathers were being ripped away. As he screamed, the men of the Red Bevy seemed to realize just what kind of horror Rylan had been fighting his entire life. What kind of enemy made him not care at all about a bunch of women on the other side of the world.

The sound of Micah pushing through the crowd threw Rylan back into his body, realizing what his crew brother, his actual family, might do when he saw what Dylan had managed. Rylan had felt the same when he had seen the bruises on Sera's body, though her own gift had settled his anger. Micah was different, though. Micah—

"Where is that bastard!" Micah seethed, pushing into the room only to get thrown against his desk by Tyrsten. "I'll kill him!"

"No, you won't," Tyrsten swore, using all of his strength to pin Micah against the desk. Micah's eyes were wild as more men came into the room, further blocking his path until Tyrsten flared his wings to dominate the space. ::"Micah, stop! Rylan needs you! Look at him!"::

It took Tyrsten's strength as a warbard and Rylan's sobbing panic to cut through Micah's rage, but he came back to himself in a rush. As vengeance gave over to terror, Rylan cowered back from Tyrsten and Raleigh as they got ready to lift him from the floor. Rylan didn't want to move. He didn't want to do anything. Gods, he just wanted to die.

"Make way!" Raleigh said, grabbing onto Rylan's arm as Ren got the other. "And get a shower going!"

Rylan clenched his jaw as they lifted him, tears streaming down his face as he was moved into the hall past Micah. His crew brother had gone white as a sheet, though the moment their eyes locked, Micah's whole demeanor changed.

Everything hurts, Rylan sobbed, knowing his brother could hear him. *Gods, it feels like I'm still on fire.*

As the two men got him out in the hallway, Micah shoved past Tyrsten to stay with him.

::I've got you, Ry,:: Micah sent, setting a hand on Rylan's back to make his bardic talent that much stronger. ::Wes is coming. Sera's gone for help. You're going to be all right.::

Rylan let his crew-brother's bardic gift wash over him, numb to all else as Micah's strength overwhelmed his mind. Legs dragging behind him, the whole of the bevy made way as Micah kept up with them, eventually trading places with Raleigh so he could start his chiurgeon's work.

Rylan's pride broke as he entered the showers, though the icy shock was almost a relief. Head hanging towards his chest, the pressure of the water seared down his neck and between his wings, but Micah was still with him. Rylan closed his eyes as he saw lanterns moving towards them, whimpering until Micah set his head to Rylan's temple to keep his focus. As terrified as Rylan was, Raleigh needed to see what he was working with if Rylan was going to survive.

By the time Raleigh got to work pulling glass shards out of blistering skin, it sounded like the whole of the bevy was inside the room. Every single one of them was on the edge of fury to realize one of their own had been hurt. Not only that, but he had been attacked inside their home in one of the most obscene ways a Kosaran could imagine. Your body was burned when it was sent to the gods, not when it was living flesh and feathers.

Just when Rylan felt like he would faint, the tension in the room suddenly sharpened.

"Make a hole!" Someone called. "Everyone! *Move!*"

A few heartbeats later, Rylan was dragged out of the icy water and turned so that Westly could set hands on him. Rylan shivered to feel the cold giving way to burning once again, but it wouldn't last for long.

"If any of you have a problem with my magic," Westly said, letting his voice carry. "Get out, now."

No one moved.

"Gods, this is bad," Westly swore, picking Rylan's head up to steady him. "Rylan, are you ready?"

"Just do it," Micah said when Rylan could only sob,

A heartbeat later, pain flared along Rylan's body again, but for once in his life, the icy feel of Westly's magic against his own gift for firestarting was a welcome relief. More than that, Westly's strength seemed to have grown dramatically in the few candlemarks they had been apart, though with the look of the lover's mark on his neck... If Westly had come into his power, then this miracle that was tearing through him was just the start of his crew brother's true strength.

Rylan wasn't the only one left gasping as the blinding light of Westly's magic began to ebb. Westly looked worse for wear, and as Rylan shivered to feel the wild itch of his healing skin and regrowing feathers, his strength began to return as well.

All at once he was hungrier than he had ever been in his life and more exhausted than he could imagine, but he was no longer on fire.

"Holy shit, Westly," said a voice from the rear. It was Tyrsten, coming up beside them. "You're some kind of miracle."

"Please don't tell anyone," Westly panted, ducking from the praise as exhaustion swept through him. "I can't do this... I can't do this for the Warhost. I just..."

Nichi's strength was beneath him before he fainted, as was Tyrsten's, realizing he was about to drop.

"Don't tell Mother," Rylan said, leaning on Micah as Ren stepped away to give them more space. "Please don't tell Mother what happened. She'll blame herself and it was all my fault."

"None of that was your fault, Rylan," said a voice behind them.

As Rylan turned to see who had spoken, he was startled to realize it wasn't only the Red Bevy who had answered Micah's call. Fionn and his Green Bevy were here as well. They all wanted answers of who had dared to come into their home and hurt their friend.

"My brother," Rylan said, unsure how to explain just what had happened. "He wants to kill me and take the title to the House Northern estate."

"He wants to kill you?" Fionn balked. "Rylan he almost did."

"Why didn't you tell anyone?" someone else asked.

"We're all here for you."

Rylan didn't know what to say.

"I thought..." he began, truly shocked as he looked around the room. "I thought you all hated me. And Mother was helping me, so I just... Gods, she knows how important this all used to be to me."

"Used to be?" Fionn repeated, incredulous. "Holy fuck, Rylan. You care more about this shit than most of us. If you didn't, you wouldn't still be here. You wouldn't have been made Bevy Primarch, either. Lord Seventh himself sees something in you, and you think we hate you? Gods above, you're probably going to end up apprenticed to one of his Primarchs, same as Micah. You're the last son of House Northern," he insisted, and for once Rylan didn't hear a trace of contempt in the words. "We don't hate you. We want to serve with you."

Rylan's jaw was on the floor, though as he looked around the room, it was clear no one disagreed.

"Honor to the Host!" Tyrsten called beside him, setting a hand on Rylan's wing in solidarity.

"Glory to the House of the Northern Lights!" the century of his brothers called in return.

It was the ancient cry of the Warhost; the one that had inspired him as a fledgling to pledge to work towards an end to the war. Hearing it on the lips of so many of his brothers-in-arms, Rylan was absolutely speechless.

As his vision of the room blurred under the force of his tears, Micah had to resettle his grip to keep him on his feet. "They like you, asshole," he whispered, though there was affection in the words. "It's why I wanted you to come revel with us the past two cycles."

Rylan shifted to elbow his crew-brother in the ribs, only to grunt as Micah pulled him into an embrace instead. He was falling apart, and as Tyrsten went on speaking, Rylan buried his head in Micah's neck.

"Starting right now," Tyrsten called, speaking as their Tyro Primarch perhaps for the last time. "We're posting rotating shifts on our boy. Our own shadow guard for our honorary Seventh," he added, pride in his voice as he said the words. "We'll see you graduated whether your asshole brother likes it or not. Whether you like it or not, too," he added. "Our chirons can fly a litter through the Ice Winds if it's needed."

The last, as ridiculous as it was, turned Rylan's tears into laughter.

"For now, we'll put him up in Nichi's room. That's the warmest room on the floor and it only has the one exit. Nichi," Tyrsten added, and Rylan managed to look up as his friend came near. "You're sharing Wes' nest now, right?"

"I am," Nichi said, his arm still around Westly's shoulders.

"Good," Tyrsten grinned. "As for Rylan's request, no one needs to tell Mother. She's moved on to bigger things and we've got this? Right?"

"Hoi!" Called the bevies in return.

"For Honor and Glory!"

Rylan sucked in a breath as his brothers gave a rousing cheer, picking up his head as he realized the family of four he had fought so hard to keep had somehow grown into over eighty men. As Micah shifted to walk him out of the barracks, for the first time in his life, Rylan actually felt like a part of them. They had all come to his defense, swelling into the halls when all he had hoped was that Micah might somehow realize he was gone; that he was in trouble again after striking out on his own.

As they parted to let him through the room, however, all Rylan could think about was how that sliver of moonlight had saved his life. He should have been dead, but something had stopped his brother's knife. Strange as that was, it had reminded him of the whisper of wind he had felt inside his ancestor's temple. Maybe his ancestors were watching out for him after all.

CHAPTER 30: VINICIA

Saturday, 22:00

"This is all my fault," Vinicia said, pulling her mind back from the chaos of the tyro barracks. Kiernan had felt the panic surging through his Seventh's Gift as well, though he had grabbed her before she could leave the Library. The fact that she was too exhausted to shove him off had only made her more upset. Even if she had been able to make it to Rylan, she didn't have the strength to heal him—not after healing so many others the day before.

"But I did this to him," she said, washing her hands over her face. "I made him a target. If I had only thought who else might want that title instead of throwing my weight around, this wouldn't have happened."

"You can't change the past, Vinicia," Kiernan insisted as she dug her hands into When he moved to stop her from pulling at it, she froze as his touch closed the circle of power between them. He let go of her immediately, but the damage had already been done.

"I'm sorry," he said, hands held up for peace. "Vin, I didn't mean..."

Vinicia was about to scream at him to get out, to just leave the Library and stay with his Blackwings where it was safe, when she felt a shiver run down her spine. A moment later there was a knock on the door to her suite of apartments, one she had left open as Kiernan had entertained himself in the Library while she packed, and she looked up to see the silver-blue shade of Counsel Lord Weylan watching them.

"Vinicia, there are two women who have come inside Library looking for you," he said, concerned as he realized she had been falling apart.

"Inside?" Vinicia balked. "What do you mean inside?"

"Hewn let them in," Weylan shrugged. "He sent me to fetch you, so I do not know more than that."

Pulling her mind out of the tyro barracks completely, Vinicia could hear a woman's cry for help filtering down from the top-most level. As she got to her feet, however, dizziness swept through her, and it was only Kiernan's hand on her arm that kept her from falling.

"Just step," Kiernan said. "You can do that with my strength, I know you can."

Vinicia grit her teeth, wanting to protest even if the man was right. With a moment to focus, she stepped them from her apartments and onto the highest floor of the massive Library. Orienting themselves, they found where Hewn's shade was hovering next to a pile of wings.

"There they are," Kiernan said anyway.

If he explains the obvious one more time...

Vinicia silenced the thought as she pulled free of Kiernan's hand at last.

"Sera?" She called. "What's going on?"

As they reached the girls, Sera's eyes were wide with panic, but it didn't appear that they were hurt.

"She fainted on me," Sera managed, having to squint as the glow-bulbs in the Library burned brightly with Kiernan's presence. It might have been daylight inside this place, even if it was five marks past sun-down.

"They were looking for you, so I opened the door," Hewn explained, watching as Kiernan helped pick up Kaitlyn so that Sera could get to her feet. "They would have never found you if I hadn't."

"Aren't you not supposed to be able to do that?" Vinicia asked, arms crossed over her chest to keep herself from helping. She was already dizzy again with Kiernan just a few steps away. "I thought the Library was sealed to keep you all inside."

"That's what we thought as well," said another voice and Vinicia watched Counsel Lord Broc appear beside Hewn.

"Is the seal weakening?" She asked.

"More like you bored a hole in it, living here so long," Broc said, reappearing beside her. "Noventrio thinks he's the only one who can use it, but we've slipped out a few times."

Vinicia sighed but didn't press him more, especially not as Kaitlyn roused.

"Kaitlyn, love," Vinicia said, catching the young woman's attention. As Kaitlyn looked up, however, Vinicia tried not to swear as she saw her eyes had gone silver-white. "Kaitlyn, what's going on?"

"Vinicia?" Kaitlyn asked, confused as she tried to sort herself. "Where...?"

"We went into the Library," Sera reminded. "And you saw the—"

"The books!" Kaitlyn exclaimed, awake all at once. As she searched around, her eyes fell on Vinicia and Kiernan before truly realizing who they were. "And the— The Founder!" She gasped, opening her hand once again. "Oh Gods, it wasn't a dream!"

"Blood and ice," Vinicia swore, knowing the hawkeye for what it was. It was certainly small—small enough to be set in a ring—but it was a hawkeye all the same.

"Don't lose that," Vinicia said, folding the woman's hand around it for safe keeping. "He must have given it to you for a reason."

"The High Consort has a project for me," Kaitlyn said as Kiernan helped Sera to stand as well. "I'm supposed to be looking into the Consort's duty to Founder Kerowyn and how she can be released from it. She wants to know what will happen to her when Kiernan returns," she said, and then seemed to realize that Kiernan was standing in front of her. "Ah, I mean, Counsel Lord."

"Just Kiernan, Kait," he acknowledged, trying to sooth her until he faltered to realize he didn't know the other woman. "And you are Sera, I take it? Rylan's Sera?"

"Yes," Vinicia confirmed. "Kiernan, this is Seraleia du'Delton of House Windover," she said, making the formal introduction.

"Well met, Sera," Kiernan greeted. "I believe I owe you an apology."

Sera wasn't sure what to make of that, but curtsied nonetheless. "Counsel Lord," she responded.

Vinicia spoke next to shift the conversation to why the two women were here. "Counsel Lord Hewn said you were looking for me?" She prompted.

"We, ah," Kaitlyn began, looking to Sera for support.

Sera took her hand, but both remained anxious and pale.

"We found out who is going to take the shot on Counsel Lord Kiernan tomorrow," Sera said, and Vinicia was glad the girl cut to the quick. "Him, whoever he means to name as his Counselheir, and Rylan."

Now their hesitancy made sense. These were not light allegations.

"Where did you hear this?" Kiernan asked carefully.

"Wenda told us," Sera answered and then looked to Vinicia. "Wenda is the crew leader that was trying to kill me when you came to get me from House Northern. She and the others are the ones being adopted into House Kirath."

"I remember," Vinicia confirmed. "But why did she tell you such a thing? Is she still coming after you?"

"Oh! No," Sera said, seeing her mistake. "We, ah, I mean Micah and I, we…"

As Sera hesitated, Kaitlyn found her voice again. "Dylan, Rylan's first-brother, seems to think that if he kills Rylan, his claim will be stronger when the case is made for the title. Killing you, Ser, earns them the right to be part of House Kirath when it forms, but if they can kill your Counselheir, then there is some sort of bonus. It is all blood money and foul, so I am not sure."

That was an incredible understatement of the truth.

"And Rylan?" Vinicia pressed, glancing at Kiernan. "What does any of this have to do with Rylan?"

"Rylan has the best claim to the title for House Northern," Kaitlyn said. "But Dylan can also claim it and sell it to House Kirath. If Rylan is dead, though, then the Estate can go to Dylan uncontested."

"But Dylan was the one who beat up Rylan and turned him into the guard for the bounty before they came after me," Sera said. "Someone told them they can't kill Rylan until he has it, but that won't stop Dylan if he has a chance to take it."

Vinicia felt like she was getting whiplash looking between the two women.

"So what happened tonight?" She insisted. "I know something happened in the barracks. It is over now, whatever it was, but there is a reason that I draw a hard line between House politics and Tyro training. There is a reason you should as well, Kaitlyn, if you are taking over for me."

"Of course, Mother," Kaitlyn said, standing taller with the command.

Seeing the tension between the two women, Sera answered this time. "Dylan was in the Palace with the House Kirath flock this evening," she explained. "When he came into Windover, he was taunting Rylan, so Rylan went back to the barracks to get away from it. But when Wenda started talking to us, she said that was where Dylan was going to find a good place to line up the shot on you, Ser, for tomorrow. Micah took the Red Bevy boys back to the barracks when we came here, so they must have found him."

"Yes, I heard the call myself. He can apparently call to the Host no matter my attempt to block him, and the tyros have dealt with the situation," Kiernan said. "Vinicia, you know that. You also know there is nothing you can do right now."

"I know there is nothing I can do," Vinicia snapped, pulling away from him. "I do not need to be reminded."

Kiernan raised his hands for peace, taking a step back as he dropped his wings low. Fragile as she was, Vinicia could only look away, counting to ten in every language she knew as she tried to control herself. She would have given the world to hear her ancestor's voice once again. That calm, clever mind could always soothe her anger, but the voice had fled ever since Kiernan had joined her. If the voice never returned and all Vinicia had for a companion was this man for the rest of her life, she might not make it.

"Thank you so much for telling us this, both of you," Kiernan said. "One thing I don't understand, however, is why this Wenda person told you at all. What is in it for her to reveal their plan? Does she want something in return from you?"

"She was, ah," Sera began, stumbling through her thought. "I mean, Micah and I—"

"They used their bardic magic," Kaitlyn said, interrupting. "That's why we wanted to find Mother. She might be the only person who would believe us."

Sera paled to realize everyone was suddenly looking at her. "When we were fledglings," she began, hesitant. "My mother taught Micah how to play and taught me how to dance. She was Ehkeski, you see…"

"Just what do these abilities do?" Vinicia asked before they got the girls' life story.

"They work together," Sera answered, pressing the tips of her first fingers together as if to demonstrate. "Micah plays his music, I perform to focus everyone's attention, and then he suggests that they be more friendly towards us. The better a reaction I can get from them, the stronger Micah can press them into doing what we wanted. Tonight we were just trying to make sure the House liked us since the other crew was there. The problem is that we built up so much power between us that when the dance was over, Wenda was near moon-struck with Micah. She just came up to us and started hanging all over him, and Micah suggested we could help if she let us know what the plan was. She came right out and said it."

"Well, all right then," Kiernan said, exhaling slowly. It was one thing to distract yourself from the idea of assassins. It was an entirely different thing to know who they were and when they were coming after you.

"You believe us?" Sera asked, surprised.

"I was an empath long before I was a Counsel Lord," Kiernan confided. "That's one of the reasons I could be a Seventh. Founder Noventrio enhanced my talent into his Gift when I became his Counsel Lord. So yes, I believe you."

Instead of being consoled, though, Sera just chewed her lip.

"Kaitlyn," Vinicia pressed, her tone gentle but firm. "You mentioned that Founder Noventrio appeared to you? Did he give you the godseyes? Could you both see him?"

"I couldn't see anything until I came inside the Library," Sera said into the silence. "But I could hear them. That older one's voice... It sounded like the Ice Winds."

As Sera shivered with the thought, Kaitlyn reached around the girl with a wing to offer her support.

"Windover has never had a Seventh Counsel Lord in our family," Kaitlyn added. "I shouldn't be able to see him. I shouldn't be able to speak with him. Not a Founder..."

"Noventrio is stronger than he lets on," Kiernan explained, and Kaitlyn didn't like the uneasiness in his voice. "When I took up the Seat, I didn't have a Counsel Lord in my line either," he said, taking hold of his hawkeye. He closed his eyes, concentrated, and then opened them again to reveal the double godseyes of his own secondsight. "But I was given the same sort of Gift, if for a different purpose."

Kaitlyn looked ready to faint again.

"Kaitlyn, did you have the start of a Gift before you came in here?" Vinicia asked gently. "Noventrio can only work with someone who is gifted in their own right. He can enhance and focus it, but not grant it from nothing."

When Kaitlyn looked down to the floor between them, Vinicia was sure she was right.

"My eyes had been hurting a lot lately," she admitted. "When you went to help Micah, when Sera was dancing... I didn't know what it was. I thought I was just getting headaches like my mother when she was my age," she admitted. "None of my stories say anything about developing a secondsight. Anything like that is held closely by the priesthood."

Kiernan let out a breath, looking around the massive library before blinking out of his godseyes. "If you walked in with a Gift like that, it is no wonder Noventrio took you for his own," he said. "It is a very rare thing for anyone to see a Seventh's shade, but Noventrio is an opportunist if I have ever known one. If it was becoming active, then he only had to focus it and lock it into place."

"That is what they say about a priestess gaining a godseye," Kaitlyn said, her confidence building. "That it comes from an ancestor's blessing. But why would a Founder I have no connection to give me a double godseye?"

"Because you had strength enough for them," Vinicia answered. "A left-sided godseye allows clergy to see the spirits of our ancestors on this side of the veil. A double godseye means you can see the spirits of all ancestors or perhaps the elemental flows, like I can. Whatever this is, your irises shouldn't go grey like Consort Lenae's, however. That is Founder Kerowyn's blessing to her High Priestess, though if you serve on Lenae's new Court, I suppose you may also be touched by her Founder's power. Let us hope they brown when you don't have them active."

"So it was magic that I saw when Sera was dancing," Kaitlyn said, glancing to the other girl with a cautious smile.

"Most likely, yes," Vinicia answered, though it looked as if Kaitlyn's wonder was short lived.

"Founder Noventrio said I wasn't to go to any temple other than his, which I assume is this place," she said, uncertain now. "He said he wanted you to teach me instead. Can you do that?"

Vinicia didn't know what to say. Tomorrow she and Kiernan would leave for Illiandria, and Kaitlyn was to stay here and take her place. But if the tyros wouldn't be back until spring, Kaitlyn could come with them to Illiandria. Well, not with them through the pillars, but she could likely make it on the gondola network before winter truly set in.

"Or Westly could teach her," Kiernan suggested. "He has the secondsight as well. She could learn a lot from Westly over the winter."

"Possibly," Vinicia hedged. "But if Noventrio sent her to me, then it may have more to do with my presence in the Library than just secondsight. I will check with him come dawning."

"Because there is nothing to be done about it now," Kiernan agreed, his words a warning. "Vinicia, we should get you back into your tree. You were doing better when you were resting."

"Tree?" Kaitlyn repeated, suddenly remembering the enormous tree that was enclosed by the Library. "Is that your hearth tree?"

"It is Founder Noventrio's temple tree, but it serves for a hearth," Vinicia answered. "It is also where I have lived as Barracks Mother, so you will need to find different accommodations."

"I should think so," Kaitlyn said, attempting a laugh.

As she looked to Sera, Kiernan took charge of the situation. "Thank you for coming to tell us, ladies," he said, giving them an exit. "Vinicia and I can handle things from here."

"Of course," Sera said, standing to leave.

"And no more magic around this one," Vinicia added, gesturing to Kaitlyn. "Not until I've had a chance to speak with Westly. I think you may be receiving the overflow from him, since you spent so much time together. You and your brother. Do you think you can manage that?"

"Yes, Mother," Sera answered. "As long as you take care of yourself."

Vinicia bit back her response, knowing the words for kindness. Kiernan she would snipe at, but Sera clearly meant her no ill will.

"Good winds to you both," Vinicia said instead, finding the strength to rise and escort them to the exit.

"And to you, Mother," Kaitlyn said, and then both girls gave soft courtesies before taking their leave.

When the door was shut and sealed again, Vinicia looked back to Kiernan, only to find him pensive.

"Vinicia, if they mean to attack Rylan, I should have a guard set on him," he said. "A Blackwing guard until a Shadow Guard can be appointed. Roder will want to have Blackwings on him anyway, though he may prefer the boy dead rather than named my Counselheir."

"He has the tyros," Vinicia said, shaking her head. "If you mean to save announcing his position until he has graduated, then you cannot play your hand. Dangerous as it is, he has a century of men with him to protect him."

"Yes, but they may only think to protect him from those crewmen," Kiernan insisted.

"They are protecting him from the Houses," Vinicia said, moving past him to return to the canopy so they could make their way down. "And for all their noble blood, they know how serious that game can be."

"True," he acknowledged, joining her. "In the end, Rylan is in no more danger than he was yesterday or the day before."

"We should keep an eye on him tomorrow, though," she admitted, feeling the weight of the world on her wings. "I could do it, but I would have to split myself in two to stay by your side."

"I mean to spend the bulk of the day with Lenae, if that is any help," Kiernan offered, following a pace behind her.

He was giving her space, but for as much as she wanted to be alone, being without him seemed impossible now. For as horrible as she had felt just a few dawnings before, his subtle company made her feel worlds better. He clearly felt the same, since it had been her power burning him up after he had taken off his hawkeye. He was cooler now given the lesser strength of the true Seventh's hawkeye, but it pooled in him all the same.

Vinicia let out a long breath. "I was thinking of sending Sera out into the winds with Rylan to watch over him," she said, hesitant to broach the subject, but confident in it nonetheless. "She may be able to guard him in a way none of the tyros could."

"It has worked for me," Kiernan said, and the smile he wore as he joined her at the edge of the canopy was a balm to her frustration.

"Behind every great man is a woman worth twice his weight in salt, eh?" Vinicia returned, only to be confused by the look he gave her. "What?"

"Of course you would quote a Lan'lieanan treatise on warfare to make a point," he said, laughing as the tension between them eased. "You really are something else, Vin."

Before she could do more than stare confusion at him, Kiernan offered his hand so she could Step them back into her suites.

Vinicia took it and when she opened her eyes again they were standing in her apartments. As he turned to find where they had left their evening meal, Vinicia went to close the door to the Library.

That done, she shifted to rejoin him at the table, only to realize how cold she had gotten being outside the tree. That cold had made her so sick in the days before she had met him, as if lacking the energy of her tyros in the barracks was like stripping off every bit of protection she had against the Ice Winds. Now, just standing in this place with him, she could not deny how he simply radiated power.

Every touch, every movement... Even the curious look he turned on her felt like he was holding out a hand, offering it to her if she would only accept. The duty to his seat was a compliment to her own purpose and his mere existence made standing in the torrent of the rest of her life that much easier.

She hated it so much.

It was an infuriating thing to have to need anyone in her life after so long doing without, while at the same time a relief to know she could lean on someone—anyone—for even a moment. Clearly she was her own woman and she could handle herself, but he could also gift her the fuel that she desperately needed. For all she had healed him when she had fractured his knee, she could gift him her own power at will, but it took Kiernan himself to close that circle through Noventrio's shield against her. Curious as she was to understand the true nature of that bond, she was still hesitant to touch him. Just being around him was heady enough.

Then again, if the power I ground pools inside this tree for Noventrio's use...

Vinicia came back to herself in a rush only to find him studying her.

"What?" She demanded.

"There is such a change in you when you are in this place compared to out there," Kiernan observed. "Especially with the door closed."

Vinicia shrugged. "I close the circle of my own power when I am in this place," she explained. "When less can escape my control, I'm not nearly so exhausted."

And yet I am still suffering, Vinicia thought, hanging her head as she moved to join him at the meal. *An idiot dying of thirst while sitting in a well of my own making.*

Kiernan's eyes were unreadable as she joined him, though he still offered her a smile. "And here I thought it was because you were as resigned to being alone as I was. It meant a lot when Kreychi offered to spend the day with me, reminding me I didn't have to be that way."

"I have always been this way," Vinicia insisted, far too proud of that fact.

"Not when you were with our squad," Kiernan reminded. "I remember you, Kehvin. When the three of us didn't know something but you did, you would light up about it. You would also go on for a candlemark if we let you, but it was fascinating. You had prepared for classes and we knew it was your whole life. It has continued to be your whole life," he said, the note of sadness in his words finally making her look up. "I am sorry that I am changing that for you. No one ever gave you the choice."

Vinicia wasn't sure what to say. Exhausted as she had been, she hadn't had the time to look at her own emotions at all. Kiernan, however, was showing he was an empath so much that it was almost frightening.

"And here I thought I just didn't sleep well having a strange man in my apartments," she managed, poking at the last of her meal. She wasn't about to eat any more of it, not with him sitting there. His strength was fuel enough.

Kiernan's smile only grew, watching her. "I do hope I am helping, being here with you," he said. "Even if I have no idea how it works."

"Does it matter?" Vinicia shrugged, giving up the fork as she sat back.

"I suppose not," Kiernan said, finished with his own as well. He had eaten every scrap. "Though I would have understood if you hadn't slept on my account. The Library is a rather solitary place and I can't say I ever entertain people in my own suites. I just..."

Vinicia hated herself as she watched him hesitate. Clearly, he would have been used to being alone. Having been part of his squad in the tyro system, she knew how lonely he had become every time Lenae had to attend a Court function without him. Kreychi, though? Kreychi had been so much worse when Kiernan had graduated.

"I thought you said you spent yesterday in a nest with Kreychi," she said, looking back to him at last.

"Ah, yes," he admitted. "That was a onetime thing, I'm afraid, and I spent four cycles trying to avoid it. Not that I regret yesterday, of course," he added. "But Lenae was right. I was hurting him, letting him hope it would ever be any more than it was."

"I will say I was glad when he became your wingmate on the Plains," Vinicia said.

"Even when he left my service, he never truly stopped," Kiernan said. "I realized that last night. He has always been in love with me, sure, but that isn't what being a wingmate means," he said, paling as remembered what Lenae had insisted Vinicia was to be to him. "At least, that isn't what it means on the Plains."

"You think I don't know that?" She scoffed as he shifted away from her. "I don't have to go to the War Plains to understand that love between men at war can be shared differently than love between people at home. Not that I've ever... I've never been with anyone," she said in an embarrassed rush. "So what do I know?"

"What do you want to know?" He asked, and the innocence of the question made it so much worse.

"Nothing," she said. "I know the stories, Kiernan. It's not safe for me to take a windwalker to nest. I would just kill you."

Kiernan studied her for a long moment, wondering at her panic until he nodded to himself. "Vin, there is much more to intimacy than what you have walked in on in the barracks," he said, and she could tell he knew the risk he was taking in speaking so candidly. "And for all Lenae never wanted me to take Kreychi back into my nest, it was his unrelenting companionship that made him my wingmate, not the physicality we shared. That was the danger in it, because he wanted to remain with me when he should have been living his own life."

Vinicia felt like a fool, not having considered that truth.

"Our partnership can have that same intimacy," he went on, his voice quiet in the moment. "Poetry or not, I knew I would be burned out by the power of a Founder because of my Gift, but now I realize the power belongs to you. If you mean to help me achieve peace with it, then I want to give it to you. At the end of the day, all the power I ever had as the Seventh Counsel Lord came from you."

Vinicia's breath caught as she realized he had extended his hand towards her. She already knew what it was to touch the power at the core of a windwalker, and she absolutely couldn't take it. The one time she had tried with Hewn, she had nearly killed him.

But you wouldn't be touching the core of Kiernan, sobbed the starving part of herself. *You are touching your power in him, which is different. You knew it the moment you healed him that he could fill you with life and you basked in it. Father made him s channel for you, just as he was remade for your mother. Why can't you just believe in him? In what he could be for you?*

"I could kill you," Vinicia said, searching Kiernan's eyes for the fear that should have been there.

"Or you could not," Kiernan insisted, hand still offered to her.

Vinicia hated herself as she closed her eyes, reaching to take his hand as she braced against the backlash. When nothing happened, she opened them to find him sagging with relief. His hand was burning up in hers, though as she gripped onto him, a surge of warmth filled her as it drained from him.

"Great Matron Celenae be praised," he whispered, sending a prayer to his shelf-founder for all the peace the touch had given him.

"Kiernan?" She asked as the silence grew thick between them. "Are you all right?"

"Now I am," he said, shifting her hand in his grip to squeeze it in thanks. "The past few days have felt like walking in a nightmare, but it is a relief to be around you. You calm the fire in me," he said, taking a steadying breath. "Whatever it is you need, whatever it is I have, Gods, it just feels good to be rid of it."

Vinicia exhaled slowly, embarrassed to realize she wasn't the only one who might benefit from the exchange. After a few more moments, Kiernan released his grip on her hand, shifting to press back the braids of his warcrest as he collected himself. The poor man looked like he had flown a lap around the Palace in the Ice Winds, though he was better for it in the end.

"I always knew I had a Gift," he said, resettling his wings. "But after Noventrio, it got to where if I didn't use the power I felt as if I had drunk ten cups of caffea. It rattled me on the inside, made me angry and self-obsessed, and I would have so many other people's thoughts in my head that it could take days to sort myself out. I might have hated the Gift, hated the perversion of the empathy that had made me excel here in the Delton Academy, but it was my duty to end the war. The ends justified the means."

"Until they didn't," Vinicia said and there was no judgment in it.

"Until they didn't," Kiernan agreed, letting out a long breath. "Until I gave up entirely. But you pieced me back together and now I know why I felt the way I have for cycles," he said. "Kreychi helped me through the worst of it, but he flies his own winds now, same as I do. I was honored that you might stand beside me, especially since it meant I could stand by you."

Vinicia looked away, awkwardly trying to avoid his praise. Hewn had said the same thing about her being able to help him and she had loved him for giving such meaning and purpose to her life. Now she wasn't sure how to feel, taking the same sort of compliment from Kiernan.

Then again, from the heavy wear in his dirty-blonde warcrest to the hazel in his eyes, she could not deny that he reminded her of everything she had loved about Hewn. If anything, Kiernan had more of the vibrancy of hope about him, which was something she knew Hewn had lost after the Fall of Kirath. It was that vibrancy that resonated with the emptiness inside of her and as she tried to bring up her shields, she had to admit she didn't want to. Not only that, but she was basking in his singular presence.

Gods, what is wrong with me?

As they watched one another in silence, Vinicia thought back to what she had been like at Westly's age when Hewn had first offered himself to her. After one offhanded comment about letting her attempt to touch the power in him, she had been an absolute wreck for a fortnight. Not only could she not keep her shielding in place, but whenever she so much as thought of him, she fled the Library back into her father's room for sanctuary, only to realize that it was Hewn's room now.

I was so sheltered back then, she thought, flustered. Despite it, though, Hewn had been so patient with her, suffering through her nerves until she knew that she just could not handle it. But yesterday morning she had proven to herself that she was more than capable of handling Kiernan's attention on her.

And his hands, and his power, and his breath...

Vinicia chewed her lip as she refused to even think of the word 'kiss'. It was that intensity of emotion that was sparking the Wellspring in her and for all that she loathed to admit it, Kiernan could probably light a fire in her to set the entire shelf ablaze. Just one night with him might set her leagues ahead of Westly for power, if she only had the nerve.

Taking a lover was the only way she knew she could raise the energy she needed without the ability to draw from her tyros, but taking a partner could be different. They could share power without that physicality, couldn't they? Even if it wasn't as strong, it would still balance the energy between them and if she lost control of herself, Kiernan would be at no risk at all. It would just be the energy of the tree she pulled through him—her energy—and he was used to that power after seven cycles of it fueling his Gift.

So what am I so afraid of?

Vinicia took a deep breath as she pulled out of her thoughts, watching as Kiernan do the same.

"Gods, but it has gotten late," Kiernan said, looking to the timecandle she had burning in the room. "Shall we turn in? We will have a long day tomorrow and we should have some true rest while we can manage it."

"Of course," Vinicia said, shifting from where she had curled up on the lounge.

As he collected their meal trays, she covered her mouth with a hand as she yawned. When he had the mess stacked, meaning to set it to the side, he came to his feet and offered his hand to her to assist her in doing the same. As she shifted to do it on her own, she hated the crestfallen look in his eyes. He had only meant to be polite and it hurt him to be refused again. It hurt her as well that she didn't have the courage to accept such a simple thing.

Coming to her feet, Kiernan began to explain how he would make a floor nest again when Vinicia realized her vision was blurring.

"Kiernan?" She breathed, willing her eyes to steady as she flared her wings to keep from falling. It didn't help, and Kiernan wasn't fast enough with his arms full of their meal to do anything but watch.

As she hit the floor, barely catching herself on her hands for all the weight of her wings, the pain of it shot through her like a lance. Laying there beside him, humiliated and exhausted, a part of herself fractured as she realized what all of this could mean. For all that had happened to Rylan this evening, for all that had happened in the few days before that she had managed, it had only been her strength as a kindred that had kept any of them alive. That strength was gone now, pooled in the man who wanted nothing more than to give it to her.

Kiernan didn't touch her as he came to his knees, trays set aside in his panic. He respected her, but there was anguish in him as he held out his hands.

"Vinicia, *please* let me help you," he begged, the force of his concern scattering the pieces of her shattered pride. Tears in her eyes, she dropped her head against the floor, releasing every shield she had thought to keep up against him.

Kiernan felt it at once, sagging with relief as the great wealth of her pooled power left him in a rush. When she looked up again, pressing against the weight of her wings, she found his offered hands and took them like a lifeline.

"Hewn said I was dying," she confessed, on her knees before him. "All the ancestors say I am dying because I will not cycle power, but I don't know how. I don't know how to do it and not kill you. Kiernan, I'm so afraid—"

Vinicia gasped as Kiernan's strength lifted her onto her feet, pulling her into an embrace.

"Vinicia, we all need help sometimes," he said, his words a whisper against her hair as his strength flooded into her.

"But I am such a fraud," she swore, hating the truth of it. "I failed Hewn and yet I am supposed to help you? *How?* I can't even help myself..."

But Kiernan, wasn't having any of it, cradling her against him as she began to shake with unshed tears. " Vinicia, the Gods alone know I would be dead without you already. All I want is to help you. If you mean to guard me, at least let me take care of you so you can."

"But I am no better than a loralae," she said, her voice breaking around the word. "Kindred that I am, I was made to devour the souls of men. I am a sorceress and a demon, not the woman you think I am—"

Kiernan's scoff of laughter as she hid her eyes against his neck was a genuine surprise.

"Vinicia, you are a gift from the Gods themselves," he insisted, one hand shifting against her lower back to hold on closer. "When you gave me your hawkeye and healed me, you saved my life."

Vinicia couldn't argue with that.

"As much as your father might mean for you to go with me," he said, his hand shifting higher to cradle her head against him. "You are the one who has to take that step. Are you a peacemaker, Vinicia, or will you stay here and pray someone else finds a way?"

The soft sound of protest she made in her throat seemed to entertain him. Glowering even if he couldn't see it, she wrapped her arms around his waist, if only to better stand with strength. As he shifted his weight to hold her steady, her breath caught to feel the spark between them. No matter the balm it was to feel what he radiated and held for her, the friction between them was a lightning flash of something even beyond that power. Something more than one person could have done.

Vinicia wanted to argue with him, but she knew he was right. Then again, the only reason she could was because her father had made him a channel, but maybe that was okay as well. Maybe all of this was truly in their best interests, manipulative though it might otherwise seem.

"And from what I can tell," he went on, pulling back to look at her as his voice dropped to a pleading whisper. "You are the only one who could possibly keep me safe going through the Eihwaz. Kindred that you are, I never thought to stand a chance, but now? Now I might actually come out of this alive. Vinicia—"

As his voice broke, Vinicia pulled back to find the eyes of the most powerful man in Kosar lined with silver.

"Vinicia, will you come with me?" he asked. "You are one of the very few people who knew me before I became a monster at war. I can't tell you how honored I would be if you would actually choose to come with me."

Vinicia's breath left her in a rush as she embraced him. "I want to go with you," she confessed. "Gods above, but I want to go home. I lived in my mother's grove for seven cycles and I can't remember it at all..."

Kiernan's grip around her was incredible as they clung to one another with the desperation they shared. They would be stronger together, that much was clear, but there was something more as well. Holding onto him, breathing him in, it wasn't long until Vinicia felt a spark of power stirring between them. No matter the balm of his presence, there was something even beyond that. Something more she could almost touch, but only because the two of them were solid in their purpose now.

And then, like the sun breaking through a terrible storm, she felt the wellspring igniting in the space between them.

Affection is a dangerous, delirious thing, she thought, shivering as she felt his hand slide against the small of her back. No matter what High Consort Lenae had encouraged between them, Vinicia hadn't realized just what that spark might feel like. Ravenous as she was for power, the desperation in her wanted to rip him apart just to find the true source of that strength—to know it just for an instant for how strong it was by comparison to anything she had ever experienced.

Feeling her stiffen against him as she panicked, his tight hold around her softened to a caress. He didn't want to lose this moment of trust with her, even if she was struggling to keep from gorging on his power.

Kiernan held that power, yes, but he was only now becoming a sorcerer. While he was talented, he was dangerously untrained. If she took hold of the energy he wielded, she might rip out his soul instead of drawing free the Wellspring energy that had ignited with their commitment to one another.

"Everything all right?" He asked, shifting to set their foreheads together.

"I don't want to hurt you," she said, hands shaking as she tried to keep herself from clawing at his skin. "Gods, Kiernan. I'm terrified I am going to hurt you. I—"

"You would never hurt me," he insisted, cutting her off. "Or you would not hurt yourself so much trying to make certain of it. So, please," he pleaded. "Take this from me."

Vinicia flushed as Kiernan pulled back, settling his lips against her brow as he projected something towards her. He was doing all that he could think of to share the strength of his Seventh's Gift and it staggered her to realize she couldn't take it.

"But I don't know how," she confessed, her breath quickening as she searched for a way through the shield that had risen between them. Was it hers or his? Was she blocking herself or was he taunting her? "Gods, but I can't figure out how to even begin."

Now Kiernan pulled back to look her in the eye, unphased by her panic. "If your Seventh's Gift is anything like mine," he said, projecting calm over her with pure bardic strength. "You should find me right below you in the pattern."

"Below..." She said, though time seemed to slow as she realized what he meant. All her life she had focused her Seventh's Gift out from herself, reaching to find her tyros overhead like her ancestor had explained, but if she felt where her strength flowed from, rather than where it went...

Kiernan's aura matched that of the Great Tree almost exactly.

"That's a promising look," he said, hazel eyes shining with hope.

Feeling his strength and knowing what it was, now it made sense. Kiernan wasn't overflowing with power, he was the key to everything she had ever gathered on the shelf. Like a hawkeye guarding the Library, the power that fueled his Gift were the books inside of Noventrio's temple, but the man himself was her key. If she could just see the difference in him, she could use one to access the other. If all she touched when she reached inside of him was her own power, she would not devour his soul.

"Can I try something?" She asked, finally sharing his hope.

"Of course," he said, curious but clueless as she set her left hand against his chest.

Calming herself, Vinicia closed her eyes and felt for the energy pooling just beneath his skin. When she could feel it shifting under her touch, swirling as she flexed her hand to draw it out of him and back into herself, she knew she was onto something. Unfortunately, the more she tried, the harder that shield seemed to build, until she might have been pulling against the great crystal roof of the Library.

When she opened her eyes, Kiernan own were glassy as he struggled to stay on his feet "I'm guessing," he managed, panting in the moment. "Whatever it is... Didn't work?"

"It almost did," she admitted, flushing as she remembered the truly erotic feel her magic could have on windwalkers.

"Were you trying," he said, still gulping down air. "To take power from me?"

"Not exactly," she said, wincing., "Just through you, but I cannot tell where you end and my power begins. I can see it in you, but it is blinding me. There is so much of it, all I see is light."

"So you need some action from me then, to set it apart?" he asked, and the smile on his lips made her heart start to race. "Something to make certain you know what I am inside all of this?"

"Something like that," she hazarded. "Why?"

"I have an idea," he said, releasing her from the embrace, if not by much. "You distinguished between that power when you healed me, so why don't you start from there?"

Vinicia couldn't help but laugh. "But you're not hurt."

"Would you prefer I let you break my knee again?" he asked, meaning it for a joke only to take up her hands with his own to reassure her. "Or you could stomp on my foot, if you must. Honestly, I'd prefer that to fighting you with a dragon pole."

"No," she countered. "No, I understand what you mean. I had to cycle power through your body to see how I had harmed you before, and I can do that again. It is... It is a good idea."

"It is one idea, at least," he agreed, squeezing her hands to stop their trembling. "If it doesn't work, we can try something else."

Could it really be so simple? Vinicia thought, closing her eyes as she flexed her hands in his to ignite the press of power between them. *My ancestor said I would have to cycle power through a grove, but if I only have to cycle it through him...*

Vinicia's eyes flew open as she realized she could already feel two distinct energies in the man. Not only could she feel the tree, but she could sense Kiernan taking hold of the power between them as well. This was his Gift coming to life, shifting that power towards her with intention, and the strength of it was incredible. After a few moments of his own study of her, Kiernan's spirit pulled back and it was only the starlight power of the Great Tree shining between them.

Separate and distinct now, Kiernan was a deep azure and indigo shadow beyond, as self-possessed in this place as he had ever been in her presence. Realizing his Gift had searched through her like he might search the Warhost, realizing that she had reached through him in the same way, her breath caught to feel the incredible energy of the tree spinning through them both.

In through her left, across her chest, and out her right...

In through his left, across his chest, and out his right...

Vinicia felt the ground drop out from under them as the press turned into one constant flow and she was able to spread out the singular line of power into a shield that contained them both. As the euphoria of the exchange grew, the intensity of the moment crackled like fire between them and Vinicia realized what it was just as Kiernan slipped his hands free of her own.

"Do you trust me?"

"About as far as I can throw you," Vinicia breathed, struggling to steady herself.

"Good thing I'm coming closer."

Vinicia felt the whisper of his pleasure as he pulled her into a truce embrace, breathing in the scent of her hair. With the press of their bodies and the heat of so much energy between them, she was floating in space, bouyant and weightless as he held her in the center of his strength.

As the world fractured in her mind, the chasm in her buckled as he took their shared power into his singular control. Not willing to let it go without a fight, she snaked her arms around his neck, pulling him closer and clawing back the power he had stolen. As the struggle between them sparked true Wellspring in the exchange, Kiernan's set his lips on her own and the shock of it sent the power raging into him once again.

Devastated by the loss, Vinicia grasped onto his warcrest with strength, returning the kiss and shattering the struggle between them into beautiful, terrifying life. As he crushed her against him to hold them steady in the torrent, she was again floating in space. Caught in the intensity of the moment, Vinicia had no idea where the line between herself and Kiernan should have been drawn, and she didn't care at all. She was one with him, one with all the power he held for her, and the Wellspring flooded into her in a way she had never thought possible.

When he pulled away to breathe, Vinicia stayed close, gasping against his neck as the Wellspring left them both at last. With that power to sustain them, Vinicia's knees went weak and her awareness sang with the feel of it under her skin. This is what she needed, this raw and violent chaos, and as Kiernan kissed the side of her neck in thanks, she realized just what kind of channel Kiernan could be.

Everything she could feel in him was her power now, pure and blinding white. There was nothing to take from him because he gave her every part of himself, gifted it to her with strength. Strong as he was as a Counsel Lord, that strength now had somewhere to go and the purpose it served brought her to life as easily as it had helped send so many others to their deaths. Reclaiming that strength, turning the greatest weapon of the Warhost into the one thing that might save it meant more than she could ever hope to explain.

As he chased after her kiss once again, hands skimming over every curve of her body, Vinicia had never been so glad to do exactly as she wanted in all her life. She could feel that power in him at once, feel the relief in him to be rid of it, and as she pulled it into herself, the core of who and what she was began to shift from gnawing decay into brilliant life. Better yet, as they stood together, Vinicia was shocked to feel the power pooling in her. The more the energy of the Great Tree returned to her control, the more she could feel her reserves filling with it, and the more that power began to cycle for the first time in her life.

Tears in her eyes, she felt Kiernan's grip soften to tenderness as he held her. Truly, there had never been anything to fear. This wealth of power, this very primal act, it was everything she had denied about herself. Consumed by his embrace, yielding to it, she knew now that every sliver of energy she had stolen, every life she had ever touched to heal, it was nothing compared to this. It would never be anything ever again compared to this.

"You have one hell of a kiss," Kiernan said, panting for a breath as he pulled back to look at her.

"I had no idea," she said, weeping even as she smiled. "Kiernan, I had no idea I could feel like this…"

"Feel like what?" He asked, shifting to brush her tears away.

"Alive," she confessed, heart pounding to see the look of understanding in his eyes.

"All that from a kiss?" He said, ducking his head to set his lips on her neck once again. As she gasped with the feel of it, his hands dropped lower, gripping at her hips to pull her against him. "You realize I can do better than a kiss, yes?"

Vinicia's breath caught as the power between them sparked with just the thought of what he might be offering. Hard as his body was against her own, he knew exactly what he meant. Before she could answer, though, she felt his lips brushing against the shell of her ear.

"Is that a yes?" he whispered. "I have been told it is polite to ask."

What would my ancestor say? Vinicia thought, lightheaded as he stole the power between them. For as much as she wanted him, the power he held pressed against her senses made her feel that gnawing emptiness so much more.

"I don't know what you're offering," she confessed, mortified even if it was the truth. "I want to say yes, but..."

"But nothing, Vin," he said, kissing her temple. "I am offering myself, however you want to take me. We can do whatever you're comfortable with."

"You don't mind?" She asked.

"Every moment I have ever had with Lenae has been quick and stolen," he said, moving a hand to cup her cheek as he pulled back to look her in the eye. "If I had the choice, I would rather savor every moment we have and go as slow as we can manage."

"I don't know how much of you I can handle at once," she said. As Kiernan made a face that looked as if he was swallowing laughter, Vinicia's cheeks heated all over again. "What?"

All he said, though, was: "You will understand soon enough, you beautiful bowen."

With the energy ignited between them, Vinicia yielded to his embrace, overwhelmed by the feel of his lips on her own. Still, knowing he would follow her lead had turned the hesitant spark between them into balefire. Terrified as she had been moments before, now she never wanted it to stop. With the world outside of their embrace collapsing to the feel of his body and the magic of the Wellspring between them, Vinicia sent one last prayer into the void.

::I hope I do you proud, ancestor. Wherever you are.::

VOLUME 4: FOR HONOR AND GLORY

Woe to him who wants the world to burn,
just so he may warm himself.

CHAPTER 31: THE LORALAE

Sunday, 05:30

Lora exhaled slowly as she came awake, disoriented for all the comfort beneath her. Rested as she felt, she could easily take on the world, but first she had to figure out where in it she was.

Wherever it is, it is warm, she knew, cracking an eye open suspiciously. When she saw she was not within the Cells that had been her home for so long, she bit the inside of her lip to see if it would go away with the shock. When it didn't, she took a deep breath of the humid air around her and dreamed of the sea.

In her long life, Lora had woken up in strange places far more than she wanted to admit. She would be going about her business one moment and then succumb to her dryad compulsion in the next. Only after the bloodrage had run its course would she come back to herself, done with her task and covered in blood. Considering that the only thing around her was an ivy-covered hollow, this morning was nicer than some others she could remember.

After discovering this glass garden during her search for the kindred, it had been almost too easy to add to her Suggestion that Westly stay with his highborn lover for the night, so long as that place wasn't here.

Once she had been certain the two had taken to nest, she had left the fledglings to their revel and come to this place.

Figuring the sapling was still distracted, Lora had half a mind to fall back to sleep, but the more she came awake, the more excited she became. Even if yesterday's plan to talk with her beloved had failed, today's plan would most definitely succeed.

Given the graduation of Vinicia's beloved tyros, all Lora needed to do was nudge one into just enough trouble to pull the woman away from the Seventh. Once that was done, Lora could talk to her, explain her subterfuge these past for cycles, and they could sort out the confusion between them.

Smiling despite herself, Lora pulled out of the nest as her mind raced with all the things she needed to do before she got on her way. At the moment, she was overly thirsty, still starving, and weak after so many cycles of nothing at all. With a bit of searching, she found the pile of foodstuffs she had gathered from the revelers the night before. She had looked for any sign of fish in the grand expanse of food, but these mountain idiots would rather kill an ox to eat it than put it to work. That had left her with the green, spear like vegetables that had packed together nicely and a hoard of apples and cheeses. As the last two would weigh her down during a long flight, she reached for the first apple and willed herself to her feet.

Biting into the apple, Lora preened through her feathers and hair with one hand as she made the fruit vanish with the other. Once she had straightened herself out, she ate the rest of the core and then moved into the greater part of the garden to find the pond. She was sure that Westly must use this as a bathing pool, since disrobing among the other tyros would make him vulnerable. To the best of her knowledge, Kosarans had about as much love for the half-breeds as her own people did. That made it even more odd to find two of them in the Palace, but stranger things had happened in the Matriarchs' Court. Who was she to judge?

After stripping down to her skin, Lora moved the pots of submerged plants to one side and then lowered herself in to the warm, silky water. She took a deep breath and then slipped completely under, wings and all.

Like calls to like, she remembered her dryad saying. *Water will heal you, but too long underneath and it will drown you as well.*

In this moment, she almost didn't care. Instead, she drew the water's energy towards her and opened her mind as it rushed inside, filling the great chasm that had been created in her reserves of energy. She had expended nearly half of what she could hold over the past day in obfuscation, which she blamed more on being out of practice than on need. She had to admit, though, being in captivity had increased her ability to store energy tenfold. Need was by far the greatest teacher.

Once she felt full to bursting, Lora exhaled in a torrent of bubbles and surfaced for air. As the water slid from her skin and oily wings in a great rush, she watched as the drops radiated with power before returning to the pool. With the feel of it humming all around her, she couldn't remember the last time she had felt more alive.

Drawing herself out of the moment, Lora moved away from the center of the pool and settled herself with her wings flexed over the side to hold her steady. After a bit of searching, she found the small bar of what she hoped was soap hidden among the leaves and set to scrubbing off four cycles of filth.

A good half mark later, her skin, nails, and hair were finally respectable, and she felt whole again. She was still on-edge mentally, but being in the heart of the enemy's capital would do that to a person, and a bath and a clear view of the sky would not heal her in a matter of moments. Still, having been tucked away in the Kosaran Cells for four cycles, who was she to complain about a little luxury?

Sighing, Lora drew a hand through the milky water and then helped it along to where the sapling had built in a little spillway, letting whatever fouled water slide off as his plants cleaned away the rest. It might take time, but with the whole city distracted, she had it to spare.

Given the past four cycles, her life hadn't exactly been that bad. Here, at least she had the comforts of a nest, a few books the Guard would allow her, and visits from members of the Kosaran military intelligence to occupy her time. Initially, she had been hounded by the Dragon Lord himself, but given that she was coming off the worst bloodrage in her life, that was all she could remember.

When she had finally dried out, he had thought to try again, but she honestly couldn't be bothered. The man had dishonored her by taking her for a trophy, and if he wanted to redeem himself, he would kill her. The Great Mothers alone knew how much she had wanted to die that night, not that they remembered their daughter.

When his interest had waned, her care had been given over to the man who probably should have held her in the first place: the Kosaran Fifth Counsel Lord. A monster of a man, Loraleia had been less than thrilled to have the attention of the Raven Lord turned on her with such ferocity. The man was *still* seething about the attack on his Kirathy shelf and despite Lora's insistence that she had not been there and had nothing to do with it, he wanted information. She was the only woman he had ever set hands on who had been both kyree and loralae, if somehow recovered, and she was a fantastic source of information about the sorcery to be found in the Vals.

Given how little loyalty she had left for her wingsisters, she didn't mind speaking with Roder or his Blackwing Fumentari. They could at least converse in the old tongue, which was good since they were otherwise immune to her mental magics. The one time he had ever asked her to explain how the loralae were made, however, she had refused. Not only had the dryads who had made her silenced her tongue on that matter, but no amount of torture would ever match the utter devastation the dryads had put her through when they had changed her. Everything paled to the feeling of having an ancient creature needling inside your soul.

But where Datura turned me into a demon, this Kosaran captivity gave me my sanity back, Lora hated to admit. For twenty cycles she had been driven by her dryad's compulsion, skirting the war or assisting as necessary when she was caught up with the Vals once again. All the while, she hunted as she had been taught to do, and when she could find no dryad-kin to cut down, it was the gifted she took in their place, be they Kosaran, Ehkeski, or on the rare occasion, her own salt-sisters.

Before being captured by the Dragon Lord, that had been her life. But given her long seclusion in the High Cells, she had been able to rediscover the pieces of her soul that remained and use the water magic of the River Kir to build a shield with them once again.

When the shield was strong enough, she had begun to remember the sense of self she had lost in the Eihwaz until the chaotic swirl of voices howling around her could no longer trigger a bloodrage. Sure, she could still search and contact for the gifted, but she did so at her choosing. Instead of seeking out and destroying those powerful mental speakers, now she could simply sit back and watch them with idle curiosity. At least, that was all it had been until the silence had been pierced by the grief of the young woman she would eventually mentor: her *sha'doe*.

For a while, Lora had known that there was a mind crying out into the void, though she had been happy to ignore it for once. After long enough, though, her curiosity had gotten the better of her. In much the same way that the dryad had first spoken with her from the shadows of her mind, Lora had sent out thoughts to the woman and listened for the woman's own thoughts in return. Uncertain what she was speaking to at first, Lora had disguised herself as the voice of 'an ancestor' and had sidestepped the specifics until her *sha'doe* had forgotten to ask.

Intrigued at the mental freedom she had found in being able to speak with the woman, Lora had helped her through an incredible grief. As she did, the more she focused on that one simple contact, the more she felt like she was returning to the woman she had been before she and MiaSera had been thrown to the Eihwaz by the Val'Corps. Whether it was her own selfish desire to have a greater chance at reclaiming a life she had thought to have lost completely or, as she realized now, that she had taken Vinicia as *sha'doe* the same way MiaSera had taken Lora herself on, she couldn't say.

All she knew was that Vinicia still needed her guidance and so Lora meant to provide that to her, no matter the risk. If Vinicia did not find the courage to touch the Wellspring in her tyros, she would die just as surely as if Lora herself had slain her. That was why she had left the Cells—to stand at Vinicia's side and guide her in person—and that was still her purpose now, even if that meant aiding the Seventh who had brought her to this place as a prisoner.

After all his cowardice has done to save my body and spirit from the horrors I suffered on the Plains, I should thank the man, Lora thought, ridiculous as that seemed. *And if Vinicia feels for me what I feel for her, then I must honor the man for the redemption he has brought into my life.*

Lora glowered as sank into the cool water, holding onto her hate as if it could keep her warm. For so long she had hated the Seventh and it would not be an easy reflex to change. But if she meant to claim Vinicia as *sha'doe,* though, it would be at his side that she would find her.

For all the woman's virtues, Vinicia had still been raised as a servant to men, and breaking Vinicia of that habit might be as difficult as breaking herself free of the dryad's compulsion. All of this was made worse by the fact that Vinicia's actions came from a sense of duty and, as much as Lora hated to admit it, a love of peace. In her world, the Seventh was peace, which is likely why the woman had been trailing after him the day before.

But in my world, he is the reason for War, Lora thought angrily. If seeing him to the Lans would end it? If just taking him there would give her Vinicia in return? *I would set the world on fire for that woman,* she knew and sighed. *And if she refuses to leave him, I will walk beside the man I hate and call it the easiest trial of my life.*

Miserable and heartsick to know that yet another day stood between herself and her love, Lora pushed away from the side of the pool with a great, angry slosh. When she moved to stand however, her stomach clenched to realize that the faster she tried to move, the harder the water held her. She had been warned that the more she touched the heart of the water, the more it would seek to change her and with nothing more than water to fuel her magic in this place, the dryad's curse was now coming to collect.

Eyes going wide, Lora looked into the dark liquid for an answer and almost screamed to see bright blue scales glittering along the outsides of her legs. Lora slammed up her shields and felt a sharp jerk as all the water in the pond pulled away from her at once. Taking the chance, Lora threw herself over the edge of the pool, landing hard on her right wing as the water reclaimed the void she created with an angry crash.

Fearing the water trying to come after her again, she pushed onto her hands and knees just long enough to grab her stolen clothes and then put as much distance between her and the pool as was possible in this place.

When she had reached the roaring hearth, she spent a frantic moment sliding her hands all over her skin, forcing as much water off of herself as she could. She hesitated when she came to the patches of scales, but to her surprise, the more water she wiped off, the more they vanished. When she could slide away no more, she beat her wings into a frenzy, shaking the water away and drying herself to damp. Only then did she pick up the musty towel she had found discarded in Westly's room and get rid of the rest.

Once dry, Lora leaned over and wrapped the towel around her hair, twisting it before standing and laying the mass atop her head. Her hair had grown nearly to her hips since the last time anyone had trusted her with a blade, and of all the things she had stolen yesterday, a sharp knife was not one of them. Her armor needed repair as well and if anyone was going to have a needle and thread sturdy enough for leather...

Looking around the expansive room, Lora figured the kin's workstation was the best place to start and winged her way towards it. Successful in her small sortie, Lora landed before the sapling's workstation. While the hutch was filled with seeds and tools, the desktop itself was clear. There was also a row of drawers to the left, and a long, thin drawer just under the desktop. She tried the long drawer first but found only paper, quills, and ink to mark the bottles. Closing that, she opened the first of the drawers and her eyes lit up to see a set of polished steel sheers.

Those she claimed eagerly, moving beyond the hutch to the expanse of crystal wall that was left exposed. The grey dawn beyond hid her from view as she stood naked before her reflection, grimacing at the paleness of her copper skin. Even the tan she from her war kurta was gone, leaving her as pale and Kosaran as her idiot father, Great Mothers rest his murdered soul. After she freed herself from the towel, she pulled the wet mess in front of her, only to grimace to see how the tips of her red-gold hair were turning blue from so much of the water's energy.

That had to go immediately.

Once she had her hair collected, she flipped her head over so it was all hanging down in front of her. Sliding her hand away from her scalp, she got halfway down the length and then used the sheers to cut off the rest. When she flipped her hair back over, the length that had turned blue in the water was on the floor and the rest covered half of her breast.

Moving towards the hearth and its steady flame, she took a seat and shook out her hair to dry. As she ran her hands through it, she gathered what water she could by drawing the energy out of her hair and dropped it on the hearth to evaporate.

As much as she had wanted to cut the rest of it off, that was not the Kosaran style, so she would have to braid it for now. One less thing to hide made it easier to blend in, she reminded herself, and set to braiding the sides. When the two tails were halfway done, she styled the remaining hair into a poof on the crown of her head with the help of some nearby beeswax. That was as close as she would get to the spikes she preferred, so she let it be.

With that in place, she finished the whole thing by crossing the two braids and gathered the rest in a tail that hung off the crown of her head. If she was going to dress as a man again to get free of the city, it was best she was a soldier, rather than a civilian.

Having taken as long as she dared, Lora returned to Westly's room and found her armor. Though it was big on her now for lack of muscle, she filled what space she could with one of the sapling's woolen tunics and found a pair of fleece leggings. Both were huge on her, given his height, but the shears worked just as well on cloth as they had on her hair. First she cut out the center of the leggings and wiggled them down over her head, setting her arms through the legs to make something of a sweater above her wings. When she figured out the length she needed, she cut off the excess from the arms and then added holes for her thumbs so she could keep it in place. Now, no matter what else she wore, she would be warm.

With that project done, she wove her armor around her as tight as the weakened ties could manage and then got into her leggings and pleated knee-length kurta. Finally dressed in all the warmth she could find, Lora filled the empty haversack with her stolen goods and took what she would from the things lying around the room. Westly had little she could use during her trip, but the book on herbs of the Kosaran woods would be particularly insightful, along with a fire starter, a dull eating dagger, and a harness that she belted beneath the skirt of her kurta and down each thigh and calf. Fortunately, her hips made up for the kin's otherwise longer bone structure, so it fit her well enough.

Once she was satisfied, Lora closed the pack and settled it between her wings, taking the crimson cloak that had been hung up as a door and draped it across her shoulders. As she headed back to Westly's workbench, there was one last thing she needed, and she knew it was here somewhere. Kosarans were known for smoking the terra plant for recreation, which was lunacy as far as she was concerned. On the Plains, the terra they had was fermented into a drink called *bhang lassi* and given to loralae as it took the edge off of their new gifts so that they didn't slaughter their own sisters. The sapling would likely have it somewhere under lock and key, right?

After a bit of searching, Lora swore as she came up empty. Switching into her secondsight, she looked around the otherwise prismatic room for any sort of magical lock or trick that Westly might have used to hide it from prying eyes, only to roll her eyes. Switching back to her normal sight, she saw the massive plant sitting right next to the nest she had slept in. Granted, it was tucked along the back wall, but it was *right there*.

Squatting beside the plant, Lora began stripping off the massive leaves, muttering to herself about how far she had fallen from The Loralae that terrified the Kosaran Warhost to an idiot who couldn't even see something sitting right in front of her face. As she set the pile on the floor next to her, she hesitated as the clay pottery holding the plant finally came into view. Of all the things she had expected to see in this room, this was not one of them.

The clay of the planter was covered in an intricate, if crude pattern of dryad script along the top. Deciphering the script, she recognized it as a pattern to help things grow, and when she lifted the box away and knelt down to get a closer look, there were a similar set of sigils mirrored on the clay plate below the pot. These were no innocent scratches...

Looking back to the pile, Lora took hold of one of the broad leaves and let her mind drop into the healer's trance. The plant was structurally perfect, which only made things worse. As much as she wanted to deny it, as much as it would make her life so much easier, Westly's ingenuity was far more advanced than she had thought. Her bindings over his power wouldn't last more than a few days if he had this sort of skill.

Hopefully, I can get her off the shelf before he attempts to free himself of it...

Her need for urgency growing, Lora stripped the last of the leaves and then made quick work of drawing out the water so she could lessen the weight of the plant itself during her trip. Not that she had any idea when said trip would start or where it would go, but she knew she could not stay in the Palace of her enemy. She had already been here far too long.

Swearing at the fates, Lora set her hand against the falconstone on her left wrist, murmuring a prayer to the Great Mothers as she watched her guise shift in the mirror that the crystal wall provided. Though she was dressed comfortably in her own gear once again, the image looking back at her was a young Warhost officer meaning to observe the games. With this face, she could get into the Lower City and then all she had to do was track the young man she had met in the High Cells. Cherished as he was to Vinicia, the boy's gift for firestarting made him burn as bright in her mind's eye as Vinicia herself.

It amused her to think that this was her task: to find one man among a city when her own task on the Plains had been to find the Dragon Lord in the same sort of way. It would be good to be using her skills again, if only to enjoy the thrill of a hunt that, for the first time in twenty cycles, would not have to end in bloodshed.

Chapter 32: Kiernan

Sunday, 06:00

Kiernan woke the next morning feeling more alive than he had in cycles. Whether it had been the relief at surviving another night without the threat of death at his door or the sheer exhaustion of sharing a nest with a bowen, he was at least glad to know a new dawning had arrived. But even if Vinicia's idea of slow had kept them fully clothed for most of the night, it had taken every bit of his cunning to understand how his Gift had been turned into true spiritual sorcery by her father's meddling, and what it would take for him to bring her to bare for her.

Everything, he thought, opening his eyes to see where she still lay in his arms. *It will take everything I have ever learned controlling my cantos to not be driven completely out of my mind with the magic between us.*

If he had thought the Warhost was bad at overwhelming him these past few days, it was nothing compared to her singular attention. Strong as her own empathic gifts were, she would needle through his soul for the pleasure of it, and Kiernan wanted nothing more than to let her. He could have died in that bliss, but it was clear he could command it as well. He would have to if he ever meant to help her create the Wellspring she needed, turning a lover's torture into manifested power.

Difficult as it was, though, he still felt better than he had in cycles. If unwittingly holding this for her was why he had been so strong as a Seventh, his ability to reach into her felt like reaching into a brand new Warhost. The only difference was that her presence flitted among that power like a true dryad in a grove, elusive and skittish until his swelling presence called her back. She was enraptured by the contact between them and even if she was of two minds about it, in the end she needed his strength just as much as he needed to gift it to her or be burned alive.

Amusingly, the whole night had flooded him with ideas about how he might spend today with Lenae. Priestess that she was to Kosar's most powerful fertility goddess, Lenae channeled the same spiritual energy as Vinicia, if for Braeden's purpose as king. If Kiernan could use any part of this talent with her...

Kiernan schooled himself, knowing the wicked smirk he wore would send Vinicia fleeing for all she was still a bowen. The feats he managed with Lenae would come in time, but he was happy to wait for the moment, enjoying the fluctuation between Vinicia's shy gentleness and the ravenous, almost violent creature she could become under his affection.

With one wing in the Eihwaz and another in the high mountains of Kosar, Vinicia was both a dream come to life and an echo of the nightmare he had survived four cycles ago. Though he couldn't see her eyes, the red-gold hair she had unbound for him gave her birthright away. For as much as he gloried in the true length of it when it wasn't hidden down the back of her jacket, the color was a haunting reminder of a memory he would have rather forgotten.

Kiernan shivered with the thought of the red-haired loralae who had nearly killed him on the Plains. She and her shield-sisters had all shown the same coloring, but the source had been a mystery until now. If Vinicia was any guide, it was possible that a dryad-born Lan'lieanan woman could have been raised to kill him the same way that Vinicia had been raised to help him find peace. Then again, it was also possible that she was just a kyree that had come under the influence of something as powerful as Noventrio in her own lands, like himself.

Either way, she is dead now, Kiernan sighed, shaking himself out of the dark thoughts. *She is dead and my Consort is beautiful.*

As long as he thought of Vinicia's coloring as a reminder of the Southern Eihwaz when the leaves of the golden oaks turned a riot of bright orange and red before winter, he would be fine. That was a far better thought than a dead assassin, any day.

All things considered, Kiernan was certain he liked the idea that Vinicia would travel with him on Envoy. Cunning like a Kosaran with a Lan'lieanan's force of personality and a dryad's sense of entitlement, Vinicia was warborn in a way that would never happen twice. But as strange as she was, there was no denying how Kiernan's predecessors—including Vinicia's own father—had crafted her into being. Vinicia was their hope for victory whether she wanted to be or not, just as much as she would be Kiernan's weapon whether he had the ability to wield her or not. If he didn't, Kiernan was sure that she would wield him, and well.

Hearing him chewing on the stubble that had taken over his lower lip, Vinicia stirred and opened her eyes. After a heartbeat to see that the emerald had shifted to a soft amber-gold, Kiernan realized he was falling into them. She had transfixed him with nothing more than a glance. He only came back to himself when she looked away, and the sound of her embarrassed laughter freed him from the spell.

"Sorry about that," she yawned. "I forget what I can do when my shields are down. Here, let me put my face on."

Kiernan felt a pulse and then the energy pooled between them shifted into her control. As she collected her hair from around her face and smoothed it back, the auburn coloring flowed down to mask the bright red. When she rubbed the sleep from her eyes, though, the amber remained.

"That's one way to describe it," Kiernan said, still fascinated if not transfixed. "But your eyes..."

"What?" She asked, suddenly worried.

"They're this burnt amber and gold," he said and smiled to ease her worry. "It's striking."

"Ah... Let me try that again," she said, closing her eyes to concentrate. Kiernan felt the energy between them pulse with purpose, but the amber remained.

Kiernan just shook his head. "Don't worry about it," he assured her, not that it stopped her from rubbing at them. "Aren't full dryads supposed to have golden eyes?"

"Or violet," she admitted, if hesitantly. "But I think I would know of something like that by now for kindred."

"You are the oldest kin I have ever heard of," he pointed out, and when she started to chew her underlip, he knew she was considering it.

"Is it terrible?" She asked.

"I told you, it's striking," he said, emphasizing the compliment.

Unfortunately, she didn't seem to take it that way and curled in on herself. Kiernan left her to her thoughts as they turned inwards, knowing her for the sort of person who needed to figure things out inside her own head before speaking.

For now, he was just glad the tension between them had eased, as her unsettled fretting was a far better thing to wake up to than a barrage from a dragon pole. Even better, the feel of her pulling their shared power out of his control had been one of the most erotic sensations he had ever felt in his life, and he meant to take her to that place again. That and more, since she only seemed to hold on to the power they raised when he was certain her ecstasy had been from more than just the rush of magic between them. Bowen that she was, she didn't realize there was even a difference.

When she finally looked back to him, it was to tap a finger between his eyes. "Even if mine is failing, I can keep yours up better," she said, brushing her fingers over the start of his warcrest. "Your eyes and hair are going silver with from all my magic. You really should hold a stronger guise if you mean to hide the fact you're going on Envoy."

"What do you mean, guise?" Kiernan repeated, keeping still as her fingertips settled against his temple. "Honestly, Vin. Whatever I look like is the hawkeye's fault."

"Well, that would explain the hazel," she chuckled. "If you were born with brown eyes, then my magic is adding the green. Actually," she said, her fingers stilling with the thought. "Maybe I can just give you a guise..."

Kiernan closed his eyes, stifling a groan as he felt her magic swirling through him.

"The hair is easy enough," she said, her touch a caress as she brushed along his white hairline. "But this..." Kiernan felt his eyes burn for a moment. "There."

"That's different," he said, surprised at how she had so effortlessly woven her intent into the shielding from his hawkeye. "Thank you," he said, covering her hand with his own.

"I've had some practice," she said, and he saw her flush as he pressed his lips to her palm in thanks. When she took her hand back, her smile caught him without warning, and he slipped under her spell again. Fortunately, it only took a moment for her to realize what she was doing, and she swore as she covered her eyes with her hand.

"I'm sorry," she laughed, releasing him with some effort. "I don't know what's come over me. I am not trying to trap you."

"No, I am already quite stuck," he chuckled and set a hand on her knee where it was still folded in with his own.

"You're lucky I even remembered how Westly made a rasha nest, much less how to resize it for the two of us," she protested, flushing as his hand slid up the back of her thigh. "I never thought I would have anyone in this room, much less sharing this space with me."

"I couldn't tell," he teased, glancing to the system of piles organizing her life within the barracks.

Vinicia scowled at him. "If I am going with you to Illiandria, I don't need to do much in the way of tidying up, do I?" She defended, shifting away from him as his hand traveled over her hip and began to rise between them. For all her muscle and strength, the shape of her was as attractive as either Lenae or Kreychi had ever been.

"I said the same thing to Lenae when she walked into my disaster," Kiernan agreed, flexing a hard grip as he stalled at her chest. "Not that she believed my excuse."

"You have no excuse," she murmured, distracted as she arched into his touch. "Gods, to think it was that demon of a stone making you a monster. If I had known..."

Kiernan shifted in the nest, lifting his lips to the long length of her neck. She lifted her chin as his hand touched her jaw, keeping her head turned as he kissed her collarbone.

"If I had known..." She tried again, her free hand draping along his warcrest as her breath quickened.

"Hmm?" He pressed, his hand flowing down to her hip once again, shifting her leg to free his own.

She sulked as the movement rolled her onto her wings, not ready to be parted from him until she felt a hand sliding down her muscled abdomen. Kiernan came up onto an elbow once his arm was free, flaring his wings over them as the subtle pressure of his hand between her legs made her writhe.

"Where would you have been instead?" He asked, lowering his lips to her own as she groaned.

"Here," she breathed, hands tightening in his warcrest as she dragged him down to close the circle between them. When he just bit her lip instead, the energy pooling between them became a riot of power.

"I suppose I could have allowed it," Kiernan murmured once he set her free. She was panting now, bracing against him as he sought after her pleasure. He had to keep riding that edge for her; keep building the tension and heat between them to bring her into her height.

"We never would have gotten anything done," Vinicia whispered, though her breath caught as she dug her hands into his warcrest, arching against him. Kiernan released the power between them at once, sending it rushing through her and she took her pleasure again in an entirely different way.

Groaning with the aftershocks, Vinicia's eyes rolled into the back of her head. As he drew his hand back to hold her steady, Vinicia released his warcrest and the sulk she wore was almost more than he could take.

"That's not fair," she panted, dizzy with the sight of him. "It's not fair that you can do that to me."

"Life's not fair, gorgeous," he teased, nudging her chin to the side to set a kiss on her cheek. "Speaking of which," he added. "We should probably find a way out of this nest before I get any other clever ideas."

The smirk she wore was wicked.

Confused, Kiernan hesitated to ask, only to collapse into the nest of comforts where she had been moments before. As he heard giggling laughter behind him, he pulled back his wings to see her rematerializing amid a swarm of starlight wil-o-wisps.

"Clever enough?" She asked, gesturing to the ambiance.

"Clever enough for a kindred," he accused, flaring his wings as he freed himself from the nest the old-fashioned way.

Vinicia gave a flourishing bow.

"Gods, I've never felt so good in my life," she said, shaking her head to clear it of the lingering fog. "Kiernan, you just don't understand. The power is still moving in me. It cycles now and I don't have to struggle at all."

"It's good to feel alive, isn't it?" He chuckled, watching her move to the small side room in her supernatural apartments. This one had one of the noble House's shower contraptions installed, though he wasn't about to ask how she had made that happen.

"Speaking of alive," she said, eying him as he followed her towards the small bathing room. "Do you have any idea who you mean for Rylan's partner when he graduates? Who will be the new Sixth?"

"You're back to business fast," he laughed, stalling at the threshold as she got the water flowing.

"I always have my mind on the Seventh's business," she threw back, eying him with a mock scowl as she tossed the long length of her unbound hair between her wings. Already aroused with his own teasing of her, Kiernan chewed his lip. He hadn't joined with her truly yet, hadn't even tasted more than her lips and neck, but by the gods he wanted to. Clearly, she was high enough with a kiss and a cuddle, and he was happy to wait until she was ready to do more.

"Fine then," Kiernan sighed. "Hest'lre says he means Tyrsten for the position, but all of it is temporary."

"Someone will have to keep up the War effort while we're gone, you realize," she admonished, reaching for her hair oils where they were stored on a stone shelf in the wall. "And if you have chosen Rylan because he will refuse to wield the Host like a veteran, then you might as well choose someone before him. Like what Counsel Lord Broc did with my father."

"Excuse me?" Kiernan asked, confused.

"Oh, did I not explain that?" She said, turning to see him. Her hands were covered with hair oil and for how she stared at him... "It explains my age."

"I believe you told me your age was none of my business," Kiernan reminded, not about to hide how the sight of her made his own body react. "Have you changed your mind?"

"I am eight and thirty," Vinicia answered, though she looked as if she wanted to wince. "I've always looked about ten cycles younger than I am, which has worked to my benefit."

"Ten is modest," Kiernan laughed. "You look about three and twenty."

Vinicia just batted her eyelashes, mocking his compliment as she hooked a finger at him. Encouraged by her invitation, he pulled in his wings, entering the shower room with her. As he stalked closer, Kiernan's words were desperate and low.

"If you keep tempting me," he warned, stepping into the spray of water to set a finger against her chest. "Lenae will be quite put out."

"Have her join us, then," she said, all innocence as her slick hands trailed down the front of his torso. "Maybe she can show me what you cannot. Lan'lieanan wisdom says men can never know mastery of a woman's pleasure..."

"And they're wrong," Kiernan said, setting a hand on her jaw as he closed the distance between them. "Why do you think we're at war?"

"Oh, is that why?" she challenged. "Because we can't agree how best to find one another's tail feathers?"

Kiernan's breath caught as she took hold of him with delicate, demanding strength, and he had to brace himself on the wall behind her as she closed the circle of their power. The oils she had meant to drag through the knee-length waterfall of her hair had made her hands incredibly soft, but the rest...

"Vinicia," he pleaded, closing his eyes as she set both her hands on him. "Vinicia, you don't... You don't need to..."

"Why not?" She pouted, nuzzling her cheek against his as he struggled to keep his knees from buckling. Feeling him shudder, she pulled him close enough that her hand was pressing him along the crease of her hip.

"Blood and ice, woman," Kiernan groaned. "You're as bad as Kreychi."

"I told you I knew some things," she purred, and his heart pounded as she took control of the power between them. "Things about men. Things I walked in on as Barracks Mother."

As her grip strengthened around him, Kiernan's world collapsed to the heat they shared and the feel of her lips on his own. Strong as the woman was with her gifts, her arousal drew him in like some sort of madness. He wanted to plead with her they didn't have time, that she didn't have to do this, but...

::I want to know what kind of power your pleasure holds,:: she sent, lips brushing against his own as he gasped for air. ::What kind of power you truly have for me.::

Kiernan's hand flexed against the wall as the kiss they shared drove every thought from his mind. As she dragged him over the edge, the energy between them became a torrent of chaos and life. Struggling to stay standing, Kiernan's growl of pleasure was met with her fascinated laughter as she saw what she had done to him. What a mess she had become, because of him.

"Good thing we're washing up," she teased, and had the gall to set her filthy hands on his chest to push him away.

"You are worse than Kreychi," he complained, unable to stop himself from laughing. "Gods, and Lenae is going to ruin me with 'I told you so' today."

"Why's that?" Vinicia asked, all sparkling curiosity as Kiernan recovered.

"Because I swore to her no woman would be able to bend me away from her, and here you are," he said. "Wrapped around me like some sort of climbing ivy."

"I just want to take care of you," she said, grinning. "That's what wingmates do, right?"

Kiernan's heart spasmed at the words. "Please don't say that," he said, and from the look on his face, she knew she had said something wrong. "Not that."

"I mean to protect you," Vinicia said, trying again. "That's all."

"I know," he said, swallowing past the hard knot of emotion. "But those words— those particular words—they belong to someone else."

As her eyes went wide, realizing how deeply she had wounded him, she nodded and moved them past the moment.

"This was Lenae's idea, anyway," Vinicia defended, offering to trade places with him, now that she was clean. "And I did promise to give you back. You know, eventually."

"Eventually," he repeated, moving towards her before she could draw into herself. As he pulled her against him, chasing after her kiss, she ducked her head, but let him hold her all the same.

After long enough standing together, she looked up and the tender kiss they shared sent shivers all the way from his toes to the tips of his wings. When he gifted her that power back, she took it gladly, her whole demeanor softening.

"You make me feel like a bowen for power," he whispered against her cheek. "Like I've never wielded it at all, not compared to what you manage."

"My ancestors have taught me everything I know of sorcery," Vinicia said, smiling. "If my father has made a sorcerer of you, I suppose I should teach you, too."

"If you teach me much more this dawning, you really will have to be the one Lenae takes to nest," he said, laughing. "The Founder she serves knows more of channeling pleasure to a purpose than either of us could ever manage. I swear to you, Vin. I barely keep up."

Vinicia made a face at that, halfway between curious and embarrassed fluster, until Kiernan waved at her to move so he could clean up as well.

Oh, this is such a dangerous game, Kiernan thought, watching her twist beneath the water one final time before slipping away. Having the time to indulge in courting her felt like a luxury, but it was also like fighting a tempest for an embrace, taming a shrew for a kiss... Vinicia was every bit the dryad's child and by all the gods of his ancestral line, if Lenae said to show this woman pleasure, that is what he would do.

When Vinicia was finally clean, her body if not her mind, Kiernan pulled in his wings in the small room and let her move past him without complaint. As he moved to take his turn, though, she was spinning her hair into a rope to wring it out.

"You said you liked long hair, yes?" She asked. "Do you think you can help me set it up some way that will be good for the flight to Illiandria?"

"I most certainly can," Kiernan said, trying not to leer. "I... Have a weakness for it," he confessed and then could have kicked himself for the admission. "As the son of a weaver, I mean."

Vinicia was amused by his tone, but when she looked at him, she saw the longing he wore openly.

"You're serious?" She said, surprised again. "For braiding hair?"

"You will understand when we are in Illiandria," he said and then flushed with his own embarrassment.

Her question answered, Kiernan took his turn, only to finish and wonder just how she had meant for him to dry off. Knowing her, she had just used some trick of magic, but that wasn't exactly something he could do. Or maybe it was now, not that he knew how.

Moving into the room where her nest was located, he found her sorting through the piles of clothes that should have been stored in her empty wardrobe. Despite the illusion of soft curves under the silk shirt she had found, the tops of her thighs beneath the hem were all chiseled strength. She was as hard-bodied as any soldier, pure whipcord and muscle, and the exact opposite of Lenae.

Forcing himself back into rational thought, Kiernan refocused his mind on the fact that he had a century's worth of soldiers to graduate this day. He did not have time to lose himself in her completely. Not yet. Lenae would want her own goodbye, and the gods help him, he meant to give it to her.

Finally wrenching his eyes from his Consort, Kiernan turned to the pile of his things. "So, what now?" He asked, if only to distract himself.

"Get dressed as if we're leaving for Illiandria," she said, turning to see him, only to realize he was still dripping. With a laugh, she waved her hand and Kiernan shivered as the water on his skin evaporated. "I need to stop in the armory before we can head to the Soldier Tyros' Wing. Do you mind?"

"Not at all," he said, making quick work of the new clothing that Counsel Lord Eirik had commissioned for him: layers of silk, fleece, leather, and kavik wool. After dressing, he rolled the rest of his clothing into the bundle that he meant to take to Illiandria and shoved it to the bottom of his pack.

When he was done, he started after the hard thigh-case that protected the short-bow he had commissioned from Counsel Lord Blake, glad to finally have the chance to look at it. Unlike a normal bow, this one was supposed to use two pulleys at the end to allow the reinforced string to compound the strength. Knowing Vinicia would probably find the weapon just as fascinating as he had, he looked over to her, only to realize Vinicia was adjusting a rather conspicuous piece of leather armor. As he gaped in surprise, all thoughts of the short-bow fled his mind.

"Is that Lan'lieanan?" He asked, following the curves of armor as they hugged her body. As cleverly fitted as the Lan'lieanan kyree armor was, it was only meant for hot weather, so unless she had woolen underclothes beneath the leather pants and flight boots, she would freeze in the winds.

"It was modeled on it," Vinicia explained with excitement. "Counsel Lord Blake had one of his armorers work out the pieces for me. I have silk, shearling, wool... Even leather sleeves and a doublet attachment," she said, laughing as she gestured to the pile at her feet.

"Well, I'll be bloodied," Kiernan said, impressed as he walked over to inspect the quality up close. The whole outfit was a dull sky blue and supple, despite the stiff backing. It was also, fortunately, already laced together.

From the wealth of pieces and the leather knickers she already wore, the outfit was meant to be a full set of Kosaran flying leathers. She was lacing into the armored chest piece now, but that was meant to be worn beneath what looked like a short half-vest with the high Kosaran collar. As she had said, there were two-part sleeves as well and those laced at the elbow and shoulders to attach to the vest, turning it into a sort of half jacket that would have curved to compliment her chest.

The final piece was larger, lacing along the underside of the jacket that would cover her torso and close the otherwise open space between the two sides of the vest.

"I've never had a chance to wear all of it," she admitted, trying to suppress her excitement. "But today I can't imagine wearing anything else. Getting you out of here alive will be my tournament, it seems."

"I wish I had the same kind of cleverness," Kiernan said, picking up the jacket. "Being able to shed pieces as we move south would be a godsend."

"But you do," she said, confused. "Or did you not notice? I know Blake was trying to be subtle with sending you the armor since it's usually reserved for Blackwings, but..."

"It does what?" Kiernan asked, and then opened the doublet just enough to see the inside. While the outside was the same color as the armor she wore, the inside was a strange, mottled green.

"The seams are sealed," Vinicia said, stopping in her work to strap into the belt and thigh-harness. "But if you want to open them, you cut the seams and lace it. He just didn't want to give away the fact that you were leaving."

Kiernan gaped as he looked down to the elbow of his sleeve, realizing that what he had taken for reinforcement was actually the same sort of lacing system she wore. His didn't break down into nearly so many pieces, but it would make sleeves and a long vest.

"My father came up with the original design for the inside color, too," she added. "Once we get into the woods, we can flip the gear and wear the mottled green. For now, the blue makes us harder to spot in the air, so it should work."

"Once we're off the shelf, we should have plenty of options," Kiernan replied. "Was the idea of decoy waystations your father's as well?"

"No, that was Counsel Lord Broc," Vinicia explained. "My father just made sure there were more. The courier's guild has thanked him for the extra stations ever since by keeping them stocked. We'll only need one route and it's a route they never take. Why would they, when it's only worth using when the Ice Winds are raging?"

"Well, at least they're stocked," Kiernan said. "Though it will take us longer to get to Illiandria."

"Not so much longer that we'll have to worry about making it before winter sets in," she assured him, taking the moment to retrieve the silver Consort broach from the cloth-of-silver doublet she had worn the day before.

Once that was in hand, she found a place on her right shoulder to affix the broach with a trick of magic. That done, she was fully dressed and so picked up her haversack of supplies before sending him off to gather his own things.

"Do you have everything?"

As soon as Kiernan had quadruple checked, he was ready to go. The haversack itself was actually their blanket and bedroll, wrapped and tied in such a way that it made a sack to hold the rest of their belongings during flight. They each had a hard soled set of shoes at the bottom of the bag to give it structure and had it packed with dried meat rations and hard-baked sticks of nuts, grains, and other dried foods that would keep them flying.

The rest of the sack held a smaller bag inside of it, filled with trinkets used for guidance and other field needs.

"Are you nervous?" He asked, watching as she twisted the length of her hair, trying to think how she would set it for the flight. He was about to tell her it could easily get tucked under her haversack when she went for a knife next to her wardrobe.

"Oh, please don't!" He yelped, his urgency startling her. Of all the things that set her apart, this one was the most stunning. She was stepping out on her own for the first time in her life and she needn't give up the most obvious show of rank and status that she had earned. Many Kosaran men would have had to survive three lifetimes at war for enough to make a warcrest the length she could make now.

"But it will just get in the way," she said, practical if hesitant, and he could tell that she wasn't sure why he felt so strongly. "Do you have a better idea?"

"A warcrest," he said immediately. "You've earned it."

"You can't be serious," she balked.

"Look, you don't have to shave the sides," Kiernan said, negotiating as he watched the blade in her hand. "But I can braid it all back for you. You did say I could braid it," he reminded.

"But it would be disingenuous," she said, though Kiernan could tell she was thinking about it. "The end of my hair reaches my knees. No man in living memory has ever been at War that long."

"Your father has," Kiernan said, now having done the maths in his head.

"But I am not my father," she said, and then looked back to her hair. Kiernan flinched as she cut through the mass, though when she pushed it back over her shoulder, her hair still fell even with her hips. "This is how long I have been training, so that is what you can work with."

"Deal," he said, remembering to breathe.

"Well, go on," she said, shaking out what remained. "We don't have all day."

Kiernan grinned and had her take a seat at her wardrobe.

In less time than she expected, Kiernan was able to fashion what he had been trying to explain. Though he admitted not having time to do as many of the smaller braids as he liked, he was able to gather the hair on each side of her head into two flat braids so she didn't have to shave them. Once he had all the smaller braids set, he used them to make a thick three-strand plait from her forehead to the crown of her head. Then he pulled in the other four to finish the warcrest with a seven-strand braid that would lay flat beneath her haversack when they were ready to leave.

When he finally let her see his creation, Vinicia was overjoyed and guilty because of it.

"I don't know what to say," she admitted sheepishly.

"You're welcome works," Kiernan laughed. "But it certainly isn't required. This is just another way of recognizing you for all you have done for the Seat, Consort."

"If you say so..."

"And it's not like anyone is going to think it was your idea," he added with a laugh. "This is the braid I made for Lenae my first season as a Counsel Lord," he said before changing the subject. "So how do you feel?" He asked, stepping back as she came to her feet and she felt at the crest of braids. "This is the last time you'll be in this tree for at least a cycle."

"I haven't trained this hard, for this long, to keep living in a room no man but my father can find," she answered, motioning for him to move towards her mosaic of knots on the far wall. The fact that she spoke with such authority as to her skill made Kiernan respect her just a little more. When they neared, Vinicia reached out and set her hand on the knot at the very center.

Kiernan watched on curiously as she closed her eyes, and then the knot of the mosaic shimmered and Vinicia pulled it from where it had been stuck in the resin on the wall. This had been the knot she had said led to the Library, and she was resolved to their task as she tucked it into the smallest hip-pouch on her belt.

"For luck," she explained, setting her hand across the hole she had made in order to shift the mosaic into a door once again. It changed in a heartbeat and then Vinicia pushed it out on its supernatural hinges.

"I thought we were heading out," Kiernan said, confused.

"Something has been bothering me," she said, moving to step through the doorway. "I just want to see something before we..." Her words failed as she turned around and when she looked up to the Great Tree, she gasped. "Oh, sweet Gods."

Kiernan followed her out, only to be blinded by the intense light. Shielding his eyes, he turned to see what had startled her, only to have his own jaw go slack in surprise.

The Great Tree in the Library was blooming.

Kiernan's gape turned into a grin as he saw the once barren canopy filled with leaves that scraped against the crystal roof. More than that, there were spots of white as well, flowers big enough to see even from the ground. Kiernan had always known that the Great Tree was enormous, but seeing it come to life, it might as well have been a true piece of megaflora from the Eihwaz.

"Did I do this?" Vinicia asked as her shock changed to worry. "Did we? But how?"

"I think you know how," Kiernan said, grinning back at her as she flushed. "Though as fascinating as this is, we should still be going. You did mean to show Kaitlyn around your office before we checked in on the century, and that doesn't give us much time."

"I know," she said, duty calling her back to the day ahead. "Oh Kiernan, Kaitlyn is going to be beside herself when she sees this."

"She will be ecstatic," Kiernan agreed, setting a hand on the crest of her wing. "The girl will get to see a dryad's tree up close, which is far more thrilling than reading about them in a book."

"But Noventrio isn't a dryad," Vinicia said, confused.

"No, but you are," he said and shook her wing with the jest. "And maybe by more than half, if this is any measure."

Realizing what he meant, Vinicia took it for the compliment he intended. "I want to argue, but I suppose I can't, given this," she said, gesturing to the tree. "All right, I've seen what I wanted to see."

"Lead the way, Consort," Kiernan said as she set her hand on the bark again. A heartbeat later, he felt his stomach drop to his feet as she Stepped them on their way.

Chapter 33: Vinicia

Sunday, 06:00

When Vinicia next opened her eyes, they were in her father's roost within the Armory. Early as they were, it seemed like neither her father nor uncle had roused, though at the sound of galloping feet, she was glad that Aevi, at least, was excited to greet her. She had woken up for the last time on Palace grounds with a new life laid out before her. Knowing what that would mean, she had to say goodbye now just in case she needed to take Kiernan and leave mid-day instead of after the tournament had wrapped up.

"Good dawning, Aevi!" Vinicia greeted as the silver gryphling leapt into the air with a happy scree. "I am sorry you can't come in the tree with me, but I'm here now," she said, watching as the gryphling soared around the room. "Are you ready?"

Vinicia laughed to see Kiernan duck as Aevi came near, given that the gryphling was nearly half a stone in weight with a pace wide wingspan. Cute as she was, he was wise to not want to see what happened if he was in her way. The next time she came around, Vinicia flexed her wings down to give Aevi space to backwing across her shoulders.

"You're rather good at that," Kiernan said, impressed as he watched the gryphling put her feathered head against Vinicia's chin, nuzzling in close as Vinicia scritched between her wings.

"I should be after almost forty cycles with her," Vinicia said, kissing Aevi's beak before nudging her head back. "Though whatever father is feeding you has to stop," She laughed, moving deeper into the room. "You're getting huge!"

Aevi's only response was to nip at her eat, indignant,

As for the room itself, it was also rather large, though this front receiving area was the main living area. There were more apartments in the back, which is where she usually found her father hiding among his notes and journals. Just because he couldn't see with his eyes did not mean he couldn't read with secondsight. As it turned out, Aevi could see just fine, and her mother had shown him how to see through Aevi like Kiernan himself could see through the men of the Warhost. It was the only way the three of them had made it out of the Eihwaz alive.

When she heard the answering call of 'Just a moment!' From her father's back rooms, Vinicia looked to Kiernan, only to find him staring at the enormous map of the War Plains that spanned the far wall. Given that he was in his flight lenses, Vinicia didn't distract him, knowing he was reading through her father's scrawl of notes. She had gotten lost in it countless times before, but having someone distract you was always disorienting.

Taking a breath to steady herself, Vinicia looked around the cluttered room and the lifetime of her father's collection. Most of the items were from the Estate on the Kirathy shelf that both her father and uncle had brought with them when they had become Counsel Lords, all black lacquered wood with crimson accents where they weren't faded with time. There was an altar here as well to Great Matron Seres, the Founder of the Kirathy shelf, and though she had never been consecrated to the Goddess of their Ancestors on Kirathy soil, Vinicia hoped that the six-winged Founder knew of her. She had tried to Honor the Founder's memory as best she could from her hiding place in Delton, but there was only so much she could do caring for the Tyro Legion as the Founder herself cared for the other eight Legions who used her Shelf for their Citadel.

With a whispered prayer as she dusted the small shrine, Vinicia hoped she would be able to serve as her own father had, bringing Her glory in the process no matter how far she was from both her homes.

Vinicia came back to herself as she heard shuffling feet in the distance and smiled to see her father with his hand on the room's threshold, taking in the sight of her.

Eirik was dressed in all the warmth that coin could turn into fleece and finery, though she was glad to see he had polished his ancient Seventh Counsel Lord's pauldron to celebrate the day. Unlike the one Kiernan wore, when her father had returned from the Eihwaz with Aevi as a companion, he had altered the piece to have a support in the back that helped stabilize Aevi's weight. She could and did ride on Vinicia's shoulders often, but given so many cycles unable to fly, Eirik's aged grace and precarious balance was greatly assisted by the accommodation of that perch.

Hearing Eirik clearing his throat, Kiernan came out of his flight lenses. He had been staring along the River Kir near to Boatswan and the Lan'lieanan stronghold of Tor'Kirin, which was as far back as he had pushed the front during his own time as acting Seventh. Given that it was also where they meant to come out of the woods, it made sense he was updating the small notebook he had pulled from the thigh-pocket of his flight harness that he had worn this dawning. Like Vinicia herself, Kiernan had stored the rest of the harness in the haversacks they both carried.

"Did you enjoy your first day in the sun, daughter?" Eirik asked, gesturing for them to sit at the lounges before a cold hearth.

"About as much as a fish enjoys drowning in a river," she returned, which only made him laugh. "I have lived in the Palace all my life and never wanted to be in that place. I am glad I only have to do it once."

"That bad, eh?" Her father chuckled. "I never did like Court either," he admitted, finding the back of his favored chair with ease. As he settled into it, wings relaxing onto the built in supports, Vinicia caught Kiernan looking to the wood piled beside the hearth as if he wondered just how long they would be here.

Trapped in his secondsight or not, Eirik noticed.

"Vinicia?" He said, head tilted towards the hearth.

Vinicia looked away, gesturing towards the wood pile to stack it like he wanted. A moment later, her father snapped his fingers, which took his hand through the subtle sign for fire magic as he pointed towards the hearth. Kiernan managed not to jump as the wood sparked to life, his eyes full of a new respect for Eirik with the show of Talent.

"Father," Vinicia warned. "Please do not tell me you had me bring him here just so you could show off. I have things to do before we leave."

Chuckling to himself, Eirik's attention went to Kiernan as he watched them both warily.

"I can't do things like that, can I?" He asked, uncertain as he perched on the edge of the lounge. "You said you made me a sorcerer and I—Ser, what did you do to me? How did you do anything to me?"

These were the questions Eirik seemed to expect. Taking the moment to let Kiernan settle, Eirik's white-eyed stare turned to him with seriousness. "A windwalker cannot be made into a greenman without passing through a hearth tree," he began. "And for all you might have stayed in her apartment last night, I dare say that does not count. No, all you have is bardic strength, though you may be second to Noventrio himself, for all my meddling."

"So, what have you done to him?" Vinicia insisted. "Surely just wearing my hawkeye did not make it so he can let me access the energy of the temple tree..."

"Wearing your hawkeye let him grow his Gift for mental magics far beyond Noventrio's control," Eirik explained. "And because of that, the excess he wields can be used for your purposes the same as it can for Noventrio's. Granted, Noventrio will be furious to realize you can reclaim that power now, but there is nothing he can do. Servants that we three have been to him, he may not harm us for all we do to work towards the peace that he promised to Great Father Tralmis."

"Great Father who?" Vinicia asked, confused. Kiernan didn't seem to understand either, though he was willing to hear more.

"Tralmis," Eirik said, though from his smile, that name was likely all he would give her. There was a reason she had read most of the Library in her youth, searching for answers to questions her father knew, but refused to provide.

Vinicia refrained from rolling her eyes. They didn't have time for this, and he still hadn't answered her question.

"Vinicia," her father said, shifting in his seat as he faced her more fully. "Our ancestors themselves knew that the end of a war is a thing long crafted, but as a Seventh I came to understand that Founder Noventrio is the architect of the war, not of peace. Pact-bound or not, he has spent two thousand cycles burning the life out of the men who serve him, hoarding what is left of us in the temple you call your home. All the men before me who have carved a path through the Eihwaz have done so hoping they might find someone who could free us from that cycle," he said, choosing his words carefully. "I was the last piece of that first step, exchanging my life in order to see you born in your mother's grove, but the cost was worth it. You were worth it, for all you have the strength to work for our peace in a way none of us could have ever hoped."

"What do you mean, exchanging your life?" she asked, confused. "Do you mean your sight? Your—"

"My life, daughter," Eirik interrupted, and there was an easiness to his voice that undercut her panic. "I told you I have made Kiernan a channel, but I was taken into your mother's hearth and changed. When I came out the other side, I was a part of her—a part of you—and the strength I have syphoned from Noventrio's tree has helped you survive in this place."

"You are a greenman, then," Kiernan said when Vinicia couldn't speak the words. "Vinicia's greenman?"

"I am her mother's greenman, but I serve her daughter as well," Eirik said, pleased he had realized it. "Though I must say, you seem to be doing well enough without me this dawning, girl," he said. "The Wellspring looks good in you."

Vinicia flushed, absolutely unable to look at Kiernan.

"Is that what I am meant to do for her on Envoy, then?" Kiernan asked, and Vinicia's heart skittered to hear the eagerness in it. "Be her greenman?"

"In a manner of speaking," Eirik chuckled, glad to see he was not against the idea. "I am not arranging a marriage, however. All I mean for you to be is a channel for her as she guards you through the Eihwaz. The power of Noventrio's temple passes freely into you as you use your gift for the Seat, but it will wane once you name your Counselheir and gift him the hawkeye. The further you move from Delton, the more she will need to cultivate the Wellspring from the acts between you, rather than from any access to her stored power. You understand my meaning, yes?"

"I believe I do," he said, glancing at Vinicia with a smile that would have melted her heart if she hadn't been blushing so furiously. It wasn't like she didn't want to share a nest with him again, but to think she would have to...

::We can go as slow as you like,:: Kiernan reminded, his words a soft, subtle whisper into her mind as he spoke with pure bardic strength. ::Or I will show you other ways to be intimate outside of a nest. I gave you my word, Vinicia, and I mean to keep it."

Vinicia's heart was racing with just the thought. When she finally smiled in return, close to giddy with the way he pulled power to himself as she watched, when he reached out a hand to her, she took it immediately.

"I can see this is going to work out just fine," Eirik said, startling them both back to the present.

"Yes, father," Vinicia admitted, releasing Kiernan's hand. "I believe it will.

"Oh, for the cycles I spent with your mother," Eirik said with a nostalgic sigh. "I had feared you would rather get your heart racing with a dragon pole than a man all the days of your life, but there is hope for you, yet."

"I haven't had the chance to find out either way," Vinicia said, equally candid. "But I like him better after our sparring session, so there is that."

Kiernan grinned back at her, near to laughter. "And I love a woman who can hold her own in a debate. For as much as you have read and as much as I have studied, we should have plenty to talk on for the long walk through the Eihwaz."

Vinicia's lips twisted in a smile as she thought about that. Certainly Kiernan held strength for her, but he was also a true friend and one she had made as a tyro in the barracks. He understood not only who she was but what she was and there didn't have to be any explaining away what made her unique. He wouldn't mind the magic, either, given how much easier it would be to travel with her as a companion. If nothing else, she could heal walking blisters without thinking twice.

"So he is a channel for me," Vinicia confirmed, looking to where Aevi was churring happily on her shoulder. "Is that all you meant to tell us, father?"

"That was the first of it," he said, and Vinicia frowned as Eirik began to unbuckle his heavy rank-pauldron. "The second was to say that the Seventh's Path through the Eihwaz will take you to your mother's grove. Heatherwood stands guardian over the end of that path where the Southern Conclave begins, but as for how you will get there..."

Vinicia wasn't sure what to think as her father came to his feet, walking towards her with the pauldron in hand. Seeing him move, Aevi shifted across her shoulders and then stepped onto the back of the lounge to be out of the way.

"Father?" Vinicia asked, ducking her head as he set the pauldron over her shoulders. "What are you doing?"

"You need this far more than I do," Eirik said, adjusting the weight across Vinicia's shoulders. "Aevi has always been your familiar, no matter how she may have served me in this place, but those talons are sharp if you mean to walk with her. It is time that she began to serve you as she was meant to do all this time."

Vinicia put her hand over the pauldron to keep it steady as she looked down to the gryphling, only to see intelligence shining back in the bright emerald eyes.

"But father, this is your—" Vinicia stammered and then almost jumped when she felt Kiernan tap her shoulder.

"May I do the rest?" He asked. She nodded, her mind blank as he reached to buckle the double straps around her chest and wings. When his hands went to the laces that held the wrap of the quicksilver against her arm, she just closed her eyes. Having him so close, having him touching her made her feel as if the heat of the sun was warming her at mid-summers, but she had no idea how to react to the fact that he was putting her father's pauldron on her shoulder. Granted, it was ancient and barely recognizable as a Seventh's quicksilver, but it was his pauldron all the same.

"It looks good on you," Kiernan said, touching her hand over the pauldron as he finished.

Aevi gave a loud squawk when he moved away, hopping onto Vinicia's lap before crawling across her shoulders. Vinicia flexed her wings back to let her get onto the leather shelf. As the gryphling draped her paws over Vinicia's right shoulder, she pressed her beak against her jaw in a churring hug.

"This is why I asked you here," her father said, setting a hand on her hair as she closed her eyes, overwhelmed in the moment. "To gift you this and to let you know that the next few dawnings will be a struggle for you. I will make certain you can leave this place, but you must take his help as you continue to the Eihwaz. Take what breaks you require, take what comfort you need in him or Aevi or whomever else you may cross, but know that his gift supports you just as much as you support him. You both have a duty to the Seat, but your life is more precious to me than any gain we may make towards peace. If you are to survive this, you must trust yourself and the strength you have. You cannot deny it any longer."

Before she could respond, Vinicia had to steady herself against the force of love that flowed in from her father's hand. For all his manipulations and meddling, this one touch sang in her in a way she wasn't sure she could ever describe. It was almost as if she could remember her mother doing it, but so much of her life had been a blur that it was hard to distinguish from the cycles of dreaming.

"I cannot deny anything wearing this out in public," Vinicia managed, laughter in her voice for all she couldn't believe what was happening. "But as long as Aevi knows where we need to go. I am sure we will manage."

Kiernan's laughter followed her own and he stepped back. "Roder's Blackwings are going to lose their minds when they see you in a pauldron *and* a warcrest," he observed. "Not to mention the tyros."

"After they way they treated me during their feast, I think I will survive," Vinicia agreed, wiping the mist of tears from her eyes before they fell. "Gods, is that all, father?" She laughed. "I cannot survive much more of this."

"That is all, daughter," Eirik chuckled, shifting back so that Kiernan could help Vinicia to her feet. It took a moment to adjust under Aevi's weight, but the gryphling was churring happily after a few moments. Kiernan's smirk left no doubt in her that, while he loved the sight of her in it, he would also love the sight of it piled on the floor beside another shared nest.

After a moment, Eirik cleared his throat, realizing they had gotten lost in one another again. "You will see Shayan at your little celebration, but do not feel as if you need to stall your leaving on my account," he said, embracing her with strength. "Good luck to both of you."

Once he was done, he turned to Kiernan, clasping his outstretched hand with both of his own for all the duty of the Seventh's Seat now rested squarely on his Counselheir's wings.

"Shall we?" Kiernan asked as her father released him, turning to shuffle back to his private rooms.

"I think we shall," she agreed, though she ducked her head to hide her smile as he approached. "Counsel Lord."

"Consort," he echoed, wrapping his arms around her as Wellspring sparked between them. As his lips met her own, the kiss they shared set her heart on fire and she Stepped them both into her office without so much as a warning.

As they came out of the twisting movement, Vinicia snaked her arms around his neck as Kiernan's own tightened at her waist. Wings pressed back against the hard wooden door, Kiernan made a temptation of himself, drawing in as much of her power as he could while he stole her breath away. Relenting at last, it was all Vinicia could do to control herself as she stole that power from him. All she could focus on was the idea of asking the man to find her tail feathers here and now.

Instead, somehow, she managed to stop them both when Kiernan set her hips on the low desk. Amazing as it felt to trade power, that ravenous part of her still refused to let him step away, legs wrapping around his hips until he had to reach behind her to brace himself on the desktop.

"Praetor Ivan is going to lose his mind," Kiernan panted, his words a hot rush of air against her cheek as his hand gripped her shoulder. "Losing me so often."

"Just as long as we don't lose our senses," she said, her attention caught by the silver gryphling that sat on the desk, watching them. "Kiernan, I—"

Kiernan's finger on her lips stopped her apology before it could start, and she was flushed with as much embarrassment as arousal as she unhooked her legs from around his waist.

"I don't know what's come over me," she explained. "I just can't get enough of you."

"And I can't think of anything beyond turning you over and fucking you on this desk," he managed, the words a strangled growl as he fought for self-control. "Last night was incredible, but tonight?" he said, his words a whisper as he shifted to set a hand at the apex of her legs. "Gods, as soon as we're in the pillars, I mean to make you sing."

Starlight burst to life in the air around them as Vinicia saw the raw desire in his eyes. Ravenous as she was for him, it took all her will power not to move as he backed away from her.

"Holy Matron, this is insane," he swore, looking to the ceiling as his wings hit the hard wooden door. "Gods, I haven't felt like this since I was eight and ten chasing under Lenae's skirts for the first time."

"It's the magic," Vinicia panted. "Gods, it's just the magic."

"Don't you dare blame this on your bloodline," he said, dropping his eyes to her again with seriousness. "You are gorgeous, powerful, and impossibly strong. The only other woman alive to match you is the woman I have pledged to take as a wife, and I would burn the world to set her free."

Vinicia slid from the desk as he stared her down, refusing to let her make any further excuses.

"Indulgent as this feels," he went on, looking away as he adjusted himself and got his clothing back in order. "Trust my Gift as an empath that the core of this is true emotion. The connection between wingmates always is. Sex is just..." He said, stalling as she chewed her lip. "Just a by-product of that."

"Liar," she laughed, glad the potent energy of the room was clearing as they kept apart.

"Okay, a very pleasurable, amazing, incredible by-product of that," Kiernan admitted, laughing as she smiled. "And I will show you everything it entails tonight."

"You promise?" She purred, gripping onto the desk behind her so she wouldn't stalk towards him.

"I promise," he said, hand to his heart. "But for now, we have folks waiting on us, remember? Kaitlyn and Sera?"

"And Lenae," Vinicia acknowledged. "I did say I would give you back to her, eventually."

"You did at that," Kiernan agreed. "It is only for the day, however. Tonight…"

Kiernan's hungry look made her regret every ounce of self-control she had ever cultivated while hiding in the Palace. What the man had done to her with only a few fleeting touches the night before still sent shivers up her spine, and as his eyes raked over her, she could only wonder at what tonight would bring.

Still, Counsel Lord and Consort that they were, they both had their duties.

Exhaling in a rush, Kiernan broke the spell between them as he turned towards the door, hearing movement in the hallway. As the wil-o-wisps began to fade, Kiernan pulled the door open to reveal Consort Kaitlyn about to knock with Dame Seraleia standing beside her. Kaitlyn was dressed in her purple and silver court garb, though she had a heavy flight cloak for the outside winds and a round, furry hat over her mass of golden curls. Sera was layered much more heavily in winter gear, though it was all Windover black and gold. Her hair was covered as well, tucked beneath what looked suspiciously like a soldier tyro's flight hood, if with an added trim of fur.

Both girls were beaming with a secret smile that nearly set Vinicia blushing. If Micah was already a powerful warbards, just what could his twin have sensed from the hall? When her knowing look flitted to Kiernan and back to her, the sense of overwhelming approval nearly made her turn scarlet.

::We could come back if you two are busy…:: Sera sent, her voice a whisper of mind speech that easily rivaled Micah's own.

Vinicia had to look away as her face lit on fire. Likely hearing the girl as well, Kiernan came to her rescue, allowing her to recover herself as he greeted them.

"We come bearing gifts," Kaitlyn said, though Vinicia's mortification continued as she realized the young woman was blinking away her godseyes. If Sera had sensed them clawing after one another with her bardic talent, Kaitlyn had likely seen the power sparking between them in the room.

"You are a goddess, Kait," Kiernan said, waving at them to set down the tray of food and caffea as Vinicia made space.

"Not at all," Kaitlyn returned.

Behind her, Sera was peeking past her wings, struggling to keep the tray level as her mouth fell open to see the gryphling on the desk.

"Sera," Vinicia said, making the introduction. "This is my familiar, Aevi."

Realizing she was the center of attention, the gryphling shifted to sit on her haunches. Silver fur puffed against the cool air of the room, the vain little creature had her wings flared just so, neck arched as she flashed both women a mischievous look.

"Oh my gods, she is so *cute!*" Sera blurted out. "Look at those pointy feet! And her wings! Oh, she must weigh—"

"Half a stone," Vinicia said, and Kiernan was able to scoop the tray out of her hands before she dropped it. Sera's attention was completely lost to Aevi as she came up onto her paws, tail flipping behind her to send the large puff on the end flitting about.

"I told you she was adorable," Kaitlyn added.

"She is also very friendly," Vinicia chuckled. "You can pet her if you like."

As both women came in close to say their sal'weh, Aevi moved to the edge of the desk, happy to have her feathers ruffled. Meanwhile, Kiernan set the tray on the table behind the desk, moving the bowls, cups, and spoons so they could be used. When everything was out of the way, Vinicia was amused to see Aevi's beak rising in the air, sniffing after the large wooden plate that Vinicia had taken from the tray to set on the floor. Unlike the others, this one was still covered.

::Well, go on,:: Vinicia encouraged, hoping the gryphling could hear her. Her father had said that the gryphling had once been able to talk to her mind-to-mind in some small way when they had been in the Eihwaz, but she could not remember doing so herself. With how she was feeling this morning, though... ::That one's for you.::

Aevi's eyes went wide as she looked straight at Vinicia and sent back: ::Open!::

Vinicia's heart filled with joy to hear the word, soft and subtle as it was, and lifted the cover up to reveal a thick fillet of raw fish. Aevi's happy scree filled the room as she reared on her back legs and pounced on the plate as if she thought herself a fox. Once it was 'dead', Aevi started tearing into it with the sharp hook of her beak and the rest of them might as well have vanished.

"Get it, girl!" Sera said, grinning as the four of them tucked into their own meals.

"She's lucky she's cute," Vinicia laughed. "She's broken more than one plate doing that before."

"It's too bad you didn't have her with you as Barracks Mother," Kiernan said, amused as he watched the gryphling. "I believe she could teach the tyros a thing or two about proper foxdrops."

"Only the dropping part," Vinicia said. "She won't get up until that fish is gone and she's not going to keep dropping until I say stop. The tyros however..."

Kaitlyn seemed to be keeping mental notes as the two went back to their porridge. "The Kitchen Mother told me you usually picked up food to take up to Aevi before turning in," Kaitlyn explained, switching to her caffea. "But since you didn't come last night, she figured the gryphling would be with you and hungry."

"She would be right," Vinicia said, thanking her again. "As you can see," she added, laughing as Aevi started on her second fillet.

Aevi was halfway through her meal when Kiernan was done, exchanging the bowl for the caffea with his thanks. The rest joined him shortly after, though as they sipped the warm, bitter liquid, Vinicia gestured around the office.

"The tour is rather simple, I'm afraid," she said as Kaitlyn looked around. "Two-thirds of the room is taken up by reports that I've made regarding the current tyros, though I could only do that because of who and what I am. I doubt if you will do that for Aaron going forward."

"I won't," Kaitlyn confirmed. "Counsel Lord Aaron said he wanted to move the reports into his suite so I can have the space for new books. I am to help him with the overall structure of the tyro program, here and throughout the mountains. He thinks what you've done here in Delton will work in the other tyro academies if it can be codified."

"Oh," Vinicia said, surprised and more than a little touched. "I didn't realize..."

"That you've had quite an impact," Kiernan said as she hesitated, toasting her with his caffea. "Ten cycles she's overseen the officers that the Seventh Counsel Lords have used at War, and she doesn't think she's done a thing to improve it."

Vinicia made a face at him, but it was useless. It didn't affect Kaitlyn or Sera, either, though they both seemed to know what he was getting at. Exhaling in a rush, Vinicia looked down as she felt Aevi rubbing her head against her knee, begging to be picked up. Taking the moment to gather herself, Vinicia picked up the gryphling, though she didn't fight to go any further than her arms. Instead, she just churred against her chest, letting Vinicia hold her like a shield against the others.

"I've always looked up to you, Mother," Kaitlyn said, seeing right through her. "Vinicia," she amended. "I have wanted to be like you and now that you are going, I find myself walking in your footsteps. You made my new life possible," she said. "Thank you for that."

Vinicia didn't know what to say.

"You're thanking her for getting to play nursemaid to eight hundred sweaty boys?" Sera laughed, seeing her unease. "Oh, sweetness. We need to raise your standards. I can barely stand my three."

As Kaitlyn gaped, taking her seriously for a true heartbeat, Vinicia and Kiernan's laughter filled the room. Sera's own grin followed close behind until Aevi, caught up in their excitement, wiggled out of Vinicia's arms to prowl around the desk.

"Speaking of unpleasant things," Vinicia said. "I am sorry about not being able to bring your mother's book with you. If I had known it was there, I would have taken it as well, of course."

"It's okay. I know where it is, so I can just run in and get it," Sera said, pressing down the gryphling's crest feathers before reaching the start of the silky fur at her shoulder blades and wings. Clearly, she had found the right spot when Aevi made a sort of half-chirping, half-purring sound of pleasure. After long enough, Aevi was pressing so hard into her hand that Sera realized she was about to slip into her lap.

::I've got you!:: Sera sent and Aevi sent back a 'huh?' just as Vinicia blinked in surprise.

"Can you talk to her?" Vinicia said, watching as Sera scooped the confused gryphling into her arms.

Once Aevi realized just who had spoken to her, Sera got her right arm under the gryphling's back legs and her left was holding her against her chest. Before Aevi could protest, Sera started to scritch between her wings and Aevi thunked her head against Sera's cheek before snuggling in close.

Beside her, Kiernan looked as if he was trying not to chuckle.

"Of course I can talk to her," Sera laughed, kissing Aevi's beak. "I can talk to most animals. Micah can't, but he's all about telling people what to do. I listen," she said, making a face at Aevi as she drew back, inspecting her with one bright emerald eye. "It's the only way I kept all the creepie crawlies out of our space as a crew. Rylan hates them," she added with a laugh. "He can deal with rats, but a spider? A centipede? He'd literally die."

As Vinicia tried not to laugh, Sera's grin was wicked.

"But I can barely talk to her," Vinicia said, more than a little confused. "And she's my familiar."

"And her brother is loud enough to be a Preem," Kiernan reminded, which only made Vinicia roll her eyes.

Sera just shrugged. "Aevi says you'll get better with time, though," she added. "Right now it is my gift that lets me hear her, rather than yours. She says your reserves need to be full, though Aevi...." Sera's eyes shifted to Kiernan with a subtle smirk. "Aevi says he is good for you."

"Perhaps you should take her with you, then," Vinicia said, watching as Aevi preened at the braid that was tucked beneath Sera's flight hood. "I mean to keep her with me to take people's eyes off my pauldron until this starts, but afterwards I was sending her to watch over Rylan and his command cadre.

If you can talk to her, I would feel far more comfortable about you being in the city by yourself."

"I'm not exactly by myself with a century of Rylan's boys ready to help me get my book back," she said, shifting Aevi's weight onto her hip to hold her better. "But I suppose four eyes are better than two. Can you be sneaky, princess?"

Aevi's gaped-beak grin bobbed along with Sera's bounce.

"We're agreed, then," Sera confirmed, letting Aevi push out of her arms at last.

"Speaking of your boys," Vinicia went on as Sera started on her caffea. "I know you were in a panic the night before, but I have not heard a whisper of that sense. Is everything all right?"

"Of course," Sera said, smiling innocently over the rim of her cup. "Rylan threw a fit when everyone came to rescue him, but it mattered that they cared. He knows he has a crew of eighty now, not just the four of us. When Kait and I went over last night to check in, the whole century was bonding over it. At some point, Micah explained that Dylan's boys had come after me as well, which was why you didn't care I was here. When I came in, they all started to promise they'd get the guy for me, only to realize that I planned to go back in myself."

"How many of them proposed to you on the spot?" Kaitlyn asked, laughing as Sera rolled her eyes. "Was it five?"

"At least!" She sighed, though she didn't seem to mind as much as she let on. "It took a candlemark just to make them promise to be ready to help me after they finished their war game. Honestly, I don't give a shit about Dylan anymore. I just want my book back and this little girl," she added, giving Aevi another scritch. "You will be far more helpful than a bunch of smelly boys, huh? Won't you?"

Vinicia exhaled a laugh as Aevi's churring began to overpower the room.

"I told you the tyros would be fine," Kiernan reminded, if cautiously. "The hard part is letting them out of the nest to see if they can fly."

"Out of the nest and into the fire," she said, sighing. "I am glad for it, though. If you do need my help, Sera, you or him or anyone, please let me know. I will not have one of the best young men for this Warhost lost over ancient history."

"Of course, Mother," Sera said again, though Vinicia wasn't sure if she trusted the way she and Kaitlyn traded looks. Kaitlyn, she knew, would at least tell her if something had gone terribly wrong, and if they had said it had not...

"Well, if that's decided," Vinicia said, looking back to Kiernan. "I suppose we should be off. You can leave the tray just outside the door and someone will collect it."

"Lead the way, Consort," Kiernan said, coming to his feet as Kaitlyn turned to open the door behind them. Once they had the trays gathered and folks were filing out, Vinicia gave Aevi a sour look.

"You will keep her safe, correct?" She asked.

::Yes,:: Aevi said. ::I like Sera. She's salty.::

::Salty?:: Vinicia echoed, but the gryphling was as bad as her father for not explaining herself. Instead, she sat on her haunches as Vinicia twisted, pulling back her wing to let Aevi crawl onto her shoulders. With her front paws draped on her left shoulder, the pauldron braced against her right wing, supporting what weight Aevi couldn't balance on her own with the little shelf her father had added to the back. Clearly, the piece was no longer made for flying, but Vinicia was glad to have it if Aevi was to be her constant companion once again.

When all four of them were in the hallway, Vinicia closed the door behind them, only to realize they weren't the only ones present. Just past the entrance to the Great Mess itself, Counsel Lord Aaron was stepping out of his own office. He was dressed in full kama today, though it was hard to see beneath the fur-lined over-jacket he wore. With the same wide sleeves, the hari was the best way to control the flowing formal robes in the wind they would face today.

Once he was free of the room, Lord Fourth and Lord Fifth moved out into the hallway as well, though like Kiernan they wore no kama. Today was the one day the top tier of the Warhost worked, and that was reflected in the leather of their Warhost uniforms and the heavy, sculpted Counsel Lord pauldrons.

Seeing them, Kiernan raised a hand, though Vinicia had to stifle a laugh as the Blackwing entourage around Lord Fifth moved to fall in around Kiernan. Lord Fifth himself had nothing but a hard, angry look for the four of them, but he didn't say a word. Instead, he turned his quiet, biting remarks on Praetor Ivan beside him, who was in charge of the men. As three of the four men moved off, Hest'lre waited for them, considering her hair, pauldron, and gryphling with interest.

"You've accessorized," he greeted as Vinicia shifted beside Kiernan.

"I had to twist her arm to let me," Kiernan defended, even if his pride shone through for all she wore. "We're going to fight the Ice Winds this afternoon and I'd rather not have to deal with the rat's nest the flight will make of her hair if we left it loose."

"Which I appreciate," Vinicia admitted.

Before she could say anything more, however, she felt her skin prickling as Micah's voice echoed in her head. No matter the distance between their small party and the muster point on the flats before the Palace, he was calling with true strength.

::"Fall in!"::

"By the Gods, that boy is louder than you," Hest'lre swore, looking to Kiernan as he put a hand to his head.

"Decius told me he wanted the boy for his personal apprentice," Kiernan said. "It was the last message I got from him on paper."

"Now I suppose he will start as a preem for your Heir?" He returned, only to quiet up as Kaitlyn and Sera appeared just past Kiernan's wing.

"Tyro Micahleia could teach lessons to Preems, I think," Kiernan said. "But there is no amount of training for raw talent with these things. Whatever your gift, you just need the will to use it. If you have that, you can take on the world."

CHAPTER 34: MICAH

Sunday, 07:30

With the wind on the open flats in front of the Palace doing all it could to freeze him, Micah's stomach twisted in an anxious knot. He was going back into the Streets again, back into the Ice Winds that had nearly killed his sister, and as he stared at the open sky over the Lower City, today he knew it would come for him.

If I never had to feel these winds again, it would be too soon, he thought and shook his knees to generate some warmth for himself. Sera would have laughed and said he was dancing, but her shimmy and his staying warm were quite different. The only real dancing he had ever done without her was his practice for the Winter Solstice and all he focused on were the muscle isolations. It was Sera who performed for others, not him.

And Sera must have told Kaitlyn something for her to know to ask about an uumi, he thought, wanting to be upset but too happy that his love and his twin were getting on so well. Micah would show her what that was soon enough, but not because Sera had told her to ask.

"Can we start, already?" Micah complained, impatient to be done. "If this is the first day of the rest of our lives, I'm ready to get on with it."

When Westly looked over at him, Micah knew he wasn't fooling anyone. No matter how tough he tried to act, he hated the cold just as much as Sera did, and likely for the same reason. So as Micah rechecked the ties on his flight cloak and tried to settle the shearling cap about his ears again, he almost jumped when he heard Sera's voice in his head. She had moved again, now somewhere off to this right near the pavilions where the Counsel Lords and their helpers were staying out of the wind.

::You'll be sweating off that hat in no time,:: Sera sent, trying to be encouraging. ::And I will be right there with you, I promise.::

::What do you mean you'll be right there with me?:: Micah asked, leaning forward so he could see down the ranks to where Sera was waving.

::While you boys do your war game, I'm going to go in and get mother's book. Given where you're setting up, I'll be close enough to keep your Gift steady,:: Sera explained and Micah gawked to see a gryphling held in her arms like a fussy fledgling.

::I never agreed to this plan, you know,:: he scoffed and then came back to his Easy On stance next to Westly. ::What's that thing going to do with you, anyway?::

::Rip the face off anyone who gets too close to me,:: she sent smugly, catching up one of the gryphling's taloned paws to wave at him. ::Or she can fly back to Vinicia if I get in trouble, which I won't. Just like you boys didn't get into trouble last night.::

::You better not get into *that* kind of trouble,:: Micah shot back as Sera hid her face against the gryphling's neck. ::Mother doesn't suspect anything, does she?::

::She does, but she's distracted,:: Sera said, glancing where Vinicia and Lord Seventh were speaking with Lord Fourth. ::Very distracted.::

::She took him to nest?:: Micah sent, snorting with stifled laughter. ::Seriously?::

::They make a nice set, don't they?:: Sera smirked.

::About as nice as Wes and Nichi,:: he grinned. ::You know, for growing up in a brothel we know a whole lot of bowen,:: he added, and was rewarded with a burst of amusement in return. He had known she wanted to be more than a crew-sister to Rylan for ages, but Rylan was seriously clueless.

::Thank your boy Tyrsten for that,:: she sent in return. ::He's the reason Ry finally said something.::

"She saying something about me?" Rylan asked, knowing the look Micah was trying to hide.

"Maybe," Micah said, glancing past him to where Tyrsten stood watching. "Though I'm not sure I want to thank Tyr for helping you realize you wanted to fuck my sister."

"Me?" Rylan balked. "She's the one who wanted to find my tail feathers. It didn't even occur to me to ask her and now she won't keep her hands off me."

"Not that you seem to mind," Micah threw back, feigning offense.

"Of course not," Rylan defended. "She's brilliant and clever and holy shit, there's this thing she does with her hands. I mean—"

"Enough!" Micah laughed, cutting him off as Tyrsten and Nichi snickered. "I don't want to know what Sera does to you in a nest. As long as she's happy, that's all I care about."

Rylan just laughed, looking back to Tyrsten.

"You're welcome," Tyrsten said to both of them.

Having heard most of the exchange, Sera was laughing to herself when Vinicia came over to retrieve the gryphling. After a bit of fussing, the thing crawled onto her shoulder and huddled close.

::Mother's heading over,:: Sera sent, waving as Vinicia moved into the biting wind.

"Mother is coming over," Micah echoed as Vinicia neared.

Seeing her fully now, Micah had to double-take as he saw how her long hair had been done up into something that looked suspiciously like a warcrest. She also had a massive pauldron on her left shoulder that wrapped around her arm like a quicksilver. It was clearly meant to support the silver gryphling, but the sight of both put up the hackles of half the tyros behind him.

As the ranks of their bevy came to attention in echo to their command cadre, the thoughts quickly shifted to speculation of whether she had spent the night with Lord Seventh.

"Consort Vinicia," Tyrsten greeted, his affection for her obvious as he saluted.

"Praetor," she returned, giving a veteran's salute in response.

As Tyrsten preened, Nichi and Tyrsten's brother Ren showed their respects, but not nearly with so much vigor. He and Rylan saluted as well, and neither were surprised when she stopped in front of Westly.

"How are you feeling this dawning?" She asked, getting a closer look at his eyes that had gone from emerald to chestnut overnight.

"Wonderful, Mother," he said, looking into hers with equal interest. "How are you feeling?"

Micah frowned for a second before he realized Vinicia's eyes had gone from dark brown to amber with hints of gold.

"Whatever do you mean?" She asked innocently.

"You seem to be full of energy today," Westly said. "That's all."

"I did have a good night in my nest for once," she said, smiling ever so slightly. "Perhaps that is all I needed."

So she had taken Kiernan to nest! Micah could have sworn Sera had been joking.

"I appreciate the pendant, however," Westly went on more quietly. "Though I was surprised to see the change."

"As was I to see my own," she admitted and moved her hand to his temple briefly. After a moment she drew back with a frown. "I'll need to teach you how to set a proper shield with it, though," she said quietly. "It looks as if the one your mother wove into your stone may be too strong."

"I didn't realize that was possible," Westly said, surprised. "I had thought—Well, last night I gifted it," Westly said, trying not to look at Nichi beside him. "Rather than wearing it myself."

"Likely a good idea," Vinicia said, and Micah breathed a little easier as she stood tall once again. So did Nichi, for that matter. "Come talk with me after the tourni, eh? In the meanwhile, try not to over-exert yourself. That goes for all five of you," she added, speaking a little louder. "You may be in command now, but I do not want to find you in the Green because you attempted to do everything yourself. I taught you better than that. Understood?"

Rylan's salute, echoed by the others, was answer enough.

With that, she looked ready to leave, though she crooked a finger at Rylan to call him closer. "For luck," she said, setting the tip of her first finger on his brow. Rylan shivered, but the heavy tension radiating from his crew-brother faded as her eyes shone briefly with gold.

"You too, Micah," Vinicia added and touched his forehead as well. Micah shivered, feeling a pressure he hadn't known he had been under suddenly lifting. All at once his stomach released from its knot and the heavy press of minds on his Gift ebbed back to tolerable.

"There she goes, playing favorites," Tyrsten sulked, and Micah nearly laughed with the look of jealousy he was failing to hide.

When Vinicia crooked a finger at him, Tyrsten set his hand to his chest in a gesture that said: *Who, me?* The joke was on him, since when he moved closer, she reached out a hand and rather than touching his forehead, caught up his chin and planted a kiss on his brow before he could blink twice.

Tyrsten was absolutely star-struck when Vinicia stepped back, and more than a few of the tyros who had been watching couldn't help but jeer good-naturedly.

"For luck," Vinicia said, moving to take her leave. "Good winds to you all."

"She kissed me!" Tyrsten declared, gaping at Nichi as he watched her walking away. "Did you see that? The blicing woman kissed me!"

"Congratulations," Nichi said with an evil grin. "You're not a bowen anymore."

Tyrsten's eyes went wide at that, but just as he turned to give Nichi what-for, the crowd near the pavilions stirred. Micah followed the noise, only to see the outline of the four Kosaran Warlords rising over the crowd.

With Vinicia well and truly gone, their cantullus proctors settled into their place behind them near the edge of the shelf. Vinicia joined them, returning to her work as Kiernan's personal guard. Given the gryphling, warcrest, and armor she likely had beneath her legion blues, any man that messed with her was asking to have his wings ripped off. The title of 'Dragon Lady of the Warhost' might have started as a joke, but for all her station now, it was the truth.

"She knows she is a woman, right?" Ren asked, looking between Tyrsten and Nichi as they waited. "I mean, I know she's spent cycles in the Tyros' Wing, but that warcrest? That pauldron?"

"But nothing," Rylan challenged. "She's earned it, dealing with us for a decade. It's her father's anyway."

"Her what?" Tyrsten gawked, catching everyone's attention.

"Her father is Counsel Lord Eirik," he said, as if it should have been obvious. "He's the only one who ever survived an Envoy, and he came back with that gryphling. Gryphlings are dryad familiars." When all anyone around him could do was gape, he just rolled his eyes. "Gods, don't you people pay attention?"

"Rylan, are you saying Mother is a kindred?" Tyrsten asked as the attention of the whole bevy turned to look at her.

"If she wasn't, that gryphling wouldn't be anywhere near her," he scoffed. "Besides, you saw what Wes did for me last night. Imagine what she could do for Lord Seventh, no matter who came after him. Warhost? Assassin? Dryad? He might actually make it to Lan'lieana with her by his side, and they'll at least talk to her. It's blicing brilliant."

Realizing just how much Rylan had pieced together that had gone over everyone's head, Tyrsten closed his gaping mouth.

"I hope you're right," he said, coming to attention as the fanfare for their graduation tourni began. Taking a breath, Tyrsten looked forward and made the call to bring the century to order: "Wings up!"

Eyes locked forward, the men of both the Red and Green Bevy came to attention as the Counsel Lords processed into position across the flats. Fourth Counsel Lord Blake was the first, a blacksmith by trade who used his time outside of classes to further develop the kingdom's weaponry. The next was Fifth Counsel Lord Roder. Once the graduation was over and the new Lord Seventh was named, he would disappear back to the Citadel in Kirath to take command of the Vanguard once again.

Bringing up the rear was Counsel Lord Hest'lre, who oversaw the Home Guard, and their Headmaster, Second Counsel Lord Aaron, whose Soldier Tyro Legion spanned the Kihara range and produced the overseeing officer corps for the War effort. While many of the men who served were from the middle court of Kosaran society, coming from neither a Guild nor a House, those chosen to train in Delton were the truly elite among them. Dedicating four cycles of their lives to the art of war, the boys who studied at the Delton Academy graduated to become emissaries of the Seventh Counsel Lord on the Plains. As a result, while their headmaster wasn't a Warlord in name, he was undeniably responsible for the future success of the War and a cornerstone of the Kosaran military.

As Counsel Lord Aaron took the stage, their full century of graduating tyros saluted as one, and the sound resonated with effect despite the howling wind. Those family members who had gathered for the start of the tournament hushed to hear. Fortunately, as Lord Second had also been a warbard, his voice travelled with acoustic precision despite the wing-rustling of those who listened.

The Gift granted to the Warhost through the Seventh Counsel Lord was supposed to be a trick of the wind and the ear, making it so a warbard could project the sound of his voice effectively, but Micah knew better. Given his own gift and his time studying with the cantullus professors, Micah knew he wasn't just speaking into the wind, he was speaking into their minds. He had used that Talent as long as he had been alive, though if the Warhost wanted to call the same talent a Gift of the Seventh Counsel Lord, who was he to judge?

"For most of you, the journey to this place began eight cycles ago when you first challenged these winds to prove you were a worthy tribute to the crown. Though you had only just given up your apron strings, you threw yourself from these cliffs, terrified that you might fall. When the wind carried you up into safety, you chose to return, fighting your way back so that you would have the chance to stand here now.

"Four cycles ago you entered the floor of the great Halls of Learning that support the barracks, ready to become men. In your testing, you showed you had a worthy mind, and in the Armory you learned to hold a crossbow and aim it well. When you had proven you could fly, you moved into the balconies of the Great Mess to watch over those coming after you and to sit at the feet of your elders who were yet higher up. These last two cycles you have spent honing your skills, finding your place, and realizing your own potential.

"You tyros yet to war, you eighty strong men who have so honored your ancestors, know you stand at the precipice of Glory. At this time of trial, we send you out on your own so you may show us your strength. We have trained you to adapt and overcome your weaknesses in all things so that you may return to us whole and hale. If you learn nothing else from this place, know that the most important part of your training is not in fighting the battle itself, but in returning home. We fight for the Glory to be found at war, for the Honor of our forefathers, and for the promise of returning home once again.

"The end of a war is a thing long crafted, handed down from one Seventh Counsel Lord to the next, in a cycle stretching to when the gods were men," Lord Second said, pausing for emphasis as he quoted the sacred text. "May your ancestors stand with you now. May they guide your thoughts, give lift to your wings, and grant you the strength to persevere. For Honor and Glory."

"For Honor and Glory!" They called in return—even Rylan—coming to full attention with a one-up, three-down stomp of a salute that felt as if it could shake the Palace itself.

As much as Micah knew Rylan hated this place, a part of his crew-brother had always wanted this and Micah was glad to be able to fight at his side, Princeling that he had been, Rylan still wanted to prove himself as the last bastion of hope for a legacy his family had all but abandoned. That chance had been stolen from him as a fledgling, but fate had handed him a second try. Now, with the rest of his worries set aside, Rylan had the chance to take it and Micah would make certain that he did. They were no longer on the streets, and if Micah had to sit on Rylan's wings to stop him, they would never go back.

"Then ready yourselves," Lord Second ordered, and turned to Counsel Lord Kiernan who was waiting beside him. "Lord Seventh has your first assignment as soldiers in His Majesty's Warhost."

As they exchanged places, the excitement among the gathered tyros was an energy like no other. Eighty determined men stood at attention before the Warlords of Kosar, dressed and ready to become soldiers. As Counsel Lord Kiernan took the stage, the great, overwhelming force of the man's Seventh's Gift could be heard clearly above even the howl of the Ice Winds.

::Each cadre has four candlemarks to take and hold as many positions throughout the city as they can,:: he sent, his voice full of such powerful resonance that it set Micah back on his heels. ::Once the noon bells toll, report to Counsel Lord Aaron at the edge of the lower shelf. At half past noon, you will return here. No exceptions. Understood?::

"Hoi, Lord Seventh!" they echoed, and Micah felt a shiver of excitement as he heard the wings of the men behind him unfolding.

::"To arms, soldiers!":: Counsel Lord Kiernan bellowed, and the game was on. ::"Go find your Glory!"::

CHAPTER 35: THE LORALAE

Sunday, 08:00

Given the milling crowds that had gathered on the Palace flats, Lora was confident her disguise was solid. Watching as the young men raced to fill the Kosaran sky still made her skin crawl, though, bringing back memories of almost thirty cycles spent on the War Plains. Lora herself had never been part of the heavy-weapons wielding Val'Corps who would counter this kind of high, hit and run offensive, but she had still seen it. Lithe and fast as these men might be, her Cori sisters were experts at dragging them out of the heights for a proper fight whether they liked it or not.

Herself, Lora had been part of the Val'Kyr; a kyree warrior who had specialized in gathering intelligence and mounting subtle, precision offensives that gutted the men's ability to launch like this at all. Her *sha'dara* had been a Commander among them when Lora had been brought into the Vals, leading an entire Flight of such women in operations that assisted the Great Tor Mothers in their varied objectives. Seven glorious years she had served with MiaSera, fighting to knock these violent indigo streaks out of the sky as they searched for one man among them: the Kosaran Dragon Lord.

Cut off the head of the Dragon and the Warhost would fall.

Lora sucked her teeth as she looked around the gathered folk, almost amused by what she meant to do today. She knew exactly where the Dragon Lord was, but for all the Vals had turned her into a monster, she would never target him again. Not for them. The Vals had abandoned her, so she would abandon them as well.

And he's dead anyway, if he's going into the Eihwaz Forest to avoid the War, Lora thought, letting her eyes shift to her darkwater secondsight. *The woods will kill him as fast as it killed me, and no dryad means to turn a man into a weapon.* That was why she had to get to her *sha'doe*, after all. Vinicia would follow him into that forest in search of peace, but Lora was not about to let the woman kill herself for the Dragon Lord's idiot plan.

As the light of the world inverted, Lora looked through the mire to where the bright crimson spark of the young tyro Vinicia favored was glowing in the stagnant power around them. There was a bright green spark beside him as well, the young kindred Westly, and another deep azure of Rylan's friend beside him. They would be easy enough to follow, though she had to wait as they sent their companions into the wind before them. Unlike the Vals, Kosarans always led from the rear where it was safe.

Unfortunately, however, as the tyros cut through the massive updraft to begin, the noble spectators were already turning towards the warmth of the Palace. As they moved, Lora's own cover began to dissolve and she frowned to realize there was almost a trinae of Blackwings now posted on the flats, all of them hovering conspicuously around both Lord Seventh and her *sha'doe*. Worse, their Raven Lord was standing with them as well, speaking in low, angry tones that had nothing to do with the war game.

As Roder turned in her direction, still giving orders to his men, Lora was able to catch the man's growling words:

"I don't care what the Guard says," the man snapped, his wings flaring with anger as he turned on the Praetor who had spoken last. "That man had served near her long enough to know poisons do not affect her. Not as they should. If you and your men do not find that woman *now*," he said, pausing for emphasis. "I will have your wings for trophies before these idiot tyros return."

As all four of the Blackwing Praetors came into a crisp salute, the Raven Lord turned from them, stalking past the Dragon Lord and her *sha'doe* with murder in his look.

"Leave and be gone, Hawkeye," he swore, and loud enough for the world to hear. "It is not safe."

As the bustle began again, Lora sighed with the confirmation that the one man she had hoped would believe she was dead obviously didn't. Now she really needed to get off the Palace shelf. So as Roder stormed back into the Palace, Lora disappeared as well. Literally.

Moving from the place she had taken up watching the festivities, she had one last glancing look at her gorgeous *sha'doe*, finding her strength in the moment.

Soon, beloved, she thought. *But first things first.*

Lora was about to turn away entirely when she saw her *sha'doe* handing over her gryphling companion to a young woman who was dressed far more warmly than the nobility around her. Looking closer, Lora realized the girl was in fitted flying leathers, though instead of the tyro indigo, hers were black with burnished gold piping. It was Rylan's Sera, moving with the gryphling towards an easier part of the updraft.

Lora chewed her lip, hesitating. If the girl was going into the city, she was likely going to follow her order-singer of a twin brother. If that boy was near, Rylan wouldn't be too far off. Trusting her instincts, Lora shifted her step to take off after the woman.

Half a candlemark later, with the thunder of the Kosaran people roaring around her, Lora finally gave up her chase.

Damn, that girl is good, she thought, hands on her knees as she panted for a breath.

Sera hadn't realized she was being followed, she had also dead-dropped from the height of the shelf through that gale, only flaring her wings to soften her landing as she moved into what Lora could only assume were the 'streets' she, her twin, the kindred, and Rylan had called home for cycles.

For Lora, that meant she was at the base of the Palace shelf, glad to have not ripped her wings off attempting the same trick. Fortunately, the girl had put down next to the River Kir, so instead of panting in the open street, Lora had tucked herself inside the small cavern where the glacial waters that began the River Kir exited from beneath the Palace shelf. Fortunately for her, it wasn't sewage from the Palace, so while it was frigid, at least she didn't have to smell the filth.

After taking the moment to calm her breathing, Lora realized the roar of the water was only part of the sounds around her. Coming further forward, she looked up to see an enormous crowd of Kosarans lining the bank of the half-frozen river, all of them bundled against the cold and looking at the bridge spanning the width of the river just above her. Knowing that she would be spotted if she moved, Lora slinked back into the shadows and sighed. She was going to let whatever it was they were waiting for happened before she could leave. Hopefully, Sera was waiting for the same thing...

Neither of them had to wait for long. Just as she got herself settled, the onlookers' attention was caught as a man dove off the bridge and started down the length of the river with metal rings covering his arms.

What in the world...?

Lora shifted into the vision she would have used when flying and watched as the man continued down the river, setting the rings on floating buoys before stopping over a bridge to toss a few into the crowd, much to their delight. After that, he started down the river again, dropping the rings as he went.

Is this their tournament?

After a good ten beats, the white-clothed man reappeared, this time free of his rings, and that seemed to be a signal for the crowd's enthusiasm to start in earnest.

Glowering, Lora looked up to the edge of the bridge as she waited for them to get on with it, and then someone up above started a countdown.

"Three! Two! One!" They chanted until there was a sharp crack of a whip and their screams overtook any sense of words at all.

A heartbeat later, Lora saw the white-clad tyros diving off into the air above the river and quickly counted two squads of boys, half marked with green and the other with red. As they cut through the open air, they pulled into the triangular formations Lora recognized from the Plains. Once they were set, they began to muscle in on one another, making space for the nimbler teammates to chase after the rings from the buoys and surrounding crowd as they raced down the river.

As the crowd turned to watch the tyros moving away from them, Lora saw Sera jogging on foot down the street, with no one other than Lora herself the wiser.

Following the woman, she glowered at the stilted buildings that kept Delton from drowning in snow. The whole world seemed inside-out to her, as the idea of building a city on the flats was the exact opposite of how her people burrowed into the mountains and cliffs of their own islands.

Under the circumstances, if the images she had of the stilted city from tyro Rylan's mind were true, it would be perfect for both her and Sera's purposes. Not only would staying beneath the buildings keep her away from the veterans, but it would also keep her out of the wind as well. Those winds were brutal enough, given the dropping temperatures. Regardless of the sun rising in the sky, the world felt colder than it had the day before and the lingering fog that haunted the buildings would freeze by mid-day if it continued. Clearly, Vinicia and her Dragon Lord would want to leave at the conclusion of the tournament, but that meant Lora had very little time to pull her attention.

Following the girl down the gently curving street, one thing continued to gnaw at her. Why had that idiot ancestor been so concerned with a rogue source of power in the city? At first she had assumed the source was the other dryad-kin, but with him bound there hadn't been a change at all. That meant the one overflowing was possibly the rebellious tyro she had met in the High Cells, Rylan, especially considering how he was glowing like the sun at solstice.

Just like the bloody Dragon Lord, Lora muttered. *But why in the winds do I even care? He is just another boy in a sea of men I am supposed to hate, even if Vinicia loves him like a chick from her own body.* The only thing that made sense was that he cared deeply for the girl who reminded Lora so much of her own *sha'dara.*

But she only looks like MiaSera because it has been cycles since I have seen any woman from the Lans, Lora argued with herself. The girl had even said her mother had been Ehkeski, which MiaSera most certainly was not. By all rights, Lora shouldn't care. But she did. *Great Mothers, what is wrong with me?*

Stalling as she came to a crossroad, Lora exhaled her frustration in a soft puff of white. Looming in front of her was a large stone building that rested against the sheer cliff of the Palace shelf. Looking to the building proper, she saw the entrance was at least two stories up and covered with people watching as the tyros swarmed the city.

She had hoped to pass under the buildings and stay away from the tournament entirely, but—vexingly—someone had boarded up those spaces.

Worse, in the time it had taken Lora to catch her breath and look around, Sera had completely vanished.

Blood on my ashes, sha'dara, Lora swore, stepping out into the street more fully. *If this is not your daughter, she should have been!*

Sighing to herself, Lora blinked into her secondsight, letting the colors of the world invert to darkness and vibrant lines of moving power. There was little to nothing on the ground level, thankfully, which made the brilliant azure streak of the young woman come alive in her mind. She was still on the ground, though, which was odd.

Lora blinked out of her secondsight, realizing there was a large set of stairs that came down to street level a little way off. Approaching the stairs with an eye for hidden entrances, Lora moved closer to the white-washed wood paneling to see if she could find a place that could be pushed in for a hidden door. When that failed, she looked back to the stairs themselves.

If this woman had spent most of her youth on the streets in a gang, small as it might have been, then it was possible there were territory markings Lora could find. This time, she moved back under the stairs as if she meant to hide from the rest of the street, and then peeled off one of her stolen gloves to feel along the wood at eye level for any subtle markings.

She found what she was looking for after a moment and then had to stand on her tiptoes to confirm that the mark was intentional, rather than accidental. Being a head shorter than most Kosarans made her task annoyingly difficult, since the markings were at eye-level for any of them, but almost out of reach for her.

There is an entrance here somewhere, she decided, following the level of the marks to the panel against the boarded-up wall. Hesitantly, she put her hand on the planks and gave a shove...And a whole section of the wall swung out, just barely. That was promising. When she pushed a second time, she caught the bottom of the door with her foot and was rewarded when the weight of the door was assisted by some kind of counterbalance on the other side.

Pleased with her success, she slipped beneath the door and let it down gently behind her. As the door dropped into place, she found nothing but a tight walkway lit by what light came in through the slats of the wooden wall.

This works well enough, she decided, and was glad for the chance to be out of the wind. Shoving her glove back in place so she could feel her fingers again, she centered herself and blinked into her secondsight. Unlike a priest's single-sided godseye which allowed a person to see stagnant energy or the double godseyes that her *sha'doe* would use to see active, moving energy, Lora's darkwater sight allowed her to see the movement of elemental forces in conflict. Under her compulsion, it had allowed her to find the flows of power as they were pulled through a kindred dryad or other strongly gifted individual. Given that Vinicia had only known of herself and the sapling Westly, Lora guessed they would be the two strongest flows on the city-shelves, with the Seventh coming a close third and now Rylan, whose glow made her come out of her sight or be blinded.

Sighing, Lora touched the falconstone on her left wrist to shake off her guise. The boy knew her as her true face and, for all she had shown herself to the girl the night before, there would be no hiding from either of them. Whether they would speak with her now, she had no idea. All she knew was that she needed to draw Vinicia away from her Seventh somehow, and her *sha'doe* had strained herself for both of them in the past few days. Loyal as the woman was, she would do it again if need be.

But will she forgive me if I am the one that hurts them? Lora thought, hating herself, even if she knew she would still want to do it. Sera looked too much like her dead mentor, and Rylan? He might as well have been the shade of Sera's heart for how much Lora knew she loved the boy. She had to, to earn the kind of devotion he had shown for Sera in the High Cells.

Letting out a slow breath, Lora moved closer on silent feet as she heard the passionate exchange between them finally coming to a halt.

"I told you I could find you, soldier boy," Sera said, her voice a sultry whisper in the quiet.

"You knew where I was going," Rylan defended, and Lora came to a stop where she could just barely see the two of them. Wrapped up in one another, she couldn't see their faces for the curve of their wings, but his touch was tender as it rested on her waist. "And I know where you are going. You can wait to go with us," he insisted. "Once this game is over, I'll go with you myself."

"You know you can't do that," Sera admonished, pulling back from him to glower. "Dylan won't let you live a third time."

"He didn't mean to let me live yesterday," Rylan insisted. "But Westly had my back."

"That's even more reason for you to not get yourself in trouble," she insisted. "If you get hurt and Wes can't handle it, then Mother is going to try to help you, leaving Lord Seventh on his own. Do you want to be the reason he gets killed? The reason a Seventh gets killed?"

Rylan had no answer for her, which seemed to make her point. Instead, he turned the question on her.

"Tell me why I'm supposed to let you risk yourself, then?" he insisted. "What's so special about this book? I know it was your mom's, but you can't even get it open."

"It's still important to me," Sera insisted. "It was the second thing she told me. Don't leave your brother and don't lose the book. To the winds if I know why, but I promised her Rylan. By her blood and ashes, I promised to keep that with me."

Lora's heart lurched. This girl's mother might have been Ehkeski, but from the way she talked, she was from the deep south if that was true. How did this girl get so far into the mountains to be born in Delton? Had her father been a Blackwing like Lora's own? Clearly, this book had answers not only for Sera, but maybe for Lora herself.

"Fine," he sighed, letting his head drop forward as she pulled out of his arms. "If you're really going to do this, then I know I can't stop you. I just wish I could help you."

"I wish I could help you, too," she said, touching his chin to raise his eyes back to her own. "You play your war game, sweetness, and I will play mine. Okay?"

Rylan didn't say a word, just let her come forward to set their lips together. After a few heartbeats, his hands cupped her backside to bring her closer and Sera laughed against his lips. "I'll let you in my nest again when you've got your pauldron, soldier boy," she said, kissing him one final time. "Not before."

::If you would both just stay put, I will bring all of us to House Northern.::

Lora's breath caught as the sound of Micah's voice resounded in the area. It was a directional burst, a monstrosity of Warhost mind-speech, but it meant Lora could hear him as easily as the other two.

::Then Sera can take the book back, we can fly the winds, graduate and get out of this place.::

::Or I can get in and out without you needing to use eighty men who have better things to do to accomplish a one woman job,:: Sera sent back, her message whisper soft if still with the same whip-crack of command Micah's held. ::Don't think I don't appreciate the gesture,:: she went on. ::But I can do it myself.::

::I'm not saying you can't,:: Micah argued. ::I'm saying you don't have to do it right blicing now. That's all. We can go in with you.::

"Sera," Rylan pleaded. "I don't want to lose you. Not again."

::If it makes either of you feel any better,:: Micah sent, unable to see how the softness in Rylan's voice has started the affection between them again. ::There are some of Fionn's men around you, but I think they're lost,:: Micah said, his mental voice fading as his attention shifted away from their conversation. ::Well, maybe not lost,:: he said, coming back more strongly. ::I think they're actually watching House Northern, which isn't a bad plan, to be honest.::

Sera pulled back from the kiss with a sulk, even if Lora was glad to hear of their problem. She had a problem, too. If she could make their problem her problem without startling them both...

The plan was to get Rylan into just enough trouble so Vinicia would come down here, Lora thought, wondering at just what this business with House Northern was about. All things considered, it was as good an opening as she was going to get with limited time.

Glancing down at herself to straighten her kurta, Lora cleared her throat outside the door where she had been spying. The two froze in their embrace, though both were looking towards her.

::Nashtae, Rylan. Sera,:: she sent, pitching her mental greeting for them both. ::I'm about to step into the doorway. I did not wish to startle you.::

Rylan had his crossbow on her the moment she appeared. Sera, standing beside him, had two wing-blades drawn.

"How did you...?" Rylan said, gaping as he recognized her. "But you were a prisoner."

::I was,:: Lora agreed. ::Past tense. Now I just want out of this city and I could use some help. You two sound like you need help as well, getting a book? How about a trade?::

"I know you," Sera said, her guard with the knives dropping as she recognized Lora as well. "You came over to me after I danced, but then you disappeared."

::One of the perks of the job,:: Lora said, head tilting as she touched her falconstone to shift into the chiurgeon guise she had worn. When she shifted back, Rylan's mouth had fallen open, but Sera was looking at the bracelet on her own wrist in awe.

"You're not still going after him, are you?" Rylan asked. "The Lord Seventh?"

::Do you think I'd be down here if I was?:: She asked in return. ::No, I'm done with that. Like I said, I just want to go home.::

"Oh," Rylan said, frowning at her. "What are you doing down here, then?"

::It's bloody cold out there if you hadn't noticed,:: she sent, giving him a flat look. ::What are you doing down here? I thought you were supposed to be in charge of this war game or something.::

"One of my friends can talk to me like you can, so they stuck me down here to keep me safe," Rylan confessed. "If the other bevy finds me and can take me in, they'll get an automatic win."

::Sounds like you need a bodyguard rather than a hiding place,:: Lora said, crossing her arms under her chest. ::Is that why you're here, girl?::

"Maybe I should be, if women like you are prowling around," Sera said, bringing up her guard again.

"Sera," Rylan scoffed, dropping his crossbow as he put a hand out to call her off. "If she wanted to kill us, she wouldn't be talking to us."

::He has a point,:: Lora said, hands still raised in peace before her.

"What do you want?" Sera demanded.

::I want to get out of the city,:: Lora said again, which wasn't a lie, even if it wasn't the whole truth. ::And if you're about to go steal something from a bunch of highborn, then I don't mind helping so long as I can take the provisions I'll need.::

Rylan laughed at that. "You could steal everything from those kestrels and I wouldn't care," he said, honestly considering her offer. "Sera, where is the book?"

Sera's gaping surprise wasn't the answer he was looking for, though Lora saw the woman's objections crumbling. ::I see the sea in you, girl,:: she whispered, sending the message to Sera alone. ::And you see it in me, too. For the first time in your life, perhaps, but it is there. You do not have to live like you have, hunted and hiding and shamed for the strength in your spirit. I can take you out of this place when I go.::

Sera swallowed around the knot in her throat, looking to Rylan as Lora's thoughts overwhelmed her mind. If Lora could not have Vinicia, saving this girl from the mountains would be consolation enough. The twin might have issues, but it was far easier to convince a woman to seek her own power than it was to tell a man he had to step back and stand down.

"Sera, she can get you inside and out without a problem," Rylan was saying, his words an echo beyond the intensity of the moment between them. "All you want is the book, right?"

"Right," Sera managed, shaking herself to shove Lora from her thoughts.

"Come on, then," Rylan insisted, setting a hand on her wing. "The faster we do this, the faster it can be over. I still have to fly the Ice Winds and I want you safe."

::Lead the way, son,:: Lora sent, stepping back to let Rylan pull Sera along behind him.

CHAPTER 36: MICAH

Sunday, 13:00

"**D**amn it," Micah swore, startling Tyrsten who was standing beside him in the tactical operations command for the Red Bevy. "They're moving."

"I'm surprised it took them this long," Tyrsten said, equally annoyed. "Are they going to Northern?"

"Of course they are," Micah said. "Rylan's not about to let her go there alone. Go in, sure, but he'll have her back."

"Will they come out of the streets?" Tyrsten asked. "To get there, I mean."

"I don't think they're that stupid," Micah sighed, focusing on where Sera had been. ::Sera, you're staying underground, right?::

::I'm not stupid, Micah,:: Sera sent, and he could feel the eye roll. ::We'll be fine.::

Micah blinked into his flight lenses, looking to where Fionn had a squad of five tyros watching the area where they suspected Rylan had gone. They were picking up and moving as well, though it looked like it was only because they had spotted the gryphling that had been with Sera.

Micah grimaced and looked at Tyrsten, hating how all the shit with Dylan was bleeding over into the war game. He wanted to just tell Rylan to give himself up so the century could get back together and deal with the House Northern problem, but Rylan would never stand for it. Competitive as he was, he absolutely refused to lose on either front.

"Tyr, I have a bad feeling about this," he said, coming out of his flight lenses. "Are you okay with me going over with a squad? I can still reach everyone and your Gift is strong enough that you can check in with me if you need. I just—"

But Tyrsten wasn't paying attention. Frowning, Micah looked to where Tyrsten was focused in the distance and laughed. "No shit! Is that what I think it is?"

Tyrsten started cackling as Micah felt one of his stronger warbards reaching out to him with the news.

::We've got him, Micah!:: The tyro confirmed. ::Fionn's in the bag.::

"What'd they say?" Tyrsten asked, realizing Micah was looking through him as he sent back his wordless acknowledgment.

"He's in the bag," Micah repeated, relieved beyond imagining. "I can't believe we worried this whole time about Rylan when Fionn was stupid enough to fly into a blicing trap. He really loves puff pastry that much, huh?"

"Sera's idea was brilliant!" Tyrren cheered, coming in fast to join them on their rooftop. They made space for him to backwing and he set down without a problem. "And I blicing told you. He got in as much trouble as Rylan did this cycle, just with the kitchen and not the guard."

"Get to Rylan," Tyrsten said, waving Micah on. "When we're set, I'll send the rest of the bevy to back you up. "

"Hoi," Micah said and grinned. Fight as they might in the war games, if you caught their Primarch, your side won, hands down. Rylan was right to make that a priority. Even crews would back down if you took their leader.

"And take your heavies," Tyrsten added. " I suspect they can do the most damage out of all of us, anyway."

"Will do, Tyr," Micah said, and then turned and jogged to the end of the roof the cadre had been using as their headquarters. Before he got into the air, he closed his eyes and 'found' where his contact was in the heavy group, a tyro named Jerren, and reached out to him with a mental touch. When Jerren realized what was going on, Micah got a confused but curious sensation in response.

::I'm heading over to you,:: Micah sent, letting his cheer bleed through. ::We have Fionn in the bag, so I need to use you lot to go back up Rylan. Meet me near House Northern?::

Micah got the sense of Jerren acknowledging the message with a mental salute. That done, Micah unfolded his wings and leapt off the roof, slicing through the air until he could get the lift he needed. When he was soaring into the open sky, he banked left and started for where Rylan had been holed up in their old crew den.

When he got to the height he wanted, Micah concentrated and was able to pinpoint where Sera was making her way through the under city, trying to be unobtrusive even if it seemed like she was being tailed. Aevi had come out of the streets at her suggestion, giving Micah the true signal of her position.

::Sera, is Rylan with you?:: Micah called, wrapping the thought with all the relief he felt. ::The game is over and I'm rallying the bevy on Northern.::

::He is,:: Sera sent back. ::And I won't let him in the Estate. I promise.::

::Just be quick about it,:: Micah went on. We need to get the boys to the edge of the shelf for the Ice Winds run and the more we can rest, the better.::

::Hoi!:: She called back, as comfortable with Warhost word as any of the tyros.

Shaking his head to hear it, Micah caught sight of Jerren on his right. "You trying to get sent to the front, Mike?" He laughed, winging his way to Micah's side as the others fell into a V behind them. "The whole shelf can hear your calls."

"No," Micah scoffed. "But there's nothing I can do about it now. I'm not going to put Rylan at risk just to avoid a promotion. Speaking of which," he said. "This might be a real fight we're heading into. Are you boys ready?"

"Of course we're ready," Jerren said as one of the others took up the lead position, breaking the wind to give Micah an easier flight so he could talk. The other three were keeping Watch over the ground they were devouring, as their actual position was meant to do. A whole squad of watchmen with heavy crosses was almost unheard of, which is why Micah had wanted them all together.

That, and to have them on hand for just this reason, Micah knew. The fact that they were using the time mid-flight to strip their bolts of the protective padding meant the world to him.

"I don't want to get into a fight if we don't have to," Micah insisted. "So if you guys can keep in the area until everyone gets here, I'd appreciate it. I'm going to try and get to his position without alerting anyone, but if you see guys pouring out of that red-roofed estate," he said, gesturing. "That's your signal to come in. Sound good?"

"The rest of the century will be right behind us," Jerren said, knuckled his forehead for a mid-air salute. "Rylan is our brother, too, Mike. The Host protects its own, especially from asshole nobles."

"He knows," Micah said, returning it before refocusing on his flight. Once he and the others were into their flight lenses, Micah found the gryphling flitting between rooftops in a way that made him think Rylan had stalled.

::Boy Sera!:: The gryphling called and Micah felt the bright, anxious voice enter his mind with urgency. ::Other Sera is here to help.::

::Other Sera?:: Micah asked, startled to hear the gryphling at all. ::What do you mean? Is there someone else with them?::

Micah winced as he felt a wave of uncertainty in response.

That can't be good, Micah sighed and used the feeling to drive himself harder through the cutting wind as he crossed to the east side of the city-shelf. *And neither is this,* he thought, feeling the sharp pricks of pain that meant the rain was starting to freeze. That rain would quickly turn to ice, and they all had to make it back to the Palace shelf before it started. Anyone caught outside would soon be covered in a sheet of it, and trying to fly in that was nearly impossible, even if it had made for some of the more badass stories of graduates to come out of the academy.

Micah shivered as he forced away the image of how he and Sera had found their mother so many cycles ago. He was going to fight those winds and win if it was the last thing he did.

::Sera?:: He sent, reaching out to her with all the strength he could muster. ::Sera, where are you?::

When he heard nothing in return, he started to panic, but then her reply surfaced in his thoughts, echoing as if they were yelling at one another down an infinitely long hallway. This was the very end of their range.

::I'm at Northern,:: she sent. ::I'm going in, but I need to hide. I'll meet you and Rylan in the temple when I come out.::

::I see it,:: he called, cutting his wings back as he saw the four-story building in the distance with his flight lenses. ::I'm coming.::

Trying not to think of how strong his gift would become with her gone, he angled towards the Estate as he made his approach with the heavies beside him. Unlike the Lower City, this part of the Delton shelf was a large ring of gardens and land meant to be a buffer between Palace affairs and the work of everyday Delton. Micah had never been beyond this wall until his tyro training had taken them into the woods on the mountainside for extended sorties, but the fact remained the same. He had never been inside one of the Great Houses and he had no idea where to look for Rylan in such a place.

That's when he saw the towering temple just to the north of the building itself and a man in white Warhost gear with a red sleeve skulking at its base. For all the temple's former glory, it was just stonework now, and he could see Rylan as clear as day as he ducked inside the structure. Sera was taking off in the other direction, hurrying towards the building. Someone else was with her as well, though he had no idea who it could be.

Realizing they meant to go in the rear, though, Micah had an idea.

::Boys, see if you can set down on the other side,:: he sent, looking over at Jerren as they caught sight of Rylan as well. ::Pull them to the front. Rylan!:: He called, seeing his crew-brother flinch in the distance. ::We're going to create a distraction. Don't do anything stupid.::

Rylan made a rude gesture at him, though it seemed to be just his frustration as Micah watched him pace in the small space of the temple. He had done five laps of the structure by the time Micah came into the yard, backwinging just outside the temple as his own boys set down on the front lawn of House Northern.

"She said it's just inside," he insisted, wringing his hands as Micah joined him. "She should be right out."

"Who is in there with her?" Micah asked and stepped up to his crew brother as he wrung out the freezing rain from his tyro crest. Fortunately, the temple let them see both the side door Sera had gone into and the front gardens where the heavies had landed at the same time.

"A friend," Rylan said, keeping his focus on what Micah assumed was the doorway into House Northern. "If she's not okay, I'm going to murder him."

"Not before he and his boys murder you," Micah said, grabbing onto his arm as his pacing took him outside the temple.

Unlike the Lower City, these Estates had been sculpted from the same bedrock the Founders had cut away to create the great city-shelves. That meant that they were all grey stone and iron on their exterior, even if the insides were said to be nicer. With the way it was starting to pour, the building and the clouds behind it were all darkening to black.

As they both stewed in their anxiety, Micah cursed as he saw one of the two heavy front doors open, and then swore aloud as he saw Sera tearing out from the back of the House.

"There she is!" Rylan said, running out to greet her as Micah attempted to grab his wing. He never had been able to stop the idiot in the two cycles he had escaped the Palace, so he wasn't sure why he thought he could do the same now.

Swearing, Micah saw the person coming out was only dressed as Sera had been, and as she stopped to uncover what she held in her hands, Micah's heart stopped. It was a crossbow.

::"Rylan drop!":: Micah screamed, realizing just after Rylan did that the woman was his old Crew leader, Wenda.

Rylan threw himself towards the icy gravel on instinct, dodging the bolt meant for him with a heartbeat to spare. As he pushed to his feet, sprinting into the fray, Micah threw his voice towards the tyros he could feel streaking towards him through the city.

::"Eighteen!":: Micah called as he ran after Rylan, his own crossbow pulled up. ::"It's a blicing trap!"::

Micah could have killed his brother as he skidded to a halt in front of Wenda just as she reloaded, though he managed to knock the crossbow to the side to send the bolt sailing into the distance. Rylan wrenched it from her with his greater strength, knocking the woman over the head with it. As Wenda dropped, Micah finally caught up with him, throwing his arms around Rylan from behind before he could do more than turn towards the building.

"How nice of you three to join us," Dylan said, standing in the doorway with Sera in his arms, a knife at her neck to keep her from squirming out of his hold. "I don't know whether this is worth the trade, though. My brother's life for this one's?"

"What do you mean, three?" Rylan asked, and Micah turned to see Westly backwinging down behind them.

"I'm not about to let that asshole kill anyone," Westly said, his voice an angry growl as the century closed in around their position. From the way the crewmen hesitated, looking wide-eyed at cobblestone courtyard, Micah suspected the men of their Tyro century were finally joining them.

"Such harsh words from a kindred," Dylan tsked. "All I want is his signature. He knows that as well, but he just insists on keeping it from me. Sera?" He asked, letting the knife at her neck draw blood. "Do you know why he'd rather see you die than sign a piece of paper?"

"Fuck you, Dylan," Sera spat, even as she pulled back from his grip. For all his height, only her grip on his arm was keeping him from suffocating her. There was nothing she could do about that knife.

::"Let go of her,":: Micah ordered, realizing he had drawn his heavy crossbow up between them only after he had moved.

In the back of his mind, Micah heard someone screaming at him to stop. Or was that Rylan gripping on his wing to pull him back? It didn't matter. None of that mattered. Sera's panic in his mind was more than he could stand.

"I don't take orders from warborn trash," Dylan sneered, and Sera screamed as he leveraged his grip at the base of her wing to stop her squirming. Obviously, he thought Micah wouldn't shoot while he held his sister as a shield; obviously, he had no idea how good a shot Micah was.

::"Let. Her. Go!":: Micah seethed, heedless of everything but Dylan and the sound of the rain roaring in his ears. His gift was fracturing inside of him, swelling with the panic all around him. "Let her go or I'll—"

"You'll what?" Dylan asked, laughing in his face. "Kill me? I don't—"

The next thing Micah knew, there was the sharp snap of a bowstring and Sera burst free of Dylan's arm as he clasped a hand over the surge of red streaming down his face. A moment later, Micah felt someone dragging at his wing and he was stumbling backwards as Sera ran towards them. As he dropped the crossbow, it was only then he realized that his bolt was still drawn. The shot hadn't been his after all.

Micah's heart was pounding as Sera grabbed him as she went by, tearing at Rylan's arm as the courtyard filled with the sounds of firing bolts.

::"FLY, you idiots!":: Sera screamed, commanding the tyros with a strength to rival Micah's own. ::"They have warshot!"::

Micah came back to himself in a rush as he unfolded his wings, and both he and Rylan were flung out of their shock. As he found his feet, the whole of the century was swarming House Northern. Westly was at their lead as he lifted the stones of the courtyard with his magic to hurl them towards the crewmen. That, above all else, sent the crewmen scattering in terror.

When the last of their warshot landed, though, Micah felt a dagger-sharp pain lancing through his back. As the world turned into a blur of ice and pain, he was sent sprawling into the courtyard, head crashing off the wet ground. When he finally came to a stop, sucking in a breath, all he could see was Rylan pulling two wingblades from beneath his tyro-armor.

Putting a hand to the earth, Micah tried to push himself back up, but the searing pain had him collapsing a second time. Rylan set himself in front of Micah, meaning to defend him as Westly's magic filled the courtyard.

Out of options now, Micah closed his eyes and focused, trying to feel for the one person he knew might be able to stop this madness. Gritting his teeth, Micah brought his Talent for bardic magic to life inside his mind, honed it with every skill he had ever learned from the cantos at the Academy, and called for help from the one person he knew could hear him.

CHAPTER 37: VINICIA

Sunday, 13:00

One moment Vinicia was taking her ease in the Counsel Lords' suite speaking with Kaitlyn about her duties as Barracks Mother, and in the next she knew something had gone horribly wrong.

::Aevi?:: she called. Aevi had been meant to raise this sort of cry for her, but that hadn't been who she heard. No, it had sounded like Micah.

Reaching towards the gryphling's presence in her mind, Vinicia's blood ran cold. Aevi was racing towards her location in a blind panic, flying hard to get within range to raise an alarm. Speechless as she was, she was clearly terrified.

"Is something wrong?" Kaitlyn asked, worried as Vinicia came to her feet.

"Tell Hest'lre to send the Blackwings to Rylan," she said, readying herself to Step. She could almost hear the cry again, but if it was Micah, he was reaching out with a wild, panicked strength. She couldn't pinpoint his location if he couldn't focus his call.

As Kaitlyn rushed to do as Vinicia had asked, Vinicia closed her eyes and spread out her awareness over the city. Most of her tyros were racing towards their Headmaster at the far edge of the shelf, but that wasn't where this call had come from. From what she could tell, there was a gaggle of tyros somewhere inside the wide swath of green that bordered the Great Houses. She knew House Northern was on the east side of that, but there were so many minds she recognized in the city. Ten cycles of training officer candidates meant she had shared energy with almost eight hundred men, not to mention all the people she had met as a tyro. All of the people Weylan, Hewn, and her father had worked with as Sevenths. A legion's worth of Seventh's men were in Delton right now and she just—

::MOTHER!::

With her power already gathered, Vinicia launched herself at the call. Reckless as the move was, she exploded into starlight as she was wrenched out of the material world and dragged towards the panic. Never in her life had she Stepped so far at once, but with all the power Kiernan had gifted her the night before, she clearly had the strength for it.

When she came back to the living world, though, she collapsed in a heap. The only thing that stopped her from losing her stomach was the sensation of her ancestor's presence suddenly reappearing in her mind. No, it felt as if she had suddenly moved towards her ancestor physically. As she was struck by the fear that she had been pulled across the veil as one of her tyros had died, there was a sudden voice in her mind.

::Vinicia?::

::Ancestor?:: She sent. ::Is that you?::

::Yes and no,:: the spirit returned, with a hesitancy Vinicia recognized meant that her simple question needed a complex answer. ::But I have something very important to tell you.::

Vinicia groaned, pushing to her hands and knees to get off the icy cobblestones as someone came to a stop just in front of her. Will all her nausea, though, it was a struggle to lift her head.

"Si vobis bene?" a woman asked, speaking the Old Tongue of all things. *Are you good?*

::Look up,:: her ancestor prompted.

Vinicia did, only to see a dead woman extending her hand. Wings flared to protect them from the icy rain, Vinicia was caught in the woman's bright, sapphire stare.

Kiernan's kyree?

"Meum nomen est Loraleia Lan'Tessa," the woman said, and Vinicia gaped as the musical cadence could have matched her ancestor's song for song. ::Not 'Kiernan's kyree'.::

"What...?" Vinicia replied, stunned as the words in her mind shifted to emerge from the woman before her. "What's going on?"

For the past four cycles, Vinicia had trusted that mental voice and everything it had told her about her Gifts. It had never been wrong, no matter how many times Vinicia had doubted it, but now that same voice was coming from a woman standing right in front of her...

As her mind tried and failed to stitch the two together, there was love in the woman's sending. ::I told you I wouldn't make you walk your path alone, *sha'doe,*:: Lora sent, and then took a step closer so she could touch a spot just between Vinicia's eyes with affection. "Ego non relinquas, dilecta." *I did not abandon you, beloved.*

Vinicia gasped as she realized the ancestor she had thought lost was the living, breathing woman before her. She hadn't crossed the veil to join her ancestor, her 'ancestor' had never been dead at all.

"You're alive!" Vinicia accused in the woman's own tongue, gaping. "How long have you been alive?!"

"Some five and forty cycles now, I think," the woman returned, stepping back to watch Vinicia flailing with her sudden joy.

"Why did you never tell me you were alive?" Vinicia said, taking the woman by the shoulders. "Why didn't you tell me who you were?"

"You were better off thinking I was one of your spirits," the woman said, uncomfortable with the confession if not with the touch.

"I have known enough dead men to last ten lifetimes," Vinicia said, smiling so broadly that it hurt. "By the Gods, you're alive! You're real!"

"That I am," the woman agreed, and before the awkwardness of the confession could take either of them, Vinicia released her shoulders and embraced her fully.

Lora returned the embrace with real affection and Vinicia flushed to remember what she had said to Kiernan the night before. She had never had the chance to see how she felt in the arms of a woman, but she was certain now. If Hewn had been a candle and Kiernan a bonfire, to her, this woman was the daystar on Summer Solstice.

As the surprise of the moment settled into something more real, Vinicia relaxed her hold. Standing together in silence, she could feel the emotions surging along the bond they had shared for so long. It was a powerful mix of regret and redemption that Vinicia didn't quite understand, but there was love as well. It was just as strong and insistent as Vinicia had felt the day before, and absolutely incredible.

::What was your name again?:: Vinicia asked, speaking mind to mind to not spoil the moment.

::Loraleia,:: the woman said, exhaling a weary laugh. ::Though I haven't been called by that in an age. Thanks to my *sha'dara* and the fates, I have been called Loralae some thirty cycles now."

::Lora, then,:: Vinicia sent, pulling back. ::For you are no river demon to me.::

For a moment, Lora's smile cracked through her otherwise humbled demeanor and Vinicia smiled back without reservation.

::I might agree with you,:: Lora sent, almost amused. ::It has been an age since I have given into a bloodrage and even longer still since I felt compelled to seek out your kind,:: she said, suddenly full of sadness. ::By all the Great Mothers, I had known dryads could send thoughts into the conclaves, but kindred just scream into the void.::

::Scream?:: Vinicia realized, her joy banked by the subject they had touched on. ::Oh, like this.::

::Yes and no,:: Lora said, hesitating. ::For me, it is a curse. I can hear anyone within a league of me physically.::

::Are you kindred, too?:: Vinicia asked, realizing the woman's knowledge could easily be explained if she was. ::I've never seen anyone in my life with hair like my own.::

::No, sweetness,:: Lora said, and though there was affection in the word, her look darkened all the same. ::I was drowned in sorcery by the dryads of the Southern Conclave to look and act as I do, and it was not by choice,:: she said. ::I will tell you of it later, but it is not important right now.::

::Does that mean you will come with us?:: Vinicia asked, suddenly afraid of finding this woman alive, only to lose her in the next breath. ::Kiernan and I are going on Envoy to Lan'lieana this spring. He meant to ask you to act as his guide, but we thought you were dead. Knowing who you are now... Lora, it would be my honor to take you home.::

::I do not mean to lose you to that man so easily,:: Lora said, and Vinicia could feel the sudden, rabid jealousy in her thoughts. She stilled it, however, as she took Vinicia's hands in her own. ::I will go with you, but it will be you I guide, *sha'doe*. Not him.::

Vinicia could live with that.

As her smile crept back into her cheeks, Vinicia had to look away as she realized just how absolutely beautiful the woman was. Her head was spinning with joy, and Lora looked more than happy to just be with her in the moment.

But wasn't there something she was forgetting?

A heartbeat later, the agony in Micah's mental call drove every other thought from her mind.

::*MOTHER!*::

Vinicia Stepped instantly.

"Oh, thank all the Gods," Micah sobbed, his relief palpable as his bardic magic sizzled off her shields.

::I'm coming to help,:: Lora sent with urgency.

"What's going on?" Vinicia said, her vision a blur of white power as she settled into the new location. "Micah, what happened?"

"I got shot before I could get enough air," he answered, somehow on his hands and knees despite the arrow lodged in the base of his wing. "They left me to go after Rylan, though. Mother—"

Micah's words cut off with a strangled gasp as Vinicia freed the arrow from his wing. Pressing her hand to his back, she healed the massive wound before he lost any more blood.

"Where are they now?" Vinicia asked.

"He took cover in the temple," Micah panted, letting Vinicia haul him to his feet. "I told them to run, but—"

PAIN!

Vinicia's head whipped up with the burst of agony searing along her Seventh's Gift. A heartbeat later, she heard a scream ripping through the icy wind from somewhere just around the building.

Rylan!

Vinicia Stepped again without thinking and this time managed to keep her feet. As she settled into the space, though, the violent resonance in the temple had her doubling over for an entirely different reason. As good as she was with working blood magic, to be hit with so much of it at once had her tasting bile.

Throwing out an arm to catch herself on the threshold, Vinicia found Westly and Rylan amid a pile of downed crewmen in the stone temple. Westly was still on his feet, moving to catch Rylan as he staggered backwards with the force of the heavy bolt lodged in his chest.

Vinicia's heart was in her throat as she followed the bolt's path back to House Northern and the man who stood braced against the building. No matter the icy rain and the blood streaked down one side of his face, there was satisfaction in his look as he collapsed to his knees. How the man had made it this far with such a wound, Vinicia had no idea, but as the crossbow slipped from his hands, she knew he was no longer a threat.

Rylan, though?

::Sha'doe?::

Vinicia flinched as she felt a hand on her wing, though when she realized Lora had come up beside her, she breathed again.

"I can't go in there," Vinicia said, still fighting bile with even the thought of stepping through the threshold. "Lora, can you help him?"

Lora's look followed her hand to where Westly was laying Rylan onto his wings in the center of the temple. Pale as the kindred had gone, there was true terror in his look as blood poured out of Rylan's chest.

::Oh, Great Mother of All,:: Lora swore, releasing Vinicia's wing as she rushed into the space. ::Sapling!::

Lora vaulted the circle of bodies with a beat of her wings, startling Westly in the moment. As the kindred looked up, though, Vinicia's mouth fell open to realize he was staring at his own hands in horror. Clearly, he had been drawing power to himself, but Vinicia couldn't feel any movement at all. Instead, his body was glowing with a strange set of bind runes, all of it tight against the kindred's skin. Apparently the 'shield' she had sensed on the Palace flats wasn't a guise at all, but a binding against his power.

With some effort, Vinicia changed over to her secondsight to see the true extent of it, only to watch him struggle to draw the energy through a complex web of bind runes. No matter how he tried, he could not release the power that had once flowed so freely between him and his crew brother.

::Sapling, stop!:: Lora called, coming to her knees on the other side of Rylan's lifeless body. ::You will burn yourself out!::

But no matter the grip she had on Westly's tyro armor, his thoughts were all inward. Clearly he was pulling strength into himself, which only made the runes grow brighter. Swearing aloud this time, Lora let go with one hand, and Vinicia nearly screamed to watch the woman draw back a fist. A moment later, Westly was slumping to the ground beside Rylan.

::He's just knocked out,:: Lora swore, explaining before Vinicia could even ask. ::I can fix this, though. Gods, I have to. I just... You're going to have to take this in, *sha'doe*. If I tried to hold this much power, I would turn into a loralae again.::

Vinicia picked her jaw off the floor, watching as Lora set a hand to her left wrist. There was something there, some focus, and as Lora's skin lit up with crimson runes, Vinicia felt the resonance of the blood magic shift.

::Vinicia!:: Lora called, demanding her attention.

Glad she had spent so much of her life living off ambient power, Vinicia opened herself to the energy suddenly surging in the area. The nausea she had felt reaching this place was receding, leaving only the heady feel of a raw, crimson power that felt like Lora. Suddenly thankful she had burned so much of her reserves Stepping halfway across the Delton shelf, Vinicia opened herself to the energy and began to draw it in.

A heartbeat later, realizing she could feel Rylan's spirit pooled among the dead energy, both she and Lora froze.

"No," Vinicia breathed, terrified. "No, he can't be..."

::He is not dead,:: Lora insisted, coming onto her knees with her hand outstretched. ::Give me your hawkeye, and I can hold him apart. I can do that much at least.::

Vinicia didn't think twice, stripping herself of the stone. Lora caught it in one swift motion, pressing it to Rylan's chest as the runes flared along her skin again.

::The power you are about to take in is too much for you to use at once,:: Lora said, sapphire eyes flashing in the moment. ::Promise you will send it into that hearth tree instead. Fill your reserves, yes, but take that strength and conquer the rest. Do you understand me?::

::I think so,:: Vinicia sent back, drawing herself up as she focused her mind. In that first panicked Step from the Palace shelf, she had been everywhere and nowhere at once. If she was going to reach the Great Tree, she would have to go back to that place in her mind, if not with her body.

::Believe in yourself as I believe in you, *sha'doe,*:: Lora sent, flooding the connection between them with love and unrelenting confidence.

With that crimson power roaring to life inside of her again, Vinicia felt the stagnant energy of the temple shifting into her control. As she forced her will on top of it, pulling it in to herself with all the strength her love for the young man could manage, she could feel a maelstrom coming into focus just between her hands. With it spiraling through her, fighting to manifest, Vinicia brought it all to a focused point.

Just as she started to send it towards the Great Tree, however, there was a whip-crack of sound through the temple. As her eyes flew open, she staggered with the feeling of the crimson power shifting out of her control.

"I should thank you, sapling," an ancient voice said, and Vinicia's heart stopped as the shade of Founder Noventrio shimmered into being at the edge of the space. As he flowed into true corporeal form, Vinicia's knees turned to water, realizing the incredible power she had gathered had all gone rushing into the Founder. "It has been an age since even my own family brought me such a potent sacrifice. Without this, I never would have been able to Step outside of my wretched prison."

Prison? Vinicia thought, worried as she saw the pleasure in Noventrio's eyes as he took in the devastation.

Every time she had seen him before, Noventrio had appeared to her as something of an elemental spirit, if the War itself could have a spirit driving it. At this moment, though, the Founder was made of flesh and feathers. As he flexed two great white wings, Vinicia could see the echo of seven others spiraling behind him, some set at such awkward angles that her mind refused to focus on them. This was a war god walking the winds among men, not some mere Ancestor Seventh, and the dark shadow of power roiling at his feet was ominous.

As Noventrio looked towards Rylan, the Founder's hunger was plain.

"If Kiernan means to name this one, I will take him now," Noventrio observed, stepping fully into the temple for the first time. Seeing Lora over his body, his eyes narrowed with contempt. "I do not mean to lose someone strong enough to become my vessel to vultures."

And then, without so much as a wave in her direction, Lora went flying backwards in the temple, only coming to a stop when she slammed against the far wall. Vinicia flinched, halfway to her feet again, only to feel the Founder's ire as his look swung to her.

"Long as you have gnawed at my roots, sapling," the Founder said, wings flaring into the space. "There is nothing you can do to oppose my will. All the power you have ever controlled belongs to me."

And then, as if to demonstrate, Noventrio pulled all of the power in the temple to himself, leaving Vinicia gasping for as she fell to her knees.

"You, however," the Founder went on, addressing Rylan's unmoving form. "You have already pledged yourself to me, and because of that..."

Vinicia could do nothing as the Founder made a gesture towards her beloved tyro. Heart aching, she watched as wil-o-wisps exploded throughout the temple, raining down on the two men as Noventrio dissolved the arrow that had lodged in Rylan's chest. A breath later, Noventrio closed his eyes to focus, letting Vinicia see the truly mortal wound he had taken. Even if she had been able to get to Rylan's side, she knew a healing of that magnitude was beyond her ability. With a Founder's strength, however...

Rylan's eyes opened with a start as he rasped for a breath, terror giving strength to his wings as he got to his feet. As he searched around the room to orient himself, he saw the bodies of the crewman, Westly beside him, and then Vinicia on her knees at the temple's edge. Finally looking to the man before him, Rylan's eyes went wide with a Seventh Counsel Lord's secondsight, taking in the violent swirl of the nine-winged Founder looming over him.

As Noventrio reached for him, however, there was a sudden flash of light and a hiss of violence reverberated through the temple.

::Do you think that wissse, windwalker?::

The shock of the voice seemed to wake Rylan out of his stupor. When he backwinged out of the Founder's grasp, Vinicia found the strength to get to her feet as the shadows of the temple began to roil. With the dark wisps of power surging towards him, the Founder flared his wings—all nine of them—into the mortal world.

"This is no business of yours, wyrmling," the Founder hissed back. "Be gone!"

Utterly confused, Vinicia watched the shadows gather in a thunderhead of billowing smoke. Given the intensity of power now roiling in the space, both Rylan and the Founder took a step back. As the column thinned out into a sinuous silver line, Vinicia's heart stopped to realize one of the peaks was taking on true form, solidifying into a square lion's head while four taloned claws that would have made a harpy jealous stretched out from the body itself. In its final shape, it was a creature straight out of a tome: the quicksilver dragon that had been used to herald every Seventh Counsel Lord of Noventrio's line.

::I am here becaussse of your actionsss,:: the quicksilver hissed, rearing its head at the Founder. ::Father sayss you ssstretch yoursssself thin and now I know why. You may fool your kin, but you will not fool usss. You do not need thisss one, not with the three you already claim.::

Surprisingly, Noventrio tsked and looked away. Vinicia had never seen the Founder chided, much less anything other than sure in himself.

The quicksilver saw it too, pressing its advantage. ::You know if you fail Great Father Tralmisss for sssome bit of greed thisss day, I will be the leassst of your worriesss.::

Noventrio glowered, but when his look went to Vinicia it darkened with anger. In the next moment, both the Founder and his power were gone and Vinicia let out the breath she hadn't known she was holding.

Rylan, on the other hand, was standing completely still as the ash grey quicksilver shifted in the wind, coiling itself around the greater part of Rylan's body before settling its head on Rylan's left shoulder. Of all things, the quicksilver looked content, even if Rylan did not.

About that time, the rest of Rylan's cadre—Micah, Nichi, Tyrsten, and Tyrren—had made their way back to the temple. There were others circling around outside, Blackwings from the look of them, working to send the Eighteenth Century Tyro Legion towards the edge of the shelf, given the break in the rain. They knew as well as Vinicia did that this had not been one of the conflict spots for the tournament, even if she was the only one who knew why they had come.

As Vinicia made herself take a deep, steadying breath, Lora caught eyes with her from the far side of the temple. Hand to her left wrist, her words were quiet even mind-to-mind. ::I should not be here,:: she sent. ::Not as I am.::

A moment later, the air around her shimmered with power, and when Vinicia blinked, Lora was a different person entirely. Now she wore the guise of a Palace guard, appropriate if unneeded with so many Blackwings around. Layered into the shielding was something that made it hard for Vinicia to focus on her at all, save for when Lora looked up and caught her with the blue of her eyes.

::When you are free of this place with your Seventh,:: she promised, taking one of Vinicia's hands in her own. ::Call for me and I will join you.::

::It won't be long,:: Vinicia said in return. ::We leave from the east side of the Palace once they are graduated.::

Lora nodded, pausing for a moment as if she wanted to say more, but then raised Vinicia's hand to her lips. ::Take care, *sha'doe*,:: she sent, and then turned and was gone.

Vinicia watched her go with a powerful sense of longing. There was something truly incredible waiting for her on this Envoy, that was for certain. Pulling her attention back to her tyros, she found Westly had finally come to his feet, though he was gathered with the others around Rylan to stare at his strange companion.

"What is that?" Tyrsten asked, watching as the creature condensed to become fully opaque as it perched atop Rylan's shoulders.

"It's a quicksilver," Nichi said, awed as he looked between the creature and the carving of the same thing in the temple. "I didn't think they were real."

Vinicia steeled herself as she moved up to Rylan, taking hold of the hawkeye Lora had hung from his neck.

"What is this?" Rylan asked, his voice breaking as he looked up at her. It was clear the hawkeye in her hands terrified him more than the dragon that had just saved him from becoming the Founder's avatar, whatever that was. "Mother?"

"It belongs to me," Vinicia said, helping him lift it from around his neck so she could take it back.

"But why did I have it?" He insisted.

"Because I was trying to save your life," she answered.

"And the Founder?" he asked, though from his tone he clearly didn't trust what he had seen.

"Did it for me," she said, not that she could explain how.

::No,:: the quicksilver hissed, curling the long length of his tail around Rylan's neck protectively. ::Kenrhysss meant to sssave his body only, not hisss mind.::

Vinicia narrowed her eyes at the creature. All of her tyros were terrified, so even if she felt the same, it was up to her to remain calm. "Explain," she said.

::Kenrhysss meant to make him an avatar,:: the quicksilver said, its head shifting on its long neck as it studied her. ::A vesssle for himself to walk the mortal realm, as Aluvinor ssstill doesss. It hasss been an age sssince one of thisss line hasss been so vulnerable to hisss power.::

"But you stopped him," Vinicia said, impressed. "Who are you?"

::Guardian,:: the dragon said. ::Great Father Tralmisss pulled me from the windsss to ssstand guardian over the lasst ssspark of the northern lightsss.::

Vinicia let out a slow breath as the tyros around her gaped, looking from Rylan and the quicksilver to the looming image of Founder Noventrio and the dragon that dominated the otherwise empty temple space. Gods, but she had so many questions for her father the moment she was back on the Palace shelf. Right now, though...

"You got a name?" Rylan asked into the silence.

::Kohlandriousss,:: the dragon hissed, radiating affection towards the young man. ::Sssal'weh, foundling.::

Foundling.

"Kohl, then," Rylan managed, forcing himself to smile. "You're not going anywhere, are you?" he asked, looking up towards the looming image of Noventrio and his own guardian within the temple.

The quicksilver's impressive talons flexed against Rylan's tyro armor as it answered. ::You are to ssserve the peaccce that was promisssed,:: it said, and Vinicia was surprised when the dragon's attention turned to her. ::Yesss?::

"The peace that was..." Vinicia started to say, only to realize the creature was staring at the hawkeye she held. "Oh, gods. Yes. That. No one knows about that yet, Kohl."

Not being a complete idiot, Rylan's eyes went wide as he realized what the dragon meant. "Mother?" he still managed to ask, terrified he was right. "What is he talking about?"

Given the worried looks on the rest of the tyros standing with him, Vinicia swore to herself. After everything that had just happened, he deserved to know the truth.

"Yesterday, Lord Seventh told me he had chosen you to be his Counselheir," she confessed. "He is going to announce it after the Tourni, but given the wound you took, it took Founder Noventrio himself to heal you. He was about to claim you for the Seat when Kohl appeared."

Rylan's look went back to the mountain dragon with new respect.

::You have the sssspark he needs to reenter the world,:: the quicksilver answered, shooting forward in a moonlight swirl around Rylan's wings in an unmistakably affectionate pattern. ::But I protect the sssspark. The lassst sssspark of windwalkersss created from the northern lightsss. I hope you do not mind...::

"No, I don't mind you saving my life," Rylan said, which seemed to please the thing.

::Are you going to stay with him?:: Vinicia asked, doing what she could to speak with the quicksilver alone.

::Yes,:: it repeated, and the intensity of its response made Vinicia think it might mean for the rest of Rylan's natural life.

Given the reaction of Rylan's closest companions to the thing, Vinicia winced. ::Then you should know that if you mean to protect him, you cannot stay formed like you are,:: she said, trying to be tactful. ::You will draw much more unwanted attention to him if you do.::

The quicksilver considered her and then doubled its head back on its long neck to see Rylan once again. After a moment, it snaked itself around Rylan's arm even more, and Vinicia felt the wind pick up as it shimmered with power. A moment later, there was a soft flash of white and the quicksilver itself was gone, replaced by a suspiciously detailed drawing of a similar creature sketched along the leather of Rylan's red tyro-armor.

::Better?:: It sent, and Vinicia had to admit that it was.

With its head and front talons resting on Rylan's shoulder and the rest of its long body wrapped around his arm, she realized what the quicksilver had done. The effect was not lost on the others, either.

"Damn, Rylan," Tyrsten said, peering at his arm.

"This can't be happening," Rylan breathed, unfolding and refolding his wings to get ahold of himself again.

"It is, and it is not over, either," Vinicia said, catching everyone's attention. "You boys still have the Ice Winds to fly. Micah, how are you doing?"

"I could eat an entire yak," he muttered, pushing off the threshold where he had been resting. "But I'll survive."

Beside him, his returning twin looked no better. From the hard grip she had around the massive book in her arms, though, Vinicia knew her own struggle had been just as hard-fought. Bloodied as she was, it looked as if none of it was her own.

"I'm glad to hear it," Vinicia said, looking up as a cheer rose in the distance. Just beyond the roofs over the southern part of the city, one of the two bonfires was being kindled. When both were lit, the flight against the Ice Winds would begin.

"We may be the last tyros in," Tyrsten said, unfolding his wings. "But we will be soldiers this day if it's the last thing we do. Right, Rylan?"

"After all this, we better be," Rylan answered, following his lead. "Sera, go get warmed up with Kait, We'll see you soon."

Sera just nodded, exchanging a quick kiss before following him out of the temple. As the other tyros left as well, Vinicia gave them the space they needed to throw themselves back into the winds. They did not need a Mother's insistence to get out of this rain.

Once they were gone, Vinicia gave herself a moment to breathe, even as she reached out with her mind towards her meddling father. If anyone knew who this Great Father Tralmis was, it would be him.

::Vinicia?:: Eirik sent back, curious why she was making the contact. ::Everything all right?

::Who is Great Father Tralmis?:: she asked, sending a burst of heat and fire through her sodden clothes to dry herself off. She was too exhausted to Step back, and she would have to use her wings or walk at this point.

::I believe he is one of the Greater Fae that control the Northern Winds in the Kihara. Father Borealis controls the eastern winds and Mistral controls the west, but the Great Father is over all of them. Father Noventrio was the name of the dragon that served Founder Kenrhys of House Northern, but he vanished after the Founding of Kosar. Kenrhys has gone by the name ever sense, not that many remember. Why?:: her father sent back, unreasonably excited by the name. ::Did you meet him?::

Did I meet him? Vinicia rolled her eyes, launching herself into the torrent of the Ice Winds raging over the city. ::No, but I did meet a wyrmling named Kohlandrious,:: she sent back. ::Ever heard of that one?::

::Can't say that I have,:: her father mused. ::What is it like?::

::I'll tell you when I get back to the Palace,:: she said, sighing. ::Right now I need to focus.::

::Have fun with the Ice Winds, daughter,:: her father chuckled. ::It's about time you flew them properly. If you mean to set out on your Envoy, it's best you do so as a proper Seventh.::

Proper Seventh, she scoffed, if only to herself. *Gods forbid I ever do anything to gain the attention of dragons. Kiernan's attention was potent enough, and he was only the Dragon of the Warhost.*

Chapter 38: Kiernan

Sunday, 14:00

"Kiernan!" Hest'lre called, his annoyance clear as he pounded on the door he and Lenae had been hiding behind for most of the day. "The tyros are about to hit the Ice Winds. Get dressed!"

"I hear you!" Kiernan called back, though he had no intention of moving. He couldn't, really. Lenae had him quite trapped.

When the heels of Hest'lre's boots had clicked away from the door, Lenae set her lips on his again. As he melted into her kiss, he slid his hands to the base of her wings and the world went dark under the waterfall of golden curls.

Close as she was to finding her pleasure, Kiernan reveled in the rush of her desperate, gasping cries echoing in the empty room. For so long they had traded love in secret, but today she sung for him, knowing this would be the last in what would feel like an age. When the moment finally took her, Kiernan had to steel himself to not find release as well.

Gods, not yet.

"Your turn, Kier'n," she purred, already shifting to be free of him.

The sound of his name on her lips gave him strength enough to bring them to the edge of the nest, but he stalled there to trade a kiss that was far softer than any other thing they had managed all day. He had forgotten how much he loved the slow, tender exchange that came with newly mated physical intimacy, and as his touch turned soft to match the kiss, Lenae nipped at his lower lip.

When she pulled back to see him, perched on his thighs with love in her look, he couldn't help but laugh. "This whole day has been my turn," he objected. "Would you hate it if we just…"

His words fell away as Lenae's hands slid down his torso. She clearly wanted more, and as much as he loved her, as much as he loved assisting her in the worship of her Founder when they shared a nest, he could tell it was intensity she needed.

Fortunately, the heady look in her eyes as she took him firmly in hand had him reconsidering what he wanted. Priestess that she was to Founder Kerowyn, she did it almost without thinking, calling to him with a siren's song that gripped his soul as powerfully as Vinicia had the night before. Transfixed by her radiant glow, Kiernan's tenderness began to harden to true purpose.

"How do you want me, Kier'n?" she asked, resettling her wings to frame the hourglass glory of her naked skin. As she drew herself up, both of her slender hands now massaging at his length, Kiernan's want for tenderness fled entirely.

"You know I love it when you're on your knees," he said, shifting his legs to urge her to stand. She released him for a moment, coming to her feet, though she found him again as soon as he was standing. Reaching for her as well, he let his fingertips brush the traces of their love as they swirled over her skin.

Fifteen cycles he had served the Warhost as both a tyro and an officer, and in all that time he had never left a mark on her. Their love was a secret, had to remain nothing more than a rumor, but Lenae had walked through his door this morning with two requests:

Honor me with a memory of your hands on my skin.
Let me Glory in the scandal of it while you are gone.

And so he had. Gorgeous as she was, everywhere his lips had touched, he had found a way to emblazon the love they shared. After four solid candlemarks, she had subtle shadows flowing around the side of her neck that her court clothing would never hide, alongside her breasts that were so unbelievably tender with her growing chick, and down the inside of her thighs. Those she wanted most especially, given how she had told him of being so coldly inspected by the King's chiurgeons.

Their concern was for the Heir, not for her, and they all knew just how little Braeden cared for her. How much Braeden despised her, given all she had done during her time as Consort before he had come of age. Braeden was now King, Avatar of their Ancestors, but for those precious cycles Lenae and her Founder Kerowyn had reigned over Kosar. Lenae would fight Braeden for any influence at all during the days of her pregnancy, but it was worth it. She had enacted so many good programs throughout their kingdom, building a world where she and Kiernan could be together, and she wouldn't stop fighting just because he had left on Envoy.

Lenae stepped back after Kiernan had seen his fill, a determined look in her eye as she turned them both in a swirl of movement. Once she was before the nest, she set her knees at the edge and her smile was eager as she looked back to him. Caught up in her silvered stare, Kiernan gloried in the feel of her round hips, tracing her curves with one hand until he bent forward to kiss the downy between her wings.

Her eyes lidded as his hand slid further up, pressing her into the nest as he took a fist-full of her gorgeous hair.

"Is this what you want?" he asked, his words soft as he tested the slickness between her thighs.

Lenae's wings dropped low with the touch, but it was the heat of her arousal sizzling along his empathic gift that was the most exquisite.

"Or is this not enough?"

Her low moan as he added to his affection nearly had him seeing stars. She absolutely didn't want him to stop, but she also wanted more. She always wanted more.

"I could stop," he said, starting the slow work of sliding free. "Hest'lre did say the tyros were on the wind..."

Lenae started to look back at him, but Kiernan's unsubtle grip on her hair made her breath hitch as he held her steady. As he shifted his weight forward, she was forced to brace herself better in the nest and he used the distraction to take hold of himself.

"Or do you want this instead?" he asked, and the low tone in her throat changed to pleading as he seated himself at the entrance to her core. "You have to tell me what you want."

"I want you, Kier'n," she breathed, her hips lifting for him as she pressed her wings low. "Gods, Kier'n, please..."

Groaning to hear the break in her voice, Kiernan released her hair as he pressed into her. Lenae's slow hiss of pleasure had his mind sizzling all over again, and when his hips were pressed hard against her own, she held still in the moment. Deep as he was, Kiernan closed his eyes and flooded the incredible need he felt into her. Vinicia had taught him that trick, had shown him how to turn someone completely inside out with his Seventh's Gift, and Lenae's prayer to her Founder made her love for him clear.

"Bless me with pleasure, bless me with pain," she breathed, sliding into the sacred headspace she needed to truly worship her Founder. "Bless me with chicks that will carry your name..."

As her eyes closed, Kiernan felt the incredible power Lenae said she wielded for Braeden suddenly pulsing through the room. Head dropped forward, Kiernan's heart was racing as he realized Lenae was deep into one of her trances. Whatever she was doing, it felt like Vinicia taking control of the power between them and he had to use her hips to steady himself in the moment.

Soul to soul with her in the press, Kiernan felt the Warhost swelling into his thoughts as Lenae's grip on his power grew. Granted, everyone in the Kingdom was focused on him at the moment, wondering who he would name his Counselheir, but that didn't matter to him right now. The only thing in the world that mattered was the slick heat of her sex clenched around him as she opened herself to her Founder. When her words shifted from prayer to pleading, her eyes flashed a brilliant silver as she looked back to him.

She was begging him to take his pleasure in her. To fill her, no matter Braeden's chick. She wanted to be utterly ruined by him, driven to the edge of reason by his massive, aching...

Kiernan shook the Host from his mind as he moved within her, the low moan in her throat calling him back to the memory of when she had first arrived. After a quick kiss at his door, she had moved them to his oaken desk, taking a seat as she had done the day before, only to spread herself before him. That temptation had been an apology for earlier when she had been too upset with her upcoming announcement to find any joy with him at all, but he had torn open the threadbare fabric she wore beneath her court garb and feasted on her all the same. When he had come up for a breath after finding her pleasure, she had stunned him by pushing him back into that chair, falling to her knees in a pile of silk and lace to take after him as Kreychi had done the day before, swallowing him whole.

Gods, Kreychi would have been jealous of how Lenae hadn't gagged once, but he would have taken a wife to know the rest. To realize how he had steeled himself to not finish as the man preferred, instead ripping off what remained of her clothing and laying her face-down across his desk. Then, what had started as a moment of teasing with the sharp crack of his hand across her ass had moved onto her begging for more, but it hadn't ended there.

Coming into his room, she had asked him to leave his lover's marks, but he had always wanted to join with her like he might join with another soldier on the War plains. To take after her like he so often had with Kreychi, no matter the admonition against it in the mountains. With her enthusiastic consent, he had taken her in the veteran's way and Gods how she had screamed for all the new-found pleasure of it.

With Kiernan spent for the moment, they had collapsed in a heap only to laugh, swearing at themselves for never thinking to do that before. No matter the twenty cycles they had shared a nest, they were always thinking of new ways to please one another, and now nothing was taboo.

With that simple regret turning to introspection, their intimacy had shifted to an emotional release as Lenae lay in his arms, sobbing as she confessed to a thousand things she hated about having to keep him at arms length for so many cycles. For all the asinine political games they had been forced through during their time serving Kosar in their own ways. For an entire candlemark, they had laid in his nest, grieving for every cruel thing the fates had done to them until Kiernan's anger and Lenae's overwhelming frustration had them taking after one another again.

By love or by spite, they had drowned themselves in one another until Lenae's pleasure had him seeing stars and his empathic Gift had fractured under the intensity they shared. Until he had lost himself a second time in her, only to feel the power of her Founder called into the sacred space they had made of the room, granting him this third wind.

Priest that he was to Founder Noventrio, Kiernan had found a way to seize the chaos of the Warhost in his mind, turning it into an intensity that had Lenae weeping for an entirely different reason. Tender as they had been before, now she was begging for a love that was hard and fast. If this was the last chance Kiernan would ever have to worship with her, he would make certain she knew how everything he did was for her if it was the last thing—

Kiernan ground his teeth as the Warhost flared into his mind, fighting for his focused attention. The tyros were halfway to the Palace now, streaking towards him, and his unguided preems were demanding his attention. Where was the cadre they had expected to report to? Were the rumors of Kiernan's madness true? Who was he going to—?

Kiernan's fury overrode their asking and he panicked as he heard Lenae's gasping release. He had driven so hard into her that the pressure alone had somehow found her pleasure. How had he missed that?

Oh, fuck all of you...

Growling with determination, Kiernan withdrew from Lenae's slick heat almost completely, using the respite to open himself to his Gift. When she was calling his name again, desperate to be joined to him, only then did he mount her with strength. Taking the fullness of him in one savage motion, her legs buckled and it was her wings holding her in place as her arms gave up their bracing.

Poised between his beloved and the Warhost, power flooded into him and he took after Lenae with a wildness he had never felt in his life. Lenae was lost to it in an instant, silent with her overwhelming pleasure. Given the wellspring he had raised with Vinicia the night before, Kiernan could see how the raw emotion he shared with Lenae was such a powerful counter to the rage of the Warhost. Now, seeing the potential of the power they raised as only a sorcerer could, for the first time in his life, Kiernan knew exactly how to channel that strength into Lenae herself.

He knew his focus was working when Lenae shuddered beneath him no matter her trance, wings pulling in as she gave herself over to him completely. Close to hitting his height, Kiernan released her hips and gripped at her wings instead. Given the renewed angle and intensity, Lenae screamed as he poured the ferocious intensity between them into his Seventh's Gift.

No matter how much the Warhost hated him, he loved her more.

No matter how much they wanted to kill him, he lived for her.

No matter how much his Founder pursued war, Kiernan would bring back peace for her.

With her orgasming around him, Kiernan reached for the diamond-studded night sky of his Seventh's Gift. Opening himself to it, to the incredible love they shared, and Kiernan followed her over that edge. This love was why he fought so hard, and he would compel them to *feel* it, to make them want to die to protect it, just like he did.

The absolutely stunned silence of the Warhost in the next moment was as incredible as it was obscene. As he gulped down air, releasing her wings to drape over her low back, his strength left him in a rush. When the blistering force of his Gift began to ebb, he heard Lenae's rasping breath, and when she finally unclenched from around him, his soul reentered his body.

"Did you just...?" She accused, and the wicked smile on her lips was his entire world. She had asked him to honor her with marks of glory that might be seen outside of a nest, but to proclaim his love for her through his Gift? She might never let him go on Envoy given the look in her eyes. Gods, if he didn't think fast, she wouldn't let him go without a fight, and Hest'lre would have to separate them like two tyros in a barracks brawl who would soon be wingmates...

"Our love is the worst kept secret in Kosar," he said, doubling down on the moment. "Let them know."

Lenae had tears in her eyes as he smiled back at her, pressing against her hips so he could stand once again. As he came to his feet, he smoothed a hand across the fullness before him with true affection. She might not be able to sit for an entire solar cycle given all the ways he had pleasured her, but as her eyes lidded, he knew she had loved it. She had wanted him inside of her, all over her, and Holy Gods, he was going to miss her...

"I am going to miss you so much," she echoed, exhausted but utterly in love.

Kiernan gave a soft laugh as he tended to the mess he had made, finally nudging her forward so she could tuck her wings in and settle into the nest in an exhausted heap. As Kiernan joined her, wiping sweat from his brow for all the Warhost still burned under his skin, she kissed his forehead and cuddled close.

"I will return as soon as I can," he promised, lacing their hands together. "You know I will."

"But what am I supposed to do without you?" She whimpered. "Braedon barely looks at me, let alone touches me for longer than it takes to set his seed in my flesh. Now that I've caught his chick..."

"Braedon is a useless fool," Kiernan said, struggling to keep the anger out of his tone. Given Lenae's own anger, he didn't want to inflame the moment. Lenae took her role as a priestess to Founder Kerowyn very seriously, and Kerowyn was a more than a means by which Founder Aluvinor continued to be present in the world. To have Braeden deny Lenae the ability to worship her goddess as she should was not only obscene, but personally insulting.

Given Lenae's own slow breath and grip on Kiernan's hand, she was his in the moment. "We will have our own, soon," Lenae said, drawing his hand against her abdomen.

As Kiernan reached out his other hand to caress her cheek, the promise it held seemed to steady her nerves. He was about to say something more when both of them flinched, hearing Hest'lre calling Kiernan's name with unsubtle urgency.

"I'm coming!" Kiernan called back, swearing for patience. "Gods, I'm coming."

"You never double up that fast for me," Lenae pouted, and Kiernan's eye roll did nothing to stop her teasing. She had always countered his stress with humor, and she wasn't about to stop now.

"No, that is your specialty," he laughed, releasing her hand as she pressed onto an elbow. When she was ready, Kiernan extended his hands, letting her unfurl her wings to be free of the large nest. As she moved to find her clothes, he did his best to memorize every glorious part of her all over again.

When Lenae had first arrived with her entourage, Hest'lre had insisted they have some time alone. Now realizing that 'some time' had become the entire tournament, he was surprised his exhaustion hadn't gotten the better of them like it had with Kreychi the day before. Granted, he knew it was their last moment alone before he left, but that just made hurrying back to their duty harder than it had ever been before.

Everything is my last today, he thought, hating the pressure of it. *Last tourni, last meal, last stolen moments...*

When Lenae was done, Kiernan got himself to the edge of the nest. As he massaged his weary legs, he was glad he would be flying for the rest of the day. Tonight he would find himself trapped under a wholly different woman, and he did not mean to disappoint her. Lenae might be ravenous for his affection, but bowen were absolutely insatiable.

"I think you'll need these," Lenae said, dropping his small clothes across his lap as she found him dreaming. When she kissed his forehead like a chick, though, he snaked an arm around her legs, reminding her he was no such thing. As she ran an affectionate hand along the thick braid of his warcrest, he ran his fingertips along the backs of her tender thighs.

"Promise me you won't restrain yourself with Vinicia," Lenae whispered as he kissed the soft flesh before him.

Looking into her bright silver-grey eyes, he loved her even more. "Did I not tell you?" He said, surprised. "Last night..."

But Lenae wasn't listening, already rehearsing some speech in her mind as she came to her knees before him.

"I know you love me," she began. "But it won't be her magic driving you mad in that forest, it will be those hungry dryads. If you have affection for her—any affection—you must use it to guard yourself." She was earnest now. Insistent. "Use it, use her, use anything you must. So many Sevenths have fallen to them, and I just couldn't bare it if... If..."

Her words stalled as Kiernan leaned forward from his seat on the nest. "Love of my life," he said as she blinked. "Vinicia is a bowen. I will need time to ease her into the feats we two manage, but we are well on our way. I promise."

"You are?" Lenae asked, and then her eyes went wide with excitement. "Oh! You must tell me everything! Was it amazing? Was it magical? Was it—?"

Kiernan set a finger on her lips so he could answer. They had both spent nights wondering what it would be like to take a kindred dryad to nest. Well, they had wondered what it would be like to take a kin to nest *together*, but some things in life were meant only for dreaming. Or maybe not, given Vinicia's teasing this dawning...

"It was more amazing than either of us imagined," he answered. "Though she swore she would give me back to you each time we rested, only to keep saying 'eventually' before starting after me again."

"Eventually?" Lenae repeated, giggling as Kiernan grinned back at her. "So you think this will work? Her traveling with you? The Gods know men fight for wingmates on the Plains, but the same must be true with her in the Eihwaz."

Kiernan gathered his thoughts as she looked at him. If this was the last he would see of her, he would have to leave her with a strong assurance. "You were right to think a woman by my side is worth ten men," he said. "Now I will be coming home before your chick is fledged."

As Kiernan moved to stand, there were tears in her eyes and he knew it for relief. Though Lenae was fragile here with him, she would be strong outside these walls. That strength was his own and it had moved even the Gods from her path in days past.

"So, what do you think of her?" Lenae asked, turning to dress as Kiernan stood. "I mean, outside of a nest," she added, still grinning with the thought.

Kiernan considered the question before he spoke. Vinicia was like Lenae in a way no other woman had any right to be, having trained at the Palace. Though while Lenae had been taught the ways of a priestess so that she might assist Braeden, Vinicia could wield a temper that would make even Noventrio proud.

"She is viciously loyal," he said at last, finding his way into his gear. "And as dedicated to the Seat as I am. Perhaps more, given her father. She can also be timid after a lifetime in hiding, but every so often the Barracks Mother comes out and I can see why the tyros like her. She has a mouth like a soldier when she forgets to hide it."

"Aaron says she's as much of a terror as you are about getting her way," Lenae grinned, finding humor in her gossip.

"She is more like you than she is like me," Kiernan corrected, though from the jealous look Lenae tried to hide, maybe that wasn't the best comparison. "She is fiercely protective of her tyros, but works the system to get her way. I just bully my way through with the prerogative of my Seat."

"As long as she is fiercely protective of you, I suppose I will allow it," Lenae conceded.

As Lenae tugged at the last of her laces, Kiernan moved behind her to brush out the heavy length of hair that she had unbound for him. Lenae held still while he did his work, remembering her whispered promise of wearing it only in his seven-strand braid until he returned. When he was finally done, she turned to embrace him one last time. Kiernan held her close as the fear of never seeing her again turned his stomach to stone.

They only stepped apart when Kiernan heard a new voice shouting in the main room. There was worry in his tone and as Hest'lre opened their door unannounced, Kiernan knew they could not stay any longer.

"I would ask if you think you're ready," Hest'lre greeted. "But any man who can entertain a woman for half a day is strong enough for the Ice Winds twice over."

"Two women," Lenae corrected as she exited the room, leaving Kiernan to stare at his partner in full scarlet embarrassment.

"Two?" Hest'lre asked, now keeping Kiernan blocked inside with his wings until he got an answer. He knew as well as Lenae did how incredibly out of character it was for him. "Does she mean Vinicia?"

When Kiernan couldn't look at him, Hest'lre sputtered with laughter.

"Gods, man," he said, refolding his wings to clear the hallway. "She tries to kill you one morning, and you take her to nest the next? Maybe you *can* end this war."

Kiernan grabbed his packs from where he had set it next to the door and moved past his partner with a groan, only to flush a second time as he realized Consort Kaitlyn had heard the bawdy compliment. She just seemed amused, which was probably for the best.

As Ninth Counsel Lord Shayan came in from the balcony dressed in the full regalia of his Seat, Kiernan tried to regain his focus. It was one thing to joke with his Sixth, but Vinicia's uncle wore the full gravitas of his seat in a rank pauldron that rivaled his own for craftsmanship and a full braid of law-speaker cords besides.

"You wanted me to hold on to these for you," the elder Counsel Lord greeted, folding back his cloak to reveal their Counselheirs' rank-pauldrons. All three were made from the same thick hide of leather, as was tradition for the naming of a Seventh's Counselheir. All three were also wrought in exquisite detail, which befitted a Counsel Lord for the King.

The first matched the one Kiernan wore, a quicksilver dragon that seemed to have writhed up the wearer's arm so that its head could rest on his shoulder. The second matched the one Hest'lre wore, an armored Warhost pauldron with a built-up gorget and a gryphon standing rampant on its rear claws. The third was arguably less exciting, though with Kiernan's greater knowledge of the Eihwaz, it was the most intimidating among them. Shayan's pauldron had been crafted to look like the bark-skin armor worn by their Founders during whatever great cataclysm had destroyed the War Plains and forced their people into the Kihara two thousand cycles ago.

To Hest'lre, the new Ninth Counsel Lord's pauldron might as well have been made of platinum. Unlike Kiernan, when he named his Counselheir, Hest'lre would immediately be raised to the Ninth Seat so that Shayan could retire. After almost fifty cycles, it was long overdue.

"I only need the one," Kiernan said, taking the rank-pauldron meant for Tyro Rylan from his extended hand. "Once Rylan returns from the far end of the Palace, I will name him Heir and leave."

"And if Rylan refuses?" Hest'lre asked for the hundredth time, coming to take the rank-pauldron meant for Tyrsten. His eyes went wide, though, when Shayan tried to offer him his own new pauldron. When Hest'lre paled and palmed a warding circle before him, Shayan just chuckled. Alexandrians might be superstitious, but Kirath-born men were not. Only Hest'lre believed it was bad luck to touch the pauldron before it was truly his.

"Rylan will not refuse," Kiernan insisted. "But the kingdom is already in good hands between the two living Sevenths on this shelf already."

"Two? Try four," Hest'lre laughed, incredulous. "As far as I'm concerned, Vinicia is a legacy," he said. "She wears a hawkeye and a pauldron, and is just as intolerable as you. With her and her father, Rylan makes four."

Kiernan exhaled his own laughter, not sure how else to react. He was right, after all.

"Eirik is expecting to speak with you before you leave," Shayan said, looking around the group of them. "And you should not be here, Your Grace," he added to Lenae. "Braeden's men have been in a fit all day for the scandal it is to have you here."

"I have served my purpose with him," Lenae returned. "The next I mean to see the man is when I hand him his chick and not before."

Counsel Lord Shayan gave her a steady look and Kiernan saw the resolve in her they had all come to expect. How long it would last without Kiernan around no one knew, but it was here for now.

"Either way, you will likely want to change for the weather, Your Grace," Kaitlyn said and Lenae sighed, taking the cloak she had worn for the trip to the Counsel Lords' suites.

"Do you need an escort, too?" Hest'lre asked, drawing Kiernan's attention back.

"I think I can safely cross the yard now that the sleet has stopped," Kiernan said. "But you can keep an eye on me if you'd like."

"Knowing my luck, I'd just watch you die," Hest'lre said and then caught himself and turned to Lenae, an apology on his lips.

"It's all right," Lenae said, even if she had paled. "I'd rather you were relaxed and ready instead of worried about me."

Hest'lre had no argument for that.

When she and Kaitlyn were ready to leave, Lenae walked back to him and took his hands.

"Come back to me, Kier'n," she whispered, kissing his palms for luck.

"Always," he answered, and kissed her palms in return.

That done, Lenae turned away with determination and Consort Kaitlyn fell in behind her, joining the entourage of guards that had been waiting. By contrast, Kiernan looked to Hest'lre and Shayan with a nod, and then the three of them moved towards the balcony. There was no going back now.

Stepping out onto the wide expanse, Kiernan was surprised to find Vinicia's gryphling waiting for him on the ice-coated railing. As Aevi turned her head towards him, she flapped as if to say: It's about time.

"Better late than never," he told the impatient thing, taking a moment to secure Rylan's rank-pauldron beneath his cloak. "Is everything all right now?" He asked, since that is where Vinicia had gone off to while he was with Lenae. Aevi bobbed her head and then puffed out her feathers, shivering for a moment. The sleet had stopped, but it was still frigid.

"Shall we?" He offered, as Hest'lre and Shayan joined him at the railing.

Aevi bobbed her head again and then turned on the banister to launch herself into the wind. Kiernan watched her climb with more power and precision than he could ever hope to achieve and then, right in the middle of the Ice Wind gale, shift to dive straight towards the Armory. She knew the trick of slipping the wind just as well as any Delton graduate, that was for certain.

"After you," Kiernan said, gesturing for the other men to step off first.

Hest'lre gave him a nod before turning to where the platform and pavilions had been moved for the conclusion of the tournament. Shayan nodded as well, though Kiernan would follow him after a moment of peace. This was the last time he would leave his balcony. If he returned—*when* he returned—he would be a different man entirely. Older. Wiser.

Kiernan gathered his courage around him and was about to follow the gryphling when he suddenly felt an icy hand on his wing. Panic shocked his senses to alert, but when he turned to defend himself, what he found wasn't what he expected.

"How goes the war game?" Counsel Lord Broc asked, as if it was no such strangeness for the shade to have wandered so far from the Library.

"Ah, fine?" Kiernan answered, shifting into his secondsight to properly see the man. "How are you...?"

"There's a wealth of magic in your Counselheir," he said, cutting Kiernan off. "More than I expected, honestly. I suppose he is a good pick, after all."

"Wait, what?" Kiernan demanded. "I thought Eirik—"

And then from nowhere, Kiernan heard the suffering sigh of Counsel Lord Hewn moments before he appeared.

"Broc," Hewn said. "Give the living their peace. This world is not meant for us."

Kiernan looked between the two spirits, mouth agape.

"But the man needs to know!" Broc insisted. "It would be wildly embarrassing for him to be the last to know."

"Hewn, what's going on?" Kiernan repeated. Neither shade had ever made it this far from the confines of the Library before.

"Noventrio," Hewn said simply. "He left the Library."

"Of course he left," Kiernan said, shivering in the icy cold. "He guides the Ice Winds."

"No," Broc insisted. "He has left entirely. He went out to claim your Rylan as a… what did he call it? A vessel?" When Hewn nodded, he went on. "Some of the ancient Sevenths were in a fright over it. Said it hadn't been attempted since Counsel Lord Tolland's time."

"But how can he do anything to Rylan?" Kiernan balked. "He hasn't even been named yet."

"This is why we wanted to warn you," Hewn said. "One moment he was with us on top of the Library and then there was a surge in power. The next thing we knew, he went full corporeal, wings and all—"

"He has nine, you know," Broc added, distracted but impressed. "The only other Founders with that many are the King's and the Consort's."

"I am aware," Kiernan assured him. He remembered quite vividly the first time he had seen Noventrio in all his glory. 'Nine winds' and nine wings, indeed.

"We started to worry when he began cackling about patience winning the day," Hewn went on. "He was both more lucid and more mad than I believe I have ever seen him, and then he vanished. Things took a turn for the worst when he came back to us. Something had stopped him from getting his way and he was absolutely furious."

"So we wanted to warn you," Broc concluded.

"By coming outside of the Library yourself?" Kiernan asked.

"Where the Dragon goes, the rest will follow," Hewn sighed. "The door has been open since you, well…" He smiled, which was surprising given their talk. "Since you spent the night with Vinicia. Granted, the physical door is still locked by Noventrio's greater hawkeye outside the Library, but the seal is broken. We've been watching the event all morning. You may have noticed if you hadn't been—"

"Nice touch using your Seventh's Gift at the end, there," Broc smirked, elbowing Kiernan in the ribs no matter if he couldn't feel it. "As for us, though, we're just out stretching our wings," he went on, doing just that. "With the power you two brought into the Library last night, it's the first time some of us have been out in hundreds of cycles."

"With what power she focused just before Noventrio returned, however," Hewn said, hedging. "We may go where we will at the moment."

"Can anyone see you?" Kiernan asked, knowing that he wasn't in any position to stop one ancestral Seventh from going where he wanted at the moment, much less all of them.

"Only the clergy," Broc answered with a dismissive wave. "And only if we are related to them. I don't expect many can, since as Eirik is the only one among us who has living offspring."

"How many of you are there?" Kiernan hazarded to ask.

Hewn just pointed to the courtyard. "They wanted to see the tyro graduation," he explained. "And so they shall."

"You can't begrudge us that much," Broc defended. "This was our duty once as well, you understand."

Kiernan grimaced as he looked out over the field. Most of the courtyard had been strung with canvas to shield the families of the competing tyros from the worst of the weather, but the veteran praetors who didn't mind the rain were eager to lay claim to the men they were being assigned out of the Eighteenth Tyro Century. Among those men were scattered the silver-blue fog of the Ancestor Sevenths, with one spirit for every ten of them. To say the war with Lan'lieana had been going on for a long time was an understatement, but the sea of Sevenths brought that to life visually.

Two thousand cycles of madness that I mean to bring to an end.

As Broc moved past Kiernan to glide into the melee below, Hewn sighed one final time. "He has such a flare for the dramatic."

"It's the thought that counts," Kiernan assured him. "Thank you, Ser."

"I do what I can," he said, though he seemed as hesitant about the whole ordeal as Kiernan. "Perhaps there won't be enough to sustain this when you have gone, but I would take your Counselheir with you just in case. It is not an exaggeration to say that the ancient Sevenths were absolutely terrified when Noventrio came back."

"Take Rylan to Illiandria?" Kiernan said, confused. "Or do you mean for him to travel on Envoy with me, like Broc did to Eirik?"

"So you know about that, too," Hewn said, wincing. "Honestly, Kiernan. If you mean this to be the last Envoy, then take him to Illiandria and teach him all you can of your gift this winter. Hest'lre can manage being Ninth while training a new Sixth with Shayan to help him. And with Vinicia gone, you know Shayan will worry himself sick without something to do. As for you," he went on. "You should get out of here as soon as you can. As angered as Noventrio was when he returned, I fear the trouble he might make if you remain within his reach for too long."

Kiernan didn't doubt that either and set his right fist to his left breast in a salute Hewn readily deserved. For as short as his time had been in the Seat, he seemed to have made it his duty to keep the others cooperating with Kiernan as much as he could manage. Hewn returned the salute, and then followed Broc in a shimmer of light.

When both were gone, Kiernan looked to the Armory, only to find Eirik flaring his wings to get his attention. Kiernan responded in kind and dropped from his balcony into the Ice Winds without a second thought. With a little effort, he slipped through the gale and landed on the roof deck next to the elder Counsel Lord.

"Can you see them, boy!" Eirik greeted, as if this were some fledgling's game of hide and find. "There must be over a hundred of them!"

Beside him, Counsel Lord Shayan was just distraught. "Can you see what he is looking at?"

"The Ancestor Sevenths," Kiernan explained. "They have the strength to step out of the Library, it seems. Apparently when Vinicia and I, well... We made the tree bloom last night."

"Ah, yes," he said with excitement. "Excellent. I was hoping I did not have to make a task of it. If you have any questions, however, Aevi should be able to help you."

"The gryphling?" Kiernan asked, surprised.

"She may not be able to talk to you mind-to-mind yet," Eirik said, though he looked annoyed at that fact. "But once Vinicia has moved enough of her power through you, Aevi will find her voice again. She can vocalize some things, though she only does it when begging for treats. Isn't that right?"

Aevi was all innocence.

"Until then," Eirik went on, shaking his head. "Do you have any questions for me?"

"What do I do if one of us is hurt?" Kiernan asked, which seemed obvious. "If we can't..."

"A bruised wing never kept me out of a nest, lad," Eirik chuckled, and then Kiernan saw his eyes focusing just over his wings. "She is quite the healer, though, so I am sure you will be fine."

Kiernan had a second of warning before he heard the rush of air on feathers behind him and stepped next to Eirik to give whoever it was room to land. Much to his pleasure, he saw it was Vinicia behind him, her cheeks bright red from the ice in the wind. A heartbeat later, Aevi left her perch on the balcony railing and Vinicia flexed her wings away from her shoulders so the gryphling could land along her favored pauldron.

"Oh, that was worth every bit of waiting," she laughed, out of breath but smiling from ear to ear.

"Isn't it, though?" Kiernan grinned, envying the way she radiated strength after such a hard flight.

When Vinicia couldn't seem to stop looking up at the peak of the roof, Kiernan looked as well, though all he saw was a man of the Palace guards. "Was there something else?" he asked, drawing her attention.

"Yes and no," Vinicia said, her smile deepening to real joy as she turned to see the tyro century following her through the Palace updraft. "But I'll explain when we have more time."

"Fair enough," Kiernan said, watching as Aevi nuzzle in against Vinicia's neck. As she returned the affection, Kiernan looked up to see someone else was coming in to join them. His own smile deepened as he saw just who it was. "Sal'weh, Kreychi," he called as they all shifted to make space once again.

"Kreychi, Kreychi..." Eirik said, thinking aloud as Shayan guided him back. "Who is that, again? The Windover heir?"

"He's their Patriarch now, father," Vinicia answered, with a look to Kiernan. "He was inducted into the House of Lords two days ago," she added and then moved up next to him so she could kiss his cheeks in greeting.

"That explains some things!" Eirik said, looking past Vinicia. "I did not think a House Lord had any business up here, but I suppose he is all right."

"You can see him?" Kiernan asked in surprise. If Counsel Lords were leaving the Library, then the man might as well get his sight back.

"No, but Aevi can," Eirik said, and Kiernan realized Aevi was peering between Vinicia's wings as she kept an eye on the air around them.

"Forgive me, Sers. Consort," Kreychi said as he landed beside them, a touch concerned as he faced two living Seventh Counsel Lords and a Seventh's Consort. "I would have sent someone to you sooner, but I just got the news. I thought it better to simply come myself."

"What is it, Kreya," Kiernan asked, making room for Kiernan's fumentari guard to land around them. Disbanded or not, Kreychi was taking no chances.

"We have cleared the Barracks and the Sires' Wing of intruders," Kreychi said. "But from my sources, the price on your head continues to soar. The first bid we were able to stop, given that it was just some Illiandrian fool upset about a ringing?"

"My sister," he said, dismissive. "More than a few men in Illiandria would rather I not put my backing behind her, remember?"

"Right. Well, he is cooling his wingtips in the Cells," Kreychi confirmed. "The second was that pewter mess and just some hot-headed noble. He says he was having a bit of fun when he saw you walking blindly back to your room. He got ten crowns off some Yaltanan who dared him to get the blade on you. We have both of them in the Cells as well."

"And the third one?" Vinicia pressed. Obviously, this was the more serious concern. "Was it from the families who mean to start this House Kirath, like we thought?"

"It did come from House Kirath," Kreychi said. "They've hired out the job to crewmen that have been squatting at the House Northern estate, but the Gods alone know who they mean to do it. I can't — Kiernan, there is nothing more I can do," he said, real fear showing in his eyes as the world around them fell away.

"Kreya," Kiernan said, stepping closer to the man to draw his focus. "I promise you, I will leave as soon as I name my heir."

"And who is that?" Kreychi asked. "You know I have my House to manage—"

"I know," Kiernan said, stopping him before he could apologize. Of all the men who had worked for him in his life as a Counsel Lord, Kiernan knew how valuable Kreychi would be as a consultant for Rylan's new Shadow Guard. "And I promised you I would not take the Seventh from your House, remember?"

Kreychi nodded, still braced for the information.

"I am naming Tyro Rylan," he said quietly. "He already knows."

"But he already has a mark on his head," Kreychi balked. "Just who do you mean for his Sixth?"

"Tyrsten," Kiernan answered. "That is why he was not made a Praetor over a bevy for the tournament. I wanted to be certain they could work together."

Now Kreychi gaped openly. "I knew you were impressed by him, Kiernan, but I thought you wanted him as a Shadow, not for—Are you certain? I mean, he isn't going to inherit a Branch, but you could have warned me."

"Not without you figuring out my heir," Kiernan said, as if it would be some sort of consolation. "But with your family here in Delton and Hest'lre to guide him, he was the strongest candidate that could work with Rylan."

"Oh, I'm not doubting you," Kreychi laughed, his Alexandrian pride shining through. "Of course he will be a great Counsel Lord, but he's still untested. How can you expect him to lead without seeing the war at all?"

"Honestly?" Kiernan said, and Kreychi nodded. "I mean to come back."

And after saying it, for the first time in his life, Kiernan actually believed it.

Kreychi's faith was unflinching. "If Tyrsten can convince a woman in heat that he's her one true love," he said, laughing. "I'm sure he can convince a hundred thousand veterans to help Rylan end a war if you take too long."

"To end the War," Kiernan repeated, reveling in the sound of it. "That is the plan."

"The best laid plans never survive the paper they're written on, you realize," Vinicia warned. "Why don't we get you to Illiandria first?"

"She is wise, this one," Kreychi laughed, nodding at Vinicia. "As for Tyrsten, you have my blessing."

"Thank you, Kreya," Kiernan said, gripping his forearm in solidarity. "That is exactly what I was hoping to hear."

"Do you mean to name Rylan now, then?" He asked, with a glance at the suspiciously shaped bulk at Kiernan's hip.

"I do," Kiernan smirked and then didn't release Kreychi's grip as a new idea came to him. Kreychi was technically both Rylan and Tyrsten's superior in the Warhost until they were elevated to Counselheirs. "Though I would ask one last favor of you, if you wouldn't mind..."

"Another boon?" Kreychi hazarded.

"I only want to make certain you retire before I leave on Envoy," Kiernan said. "Truly, this time."

"I'm listening," Kreychi said, finally releasing his hand.

Vinicia was watching the two of them conspire with honest curiosity, so he waved at her to follow them inside Eirik's suite. His Shadow Guard he left on the balcony, but everyone else slipped back inside the armory for one last task.

CHAPTER 39: RYLAN

Sunday, 15:00

"Great Matron Celenae be praised," Tyrsten said, and Rylan watched as his friend kissed the barren ground of the Palace flats with a prayer to his Shelf-Founder. "We made it. It's over."

"Over?" Rylan said, passing Tyrsten to land just ahead of him. "We just got to the blicing starting line."

"Let him have his joy, Ry," Micah said, landing hard as he set down halfway between them. "Once he realizes he'll have to trade his flock of court daughters for a wingmate, you'll never see him happy again."

"Are you offering?" Tyrsten grinned, pushing onto his knees only to have to duck again as his brother Ren passed close overhead. "Because you're pretty enough that I might take you up on that."

"Nice try," Nichi called, panting as he set down with Westly close by. "You'll be celibate your whole commission if you go after him. Two cycles and all I ever got was a taste of his terra."

Tyrsten raised an eyebrow at that and then laughed as he saw Micah rolling his eyes. "Micah, you tease!" He said, getting back to his feet. "I thought for certain you two had already..."

"I said I'd fuck him on the War Plains and not before," Micah answered, preempting Nichi's response. "He knows that as well as you do."

Tyrsten cackled as he looked back at Nichi, though he had to duck when Nichi went to hit him with a wing as he passed by.

"Knock it off, you two," Rylan called, starting towards where he could see the chirons had set up their blockade at the entrance to the Chirons' Wing.

Just before the Eighteenth Tyro Century had pitted themselves against the Ice Winds, they had dropped the weapons and gear they'd worn for the past five candlemarks. Now all they had to do was get out of their tyro armor, sweaty and soaked as it was, and give it to the chiurgeons. Once that was done, they could pick up their Warhost jackets from where they had stashed them before mustering for the tournament.

Fortunately, although his command squad had been the last to arrive on the platform at the south end of the Delton shelf, they were some of the first tyros to make it back to the Palace flats. Vinicia had been the first person to return, though Rylan figured she'd used some trick of magic to give herself a boost. While some might see that as cheating, cheating usually meant winning in his book, so he didn't fault her for it. Sera had wanted to fly the Ice Winds as well, but she had been sent back to the Palace flats with a stern look from the Blackwings who had closed in around Rylan. They had not meant to fly the Ice Winds either, trusting the flight to keep him safe, but once he was on the shelf he had been told to expect a detail.

As they came underneath the warming tent next to the Chiron Tyros' Wing, Rylan tried not to jump when he saw the two Blackwing men waiting for him. Set apart from the chirons with their flared, black-enameled rank pauldrons, those two were the only ones in the tent carrying steel. Seeing him, the two men brushed their right hands over their pauldrons in salute. It was subtle, but it still made the pit of Rylan's stomach turn to stone.

This was really happening.

Seeing it as well, Micah, Nichi, Ren, and Tyrsten all glanced at Rylan as they stripped out of their white jackets, dropping them into a pile before shaking off their wings.

"Come on, guys," Micah said, herding them towards the door. "We'll be warmer with dry clothes and our Warhost jackets are inside."

Rylan took a steadying breath, ducking his head as he followed the others into the Chirons' Wing. It was worse inside, and all six of them had to pull up short as a group of men in black uniforms suddenly fell in around them.

"Rylan, Ser?" Said the leader among them, a blond-haired man with a warcrest falling between his wings. Unlike the Blackwings outside, this man's uniform had the seven silver slashes of the Shadow Guard on his right forearm and left calf. He also had a heavy praetor's pauldron with the Lord Seventh's quicksilver concho pinned to his left shoulder. That meant he was not only Praetor, but a First Praetor, and second in command to Counsel Lord Kiernan's fumentari.

"Uh, that's me," Rylan managed.

"And you are Tyro Micahleia, Tyro Andronicus, and Chiurgeon Westly," he said, naming them in turn. Once they nodded in confirmation, he looked between the two Borean brothers. "Which one of you is Tyrsten?"

"That would be me," Tyrsten said. "What's this about, if you don't mind me asking, First Praetor...?"

"Lyonel, Ser," the man said, trading a look with the other three around him. "You five are to come with us for your assignments," he said, vague for all the attention they were gathering.

Realizing the tension, Tyrren tucked his wings in as he stepped back. "Why don't I go help Raleigh?" he said, bowing out. "I'll catch you guys when we line up for the procession."

"That's a good idea, Tyro," the Blackwing First Praetor said, bowing his head.

Rylan wanted to be sick. All he had wanted to do was graduate and put his head down and now this? The only thing keeping him on his feet right now was the strange tightness over his left shoulder. Given his nerve, he wasn't sure if that was the quicksilver around his arm or the impending doom of the day.

"If you'll come with us," Lyonel said, stepping back to open the way. Just past the man, Rylan could see two Blackwings posted as sentries at a door just at the end of the hall before the Glass Garden.

Do I have a choice? Rylan thought, miserable as he and the others followed the men into a small, intimate sort of lecture hall used by the Chirons. Unlike the Soldier Tyro lecture halls with their tiered seats and vaulted spaces, the Chiron room was furnished with nine low marble tables meant for whatever herb or animal work needed to be done. At the moment, those tables held new uniforms for the five of them, three in the same black and silver that the First Praetor wore and two in deep Warhost indigo with silken kamas.

"Please change and be ready, Sers," the First Praetor said, lingering at the door. "In ten beats, someone will be in to brief you about the graduation event. Hoi?"

"Hoi, First Praetor," Tyrsten said, as he was the only one who hadn't swallowed his tongue.

The five of them changed in silence, if only to be out of the rest of their frigid gear. Rylan and Tyrsten took longer given the kamas, but both had grown up wearing them for festivals, so they knew how they went on. Micah was taking out his frustrations on the strap of the black flight harness that had come with their uniform. Given his height, he always needed to adjust them.

"I guess I don't need to fight to stay near you," Nichi said, looking to Westly once he was changed.

"Your brother was the Primarch of Kiernan's Shadow Guard," Westly said. "I suppose it makes sense Kiernan would want you to follow in his place."

"Yeah," Nichi said, still a bit stunned. "I guess I can't say I'm surprised, but I've never heard of a chirurgeon in the Shadow Guard."

"Neither have I," Westly agreed, looking to Rylan. "But it's not a bad idea."

If Counsel Lord Kiernan had a kindred for a companion, then it made sense he wanted one for Rylan as well. What better place to obfuscate him than in the Shadow Guard?

Rylan just wished he had a flight hood he could pull up, no matter the finery he wore. *Why can't I just have a normal life for once?* he wanted to know. *Kicked out of a House, growing up on the Streets, shoved into a tyro uniform halfway through the program... Counselheir before I'm even a soldier. Blood and ice.*

::It won't be so bad as all that,:: said a gruff mental voice and Rylan shuddered as he felt the quicksilver shifting beneath his kama. The thing had promised to stay hidden while they were changing, but now that he was in his Counselheir's uniform, Rylan could feel the thing nosing around again.

A moment later, Rylan yelped as he felt it sliding down his arm, but when he looked for it, all he saw was a hint of grey smoke as the thing settled into the outline of a dragon across the wide silk sleeve. ::I can keep a better watch here.::

Just try not to move, Rylan pleaded, looking back to his squad mates as they finished with their own uniforms. *The last thing I need right now is even more attention.*

"These are cut almost exactly like the Windover Blacks," Nichi was saying, trying to give the moment some sense of normalcy despite the seven bands of silver on their right forearms.

"They have to buy the leather from somewhere, don't they?" Micah said, stepping next to him as Tyrsten smoothed down the flowing fabric of his kama. Everyone else in their century would have had a kama as well, and it was only the Shadow Guard who never wore them. Shadow Guard were always working, and they made certain they were known.

"Maybe," Rylan replied, feeling sick to his stomach.

Why was Tyrsten in here? He knew Century Primarchs were usually given some sort of acknowledgment at graduation, so that could make sense, but shouldn't he be out with the others? Maybe they wanted him in here since he had seen the quicksilver, but Tyrren had also known and they had sent him away.

For as long as it had been since they had been left to change, Tyrsten chewed his lip as he looked to the door. "Shouldn't someone have come by now?"

"It has been longer than ten beats," Nichi agreed, watching him move for the door. "And we heard everyone moving to muster as we were changing. Shouldn't we—?"

Rylan flinched as he heard the high, keening note shared by a choir of warbards calling for attention nearby. Looking to Micah, Rylan saw his brother's far-away look and knew he was listening in to some sort of call. A moment later, there was noise in the hallway, and the anxious chatter of their tyro brothers went suddenly quiet.

"What is it?" Rylan asked.

"They're postponing the tyro draft," he reported, blinking as he looked back to the five of them. "They just told the Warhost officers that it's going to happen tomorrow."

"What about now?" He pressed. "About us?"

Micah just shook his head, though from the noise they could hear in the hallway, the Eighteenth Century of the Tyro Legion was processing into the Long Hall. From there, they would exit into the courtyard and be presented to the Host.

"Do you think they forgot about us?" Tyrsten said, moving for the door to look out.

He came to an abrupt stop as the door pushed inward before he reached it. Someone, it seemed, had finally come to collect them. Just who it was, though, had them all gaping.

"Sal'wehte, soldiers," Patron Kreychi greeted, dressed in the full regalia of the Primarch's position he had once held in Counsel Lord Kiernan's fumentari. That was to say, he was dressed in the same head-to-toe black with seven bands of cloth-of-silver. He was also armed to the teeth, a fact that made even Nichi have to see Kreychi for the warrior he had been long before returning to govern his House.

The most striking addition, though, was the change to the man's platinum hair. Though the sides of his head weren't shaved, Counsel Lord Kiernan's handiwork was evident in the way Kreychi's hair had been re-plaited into an intricate warcrest. Craziest of all was the fact that the end of the length hit just between the man's wings. At that length, Kreychi was saying he had never stopped working for Counsel Lord Kiernan at all.

"Kreychi?" Nichi managed, shaking his head as Tyrsten backed away to let him inside the room. "What are you doing here?"

"I've been sent to collect you flock for graduation," he said, holding up the Prefect pauldrons they had all missed as he had entered the room. "I thought the uniform would have given it away."

"But why are you dressed like them?" Tyrsten asked, baffled to see him setting the bundle on the table. "You're our Patriarch now."

"If you think for one moment that I ever intended to give up my bow or blades until the last possible moment," he said, waving for Micah, Nichi, and Westly to take one of the three pauldrons he had set down. "You are mistaken, cousin."

Still confused, the three moved towards the table Kreychi stood at, picking up the pauldrons in turn. Before they could step back, though, Kreychi caught them with a look as he reached to the small of his back to pull two folded-steel wingblades free. Moving closer, Rylan's eyes went wide to see them, knowing just how much something with that kind of craftsmanship would cost. Compared to the two heavy blades he carried from his days on the streets, they might as well have been made of diamond and gold.

All of them watched as Kreychi flipped them forward to hook them around his thumbs before moving them both into one hand. With a look of pride, he offered the set to Nichi. Nichi took them in stunned silence, and Kreychi was glad to be free of the first of his burdens. As he began to pull out a second set where they were hidden behind his thigh pouches, Tyrsten recovered.

"So my father was right. You haven't taken a wife because you were still working for Counsel Lord Kiernan," Tyrsten scoffed, watching him hand the dark-steel blades to Micah with the same look of pride he had for Nichi. "But are you really giving up the game, or is this a double feint?"

"I mean to retire for true this time, Tyrsten," Kreychi said, reaching into the bindings at the left cuff of his jacket. A moment later, he pulled out a stiletto, still sheathed, and extended it to a very confused Westly.

"I once heard a story of a chiron who kept a man from dying with this knife after a bolt sailed clean through him," Kreychi said as Westly took it. "With your talents, you may know more of what to do with this than any of us ever did."

When Westly pulled the stiletto free from the sheath, his mouth fell open in surprise. "Is this living steel?" He asked. "Actual living steel?"

"It came from our great grand-sire's wingmate," Kreychi explained. "One who had your coloring."

The look on Westly's face was priceless.

"No one at Court will ever trust you again showing up like this to graduation," Tyrsten insisted, and his gesture included both Kreychi and the men who were meant to take his place. "This is it. This is the end."

"Every shadow must recede when the guiding light of their Seventh takes to the Eihwaz," he quoted, starting after the laces on his right wrist.

"But what's that got to do with me?" Tyrsten protested. "I mean, I'm their century Primarch so I could lead them out, but—"

"Tyrsten," Kreychi said, separating the tooled leather at his wrist to reveal a heavy gold chain hidden beneath. Once he had the clasp free, he pooled the chain in his palm slowly, making it obvious that the tube of gold surrounded a bright core of silver. When he looked back to his cousin, it was with a seriousness that surprised them all.

"In all my time in Kiernan's shadow, it was to Counsel Lord Hest'lre that I reported," he said, and the realization dawned on them as Kreychi offered Tyrsten the chain of office. "I had meant to bring you into the Shadow Guard when Kiernan left his Heir with us, both you and Nichi," he added, with a look to his younger brother. "But if Lord Seventh means for Rylan to take his place, I can think of no better man to guard his back."

"Lord Seventh wanted to know if I could work with someone," Tyrsten realized, his hand shaking. "Is that why I wasn't Primarch of the bevy? Am I his—Ry, am I your—?"

As Tyrsten gaped, Rylan forgot to breathe. *Did I look like that?* He thought, numb. *Terror and anger and panic all at once?*

If Rylan's stomach had been in knots before, now it turned to stone. That chain was the Sixth Counsel Lord's favor, passed on to the man he felt should stand as the Primarch of Lord Seventh's Shadow Guard: a braid of heavy gold guarding the only hope of fragile peace.

"I think you're my Sixth," Rylan managed, his words echoing in the stunned silence of the moment.

Tyrsten blinked once, looked from Rylan to Nichi, back to Kreychi, and then snickered, obviously trying to stop himself. A moment later, he snickered again and then he fell to his knees, roaring with hysterical laughter. Rylan took a step back, worried his friend's mind had just cracked until he realized that Tyrsten was truly and honestly laughing. He couldn't believe it, but then again, neither could they.

The longer it went on, the more Rylan had to grimace at the awkwardness, but when he matched eyes with Micah, his own laughter began for real. Tyrsten's humor had always been infectious, but now it was a plague. The whole idea of men who had never been to war being raised to lead the Host was so ridiculous, all they could do was laugh.

Hearing the tenor of the drums changing beyond the doors, Tyrsten wiped the tears from his eyes, taking Rylan's offered hand to get back to his feet. As Tyrsten finally took the chain from Kreychi, Rylan saw Micah waiting for him to make the obvious connection. What Tyrsten said, though, surprised him.

"Give this to your sister, eh?" He said, still chuckling. "You never could stop Ry from leaving the shelf."

"Neither could you," Micah countered, shaking his head as he caught the chain Tyrsten tossed at him.

"Sera is the only one he ever listens to," Westly agreed, watching as Micah clasped it around his neck before tucking it under his high collar.

"It's time, boys," Kreychi said. "Let's not keep them waiting."

For all the fanfare that had sounded for the Tyro Legion as it processed into the courtyard, the deep, rolling thrum of war drums seemed to resonate with the tension in the air. Rylan heard the first inhaled surprise as Kreychi moved past the threshold and into the courtyard full of Warhost officers. If the cut and color of his uniform hadn't placed him, the warbard's hail put everyone on notice:

"Give Hail, all you men of the Host!" The man cried out, and Rylan squinted as the keening sound whistled inside his head, only to be sucked away by the icy touch of the stone on his chest.

"Give hail to the coming of Krecentius su'Alexandria, Cadre Primarch of the Shadow Guard Fumentari for Seventh Counsel Lord Kiernan su'Illiandria. Guardian to the man he means to take up his Seat: Counselheir R—" the man stopped mid-call, cursing as he re-read what it was he was calling from. "Wait, are you shitting me?" A beat later, he cleared his throat as he caught his place again, speaking louder as if to make up for his slip. "Seventh Counselheir Rylan su'Delton of the House of the Northern Lights."

Kreychi had timed it perfectly. Rylan stepped through the threshold at the exact moment everyone's eyes turned to find them. The silence that overtook the packed courtyard was deafening, making the drums that much louder by comparison. Rylan somehow kept moving. Tyrsten, a step behind him, never faltered. Knowing him, he was grinning like a cat in cream.

When they were halfway between the Long Hall and their destination at the end of the gathered masses, the warbard seemed to remember that he was supposed to be saying more and picked up his call once again.

"Hear me, men of the Home Guard," the warbard called, disbelief still evident in his voice. "Hear me and know that, named with him this day is the man who will take up the mantle of the Sixth Counsel Lord, Sixth Counselheir Tyrsten su'Illiandria of House Windover, Borean Branch."

Silence followed this as well and as the drums continued their thundering roll, Rylan let his eyes slip from their forward lock and saw that Counsel Lord Kiernan and Counsel Lord Hest'lre were waiting at the center of the platform with rank-pauldrons in their hands.

Not sure what was supposed to happen, both he and Tyrsten followed Kreychi until they were positioned in front of the two men. Arriving, Micah, Westly, and Nichi pivoted to face the audience, already acting as Rylan's guard.

Finally, when Kreychi moved to give his right-fisted salute, Rylan and Tyrsten followed with tyro-perfect precision.

"Counsel Lords," Kreychi began with respect. "I trust in the wisdom of your Seats and the strength of your convictions to bring out the men you judge them to be. I am beyond honored by the commissions they have received."

"Primarch," Kiernan acknowledged, returning his salute. "The honor is mine. Your service these long cycles have been invaluable, and I take it as a show of trust in my mission that you would gift so much of your House into the service of the crown."

"For Honor and Glory!" Kreychi replied, saluting a second time.

"For Honor and Glory," Kiernan agreed, and then stepped back into his ease as he looked to Hest'lre.

"Soldiers," Hest'lre commanded, speaking to Rylan and Tyrsten directly. "Wing up and report."

With only that for prompting, Kreychi fell back into rigid attention. As he pulled in his wings, Tyrsten and Rylan unfolded theirs, lifting off the ground together in an impressive show of readiness. Tyrsten winged his way to the left beside Hest'lre, and Rylan, having known how this ceremony was performed since he was a fledgling, went to Kiernan on the right. Back to back, the two Warlords would name their Counselheirs so that the Heirs themselves would know to have one another's backs in the cycles ahead.

When he landed, Rylan saw his three friends were looking out into the crowd, already acting as his guard.

::I haven't forgotten that it's Dylan's crew that was after Kiernan,:: Micah whispered, feeling his curiosity. ::They will be after you the moment you put on that pauldron.::

Dylan is dead, Rylan reminded him, taking a deep breath as he looked to Counsel Lord Kiernan.

::So we have kicked the hornet's nest,:: Micah said darkly. ::They will all be after you now and I don't mean to let them have you.::

In the moment he had glanced away, Kiernan had traded the rank-pauldron he had held for a piece of parchment and a flatboard from the other Counsel Lord who had joined them at the front of the platform: Supreme Justicar, Eighth Counsel Lord Lucien.

"I need your signature," the older man said, handing Rylan a glass quill that was already wet with ink. Rylan took it and the long piece of parchment. "This states you accept the commission as Counselheir to the Seventh's Seat. With your signature, any and all debts held against you are forgiven, no matter who holds them. We will work out the rest of the details over the Winter. Understood?"

Rylan signed it immediately, as near to hysterical as Tyrsten had been to know how one trail of ink in this moment could set Sera free of the boon it had taken to save her life. Even if it meant his own in return, if that was what it took, he would gladly give it.

Counsel Lord Lucien looked over the signature, took the quill and signed it himself before turning to Kiernan to finish. Once it was complete, he nodded in approval and then handed the pauldron back to Kiernan. As he moved to Tyrsten to perform a similar task, Rylan realized Kiernan was starting at the laces on the obscenely intricate rank-pauldron.

"I knew you would never go anywhere without your crew," Kiernan said quietly, not looking up. "As your fumentari, they can go anywhere with you and do anything for you under your authority."

As the last lace came free, Kiernan did look up. "You were right," Rylan confirmed, not wanting to give his thanks, but glad the man currently in command of the Warhost was not completely dense.

"Under the circumstances," Kiernan went on, pulling open the molded leather a few times to work it. "You will all need to come with us to Illiandria for the winter. Vinicia and I should be able to teach you enough about the Seventh's Gift so that you can protect yourself from the Founder."

When Kiernan gestured for him to turn to his left to let Kiernan set the rank-pauldron against his arm, Rylan did so without question, only to realize he was staring at the massive crowd that had turned out for graduation. Every single one of them was staring back at him, and Rylan shifted back on his heels with the weight of their watching.

With the sun still strong in the west, the Kosarans before him were every color from indigo to sky blue that he could have imagined, hanging out of both the Sires' Wing and Soldier Tyros' Wing in equal measure. It was only then, seeing everyone staring at him, that Rylan was able to come out of his own head to realize just what was happening. With Kiernan tightening the laces of the rank pauldron to his left shoulder, the roar of the crowd in front of him was only in his mind. The Warhost was coming to life inside of him, surging forward as it carved out space for a mental gift that he had only ever discussed in theory as a tyro at the Academy. In the same breath, his eyes watered and burned as the world before him shifted, and he was truly lightheaded as the Warhost officers before him blurred to reveal a massive choir of silver-blue shadows standing at the head of the gathered crowd.

At the very front, standing beside Micah, Westly, and Nichi, Rylan's jaw went slack as he saw Counsel Lord Hewn giving him a soft salute.

::I was not wrong when I said we expected great things from you son,:: the ancestors said.

Rylan nearly staggered as Kiernan set his hand on Rylan's pauldron, grounding the Gift that seemed bent on devouring his mind. As Rylan remembered to breathe, the man's attention turned to the Warhost officers before him.

::"My last order to you is this, brothers: keep faith with my Counselheir so he might keep faith with the Gods that guide us,":: Kiernan said, wings flaring as he addressed the Warhost one final time. ::"Honor to the Host!"::

::"Glory to the House of the Northern Lights! ":: the Warhost responded, and the intensity of the words staggered him a second time.

Strange as his appointment was, these men were accepting it.

When Kiernan left for the Eihwaz, he was going to be the Seventh Counsel Lord.

Standing before every officer available for the Nine Legions of Kosar, he had just been named the Seventh Counselheir.

Rylan looked back to Kiernan in a daze as the man tightened the laces of the pauldron beneath his arm. A moment later, Rylan felt the quicksilver slipping out from underneath and the barely concealed look of surprise on Kiernan's face told Rylan he recognized the dragon.

"Holy Matron," Kiernan breathed, taking his hands away carefully. "Is that...?"

Pleased to see the carved version of itself now covering Rylan's arm, the quicksilver slithered into the crevices, giving the whole thing a glittering sheen beyond what the leather smiths had managed.

"It stopped Noventrio from giving me wingbars right there in the street," Rylan said, looking to the man's own abused pauldron. "It said Great Father Tralmis was angry with Noventrio for naming so many Sevenths at once."

"Huh," Kiernan said, still stunned. "We'll have to talk about that more later. For now—*Fuck!*"

The last was a whispered curse, and Kiernan shoved against his chest just as the quicksilver cinched around his arm, twisting him further. As Rylan caught himself, he opened his eyes to find Kiernan staggering backwards, clutching at the heavy crossbow bolt that had appeared in the hollow of his throat.

If he hadn't shoved me—

::You would both be dead!:: The quicksilver growled, and Rylan turned to find the courtyard in chaos.

As he heard Vinicia scream behind him, the attention of the Warhost swung to the only empty window of the Soldier Tyros' Wing. When he switched into his flight-lenses, he saw his brother's left-hand man, Oren, dead-center in the window, readying a second bolt.

"Oh, you asshole!" Rylan swore, already sprinting for the edge of the platform. As the world around him erupted in panic, Rylan clawed into the open sky. "Can you get into that window?" Rylan demanded of the quicksilver.

::What do you want me to do?:: The thing asked, confused but eager.

"Help me!" Rylan cried, flinging his arm in front of him.

::Like I did lassst night?:: The little dragon hissed, taking off in a rush of wind that helped Rylan get into the air.

"That was you?" Rylan balked, only to hear a crank-style crossbow being fired a heartbeat later. As Rylan twisted in his flight, pulling in his wings to make a smaller target, he saw the bolt shatter as the quicksilver devoured it mid-air. Oren saw it as well, dropping the crank-bow to make his escape as the shutters and glass he tried to close exploded into shrapnel.

When he was close enough, Rylan gave himself one last powerful beat and then tucked and rolled into the wind again, diving inside the room with just enough time to come to a wing-straining stop a hair's breadth from the opposite wall.

::He'sss getting away!:: The quicksilver hissed, swirling in a furious mist just past the threshold of the room. ::What ssshould I do?::

"Follow him!" Rylan shouted, pushing away from the wall so he could do the same. As the quicksilver swelled in size to move faster through the air, Rylan started after it in a vengeance, only to get half strangled a moment later.

"Where are you going?!" Micah demanded, and Rylan had a heartbeat to protect himself as Micah threw him down on his wings.

"After Oren!" Rylan swore, pulling in his wings before Micah could step on one to keep him pinned to the ground. Micah glared at him as he came onto his feet. "I mean to end this now, not give him another chance to set up a shot."

Micah looked ready to argue, but held his tongue as Rylan saw Nichi making a careful landing on the glass-strewn window. "Why are you both just standing there?" He demanded. "Which way did he go?"

"Towards the washroom," Rylan said, pointing. "Kill that bastard!"

"We'll cover the armory side! Go!" Nichi said, twisting to dive out the window. A heartbeat later, another body landed hard on the side of the building and pushed off again, likely Westly.

"What is wrong with you?" Rylan demanded. "Don't you trust me?"

"Three days in a row you have almost died trying to kill them," Micah swore, yanking open the closet in the room to grab the crossbow hanging inside. "Just let me do it."

"We'll do it together," Rylan swore, realizing Micah was picking up Oren's warshot bolts near the window. By the time they were both in the hallway, the crewman was obviously gone, but from the way people were staring at a room halfway down the building, he hadn't gone far.

"Out of the way!" Rylan bellowed, which had them ducking back into the rooms they had been using to watch the graduation.

As the hall cleared, Rylan swore again, diving to the ground and yelling "DROP!" As he saw Oren coming out with a new crossbow of his own. Two cycles of flinching every time the Barracks Mother or one of their Professors had them on the floor doing foxdrops may have just saved their lives.

Realizing he had missed, Oren took off down the hallway again. Rylan stayed down, knowing Micah was going to take his own shot, but after the first one was out, Rylan was back on his feet. As he gave chase down the hall, there were wisps of dark mist following in Oren's wake.

::Dammit, dragon! DO something!:: Rylan swore, though he nearly tripped to realize he was speaking with bardic strength. For the first time in his life, he could feel the words pouring out of him like their cantos had said it would once he served the Lord Seventh. Staggering in mind, if not in body, he soldiered on as a lion-headed snout formed in the mist to stare back at him. ::Trip him or bite him! Anything!::

The dragon wasn't confused . ::I can do that?::

::Of course you can!:: Rylan Rylan wanted to scream, clenching his fists around the wingblades as he saw Oren duck off to the right. Both he and Micah slowed to stagger their footsteps, taking away his chance at timing a shot while they figured out what they were going to do.

::But Father sssaid I was to protect you, not harm windwalkers,:: the quicksilver sent back, confused. ::Guide you, but do no harm.::

::Well, I am about to put myself in danger::, Rylan thought, glaring. Obviously, if he was going to be followed by a supernatural creature, it would be absolutely useless. What he wouldn't give for Vinicia's gryphling right now, with that beak and talons.

::Why would you put yoursssself in danger?:: the quicksilver grumbled. ::You are a peacccemaker.::

::Because he's trying to kill me!:: Rylan thought, realizing as they neared the center of the Wing that Oren had probably run into the dayroom to reload. And then Rylan got an idea. ::You're next to him, right?::

::The bessst way not to get killed isss not to fight,:: the dragon grumbled. ::Two thousssand cccccycles and you creaturesss ssstill haven't learned.::

Rylan grit his teeth, knowing the dragon was right. The problem was, they were in the middle of a fight right now. How was he supposed to not fight if—

Rylan swore as he got an idea.

::You're next to him. Right Kohl?::

::Yesss,:: the quicksilver said. ::He's crouching behind thisss big table thing.::

Perfect, Rylan thought. *He's right near the walkway.* Without looking back, Rylan brought his right hand up in an arc from left to right, signaling Micah behind him that he was going up and over. ::When I give you the signal, can you show yourself to him?::

::But the Earth Mother said not to,:: the quicksilver protested, which must have meant Vinicia. ::You have told me not to since I revealed myself to you.::

::You're just 'guiding' him into the walkway for me, Rylan assured the thing. I promise Mother won't be upset.::

::It's your tail if she is,:: the quicksilver sulked. Clearly, he didn't like this plan. ::Just tell me when.::

Taking a few deep breaths, Rylan set himself and then started to sprint down the hall. Micah stayed where he was, already aiming. If all the cycles of fighting on the streets were worth anything, if all that struggling in small spaces and tight quarters was to be useful, this is when it would count.

::Do it!::

Oren's ear-piercing scream was priceless as he stumbled out of the study area with his back turned to the greater part of the hall. Seeing his chance, Rylan shifted to the left, gathered himself, and then leapt up into the air. With his feet on the wall, Rylan took two steps and then twisted up and over Oren, who was staring down the huge, ashy quicksilver as it roiled in the air in front of him.

Blades in hand, Rylan dropped to a knee to stop his spin and ducked as Micah's shot went off. Oren's second scream was one of pain and Rylan saw blood pouring down his wing as Oren's own crossbow fired harmlessly through the empty room. A beat later, Rylan heard Micah launch as well and braced himself for the impact. When he felt Micah crash into Oren's head and shoulders, dragging him across the crest of Rylan's flared wings, Rylan pivoted with the force and drove his wingblades into Oren's body as he pressed out of the crouch.

Rylan came back to his feet just as Micah twisted to land, which was much more easily done in the small space given his friend's lesser height. Coming to their feet, it was obvious from the open gash on Oren's gut that he would no longer be a problem.

As the rush of the fight burned in his veins, Rylan felt Vinicia's hawkeye going cold against his chest. It stopped just as soon as the quicksilver swirled back around him in a fury. Micah didn't seem to notice or care, though when he looked up from Oren's corpse, it was only to toss the borrowed cross and bolts to the side of the hallway, muttering about putting an end to a man who had haunted his sister for cycles.

Rylan was just glad to know that the assassin paid to take down Kiernan and himself was dead, and if anyone had backed him up, they had run instead of meeting Oren's fate. Exhaling in a rush, Rylan dropped the two wingblades at the man's feet and his hate with it.

Joining Micah on the other side, they looked at each other as the quicksilver swirled around them. No matter the chaos raging outside, both he and Micah knew the underlying trust between the two of them was as unshakable as the bedrock of the mountains. Still, that didn't mean Rylan didn't do things that completely pissed him off.

"I won't run off like that again," Rylan said. "I give you my word."

"You can't promise something like that," Micah argued, looking sideways at him. "Not with what you're going to be."

"Then make me," Rylan said, meaning it as he watched his brother taking on the mantle of a true Shadow Guard officer. "You can do that, can't you? Compel people?"

"I wish," Micah said. "I can nudge you in the right direction, though I do it better with Sera's help."

"Then I want you to do it," Rylan insisted. "Both of you, working together. Figure out the words you want to use so I can't wiggle out of it, and I'll let you do it to me," he said, looking down to where Oren's body lay as he realized it could have just as easily been his on the floor. "Mike, I could have died. I could have gotten you killed. He could have been waiting for us with the rest of the crew in that hallway and I just flew in there blind. Gods, why can't I ever listen to you?"

It took Micah actually turning him away from the sight before Rylan realized he was shaking. As Micah set their heads together, projecting his calm over Rylan's growing panic, the adrenaline of everything that had just happened took him by the throat.

"Breathe, Ry," Micah said softly, and Rylan could feel the hands on his hair, working calm under his skin no matter how badly he wanted to fight and flee. "It's over. We made it."

"If Kiernan is dead, I'm already the Counsel Lord," Rylan said, hearing the strain in his voice as his eyes burned with tears. "Seven cycles. That's all I have. Then I'm going to die. They're going to kill me. They're going—They're going to—"

Gritting his teeth, it was all Rylan could do to keep from sobbing aloud. Micah's strength redoubled as he gave up his hold to embrace him fully.

"Not while there is breath in my body," Micah said, and Rylan could hear the strain in his friend's words as well.

"Nor ours," a new voice added, and Rylan didn't have to open his eyes to know Nichi had joined them. Westly was there as well, and Micah hugged him tighter before releasing him so all four of them could huddle up.

"Do you really think the other Sevenths would have approved of Kiernan being given Vinicia as a bodyguard, or you being given me, if we weren't meant to keep you alive no matter what?" Westly said, his wing stretching to curl around Rylan's own.

Rylan wanted to believe him. Knowing as much as he did about the Sevenths, it was not something he could say had ever been done before. But for as much confidence as they were trying to radiate, he couldn't overcome the raw hollow of fear that kept burning away at his hope. Worse, new as his Gift was, he could feel the confusion and shock of the Warhost rising like bile in the back of his throat; could feel their anger and hatred like a wildfire tearing through his veins...

When he looked down to gather himself, Rylan hissed with pain as that fire inside of him began to spread from his chest and out into his wings. As he dropped to his knees, spasming with the intensity of it, all three of them stepped back with shock and honest horror.

"You're getting wingbars," Nichi said, shielding his eyes as the whole corridor flashed with white.

A heartbeat later, Rylan heard Nichi collapse beside him and then Micah fell as well. Rylan tried to say something—anything—only to realize that everything in the world seemed to be sliding northwards.

CHAPTER 40: VINICIA

Sunday, 16:00

"**N**o!" Vinicia screamed, watching in horror as the chirurgeon with his hand on Kiernan's throat drew out the bolt meant to slay him. "No, he's not dead!" She pleaded, struggling against the men who had thought to restrain her when Kiernan had fallen. "He is alive! I can still save him!"

"Be quiet, woman," Second Counsel Lord Gallen snapped, looking over to her as his chirurgeon team backed away. "You are embarrassing yourself."

"Vinicia, please," Hest'lre said as he neared, flaring his wings as he came to stand between her and where Kiernan had fallen. "Do not give Lenae hope like this."

His insistence only made her strain harder, and she planted her feet against the podium and rooted her place with earth to keep from being dragged back. The men hanging on her did not relent, but they did flinch when there was a sudden burst of bright light in front of them.

Vinicia could have cried to see Westly appear at Kiernan's side, scattering the chirurgeons lingering around his body. In the shock of the moment, Westly pulled a stiletto from within the sleeve of his left arm and plunged it into Kiernan's body.

"Westly!" She cried out, horrified. "What are you doing?"

"Saving him," Westly called back, flaring with power.

In her secondsight, Vinicia gaped to see how the dagger had somehow pinned his spirit to the earth, no matter how it had been drawn towards the Library. What was left in him shuddered and was still, but she knew the fragile power was still spinning. He had bought her time, and now she had that moment to fight.

So as Westly hovered over Kiernan's body, Vinicia looked to Hest'lre with determination. Alexandrians were terrified of magic, weren't they? Well, he was about to be terrified of her.

"This is exactly why Lenae asked me to stand with him," Vinicia said, letting her shields shatter to reveal her red-gold hair and bright amber eyes. Hest'lre fell back a step to see her, his own going wide. As he stammered a reply, Vinicia gathered her breath to scream once again, redoubling it with power.

::"LET ME HELP HIM!"::

As the echo of her demand rang in the courtyard, the burst of bardic magic sent the men on the podium to their knees, Hest'lre included. The two men on her arms simply collapsed, knocked unconscious with the whiplash of force. As the feel of a few thousand men before her recoiled, Vinicia reached out along with her Seventh's Gift to make certain she had a hook in every military mind on the shelf. Knowing their reaction to her magic, fearing Kiernan's certain death without her help, she wrenched what energy she could feel out of their control.

No one would act without her express command.

No one would move unless she gave her permission.

Giving no direction at all, Vinicia watched in morbid fascination as the bodies began to fall before her. They had stopped, everything had stopped, and in the silence that followed, all her hate and rage turned into a clear purpose in her mind. This was the dangerous back edge to the gift she had used to heal for so long, but if Kiernan's own men meant to kill him, she would kill every single one of them to bring him back to life.

With the fate of the Warhost in her grasp, all she had to do was pull Kiernan's spirit back from the Library and put it where it belonged.

Kiernan was her charge. Her responsibility. Her Seventh. He was hers, body and soul. He did not belong to Noventrio and he never would. Noventrio might have taken Hewn from her, but he would take Kiernan over the dead bodies of four thousand of his own men right here in Delton.

It would be the Fall of Kirath all over again, with only one woman to blame.

As the destructive potential roared to life with the slaughter at hand, Vinicia pulled the chaos into herself with a wild sort of greed. Just the night before, she had realized she needed Kiernan in order to complete the circle of power between herself and the Great Tree. Without him, whatever force that trapped the ancestors in the Library was the same shield that had kept her out of it for so long. But with Kiernan's spirit behind that shield, would he be able to grant her access? Would he have to, now that she held the strength of so many in her control? With this, she should be able to pierce that stronghold and rip him free.

Vinicia took a breath to focus and regretted it instantly. Met with a wave of utter revulsion, the energy writhed in her grasp and she felt the stolen power bucking her control. It was only as she struggled to keep hold that she realized the maelstrom of angry minds inside, all screaming for vengeance. All demanding their freedom. The will of the Host to survive was impossibly strong.

It took everything that Vinicia had to stay on her feet as the spirits clawed at her. No matter her valiant intent, those minds were struggling in their last act of confusion or panic as they realized just what kind of monster had been standing before them.

Oh Gods, what have I done? I can't use this. I can't—

With everything happening at once, Vinicia gasped aloud when she felt a touch on her brow and opened her eyes to find the woman who had taught her so much standing before her. If anyone could help...

::Stay calm, *sha'doe*,:: Lora commanded and Vinicia fell into the deep blue of her eyes. Recognizing the Suggestion for what it was, she willed herself to submit.

"Lora, what have I done?" Vinicia asked, gasping on the edge of madness. Was Kiernan worth so many lives? Was one man ever worth the sacrifice of so many others? "It is too much. I've never taken so much. This is why I never wanted to take in so much."

::If you had listened to me, this would be no task at all,:: Lora said, though there was no judgment in it. ::But this is what they made you for. This is the kind of power you were meant to hold, I swear to you.::

"But what do I do with it?" Vinicia asked, letting Lora take up her hands to guide her from the pile of men that had been restraining her from Kiernan's side. "How do I do anything with this?"

"He's not dead," Westly said aloud, even though he knelt in a pool of blood. "I got him into some sort of stasis, but I can't find his spirit. I can't even feel it..." he said, only to look up and see Lora hovering over him. Before he could speak, Lora was already answering his question.

::I'm not going to punch you again, sapling,:: Lora answered, pushing back the hood of the cloak as if to disarm herself. ::But I have been her teacher and yours, through her, for cycles now. All you need to do is keep the energy of his vessel moving and she can have the chance to save his spirit. You can do that much, can you not?::

Westly's mouth clicked shut as he nodded.

::Well, get to it!::

Westly actually flinched as Lora rolled her eyes, setting to his task.

Vinicia tried to give him a weak smile, amazed to see the blade at work but horrified to know just how close she had come to failing him. For all her charge to keep Kiernan safe, for the second time in three days she was dragging him back through the veil.

Lora seemed to recognize her unease and set a hand on her wing, forcing her to focus.

"Lora, what do I do?" Vinicia asked. "If I let them go, they will kill me—us. All of us."

::You will have to skim from it, *sha'doe*,:: Lora replied, and the irony of the instruction was not lost on her. ::It may be your crutch, but you are a master at it.::

"Skim the Host," Vinicia acknowledged as the power roiled inside of her. Even with a lifetime of practice, though, her tyros had always trusted her. This stolen power was so volatile that she had no idea where to even begin. Take too much from one place and an entire soldier would perish. How she was supposed to wield any of it, much less focus it into a weapon, was beyond her.

And then Vinicia felt the heavy weight of her gryphling landing on her shoulders. A moment later, she felt the energy within her settle and she could think clearly once again.

::This is not how Grave magic works,:: the gryphling argued, staring down Lora as she flexed her talons against Vinicia's pauldron. ::Whatever magic you take on this scale must pass through a tree to be focused and reformed. You are not a Founder. Your vessel is not enough to purify this kind of living magic, not without killing yourself in the process.::

::Do you want him to live?:: Lora sent, glaring at the gryphling. ::If you want him to live, do not think to tell her what she cannot do. No matter what I have tried to teach her, she has always done this—tree or no.::

As her two companions argued, Vinicia reached out for the Great Tree. Perhaps if she flooded the system, she could shatter the shield of Noventrio's influence entirely. Like an ice damn bursting in spring, she would force her way through. That was more her nature than even this idea of skimming. As she brushed that power, though, she flinched as she felt Noventrio himself swelling into the area around them.

"Be quiet, both of you," Vinicia hissed, watching the silver shimmer of power that hailed the Founder's coming. "We will all die if I do nothing but stand here."

"As you should," Noventrio said, furious as he materialized at Kiernan's feet. "Release your hold on my Host this instant or I will sever you by force."

"Kill me and I will take all of them with me," Vinicia demanded, holding her ground in the face of his greater power. "All I want is Kiernan's spirit returned."

"Do not think to make demands of me," the Founder growled. "I have suffered you in my temple long enough."

"Your temple has been powered by my workings for the past thirty cycles," Vinicia said, her anger giving strength to her determination. "For all I've given you, I have asked nothing in return. All I want is Kiernan's spirit, so we can do your work. This is all in service to the Seat."

"You have done nothing more than gnaw at my roots, sapling," the Founder said and Vinicia watched as he looked to the man sprawled at his feet. "If you want him so badly, follow him across the veil so I may be rid of you both."

"You would like that, wouldn't you?" Said a new voice and Vinicia gasped as her father appeared in a flash of white light beside them, garbed as Kiernan was in his Warhost kama. "To be rid of everyone who came after me?"

"You!" Noventrio hissed, wings flaring for all his anger at the elder Seventh. "You should be dead ten thousand times over for all you have done in opposition to my will."

"Kill me then," Eirik challenged. "Oh wait, you can't," he amended, cackling as Noventrio stared daggers through him. "Your wings are tied in this one thing, aren't they? You cannot kill us because we serve a purpose greater than your own. Worse, you cannot kill her for the decade she spent in service to your gaesh. No, the only power you have is politics and waiting for us to die."

"Silence!" The Founder roared. "You thought to pit her against me, but she has only set me free from the prison my brothers made to bind me. One more act of power from her, one more attempt at passing energy through my temple, and I will have the strength to take the firestarter for my true avatar. Through him, I will put an end to you both."

Vinicia wasn't sure what to think as Noventrio turned from them, flaring his wings with a crackle of power. A moment more and he was gone, though the fury he left in his wake still made her sick. Tied as she was to his hearth tree, she had always known the Founder's moods for good or ill.

When he was truly gone, Vinicia turned to her father for an explanation, only to realize his eyes were free of their clouded white. For the first time in her life, the true coloring shone through and she was staggered to see the chestnut in him.

"Father," Vinicia asked, not sure what was happening but terrified all the same. "Father, what is going on? If he does not mean to stop me, can we save Kiernan?"

"Yes, love," Eirik said, moving to stand near to her as he extended his hand. "With my help, you can."

He paused when he saw there was a woman standing behind Vinicia as well, though when he realized what the woman was, he seemed strangely delighted.

"You are Kiernan's loralae, yes?" Her father asked, looking directly at Lora.

Lora shifted uncomfortably behind her, but nodded.

"Can you bind my daughter the way you were taught to do on the Plains?" he asked. "Bind her from all but her Seventh's Gift?"

Vinicia's confusion heightened as she realized Lora was terrified of her father.

"Do it then," he instructed. "If she is bound, she will not kill the Host and the rest we can do without your help."

Lora had one moment of hesitation before her will buckled. "Serviam, Viridis." *I will serve, Greenman.*

"What is going on?" Vinicia asked, watching the woman back away.

"All men live for the day we pass on our power to our kith, my love," her father said, taking her hand. "I will pass my legacy onto you, but not before I set you free from that beast. This much I promised your mother. It is why I held on to so much of her strength for so long, even if it meant I could barely see your face."

As she caught up his hand in hers, Vinicia felt the raw energy at her father's command as he opened himself to her touch. There was a wildness to it that she had never felt before and as she looked into his eyes, she saw a bright violet power flowing between them. It was her mother's power, she realized, supporting her through her father's influence during the time she had been outside of the Eihwaz. 'More dryad than windwalker,' Kiernan had said this dawning. That was nothing compared to the power her father meant to use to free her from the grip of a Kosaran Founder.

Can he do that? Vinicia gaped. *Can my mother do that?*

::Eirik was taught to channel Heatherwood's power the same way he has made it possible for Kiernan to channel for you,:: Aevi said, and Vinicia realized that in the chaos of what was happening, the gryphling had left her shoulders and curled protectively around Kiernan's head. ::But you will have to reach through him to reclaim Kiernan's spirit. Mother says you can reach through all Sevenths, but since your power had to be in the Founder's control for so long, she feared he would never let you go. You changed that last night,:: Aevi said, radiating with pride. ::When you took your Seventh to nest, he linked that power back to you at last.::

Vinicia's face went scarlet as the memory of the night before surged into her mind. As Aevi's bright emerald stared back at her, she looked away in embarrassment, only to realize Lora's presence. Lora was too focused on her task to bother reading thoughts at all.

::Do you consent to this binding?:: Lora asked, quiet even mind-to-mind. ::It will block you from any power not related to your Seventh's Gift.::

Vinicia didn't have to think twice.

"Do it."

Lora sat back on her heels, palms pressed together before her sternum as she closed her eyes. A moment later, the air around them prickled like a storm and then Lora swept her hands in a wide circle, out and up and then crossing at the wrists to return to the place where they had begun.

It seemed like nothing at all had changed until Lora opened her palms, wrists together, and shoved them both towards Vinicia with a hiss of air and intention.

Vinicia saw stars as the force of the binding wrapped around her. It took a few heartbeats for the icy sensation to clear, but as quickly as the power of so many souls had appeared at her fingertips, now it was gone. Except, it wasn't. It seemed as long as the shield held her power as a kin segregated from her Seventh's Gift, it would have to work. It was her only chance at bringing Kiernan back.

Vinicia opened her eyes as she took a steadying breath, confirming the block was in place with a small nod. With her mind firmly settled inside that stillness, she lowered herself to her knees to take hold of the stiletto Westly had at Kiernan's throat.

"What is this?" She asked, realizing as she touched it that it felt almost as pure as the Wellspring she had known in Kiernan's arms.

"Living steel," Westly said simply. "It is shifting the grave magic running through him back to grove, keeping him alive. If you can bring his spirit back into his body, we have a chance."

"So be it," Vinicia said, looking at her father when she was resolved to the task. "What do you need from me?"

"Like calls to like, Vinicia, and blood calls to blood," he answered, extending his hand as she waited for his guidance. "As I go, I will open the way for you. That way will always be open for you, once I am inside, that much I can promise. Your mother made certain of that."

Vinicia covered Westly's hand on the blade at Kiernan's throat with her right hand, leaving her left in her father's as the cold reality of what he meant to do settled over her heart.

"Are you sure?" She asked, her throat tight around the words.

"You will not survive if I do not," he said, squeezing her hand with affection. "After all these cycles, if you do not leave the shelf now, you will fall just as surely as he has. It is his strength you need to leave this place and he needs your strength to set the rest of the world free."

Vinicia's breath caught as she squeezed her father's hand, though as her tears fell, she opened herself to the power she could feel resonating in him. As she pulled it into herself, it was a terrifyingly easy task to send it towards the Great Tree. Noventrio wanted her father as surely as he had wanted Kiernan, and he would not stop this slow suicide.

As her father's hand began to go cold, she let the pull of the Tree take over the flow and followed it inside with her mind. With her mental search, she felt for Kiernan like he was one of her beloved tyros until the spark of his spirit surged into prominence. Slowly, very slowly, Vinicia wove the power that had been shared so intimately between them the night before into a shield that covered the core of who Kiernan was beyond that power. With his essence now firmly in hand, she turned her attention through the otherworldly space to find the way back.

Despite all of the frustration and single-minded purpose, despite the strength of trading one life for another with the magic she wielded, Vinicia was horrified to come to that edge, only to find it sealed over with crystal. No matter how many times she had been inside this power, no matter that she had given the Founder all of this power in the first place, she could not pass through it without Noventrio's consent.

Vinicia opened her eyes in the true world again, her hand flexing around the dagger in Kiernan's throat. Beside her, her father stood as pale as a shade, though his spirit shimmered with the amethyst of her mother's power churning inside of him.

"Your mother taught me many things," he said simply. "How to be a channel for her power was the very first among them. It brought you into this world and it will bring Kiernan back as well. When I am gone, he will return. Have faith, my love, and fly free."

Vinicia closed her eyes again as she felt him slip away, and the backlash of her mother's power entering the Great Tree rocked the very foundation of Noventrio's hold on the shelf. For an instant, a hair's breadth, the whole shield was gone and she ripped the dagger free of Kiernan's throat with a scream of grief and rage.

Not a moment later she felt Kiernan spasm beneath her hands, and as that energy doubled back on her, her father's spirit lodged into the bore they had made. Now and forever, if she needed the power of the Sevenths who meant to support her, she would find her father standing guardian over her access. He had given his life to make absolutely certain of that.

Vinicia opened her eyes to see Westly stitching Kiernan's body back together with his own talents. Kiernan's power was starting to pulse in him, and the weight of her father's sacrifice fueled her resolve to see Kiernan live, she brought the power in the Tree itself to bare for Westly's working. This time it would not be like Hewn.

With her power cycling through the massive hearth and Westly's skill crafting it to purpose, it wasn't long before they had Kiernan roaring back to life. Vinicia wanted to scream in triumph as Kiernan's lungs filled with air for the first time in almost half a candlemark, but the only sound that escaped her was a strangled sob.

Her father had given his life to see this done. Her father had given his life to set her free. All she could do now was watch as the shade of her father shimmered in front of her, right next to the very men he had plotted with to make this moment a success. In addition to freeing Kiernan, it seemed as Noventrio's grip on the ancestor Sevenths had weakened that much more.

"It's about time, you old bird," Counsel Lord Broc greeted, shaking the man's hand with vigor. Counsel Lord Hewn greeted him as well and then looked to Vinicia with a pride she hadn't expected.

"I believe you have come into your own at last," he said with a smile.

Vinicia couldn't say anything in return, could barely see them for her tears.

"I could not be more proud of you, daughter," her father said, projecting love with every part of his being.

"We will do what we can to stall Noventrio," Broc added. "He may be free of his prison, but he will not have the strength to claim the Counselheir for some time. We can do that much, at least. Those of us who truly seek peace will stay with you until that peace is won."

Vinicia nodded to acknowledge them and then scrubbed at her eyes as they disappeared in a shimmer of light. When they were gone, it was all she could do to turn back to the chaos before her, unsure where to even start. For one, her body was covered with blood and her face with tears, and then she realized both Lora and Westly were kneeling quietly beside her. Vinicia had almost forgotten their presence with so many others held in the unnatural stillness.

"I'll go fetch some water," Westly said, seeing the significant look between the two women.

Vinicia sagged with exhaustion as he stood to leave, and she dropped her wings low as she looked to the sky to find her strength.

::You have done enough, *sha'doe*,:: Lora sent and as Vinicia's vision dazzled between blackness and stars, she could not disagree.

::You need to release the world back into its own working,:: Aevi reminded, even as she glowered towards Lora. ::Though it will be like ripping a bandage free of a wound for all the skill with which these bindings were placed.::

::I can hear you, cat,:: Lora sent, exchanging insult for insult. ::And do give me more credit. I only did as her father asked and I did not set the seal as firmly as I set the other one.::

::You shouldn't have set a seal on Westly at all,:: Aevi snapped back. ::You should not even know how.::

::Enough,:: Vinicia sent to both of them, even if she found comfort in their bickering. Against the cacophony of angry, fearful voices echoing in her mind, they at least made sense. ::I just need to catch my breath.::

::You need more than that,:: Lora chided and Vinicia looked up as the woman moved around Kiernan's unconscious body. When she offered her hand, Vinicia took the help to stand, and then Lora walked her to the edge of the platform so Vinicia could take a proper seat outside of the blood. As they moved, Aevi made her way back to Kiernan to curl protectively at his side, ever vigilant.

Vinicia let out a long, exhausted sigh as Lora gathered her in an embrace. With the world shielded from her, it wasn't long before Vinicia was shaking with the weariness of having to keep going despite the shock of all that had happened. As the great wave of grief swelled inside her, she buried her eyes against Lora's neck.

Tears will do nothing to help me right now.

Tears are nothing but a weakness and a curse.

But as Lora stroked down the crest of her braids, it didn't matter what she thought. After a few moments, her lungs were burning as she refused to breathe.

::Do not think to hold back the ocean when the tide is rising,:: Lora whispered. ::It will destroy you regardless.::

It was the first thing Lora had ever said to her after Hewn's death and coming back full circle, it set her free once again. As Vinicia was wracked with sobs, she clung to the woman and completely fell apart. The moment didn't last for long given everything that still lay before her, but she cried herself hoarse before Lora let her find a handkerchief.

::Better to cry a river than drown in the ocean, *sha'doe*,:: the woman consoled as Vinicia composed herself.

When she could breathe again, Vinicia looked up with a hesitant smile. ::You keep calling me that... Shadow? What does it mean?::

:: *Sha'doe*,:: Lora corrected, leaning on the end of the word. With it, she projected the image of two Lan'lieanan soldiers standing together, one noticeably older, with her forehead resting against the younger woman's. It looked a lot like the two of them, if only because of the trick of youth in her mother's blood. ::It can mean many things to many women in the islands, but is most often used for those who live as officers in the Vals. Cherished student, *shae doe*, to cherished teacher, *shae dara*.::

::What does it mean to you?:: Vinicia pressed, still scrubbing at her eyes. ::Why are you doing this? Why are you helping me?::

Lora crooked a finger at her and Vinicia leaned forward once again, flushing without really knowing why. Short as the woman was, with Vinicia sitting on the side of the platform and her standing on the ground, they were actually of a height.

Vinicia looked down between them as Lora's hand came up to cup the sides of her cheeks and when she set their foreheads together, she could feel the woman's breath against her skin. ::When I met you, I wanted to die,:: she said simply. ::Knowing you has made me want to live. I would do either for you now, whichever you prefer.::

Vinicia had tears in her eyes again as Lora set their lips together. Gentle and slow, the world and all its chaos melted away into the silent exchange as she was filled with the pure, unadulterated joy of finding the other half of her heart.

Vinicia was breathless when Lora pulled away and her easy smile made Vinicia's heart ache. For so long she had known the love behind that smile, but to see it now was miraculous. Her ancestor was real. Her love was real. Of all the spirits she had ever known, Lora had always burned the brightest.

::What do I call you?:: Vinicia asked shyly.

::*Sha'dara*,:: Lora answered, leaning on the end of the word the same way she did for *sha'doe*. ::I will tell you more as we travel, but this is my promise to you. Wherever you wander, I will always be there. Whenever you are unsure, I will guide you. Whenever you are in need of me, I will be worthy of you. This I swear.::

Vinicia was taken aback to hear such passion of purpose meant solely for her. She had never asked for this, had never thought to know it for all that she was, and yet now she knew that the partner she had needed for so long had been at her side the entire time. The love she had thought to feel for an ancestor dead and gone was here in this life, standing before her with hands and heart offered without hesitation. It was almost too much.

Before she could do more than open her mouth to speak, Lora's hand lifted from her cheek and she flushed again for the desire that must have been so plain on her face.

::I will see you again soon, *shae*,:: Lora sent, her first finger pressed lightly between Vinicia's brows. ::But you know as well as I do that I should not be here when these men wake. They will assume I was the one out for his life, rather than one of the few helping you piece it back together, and then where will we be?::

Vinicia closed her eyes to revel in the love flowing into her from that single touch, knowing she was right. After so many cycles, she was always right.

::Gather your flock quickly and be on your way,:: Lora said, looking to where she meant to fly. ::I will watch for you to pass over the edge of the city and will join you when your wake is clear.::

::Of course,:: Vinicia said, chewing her lip as she struggled to look at her fully once again. For all the fantastical things in her life, her own bloodline included, why was it that being around this woman felt so absolutely magical?

::*Sha'dara?*:: She asked, hesitating over the foreign title.

::Yes?::

::Thank you,:: Vinicia said, with a guilty sort of smile.

::That title on your tongue means more to me than all the thanks in the world,:: Lora said, her serious face transforming into the beautiful, dazzling smile that Vinicia had suspected could lie beneath.

Vinicia flushed as Lora stepped back, a knowing look in the woman's bright blue eyes. A moment more and Vinicia exhaled a laugh, smiling back with the same enthusiasm. As Lora got onto the wind, Vinicia took a deep breath and sighed. Everything would be all right, eventually. For now, this was good enough.

CHAPTER 41: ENVOY

Sunday, 17:00

As Lora disappeared over the top of the Armory, Vinicia looked to where Kiernan lay cradled on his wings. Aevi was still curled up next to his head, churring her quiet comfort as Vinicia prepared to face the stagnant chaos. Last night Kiernan had shown her why she could not do everything on her own, and seeing him now, she knew he was right.

But who can help me with this? she wondered, looking around the platform at the Counsel Lords, Shadow Guard, and other men who had been present for the graduation ceremony. She would have to release Hest'lre and Kreychi to let them know Kiernan was alive, but it would be better if she could rouse Kiernan first. Kiernan would likely rouse with Lenae's help, though having her panicked might set off Kiernan...

Had Lenae even seen the arrow? Vinicia wondered, searching the balcony that was built into the Long Hall for the royals' use during these events. Yes, Lenae had seen. She looked to have gone half-mad with her own grief, collapsed against the balcony railing with Kaitlyn and Sera at her side. Given how Kaitlyn had come under Noventrio's influence the day before, it would be wise to take her to Illiandria with them. Given Sera's control over Micah's wildly strong bardic gift, she would be needed as well...

Sisters-at-arms first, then, Vinicia decided, squatting down to set her hands in the unnervingly large pool of Kiernan's blood at her feet. Drawing the energy into herself, she took solace in the fact that her use of the magic would at least leave them both clean.

Once she had the power gathered, Vinicia turned to the men laying on the main platform and used the unstable strength to move them aside for space. When they were set to the side, she turned her attention to the balcony again. Blinking into her second sight, she searched for the core of the women and then tugged ever-so-gently to awaken them.

Lenae's terrified scream brought Sera and Kaitlyn out of their confused slumber in a rush. Given their last moments, they immediately grabbed the Consort, only to gape at the devastation around them.

"Kiernan is alive!" Vinicia called, waving from her place at the center of the chaos. "He is all right, but very weak. Lenae, I was hoping..."

Lenae was already on the wind.

"Gods be good," the Consort breathed, landing in the space Vinicia had made only to rush past her and drop to her knees at Kiernan's head. As Aevi scampered away to make room, Vinicia greeted the two other women.

"Mother," Sera asked, eyes wide as she landed on the platform. "What's going on?"

"She created a Silence," Kaitlyn said, awed as she looked from the Counsel Lords slumped in their seats to the ranks of tyros and officers in the courtyard. "It is like the transfixion when you dance, but..."

"Way bigger?" Sera guessed.

"I am in control of it," Vinicia assured them. "But I need your help before I can release everyone. I am doing it in stages for now, and you three I trust more than anyone in this world. Can you help me?"

"Of course," they both answered at once.

Vinicia exhaled a weary laugh, looking to Sera first. "Sera, I need you to find the boys."

"Rylan took off after Oren," the girl said with confidence, already unfolding her wings to fly. "Micah told me they took him down just before this 'Silence' happened. Rylan was getting wingbars and then everyone was dropping."

"And now you know why," Vinicia said, looking back to Kiernan. "If it wasn't for a number of things, neither of them would be here. I will explain it in time, but he is hale and whole, as you can see. Westly went to get water, but the boys..."

"I know where they are," Sera said, taking off at a run for the edge of the platform.

"Bring them here," Vinicia called. "And tell them to pack for a flight to Illiandria with as much food as they can carry!"

As Sera spiraled around to salute her mid-air, she looked back to Kaitlyn to find her waiting patiently.

"What do you need from me?" Kaitlyn asked, gathering her courage.

"I need you to come with us to Illiandria," Vinicia said, not knowing how else to break the news. "What I have done has angered Founder Noventrio and it will not be safe for you here for a while. It need only be for the winter," Vinicia added, realizing Lenae had meant to use Kaitlyn as a resource as well.

"But—" Kaitlyn protested, only to stop as Lenae tsked from behind the two of them.

"We will figure out your service come the spring," Lenae said, looking up from Kiernan's face for a moment. "I will handle any issue that comes up, even if I have to boss around a few tyros myself with a belly full of chick."

Kaitlyn looked horrified at that, which only made Lenae's point. Trying to do anything 'normal' in this moment was as ridiculous as doing the obvious.

"Okay, then," Kaitlyn said, looking back to Vinicia. "Should I go gather my things? My things and Sera's, I'm assuming?"

"Yes," Vinicia agreed, glad for the young woman's competence. "Feel free to raid the tyro's supplies for anything you cannot find yourself. Just be back within half a mark."

"I'll do my best," Kaitlyn said, giving a small courtesy before she rushed off in the opposite direction.

"How is he?" Vinicia asked, moving to join Lenae.

"Alive, thanks to you," Lenae said, taking her hand and kissing it as Vinicia sat on her heels beside them, wings tucked back for balance. "Although he looks the same as he did one summer when he took ill with a wasting sickness," she went on. "He couldn't keep anything down for a fortnight until it passed and then it took moons for him to gain his strength back. You aren't any better, mind you," Lenae added with a hard look. "Will you two be able to make it through the pillars? I could keep you all in an estate on the edge of the shelf until you can recover."

"We will manage," Vinicia said, giving her a weak smile. "What energy I need, I will make up with rest. I take it he told you of the night we shared?"

"He did," Lenae said, genuinely happy. "And he told me that he can raise power for you. Priestess that I am to Founder Kerowyn, I understand more than you know." Given Vinicia's look of confusion, she exhaled a soft laugh. "I am used to channel Braeden's ancestral power in much the same way."

"I am sorry to have to use him," Vinicia said, wincing at the word. *Use.* "But with my mother's magic, I can pass on the strength he helps me reclaim to others. We will recover faster than anyone would expect."

"I am certain you will," she said, full of a confidence. "So long as you cherish him in the act, I am sure he will thank you for every moment of it. Please, Vinicia, if you are my friend, take care of him for me."

Vinicia ducked her head, hiding her own smile. Somehow, she had gained so much this day: a friend, a wingmate, and a partner from across the veil. Incredible as it all seemed, she knew she cherished them all in their own way. For all she had thought herself alone these past thirty cycles, she was also confident that it had all been a lie. There were so many people who supported her now and she could not deny it.

"Kier'n has been studying dryads and their kin since he took the Seat," Lenae went on, stroking down Kiernan's warcrest as he stirred. "So he is quite educated on their wants and needs. Aren't you, beloved?"

"Hmm?" Kiernan breathed, his eyes opening to dreamy slits as he realized his head was in Lenae's lap.

"Vinicia will take good care of you while you are on Envoy," she said, her voice wavering as he shifted beneath her.

Vinicia breathed easier as Kiernan came more awake, stretching muscles that had gone cold.

"I told you she will," Kiernan assured her, reaching a hand up to cover his yawn, only to stop as his hand neared his throat.

Vinicia braced herself as his eyes flew open, realizing the empty, silent sky overhead.

"What happened?"

Lenae gave him space as he rolled to his side so he could come off his wings.

"Too much to explain at the moment," Vinicia answered. "Just know that your assassin failed, my father saved your spirit, and I ripped you out of The Great Tree before Noventrio could claim you. Westly managed to heal your body, so he should get most of the credit," she added, looking up to see the kindred sitting with his head in his hands nearby, recovering his own strength. "Without somewhere to put you back, I have no idea what I would have done."

Kiernan swallowed as he realized the rest of the world was unconscious as far as he could see.

"When they wouldn't let me help you, I drew them into a Silence," Vinicia explained, glad she had a word for the phenomenon. "Counsel Lord Gallen set his guards on me."

"I can't say I'm surprised," Kiernan sighed, coming to his feet as he saw what she was speaking about. "Not that it matters. Can you wake people one at a time, then?"

When she nodded, Kiernan moved to squat on his heels next to Hest'lre. Vinicia came into her secondsight, brushing the shield in order to find Hest'lre in her bindings. As she did so, she felt a tug in the back of her mind and heard Sera's mental voice yelling that she had found the boys.

::When they have their gear, tell them to go into Counsel Lord Blake's office in the Armory,:: she sent back, feeling the nauseating strength of the blood magic boosting the sending. ::There is a weapon's cabinet with prototype short-bows. They'll have wheels on the ends. You can't miss them. Each of the boys should take one, but if you see something you like, take it as well. Bring all the bolts and arrows you can carry.::

::Yes, Mother!:: Sera called back with a little mental wave.

Satisfied that they would not wake in a panic, Vinicia released her favored tyros as well: Rylan, Micah, and Nichi. For that matter, she should probably release Tyrsten, though he was in a heap next to Kreychi. When she had all the threads she meant to pluck gathered in her mind she released them from the spell.

Hest'lre came awake in a gasping panic. As Kiernan saw to him, Vinicia moved to be close at hand for Kreychi and Tyrsten.

"Kiernan?" Kreychi asked, coming awake all at once to find Vinicia offering him the hand he needed to stand.

"Everything is taken care of, Kreychi," she said, only to see true terror in his eyes. As Vinicia flushed, realizing if her hair had gone back to the red-gold given the bindings, he likely thought she was a loralae. Refusing her help, he got back to his feet and moved towards Kiernan.

Vinicia let out a slow breath, taking the moment to reset her guise before she went to help Tyrsten. In all the chaos, the young man couldn't seem to get his wing out from under the chiurgeon who had failed to do Kiernan any good. Once he was free, though, Vinicia helped him back to his feet.

"Am I really going to be the Sixth Counsel Lord?" he asked, looking around the courtyard in shock.

"You will," Vinicia said. "Though I expect you will have a long tenure. It will take more than some hotshot with an arrow to kill a man I mean to protect."

Tyrsten exhaled a laugh to hear her humor, still unsure in the moment.

"You will have a lot to learn to fill Counsel Lord Hest'lre's Seat, but my uncle can help you just as much as Hest'lre can," Vinicia said, remembering that she would have to wake Shayan as well. Of all these men, she had to be the one to tell him how her father had fallen.

"Ninth Counsel Lord Shayan?" Tyrsten said, amazed. "I guess Rylan was right when he said you were the dryad daughter of Counsel Lord Eirik..."

"He was," Vinicia said, which made him blink a few times to look at her anew.

"Oh," Tyrsten said, distracted as a group of flyers circled overhead to find a place to land. With the gear they had strapped all over themselves, they needed a bit more space than usual.

"Nichi, did you know she was dryad-kin?" Tyrsten demanded, watching them land.

"Of course I did," he said, and the group of them looked glad to see that they had not dropped into panic.

"How long have you known?" Tyrsten asked.

"Two days?" Nichi said, looking to Micah.

"I've known for three," Micah said, shrugging.

"Four days and a wake up," Rylan said, though there was irony in his tone. "I didn't actually believe it until she started bossing Counsel Lords around, though."

Sensing his crew-brothers returning, Westly came to his feet to join them, only to see her. "Are you okay?" He asked, his eyes in his secondsight as he looked at her. "Your power is still bound."

"I will break the bindings as soon as we mean to leave the shelf," she said. "That will release everyone from this Silence as well, but it is safer this way."

"Good," he said, hand raising to the slowly purpling bruise he had gained from Lora's fist earlier. "Because it looks exactly like what got me into trouble with Rylan and I cannot handle that right now. I barely broke free of it before we flew the winds."

"I think you might be surprised what you can manage," Vinicia said, hearing Lora's own words coming out of her mouth. "I know I was, doing all this..."

When Westly gave a soft laugh, Vinicia turned to look at the group scattered around the podium. "Circle up, boys," she called and was amused when not only her former tyros began to move, but Kiernan, Hest'lre, and even Kreychi.

"Kiernan says you mean to gather your things and leave before you lift this..." Hest'lre began, gesturing to the unconscious folk around them.

"It's called a Silence," offered a voice from behind them, and the circle opened just next to Micah and Nichi to allow Kaitlyn in with the gear she had brought for herself and Sera.

"This Silence, then," Hest'lre amended, looking to Kiernan.

"The first way station is only three candlemarks from here," Kiernan said. "If we leave now, we can make it before it's too dark."

"Will you be able to manage the waystations fast enough with a group so large?" Kreychi asked, worried as he realized just how heavily his own House was represented.

"We cannot take the gondolas and think to survive another attempt, even if one would-be assassin is dead," Kiernan said, thinking aloud. "But if we take the route through the waystations at a slower pace and gather provisions along the way, we should make it to Illiandria by midwinter."

"A whole moonturn?" Rylan balked.

"There are no updrafts where we're going," Nichi explained, though he didn't look happy about it. "I used to hunt the pillars between Alexandria and Greying, and it's just like this."

Rylan's objection didn't change, but his understanding silenced his protest.

"Even if Nichi will be able to hunt and trap for you on the flight over, that's still eight flyers," Kreychi added, worry marring his face.

"All of them untrained for a flight like the one you mean to make," Hest'lre said. "But if you take Henrick and Lyonel, that will be a proper decanus and you can serve in shifts. The girls can organize your supplies, and the boys are can be taught how to act as proper shadow guard."

They had spoken at length about Kaitlyn's attachment to Founder Noventrio's power this afternoon, and from Kiernan's look, he was explaining it in detail mind-to-mind. When Kreychi ducked his head, deferring his objection, Kiernan went on.

"We're settled, then?" Kiernan asked, looking to Vinicia.

"I will leave them for you to brief," Vinicia confirmed, closing her eyes to wake the two men with a targeted thought. Hest'lre nodded before moving from their group to help the men find their bearings.

"Traveling during the snows will also keep you hidden from any rescue should something go wrong," Kreychi said and it was a fact he seemed to hate.

"We will have two dryad-kin with us," Kiernan added, with a small smile to herself and Westly. "If we can survive the pillars, we can survive the Eihwaz, right?"

"I think I'd rather have a plant kiss me to death than freeze my wings off where no one will find us," Rylan muttered, and there were more than a few who agreed with him. "But Mother, what are these?" he asked, setting a hand on his left thigh where a strange, wheeled short-bow was secured. "I know we should carry bows for distance shots, but how do these even work?"

Vinicia relaxed just a touch as she extended her hand. "My pet project," she explained. "I have been working with them for two cycles at Lord Fourth's request, not realizing they were meant for Kiernan's Envoy."

Rylan handed over the bow with her asking, and then stepped aside as she put the arrow to the notch. With the covered walkway between the armory and the tyro's wing being a good two hundred paces off, she took a breath, brought the bow up as she blinked into her flight lenses, sighted a fluttering banner, and let the arrow fly. A moment later, the hard thunk of the arrow tacking down the banner into a wooden crossbeam made the men around her gawk.

"That's not even all of the draw, mind you," she said, handing the bow back to Rylan. "I'm sure you'll do fine."

"Yes, Mother," Rylan said, and she laughed as the group of them look down to the new bows they carried with respect.

"All right," Vinicia said, ready to be done with the shield against her greater strength. "I still have one person to wake here, but if the rest of you could gather on the Soldier Tyros' Wing, I would appreciate it," Vinicia said, trying not to look at her uncle.

Fortunately, no one asked for an explanation, though Lenae, Hest'lre, Kreychi, and Tyrsten took themselves off the podium and away from them instead of flying up with the others to make final arrangements. It was only when she heard the soft whisper of wings beside her that Vinicia realized Kiernan was moving to stand in front of her. When he set a gentle finger under her chin, Vinicia looked up and waited for him to speak.

"Hest'lre is close at hand," he said, looking to where her uncle sat slumped in his chair. "He is Shayan's Counselheir as much as Rylan is mine."

Vinicia nodded and followed his gaze, only to have her vision water as she realized what had happened all over again. To save Kiernan's life, she had killed her own father. She had taken his power and traded it for Kiernan's, knowing what would happen. Eirik had known as well and he had made the choice to act, but it didn't lessen the blow.

As the flood of emotion swelled inside her, Kiernan pulled her into a gentle embrace. Considering all that she and Kiernan had been through together under the legacy of the Seventh's Seat, there was no denying that he could understand having to surrender another Seventh to the war god that seemed intent on devouring them.

As she stood in Kiernan's strength, she sent a trickle of power into her uncle, who woke to much the same confusion that the others had shown. After realizing the world around him was silent and asleep, he saw Kiernan standing before him with Vinicia in his arms.

When Kiernan pulled back so they could see one another, it was clear that her uncle already knew. For all she had managed not to weep before, as Kiernan released her, she fled into the arms of the very last of her Kosaran family. For all her father had hated tears, Shayan had never hidden his pain. As far as Shayan was concerned, it was either weep or grow numb to every other feeling in the world.

"Damn him!" Shayan swore, furious as he crushed her against him. "Damn him, I told him not to make you do this! I swore I would kill him myself if he—Gods, Vinicia—Vinicia, I am so sorry. I never wanted this for you. I never wanted any of this for you. After everything that happened with Hewn, I did not think you would survive it."

Swallowed up by their shared grief, neither one of them knew when Kiernan disappeared, but Aevi was nipping at her heels by the time she was fighting to breathe once again. At that point, Vinicia realized that even her uncle was having trouble and she had to force herself back to calm.

"Come on, love," Shayan said, setting a hand on her mock of a warcrest as if he meant to tousle unbound hair. "We've made quite a mess of ourselves, but you need to be off."

"I will release everyone before I go," she said again. "I am sorry that you will be the one with the burden of putting right the chaos we leave."

"What chaos?" He asked, waving for the men standing off to the side to join them on the podium once again. When Kiernan, Lenae, Hest'lre, Kreychi, and Tyrsten joined them, he went on. "All I know is that Kiernan's assassin failed, and in the confusion afterwards, you and Kiernan left with the Counselheir and his new guard. No one need know about my brother but me," Shayan said, giving her a weak smile. "No one will remember I exist at all once I step down, though I appreciate the project you have left me with, setting up a library in his honor on the House Northern estate. That will be young Rylan's, beloved. I will make certain of it."

Vinicia scrubbed at her eyes, taking a deep breath before nodding to Kreychi and Hest'lre in turn. Their thanks for keeping their brother, friend, and confident alive despite all odds was much the same: complete and eternal.

Kiernan did so as well, though he ended with Lenae in his arms, their wings fanned out for one last private moment before they parted.

When Vinicia and Kiernan finally joined the others on the Armory, it was quick work to strap into the gear they would carry for the long flight ahead. With Aevi sitting perched on her shoulder, the only thing she had left to do was pull against the wealth of power she could feel just beyond her shields. Lora had said that would shatter the binding and send it back into the possession of their rightful owners. Hopefully, it would also take the memory of just what had happened to Kiernan so they would have less to explain in the coming fortnight.

The group of them quieted as Vinicia moved to stand at the edge of the armory's roof deck. Gathering herself, she held her hands out towards the sleeping masses, feeling for the lines of energy that she had established over her lifetime. Though it wasn't the first time she had returned borrowed energy to its source, this was certainly the most important.

Closing her eyes, Vinicia reached out with one hand for the reserves she had within the Great Tree and primed herself as if to deposit all the power she now held inside. With the other hand, she felt for the bindings, bracing against the ricochet of energy that would soon occur. With both in her mind, she sent a thin stream out from herself and back towards the people below.

There were gasps behind her as the bindings launched its opposition to her intent. As she opened herself to the life around her, she used the bindings as a guide to rain down the stolen energy into the lifeless forms. Once the connections were made, she strengthened the flow and then opened her eyes to watch as the bindings shattered under the force of power passing through it. Tense as the moment was, she still smiled to see the wil-o-wisps forming all over the Palace grounds, soaring towards the Warhost like an ethereal rain.

As the last of the overwhelming power bled away, Vinicia took a deep breath and looked to her companions, ready to leave. Why she had expected to find them in anything other than respectful silence she couldn't say, but the sight of them waiting for her to put her pack on meant the world to her. With the power she held, she could have massacred the heart of the Kosaran Warhost, but she was a peacemaker, through and through. They all were now, given how far they had come because of one another.

As she secured her pack, Vinicia looked to the roof where Lora still crouched, watching over the Envoy in the guise of the blue-eyed Kosaran guard. Unable to suppress her smile at seeing her dream come to life, Vinicia hid it in Aevi's side, turning to nuzzle the gryphling as she scritched at the base of her wings. Once Aevi was well and truly churring with content, Vinicia shifted to tip the gryphling off her pauldron and into the open sky. The rest of her party took that for their cue, stepping up to follow her.

Kiernan was the last, and though he didn't say a word, he seemed to know what she was thinking. Both of them had come so very close to death this day, but they had made it out alive. Now, knowing they were setting out on a journey they had always been meant to take, they were nervous beyond imagining. No matter their fears, though, it was worth the risk.

The Seventh's Peace was worth the risk.

"We made it," Kiernan said, taking up her hand to kiss her knuckles as he unfolded his wings.

"Now we just have to make it back," Vinicia agreed, letting his strength fill her one last time.

"Too easy," he said, and laughed.

Kiernan grinned as she unfolded her wings to match him and together they leapt into the open sky, riding the Ice Winds one last time. When they were deep into the wind, they banked east, soaring over the embattlements as they turned towards Yaltana and the Illiandrian peak beyond. As they came out of the space over the Delton shelf, the sky was open and clear as far as they could see.

EPILOGUE

THE DRAGON AND THE LORALAE

This was going to be their last push, Lora was sure of it. Just finding this man among the Warhost had taken the better part of the fighting season, but with the nine of them set to it, nothing was impossible. Since they had found him, though, they had spent a solid fortnight attempting to get a handle on the guard rotation, sortie schedules, and other movements within the camp with little to show for it.

Lora looked up from the embers that remained of their fire and saw her wing-sisters were resolved to their task. They didn't need words between them, not for this. This was the culmination of every part of their crafting. They were each the last of their initial group of loralae, resilient despite the compulsion that had driven so many of them to death, and in coming together now they were stronger for it. There was no sorcerer more powerful on the War Plains than the Kosaran Seventh Counsel Lord and it had been the call to his power that had drawn them into this elite clutch. It would take women of their caliber to bring him down, if only because it would take all of them just to get close.

Still, no matter the magnitude of the target, the incessant hum of their compulsion was the same. Kill or be killed. Kill this man or die trying. Kill him and it would all end.

To seek, to find, to lure, to bind,
Feel the power with your mind.
Hair of emerald, heart of gold,
Find the ones that Mother scolds.
By kindred speech or gifted thought,
Lure the ones who remain soft.
With your power revealed in truth,
Bind your target, strike it through.

::Warborn,:: their leader said, looking her in the eyes from across their circle. ::You are last among us and will be last among them. We will open the way for you.::

Lora's heart began to race. ::But I—::

::Do not think to escape your fate,:: the woman sent, cutting her off. ::You are the strongest among us because you share conclave with him. We give you the chance to redeem yourself by being the one to strike him down. Kill this man and the Great Mother will welcome you back to the blood. You know this is true.::

Swallowing hard around the knot in her throat, Lora nodded. She knew as well as they did that her Kosaran father was the only reason their clutch had any hope of success. She could feel Kiernan where they could not, but their combined strength had heightened her power, making it possible for her to pinpoint his location among so many others. When they finally struck, she would have their collective power at her command in order to destroy him.

When Lora nodded, the eight women around her moved to stand. All their life they had known that a woman's power rested in the blood of her sacred cycle, but the loralae had been made to wield that power beyond herself. How to gather it, twist it, and use it for a purpose that might rival the power of creation itself. Tonight, one by one, they would enter the encampment, strike down the men they found in their way, and use their spells to take the man's form for their own until they were discovered and slain as well.

All of served one purpose: sending power through the hive they made into Lora who would use it all to destroy the Dragon Lord. As her wing-sisters moved into the darkness of the night, Lora opened her palm above the fire and called from the humid air around them the water she needed to drown the embers.

When the last had gone, Lora looked up into the moonless sky and her vision turned to blackwater and the burn of useless tears. These women had come here to die. After twenty cycles of being driven around the Plains as a loralae, the grief she felt only enhanced the sight, bringing to life the trails of violet energy her sisters left in their wake.

When Lora searched ahead of them in the camp, she found the Seventh's sun-bright power that was their goal. So very much like them, the Seventh Counsel Lord had been forced into his Gifts as well. The Southern Conclave had known that and sought to turn it against him as they had against so many others. Balefire killed men just as easily as arrows and stone, and it had been taught to all of them to ensure this one man's destruction.

Standing in silence, Lora waited until the first burst of energy flowed back to her through their hive of power. Knowing her sisters had crossed the point of no return, Lora began to move. Soon enough that borrowed blood would redouble as her sisters were sent through the veil and she did not mean for them to die in vain. If she was to be the reason for the end of any number of lives this night, it would most certainly include his.

Seventh Counsel Lord Kiernan started awake as he felt a burst of power just beyond his senses. Closing his eyes, he drew his mind to focus and called up the lines that connected him to all of the men in his encampment. That was the nature of his Seventh's Gift, the ability to see into the mind of his men and view the world through their eyes. As he had been told by the predecessor to his seat, Seventh Counsel Lord Eirik, his unusual strength as an empath had been the reason their Seat-Founder had taken an interest in him. Eirik hadn't been wrong, and the Founder himself had instructed him in the use of that Gift. At the moment, all of his senses were telling him there were enemies among the encampment, and Kiernan winced as he felt the associated lives being ripped out of his control.

These were no simple killings, but murders done in surprise and shock, and as he searched to figure out a pattern, he realized he could feel a distinct *other* stalking through the camp as well. Somewhere among them there was a warborn woman, and the power he was losing was being folded into hers as she followed her dying clutch into the camp. She was strong, of that he had no doubt, but he was stronger.

In his three cycles as Seventh on the Plains he always had been and, with a prayer to his ancestors, he always would be. No fly-by-night assassin would stop the force of his campaign to end this war once and for all.

Pulling his mind back from his search, Kiernan sent a pulse of alarm to his most trusted men. A moment later, the flap of his pavilion moved and the Primarch of his fumentari guard stuck his head in.

"I'll see to the short patrol," Kreychi said, pulling back his flight hood so Kiernan could see his platinum hair. "Ambrose is seeing to the men around this pavilion. Don't do anything stupid, lover."

No matter the intensity of the moment, Kiernan exhaled a laugh. "Yes, Kreya," he replied and set his fist to his heart in salute. Kiernan trusted this one man above all others and though he didn't need the reminder, he also did not mind reassuring the man who shared his nest that he would not make himself part of the problem. Hearing him, Kreychi turned and was gone, letting the heavy flap fall against the side of the pavilion once more.

Closing his eyes, Kiernan let his senses flow above the camp, layering the mental image of the tents over the minds that he could feel with his gift. This way, he could understand the approach the women were taking and nudge a few men into or out of the path of the violet auras as best he could.

Lora wanted to scream as she felt the last of her sister's pass through the veil, fighting the backlash of power as it threatened to overtake her. Even knowing this was going to happen, there had been no way to ready herself. No woman could prepare for the power of so many pooled so densely in one mind.

Still bent over the man she meant to wear as her final mask, Lora closed her hands around the gaping wound in his neck. As his rage at dying flooded into her, burning up her left arm, across her chest, and back down her right, she completed the circle of power. Finishing the spell, she took her right hand off his neck, pressed her palms together, and covered her face with her hands. As the man's lifeblood burned against her skin, the corpse she kneeled over suddenly transformed into the woman she knew herself to be.

"Ambrose!" Came a cry from behind her, not half a moment after she knew herself to be changed. "Have you downed her? Is that—?"

Lora came to her feet, hand still holding her knife.

"Blood and ice," he swore, stopping short as he saw the image Lora had transferred to the corpse. "Another loralae? I haven't seen so many of these monsters since Kirath."

Lora held her tongue, not that the man noticed. He was gawking at the wound that had half-severed the man's head from his body.

"Primarch just went to check in with Lord Seventh, but he's making rounds now," he said. "Go get cleaned up so you can make the report that you took the last one down."

Lora set her right fist against her left breast with the Kosaran salute and turned before the man could demand a response. She didn't follow his orders, though, instead heading straight for the beacon that was her final target. This was her last walk, her last moonless night, and she did not mean to see it wasted by a spell done in haste.

With her hand set against the wrist-cuff on her left arm, Lora activated the falconstone to amplify the spell that would end the man who had slaughtered so many of her sisters.

And then, finally, she could die.

Kiernan stopped in his pacing as the canvas flap rustled behind him.

"Ambrose?" He called, blinking out of his secondsight as the man came inside the tent. As much as he respected the man's abilities, he was still Alexandrian and had fainted the last time he had walked in on Kiernan's white-eyed stare. "Gods, man. What's going on out there? I can't keep anything straight anymore."

As Ambrose moved into the tent, wings flared just enough to keep the blood that covered him off the canvas itself, Kiernan realized something was wrong. As superstitious as the man was about seeing Kiernan's secondsight, he was three times as fastidious about blood.

This isn't Ambrose.

Kiernan had half a heartbeat to throw up his mental shields as the creature before him laced her hands together, tips of her fingers hidden between her palms and thumbs pressed flat against the fist it made. Though Kiernan only knew a few of the hand-signs that were used to summon elemental energy into manifestation, that one had been the most important. This one combined all of the elements with the Spirit of the sorceress herself, calling to life a fire that refused to die until its target was turned to ash.

Time slowed as Kiernan braced himself, praying to any God that could hear him for a miracle. As the loralae inhaled, Kiernan felt the power enveloping her ignite, and then the inside of the tent lit up with the balefire meant to consume him.

Lora wanted to scream as she realized the dark flames she had summoned were being swallowed up by a force she could not explain. The Seventh looked as surprised as she was, standing with his arms up to shield his face. But as he realized he was still among the living, the falconstone ignited against her skin. A moment later, her control buckled under the backlash of having summoned so much power so fast, only to have it be ripped out of her control. She had meant to end both of their lives with that blast, but as the power of the spell was sucked away into the sudden void, the whiplash from the loss had her seeing stars.

It took Kiernan almost a quarter candlemark before he could stop shaking after the loralae had collapsed. It didn't matter that she looked half-dead; she was as hard bodied as any woman he had ever met at war and though most Lan'lieanans were smaller in stature, the power she wielded made her larger than life.

Hand gripped around his ice-coated hawkeye, Kiernan stared at the loralae through his secondsight, trying to understand what had happened. Though it had been balefire coming from her hand, for some inexplicable reason, all of it had been consumed by the hawkeye hanging around his neck. The thing he thought only the key to a library back in his mountain home had suddenly saved his life.

Gathering his nerves, Kiernan confirmed the woman was not dead and then clawed off the cuff on her left arm that she had used to summon the balefire. Fearing that she could attempt the same assault when she woke, Kiernan had thrown it into the bottom of his warchest before sending a mental burst of alarm to Kreychi.

His Primarch was not the only man who appeared after his summons, and more than one of them staggered to avoid stepping over the body of the blood-covered woman that had made it inside of Kiernan's tent.

"This was the last of them," Kiernan had said, praying that his voice didn't waver as he spoke. As two men stepped on her wings to pin her to the ground, he gestured to the blood covering her face.

"Kiernan, are you whole?" Kreychi asked, caught between the woman and Kiernan himself. "Did she—?"

Kiernan took a slow breath before matching eyes with his Primarch, knowing Kreychi was just as superstitious as Ambrose had been. Most of his Shadow Guard was, regardless of the fact that their Lord Seventh was a sorcerer as well. That, if nothing else, had given them an unfailing respect for his power and authority.

"I became a primarch to Counsel Lord Hewn because I survived the Fall," Kiernan answered, looking to the men who had crowded into his pavilion. "One loralae is nothing compared to that."

No one questioned him.

No one even wanted to look at him.

"This one is still alive," one of his newer men, Henrick, reported. "Should we send her to her sisters?"

Kiernan considered the woman for a long moment before shaking his head. "No," he said, making it an order. "And no one touches her. Bring one of the lift-cages in here and set her inside of it. I mean to hold her to answer for this attack."

Again, no one questioned him and in half a candlemark she was bound inside of a cage that would lift their gear back into the heights of the Kihara range. Only when the rest of his guard had been set to task outside of the pavilion did Kreychi come forward with his true question.

"Are you sure this is wise?" He asked, refusing to leave him alone with the woman, no matter her prison. "Lord Fifth has never taken a loralae alive. She should be handed over to the fumentaris."

"She meant to die here," Kiernan answered, watching as she opened her eyes in a daze. "If she has lost all hope of returning, she may tell me what I need to know."

"And that is?" Kreychi pressed, as they watched her realize what had become of her freedom.

"Who sent her," Kiernan said. "Because it was not Lan'lieana."

In less than a moonturn, Lora was moved from the Kosaran camp outside of Kelsineah to the Kosaran capital city of Delton. Worse, without her falconstone, she had been left to drown in the chaos of voices her dryad abilities allowed her to hear. At least with the stone, her compulsion to seek those with gifts had made the cantullus corps she could also hear just a dull roar.

Not anymore.

With her thoughts lost to a melee of otherwise incomprehensible madness, she had been forced to draw on the magic of the river raging on the mountain in order to create any defense at all. Once she had grounded herself from the vertigo, she realized she was being held as a spectacle before the Kosaran Court and that had made her want to kill the Seventh all over again—this time with her bare hands.

Having had to promise more than a few boons to arrange for his prisoner's safety in the High Cells below the Kosaran Palace, Kiernan had made it his mission to get the woman to speak with him. They were calling her The Loralae, if only because she refused to tell anyone her name. In truth, she couldn't tell them as she seemed to speak nothing but the Old Tongue, no matter the 'encouragement' his men had applied.

As time wore on, Kiernan recognized the madness in her that he had seen in his predecessor, Seventh Counsel Lord Eirik, when he had given over the Seat and the hawkeye that came with it. For some reason, the woman's own reddish-black stone seemed to be the key to keeping her sanity, but it wasn't like he could just give it back to her. Not when he knew what she could do with it.

Two full cycles went by without any success before his Sixth persuaded him to leave the woman to her madness and let her fall away from the Court's talk. There were already rumors of him having been bewitched by her, for love or loss, and the longer he kept up this effort, the worse it would get. Finally, though he hated to admit his defeat, Kiernan left her alone so he could move on from his failure.

He did leave her with one option, however. In another two cycles he would set out on an Envoy to her homeland, and if she was willing to guide him there, Kiernan would return the stone he knew she wanted. He even went so far as to say that she could take him as prisoner once they crossed battle fronts, as long as he was taken before their Great Matriarch as the tribute that he had made of her. That chance was more than any man before him had ever managed.

Two cycles after those parting words, so many things had changed. Though Lora still loathed the fact that she was about to accept the man's truce, there was now something very precious involved in the exchange. Because she had named the woman he called his Consort her *sha'doe,* Lora knew she would do whatever Vinicia asked of her, even if it meant helping him.

::You can join us now, *sha'dara,*::

Lora winced at the exhaustion in Vinicia's mental call, but acknowledged it all the same. It wouldn't do to make the woman worry over one more person after the day she had suffered. Even in the strange terrain Lora could take care of herself, and that fact might have been the one thing keeping Vinicia going.

::Coming, *sha'doe.*::

Lora flared her wings into the bitter cold, enjoying the gentle lift from the air she gathered. For as long as she had known of Kosar, she had understood that the Kihara range was old, but she hadn't expected this. All that remained of what may have been mountains a millennium ago was a barren expanse of open space, filled in with circular pillars of bedrock. Granted, those pillars were large enough to support small fishing villages in places, but here on the outskirts of the Delton peak, they seemed nothing more than high perches.

In the fading light, Lora could see the small copse of trees where Vinicia's companions were making camp. High as it was, she could see neither the ground itself nor the water that had carved away the soft earth of the mountains.

Lora checked the straps on her borrowed Kosaran flight cloak and stepped to the edge of the pillar, frowning at the distance between her current perch and the way station the others had reached. It had been ages since she'd been given space to fly, so after taking a moment to check the distance, she tipped over the side and was thankful for the long, broad wings she had gained from her Lan'lieanan mother.

After a five count, Lora unhooked her ankles. As she let them swing out beneath her, her wings filled with air so suddenly that her head snapped to the side as she soared in her new direction. Her wings were burning with effort as she crested the height of Vinicia's pillar and half-collapsed into the sandy pit where the others had made their landings.

With her feet on the ground, Lora let her wings go lax, crossing the tips behind her as the crests splayed apart. She hadn't the strength to hold them to any sort of posture and her back wasn't cooperating anyhow. As she started walking again, Lora worked at the buckles of the cloak-belt-thing, trying to free herself as her frustration grew. She was starting to doubt the sanity of all Kosaran women if they suffered such idiotic constraints of fashion without complaint.

I'm just distracting myself, Lora knew, swearing at her hands as she realized they were shaking. *I don't have any idea what is about to happen and all I can think is how stupid it was to pretend to be a blicing spirit—and Goddess save me, I just used a Kosaran curse.*

Lora stopped walking, laughing despite the swell of anxiety. It didn't matter that it was only in her head, she had said 'blicing' and meant it and that was just another crack in her armor.

Hands at her hips, Lora took a breath in, held it, and exhaled slowly. She cycled her breath a second time, and then a third until her hands were steady enough to finish unbuckling the belt around her waist.

I've been through war zones less dangerous than the one I walk into now, Lora thought, starting her slow walk once again. *But I wouldn't care half so much if I wasn't about to rely on that idiot Seventh for shelter and aid. The younglings I can manage, especially the two warborn, and I will shear off my own left breast if they aren't MiaSera's chicks. That costume she was wearing was straight out of the Matriarch's Court and the wrist wrap has to be Mia's stone. If they grew up thinking she was Ehkeski...*

Lora wouldn't have put it past her mentor to have sheared her wings off just to keep her chicks safe in Kosar. Relentless as her compulsion was in driving her into Kosar, it might have been her only option.

Letting out a slow breath as she rounded the dense stand of trees, Lora was glad to see the waystation looming in front of her. From here she could just make out Vinicia closing the door and then watched as she started to search around. When Lora stepped out of the shadows, Vinicia started to move, though she was close to staggering under a weight of panic even Lora could feel.

Lora's anger vanished as she jogged towards the woman in the sunset light, struck by the sharp contrast of honeyed skin and fire-bright hair as her shields collapsed. Vinicia was both devastatingly beautiful and as frail as she had ever been strong in her life. Worse, the closer Lora came, the more she realized Vinicia's reserves of power were completely gone.

As they neared, Vinicia cut to the side and Lora stalled as the woman collapsed to her knees behind one of the massive trees. She lost her stomach a moment later, though the only thing that surfaced was a sickly black bile.

::Something is wrong,:: Vinicia managed, weak even mind-to-mind. ::I can't stop hearing the violence of the Host. Everyone I touched earlier is still screaming in my mind, and my power... I tried to purge it all when we landed, but it is like tar in my veins. Everything burns, and I just—::

"Shhh..." Lora breathed, pulling Vinicia back from the mess she'd made and into her arms. With an effort, Lora raised heavy shields around them, creating a space where Vinicia could ride out the agony of her first true use of blood magic in safety.

::It will be all right, *sha'doe*,:: Lora soothed, setting a hand on the back of the woman's head. ::The feeling will fade with time. I promise.::

Whatever Vinicia said in return, Lora couldn't tell. At the very least, the sending made her relax into the embrace, and her sudden, wracking sobs gave Lora hope that this was the last of the storm.

It was full dark by the time Vinicia was murmuring through the ten thousand regrets she had from the day, and it took Lora a moment to realize they were not alone. Rather, there was a woman hovering a few paces away with some sort of handkerchief in hand, as startled at the sight of Lora as Lora was at the sight of her.

Oh, this one, Lora thought, recognizing the blonde-haired highborn that was Seraleia's friend.

"Sal'weh?" The woman greeted, hesitant as she came a step closer. "Is... Is that Vinicia?"

Lora nodded, though her attention remained with Vinicia.

::Did you not tell them I was coming?:: Lora chided with affection.

::What would I say?:: Vinicia returned, half-asleep where they were kneeling together. ::That is Kaitlyn, bless her.::

"We've been looking..." Kaitlyn went on, unsure. "We've been looking for her."

::I found her, Kaitlyn,:: Lora sent, releasing Vinicia so the woman could look up.

Kaitlyn's jaw dropped open with the words.

She can talk like Micah! The girl thought, turning her attention as footsteps sounded behind her.

"Kait?"

A moment later, Lora saw the olive-skinned boy set a hand on Kaitlyn's wing as she stepped aside to let him see.

"Who are you?" Micah demanded, his voice loud enough that it was obvious he was calling for backup.

::A friend, and you don't need to be quite so loud,:: Lora sent, her own voice a subtle whipcrack of command. ::With that gift, you'll hurt her whether you mean to or not.::

Now it was Micah's turn to start, and Lora watched a third person moving to join them as the other two moved aside. This one she knew, though it was a shock to see the boy wearing an unmistakable Dragon Lord's pauldron. She had seen the quicksilver who guarded him when it had claimed the boy, so the leather copy just seemed ridiculous. No one in their right mind bragged about attracting the attention of a greater fae.

"It is her," Rylan declared, as if he was continuing some earlier conversation. "Is Mother all right?" He asked, moving past Micah and Kaitlyn no matter his crew-brother's objection.

::Yes and no,:: Lora responded, expanding the sending for the three of them to hear. ::If one of you would help me carry her inside that waystation, I can explain.::

"Kier'n inside," Vinicia murmured, though the words were slurred and her second attempt to move her head was about as successful as the first.

"Kiernan is the reason we came to look for you," Rylan said, coming to a stop beside them. "He said he felt someone else out here, and he was right. I felt someone, too, so I said I'd take a look." There was a challenge in his eyes as he looked down at Lora. "You were the one who shot my brother, aren't you?"

Lora matched his hard stare with one of her own. ::So what if I did?::

"Were you the one who killed him after he shot me, as well?" Rylan asked.

Lora narrowed her eyes at him. ::He was a rabid dog.::

"And then you saved my life," he accused.

::Would you rather I let you die?:: she threw back. ::The one decent man on this entire mountain?::

Rylan's hard look shifted into a subtle grin with Lora's reaction. "If you ever need anything of me," he said, an uncanny intensity in the words. "I am at your call."

Lora raised an eyebrow at his tone, though when she heard Micah swearing, she realized the cause.

::I am not part of your street-crew, boy,:: she scoffed. ::I am an assassin, a loralae, and Val'Kyr until the day I die. You should fear me, not think me a friend.::

::You are none of that anymore,:: Rylan sent, and his mental voice nearly staggered her for all it's strength. ::The fact that we are all alive and standing here proves it.::

Lora glowered as the boy smirked at her.

::Are you going to help me get her to shelter or not?:: she sent, refusing to be baited. She had her *sha'doe* to worry about, and her *sha'doe* needed out of this cold.

Sensing her frustration, Rylan peeled one of Vinicia's arms from around Lora, hooking it over his neck as he flared his wings. When Lora was on a knee, they both used their own wings to gather up Vinicia's, and then they were on their feet together with her strung out between them.

Rylan led the way as they moved with her towards the shelter, and when they neared, Kaitlyn and Micah helped them pass through the narrow threshold. Inside, Lora found Sera, the sapling dryad, and his lover on their feet, shivering around a small fire on one side of the cottage. On the other side...

hand went to his hawkeye and the two guards shifted as if they meant to come to their feet.

::I claim the Pax Septima,:: she sent, making certain everyone could hear her. ::I will not harm you, Dragon Lord, if you will not harm me.::

Kiernan's shock was matched only by the sharpness with which he called off the two warfighters beside him.

"I hear you and accept," Kiernan said, formally marking the truce between them.

Lora let out a slow breath as she shifted Vinicia's weight over her neck, turning her attention to Rylan once again. As she did so, she found Westly had turned to them, his eyes gone silver-white as he looked at Vinicia,

Lora swore and ducked her eyes, another chill running through her with the memory of far too many nights spent being tortured by eyes like the ones he showed now.

"Do you know what is happening to her?" Westly asked, breaking the silence that had fallen over the waystation. "I've never seen anything like this…"

Lora just nodded, tugging on Vinicia's arm to get Rylan moving to where they might set the woman down. Unsurprisingly, the space that held Vinicia's gear was just next to the Dragon Lord, but it would have to do. This cottage was barely big enough to fit five windwalkers, let alone eleven.

Seeing her plan, Westly made quick work of freeing Lora from her own pack and belts, and she wondered if the kin recognized them for his own. When he was done, Westly and Rylan held Vinicia long enough to let Lora sit down, and then they lowered Vinicia so that her head rested on Lora's shoulder.

"Are you taking me up on my offer then?" Kiernan asked, so even in his tone that he might have been wondering about the weather. The man apparently believed in his Seventh's peace, his Pax Septima, so much that he was willing to ignore the absolute insanity that had placed her alongside him in the moment.

Lora looked sideways at him, glowering. Kosarans always took that for a yes.

As the silence hung heavy between them, Lora rested her head back against Vinicia's pack with a silent groan, Exhausted as she was in body, she still had her own reserves, and she would need to set a heavy shield around her *sha'doe* if the woman was going to survive the night. As she did so, though, the hair on the back of her neck stood on end to feel the subtle drain on Vinicia's power. Lora had known Vinicia had purged her reserves, but she hadn't realized the woman was still tied to the Delton shelf.

Looking back the way they had come, Lora let her eyes water over with her secondsight and her breath caught as she saw the woman's energy was being pulled towards the capital city. It looked almost as weak as she was, though Lora knew the hunger it would stir in the woman if it went on for too long. Lora herself had been cursed with the same sort of drain ever since she had been turned into a Loralae. For the past four cycles she had fed it water magic and ignored the cost since she had been sitting in a river. Now, though? Seeing the same sort of trickling power in Vinicia made her heart start to race.

Her *sha'doe's* breath was shallow and rasping, her skin ashen and pale as her face lined with pain. Without something to sustain her, Vinicia would not survive the night. For all the power she had gained this day, Vinicia had not been made to regenerate her bodily strength as true loralae did. Frozen with an unexpected fear, Lora nearly jumped when the Dragon Lord spoke again.

"I don't know what to do for her," Kiernan said, a break in his voice as he set a hand on Vinicia's wing.

Lora didn't need her Talents as a sorceress to know that Kiernan was full to bursting with the energy Vinicia needed to survive. She had realized just what kind of connection lay between them when she had felt true Wellspring moving on the Delton shelf the night before. Granted, she had been so repulsed that she had fled to the sapling's Garden to drown herself in Grove magic, but it didn't change the fact that Vinicia was a kindred dryad with a windwalker acting as her greenman. For all she knew of dryads, however, they had to accept that power to use it and Vinicia couldn't exactly do that if she was passed out.

"Her father warned me the next few days might be hard on her," Kiernan went on. "But something is hurting her," he added, reaching for Vinicia's wing. "I've never felt anything like it before, but it burns at the edges of my senses..."

Lora flinched as she felt Kiernan touch her *sha'doe*. Powerful as the Wellspring had been between them, that wasn't what he was offering her now. No, the power he held felt like the energy Vinicia had wielded when the Founder had come to claim Rylan's life. If the ancient creature had simply held onto that power, if he hadn't passed it through the hearth tree, then the power Kiernan was accessing for her was—

Great Mother of All, it's blood magic, Lora swore, watching as the toxic strength flowed into her *sha'doe*. Kiernan apparently couldn't sense it, but that was likely because of the hawkeye he wore. No, not a hawkeye. Not anymore.

"Take off the stone!" she hissed in the Old Tongue, recoiling from him. "Holy Mothers, take it off!"

"What? Why?" Kiernan demanded. "What does that have to do with—?"

Lora swore, cutting the man off. "Look at it, you idiot!"

Kiernan just gaped at her, though he did look down to the stone. As his jaw fell open to see the crimson streaks overwhelming the blue, she explained.

"That creature is poisoning the well of her power to be rid of you both. If you mean to help her, take it off or by the Gods of Sea and Shore, I will kill you if you ever think to touch her again."

Kiernan gripped the stone in his hand, yanking at the pendant with a force that unbent the jump-ring holding it on the kingchain. When he opened his palm to see it, Lora hated that she was right. The hawkeye in his hand was burning like a coal as it completed its gruesome transformation. No matter what it had been before, the void stone was a true falconstone now, just like the one she had been bonded to after her torture by dryads.

As Kiernan threw the stone to the far side of the waystation, Lora cradled Vinicia close. ::Great Mothers, no wonder you are hurting,:: she murmured as her blood ran cold. ::I've got you, beloved. I'm here for you.::

This time when Kiernan reached for Vinicia, Lora saw the relief in her *sha'doe's* features at once. With the circle of power between the spiritual energy of the Great Tree closed through Kiernan's Gift alone, the energy he offered her was exactly what she needed. Sick as the blood magic had made her, she could only guess at how devastated Vinicia might be as a kindred to have been drowning in it for so long. The only time Lora had felt as horrid as Vinicia looked now had been when Kiernan had taken her prisoner, and she had needed cycles to find herself again.

"The further we get from the Great Tree, the harder it will be for me to channel for her," Kiernan said, an uneasy look in Lora's eyes. "I am supposed to act as her greenman..."

"I would sooner kill you than let you lie with her when she cannot consent," Lora growled, though her voice was low for all the panic she could feel in the room. Not only would she kill the man, but for all Vinicia's need, Vinicia herself might kill him if he didn't have the strength to stop her desperate grasping.

"I would never," Kiernan balked, eyes going wide until he realized Lora's own panic in the moment. "Wait, how long will she be like this? You know, don't you?"

Lora glowered at the man. "I didn't come off my first bloodrage for moonturns, but there is no telling with her," she said. "Just be grateful I know what must be done and get us out of these pillars. If you can do that, I will take you both to the sea."

That was what the man wanted after all.

"I can do that," Kiernan insisted, hand gripping onto Vinicia's wing with strength. "On my honor, I can do that much, at least."

THE END OF BOOK 1: NO HONOR IN GLORY

APPENDICES
PRONUNCIATION GUIDE, KOSARAN WARLORDS, CHAIN OF COMMAND, AND GLOSSARY OF COMMON TERMS

PRONUNCIATION GUIDE

People

Aevi: A-vee
Braeden: BRAY-den
Celenae: SELL-len-neigh
Dylan: DIE-lan
Eirik: EYE-Rick
Hest'lre: HEST-ler-a
Kaitlyn: KATE-lynn
Kiernan: KEER-nan
Kier'n: KEER-en
Kreychi: KREY-chi (Krecentius: KREY-sin-tea-us)
Lenae: Len-NEIGH
Lora: LORE-ah
MiaSera: ME-ya-SER-rah
Micah: MY-kah
Nichi: KNEE-chi (Andronicus: An-DRON-ni-kus)
Noventrio: No-ven-TREE-oh
Rylan: RYE-lan
Sera: SER-ah
Shayan: SHAY-yen
Tyrsten: TIER-sten
Tyrren: TIER-wren
Vinicia: Vii-knee-SEA-ah
Weylan: WHEY-lan
Westly: WEST-lee

Places:

Kosar: Ko-SAR
Kihara: KEY-har-rah
Mount Alexandria: AL-lex-and-ri-ah
Mount Delton: DEL-ton
Mount Greying: GREY-ing
Mount Kelishe: Kel-EE-sh
Mount Kelsineah: Kel-sin-A-ah
Mount Illiandria: Ill-e-AN-dri-ah
Mount Yaltana: Yal-TAN-ah

THE KOSARAN WARLORDS

Fourth Counsel Lord: *Blake su' Kelishe*
Oversees the Quartermaster Corps (logistics), all Kosaran military research and
development, and the Cantullus Corps of warbard instructors for Soldier Tyros.

Fifth Counsel Lord: *Roder su'Greying*
Commands the 'Vanguard' forces on the War Plains, including the special
operations men of three specialized Fumentaris: Blackwings (Covert
Operations), Yellowings (Administrative, Political Operations), and Redwings
(War Priests)

Sixth Counsel Lord: *Hest'lre su'Alexandria*
Commands the domestic 'Home Guard' forces of enlisted men who cycle to and
from the War Plains on a 3 year enlistment/rotation. As partner to the Seventh
Counsel Lord, he makes it possible for the Legions to put Lord Seventh's orders
into action.

Seventh Counsel Lord: *Kiernan su'Illiandria*
Using a supernatural gift for farsight from the blessing of his Seat Founder, he
commands the overseeing officer corps which directs the efforts of the Nine
Legions of the Kosaran Warhost.

Chain of Command

Counsel Lord: A member of the Kings High Counsel who advises king on military matter. (Eq: Army Chief of Staff)

Cadre Primarch (CAH-drey PRY-mark): A member of a Counsel Lord's inner circle with specialized mission tasks.

Primarch: Leader of approximately 30-100 Praetors.

Praetor (PREY-tor): Leader of approximately 10 Prefects.

Prefect (PRE-fect): Leader of approximately 15-30 soldiers.

Tyro (TEER-row): A military trainee or officer cadet.

Glossary of Common Terms

1. **Blicing** (BLY-sing): A common Kosaran expression of frustration that originates from the phrase 'Blood and Ice'. The idea of your blood freezing to your wings in flight haunts both military and civilian communities alike.

2. **Cantullus** (can-TUL-lus): Also called 'Cantos', these soldiers are the officers that pass orders from the Seventh Counsel Lord into the Warhost. The strongest among them are blessed by the Seventh Counsel Lord's ancestral founder and referred to as the Cantullus Premis, or Preems. Their warbard Gift can deliver orders to the men in their chain of command without any vocalization.

3. **Chiurgeon** (kai-URGE-on): An individual who has been trained in the arts of healing, or who is training as a tyro to become as such. They are distinguished from common, first-aid healers because of this training.

4. **Consort** (CON-sort): A female companion to a member of the King's High Counsel or the King himself.

5. **Dryad** (DRY-ad): A being living in the Eihwaz Forest who is known to practice sorcery. They take no part in the war between Kosar and Lan'lieana.

6. **Dryad-kin** (DRY-ad KEN) / Kindred Dryad: The offspring of a dryad and a Windwalker (Kosaran) or Wavewalker (Lan'lieanan), known to have emerald green hair and eyes one they begin working their mother's earth magics. Without a dryad to teach them how to use their sorcery, most succumb to madness by the age of fifteen.

7. Ehkeski (Eh-KES-key): A wingless individual living on the Ehkeski Plains as part of a nomadic tribe, or in the Kosaran or Lan'lieanan nations as servants or slaves.

8. Ehkeski Plains, War Plains (EH-kes-ki): The barren, desert-like stretch of earth between the mountains of Kosar and the island kingdom of Lan'lieana.

9. Eihwaz Forest (EH-ah-waz): The home of dryads to the east of the River Kir.

10. Fledgling (FLEDGE-ling): The term for a young Windwalker or Wavewalker that is learning how to fly. The term is also used for when referencing a person who has no adult knowledge of the world, for whatever reason.

11. Fumentari (FOO-men-tar-ee): Any highly specialized group of soldiers that are overseen by the Fifth Counsel Lord.

12. Godseyes: A magical, silver-colored clouding of a windwalker's eyes. If seen in the left eye, it designates the person is a priest and can see ancestor spirits. If seen in both eyes, it designates a sorcerer who can see the flow of magical energy.

13. Harpy: A legend of Kosaran origin that is said to be a war veteran or widow has 'thrown himself to the winds' as the result of mental illness, post traumatic stress, or other reason. Harpies are said to have grown taloned gryphon legs, protruding hooks off the back of their elbows, and a black, oily feathers in place of a warcrest.

14. Kestrel (KES-trel): A small falcon, known to aggressively defend their territory within the Kosaran Mountain Range. The term is used as an insult or slur for cowards.

15. Kosar (ko-SAR): The mountain kingdom ruled as a patriarchy, who is the enemy of Lan'lieana. Known for hawk-like wings and the ability to fly with supernatural celerity at times. At war, they use long-range projectile weapons and rarely land in order to engage in combat.

16. Lan'lieana (Lahn-lee-EH-nah): The island kingdom ruled as a matriarchy, who is the enemy of Kosar. Known for duck-like wings, most have the ability to dive underwater and swim considerable distances. At war, they mostly keep to the ground, using nets propelled into the air by ballistas, shields attached to their wings, and the use of long bladed weapons.

17. Loralae (LORE-a-lie): A water demon of Ehkeski origin who haunts the River Kir that separates the Ehkeski Plains from the Eihwaz forest. The term is now used to refer to berserk Lan'lieanan warriors who are rumored to wield blood magic.

18. Rasha (RAH-shah): A weed that grows in or near the River Kir that is pliable while wet and used to contract a large portion of the furniture in Kosar.

19. River Kir (KEEr): The river which is sourced in the mountain above the city-state of Delton and flows to the end of the mountain where it spills over a high cliff and then runs as a boarder between the War Plains and the Eihwaz Forest before emptying into the ocean. (See "War Plains", "Eihwaz Forest")

20. Sal'weh, Sal'wehte (SAL-weigh; SAL-weigh-tey): Kosaran term for Hello, singular and plural respectively.

21. Terra (TER-rah): This medicinal plant is largely used for its narcotic pain-killing properties, mood stabilizing effects, and ability to suppress the mental talents of Kosaran warbards.

22. Val'weh, Val'wehte (VAL-weigh, VAL-weigh-tey): Kosaran term for Goodbye, singular and plural respectively.

23. The Vals (VALs): The common term for the military force of the women of Lan'lieana. The four distinct factions within the Vals are the Val'Corps (infantry), Val'Kyr (special operations), Val'Tara (weapons), Val'Lorus (war priestesses). Berserk Lan'lieanan sorceress are referred to as 'loralae'.

BIOGRAPHY

"Si vis pacem, para bellum."

The stories Nic tells are Epic Military Fantasy. Through a lens of a fanatical world of elemental magic, meddling dryads, and men and women with wings, it is her goal to take you inside the mind of those soldiers who fight against the overwhelming sorrow that is war without end.

At fourteen years old, she took her first steps towards a love of martial combat when she read about a young man in a fantastical world who had a duty to fight for the less fortunate because, given his knowledge and abilities, 'he was bound to try'.

After discovering genre fiction in high school, she turned that passion for fantasy sword fights into a love of the modern sport of fencing until she ended up competing in the 2000 Junior Olympics. Over twenty years later, she is now a coach herself, but she never stopped fighting, on the fencing strip or in life.

While pursuing an English degree at the University of Iowa, she indulged in the truly epic military and political history that overwhelmed the world of Ancient Rome. Realizing she could advocate for others as an academic, she attended Suffolk University Law School and became a lawyer who could defend the rights of other artists like herself. At thirty-five years old, she enlisted into the Army National Guard, becoming the public servant at the heart of the war-torn story she had been writing about for the past twenty years.

"Si vis pacem, para bellum" are the words that have driven her all her life. *Let he who desires peace prepare for war.* Armed with the knowledge of those who came before, she believes we can do better. We deserve better. Whatever our passions, culture, or creeds, love should bring us together. Peace, for all its problems, is worth a fighting chance.

For Honor and Glory!

The Three Little Sisters

The Three Little Sisters is an indie publisher that puts authors first. We specialize in the strange and unusual. From titles about pagan and heathen spirituality to traditional fiction and non-fiction we bring books to life.

the3littlesisters.com
instagram.com/3littlesistersllc
tiktok.com/@3littlesistersllc

NICOLE EDITED THIS 20 SEPTEMBER 2023

www.ingramcontent.com/pod-product-compliance
Lightning Source LLC
LaVergne TN
LVHW061225010325
804666LV00002B/6